THE SUNSHINE COVE MYSTERY SERIES

AVA ZUMA

CLEANTALES PUBLISHING

Copyright © CleanTales Publishing

First published in July 2021

All characters and events in this publication, other than those clearly in the public domain, are fictitious and any resemblance to real persons, living or dead, is purely coincidental.

Copyright © CleanTales Publishing

The moral right of the author has been asserted.

All rights reserved. This book or any portion thereof may not be reproduced or used in any manner whatsoever without the express written permission of the publisher except for the use of brief quotations in a book review.

For questions and comments about this book, please contact info@cleantales.com

ISBN: 9798529845455
Imprint: Independently Published

THE SUNSHINE COVE MYSTERY SERIES

BOOK 1-6

MAKEUP AND MAYHEM

A SUNSHINE COVE COZY MYSTERY

ABOUT MAKEUP AND MAYHEM

Released: August, 2020
Series: Book 1 – Sunshine Cove Cozy Mystery Series
Standalone: Yes
Cliff-hanger: No

A suspicious death at a party. A list of unusual suspects. A small town beauty consultant who just wants life to return to normal.

Celia's life isn't a bed of roses. As a widow with two young boys, she's only happy when her boys are happy. Her business, providing makeup products to the citizens of Sunshine Cove, puts food on the table and gives a purpose to her days.

When a former classmate drops dead at a party, Celia is confused and wonders what could have caused her demise. Her confusion is turned into anxiety when the police name her as a prime suspect. Celia regrets attending the party where she was cajoled into offering free make overs to the party attendees.

She can't think of anyone who would have wanted to kill the deceased. Still, in a town where anyone's business is everyone's business, she knows the killer is lurking in plain sight.

She can't afford to wallow in self-pity while there's a killer on the loose. Will she help to find the killer and restore normalcy to her life, her family and town or become the killer's next victim?

1

Selling makeup is easy when your client is desperate. This desperation might be due to an impending landmark event, a desire to impress or simply the need to replenish an exhausted supply. Either way, the exchange of cash for goods is much quicker when the common denominator of desperation is in play. Celia Dube was a master at discerning the varied manifestations of this desperation and was equally adept at offering the solution. She had been a beauty consultant and makeup distributor in the Cape Town suburb of Sunny Cove for the last twelve years.

As Celia watched her older son running around the kitchen that morning, she was glad she didn't have the pressure that a nine-to-five job brought to a large percentage of the working population.

"You can't wear the Superman cape to school today!" Celia said to her nine-year-old son James, who was giggling as he ran rings around the kitchen island, his arms stretched in front of him like a superhero cutting through the air at thirty-five thousand feet. She timed his run and swooped him up into her arms. As James wriggled playfully, Celia undid the cape strap around his neck and took it off. She placed him back on the floor and straightened his slightly ruffled school shirt.

"So when will I wear it?" James asked. He was a charmer, with tiny beady eyes and dimples when he smiled that she often found disarming.

"We'll do that over the weekend at the beach, okay, sweetie?" Celia replied. "Go get your brother away from the TV so we can leave," she added, satisfied that he was fully dressed up.

Celia watched James run into the living room that was painted with the orange rays of morning sunlight. His younger brother John was engrossed with his favorite cartoon, all smiles and focus. So caught up was he that when James called out his name, John didn't even flinch.

Celia reached for the remote control atop the kitchen island, which she kept close for moments like these, and switched the television off.

"Oh, Mom! It was almost finished!" John spun around to look at his mother, wearing his best version of a frown. The boys were pretty good actors, Celia always observed.

"No, it wasn't baby. Come on, we're running late for school. You will catch up in the evening, okay?"

"Promise?" John asked with puppy eyes.

"I promise," Celia replied, with one hand over her heart. John's wide smile returned. Now bounding with energy, John ran towards the front door.

"Come get your backpacks first!" Celia said as she reached for two little backpacks placed on the kitchen stools: a rugged, small khaki one for James and a new blue one for John. Her husband Trevor, a hulk of a man who served in the military, had used the khaki bag to carry daily essentials during one of his military missions in East Africa. When Trevor left it behind as he went on his last tour of duty, James had claimed it and made it his school bag, discarding the new bag she had bought him.

It had been five years, and the khaki bag had seen better days, but James would never think of getting another one. Celia didn't even want James to change it because she loved the memories of Trevor that it brought back.

John got to his backpack first, grabbing it just as James arrived. It had become a competition, as it always was with boys.

"Be careful!" she said for the umpteenth time that morning.

James slung his backpack faster than his younger brother and pretended it was now a jetpack, resuming his 'fly-through-the-air' antics to get to the door first. He opened the door, and John walked through it before James could squeeze past. Amused, Celia quickly grabbed an apple from the fruit bowl, as well as her car keys, and followed them out.

They emerged into a sunny Cape Town morning as the sun peered out through the tall trees surrounding their home. She loved the fact that they were in the suburbs, away from the skyscrapers and the concrete of the city center. When Trevor had suggested making their family home in the suburbs, she had jumped at it. Though they had good times in the big city, coming back home to the close-knit community she was familiar with was her dream for raising a family. With time, she had fallen totally in love with the practicality of it all. Here, they could take walks when needed and the boys had plenty of room to play as they explored the landscape and enjoyed the sandy beaches. It wasn't called one of the most beautiful places in the world for nothing.

Celia unlocked the Subaru station wagon, and the boys jumped into the back seats.

"Seatbelts!" Celia said.

"Check!" the boys replied out of sync as they frantically hurried to belt up.

Celia was about to switch on the car when she realized she had forgotten the bag of beauty products in the house. They were crucial to her daily run of driving around to meet clients, make deliveries and offer her expertise as a beauty consultant.

"Oh, drat," she whispered under her breath.

"Oh, drat!" James parroted back gleefully.

Celia turned back to look at him. His smile almost disarmed her again, but she needed to draw a line here.

"What did we say about talking back to mommy?"

"Don't talk back unless you ask us a question," James replied.

"Good. Let's keep it that way, okay?" she said, smiling. James nodded. Celia hoped she wouldn't have to do that very often.

"All right guys, let's get back out."

"Why?" James asked.

"Mommy forgot her products in the house. Come on, I need a pair of strong hands," she said as she got out of the car. The kids followed her to the house.

A few years ago, Celia would have left the boys in the car—what harm would a thirty second wait do? A lot. Celia had once made them wait in the car as she went back for something she had forgotten. When she returned, she found a scruffy, strange man walking up to the car. She screamed her lungs out, and he took off. Trevor, who was home that morning, came out with a gun. Since then, they resolved to always keep the boys close, and Celia wasn't about to drop the ball on that one.

She got the bag of beauty products without much ado, and they walked back to the car. Celia rarely forgot things, and when she did, she knew it could be a sign of exhaustion. It had been an intense couple of weeks running the business and a whole household with two energetic boys. As she fought to keep her wits sharp, she wished Trevor was around to help her.

"What's drat, Mom?" James asked. They were at the front courtyard of the school.

"Well, in the evening, when you tell me all the good things that will happen in school today, I'll also tell you what that is. Deal?" Celia said. James nodded. She hugged both of her sons and watched them walk up the steps and into the school building.

Celia headed back to the spot where she had parked her car and got in. Instead of driving off, she took a moment to do something that was becoming a habit: people watching. Looking on as parents dropped off their children, Celia narrowed her focus to the mothers.

Some women were office workers who needed to drop off their kids before embarking on the half-hour drive to the city center. Celia liked their trim outfits that suited the corporate office spaces they worked in. Some had office access tags hanging off their necks because they would only have seconds to race into their offices before their bosses raised hell. Savvy!

The other group appeared to be housewives. They were the ones who always had no urgency to their drop off routine; many would seek to do the final touches to their kids' uniforms while in the parking lot. They would also have separate lunch boxes for their kids and take the longest to say goodbye. Cute!

Watching both groups in action, Celia figured she was somewhere in the middle. She had the urgency and focus of the office-going women, and the motherly care and flexibility of the housewives.

She took out her notebook and looked through the list of client deliveries she needed to make. It was a day full of back-to-back deliveries, and she resolved that if it got too hectic, she would readjust her schedule and add an afternoon siesta to the mix.

First on the list was Christine Owens, a seventy-year-old feisty woman who lived close by. She had been a good client initially, but her enthusiasm for prompt payment had recently been replaced with an indifference that Celia didn't like. Celia didn't run her business on credit, but had made an exception with Mrs. Owens on her last delivery because she was a good family friend. Since then, it had been hard to get Mrs. Owens to pay up.

Maybe it was time for a change in approach.

The Macan Residences was a quiet, semi-posh residential neighborhood full of robust, identikit bungalows. A lot of older residents with a decent bit of money lived there, forming a crucial community of peers who supported each other as they lived through their sunset years. The relative affluence of the place made Celia wonder why Mrs. Owens wouldn't pay her dues.

Mrs. Owens' house was at the corner of the street. It had blue highlights to its cream walls and red-tiled roof, something Celia found odd but couldn't judge harshly. She rationalized that it could be a pricey blue color only found in Italy, perhaps, because sometimes what you think is tacky is rare and classy in other quarters.

After she parked along the street next to the house, Celia picked a small little gift bag labeled 'Maven Beauty Treats' from the passenger seat. She walked to the front door and gave it three confident knocks.

Nothing.

Celia knocked again, a little louder. Still no response.

She peeped through the glass in the door and, beyond the transparent lace curtain, she saw the form of Mrs. Owens lying on the floor, face up. She wasn't moving. Celia could hear a faint sound seep through - it sounded like music.

Celia's hand started shaking. She was getting anxious wondering if Mrs. Owens was just unconscious or, God forbid the thought, dead.

2

"Hello? Mrs. Owens! Are you okay?" Celia shouted while banging on the front door furiously.

Moments later, and to Celia's surprise, the body started moving. Mrs. Owens' left hand moved to her face slowly. She seemed to be mumbling to herself.

"Mrs. Owens, are you okay?" Celia persisted.

Mrs. Owens tilted her head to the side and asked, "Who's that?"

"It's Celia. I'm here to deliver the beauty products you ordered?"

"Oh, Celia! Give me a moment, let me come over," Mrs. Owens said, getting up gingerly. Celia stepped back from the door to compose herself.

The door lock jingled as it was opened, and Mrs. Owens appeared, wearing a big smile and beaming eyes as if nothing unusual had happened. She had her head wrap tied neatly; her face looked fresh for a woman her age, and she had that graceful aura that announced her presence. Celia was baffled.

"Why didn't I know you were coming this early?" Mrs. Owens asked.

"Well, we had a… anyway, it doesn't matter. Are you okay?" Celia stuttered as she sought to make sense of things.

"Never been better!" Mrs. Owens declared proudly.

"Why were you on the floor?"

"Oh, I'm sorry, there's this new meditation I have been listening to and I drifted off to sleep. Can you believe that?" Mrs. Owens replied with a slight shake of the head.

"Uh, meditation? That's it? Nothing else…?"

"That's it. I am as fit as can be at my age," Mrs. Owens declared.

"Oh. Okay. It must be pretty effective then," Celia said.

"Well, I am not sure about that. It's supposed to clear my mind, not make me sleep. Come on in and make yourself comfortable," Mrs. Owens said as she walked back into the house.

In the living room, Celia noted it was still as cozy and homely as it had always been. Mrs. Owens always had a penchant for memorabilia, and her home was filled with collectibles from years past. Although many were knockoffs, Mrs. Owens gave them the affection one would give to rare masterpieces. There were little sculptures, paintings, postcards, little pendant - bits and pieces that were always conversation starters in Mrs. Owens's home as she often used them to refer to past events in her life. Lately, there were fresh knitted pieces on the couch, which were not memorabilia but simply evidence of Mrs. Owens's newfound hobby: knitting.

Then Celia noticed it: the now pervasive sound of a hypnotic voice, laced with flute music, filling the room.

You are the cat's meow.

Feel the energy of the earth beneath you.

Feel the vibration of the earthworms as they

Massage the soil beneath your skin.

Let nature speak to you…

Celia rolled her eyes as the words of the audio filtered through to her. She found it outrageous, the droning voice of the narrator boring. Adding that snooze fest to the homely feel of the room, Celia understood why Mrs. Owens had drifted off into deep slumber.

"How are the babies?" Mrs. Owens asked, her voice wafting in from the kitchen.

"They are great! Just dropped them off to school," Celia replied.

"They grow so fast, don't they?" Mrs. Owens said as she returned with a mug of hot tea in hand. "Here, sip on this. Is the younger one still quiet?"

"Thanks. He has his moments, but he's doing just fine," Celia replied.

Mrs. Owens then went over to the audio player and switched it off, a merciful gesture to Celia's ears. As she returned, Mrs. Owens got into her trademark story voice, which she often did when relaying a tale.

"You know, I still remember it like yesterday. The day I came to help your mother give birth to you. You were so pretty, just like your mother, and you have passed on that beautiful face and smart mind to your babies. Especially that little boy - little Johnnie. Keep an eye on him. He will have most of the brains, I can guarantee you that."

Celia smiled, she found the thought reassuring. Debt aside, Mrs. Owens held a special place in Celia's heart. She wasn't just a client. She was a close family friend who had been the midwife when Celia was born. As Celia grew up, Mrs. Owens would visit and check on her like a godmother, and Celia had built a healthy affection towards her.

"You have a great mind too and magic hands, Mrs. Owens. Thank you for helping Mama bring me into the world," Celia said.

"Ah stop it, you know I would never have left your mother to her own devices. It was my gift to you," Mrs. Owens gushed, clearly trying to be modest but also loving the fact that her work was recognized. Celia knew that the older she got, the more Mrs. Owens needed such affirmation, and she gave it often. The older woman needed to know that the years gone by still held great significance.

Celia handed the gift bag to Christine Owens, who was smiling with excitement. Mrs. Owens took out her delivery, a matte lipstick and eye shadow that Celia had picked out for her.

"You know the ladies are calling me in for a knitting night. I want to look good," Mrs. Owens beamed.

"You're wearing makeup just for knitting night?" Celia asked quizzically.

"I'll be presenting my latest pieces, so why not? I have to live it up a little, my girl," Mrs. Owens replied with a little jig. "How much is it?"

"Twenty-five dollars," Celia replied, business-like.

"Twenty-five? For this?" Mrs. Owens seemed genuinely dumbfounded.

"Yes, plus the fifteen dollars you owe from the last delivery. So make it forty dollars."

"You must be joking. How did these become so expensive?" Mrs. Owens asked, still admiring the packaging of the product.

"Umm…"

"I shouldn't be paying so much money to look beautiful. Come on now Celia, give me a better deal."

"That's the best deal I can offer," Celia said, determined not to let the older woman get the best of her.

"I know you can give me a better deal," Mrs. Owens said as she tugged at the heartstrings she knew existed in their relationship.

"Well, I…"

"If that's the case then I better try them on and see. Keep the tea going," Mrs. Owens said as she disappeared into the bedroom.

Celia sighed and took a sip of the tea. She found it too sweet and wasn't going to ask for a fresh one. She left it and waited. She didn't have to wait long.

Mrs. Owens returned, and she didn't look flattering. She had applied too much lipstick, possibly to make her thinning lips fuller, but they now looked pudgy and crooked. The eye shadow over her eyelids was going in the right direction, but it was not evenly applied, giving her an overall Goth look.

"You always get me the best. I love these! They are so easy to use and my skin is singing songs. Don't you think?" Mrs. Owens asked as she struck a pose in front of Celia.

Celia wondered if the bathroom mirror was broken or the light was dimming because she didn't understand how Mrs. Owens liked her look.

"I…. I agree, the colors suit you perfectly," she said. It wasn't a lie - the shades Celia had chosen were perfect for Mrs. Owens's skin. The application was a different topic, and she wanted to raise her concern respectfully.

"But I think you should tone it down a bit, you know. Keep it simple," Celia found herself saying.

Mrs. Owens turned to her and said, "Simple? Why on earth would I keep it simple? My skin is singing! It's happy! And it says thirty dollars should be enough," Mrs. Owens replied.

Before Celia could protest, Mrs. Owens handed out thirty dollars to her. Celia took it. She thought it would be better to take what she could get and the remaining debt would be recovered somehow. She also needed to evaluate this buyer-seller relationship, because clients like Mrs. Owens would make her go bust, eventually.

"Thank you, Mrs. Owens. I hope you have fun on knitting night."

"Oh, I intend to. The girls will be floored," Mrs. Owens replied.

Celia almost added 'like you were this morning' but she kept it to herself. Instead, she admired how Mrs. Owens spoke, because she spoke those words with the voice and confidence of a movie star.

"Just take your time, don't rush it. And please remember, you can use some foundation." Celia said as she rose to leave.

Celia stopped at the petrol station close by to refuel for the rest of her trips. She had seven more clients to drive to, spread across town. After paying up for the fuel, she walked back to the car. Then she heard a familiar voice behind her.

"Celia?"

Celia turned to see the lively face of Rosie Williams, her former high school mate and great friend, who looked like a model from a holiday magazine.

"Oh wow, Rosie?" Celia said, surprised. Rosie walked over and they embraced.

"If it isn't the ravishing Celia!" Rosie said. She oozed charm, wit and a certain aura of calmness with the world, Celia thought.

"You are visiting?" Celia asked.

"Visiting my hometown? Girl, no! I am saving to do that in the Bahamas if I get there! I moved back home," Rosie replied.

"Seriously? Welcome back!" Celia replied. "Wow, it's been what? Five years since I saw you? You look amazing!"

"Well, you know we have great genes in my family. You look great yourself, my dear," Rosie said.

"Why did you move back?"

"Long story short, my company decided to do a merger. They cut loose the hardest workers like myself and here I am!" Rosie giggled a little. "I want to start something different in a much more relaxed setting. Jo'burg is a bit crazy, I always liked the energy in this place."

"And the holiday spots." Celia chimed.

"Have I ever denied my little pleasures?" Rosie asked. The two women laughed.

"We should catch up sometime," Rosie suggested. "In fact, how about right now?"

Celia shook her head: "Sorry, I can't. I have a few clients waiting to see me."

"What a bummer. Do you know what's cool? I'm throwing a party sometime soon. I'll invite our old friends for a proper catch up! Are you in?" Rosie asked.

"Er, thanks but I am not fun at parties," Celia replied.

What Celia couldn't voice was that she had flashbacks of all the times she had gone out with Rosie in the past. Those times, though a lot of fun, always ended with drama or commotion, and Celia was not keen on having either of those in her life at the moment.

"Well, maybe this is the universe giving you a chance to loosen up. Let off some steam. I think you need it," Rosie winked and smiled. "Trust me, this is not the usual. And I, Rosie Williams, will make it worth your while!"

Celia knew she would give in, eventually. Her gut also knew something out of the ordinary was bound to happen.

3

There is nothing as good as food cooked by your own mother. It doesn't matter which fine dining restaurant you have been to or if the world's best chef took over your kitchen for a day. None of them would be able to put together the bliss that comes from tasting a mother's soul food cooking.

These thoughts were swimming in Celia's mind as she ate her sosatie, the South African kebab. Her taste buds thanked her for each bite she took as she savored every morsel of the grilled lamb meat cubes. Her mother's secret recipe added a subtle lemon flavor to it that reminded Celia of her childhood. This always lifted her spirits.

It had been a long, tiring day, and this was just the kick Celia needed to regain an appreciation of the world. She had met all her clients except one, who suddenly became unavailable at the last minute. Such surprises happened. She bumped the client onto the next day's list.

Celia had then picked up the boys. They were elated when she stopped by their grandmother's place on the way home. They saw her almost every week, but were always excited as if it were the first time. Celia's mother spoiled the boys like there was no tomorrow.

"Are you really watching your diet or is this an exception?" Audrey Matinise, Celia's buxom, gray-haired mother peered over her glasses as she stared down at her daughter.

"This is sugar-free food, Mama. No sugar is the motto. Everything else is free game," Celia said whilst chewing a small mouthful.

"All right, it's getting out of hand now that you are wolfing them down and talking with your mouth full. You're lucky these boys are not that hungry today," Mrs. Matinise replied with a smile.

Celia smiled back. She looked through the large living room windows facing the rear lawn, where she could see the boys playing an improvised form of football with a leather ball that their grandmother had just given to them as a gift.

"They haven't discovered the magic your food has. I'm taking it in because I know from experience what it can do," Celia said with a glint in her eye.

"I know what it can do. We never age here. Our good genes don't run out," Mrs. Matinise said.

"Watch my skin glow after this! This food is the secret people are missing out on in this world," Celia said.

Mrs. Matinise burst out laughing. Celia loved the way she could banter with her mother about anything. If it wasn't for the age difference, you could easily think the two were sisters. They would talk about anything under the sun; nothing was off limits. Celia was relaxed here. Perhaps it was the years of experience working as a nurse where she skillfully comforted patients that made Mrs. Matinise so good at putting someone at ease. It was at those moments, when your guard was down, that she would ask sensitive questions.

"So, has my beautiful daughter been on a date recently?" Mrs. Matinise asked.

Celia hated these questions, but she knew she couldn't avoid them.

"Mama, we saw each other last week and I told you no," she said.

"A lot can change in a week. Heck, a lot can happen in a day!" Mrs. Matinise replied with a chuckle.

"Nothing has changed here. I'm too busy with the boys and the business," Celia said, keeping her tone as matter-of-fact as possible. Mrs. Matinise moved closer to her.

"It's been five years, Celia. He would have wanted you to move on."

"I'm doing that, Mama. I'm building the life that we envisioned together," Celia said, agitated.

Silence. It was clear that they both had a fondness for Trevor. His presence had been larger than life, and it wasn't just because of his size. His large voice filled rooms with mirth and energy because he loved telling stories and making fun of the people around him. For a big man with the tactical nous to battle an army, he had been a gentle bear to his loved ones. When Celia had gotten the call that there had been 'an incident'- that's what they called it - she had dashed to the army headquarters.

In her mind, Celia figured he might have been injured in combat, something that they had always talked about. As she drove, she had replayed the changes she would make to the house as he recovered: taking out the wheelchair from the basement if he couldn't walk, or use the crutches if it wasn't too serious. The gazebo they had built at the back that overlooked the forest would have needed some cleaning, nothing serious. He would use it when he went to get some fresh air. The first aid kit was there, the medicine cabinet was stocked with painkillers just in case, but maybe his doctor might recommend another type of drug. She had upgraded the medical insurance coverage and knew they would be safe with the expenses. Growing up, Celia had learned the many ways of nursing a patient at home by literally helping her mother out whenever one of the other family members was bedridden at home. She was ready for this moment.

Until she realized she actually was not ready. Trevor had been killed in combat. She would never hear his voice again.

She was shattered for the next couple of weeks after she got the news. Even after his funeral, which was led by the military in honor of him, she had struggled to cope. Her mother always feared Celia barely had time to mourn Trevor's death, and the fact that she had never dated again was a very clear indicator to her that Celia had not moved on. She may have retired as a nurse, but she was still in the nursing business. She was determined to ease Celia over the line.

"I'm not asking you to rush into anything," Mrs. Matinise said.

"Why didn't you remarry?" Celia countered. Her father had died of cancer fifteen years ago, and her mother had never walked down the aisle again.

"Well, have you forgotten Mr. Awesome?" Mrs. Matinise asked. Celia hadn't. He had been Mrs. Matinise's partner for years after her father's death, but lately she had not seen much of him.

"I haven't actually – where is he?"

"He's out there on a cruise ship somewhere, chasing his bucket list," Mrs. Matinise said. "I won't be waiting for him, but I still have a thing for that silly man," she said fondly.

"How do you cope?"

"Take it one day at a time. Then remember there is nothing wrong to feel that you miss a man in your life. Trevor filled a man-shaped hole in your life. Another man can do the same," she said.

"I'm not sure there's a man who can fill that shape like he did," Celia confessed.

"Maybe. But you will never know until you go on those dates," Mrs. Matinise advised. Celia could see the sense in the point being made. She just didn't have the energy to start looking.

"How's the business going," Mrs. Matinise asked, changing the subject.

"Busy. I had a very active day with deliveries, only missed one. Tomorrow we go again."

"Good, good. Take every chance you get to grow it. Save, invest. Multiply."

"Trust me, that's the goal. Going to have an empire in a few years," Celia said.

Mrs. Matinise smiled and said, "You remind me so much of my younger self. You go out and get things done. You're better at it than I was - you focus and don't let go until it comes to pass. I'm proud of you."

"Thank you. That means a lot to me," Celia said with a wide smile. She didn't mind some positive affirmation.

"On that note, I think you deserve some more sosatie," Mrs. Matinise said as she turned to the kitchen.

"Wait, there's more? Why didn't you tell me?" Celia exclaimed.

"With your rate of eating, do you think it would have been wise to share my backup plan with you?" Mrs. Matinise asked with a wry smile.

Celia laughed. Then her phone rang. It was Rosie. Mrs. Matinise disappeared into the kitchen.

"Heya, Celia! How are you doing, girl?" Rosie asked.

"I'm great thanks. Long day," Celia said.

"Don't worry, I have just the thing to make you relax a little more! So, I've come up with a date for the party. We'll have it this Saturday, from three o'clock till late. Or maybe till the night is done, who knows? You should come though," Rosie said with confidence.

"Sorry Rosie, you remember parties are not my thing…"

"Relax! It's going to be a really small group, you know. People with a good head on their shoulders. A really sober group. Actually, they might not be sober at the end of the night," Rosie chuckled, "but you know what I mean."

"Rosie, I really can't," Celia said.

Rosie interrupted her. "Okay, hear me out. How about I make it a party where the theme is makeup? You can sell your products to the guests who will come. You get to party while making money. What could be more perfect?"

Rosie had a point. A makeup-themed party would work to Celia's advantage. It was worth a shot, if the crowd was in the money. With Rosie, it most likely was.

"Hmm. Tell me who's coming," Celia said.

"I'm still building the final list but I am sure you will love it."

"I just want to know who will be coming. Come on now," Celia persisted.

"Where's the fun in that? I'll be there in case you have no one to talk to," Rosie said.

"Please…"

"Come on over, Celia. It will be a surprise you have been longing for," Rosie said, knowing she already had Celia on the hook. The game was sealed.

Celia hated surprises, and this was not going to change. Yet, she was going to go for it. After all, she had survived the morning scare with Mrs. Owens. What's the worst that could happen?

4

Celia drove up to the large mansion off Manor Street. The William's family home was still as imposing as she could remember it. The gate opened on its own as she got close, activated by motion sensors, and Celia could feel the aura of wealth seep into the car. The sound of her wheels rolling gently over the gravel added to the ambience of the whistling trees on either side of the long driveway.

At the car park were a few high-end cars: a Maserati, a Porsche and a BMW sports car. Her family station wagon was immaculately maintained and had decent power under its hood, but it was at a lower price point comparatively. She still parked next to them because she was not fazed by such opulence.

Celia was walking up to the large main door, pulling her suitcase with products behind her, when Rosie came running towards her.

"Aaand she's here!" Rosie shouted as she hugged Celia. "It's really good to see you."

"Thanks for having me," Celia replied with a smile. "Where do I set up?"

"That's why you're early, huh? Always the prepared one. Come with me."

Rosie led Celia through the large hallway that led to the party room. Celia had fond memories of her teens when she used to visit Rosie's home. She never understood how people lived in a house big enough to have its own party room.

"I remember coming here to watch movies and your father used to get us that huge tub of strawberry ice cream to dig into," Celia said.

"Oh yeah! Those were fun times! You want to check out the movie room again?" Rosie asked.

"Ah no, not now. I just like good memories."

"I hear you girl, I hear you!" Rosie said.

The party room was huge. It had a high ceiling, large windows overlooking the lush gardens outside, round tables and seats for guests, a serving area, a small dance floor, and a DJ booth. It was soundproofed from wall to wall by carpets and rugs from the William's family business; they were leading manufacturers of everything carpets and rugs, and you could tell from the quality that they knew their job well. Along one end of the wall where a series of tables with little colorful umbrellas atop them.

Rosie, pointing at the tables, said: "So we set up these spots for you and anyone else who wants to put up their products during the party."

"You said it's a small party. Why are we in such a big room?" Celia asked.

"It is a small party. Only twenty people are coming."

"So why are we in such a big room? We could easily…"

"Ssssh, watch," Rosie said. She moved to the wall that had a series of switches. She flipped two of them at once and there was a subtle whirring sound that came from the middle of the room.

Suddenly, Celia noticed the large partition panels that stood on each side of the room. The panels moved towards each other at a slow but steady pace. A minute later, the panels had joined to form a temporary wall. They were now standing in a much smaller room whose table seating was just shy of thirty people.

"There you go. Looks more like it, huh?" Rosie asked.

"I am impressed," Celia responded.

"Great! Feel at home. Need some help to set up?"

"No, it's nothing complicated, I'll be fine," Celia replied, setting the case next to her stand.

"Are you sure about that?' a familiar male voice asked from behind them, and the two women turned to see the new arrival. Standing there was the tall form of Mark Williams, Rosie's older brother. He was dressed smartly in a sweater, cotton shirt and jeans. Celia could tell he was in great shape. He smiled, activating his dimples.

"Hey Mark! Guess who's here, a blast from the past!" Rosie said animatedly.

"You mean a bombshell from the past," Mark said with a glint in his eyes. "Hello Celia. Good to see you."

"Hello Mark," Celia replied, her smile trying to mask a slight blush. "You look well."

"I am well, thank you. Yourself?"

"I'm great, thanks. Here for the party."

"Yes, Rosie told me about it."

Noticing the tension of past bonds weighing in, Rosie took her cue to leave.

"While the two of you catch up, let me meet up with the other guests. Someone should be bringing you some wine in a few, to get you into the mood. See ya!" With that, Rosie strutted off.

Celia wanted to stop Rosie from leaving, but it was too late. Why? Well, she shared with Mark an unspoken feeling of unfinished business since their high school romance, which ended abruptly.

"Rosie tells me the beauty consultancy business is thriving these days," Mark said.

"Yes, yes. It's pretty established now. It feels easier making other people look and feel beautiful." Celia said.

"That's a great thing, giving other people a better version of themselves."

"Well, it's not superhero level work, but it does make a difference in its own way I think," Celia remarked, keen to manage expectations. "What are you up to these days?"

"I run the family business now. My parents are getting older, and they asked me to leave my practice and step in. So that's the latest news," Mark replied. As he spoke, Celia noticed that his hand didn't bear a wedding ring.

"Do you like it?" Celia asked.

"Yes, I have grown to enjoy it. It's like a mission," he said. Hearing Mark say this made Celia's endorphins spike. She liked a man with a purpose.

"I'll get you that wine while you set up, okay?" Mark offered.

"Sounds good," Celia replied. As he walked away, she imagined what it would be like if she was walking next to him, hand in hand, as his wife. What would it have been like, becoming a member of this family, if they had eloped as they said they would?

At exactly three o'clock, all the guests had arrived. Apart from the occasional figure of Mark and some servers, the space was full of ladies. They were all former school mates from Happy Springs High, although there were quite a number that Celia didn't know. She could recognize Sheila, whose father ran the local pharmacy where they would go to buy lollipops. Samantha Bradley, who was Miss Happy Springs two years in a row and was still sporting her slender, model-like form after all these years. Celia had bumped into her a few times in town, though they never talked much. Karen Damonze, the local church minister's daughter who was a talented singer. She was now married to the successful banker Dennis Damonze and living the good life. The last person she recognized was Azzara Basson, who had competed for the Miss Happy Springs crown once, but lost to Samantha. She was now running her own successful catering business that catered to high-end clients like the Williams' family. She too had a stand two tables away from Celia's, with an assortment of delectable finger food for guests.

There was throwback music playing from their high school days. The guests filled the room with chatter while they talked in small groups as servers moved around pouring drinks and offering food bites. The atmosphere was alive and kicking, and Celia was ready for it. She had decided instead of offering just free samples, she would give quick makeup sessions to any lady interested in her products. If they believed in the product after seeing how good it looked on them, they would buy it. She was here to close the deal, not just show off her range.

Celia joined a group of five women chatting close to her and listened in.

"It was out of this world! A whole giraffe poked its head into the restaurant and wanted to have my breakfast," Samantha said animatedly. She traveled a lot and always had tales of her adventures at her fingertips for such social settings.

"You're lying to us, come on! A giraffe's head through a window?" Karen asked. Celia noted how Karen's hairdo was simple but elegant. Her jewelry and mannerism were that of a lady who was definitely married, but not tied down by it.

"Now why would I lie to you, Karen? Wait, I have some pictures," Samantha said as she lifted the phone she was holding and scrolled through it for a few seconds. "There you go. See! And I don't have Photoshop on here, if you care to dig in further!"

Samantha passed her phone around as each of the women took a quick glance at the photograph. There was a mishmash of reactions that included:

'unbelievable!'

'oh, he's so big and cute.'

'look at those eyes.'

'this is so romantic.'

'why is it so close to the food?'

'did you eat afterwards?'

Karen, who had stirred up this quest for evidence, didn't look amused by Samantha's evidence and resulting vindication.

"Excuse me ladies, I have to go freshen up a little," Karen said and left.

When the phone got to Celia, she was taken in by the frame: Samantha was posed with the giraffe quite close to her. She was alone, although there were two plates at the table. It was most likely that her partner had taken the photograph for her - it was none of Celia's business to know who this was because the whole town knew Samantha had never been close to marrying. Celia envied this life; it looked like the kind of place Trevor would have taken her for a getaway, as they both loved traveling and trying out new restaurants. It was one of the things she missed about him not being around anymore.

"Where was this?" Celia asked.

"It's a cute restaurant in Nairobi, Kenya. We had gone on safari there. What an experience!" Samantha gushed. Celia handed back the phone.

"I am famished! Where are those food trays?" Samantha asked.

"But I thought you just ate a whole chicken, going by the number of drumsticks you have eaten?" Celia joked.

"Did you see how tiny those drumsticks were? They can hardly be considered an appetizer! Besides, I have been on this intermittent fasting plan for the last seven days and my, oh my, the cravings I get sometimes!" Samantha said.

"You eat so much, yet we don't see where the food goes!" another lady named Melanie said. They laughed.

"It's always been the same story since high school, Melanie, it's not going to change!" Samantha chuckled. "Let me head to Azzara's table and get some bites. I'll be back."

Samantha stepped out of the group and headed towards Azzara's stand. Celia was trying to recall Melanie's face from her memory of high school girls, but she couldn't remember her. Melanie seemed quiet and organized, and possibly one of those who talked more once she had a little wine. Celia made a note to get to know her as the evening wore on. Meanwhile, Celia decided to fill up the silence with a quick pitch.

"Hey ladies, I'm selling some high-quality beauty products and wanted to give you a free makeup session. Doesn't hurt to try, so who wants in?" Celia said.

"I'm game!" Melanie was the first to say. Two more ladies raised their hands.

"All right! Come on over before the word gets out!" Celia said. Eager volunteers were a good sign.

Celia led the women to her stand. She started working on Melanie, who had thinned out her eyebrows and hardly wore lipstick. Celia decided it would be great to fill out her eyebrows slightly and apply some gloss that suited her thin lips. As she did this, she learned that her full name was Melanie Dawes. She worked as a librarian at the town library, which had been recently modernized. Five minutes later, Melanie looked at her reflection and was ecstatic.

"Oh, my word. Celia, you are a genius. How did you do that?" she asked.

"I have a knack for knowing which colors and blends would work on any complexion," Celia replied.

"You're an artist! I have to buy this," Melanie said as she struck different poses in front of a large mirror as if she had never seen herself before. Celia knew she had her in the bag.

Just then, Samantha appeared. She was stuffing two fish fingers into her mouth with gusto.

"How about me, Celia?" Samantha asked.

"Come on Samantha, we both know you don't like makeup," Celia replied.

"That's true, but it doesn't mean I don't use it. Sometimes when doing a fashion show, you just have to. Anyway, I just had a few bites, and I need a retouch. Just a little. Some powder here and there. Maybe some gloss too, just like Melanie's?"

Melanie smiled awkwardly and shrugged, "I don't mind sharing a good look."

Celia looked at the other ladies who were waiting, and they waved her on, signaling their readiness to wait.

Celia waved to Samantha and said, "Have a seat, my dear."

"Awesome!" she said, moving fast into the seat. For someone who couldn't stand makeup, Celia admired her enthusiasm.

Noticing Melanie staring at some of the products on her stand, she said, "I think you should definitely get some gloss and eyeliners plus some foundation. It really looks good on you."

"Do you have a free sample of the foundation I could try out first?" Melanie asked.

"Oh, yes. After I am done with Samantha and the two ladies, I will prep your order," she replied.

"Thanks a bunch!" Melanie said as she left to join the party. Minutes later, Celia finished the transformation work she had begun on Samantha.

"You're really good at this, Celia. I'm usually careful about what I put on my face because my skin is sensitive, but this right here is a winner!" she said.

"You're welcome. You want to buy some?"

"Buy some? Do you have packs of this stuff? Because I would like to buy in bulk and forget about it!" Samantha said confidently. Celia couldn't be happier.

"Sure, why not! I may have to get some more stock in and have it delivered to your house," she said.

"Yes, that sounds like fun. And we can catch up, I can have you over for lunch," Samantha said. Celia briefly marveled at the prospect she may be reconnecting with someone she had never really known well. They exchanged numbers for the first time, and Celia promised to call once the order was ready for delivery.

"Let's take a quick picture before the day gets wild," Samantha said. They posed for a selfie together. They must have taken eight different poses before Samantha was satisfied. "Got it!"

Samantha sauntered away into the party crowd as Celia worked on the other ladies.

Fifteen minutes later Celia was done and decided to take a short break. She walked to the now larger group of women as they flaunted their spruced-up looks. Her work had created a buzz and five other women raised their hands. Celia was excited that her effort was paying off.

"Ladies, don't do dinner before I pamper you a little. We all know that it will be hard to do that after the food and wine takes a hold!" Celia teased, and they laughed.

"We should all take pictures after this," one of them said.

"Yes, we should. Samantha is our resident photographer. Where is she?" Celia asked.

No one could spot Samantha after looking around the room, and

Celia hoped she had not rushed to the bathroom to remove the makeup - she had been careful to apply it sparingly.

Moments later, Rachel Bass, who was the daughter of one of the town's former councilors, rushed into the room, out of breath.

"Hey, which of you here is a doctor or knows advanced first aid?" she asked.

"I know first aid," Celia replied. "Why, what's going on?"

"Just come with me," Rachel said as she turned around. Celia followed her quickly.

"What's going on?" Celia prodded.

"I think Samantha has been drinking or something. She's fainted on the stairs," Rachel replied hurriedly.

When they got to the stairs, they found Mark administering CPR to the still form of Samantha.

"Have you called an ambulance?" Mark bellowed.

"Calling one now!" Rachel replied as she pressed her phone frantically.

"Stop slacking, this is serious!" Mark shouted.

Celia got to Mark. "Can I help you out?" she asked.

"No, hold back for now. Look out for that ambulance!" he replied. He was tense, constantly monitoring Samantha's face for any response. "Come on, Sam! Come on!"

Five minutes later, with Mark a little winded, Celia took over. She had learned emergency life-saving skills at the age of nine, as her mother had been keen for everyone in their household to know what it took to save someone's life.

Celia was ready for this moment. However, it was very obvious to her from the moment she touched her body that Samantha Bradley was already dead.

5

There were only twenty guests at the party, but this unexpected scenario made her more acutely aware that most of them had been sheltered from the hazards of life. They were detached from things like sudden deaths and emergencies, so most of them didn't know what to do except succumb to overreaction and anxiety.

Some women were crying, their makeup washing out under a stream of tears; others were frozen speechless; others were moving around trying to be active due to the adrenaline pumping in their veins, but were not aiding the situation.

Celia had continued administering CPR to Samantha's body for a few more minutes as she waited for the paramedics to arrive. When they got there, they did their best to revive her. They checked Samantha's pulse and vitals, attached an oxygen mask to her face before rushing her out on a stretcher to the ambulance that had drenched the car park with flashing lights. The paramedics had a brief chat with Mark before speeding off towards the hospital. Mark then broke the news to everyone that Samantha was gone, asking everyone not to text anyone or post anything on social media before he could notify her next of kin, which Celia found quite considerate.

As the gravity of the events dawned on everyone, speculation began about what happened. Had she been unwell? Had she been pushed down the stairs by someone? Was it the food she ate at Azzara's food table? Celia listened to the whispers and shook her head. The human mind always looks to make meaning out of what it does not understand, while it's always better to lean on facts. But facts can take time to reveal themselves, and human beings are not always patient.

At this point, another siren drew closer to the house, and there was reduced chatter as they realized it was the police. A policeman in plain clothes and wearing a heavy coat secured the scene. He started interviewing each person, writing their statements in his thick brown notebook. He was later joined by an entourage of officers. The place swarmed with them as the evening set in.

Once Celia had given her statement, she asked if she could leave because she needed to get to her boys. The policeman agreed, but refused to let her take down the setup of her beauty products display. Other stands, including Azzara's, were almost down before they were stopped.

"Am I a suspect?" Celia asked.

"At this point, everyone here is a suspect. This whole house and everything in it is a crime scene, so you cannot take anything out in case it is evidence," the policeman answered.

"That doesn't make sense. Then why are you letting me leave?" Celia asked.

"Well, I have already checked you. At least when I need to find you, I can find you. Your stick of lipstick doesn't have an address. On that note, please come to the station at nine o'clock tomorrow morning. Thanks," the policeman quipped and went away.

Celia walked past the huddled guests and the many police officers who were taking pictures of the scene and collecting samples. She was glad to be able to get away from it all. As she left, she saw Rosie and Mark watching the proceedings with serious expressions. She decided not to weigh them down with questions; she would check on them the next morning.

Later that night, after tucking in her sons, Celia couldn't help wondering which party guest wanted Samantha dead - and why did they choose the party as the best place to do it?

6

The next morning was a Sunday, and Celia usually used it as a day to recharge and connect with the boys. However, she wouldn't be able to do that with them for the rest of the day. She was going to be at the police station, and judging from stories she had heard, it was possible she would spend the entire day there, giving statements and answering more questions.

Celia drove her sons to her mother's house and found Mrs. Matinise waiting outside. She looked radiant in a colorful sundress that Celia had helped pick out when they went for one of their monthly mother-daughter shopping sprees. They would just randomly wake up on those days and decide if they were going to shop for clothes or groceries or the best deals in town. It was something they both enjoyed doing and gave them an opportunity to spend time together.

"Where are my boys?" Mrs. Matinise asked as the car came to a stop. The boys rushed out and gave her a hug as she laughed. "You better not push me over now."

Celia walked up to her mother and added her embrace to the mix.

"So are you finally going on that date we talked about?" Mrs. Matinise teased. For the first time, Celia wished she could say 'yes, I am!' because a date was definitely a more exciting prospect than spending a day with the local police.

Instead, she shook her head and said, "I have an appointment."

"With a client? On a Sunday morning?" Mrs. Matinise asked. Celia shook her head again. The two women locked eyes and her mother knew something was up.

"Boys, get into the house and set up the table. Grandma's got a surprise for you," she said.

"All right! Bye Mom!" the boys said as they dashed into the house.

"Bye boys, and don't eat too much of Grandma's goodies!" Celia replied.

As soon as they were out of earshot, Mrs. Matinise said, "Well?"

"I have to go to the police station. I'm simply making a statement."

"What's going on, Cece?" Mrs. Matinise asked, her eyes furrowed in concern.

"I'm okay, I just have to give a statement," Celia was trying to make light of it, but her mother was having none of it.

"Answer the question."

Celia sighed. "Someone died at the party yesterday. They're interviewing everyone who attended."

"Someone died and you're acting as if nothing happened? Is this when you tell me?" Mrs. Matinise asked angrily.

"It's nothing mom. I have to go. Let's talk about it later?" Celia pleaded.

"All right. Take care of yourself, and if you need me to come and get you, just call. Okay?" she said.

Celia nodded with a weak smile. She got into her car and drove off.

Bill Koloane was not what Celia expected her interrogator to look like. He was clean-shaven, but with a goatee that was trimmed down to precision. His bald head shone in the overhead light, and she could guess that he shaved it two to three times a week. His shirt, though having rolled-up sleeves, was well-pressed and his trousers were fitting. His shoes were so shiny you could see your reflection on them. He was clearly a man who looked after himself, perhaps a little too much for a policeman. She admired it, but on his salary, she was suspicious of his ethics.

She was tired of him. Detective Koloane had been asking her detailed questions for the past forty-five minutes and there was no letup. Celia had told him everything she knew, breaking down how events unfolded from the time she had arrived at the Williams' house to the moment the first policeman arrived and questioned her. Every bit, right up to the time she watched her sons turn in for the night.

"All right, you don't have to tell me more. I was only trying to understand the sequence of events and all witnesses are giving their accounts so we can crosscheck the information," Detective Koloane said.

"So you will come and interview my sons to prove I was home? They are not part of this," she said.

"No, we won't need to do that," he reassured her.

Atop the table where they sat in the small, sparse, gray-walled room was a small portable audio recorder. During pauses where Detective Koloane would write his notes, she could hear it whirring.

"Why would there be a makeup themed party?" Detective Koloane asked. He looked genuinely baffled.

"It was Rosie's idea. She knows how hard I work on the business. We hadn't connected for a while, and she thought it would be a great way to give my operation a boost. Introducing the product to a new line of clients is something I always try to do. This was a great way to do it," Celia explained.

"Judging from what you said earlier, you wanted to make sales at the party?" he asked.

"Yes, sharing my brand with new customers and closing sales is what I do. It's just that the setting varies sometimes."

"And you were one of the last people to interact with Samantha. Tell me this, why did you apply makeup on her, yet it's generally known that she doesn't like makeup?" he asked, his tone cutting like a knife through the air.

Celia didn't hesitate, "I was aware of it, and I asked her the same question. But she wanted to do it. Even as I met her request, we agreed to only apply it sparingly. I kept any potentially harmful ingredients away from her."

"Are you sure you succeeded?" he asked.

"Yes. I mean, I literally asked her what suited her and what didn't and she told me," Celia replied.

Silence. Detective Koloane scribbled some more notes. As the recorder whirred, she grew nervous. Why was he asking her trick questions? What was he getting at?

"Am I a suspect here?" Celia asked.

Detective Koloane looked up at her as if irritated with the boldness of her question.

"Everyone is a suspect. I think you were told that yesterday. No one has been cleared, not until we get the toxicology report from the lab," Detective Koloane said.

"Am I under arrest?"

"For now, no. Will you be arrested at some point within the next forty-eight, or ninety-six hours? Maybe," he said, matter-of fact.

"I see," she replied. Celia didn't like where the conversation was going.

"We will most likely call you in again tomorrow," Detective Koloane added.

As that played in her mind, she hoped she wouldn't need to call her mother to come get her. Then she realized that if she was arrested on suspicion of murder, she would have to call her mother to go get the boys, because she wouldn't be returning home.

7

"Nothing like a little fresh air and sun to shake off that morning," Celia said to herself as she walked down the main street.

She had survived the interrogation, but was not amused by how Detective Koloane had handled the interview. It's times like these that you look at your own record with law enforcement, just to prove to yourself what kind of citizen you have been. She had never fallen foul of the police, usually working with the philosophy that cooperating with them was better than trying to be a hero. She had never had to defend her innocence, except maybe the time when she rear-ended another driver at a stoplight, which was actually caused by her starting her car while her foot wasn't on the brake pedal. Rookie mistake.

Detective Koloane had hounded her somewhat, and she wondered if this was the same thing he was doing to each witness, just to see who would break. Maybe it was strategic in that way, but she'd also been informed that the police had no strong leads on who actually did it. They were shaking every branch as hard as they could until a fruit dropped.

As Celia walked past the large window of a coffee shop, she looked inside and saw a familiar figure. She slowed down as she tried to confirm if what she was seeing was true.

Seated in one of the better tables was Rosie, and she was talking animatedly on her phone like someone who was narrating a very exciting story. She then laughed with great mirth, and this struck Celia. Why was the host whose party was ruined by a possible murder this happy just a few hours after the incident?

Celia had to talk to Rosie, so she walked into the coffee shop. She went to the self-service counter first and ordered an Americano coffee. Once served, she walked straight to where Rosie sat. Rosie was still having her animated phone call.

"...you had better come through, my dear," Rosie said as she noticed Celia arrive. "I've got to go now. Let's talk soon and toast to this new adventure, okay? Thanks. Ciao!"

"Hey Rosie," Celia said. "Didn't think I would find you here."

"Celia! Small world they say, huh? Come on, have a seat!" Rosie said with a smile. She was having a masala tea and chocolate doughnuts, one of which was already half eaten.

"Are you okay?" Celia asked.

"Yeah, sure! I mean, a little tired after yesterday. We slept quite late because the police stayed on for hours after it happened. Told you that it would be a surprise," Rosie said.

Celia wasn't sure if Rosie was excited that it happened, or just confirming that she had a thing for attracting trouble.

"That you did, that you did. You look, er, happy and refreshed though," Celia said.

"Well, life is short. It's a new day, and my conscience is clear about the whole thing," Rosie said nonchalantly.

"How can your conscience be clear? Someone died in your house," Celia said, trying to wrap her head around it.

"Yeah, but life happens. I didn't do it, and that's the truth. They will find the person who did it, I'm sure."

"Yeah, but a life was lost. Someone you know. That's what I meant. You feel nothing about that?" Celia prodded.

"I do feel bad that it happened at my place, sure. But does that change anything? It's a pity I didn't know Samantha very well, other than the fact she worked at an animal shelter. Paws and Whiskers, I think it's called. I liked that about her, because I'm an animal lover myself. Also, everyone knows I don't handle death very well, so there's that too," Rosie said as she bit into her doughnut.

If Rosie had done it, then she had the perfect mindset of a murderer, Celia thought. But she couldn't bring herself to believe that it would be Rosie. She wouldn't have done it at a party she organized herself - that would be counterproductive to the idea of getting away with it.

"Did the cops mess up my stuff?" Celia asked.

"Oh, yeah. Don't worry, nothing was seized, except a stick of lip gloss, I think. I had one of my people pack them for you. They can be dropped off later today at your place. Just send me your address," Rosie offered.

"That would be great, thanks. Also, there were some guests at the party I couldn't remember and we apparently went to school together. Karen, I can remember. Melanie, I had no idea about her at all. Do you mind filling me in some more?" Celia asked.

"Well, Karen Summers was a bookworm in school, always in the library and scoring high grades. She's now married to the Spiro bank manager. Very stylish couple," Rosie said.

"Yeah, I know a bit about that. I could tell from her outfit and accessories that they seem to have a bit of money," she replied.

"Not a bit, a lot. Well, not as much as my family, of course, but quite a lot. They've been married for a few years and are making good moves around the place. Power couple with the perfect life," Rosie said.

For someone who knew how those circles worked, Rosie's description fit perfectly with what Celia suspected.

"Karen didn't seem too impressed with Samantha at times," Celia said.

"Karen is like that. I guess it's an introvert thing. She never mingles comfortably, so one time she's all warm and friendly, then she suddenly pulls away. I wouldn't read much into it. She does it to everybody," Rosie said. Celia agreed - not everyone can handle social situations in the same way.

Rosie continued, "Melanie Dawes works at the local library. She's a great librarian, been there a few times to check it out. Great spot to slow down the day with a book."

"Is she married?" Celia asked.

"No, she's single. Maybe the library scene doesn't have good suitors," Rosie said.

Or it's a personal choice, Celia wanted to say.

"How about Azzara? The one who runs the catering business," Celia enquired.

"Azzara is amazing. She didn't come from a rich family, but her father ran a restaurant. It's still there, I think. I guess that's where she got the idea for the catering business. She works with some of the top establishments and names here. Parties, events, you name it. She can get you the food you need to make it special. Miracle worker," she enthused.

"Those are glowing accolades. Tell me something, do you think she did it?"

"Azzara? Why would she? Other than the fact they were not really good friends in high school after the whole Miss Happy Springs thing, I don't see why. That's really not a reason to kill someone years later, right?" Rosie posed.

Celia shrugged. She agreed. It didn't make sense that a high school grudge over a fashion competition would trigger a murder years later.

"But, hey! I never thought that someone could be murdered at my house and voila! So, life is full of surprises," Rosie added with a laugh. Celia couldn't help smiling too, because the world did seem to have a twisted sense of humor.

"Yeah, not everyone is a methodical killer. I just hope that there are some clues out there," Celia said.

"Are you an investigator now? That's how much you loved it at the police station?" Rosie teased. Celia laughed.

"Don't remind me about that. Look, I have to go. Let me recover what little is left of my day. Good to see you," Celia said as she got up.

"Should I pass any message to Mark?" Rosie asked with a sly wink.

"No, not today. I'll see him when I see him," she replied.

As Celia left Rosie to her masala and chocolate doughnut feast, her mind was still unsettled. Maybe it was the pressure she was getting from the police, or her own conscience that wanted to solve this. She was determined to find answers from somewhere.

8

The next morning was slightly overcast, making it a cooler morning than usual. Though she was not superstitious, Celia hoped it was not the proverbial gathering of clouds before a storm.

As promised, Rosie had sent her driver to drop off Celia's products the evening before. Everything was intact except the ones she had used for the sessions and the single stick of lip gloss taken by the police for lab testing.

It was already mid-morning and Celia hadn't received a call from Detective Koloane. She took that as a good sign. The boys were at school, and she had already gotten an order from a long-standing client to deliver some makeup to her salon. The day was picking up nicely, and she intended to go about it as normal.

Celia went through her inventory, arranging the products her client needed for delivery. She needed to restock soon. Fortunately, the head office had confirmed that her order had been processed and she would replenish supplies the following week. She then remembered Samantha had wanted to make a big order too, and that made her heart sink a little.

Her delivery package set and ready, Celia freshened up. It was as she was checking herself for the last time in the mirror while humming a tune that she heard footsteps coming up to her door. She paused, not sure if she was hearing it right. Just then, a leaflet was pushed underneath her door. The footsteps went away.

She walked to the door and looked through the peephole to see who it was. She saw no one.

She picked up the leaflet. It read:

'Paws and Whiskers Animal Shelter invites you to an Open Week! Pop in any day of the week and get the chance to connect with the sweetest animals in town!'

She remembered that it was the same animal shelter Rosie had talked about at the coffee shop. While Celia wasn't a big believer in serendipity, she took this as a sign that she needed to go there. She grabbed her car keys along with the delivery package and left.

Driving back from the successful delivery, Celia drove up along Bay Street. It was not the busiest street, and most establishments were wholesalers. It would be easier to get a space here for an animal shelter, she figured, as the land rates would be cheaper than other parts of town. She hadn't driven for very long when she saw the large sign: Paws and Whiskers Animal Shelter. She turned into it. The front of the shelter had a decent parking area, with two Land cruiser pickups parked at the front, bearing the shelter's logo. She guessed the animals would be at the back. The shop colors were bright and designed to give you that warm, welcoming feeling.

The door jingled as she walked in. At the counter was a young receptionist, probably in her early twenties. She had a green polo shirt with the shelter's logo, and her hair was tied in a cute bun.

"Hello, welcome to Paws and Whiskers! I'm Brenda. Which of our little friends are you interested in seeing today?" the receptionist asked, wearing the widest smile. She looked genuinely happy to see a visitor.

"Er, it's my first time here so I'm open to whatever you propose," Celia said.

"Do you have a pet? Any animals you like in particular?" Brenda asked.

"I like most animals. Except bugs, bats, snakes, slugs and any wildlife that needs to be in the wild," Celia said with a chuckle.

Brenda laughed back. She took out a printed list of animals that lay next to a thick, blue folder. Next to each name was a small image of the animal.

"So this is a list of the animals we have at the moment. Most of them have been saved from cruel owners, or from the streets. Many of them were not in the best condition when we found them, but we have nurtured them well."

"The ones you have on this list are the ones you have looked after, treated and are now ready to have a new home?"

"Yeah, we can't give out the ones that just came in until we have treated them and at least helped them recover from whatever difficulty they were facing," she replied.

It sounded like a great place for an animal to get a second chance at life. Celia wondered if this good-natured girl even knew what had happened to Samantha.

"So, which of these darlings stand out to you? Which one can you recommend?" Celia asked.

"Wow, that's a tough one. I'm a little new in this part of the business. Another colleague of mine would have been perfect for this, but she's not around at the moment," Brenda replied.

"This other colleague, would her name be Samantha by any chance?"

"Yeah, Sammy. You know her?"

"Yes, we actually went to high school together back in the day," she said.

"She was great with all the animals. Sammy would tell you anything you needed to know."

"Can you tell me more about Samantha? What was she like, what work she did, that kind of stuff?" Celia asked.

"Um, well. I'm not sure I should…" Brenda started to say.

"Who's that asking about Samantha?" a deep voiced bellowed from the back.

Celia angled her neck over Brenda's shoulder as she looked for the source of the voice. She saw a hairy, bespectacled man's head pop out from behind a stack of wooden crates.

"I was just asking her…" Celia started to say, but he cut her off.

"Wrong answer. I asked you this: who wants to know?"

9

"My name is Celia Dube, and you must be the manager," Celia replied.

"Come on over to my office, Ms. Dube, and let's talk," the man said to her. Brenda pointed to a little space through which Celia walked past the counter and to the back. Hidden by the stacked crates was a door leading to a spacious, neat office. It had a wide office table full of paperwork. The walls had posters of animals and pin-ups of activity sheets. Two chairs stood next to the table.

The man, who was stocky and hairy on his arms, ushered her towards a seat. Celia eased into it while he sat across from her, training his suspicious gaze on her.

"So, what brings you fishing here about Samantha?" the man asked.

"Samantha was a friend of mine. We went to high school together. Who, may I ask, am I speaking to?" Celia posed.

"Woods. Danny Woods is my name. I own the place," he replied.

"I see. You have heard that Samantha passed away?"

Danny sighed, "Yeah. The police came by to tell me. Unfortunate."

"She had worked here for a while?"

"She was my longest serving employee. Six years she was here.

When others left, she kept going. She surprised me sometimes," Danny said.

"What kind of employee was she?" Celia asked.

"She was not what you would call the model employee. She would come late every day, always had an excuse. The most common one was 'she was held up while helping a neighbor'. It got me wondering what kind of neighbors needed her help every morning. Spent too long with one customer, even when there were queues. She was good with people – great, actually. She would charm them up and keep them coming in like nobody could. She just couldn't focus very well on the big picture sometimes. Anything goes. Talking and eating while attending to customers. I mean, everyone loved her, but I kept wondering if I would have to tear up the employee code of conduct if she kept at it," Danny said.

Listening to him, it was obvious he had never really shared his perspective of Samantha with someone else.

"But you didn't tear it up for six whole years," she said.

"Oh well, you could say I learned to work with her. She was just amazing with the animals and the people. There's no doubt about it."

"Did you get along?"

Danny's eyes narrowed as he paused, as if he hadn't heard her right.

"What do you mean by did you get along? I worked with her for six years!" Danny said, clearly irritated.

"Well, it can't have been smooth sailing all the way," Celia said.

Danny stood up.

"I think it's time for you to leave, Miss Dube," he said.

"All right." Celia stood up. "Thanks for your time."

She extended her hand for a handshake, but he didn't return the favor.

As she passed the counter, the receptionist was holding a little brown puppy in her arms. It was so cute that Celia was tempted to buy it. The boys would love a little puppy.

"That's a really cute one. What breed is it?" Celia asked.

"Hey, no more questions! Please leave my premises!" Danny shouted. He was walking behind Celia.

"So, I can't be a customer now?" she asked.

"You never were. Get. Out!" Danny said, his hairy arm pointing towards the door.

Celia shrugged. She would have snuck in a question or two, or given Brenda her card at least, so Danny's continued aggression would then be somewhat justified yet needless. Then again, maybe it was good that she hadn't gotten the chance to talk to Brenda more. Judging by his reaction, Danny may have taken it out on her. Celia walked out, knowing this wasn't over by a long shot. It was obvious that Danny Woods was riled up because he was hiding something.

10

Hi Celia. So, I have 3 pimples on my face. THREE PIMPLES. The products you sold me are doing this to my face!! Never had them since I was a teen. What do I do now???

As soon as Celia had gotten into the car, she received a text notification on her phone. The message was from Mrs. Owens. Celia took a deep breath and thought quickly. Although she knew it couldn't be her products as this was the first time in a year that Mrs. Owens was giving such a complaint, there was no benefit to having her products get a bad review. Knowing Mrs. Owens, she wouldn't hesitate spreading the word about the Maven product line 'messing up faces'.

Gathering her composure, Celia texted back:

Hello Mrs. Owens! Don't worry, I have an idea of how to get that sorted. On my way.

Fortunately, there was no traffic as she headed towards the intersection that would take her to the Macan Residences. As she waited for the lights to turn green, Celia remembered that she had an organic skin cleanser that could help ease Mrs. Owens' situation. So instead of turning right, she turned left and headed to her house. She estimated she would be there in about fifteen minutes. She hoped her quick text response would buy her some time before she got to Mrs. Owens's house.

It was as Celia was waiting to turn into her driveway that she saw him. He was dressed in all black, masked slightly by the growing avocado tree right next to the door. She went into attack mode. The intruder hadn't seen her, so as she turned into her driveway, she revved her engine and sped in. He was startled, but she was only getting started. As she closed in on the intruder, she pressed her car horn and it blared furiously. Celia could now see him in her frontal view as he did the math of how soon she was going to hit him. He did look like a deer caught in the headlights. She noticed he was slender, medium height, with athletic gear that mimicked a jogger. He was probably in his mid-twenties, but had a healthy, rugged beard.

The car's wheels screeched as she braked hard, stopping just short of the intruder. He had panicked, already anticipating the crash. He jumped atop her hood and leaped off to the other side, running as fast as his track shoes could carry him.

Celia wanted to get out and run after him, but her door jammed. She made three attempts before giving up, slamming the steering wheel in frustration. She later realized she couldn't get out as she had not switched off the central locking. A safety feature she loved, but at that moment she didn't think fast enough. He was gone.

Her hands shaky, she reached for her phone and called the police.

"Tell me again what he looked like," the detective asked Celia. She had expected Detective Koloane, but she was told he was on another call. It wasn't the norm to see flashing police lights in her neighborhood, and she could see her closest neighbors peep through the curtains with curiosity.

"Like I said before, it happened so fast. Um, he was in a black tracksuit and track shoes, as if he was a jogger. Actually, I think that was the idea. He came up here posing as a jogger. But no one in this neighborhood jogs in the afternoon anyway," Celia said.

"What else did you notice?"

"He was slender. And he had a beard. He was most likely twenty-five or twenty-six years old, not older than that."

"Did he have a weapon?"

"You mean a gun? No, I didn't see one. Maybe he had a lock pick. Those are pretty sharp. Because that's what he was trying to do here."

The detective and Celia had already checked the lock, and although there were scratch marks on it, the intruder had not succeeded. Though the lock looked ordinary, it had a three-step locking system, so he was fighting a losing battle.

"Possibly. A good thing you have a reinforced door at the back, maybe that's why he was trying to pick this lock," the detective deduced.

"You know, maybe this is Samantha's killer coming after me. They are trying to see what I have, and I have nothing. Tell Detective Koloane there's no way I did it if the real killers are after me," she said. She was getting convinced that this was tied to the murder somehow.

"I wouldn't jump to conclusions just yet. He's clearly not a very sophisticated intruder, seemed unprepared. His methods match that of a gang of young hoodlums who have been staging some house break-ins in the area," the detective replied.

"But are you sure?" she muttered.

"We are investigating, and when we catch them, we will list this house as one of their targets, see what a shakedown brings. For now, I would advise you to invest in a surveillance camera system."

"Oh wow, are you serious?"

"The world is not getting any safer. Just use the tech and it might help us catch him when… I mean, if he comes back. Though I doubt he will. He's learned his lesson," the detective said as he left for his car.

Celia sat at the corner of her plush bed, thinking. She had cried a little. It had shaken her boots somewhat, despite the fact she handled it well. Beside her was the case of skin cleanser she was about to take to Mrs. Owens. Her left hand was placed on a dark blue hard case. The case, which usually stayed in her closet, belonged to Trevor. These kinds of moments were when she felt most vulnerable, and she longed for his reassuring voice, his kisses on her forehead and his firm, strong bear hug. He always made things safe again for her and the boys.

Inside the case was the gun they had bought together. She had never used it herself, for she hated guns. It was Trevor's area of expertise, so she never really thought of it. Yet today, she felt that she needed to learn how to use it. Or at least open the case and hold it in her hand. Yet, she couldn't muster the will to open the case without Trevor around.

Tears had started rolling down her cheeks again when the phone buzzed. It was Mrs. Owens.

Celia, I now have SIX PIMPLES. This is getting serious. Hurry!

For some reason, the thought of six pimples on Mrs. Owens's face made her laugh. It was lighter in nature to what had just happened, so it was suitable comic relief.

I'll be there, sweetie! I'll get you back in shape!

Celia smiled as she texted. It was time to save Mrs. Owens again.

11

"Do you realize how many things I have missed out on because of you?"

Mrs. Owens was fuming at an apologetic Celia, who had just arrived. Celia did a quick once-over of Mrs. Owens' face and found that the pimples were quite small. They were on her cheeks, where neither the eyeliner nor the lipstick would get to, so they were ruled out as the causes. If the foundation was suspect, Celia had the comfort of proving it had never affected Mrs. Owens because she had been buying it from her for almost a year. Celia was ready to challenge this.

Mrs. Owen went on, "I was due at seven in the morning to turn up at Gladwell's for a breakfast meeting. Ha, I woke up and these pimples said 'good morning' to me instead! There were two tiny ones, but by midmorning they had grown and given birth to a third one! Speaking of mid-morning, I was supposed to be taught how to play golf by Mrs Meadows but was I there? No! Why? Because I had these three pimples who were singing 'stuck on you' lyrics to me on repeat!"

Celia sniffled a laugh without wanting to, because this was comical theater. Mrs. Owens noticed it, unfortunately.

"Celia, you think this is funny? Do you know how traumatizing it is to have wrinkles and pimples and aching bones at the same time? Well, you wouldn't know because you have neither, but sympathize with me!" Mrs. Owens ranted.

"I'm sorry, I didn't mean to play down your distress, sincerely. You know I wouldn't want anything else but the best for you. Here, let's try this right away."

Celia handed Mrs. Owens the skin cleanser bottle.

"Apply this around the pimples. Simply dab it on a clean pad and apply it around your face once you've washed it. It should be easing up in a few hours."

"So, they will be gone today?" Mrs. Owens asked excitedly.

"No, they won't be gone today. But you will see them ease up. Be patient with your skin. However, I have to say I don't think any of my products did this," Celia asserted.

"What do you mean?"

"Have you changed your diet recently?" Celia asked.

"Not really."

"Are you sure? Nothing new from the store that you don't usually eat?"

"I mean, the only thing I haven't eaten for years was the nuts my friend brought me from Egypt," Mrs. Owens replied.

"Nuts? What nuts?" Celia asked.

"You know, nuts. Peanuts."

"And when did you get these?"

"They came in yesterday morning. I maybe had one or two just to see what they tasted like," Mrs. Owens said. "They are pretty good, you should try some."

With that, Mrs. Owens went to the kitchen and came back with a bag of peanuts in hand.

Celia took the bag, and instead of taking a handful, read the ingredients on the pack. Moments later she said, "Yeah, I think it's possible you are allergic to these nuts. Don't take any more."

"Oh, come on now, they are top-notch," Mrs. Owens said.

"Well, then staying off them for a few days shouldn't be a problem, right?" she asked.

"What if I go somewhere during my free time and encounter nuts somewhere else? What then, huh? You are asking for the impossible."

"Tell me, what exactly do you do with your free time?"

"I go places, I already told you. In fact, I am supposed to go for a charity event tonight. That's why this pimple issue was so important to me," Mrs. Owens said.

"You are part of a charity? Which one?" Celia asked, surprised because as much as she knew of Mrs. Owens' generosity, she had never heard her being involved in a charity before.

"The Color Circle. We plant flowers at iconic sites that need a little more color and pizazz around them. Make the town livelier," she said with a smile.

Celia was genuinely fascinated. It sounded like a novel idea, yet at the same time it had the air of pretentiousness to it. Her curiosity aroused, she wanted to debunk her own assumptions.

"Tell me more. Where do you meet? Who leads it?"

"Oh, we meet at the site we intend to fix up, if it's close enough. If not, we get onto a bus and drive together to the location. No frills, just people and flowers. Oh, it was started by this charmer called Dennis Damonze. Quite the lover boy that one."

"Dennis Damonze? Isn't he married?" Celia asked, surprised by the lover boy tag.

"I wouldn't know to be honest, I'm just two trips in. But from what I have seen and heard, he likes the ladies in there, the younger ones of course, and the ladies love him."

"Interesting," Celia said. This new piece of information about Dennis was something worth looking into. "Do people of all ages come too? Because my boys love flowers."

"Oh yeah, kids come too. Although today's event might run a little late, so you might want to use your car," Mrs. Owens said.

"Can I take that as an invitation?" Celia posed.

"Oh heck, why not? I leave at five, so you better be here on time," Mrs. Owens said as she went to wash her face.

Mrs. Owens' car, followed closely by Celia's, drove into the car park of the Royal Heritage Fountain, a historical site that was over a hundred years old. It once housed a functioning fountain that was a key landmark of the town as it came up. Legend had it that travelers would often make a first stop at the fountain to have a drink and ended up settling in the area.

There was a sizeable group of people already there: men, women and a few children and teens. It was quickly obvious to Celia that the majority of the attendees were women in their thirties.

"How do I look?" Mrs. Owens asked after they had stepped out of their cars. She wore an elegant sundress and flats together with a sunhat, despite the fact the sun would be setting soon.

"You have asked me so many times," Celia said.

"Yes, but the light here is different!" Mrs. Owens replied. She was gently feeling up the pimples.

"You look fine, Mrs. Owens. The pimples are already getting smaller," Celia reassured her.

"I hope so, my dear. I hope so," she replied.

As they walked through the animated crowd, there were ushers handing out two flower seedlings to each attendee. Celia handed one each to her sons and took two for herself. It was as she was handing John his seedling that she spotted Karen Damonze. She was looking immaculate and polished, in a tweed jacket, jeans and boots. She was quite some distance from the main crowd.

However, Celia noticed that Karen was gesticulating wildly to someone who was out of Celia's line of vision. Karen was clearly agitated. Who was she having a tiff with?

"Come with me, boys," Celia said as she led her sons forward, slowly moving in a direction that would get her to see the other side of the heated argument she was witnessing.

Once her line of sight was clear, Celia got what she needed. It was a full-blown argument between Karen Damonze and her husband, the so-called lover boy, Dennis.

12

If gestures alone could kill, then Karen would have killed her husband Dennis with her animated hand movements. Although Celia couldn't hear what was being said, she could tell that Karen was livid. Dennis was trying to calm her down, but she was having none of it. Karen eventually threw up her hands and stormed off towards her car. Dennis watched her leave and shook his head. In the distance, wheels squealed as Karen drove off.

Dennis, still stumped by what just happened, turned towards Celia and their eyes locked. He realized she had seen it all. He took in a deep breath and walked towards Celia.

"Hello there. You must be one of the new arrivals," Dennis said, forcing his best smile possible. He was dressed in a cream polo shirt, blue camouflage pants, and had a sweater draped over his wide shoulders. His hair was cropped nicely, and when he smiled, it revealed his bright white teeth. Celia could feel the charm that he oozed.

"Yes, first time here," she replied.

Dennis stretched out his hand, "Dennis Damonze."

Celia shook it. He had a strong grip. "Celia Dube."

"Welcome to the Color Circle! And who are these little guys?"

Dennis shook the hands of Celia's sons, who were never shy of strangers. "You have some handsome boys here to give me competition," he said with a chuckle. A charmer who was self-aware of his power, Celia mused.

"Oh, the world won't be ready for them once they turn eighteen. I hope, um, things are okay between you and…?" Celia asked.

"Yeah. Sorry about that. Karen, my wife, sometimes gets edgy. It's nothing serious, just another day in the office we call marriage. I apologize for that and hope this doesn't affect your experience here today?" Dennis seemed genuinely contrite, and Celia empathized.

"Just give her time and try to reassure her that you mean well," Celia advised. "Color Circle sounds interesting to me and the boys. How do I sign up?"

"You love flowers?" he asked.

"I do, but my boys love them more," she said with a laugh. James gave her a playful nudge and she patted him on his shoulders. "What inspired you to start this?"

"My father had a home garden. Whenever he went in to check on his flowers, I would join him. I got hooked, and I guess that's partially why I started all this," he said.

"Did someone say got hooked?" a soft voice asked.

A young woman in her late twenties with long hair appeared out of nowhere, slinking her hand through Dennis' left arm. Celia was amused, waiting for Dennis to react.

"Hello Stacy. I was just introducing Celia here to what we do," Dennis said as he gave her the once over. She was wearing a crop top and fitting jeans that accentuated her curvy figure, so Celia didn't blame him for checking her out.

"Hey Celia. It's all fun and sun at the Color Circle," Stacy said.

"I'm sure it will warm us up nicely," Celia replied as she watched Dennis. He was clearly not going to move Stacy's arm away. Celia immediately understood Karen's anger.

Later that night, after Celia and the boys had returned home and had dinner, her mother called.

"Hi Mama."

"Hello darling. How did things go today?" Mrs. Matinise asked.

"It was fairly decent. I just had to help out Mrs. Owens, who thought my products were messing up her skin. I also had a few interactions with people who were at the party," Celia said. She didn't want to let on too much about the case, but her mother was keen on it.

"Have the autopsy results been released?" Mrs. Matinise asked.

"Not yet. At least, I don't know anything from the police. I actually want them to come out. It should help get me off the suspects list quite fast," she said.

"I would think so. How are you handling it?"

"Trying to be patient. Also, it's not just about clearing my name. Samantha was full of life, and I can't shake off the question of who would want her dead."

"You are not a detective, Celia," Mrs. Matinise said.

"I know, but think with me here. Azzara, her former high school nemesis, was serving snacks at the party. Could she have done something?"

"Too obvious. I mean… why would she even try?" Mrs. Matinise posed.

"Hmm. But she had an easier way to do it, you know. The motive is maybe not strong enough. Karen Damonze, another former schoolmate, was arguing with her husband tonight because he loves women. Maybe he…"

"…had a fling with Samantha?" Mrs. Matinise finished. "You would have to prove a connection between the two of them."

"Strong motive. Then there's Melanie, who I need to find out more about. Most intriguing of all is Samantha's boss at the animal shelter, Danny Woods. A man who is just full of aggression. Although she worked for him for six years, maybe something happened that ticked him off…" Celia said.

"What on earth could that be? How could he have done anything to her at the party? He wasn't even there."

"Maybe she found out something shady about him," Celia said, her eyes widening. "That's it!" she said as she paced the room.

"What are you on about?" Mrs. Matinise asked.

"What if the person who wanted her dead was not at the party that day?"

13

The next afternoon Celia was shopping at the grocery store before picking up the boys when she spotted Detective Koloane at the cleaning detergent aisle. He was dressed down as if he was off duty. He sported a checked shirt and some jeans, a far cry from the official suit she first saw him wearing at the police station.

It had been a couple of days since he hounded her at the station, and she kept replaying the interrogation in her head to see if she had implicated herself. Each time, she concluded she had been honest about everything. The truth will always win, her mother would say. However, Celia didn't like having a target on her back.

She walked up to him.

"I hear the Supreme powder works wonders on your clothes," Celia said. Strange conversation starter, but what the heck.

Detective Koloane turned to her and raised an eyebrow.

"Celia Dube. What a coincidence," he said as he went on scanning the shelf. "Why would you think I am looking for detergent, when there are other things on this shelf?"

"Just a guess," she replied.

"Well, that's not a good way to go," he said. He was clearly not in the mood for a chat, but Celia wanted answers.

"So, what's the latest on the autopsy?" she prodded.

"Nothing yet. Toxicology results take time to do in the case of poisoning," Detective Koloane replied.

"So, it's poisoning now? She didn't like, fall down the stairs and break her neck?" she asked.

For the first time, Detective Koloane smiled. "No broken necks. This is substances. So, it's either in the food she ate, the drinks she had, or the makeup that was applied on her," he said.

Hearing from Detective Koloane that she was still on the list of possible suspects really brought a chill to her spine. She didn't produce the makeup. Could it contain poisonous chemicals? What if after she had left the party, the actual killer had planted the poison on her products? What then? She could feel the shelves closing in on her, and suddenly she didn't want to be there anymore.

"Thanks for the update," she said. She dropped the empty basket she was going to use and headed for the exit.

As she got to her car, her phone buzzed. It was a text from Mrs. Owens.

Hi. I didn't have any peanuts today. The pimples are still on me. What do I do now?

Celia didn't have an answer. She turned on her car and drove off fast.

As soon as she got home, Celia got down to work. She took out her pen and notepad, then laid out every product she had used at the party, as well as those she had sold to Mrs. Owens. She started checking the labels and noting down common ingredients. She was going to have to research what her products were made of, because if there was poison in there and she didn't know about it, ignorance wasn't going to be a defense.

14

"Can we do the burger run?" James asked Celia, tugging at her skirt.

"Get your brother and then we can roll out," she replied.

"Yes! Yes! Yes!" James said, as he ran off to get John.

Ever since Trevor's death, Celia had tried to make sure she would do the activities he liked doing with his sons. Going to the park, swimming, football at the beach and going out for takeout lunches or dinners.

That Saturday, the boys were craving some burgers. They always went to Big Mike's Burger Palace for those. The restaurant had been around for years. Going there wasn't just a lunch treat; she felt at ease knowing she was doing the things that would make him smile.

When they got there, James was the first to jump out and run towards the restaurant entrance. John was a close second. Walking away from her car, Celia spotted Azzara Basson in the car park of the adjacent building. Azzara was carrying a serving tray to the back of her SUV, whose trunk was open. Celia paused and waved to her boys.

"Hey, James, John, come with me!"

"But I thought it's burger time!" James said.

"It's burger time, but I have to say hello to an old friend, so come on now," she replied.

The boys tugged along, albeit a little sluggishly as a form of protest.

"Hello Azzara!" Celia said as she got close. Azzara, who was clearly busy, looked up with a quizzical expression.

"Hi. You look familiar…" Azzara said, trying to remember.

"Celia Dube. We went to high school together. We met at Rosie's party?" she clarified.

"Oh yes! Sorry for my rude memory. Hi Celia! I would shake your hand, but well, you can see for yourself!" she said with a laugh.

Celia realized Azzara was quite personable and not as serious as she thought she would be.

"That's okay, we don't mean to interrupt," she said.

"No, no trouble at all. I was just finishing up actually," Azzara replied.

"So, you supply food here too?" Celia asked.

"Yes, they had some company breakfast meeting and asked for a few bites to keep things going. A small set up. I usually have a team with me, but they are setting up for a wedding and this is manageable for me," Azzara said.

"Oh, so you handle both individual and corporate gigs?" Celia asked.

"Yes. Mostly corporates. I make more money there, so it's my core business," Azzara said.

"Wow, good for you. I supply beauty products, so most of my clients are people. No room to do corporates, really. You're doing well."

"Thank you. Hey, every business has its niche. Anyway, if you ever have a gig or need to do an event for your clients, drop me a line. I can give you a good deal," Azzara said as she handed Celia her card.

"Thanks! I'll keep it in mind. All the best with the wedding!" Celia replied as she and the boys headed back to the restaurant.

"It's burger time!" The boys shouted as they ran towards the restaurant for a second time. A man was at the door and opened it for the boys as they got closer.

"Thank you for that," Celia said to the stranger who was still graciously holding the door open for her to get in.

"Anytime, Miss. I saw you talking to the lady at the SUV there. She's a friend of yours?" the man asked.

Celia paused, turned to him and said, "We went to the same high school. You know her?"

"Yeah, she used to supply food to a construction company I was working at two years back," he replied.

"Oh really? How was her food?" Celia asked.

"It was pretty good at first, until things went south," he replied.

"What do you mean by that?" she asked, her ears pricked up.

"One time, shortly after having her food, a lot of guys fell ill. Had to be rushed to hospital. Food poisoning, they called it. Two guys didn't make it," he said.

"Oh my, sorry to hear that. What happened after that?" Celia asked.

The man shrugged, "We never saw her again. I thought she got locked up - until I saw her today. Listen, I don't know who looks out for her and has kept her out of prison, but I wouldn't go near her food with a ten-foot pole."

15

"Does a traffic light have eyes in it?"

Celia was distracted. She was driving the boys home and John kept asking her questions about everything he could see along the way.

"Er... eye bulbs," Celia replied.

They had eaten burgers to their fill, and she uncharacteristically allowed them to have a bottle of soda each, which could be adding to the sugar rush they were having. She usually fired off answers to their inquisitive questions about everyday things without much fuss, but her mind was on overdrive. Not only was she navigating unusually heavy traffic, but she was also playing back what the man at the restaurant had said to her.

'Two guys died that day.'

'I wouldn't go near her food with a ten-foot pole.'

What he had said only proved three things; Azzara had a history of serving bad food, people had actually died from it, and she had gotten away with it. Azzara could be a cold-blooded killer who wouldn't be phased doing a number on Samantha. Could it be possible that what they thought as farfetched, a grudge from their Miss Happy Springs fallout, was true?

Celia started replaying her memories of high school. Samantha was always the happy-go-lucky one, but Celia saw another side of her when Azzara came into the picture. It had started at the lunch canteen with a war of words between the two. It got personal later that day during catwalk practice at the gym studio. The war of words turned physical, and the girls tore at each other. They had to be separated by their coach. They both had bruised faces, but Azzara was slightly worse off. People in her corner always said that if she hadn't been bruised, she would have beaten Samantha in the competition. Celia didn't see it that way. Samantha was always the more natural model, who really had a passion for it. Azzara knew she had the look and just wanted to add the win to her accolades. Passion won.

Azzara and Samantha never spoke to each other again. Until maybe Rosie's party. The idea of a long-running grudge still wasn't strong enough, Celia felt. Maybe something else had happened in recent times to revive their rivalry.

The traffic was acting up. Celia decided to turn into Bay Street and gain some time.

"Mom, why is it called a billboard?" John asked again.

"Billboard? I'm not sure. Maybe it was invented by a guy called Bill," Celia replied, knowing she was not giving her son any meaningful knowledge.

"I should invent mine. Call it a Johnboard," he mused.

The traffic on Bay Street was moving along nicely, and Celia was glad she made the decision to use it. As she drove, she spotted the familiar form of Brenda, the animal shelter receptionist, standing at the bus stop. Celia would have driven right past her if she wasn't carrying the boys, because she usually drove faster. She immediately slowed down and pulled over. She honked to get the girl's attention. Brenda came to the passenger side window and recognized Celia.

"Hey! Where are you headed?" Celia asked.

Brenda hesitated before saying, "Going towards the Baobab road."

"That's along my route. Hop in," she said, waving her in.

Brenda got in quickly, "Thanks for this."

"No problem," Celia replied. "You're off work early?"

Brenda winced at this, then said, "Yes, I took the day off. It's been a busy week,"

"I hear you. Just taking the boys back home after a lunch treat. I'm just as tired as you are, they are quite a handful," Celia said, trying to loosen her up.

Brenda attempted a smile, but it didn't come off. She nodded instead. Celia could tell there was something off, because the person she met a few days ago was warm and bubbly.

The car came to a gentle stop at the intersection of Baobab Road and Felt Road. Celia pulled over to the side, off the tarmac.

"Here we are," Celia said.

"Thanks again for the ride, I really appreciate it," Brenda said.

"You can call me Celia."

"Thank you, Celia."

"You're welcome," she replied.

Brenda got out of the car. Celia was about to drive off, but thought otherwise. She had to talk to her. She switched off the engine, put on the handbrake and got out.

"Wait for me, boys," she said as she locked the doors.

Brenda was walking slowly, her eyes on her phone.

"Brenda, wait!" Celia shouted. Brenda stopped and turned. Celia got to her quickly.

"Look, the person I met the other day was very warm and happy. You're not that person today. Are you okay?" Celia asked.

'Yeah, I'm fine, just a little tired," Brenda replied, avoiding eye contact.

"Are you sure? You can talk to me, you know," Celia offered.

That's when the dam broke. Brenda started tearing up. Celia stood by her in support.

"Tell me what's wrong, Brenda. If there's any way I can help you, I will," she reassured her.

"I... I just lost my job. I was fired today," Brenda said. Celia felt for her, and for some reason wasn't surprised. She imagined a manager like Danny Woods would be a nightmare to work with.

"I'm sorry to hear that. Why was that?"

"I usually tell the manager that he should communicate better, teach me things so I can work better. But he just expects me to walk in every day and do things, even those that I have never been trained to do. He then starts shouting at me, sometimes in front of customers, when I fail to do what he asked me to do. It was becoming a vicious cycle, and today, I had enough of his bullying and rudeness. So, I told him off and…" Brenda's voice tailed off.

"And…?" Celia whispered, putting a hand on her shoulder.

"And he fired me instead," Brenda mumbled, her voice shaky.

Celia knew about them, bosses who want you to get better at your job at the drop of a hat, but too lazy to put in the time or money to help you become the best version of yourself.

"Or maybe he wanted me to cozy up like Samantha, I don't know," Brenda added.

Celia was struck by what Brenda had just blurted out. "What do you mean, cozy up?"

Brenda bit her lip, as if gathering the strength for the words she was about to say.

"I'm not supposed to be telling you this, but Samantha and Danny had something going on."

16

As Celia approached her driveway, she was still trying to process what Brenda had just told her.

Then she spotted a figure at her front door. Instinctively, her mind flashed back to the intruder who had tried to break in. But the person moved, and she realized it was her mother. Why was she here today? Celia wondered to herself.

Once the car was parked, the boys excitedly ran out to hug their grandmother.

"Steady now boys, steady!" Mrs. Matinise said as she laughed.

"What are you doing here, Mama?" Celia asked.

"Is that the welcome I get from you?" Mrs. Matinise asked with a frown.

"I almost thought you were the perp…" Celia caught herself. She had never told her mother about the episode with the intruder. Mrs. Matinise's eyes furrowed a bit more.

"I lost my house keys at the market for some strange reason, never happened before, and here I am. The spare keys I gave you are still here, right?" her mother asked.

"I would never lose them. Come on in," Celia said as she walked to the door.

Once the boys had gotten over the initial excitement of having their grandma around, they retreated to watch some cartoons. Celia decided to start preparing dinner early, going for some chicken stew and rice.

"Do you want me to help you with that?" Mrs. Matinise asked.

"No mom, you are my guest today, so relax," Celia replied.

"Your choice. So, tell me more about this perp," Mrs. Matinise said. She was not one to let go of things, especially when she felt they might be bigger than her daughter was willing to admit.

Celia sighed. "First off, it's already handled. The police are investigating it and…"

"Just tell me what happened, Celia."

Celia moved closer, so that she didn't have to raise her voice. She didn't want her boys to know.

"I was just getting home the other day when I spotted an intruder at the front door. He was dressed in all black. It seemed like he was trying to pick the lock. I panicked, drove towards the door as if I wanted to hit him while blowing the car horn," she paused. "He took off."

"You are telling me all this now? Am I a joke to you?" her mother asked.

"Mama, please. Don't start. Nothing major happened," Celia said.

"So just because nothing was taken, no one was hurt, I should relax?" Mrs. Matinise asked.

"Like I said, it's being handled by the police," Celia insisted.

"I think I should stay the night now," Mrs. Matinise said.

"No need to. I don't want to scare the boys. It's most likely not related to the case. The police said there have been a series of house break-ins in the area. The intruder won't return - my house is hard to break into," she said.

Mrs. Matinise was unconvinced. She shrugged to show her displeasure.

"So, what else do I need to know? Tell me about this case," Mrs. Matinise said. She wanted to identify any blind spots. If someone was after Celia, Mrs. Matinise wanted to be ready to point it out.

"Well, I have two possible suspects I'm trying to figure out," Celia replied.

"But that's what you had last time we spoke," Mrs. Matinise said.

"No, this is different. Funny, these leads came to me back to back. Earlier today, while I took the boys to lunch, I bumped into Azzara. She had just served some of her clients. We chatted, nothing serious. I actually didn't think much of it until, as we entered the restaurant, a man held the door open for us. He told me he knew her," Celia said.

"Was he stalking you?" Mrs. Matinise asked, concerned.

"No, Mom! Focus! He spotted me talking to her and said he used to work at this construction site where she would supply food. One time, two people died from food poisoning," Celia said.

"Wait, what? She killed them?" Mrs. Matinise said as she folded her hands across her chest.

"Allegedly Mama, add allegedly. It's a strong accusation," Celia advised.

"If that's true, why would Azzara allegedly kill Samantha?" her mother asked.

"That's what I need to figure out. They were not the best of friends in high school, you know," Celia said.

"No, Celia. There must be something bigger that happened in their adult lives that would push that dislike for each other over the edge," Mrs. Matinise said.

"You know what? I had the same thought," she said.

"She killed two people? Wow," Mrs. Matinise said, clearly was still trying to process.

"Allegedly. We still don't have a strong motive yet if she did the same to Samantha," Celia added.

"Well, people dying because of your food is a strong enough reason, no? And why is she still out on the streets, running her business?" Mrs. Matinise asked.

"That's what I would like to know. I'll dig up something on the internet once I'm done here," she said.

"What was the next thing you got?" her mother asked.

"Ah, yes. We were driving back home just now, and I saw the receptionist from the animal shelter at the bus stop. I gave her a lift. I noticed she was not quite the bubbly, lively girl I met, so I asked her what's wrong. She didn't tell me. After I dropped her off, I went after her - you know, away from the boys listening in. She broke down and told me she had just been fired."

"All right. And?"

"And, I guess because she no longer owes her boss any loyalty, she dropped a bombshell. Apparently, her boss and Samantha, who used to work there, were having a little thing."

"What do you mean a little thing?"

"A fling! Come on, work with me here!" Celia said, careful not to get too loud.

"I get what you mean, I just wanted to be sure. So they were sharing time in the sheets, huh?"

"Yes, and now my suspicions about the manager have just gone up from fifty to eighty percent," Celia said.

"I hope you are not planning to talk to him?"

"I'm considering it," Celia replied.

"You're not a detective, Celia. How about Rosie? Is she also on the list?"

"No, Rosie is Rosie. She doesn't seem to have had issues with Samantha," she said. "The only person I have not heard much about or talked to is Melanie Dawes."

"Well, if you haven't heard about her, then maybe she's not part of the mix," Mrs. Matinise said.

"Or she might be. The best killers hide in plain sight, they don't make headlines. She's a librarian, the perfect branding for someone who needs to look as harmless as a fly."

Celia paused for a moment and looked at her watch. It read four o'clock. The library closed at six in the evening. She was feeling lucky and maybe going for a trifecta of strong leads wasn't going to be a bad idea. It would give her something to chew on later in the night as she put the pieces of the puzzle together in her mind.

"You know what? Maybe you're right. We should swap roles," Celia said, taking off the apron and handing it to her mother.

"It's about time! I was wondering when you would add some seasoning to that stew."

"I already did," she replied.

"Didn't feel like it. You can smell if it's well-seasoned. You forgot my great kitchen teachings?" Mrs. Matinise asked.

"I'll enroll back in your class when I get back," Celia said as she grabbed her car keys.

"Where are you going?" Mrs. Matinise asked.

"To renew my library card," Celia said as she headed for the door.

It had been years since Celia had been in the library, and it had changed. It was still a small one in terms of size, with just one floor to its whole layout. When she would drive past it, she had a passing admiration for the new modernized architectural design that added a sharper, wedge-like feel at the corners. Now, as she stood in front of it, she truly appreciated just how good it looked.

She walked in through the sliding glass doors and strode to the counter. It was well spaced out and quiet, like a library should be. They were using natural light and low energy bulbs for the lights, possibly to keep costs manageable. The library had shelves mapped out well across the space. Judging from the empty tables lining the center of the hallway, most of the day's readers had already left.

Standing behind the lengthy varnished wood counter was the nerdy yet smart form of Melanie Dawes. Maybe it was the glasses or her straight lips and inquisitive eyes, but Mel always looked like a genius. Celia was sure this had opened many doors for her, because Mel had grown up in a tough part of town, and for her to reinvent her destiny like this was commendable. Mel was arranging some books, which had most likely just been returned.

"Hello Mel, is it too late to renew my membership?" Celia asked.

Mel looked up, all serious. A smile broke on her face when she realized who it was.

"Celia," she said. "Well, if it wasn't some minutes to closing time, I might have considered it."

"But I think you should because it's not yet closing time," Celia countered.

"It's a bit of paperwork and it might spill over past the official hours. I unfortunately don't get overtime here," she replied. "Can I help you in any other way?"

"Actually, you can," Celia said. "You were at Rosie's party too when Samantha died. What do you remember about that day?"

"No, I really don't want to talk about that tragic party again. The police have already been here and asked me all the questions," Mel replied and went back to arranging the books.

"But I'm not the police. It's me, Celia. We can talk as friends."

"Even worse," Mel replied, working more urgently. She picked up the books and headed down the hallway. She searched out the shelves where each book belonged. Celia followed her as she tried to charm her into a conversation. Mel was having none of it.

"Celia, you are eating into my work time," she protested.

"But there's hardly anyone here. In fact, we are talking in our normal voice pitches. See?" Celia said as she raised her voice.

"I told you I'm not talking about it. Especially if you are here because you are a suspect," Mel replied.

That statement shocked Celia. Who was talking about her this way?

"Me? A suspect? Who told you that?" she asked.

"My own guess," Mel said curtly. "So please leave."

"Mel, you need to talk to me, considering I gave you a makeup session at the party," Celia said. Mel just stared back at her. Celia realized this was going nowhere, and she took out her card.

"When you feel comfortable, call me. I'll buy you coffee for your troubles," Celia said as she turned.

Mel looked at the card for a few moments. Then she said: "Wait!" Celia turned around.

"Which lipstick are you wearing?" Mel asked.

"It's the ebony black. I sell them if you want one," Celia replied.

"Um, got any free samples?" Mel enquired.

"Yeah, I actually do. There should be a set of samples in the car. Give me a minute."

As Celia walked back to her car, she smiled. If free samples were going to do the trick, then she was going to use that to get what she wanted.

17

"Wait for me at the counter as I make sure that everyone has left," Mel said.

Celia had just returned with the free samples. She found Mel had touched up her hair a little and organized her front counter desk.

"No problem," Celia replied.

Mel walked away, disappearing in between shelves as she canvassed the space. Occasionally, Celia would hear the drag of a desk or a chair, probably left out of place by some lazy user who didn't consider the place as hallowed grounds. However, Celia was fascinated by how Mel's footsteps played out. The library walls had some artwork, but neither that nor the book shelves were sufficient to bounce off the sound. Echoes rang aplenty as Mel moved around the space. Celia created her own game of trying to figure out which part of the library Mel was at, and was happy to see that her mind was sharp enough to figure it out ninety percent of the time.

"All right, we are good to go now," Mel said as she picked up her bag from the counter. Celia had seen it, but hadn't thought of looking through it; it wasn't her style to snoop around in that fashion. At least, the situation didn't really call for it. She felt she was getting closer to solving the case. Someone was going to slip up, and she would be there to pick up the pieces.

"Got the samples?" Mel asked.

"Here you go," Celia said, handing three small bottles to Mel. There were three variants of the ebony range: soft, mild and intense, with the names denoting how they varied in tone.

"Oh, this will be great! Look, I don't have a car, so do you mind giving me a ride?" Mel asked.

"Which side are you headed?"

"Actually, we could go to this restaurant not far from here. They have a happy hour with drinks at half price from five to seven. We can chat there, it's a pretty cool setting," Mel replied.

Celia hadn't pictured Mel as the type to go out for drinks, so this was an interesting discovery. Plus, she had finally convinced her to sit down and talk. The day was just getting better.

As Celia drove to the restaurant, Mel gave directions while using the car's rear-view mirror to apply lipstick. She went for the soft version first, which made her thin straight lips better accentuated. The look would work great when going for a first date where she didn't want to appear to be trying too hard.

"It looks good on you," Celia said.

"I know, right? It's not loud or brash. Just perfect," Mel agreed. "Let me also test out this intense version."

"No build up to it?" Celia joked.

"No room for middle ground in this life. It's either soft or intense, hot or cold," she replied with a smile as she went for the other sample.

Celia smiled back, although she didn't fully agree with the thought. Life was full of gray areas.

The intense version also worked on her. The nature of her lips meant the look was still strong but not too intense on the eye, Celia observed. Perfect for a formal setting or party scene.

"Your boyfriend would love that one," Celia commented.

"You've been waiting to know if I have one. Smart way of asking," Mel replied as she went on checking herself. "This is a nice one too.

So I think I can go with the soft one and the intense one for sure. It's okay if I keep the other one, right?"

"Sure, they are samples after all. Do you want to buy more of those two that you like?" Celia asked, keen to make a sale.

"Um, let me hang on to the free samples for now. See how it plays out in other settings, then I will give you a call for sure," Mel said.

Celia got the feeling that Mel got by with a lot of free stuff in her life, probably to make things more bearable. Maybe librarians didn't make as much money as other professions. She would let it pass.

They arrived at the Hobo Restaurant, a little place with a strong cabin-in-the-woods feel to the exterior décor. A lot of cars were parked out front, and through the large windows Celia could tell the place was nearly filled up.

"I hope we get a place to sit," Celia said.

"Oh, we will," Mel said confidently.

She was right. Inside, there were cubicles where most of the patrons sat because they had more capacity, privacy to hide your date and plush seats. The other areas had smaller, round tables with two seats. There were a couple of round tables free, and the two women took up one of them. It had a good view of the rest of the restaurant. A waiter promptly came to their table.

"Would you like to order?" the waiter asked.

"Yeah. A vodka shot for me and some of those tasty finger foods," Mel said, signaling Celia to order.

"White wine, please. Thanks," Celia said.

"Great, I'll be with you in five minutes. I hope you enjoy the evening," the waiter replied and left.

"All drinks are at half price for two hours?" Celia asked.

"Not all drinks. Just a few chosen ones. If they were all at half price, this place would be a madhouse," Mel said with a laugh "To answer your question, I don't have a boyfriend. At least I haven't had one in the last two weeks."

"You broke up?"

"Sort of. Let's just say he felt this town was too small for him, and he left on his bike. It had been coming, so I was like, meh," Mel said. She clearly wasn't hung up on it.

"Sorry to hear that," Celia said.

"It happens. Some of us can't keep hold of men like Samantha could."

Celia was surprised by the statement. Was it jealousy?

"What do you mean by that?" Celia asked.

"I'm sure you know this already. Everyone does. Samantha had a way with men that kept them at her beck and call. I saw her often with different guys," Mel said.

"Where did you see them?" Celia asked, her curiosity aroused.

At this point, Mel paused as the waiter brought their drinks. It was faster service than the waiter had promised, and Celia made a mental note to buy at least one drink with cash and give him a tip.

"A lot of times, right in this place. She was never shy about it, some of the men were. But she believed in loving loudly, as if she was in charge of things and not the men she was with. Most of them had deep pockets, if you know what I mean," she said.

"How do you know it wasn't just business?" Celia asked.

Mel laughed at this. "Well, the way they doted on her? It was clear to see. You are a woman, you can tell from body language the difference between a business meeting and a meet up between lovers, right?"

"You have a keen eye," Celia said.

"I guess so. That's why I like sitting here. I can see a lot of the restaurant from here. I guess it's a bad habit from the library work," Mel said with a shy smile.

Celia appreciated Mel's self-awareness. "Is this where you saw the animal shelter manager with her?"

"Yeah. That man is always here. He's here right now," she said.

"What?" Celia whipped her head left and right. "Are you serious? I didn't see him."

"You didn't know where to look. You can't see him right now, he's masked by the cubicles. But he's here."

Celia shook her head and sipped her drink.

"There's one more man who's here that I spotted often with Samantha. You can spot him if you are keen," Mel dared Celia.

Celia started scanning the place, challenged by the spatial awareness of her company. Then she spotted a familiar form. She could tell it was him, just by the sweater draped over his shoulders.

"Is that…?"

"Yep. It's the one and only Dennis Damonze," Mel announced.

18

After having a feast of the restaurant's best finger foods, Celia decided to call it a night. Two hours had passed and Mel had opened up as the evening had grown, sharing more of her woes about love, life and career. In between their conversations, Celia kept an eye on Dennis Damonze. He wasn't doing anything unusual, just enjoying a night out with friends. He had no women with him, nor did any beauty walk up to him to say hello.

As she listened to Mel, Celia had realized this was an interesting, ambitious woman who did not want to spend the rest of her life as a librarian. Mel was a traveler at heart who needed to see the world. Celia advised her of cheap ways to do this. Mel commented that she was religiously saving every last penny she could, so in twelve months' time, she'd be waving bye-bye to Happy Springs and saying hello to the outside world. Celia also knew she had one less suspect to check off her list.

As they got up after paying the bill, Celia spotted Dennis Damonze walking towards their table. He had spotted her.

"We meet again," Dennis said as he smiled widely. He shook both their hands. "I didn't know you came here," he added.

"It's my first time, actually," Celia said, "courtesy of Melanie here."

"Ah, nice. It's a pretty popular place," he said.

"So I hear. We were just about to leave though," Celia said as she motioned Mel to take the lead towards the door.

"Could I interrupt your exit for just a moment, we need to talk," he said. He seemed concerned about something, and Celia wasn't going to pass up the opportunity for more revelations.

"I'll get the bus home. Nice catching up, Celia," Mel said.

"Thanks. Text me when you get home," she urged. Mel nodded, sneaked in a quick wink at Celia and left. Celia smiled at the cheekiness.

Dennis and Celia sat back down.

"So I have been having a few bumps around my chin recently. Never got them before and they are making me uncomfortable," he said.

Celia was taken aback. She had hoped the talk would be about something more substantial.

Dennis angled his chin upwards, trying to show her what he meant. He didn't have a beard, but his stubble was evidence he used to have one. She couldn't see any of the bumps from where she was seated.

"You can come closer if you want, or touch it a little bit," he offered. For some reason Celia took what he said as flirtatious and wasn't sure if discouraging him now would make him shut down.

"Have you changed how you shave or something?" she asked instead, ignoring his suggestion completely.

"No, not really. The only thing I changed is the shaving cream I use. Well, it's the same brand, but they released a new variant that I bought," he replied.

"Then that could be it. How about you stop using it for the next two days and just wash with warm water after a shave?" Celia suggested.

"No lotion suggestions or something? I feel pretty plain after a shave if I don't apply something," he replied.

"Just do this for the next two days. We are trying to eliminate the possible cause. Adding another chemical to the skin might complicate things. Once you do that, I can get you something to help out with the bumps," she advised.

Dennis nodded. "Sounds good," he said. In the same moment, his hands reached for hers and he held them. It was a soft hold. His hands were amazingly warm and firm. She didn't expect this, but it felt good.

"Thank you, Celia. This has been making me very uncomfortable, but your advice is very reassuring," he said, his eyes locked on hers.

Celia found the moment a bit too intense and slowly withdrew her hands.

"I should be leaving now," she said

"Hey, it's three days to the weekend, and we'll be having another flower planting event at the St. Mathews church garden. We could meet up then. Come with five bottles of the product," he said.

"Five bottles?"

"Why not? Something tells me they are worth it," he said confidently. This made her smile.

"Five bottles it is. See you then," Celia said as she got up and walked to the door.

"See you then, Celia."

It was already dark when Celia got out of the restaurant. She figured her mother and kids must have already eaten dinner. Suddenly, Celia felt famished, even though she had eaten quite a few nibbles. Maybe it was all the talking that had transpired that was making her crave for something more. As she walked quickly to where she had parked, she couldn't see clearly in the shadowy car park. She bumped into someone else who was coming around a van.

"Sorry!" Celia instinctively said as she backed up to see who it was. To her surprise, it was Danny, the animal shelter manager. It seemed he had helped himself to one too many drinks.

"Argh, these people should put up some lights out here!" he said.

"Fancy seeing you here," Celia said. She knew he hadn't recognized her yet, and she was willing to push him along.

He squinted at her before nodding in realization.

"You're that snoopy lady. Dube," he said.

"I wasn't snooping around. I walked in through your front door," she clarified.

Danny grunted. "It's snoopy now that you're stalking me here."

"Don't be silly. I was meeting with a friend of mine," she said, slightly irritated.

Danny looked behind her, as if looking for the proof of her friend's presence.

"Seems like you are all alone to me," he said.

Celia shook her head. It was futile trying to convince this man.

"If I wasn't mistaken, I would say that's the same way you would look out for Samantha when you came to meet her here," she said.

Danny's shock was visible even in the dark.

"How did you..." he asked.

"I know things. People talk," she replied confidently.

"Brenda told you this, didn't she? It's good riddance that I fired her," he gloated.

"She's got nothing to do with this conversation. Were you seeing Samantha or not?" Celia asked.

Danny shrugged. "Yes, I was seeing her. So what?"

"Why didn't you tell me when I came over?"

"I didn't have to," he replied.

"What happened between the two of you?" Celia asked.

"We broke up the day she died. Didn't think it was important," Danny replied.

Celia wondered if that was the trigger that made him kill her.

"Where were you the day she died?"

"I was here. Drinking away my sorrows as they say," he said.

"You were here? What time exactly?" Celia prodded.

"Listen, I'm not answering any more of your questions. I'm here to have a pleasant evening, so this conversation is over," Danny said. He brushed past her and went into the restaurant.

Celia watched him walk off. In her mind, there was no doubt he may have killed Samantha. Especially if he found out about Dennis. A classic love triangle. She would love to see footage from the restaurant's security cameras. But that would have to wait till the next day, when things were a little quieter.

19

It was a sunny Saturday and Celia arrived a few minutes after four o'clock at the St. Matthew's church. It was one of the oldest churches in town, built by the first Catholics who settled in the area. Even after several retouches, it still retained its rustic feel and grandeur from the past.

She had gone back to the Hobo restaurant the day after bumping into Danny. The manager was not very welcoming to a stranger asking for their security footage, so she decided not to pursue it further - for now.

Celia headed towards the garden, which was behind the main sanctuary. There she found a buzzing crowd of about forty people talking and mingling. The crowd stood on the most pristine grass she had ever seen. It felt like a transgression that the church was allowing them to walk on their well-manicured lawn. But what stood out more was the fact that the crowd was more dressed up than they were the last time she was there. The social class of the attendees was on full display. The designer dresses, suits and fancy footwear suggested no one was there to plant any flowers. Celia tried to look out for Mrs. Owens, but she couldn't spot her.

However, she spotted Karen Damonze, who looked as elegant as ever in a designer blue dress and a matching wide-brimmed hat. She was talking to two important-looking men, probably bank managers. Karen waved at Celia, who waved back. Karen went on talking to her guests.

Celia approached a woman who stood alone, casually sipping a drink.

"Excuse me, I was wondering if this is the Color Circle event?" Celia asked.

"It sure is," the woman replied.

"Last time I was here no one was dressed up like this," Celia said.

The woman smiled knowingly. "You must be new. Out of every three monthly meet ups, two are like this. This is where the fun happens."

'When do you plant flowers when dressed up like that?"

"You don't," the woman said, pausing to take a sip. "If you go to the planting zone on the other side of the crowd, you will find other people doing it. They hire workers to plant the flowers as we do this other fun stuff. Kill two birds with one stone."

"I never expected that," Celia admitted.

"I can tell from your outfit. Don't worry, it doesn't really matter. Just enjoy yourself. It's a beautiful afternoon," the woman said.

"I intend to. Thanks for the heads up," Celia replied as she went looking for her main target, Dennis Damonze. She had the products with her and was really keen to offload the five bottles. He'd better be a man of his word.

She found him at the flower planting zone the woman had talked about. He was talking to one of the workers-for-hire. The workers were all young men and women, six in number. They were clearly people from the poorer neighborhoods who needed the gig. Celia rationalized it was better to give them a way to earn some cash than let them sleep hungry.

"Hello Dennis. Sorry to interrupt."

Dennis turned to see her.

"Hey Celia. No problem, I was just finishing up actually," he replied. He nodded at the worker, and the young man went back to work.

"Got something for me there?" he asked, as he looked at her bag inquisitively.

"I brought what you ordered," Celia said as she handed him the gift bag. Dennis received it and took out one of the bottles of cream.

"Looks fancy, I like the packaging," he said. "You know what? You were right. The bumps started reducing when I stopped using the shaving cream. Felt weird at first, but I got used to it."

"That's good," she said, happy that her advice was now working for male clients. She could now plan how to reach that segment of the market, which she had not really explored before.

Dennis took out his wallet, leafed through some notes and took out the cash.

"There you go," he said.

As she reached for the notes, he held her hand and kissed it. Celia wasn't amused, but she found it hard to withdraw her hand.

"Thank you. You are a lifesaver," he added.

Celia knew he was being dramatic, yet understood why he was such a hit with women. He knew how to connect with them on a visceral level and make them feel special without losing his power over them. Even though she was resisting his advances, she could tell that had the circumstances been different, she would have warmed up to him quite quickly. She hadn't felt that way in a long time.

"Why do you always say thank you in such dramatic ways?" she couldn't help asking.

"It comes with the territory. I suggest you get used to it," he replied with a wry smile as he walked away.

Celia shook her head. That business complete, she figured she might as well grab something to eat. She walked towards the gazebo, where the finger foods and drinks were being served. As she got close, she saw the woman she had talked to earlier.

"I see you have a fan in Dennis," the woman said as Celia was about to go past her. Celia slowed to a stop.

"Excuse me?" she asked.

"Dennis, he's a fan of yours," the woman reiterated.

"What do you mean, exactly?"

"He likes your work, so he's definitely going to be doing business with you," the woman said.

"How exactly do you know what business I do?"

"It's hard to miss out on the Maven beauty line if you like looking good," the woman replied.

"You use our products?"

"I used to. Haven't had a supplier in this area. Unless…" the woman left the statement hanging as an invitation.

Celia took out her card. "Celia Dube. Call me when you need something."

The woman took the card. "Abby Dwente. I'll be reaching out; you are a lifesaver."

Celia didn't know if Abby was a lip reader, because it was uncanny that she was using Dennis' line, yet she believed they were out of earshot.

"I'll be waiting for your call," Celia said as she walked off. Abby had a strange aura, in Celia's opinion. Was she Danny's assassin-for-hire? Why was she watching her every move? Although she realized that she might be overthinking things, Celia resolved to keep an eye on Abby for the rest of the afternoon.

The food serving area was simple, consisting of a few tables bearing a decent variety of tasty nibbles that included chicken wings, biltong, sosaties and meatballs. Celia wasn't in the mood to eat meat, so she started eyeing the confectionaries. Displayed tastefully were cupcakes, brownies and doughnuts.

"Never thought you had a sweet tooth."

Celia turned to her left and saw the smiling Karen Damonze watching her.

"Ah, I didn't feel like chowing down the meaty bites today," Celia said.

"That's a shame, seeing as Azzara has pulled all the stops to serve us today," Karen said.

"This setup is by Azzara Basson?" Celia asked.

"The one and only. She always comes through. What would I do without her?"

"Aren't you worried about...?" Celia started, but Karen cut her off with a casual wave of her hand.

"Nothing has been proven. Azzara has given me good service for years with no issues. I'm not going to ditch her now in her time of need," Karen replied.

"It makes sense," Celia said. Karen was right. There was no evidence at present against Azzara. However, the revelation that Azzara was behind the food setup made Celia hesitate placing anything on her plate. Karen noticed her discomfort.

"You know what? I baked a cake yesterday that I wanted to present later. I'm not sure how it came out. Do you mind being my unofficial taster?"

Celia was open to new options at this point. "Sure, where is it?"

"Follow me," Karen said.

She led the way towards the chapel kitchen, which was overlooking the garden. It was a spacious kitchen with everything you would need to do a cookout, and the church seemed to have these quite often. It was clean and organized too. Celia was impressed.

"Great space, huh? We didn't use it because we already had Azzara in mind, but when I got here, I just had to use it for something," Karen said.

Karen took out a fruitcake from the oven, which was covered in foil. She had already cut it into four large quarters. She carefully cut out a thin slice from one of the large pieces and placed it on Celia's plate.

"Forgive me. I don't want to give you too large a piece because there are forty people it needs to feed. Let me get you a fork," Karen said.

"It's fine. No need for a fork," Celia said. She had a serviette on hand for that purpose, so she saw no need to stain any cutlery. She was studying the cake slice, which looked enticing. "It looks fresh. Are those strawberries?"

"Yes, I added a few in there. I initially wanted to put in dates, but I have never tried those before. At least I have tried it with strawberries once. All right, I'm a little nervous so be gentle with your feedback," Karen said with a smile.

Celia was amused. She held the slice in her serviette and took a bite. It was soft and rich in flavor. She bit into the strawberry and loved it.

"Oh wow. You really did something with this one," Celia said.

"Okay... Is that something good or something bad?" Karen asked.

There was a pause as Celia kept chewing, keen to swallow the rest of the cake before she continued her review.

"It's good! Very nice, I love it. You know, strawberries always taste better when they are part of a cake, not when you eat them on their own. Karen, you aced it there. Let me gobble down the rest of it. Wow," Celia said as she reached for the other half.

She fumbled a bit and couldn't get a good grip of the piece. Before she could salvage the situation, the cake wrapped in serviette fell from her hands onto the kitchen floor.

"Oh, drat," Celia said as she moved to gather up her mess. As she leaned forward, she couldn't maintain her equilibrium and suddenly she was on the floor as well. She tried lifting herself but her whole body, arms and legs felt like jelly. She somehow managed to turn over and lie on her back. Everything was blurry, but she could still hear the distant sounds of people and the sound of Karen's footsteps approaching.

She saw Karen's blurry face come close to hers. Celia wanted to ask her what was going on, but her mouth could hardly move. Karen's blurry face was saying something though, and Celia forced her foggy mind to listen.

"You think you were going to come here, give my husband that silly gift in front of other people and get away with it? At our event? This is your fault!" Karen said as Celia started losing consciousness.

Celia's mind rushed to a deep, dark place. Images of her mother and her sons flashed across her mind.

Then it went dark.

20

She could hear a distant hum. Incessant, strong.

Then it got stronger, and stronger, until it was no longer a hum, but a beep. The persistent, regular beeping sound of a machine.

Her eyelids were as heavy as lead, but she summoned the little strength she had and managed to lift an eyelid. It took the whole of her being to raise the other eyelid, and Celia was finally able to see her mother, Mrs. Owens, and surprisingly, Rosie. The three were standing at her bedside.

"She's awake now," Mrs. Matinise said. A sigh of relief was palpable in the room.

"Where am I?" Celia asked in a weak voice.

"You are at the hospital, sweetie," Mrs. Matinise replied softly.

Celia looked around the room. The white and blue walls stared back at her. The consistent beep was from the cardiac monitor next to her bed. She watched the waves on its screen for a moment, then noticed the cables on her left arm.

"Why… what happened?" Celia asked. Her thoughts were in a jumble.

"Karen tried to get to you," Rosie said. "She… she gave you some of that poisoned cake," she added.

Suddenly the memories came flooding back; the cake, the serviette, losing her balance and Karen's blurry, evil smile.

"Oh my God, how did I survive that?"

"You had a guardian angel. Mrs. Owens was keeping an eye out," Mrs. Matinise said. "You didn't want to do it yourself, so I asked for a little help. Thank goodness she noticed you and Karen going into the kitchen. When she heard the commotion as you fell down, she came in and fought off Karen. The standby paramedics got to you in good time."

Celia turned her gaze to Mrs. Owens.

"Wow. I… I had looked for you, Mrs. Owens," she said.

"Guardian angels don't need to be seen, Celia. I had my eye on you, that's what matters," Mrs. Owens replied.

"What happened to Karen?" Celia asked.

"She was arrested immediately. She's at the station, set to appear in court tomorrow," Rosie said.

"Wait. How long have I been…"

"You've been unconscious for five days. It's been a long wait, but the doctor said it was only a matter of time before you came back to us. Don't worry, you'll be fine, no major damage. They caught it before it could mess you up. Good thing you didn't eat the whole slice," Rosie said.

Celia was grateful too that the cake had slipped from her fingers. Funny how mistakes can turn out to be blessings.

"But why? Why did she do it?" Celia said.

Rosie, Mrs. Matinise and Mrs. Owens looked at each other, as if wondering who should spill the beans.

"Okay, I'll do it," Rosie volunteered "First of all, Karen is a crazy woman. Do you know she wanted to beat up Mrs. Owens when she came to save you?"

"Oh, she tried but she was not going to take me down. I know how to smack you with a pan real good if I need to," Mrs. Owens said with an air of defiance.

"You two fought?" Celia asked.

"I didn't hit her with the pan, I almost did though. You don't play games with me. She pushed me off you when I was checking if you were okay or not," Mrs. Owens replied.

"Before things got too crazy, we had heard the noise and came running to the kitchen. Four of us held Karen back as she shouted all sorts of craziness. Thank God the police arrived shortly afterwards. We might have been forced to mess her up a bit," Rosie added.

"But you're still not telling me why she did this? And is this how she killed Samantha?" Celia asked.

"Same poison, different snack. You're just lucky you got a little dose of it," Rose said. "Apparently, Karen and Dennis have tried to have a baby for years, but that became more complicated when she found out about Dennis' cheating. They argued all the time, but funny enough, she didn't leave him. She couldn't take it that Dennis was spending time with other women instead of getting her pregnant. Eventually Karen snapped, and decided to kill his mistresses, one by one. She planned to kill off Samantha first, and unfortunately…"

"…she saw her chance at your party," Celia said weakly.

"Exactly. You've been unconscious this long and your brain is still in detective mode," Rosie said.

Celia smiled.

Rosie continued: "Anyway, she went to Azzara's food table and took some bites, which she poisoned. When Samantha went to get something to eat, Karen intercepted her and gave her the bites, acting like the 'considerate friend'. Once Samantha devoured them all, she didn't stand a chance."

Celia remembered how Samantha had come to have her makeup done, biting into the food. If only she had known. Celia closed her eyes. The memory pained her.

"Life is just too short. Too short," Celia whispered. Her mother reached for her and squeezed her hand.

"You're still here. You're beating this, okay?" Mrs. Matinise said.

Celia opened her eyes and nodded. Her eyes welled up with tears. Keen to lighten things up, Mrs. Owens stepped forward.

"Hey, I got something for you, Celia," she said.

Mrs. Owens took out a check and showed it to Celia.

"What's this?" Celia asked.

"I'm settling all the dues I owe you for the past year. Let's start on a clean slate when you get out," Mrs. Owens said with a smile.

Celia smiled and nodded slowly.

"I also have a debt I need to repay," a voice said.

They turned their heads to see Detective Koloane standing at the foot of the bed. He had just arrived, holding a small bouquet of roses.

"Are you here to interrogate me?" Celia asked.

"I see you still have a sense of humor. Good to see you awake. Do you accept my flowers as a peace offering?" the detective asked. The bouquet was not a big one, and the flowers could be mistaken for a bunch he stole from the hospital flowerbed, but the intention was what counted.

"Sure. As soon as you confirm to my guests here that I'm no longer a suspect," she said.

"I can confirm you are no longer a suspect, Celia. What you did, putting yourself in harm's way, was very brave, but you should have come to me with any suspicions you had," Detective Koloane replied.

"That's my girl. It runs in the family," Mrs. Matinise said.

"It sure does, Mama," Celia affirmed.

"When you get out of here, we are going to have a party," Rosie said.

"Not on my watch, Rosie. Last time..." Mrs. Matinise was discouraged from finishing her statement when Celia gripped her hand.

"Ssssh! Now what we won't do is hang on to the past. That's already taken Karen's life sideways. I wouldn't want that to happen to anyone here," Celia said.

"That sleep made you real wise, huh?" Mrs. Matinise said.

Celia smiled. "When will I see my boys?"

"An hour from now. I hope you are ready," her mother said.

"I've had five days to get ready," she said.

"Good. Focus on those boys, no more snooping around," her mother said.

Celia turned to her with a cheeky smile.

"Sorry, I have a clean slate. If there's another challenge for me, bring it on! I'm ready."

The End

EYEBROWS AND EVIL LOOKS

A SUNSHINE COVE COZY MYSTERY

ABOUT EYEBROWS AND EVIL LOOKS

Released: September, 2020
Series: Book 2 – Sunshine Cove Cozy Mystery Series
Standalone: Yes
Cliff-hanger: No

Celia welcomes any opportunity that will display her skills as a makeup artist and sell some of her products. She delights in rubbing shoulders with some of the movers and shakers in the small town of Sunny Cove at a charity event she's been invited to. When the organizer of the event, a prim and proper know-it-all, suddenly falls down dead, pandemonium breaks out in the room.

Celia is saddened when her good friend, a local librarian, is identified as a prime suspect as she provided the space for the event.

Celia had minimal contact with the deceased but witnessed her in some 'spicy' altercations with her family and colleagues. Could her rude behaviour be the reason behind her murder or something much more sinister?

Celia has been warned by a local detective in charge of the case not to poke her nose in his murder investigation. But Celia can't help wanting to solve this murder mystery as her friend is in danger of spending time behind bars if she's not exonerated.

Will she find the killer in the nick of time or see an innocent person pay the price for a heinous crime?

1

Celia Dube wasn't having the best morning.

It was one of those rare cloudy days in the suburban town of Sunshine Cove, and along with it came a chill, swept in by the cold winds from the nearby ocean.

Such dull weather was preferable to rain. Her work as a beauty consultant and makeup distributor meant that she was often driving to meet new and old clients. The rain would have made this more difficult, especially when she was trying to finish the day's work and run home to her two little sons.

The cloudy weather wasn't the reason she was having a difficult morning. She was seated in the large living room of one of her clients, Flavia Swane. Flavia was pacing around the room in anger. She spoke in a very animated way, her afro shock of hair dancing as she protested.

"Here I was thinking that we were good friends! After eight months of throwing my money at you, can't I get even a tube of that special edition you released last month as a surprise?" Flavia exclaimed.

As Celia listened, she reflected briefly on her twelve-year-long career. She often turned to her training and experience to find solutions for such situations. Always the optimist, she had quickly learned early in her career the importance of managing client expectations. She was a great marketer, but her client base grew at a slow pace due to high competition when she started. Things changed when her husband, Trevor, died, and she knew she had to improve. Her two sons needed her and she couldn't let them down. So she focused on developing her listening skills extensively, as well as taking several body language classes to learn how to read people better.

Applying these skills had made her successful. Many clients often shared positive words such as 'Celia, you understand me' or 'Celia, you are such a good listener!' which always gave her the encouragement to keep going. She was now earning a good living from a loyal client base that she enjoyed serving. For her, this job was more than selling products. It was a calling to make the people she connected with feel and look better.

"Celia, just one tube to surprise me a little. Was that so difficult to do?" Flavia asked.

Celia kept listening. She needed to be patient and only speak when the time was right. Interestingly enough, Celia wasn't a fan of surprises, so she tried as much as she could to avoid surprising her clients. Her husband Trevor had been the opposite. He lived for surprises, perhaps because his military training espoused its benefits. It was little wonder that her sons loved surprises too, but maybe that was purely down to childish wonder. She didn't mind the glee it brought to their faces when she got them goodie bags without notice. Surprises had their heartwarming perks.

While Celia listened to her client's complaint, she reflected on their relationship. She remembered that she had already given Flavia four freebies in recent months, the most she had offered any of her clients. Giving her a new one with this delivery of shampoo had never been in the cards. When it came to her clients, Celia walked the fine line between managing their expectations while putting them up on a mini-pedestal. She would always tell them in advance when she was running an offer on a beauty product she delivered, and what they would get in the deal. This way, when she showed up at their doors, she had exactly what they wanted. Some of them became fickle and wanted to change the nature of the 'gift' they were getting. While Celia sometimes kept options for this scenario, it wasn't always possible. In those instances, she either withheld it altogether or asked them to give it to a loved one who may appreciate it.

Flavia, needing to pause for a moment, stopped her rant with a big sigh. Celia saw her chance to respond.

"I am really sorry about this, Flavia," Celia said politely, "Bear with me on this one, especially since I have been quite generous the last couple of months. My memory is still very fresh. I remember how you danced around this very living room two months ago after I got you the gift hamper," Celia said.

Flavia paused for a moment, recollecting the memory.

"Yes, I appreciate that. But it was two months ago, my dear. Two months!" Flavia insisted.

Celia sighed. It was like talking to one of her sons about why eating junk food every day wasn't healthy.

"You know that as much as I appreciate your business, I can't do special offers with every delivery. So kindly bear with me for now. I'll tell you this: there will be a surprise for you next month. Guaranteed!"

"It better be the special edition, my dear."

'It's not going to be the special edition. That's a mainline product,' Celia said to herself.

"I have a few samples of a new eyeliner that's being introduced to the market. Would you like to be one of the first ones to get it?" Celia asked.

Flavia mellowed instantly.

"Why, yes! The last one I bought from another supplier was just horrible. It couldn't last a day! I walked around looking like an egg because I had no eyebrows! So please, bring it!" Flavia replied.

This made Celia smile.

"Consider it done," Celia said.

"You know what? I'm sorry for putting you on the spot earlier," Flavia apologized, putting both hands to her cheeks, "I appreciate the way you have explained things to me. Not many have your patience."

Celia was pleased with herself. "The pleasure is all mine. Can we conclude the deal now?"

She needn't have asked, because Flavia was already fishing through her gold-colored purse. Her long-manicured nails emerged with forty dollars, which she handed to Celia.

"As always, thanks for your business, Flavia," Celia said as she got up to leave.

"I'm sorry. I was so caught up at the moment I forgot to offer you something to drink. Will you have coffee, tea?" Flavia offered. It was amazing to watch the shift from angry client to courteous client, and this satisfied Celia more than any beverage could.

"No thanks. Let's push it to my next visit," Celia replied as she headed for the door.

When she got outside, she looked up to the sky and saw a sliver of sunlight peeking through the clouds. She smiled, relieved to have served her last client, and to see the sun still shining beyond the clouds. She got into her Subaru station wagon, keen to get home to her kids.

* * *

AS CELIA WALKED towards her front door, she could hear the wild cheers of her two sons coming from within. Walking in, she was greeted by a sight that had become all too familiar over the last couple of days.

John and James were standing in front of the wall-mounted wide screen television with game pads in each hand. They were playing a car racing video game, and the noise she was hearing was of them chiding each other's driving styles. They hardly noticed her arrival.

"You need to slow down to win," nine-year-old James told his younger brother.

"But you keep blocking me! We have to play another one!" John replied.

"No, we said, the winner is the winner," James said.

"You were cheating. We go again!" John insisted.

This descended into a shouting match, soon broken by Celia's shrill voice.

"All right, that's enough now!"

The two boys stopped, then ran to her, "Mom!"

They both embraced her at the same time, hugging her so tight she thought she would lose her balance.

"Ease up, little fellas. I know why you're showering me with all this love," Celia said.

The two boys stepped back.

"Where's your grandmother?"

"Here as usual!" a voice said as the approaching figure of Audrey Matinise, Celia's mother, emerged from the kitchen. She wore a colorful apron and held a kitchen towel, "Welcome home, sweetheart."

"Hi, Mom. How's it going?" Celia asked as she placed her bags down and took off her long coat.

"Pretty good. We had a good time today, didn't we, young men?" Audrey asked.

"Yes, Grandma!" the boys replied in unison.

"It looks like they are having a little too much fun, actually. How long have they been playing this video game?"

"Maybe an hour," Audrey replied.

"Have you done your homework, boys?" Celia asked. The two boys looked at each other but kept silent.

"All right, that's it. We are going…" Celia started, but her mother interrupted.

"Let them play just for tonight, okay? I'll have them in check from tomorrow. Come over, I need some help with the food."

Celia paused and caved in to the idea.

"All right, you can play for thirty more minutes," she told the boys.

"Yay!" The boys cheered as they ran back to their gaming positions. Soon, they had started a new race.

"You spoil them too much," Celia said with a sigh.

"That's what grandmas are for! I'm the good cop, you're the bad cop. The boys need both," her mother replied with a cheeky grin.

Celia followed her to the kitchen where they spent the next forty minutes preparing lunch, which they ate together.

Afterwards, the boys played in the backyard, enjoying the afternoon sun. Celia watched them from the living room while sipping a glass of warm water. Audrey walked up to her.

"Relax, sweet thing. It's the holidays. Let them loosen up and explore."

"But they explore the TV screen more than the outdoors these days. I need to find something new for them to do," Celia said.

Her mother laughed.

"They read for nine months a year, they have got to have some time to do other things in between," she replied.

It was at this point that an idea crossed Celia's mind.

"You know what? I know what to do," she said as she stood up to leave.

"Where are you going?" her mother asked.

"To see a friend of mine. I have just discovered a new activity for the boys," Celia replied with a wink.

The local community library looked immaculate in the afternoon sun. Since its refurbishment from the old drab exterior, it had become an aesthetic wonder around Sunshine Cove. On sunny days, its snazzy facade bounced off rays with its marbled walls and tall window panels. It had quickly become a cool haunt for young people. They would come and read from the wide array of books, or sometimes sit on the library grounds' benches under the shade of trees.

Celia walked into the library, which was deathly quiet, her footsteps echoing across the large expanse of the room. She arrived at the reception counter. A young man stood there, book in hand. He was waiting for the librarian, who was nowhere to be seen. They didn't have to wait long. Another set of footsteps could be heard approaching them from behind the shelves. Melanie Dawes, wearing a casual suit with her curly dark brown hair pulled into a ponytail, soon emerged.

Melanie didn't voice any greeting, smiling and nodding at them instead as she went round to the other side of the counter. Her commitment to maintain silence was impressive.

She took the young man's book and scribbled an entry into her record book, before handing it back to him. The man mouthed a silent 'thank you' and went on his way. Celia eased into his place.

With Celia, Melanie was open to breaking the rules.

"Hey, Celia. What did we say about unannounced visits?" Melanie whispered. She was genuinely happy to see her. She had few friends and the last time she had met with Celia was three weeks ago.

"That I have a special pass?" Celia whispered back in jest. "How's your day going?"

"Good, so far. Busy. The visitor numbers have been growing since we refurbished the place. It's becoming a space for human connection again," Melanie replied.

"That's great! I wanted to check in on you, and I'm glad the vibes are good. So, I remember you told me there's a kids section, right?"

"Yes, a good one. And we just added a new collection of books. You want to see it?"

"Yeah, of course. Will it take long?" Celia asked.

"Not at all," Melanie said as she walked out from behind the counter.

Just then, two people approached them from the main door. The two friends turned to look. Celia was unable to make out who it was. Melanie recognized them.

"Actually, it might take a little longer...," she said.

"Hello, Melanie!" the woman said, her voice projecting across the whole space. She was clearly not aware of where she was, or didn't care.

Melanie waved with a pained smile.

"Hello, Rachel Sablay, how are you?" Melanie whispered in response, keen to impose her rules.

Rachel wore a puzzled look on her face. "Why are you whispering?" she asked.

"We're in a library. It's standard practice," she whispered.

"Ooooh, sorry, honey!" Rachel whispered back, as if surprised at the news. "I hope that won't be the case during my event?"

"It won't be. The space will be all yours," Melanie replied.

"Great! This is my assistant, Joshua. He's here to keep notes about the things we agree on. You can take me around the place?"

"Sure, let me get my notebook," Melanie said, turning back to the counter to pick a small notebook and pen. As she walked past Celia, she raised her eyebrows in that 'here we go' way.

Celia didn't have to be told twice. She followed Melanie; although she had no idea what was going on.

2

"I sent you that email with the setup I am planning to have, right?" Rachel Sablay asked Melanie as they walked. Their combined footsteps were creating quite a bit of a cacophony.

"Yes, you did. That's why I think it's best if we use our largest space," Melanie replied.

"Ah, that's super! Keeping everything together is perfect," Rachel said.

Celia listened to their conversation as she studied the visitors. Rachel was dressed in what seemed to be a designer outfit, a figure-hugging blue dress with open shoulders. She also wore a pearl necklace, earrings and bracelet, complemented by shiny navy blue heels. Her purse was small and blue too, capping off her matching outfit. She had read somewhere that wearing a blue-colored outfit was good for negotiating a deal, because your target would be inclined to trust you more. Celia wouldn't be surprised if Rachel believed this. She was either in marketing or event organizing, Celia thought, and was well-heeled.

Her assistant, Joshua, was always by Rachel's side, keeping in step. He was dressed in regular formal wear, a well-ironed short-sleeved shirt and black trousers with shiny black shoes. He had to keep up with his boss' standards. He was keenly listening to everything that was discussed, pen and book on the ready. He also had a small portable camera hanging by a strap around his neck.

They arrived at the main space, which had a few shelves along the walls but was mostly filled with reading tables, chairs and couches. It was much cozier and ergonomically designed than it had been in the past. The interior design was excellent, with a classy feel to it. The old chandeliers had been replaced with straight and circular LED lamps strategically placed across the space. There were also tasteful pieces of graffiti along the insides of the wall, paying homage to famous writers. It was an inviting space. It was also half-full, with mostly teens or people in their early twenties deeply absorbed in their books.

"This looks perfect!" Rachel said immediately as she stepped in. They all stood and surveyed the space.

"I thought it would be. You can fit all the things you want here. We can map it out right now so that it's easier to set up tomorrow," Melanie replied.

"Sure thing. Um, is this the main entrance we will use?" Rachel asked.

"There's a double side door there," Melanie started, pointing to their left along the wall. "I don't want to rearrange other rooms in the library, so we can use that to give you direct access to this space. We can have your stewards and registration tent right outside. The door we came through doesn't need to be used."

Rachel nodded in acknowledgement. "Where are the washrooms and changing rooms?"

Melanie pointed to their right at a well-lit corridor.

"That leads to the washrooms and two smaller reading rooms usually used by study groups. It helps them focus and have discussions without distracting the other users in this larger space," Melanie replied.

"Nice," Rachel said, "So this is what I think: we should have the stage right next to the corridor. I think the space is sufficient there. It will be easier for the models in case they need to change or something. Someone has kindly donated a stage, which we will pick tomorrow. Then everything else can flow from there."

"How big is the stage?" Melanie asked.

"To be honest, I don't know. Joshua, how big is the stage Ken is donating?" Rachel turned to her assistant, who was taking photos of the space.

"He didn't say. But it's the one he uses for medium size events. I'll confirm that when we pick it tomorrow," Joshua replied, then went on clicking.

Rachel smiled at Melanie, who was writing something.

"That's one challenge of organizing these charity events. Some people donate their equipment and you can only hope they fit the purpose," Rachel said.

"It's a charity event?" Celia asked, speaking for the first time. It seemed everyone had forgotten she was even there, because they all turned to look at her.

"Yes, it's a fundraiser for the local chapter of Eye Masters International," Rachel replied as she studied Celia, "Sorry, I don't think we were introduced. You are?"

"Celia Dube. I am a good friend of Melanie's," Celia answered.

"And we work on projects together," Melanie quickly added, to which Celia shot her a look.

"Really? And what do you do, Celia?" Rachel was fishing, Celia could tell.

"I am a beauty consultant. I sell some of the best organic products in town. I also do styling, makeup and… and research, which is what Melanie was referring to," Celia replied.

Rachel nodded quietly, as if doing her math.

"Nice to meet you, Celia," she said, then turned back to Melanie, "The runway for the models will stretch down from the front of the stage. It's about ten metres long, so it will fit. Then after that we will have the seating areas."

"Along the runway or facing the front of the stage?" Melanie asked.

"Some along, some facing," Rachel replied.

"So, U-shaped, right?"

"Yes, you can say that. U-shaped sounds good," Rachel said.

"Great. You also said there will be a few vendors?"

"Yes. Just two mini-tents, nothing big. People are here to donate, not buy for posterity. The items sold there will have part of the proceeds donated to the cause," Rachel replied.

"Who's paying for those spaces?" Melanie posed.

Rachel paused, raising an eyebrow and her voice, "Come on Melanie! You know this is a charity event and…"

"Sssssssshhhh!!"

Rachel went quiet as they all turned towards the source of the sound. It was actually hard to tell where it came from, because the whole room of readers was glaring at them with possible disgust.

"Let's go to the small reading rooms, we can talk from there," Melanie said as she led the way.

As they walked off, the readers seemed to calm down, their heads returning to their books in a movement that mimicked a Mexican wave at a soccer stadium.

They got to one of the reading rooms, and it was spacious enough to comfortably hold twenty people at once with room to spare for chairs and other set-ups.

"How many models are you bringing in?" Melanie asked. Joshua's camera was click-clicking.

"Not many. Around thirty. They are all volunteers of course," Rachel said, "Speaking of models, Celia, you said that you do makeup?"

"Yes, I do. Occasionally. Not too much at events unless I am marketing my own products," Celia replied.

"Nice! Now, I have been looking for someone to help me out with the makeup bit and I have just kept hitting dead end after dead end… I know this is a little short notice, but are you open to doing this for us? The event is happening the day after tomorrow," Rachel said, giving Celia a sincere look.

Celia narrowed her eyes.

"I'm not so sure. Are you paying your key team members for it?" Celia asked, casting a casual glance at Joshua.

"Unfortunately, I can't pay you. The challenges of organizing charity events I tell you. I have to scrape for everything, but it's all for a good cause. The heart ends up rich and fulfilled. All I can say is that each model is only going to have two sets of outfits, nothing crazy that will need you to go overboard with your makeup. In around half an hour the runway bit will be done."

"But it would be at least two hours of standby makeup work, including prep and retouches," Celia murmured to herself. She would have to do it quick and early so that she could get a chance to mix in with the guests.

"Another bonus, I do my own makeup, so I'll not be calling you up with demands," Rachel said, wearing her best smile. "Please."

Celia was now convinced that Rachel was experienced in sales, because her power of persuasion was maybe at par with Celia's own. She respected that. Also, what was there to lose?

"All right. Let's give it a shot."

Rachel extended her hand. "Thank you for this, Celia. We'll be setting up tomorrow, so if you want to swing by and talk through the finer details, please come."

"No worries, I'll look into it," Celia replied.

"So, are you okay with the spaces so far?" Melanie interjected, keen to finalize the plans.

"Oh yes, Melanie. This is better than I expected, thank you. Can we talk about the other matter in the morning?"

"Sure. Let's complete that tomorrow," Melanie replied.

"Great! We'll head out now."

Melanie and Celia walked the two to the library entrance and bid them goodbye. They watched them drive off in a new model Panther SUV. As soon as they were out of sight, Melanie let out a huge sigh, as if she had been holding in her breath all this time.

"Are you okay?" Celia asked.

Melanie nodded. "Yeah. I just hope this whole thing goes well. From what I have heard, she likes a news splash at her events. The headlines are not usually good."

"I don't think you need to worry about it. You are one of the most organized people I know," Celia said.

"You don't understand, Celia. It has only been a few months since we reopened. We are already getting more visitors, which is great. The board did not want me to host this event, but I fought hard to convince them. It needs to work. So, trust me when I say the last thing we need is bad publicity," Melanie said gravely.

3

The next morning was an early one for Celia. She woke up the boys soon after sunrise so they could catch up on the homework they didn't do the previous day. She had returned to find them too exhausted after playing in the garden all afternoon, so she made a deal with them to start first thing in the morning.

They were done in an hour, and she promptly rewarded them with hot pancakes for breakfast. Later, she drove them to her mother's house. She would have loved to spend the day with them, but the charity fundraiser was on her mind. She wanted to get to the library in good time, not only to get a sense of what she had gotten herself into, but to show her support to Melanie.

"Mom, we are here!" Celia shouted as she led her sons into the living room. Audrey appeared from the direction of the kitchen.

"Where are my young men?" she asked.

The two boys ran to her, wrapping themselves around her legs in an embrace.

"Who's ready to have some cookies?" Audrey asked them.

"Me, me!" James shouted as John jumped in excitement.

"Go into the kitchen and come with one each. Only one, no more," she instructed.

The boys ran into the kitchen.

"You are going to make them fat," Celia warned her mother.

"They are sugar-free cookies actually," Audrey boasted.

"Do those really exist?"

"Well. You just give it a minute or two, you'll see," Audrey replied, "Going for that library event you talked about?"

"Yes. I want to see what is going on. There might still be time to change my mind if it's a disaster. Promise me something... no video games for these boys today. Please."

Her mother put her hand over her heart, "I promise. I got a nice jigsaw puzzle they need to solve. That will keep them busy today."

"Sounds good. Let me go now. John and James, I'm leaving now!" she shouted as she turned towards the door.

Just then the two boys appeared, a cookie in each hand. Strangely, they were taking small bites of each cookie and scowling in disgust.

"What's wrong?" Celia asked.

James looked at them, puzzled. "Why are they not sweet?"

"Because it's healthy son. Let me show you how to eat it," Celia offered. Both boys ran to her, handing over their cookies. She bit into one. She frowned, struggling to chew. It was as bland as paper, but she persisted.

"See, not bad," she said, still chewing. The boys shook their heads and ran out to the garden instead.

"What is this?" Celia asked her mother.

"I told you it was sugarless. You want more?" Audrey replied.

"No, thanks, I think I'll struggle to get through these two."

Audrey laughed. "Keep them for good luck. Let me know how it goes."

Celia nodded and left.

Celia arrived at the library to find it was a flurry of activity. The main space's layout had changed already, with the reading tables and chairs ditched for red padded chairs that could seat around two hundred people. There were workers arranging the seats in equal distances, while others set up the two vendor tents near the room entrance. The stage and runway were already up, just awaiting final touches. A backdrop with a wide screen for video projections was going up. The sound system, with smaller speakers than Celia would have expected, was also being installed around the stage. Two men were putting up a banner that read: 'Giving Hope to Eye Masters.'

Celia moved towards the stage, partially hoping to spot Melanie. She eventually did, but she was having an intense discussion with the foreman, trying to explain something about the stage's positioning that she didn't like. Celia tried to move into her line of sight, but it wasn't going to be possible, and it seemed rude to interrupt. She opted to go to see how the changing rooms were set up.

The planners had assigned different roles to the two reading rooms. The first was the designated makeup room, which had around five dressing mirrors set up. There was a seating area where models could sit and wait their turn. The second room was the wardrobe room. It was full of portable closets bearing the outfits the models would wear. It too had five stations with full-length mirrors where models could see what they looked like. This is where Celia found the models milling around, chatting.

They didn't notice her walk in the open door. Celia observed that these were not your everyday runway models from London Fashion Week. They were all regular people that you would meet in the neighborhood. There were about twenty of them, all milled around an animated woman who was talking to them in a hushed voice from the middle of the circle. The woman was wearing a brightly colored wig such that you couldn't see her face clearly as she spoke. Curious, Celia moved closer. The closer she got, the more Celia realized the woman's voice was familiar.

"And that's when the generator came on. Now, this was a really huge generator that we had at the hospital, and it was a very loud one. It startled me and my handsome doctor colleague so badly that we both lost our balance and fell into a puddle of water nearby," the woman paused to chuckle with her listeners, "So the question is: how was a nurse going to do her ward rounds soaked in mud? How would the doctor explain himself?"

The listening models burst into laughter as the woman took off the wig and waved it over her head. Celia smiled, because standing in front of her was one of her longtime clients, the ever-talkative Christine Owens. In her sixties, Mrs. Owens was a retired nurse and midwife, as well as a close friend of Celia's mother. In fact, she was the midwife at Celia's birth. Mrs. Owens loved attending social events, but Celia was still surprised to see her there.

"Mrs. Owens?" Celia asked.

Mrs. Owens was still lost in her mirth when she stopped to look at Celia.

"Celia darling! How are you?" she exclaimed in great joy as she moved to her for a hug. Celia returned her warm hug as she always did, with reciprocated warmth and a smile.

"I am fine. What brings you here? Are you making a donation?" Celia asked.

Mrs. Owens gave her a knowing gaze. Celia knew the look. Mrs. Owens had used it many times when she wanted to talk her way out of settling debts she owed for beauty products. Celia found it frustrating, yet also amusing how Mrs. Owens delayed payments, yet she was one of the well-to-do retirees in the area.

"Modeling of course!" Mrs. Owens said with excitement, "I am one of the beautiful people who will be going down the runway tomorrow, something I have never done before."

Celia couldn't help smiling. Considering Mrs. Owens' age, she always found a way to try new things.

"What brings you here?" Mrs. Owens countered.

"I'm here to help with the makeup," Celia replied.

Mrs. Owens' eyes lit up with her smile at this, turning to her listening models.

"Oh, girls, we are in for a treat! This is Celia, and she'll be doing our makeup tomorrow. She's one of the best in town, so be nice to her, okay! She's like a daughter to me!"

There were mixed versions of 'Welcome Celia' from the crowd,

EYEBROWS AND EVIL LOOKS

and Celia didn't mind it. She just did not want Mrs. Owens to start telling strangers how she was born.

"Thank you for the introduction, Mrs. Owens. I look forward to working with all of you," Celia replied.

"You are going to blow their minds away, darling! I am more excited about this charity event. Isn't it nice that we can help so many people who need eye operations?" Mrs. Owens rallied.

The models were marching around her with arms in the air as if she was now the leader of a revolution. It was at this point that Celia spotted Joshua from the corner of her eye. He was standing in one corner of the room, looking in her direction. Once he made eye contact, he waved at her.

"Kindly excuse me. I have to prep for tomorrow. See you all soon!" Celia said.

"No problem, darling, we will be good to you!" Mrs. Owens replied.

Celia walked up to where Joshua stood.

"Rachel would like to see you," he said to her.

"Sure, I would like to see her too."

They found Rachel standing next to one of the vendors' tents. She was dressed more casually, but still looked classy in a polo top, pants, and matching flat shoes. She was having a deep conversation with a woman Celia didn't know, who was wearing a skirt suit and had sunglasses on. Celia found the sunglasses an interesting oddity, to be wearing them indoors.

Rachel spotted them and excused herself from the woman. Sunglasses Woman stood back, waiting.

"Hello Celia, glad you could make it!" Rachel said. They embraced as if they were old friends, Rachel clearly keen to keep her in the fold.

"Thanks. The set-up is coming along nicely," Celia said.

"Yes, thankfully! We started early, and most of the pieces are all here, except maybe some parts of the sound kit. We should be able to do a good old rehearsal later this afternoon. You should stick around for that," Rachel explained.

"I plan to," Celia replied, "So what time do you start tomorrow?"

"The event starts at six o'clock with a cocktail and bites, the usual. Get the people warmed up with something in the system. Then the fashion show will happen at seven. You should focus on that bit. Are you able to come early?" Rachel asked.

"Yeah, I'll be here by five in the evening to get ahead of the schedule."

"Awesome, and thank you again for agreeing to do this. I hope to be able to make it up to you in the near future," Rachel replied, "Sorry, I have to go finish my chat. See you soon."

With that, Rachel left. Celia thought of going back to the reading room, but decided to linger around a bit more. As Celia feigned interest in how the banner was being rigged, she cast discreet glances at the two women.

Rachel seemed to be explaining something to Sunglasses Woman, who was stoical in her response. From her experience with body language, Celia could tell Rachel was getting impatient with the woman, who didn't seem open to her point of view. Trying to read her lips, Celia guessed Rachel was saying 'it will work' repeatedly again to the woman, who didn't appear convinced.

Remembering her conversation with Melanie, Celia wondered if Sunglasses Woman was a reporter. If so, was Rachel trying to convince her that the event would be a success?

She didn't get to learn more, as the woman abruptly turned and left. She looked dissatisfied, and Rachel was shaking her head. As Rachel walked off towards the stage, she spotted Celia and feigned a smile. She kept on her way and disappeared.

As Celia turned and walked away, she wondered if there was more than meets the eye about the situation.

4

It was four o' when Celia arrived at the library. It was the day of the event, and she was there much earlier than she had planned at the special request of Melanie. They had not managed to talk the previous day, and Melanie had called later to apologize. She wanted to catch up early before things got crazy, and Celia obliged.

The event space wasn't as busy as the previous day, because most of the setup was already done. The rehearsal had gone well, overall. There were hitches with the sound system because some key parts had arrived late from a supplier Rachel had not worked with before. The models were all novices and a crash course on how to strut the runway had taken longer than usual. Other than that, the session had ended well. Tweaks would be made before the event started, Celia observed, so there was no big cause for concern.

She found Melanie having a coffee while supervising the cleaners as they attended to the runway. They needed to ensure there were no injurious objects on it, as some models would walk barefoot.

"You better have an extra cup for me, considering you called me in this early," Celia teased.

Melanie smiled back, knowing she didn't have that. She offered her cup and Celia turned it down. "I'm joking. Everything's okay with you?"

"Yes, yes! I'm tired, but everything seems to be fine. So far," Melanie replied.

Celia spent the next hour listening to Melanie narrate how her day had gone, her highs and her lows. She had never hired out the library space for such a large event, but she wasn't particularly surprised. That was one of the hopes they had as an outcome of the facelift, that the new look of the space would attract such clients. It would be good for the long-term sustainability of the place.

"Is she paying for this?" Celia asked, keen to ensure her friend wasn't holding the short end of the stick.

"Yes. That was something I couldn't get off the deal. The board insisted on it, and Rachel agreed to it. It's a cheaper rate than anywhere else in town for a space this size. So she really had no other choice," Melanie replied.

"Good. For a moment, I was worried there. But it seems like you are getting the hang of it actually," Celia said.

"Sure thing. Speaking of Rachel, she's supposed to have arrived by now," Melanie said as she checked her phone. She dialed a number, and it went through. "Hello Rachel... yeah... so far so good... two minutes? All right, see you soon."

"She's close by?" Celia asked.

"Seems like it."

The two waited, and ten minutes later there was still no sign of Rachel. Then Celia caught the sound of loud voices coming from the room entrance. They looked at each other and headed for the entrance.

As they got outside, the voices got louder, leading them to the car park outside, where Rachel's Panther SUV stood. She was standing next to the open passenger door, shouting at the unseen driver.

"Do you think I have the time for this? Do you think I do?"

"You always have time for everything else, why not for your son?" a male voice shouted back from the inside of the car. Celia couldn't see who it was.

"Don't you dare question my parenting skills in front of strangers, you hear me? Not here, not now!" Rachel hit back.

As she spoke, Melanie had already reached Rachel, and tried to pull her away gently. Rachel did not budge, so Melanie stood in between the couple instead.

"Excuse me, we have a long evening coming up and this is supposed to be a safe space. Please, let's stop this!" Melanie pleaded.

Rachel reached into the passenger seat and got her purse, then walked off into the event space.

"Are you staying for the event, sir?" Melanie asked, facing the driver.

"Yeah, of course I am," the man replied.

"Good. If you are attending the event, I kindly ask you to park over there," Melanie said, pointing to a parking spot closer to the live fence and away from the entrance, "We will need this space open for other drop-offs. Thank you."

"No problem," the man said. Melanie closed the passenger door, and the car drove off towards the parking spot. Celia was impressed by her friend's handling of the situation.

"Good on you, Mel," she told her. Melanie just shrugged.

They both waited for the man to get out, because getting a good look would make it easier for them to keep the two apart. The man walked up to them wearing a corduroy coat and a simple shirt and pants. Dark tan shoes completed his look, and he walked with an energetic gait. Despite his almost cowboy look, he was neat. He was clearly older than Rachel and was probably a warm personality in another context. In this one, he was trying to shake off an angry frown.

As he got to them, he offered a hand to both.

"Frank Sablay, Rachel's husband. Sorry for that. It's a minor thing which we took too far. I promise to keep calm," he said sincerely.

"I'll appreciate that. I'm Melanie, this is Celia. Let me show you to your seat."

Melanie led the way inside.

With the clock ticking, Celia decided to go and prep the models.

As she walked to the room, she saw Rachel busy checking every single detail of the setup, her assistant Joshua in tow as usual. Rachel wasn't dressed for the event, and Celia figured she had a change of clothes stashed somewhere. Joshua, on the other hand, wore a bespoke suit and looked very polished.

For the next two hours Celia attended to the models, doing touch-ups to match what they were wearing. There was often a break in between as she waited for them to get their outfits. Celia noted that the clothes followed an earth-centric theme, with tributes to water, soil, plants and animals. This was mainly illustrated by patterns and colors mimicking the themes, with occasional out-of-the box design touches here and there. As Rachel had assured her, there was nothing really risqué except the body hugging outfits that accentuated some of the more curvy models' bodies.

When Mrs. Owens came to have her makeup done, she was wearing a long flowery dress with larger-than-normal shoulders. She walked in, shaking her shoulders from side to side in dramatic fashion.

"I'm the peacock of the bunch," she declared with pride as she settled into the seat.

"You always have been, Mrs. Owens," Celia said.

"Well, this is the higher version of that! So you better work your magic on my face, darling," Mrs. Owens replied with a laugh.

"I'm going to make you the star attraction that you are," Celia promised.

When Celia walked back to the event space after finishing the first round, it was already packed with people. It was filled with the chatter of conversation, clinking of glasses, laughter and the background sounds of music. The place had come alive, and there was a strong sense of camaraderie.

Grabbing a glass of fresh orange juice, she slowly walked around the space. She spotted Rachel again, who had changed into an immaculate red evening dress. She was all smiles, and the stress was gone. She was talking to a tall man in a tweed jacket, clearly enjoying the conversation. Celia was happy to see this, then got curious when

EYEBROWS AND EVIL LOOKS

Frank came into view to whisper something in Rachel's ear. Rachel frowned, then shook her head, clearly not agreeing with what Frank had to say. He went on whispering to her, but Rachel was no longer listening. Frank gave up and slinked off into the crowd. Rachel rediscovered her smile and went on as if nothing had happened. Celia made a note to keep checking in on them. Fireworks from those two were the last thing the event needed.

"LADIES AND GENTLEMEN, thank you for making time to attend this fundrai…"

Rachel started saying when the microphone got cut off. She was standing in the middle of the runway, in clear view of all the guests. She turned to look at the sound engineer who was frantically checking his cables. He gave her the thumbs up and she turned back to her guests with a smile.

"Sorry about that. They say don't tell a printer or microphone that you need them to work urgently, that's when they start misbehaving," she joked, her guests joining in with a good laugh.

"As I was saying, thank you very much for attending this event. And now I would like you to take your seats. We have a great fashion show for you. So get comfortable and enjoy!"

The fashion show was a good experience for everyone, with the models strutting their stuff with great confidence. No one was stiff or tense, possibly because it wasn't a competition. Everyone seemed to have discovered the secret to having fun, and they ran with it. Mrs. Owens herself pranced around looking her best self. Celia resolved that in her golden years, she would live her best life just like Mrs. Owens was. Great cheers came from the guests, a good sign that they had warmed up to the evening.

As she enjoyed the sight, Celia noticed Joshua make his way towards the entrance. He was slightly disheveled, his coat unbuttoned and his tie hanging loose. His face was stern and cold, clearly not in the mood to talk to anyone. He moved quickly through the crowd and then left. She wasn't sure if he had just gone to get some air. When she looked around for Frank, she couldn't spot him.

Celia managed to do quick touch-ups in between the clothes

changes and reemerged just as the models did their final lap of honor. They lined up along the backdrop, and Rachel appeared, walking the full length of the runway similar to the models. As she did this, the guests stood up to give a standing ovation. Rachel beamed with a warm smile as she bowed in appreciation.

"Thank you, thank you very much," Rachel began. "Can you give a big round of applause to our models as well," she requested as she turned to the models. They, too, bowed in appreciation as they were showered with claps and whistles from the guests. Celia remembered her mother had asked her for an update, and she took out her phone to send a quick text.

"We are all very humbled by your support," Rachel went on. "We don't usually get this kind of reaction at our events so you have been very gracious guests, and we salute you! Please take a moment to…"

Rachel's voice got cut off again. Celia, still on her phone, kept typing until she heard a collective groan from the guests. She quickly looked up and wasn't able to see what was going on because everyone was on their feet, blocking her view. Instead of Rachel's voice, there were growing murmurs and shouts.

"Call an ambulance!" someone shouted.

Celia tore her way through the crowd towards the stage. When she got there, she realized that it wasn't the microphone that had been cut off. Sprawled out on stage, at an awkward angle after her collapse, lay the motionless body of Rachel Sablay.

5

"This is so sad. Really sad," Celia said, her voice cracking with emotion.

She was watching the paramedics attend to Rachel's body. The paramedics had confirmed her demise five minutes earlier, but Celia already knew this. She had managed to reach Rachel, and having checked her pulse, she knew she was gone. Despite the fact she had not known her well, she struggled to compose herself after that. She sought out Melanie, who was having it worse.

"I can't believe this is happening," Melanie whispered as she stood next to Celia.

"Same here. It's like a dream. It's all too surreal," Celia replied, putting one arm around her friend. "Hang in there. I can't believe it either, but I am here for you."

"Thanks, I really need that, because I don't know what to do next, or what I'll tell the board. Are the police here yet?" Melanie asked.

"Right on cue, there they are," Celia said as she saw several police officers walk by. Some went straight to where Rachel lay, while the rest started directing people where to stand. A senior police officer soon appeared on the stage. He was holding the microphone while wearing gloves.

"Good evening, everyone. I am Corporal Jeff Watson from the Sunshine Cove Police Department. This is an unfortunate incident and we urge you to remain calm. Our officers are all around this place and we request you to cooperate with them, because we will be doing short interviews with you. We kindly ask for your patience," he said. He then came down the stage.

Murmurs spread across the room. Celia turned and saw officers directing people to different corners of the large space.

"What does that mean?" Melanie asked.

"We are all witnesses, and they just want to get a record of what happened as part of their investigations," Celia replied.

"Two hundred interviews is a lot. We might be in for a long wait," Melanie said.

"I guess that's why they have already started," Celia replied.

Celia's gaze fell on the man in the tweed jacket. She had spotted him talking to Rachel earlier that night. A police officer was already interviewing him. Celia noticed that the man kept drying his eyes with a handkerchief as he spoke, clearly shaken.

"I wonder who that is," Celia whispered to herself.

"Excuse me, are you one of the organizers of the event?" a voice asked, interrupting her train of thought. She turned to find a policeman facing them. He held a small notebook in his hand, a pen at the ready.

"No, I am the librarian," Melanie replied, "I hired out the space to the organizer who is now… um… who is now gone."

"I know this must be difficult for you. However, I need to ask you some questions, I hope that is okay?" the officer politely said as he flipped a fresh page on his notebook.

Melanie nodded. The officer then cast his eyes on Celia.

"Kindly excuse us for a few minutes," he instructed her.

Celia looked at Melanie, concerned about her friend's wellbeing.

"It's fine, I can handle it," Melanie replied.

"Okay. If you need anything, I'll be just five steps away," Celia said. Indeed, she took five steps back. She wanted to keep an eye on Melanie and the events elsewhere at the same time.

EYEBROWS AND EVIL LOOKS

Apart from the police and paramedics, Celia noticed that everyone was in a state of shock at what had just happened. Some were in tears. Others stood shaking their heads in disbelief. A few people chatted. Celia's eyes went back to the group next to Rachel's body. Rachel's husband Frank was standing there looking disheveled as a police officer interviewed him.

Celia studied him, noting that he did not look emotionally shaken.

She thought that maybe he was still in shock, trying to grasp what had just happened. Was he numbed by the anger from the argument he had had earlier with his wife? She couldn't tell. Celia's eyes turned to another part of the space where the police were setting up three tables. She soon saw guests line up in front of the tables, a clear strategy to make the interviews move along smoother, and hopefully they would all be getting home sooner. Just then, out of the corner of her eye, a tall familiar figure approached.

"We need to stop meeting like this," Detective Bill Koloane said.

Celia managed a smile. He wore a long brown jacket and had his bald head shone under the overhead light. She found him attractive for a reason she did not fully understand, although he was a police detective. Seeing him also brought to her another memory, which she had hoped to forget. He reminded her of the death of Samantha Bradley, which happened months earlier. A former high school mate, she was poisoned at a party that Celia had the misfortune of attending. Crossing her fingers, Celia prayed that this wasn't a bad omen for what had just happened to Rachel.

"Detective Koloane. Why am I not surprised?" she replied.

"Duty calls, as usual. This is a sad evening."

She sighed, "Yes. Life is short."

"How are you coping?" Detective Koloane asked.

"I am okay, sort of. A little shaken. A sudden death always makes you pause and think. I was helping with the models. I barely knew her. But I liked her strong desire to give back to the community."

"That's a noble mission that didn't need to end like this. Did you see what happened?"

"Sorry, is this my interview now?" she asked, noting that he wasn't writing anything down.

He smiled. "No, it's not. It's a friend checking on a friend. Once the officer is done with Melanie, he'll attend to you."

"Good to know... and thank you for your concern," she replied. His sincerity warmed her heart.

"I also don't want to spook you, but we first met when someone else had died," he reminded her.

Celia had hoped he wouldn't bring it up.

"Yes, I remember. I wish it were under different circumstances. I hope you are not here because..."

Detective Koloane got her hint and shook his head.

"Ah, no! No, it's too early to say. It looks like natural causes. We will have a better picture after the autopsy," he clarified.

There was a brief and awkward silence between them.

"All right! Let me get back to my people. Take care of yourself," he said, and walked away towards the stage.

Celia's eye caught sight of Melanie, who was walking back from her police interview. She was wiping tears from her eyes. Celia went and hugged her.

"How did it go?" Celia asked.

"Well, pretty straightforward. I just told them everything as I had seen it. She fell without warning, had no sign of illness earlier that day. There was nothing more to say."

"Are you okay?"

"Well, I am better now if that's any consolation," Melanie replied. Then she shook her head. "You know what? I am not actually. This was supposed to go well. This is such a tragedy, honestly! I can't imagine how Rachel's son will take it."

"Yeah. Her husband looks spaced out. I wonder what Joshua will do when he finds out," Celia said.

"Where is he?" Melanie asked.

"I don't know. I saw him leaving earlier in the night. I haven't seen him since," Celia replied.

Melanie frowned as her eyes focused on something behind Celia. "What do you think is going on over there?"

Celia turned and saw what was catching Melanie's attention. At one of the vendor tents was Sunglasses Woman - only she wasn't wearing sunglasses. She wore prescription glasses instead, which revealed her intense, piercing eyes. Dressed in a knee-length evening dress which had a simple flower pattern, she was talking to a man in animated fashion as he tried to calm her down. She pulled out a carton from under her presentation table and started placing in it the health food products she had on display. The man moved to stop her, but she resisted. Melanie walked towards them, with Celia behind her.

"Is everything all right here?" Melanie asked.

The man and Sunglasses Woman turned to look at Melanie.

"Everything is fine. We are just..." the man started.

"Taking away the product," Melanie finished his sentence, turning to the lady, "Dani, is he bothering you?"

Dani glared at the man, and then said, "No, I was just preventing him from doing that."

The man shook his head and sighed.

"I think she's saying you need to leave her alone," Melanie told him.

"I am not bothering her! We are business partners and I am here to help her," the man replied firmly.

"But I already told you I can handle this on my own, Martin! You don't have to be here," Dani said as she placed more of her products into the carton. Even in her anger, she was arranging them carefully, Celia observed.

"I do, because the cops told you not to touch your products! Remember that?" the man protested.

"Yeah, but I am done with my police interview, no? I need to leave this place," Dani retorted without stopping.

"Okay, you win!" Martin replied, stepping back with his arms folded over his chest in frustration.

"Did the police tell you that?" Celia asked Dani.

"Yes, but that was before the interview. I presume once that's done I can go," Dani replied.

"Hmm. If that is the case, I am afraid that Martin is right," Celia said.

"Thank you! Can you please talk some sense into her?" Martin said.

"What on earth are you talking about? They are my products. I have to use them tomorrow for another business transaction," Dani replied.

"I think it will be best if you leave them where they are. The police need them for their investigations. Trust me, you will find them intact once the police are done," Celia explained. She was tempted to say she was speaking from personal experience, but she was still determined to push the memory of Samantha's death to the back of her mind.

"When will that be?" Dani asked.

"Most likely tomorrow. You just have to be patient," Celia said calmly. Dani paused, thinking.

Melanie moved towards her.

"Dani, remember that I'm the librarian. I run this place. As soon as the police are done collecting evidence, I'll call you to come and pick them up."

As Melanie convinced Dani, Celia noticed to her right the form of Mrs. Owens. She was talking to someone hidden from view by another small group. When the group moved, Celia was able to see who Mrs. Owens was talking to, and it was the last thing Melanie needed. Mrs. Owens was talking to a female news reporter, who was accompanied by a cameraman behind her.

"Hey, Mel. Give me a moment, I'll be back," Celia said as she moved through the small groups towards Mrs. Owens.

"This is so terrible! This beautiful young lady invited me to my very first fashion show. You see this beautiful outfit I am wearing?" Mrs. Owens said with great conviction. "It was such a beautiful night. Everything was going so well. This is a terrible loss!"

"And did you see anything backstage that was suspicious?" the reporter asked, pushing the large branded microphone towards Mrs. Owens.

"Well, I didn't see anything crazy. Some girls were spreading some crazy rumor that Rachel and her husband had a big fight. But if it was a big fight, why didn't I hear about it?"

"Are you saying that her husband might have...?" the reporter asked. Celia cut her off, grabbing the reporter's microphone.

"Hey, what are you doing?" the reporter shouted.

"The interview is over. Kindly leave the premises," Celia ordered as she pushed back the reporter and her cameraman. The camera lens turned towards her, and Celia promptly covered the screen with her hand.

"You can't harass my cameraman!" the reporter complained.

"And you can't harass my guests! Please leave the premises!" Celia said with authority. The reporter hesitated.

"Stop filming, Andy," she said to her cameraman.

"Oh, come on...," the cameraman replied.

"Just do it," the reporter insisted. He stopped recording and lowered his camera to his side.

"You can't kill a story," the reporter said.

"Please don't threaten me, otherwise we will take you to court!" Celia said, surprised at her own courage. The reporter then turned on her heel and they both left.

Celia turned back to find Mrs. Owens holding her head in her hands.

"What have I done?" Mrs. Owens asked.

"It's not your fault. It was only a matter of time before the circus comes to town," Celia reassured her.

Yet, even as she said this, Celia feared the worst.

6

Celia looked for Mrs. Owens in the crowd, keen to give her a ride home to ensure she was safe. Two hours later, the police had finally allowed the guests to go home. Celia knew that her mother would never forgive her if she left their family friend alone at that hour.

Mrs. Owens was tired but lively when Celia dropped her off.

"You know I am way too old to be getting home at this hour," Mrs. Owens said with a chuckle.

"I am just glad you are able to sleep in your own bed after the night we've had," Celia said.

"Do you want to stay on? I have some pie we can eat together," Mrs. Owens offered.

"No, let me be getting home now. Mother will be a little worried," Celia replied, "Oh, and please don't tell her about Rachel's death."

"Why not?"

"I want to share it at a better time, just not tonight," Celia said.

"Fair enough. Have a good night!" Mrs. Owens said as she walked to her front door. Celia waited until she saw her get into the house before leaving.

She drove into her mother's driveway some minutes before

midnight, exhausted. She unlocked and opened the main door slowly, just in case her kids were asleep. Once inside, she switched on the lamp to keep the light low, and threw herself on the couch.

The hallway light came on as her mother Audrey emerged dressed in pajamas.

"Hey Cece. How was it?"

"It was a busy night," Celia replied, "Are the boys asleep?"

"Yes, of course. They hit the sack at nine just as you asked. No video games in sight," her mother replied. "You managed to get some new clients?"

"Not really. There was a lot going on. With these events, you win some, you lose some," Celia replied, careful not to hint at anything about Rachel's death.

"Would you like some food? I made some roast chicken and pasta for dinner," she proposed.

"Yeah, that would be nice. Thanks," she replied with a smile.

"All right, I'll be with you in five minutes," she said as she headed to the kitchen.

Celia felt the drowsy pull of sleep inviting her to shut her eyes and call it a day, but she could also feel the pangs of hunger beating a loud symphony in her belly. Since she didn't want to wake up in the middle of the night hungry, she was going to wait for those five minutes.

Audrey came back to the living room and pulled the coffee table closer to where Celia was.

"I always used to tell you that it's not good to eat dinner late. It messes with your system," Audrey said.

"And with your waist," Celia added. They laughed.

"That too," Audrey replied. She returned to the kitchen and came back with a hot plate of food and some fresh orange juice.

"I'll fix you some hot tea if you want," she offered.

"No, I'll be fine. Thank you, Mom, you are the best," she replied, digging into the meal. As soon as she took the first mouthful, she realized just how hungry she was. She bulldozed her way through the meal in less than ten minutes, to her mother's surprise.

"They must have rationed the snacks there, huh?" Audrey said in jest.

Celia leaned back into the couch to get more comfortable.

"It happens sometimes. That meal was heavenly. I appreciate you," she replied.

"Do you appreciate me enough to tell me the truth?" Audrey asked.

Celia sat up again, wondering what her mother was getting at.

"Tell me what happened at the event," Audrey said.

"How did you find out? Was it on the news?" Celia asked, hoping the reporter had not made good on her threat.

Her mother shook her head.

"Christine called me about twenty minutes before you got here."

Of course, it had to be Mrs. Owens, Celia thought. Her request for silence had clearly gone unheeded.

"I didn't want to worry you," Celia said.

"I know that. But I would have still found out anyway," her mother replied.

"To be fair, I wanted to tell you tomorrow."

"Now that I already know, was it a murder?" Audrey asked.

"No, it looks like natural causes."

"I see," Audrey said, "My prayers go out to the family."

"Same here. I am sorry for keeping it from you. Can I ask a favor?"

Her mother nodded.

"I need to help Melanie get the library back in shape tomorrow. Can the kids stay here in the meantime?"

"Sure, I wouldn't have it any other way," Audrey said, "I want a favor too."

"I am listening."

"I want you to tell me what's going on with you upfront. I would have preferred to find out about this from you, Cece," Audrey said.

Celia nodded, "I'll do my best. Thank you for tonight."

As her mother left for the kitchen, Celia knew honoring her mother's request wouldn't be easy. Celia always shielded her family members from such information, and she wasn't sure she could shed

EYEBROWS AND EVIL LOOKS

off her protective nature. This thought kept playing on her mind until she dozed off.

However, Celia did not sleep much that night. She was up by four in the morning, still thinking about the previous night's events. It wasn't every day one witnessed the demise of someone they knew, and it had left an effect on her. She made herself some tea to calm her nerves. She dozed off again. Her son, John, gently tapping her shoulder, woke her up.

"Wake up, Mom!" he said to her as she opened her eyes.

"Hey champ," she replied.

"Can we go with you today?" he asked.

"Go where, son?"

"You told grandma you were going to take us to the library," he replied.

"Oh. Yes I did…" she started, knowing she had to give a careful answer, "And they made it look very cool and fun to hang out in. But they are fixing a few things first."

"What things are they fixing?"

Celia paused for a moment, thinking of the best way not to lie.

"They recently had an event there, and they had to rearrange things. So now they will arrange things back to how they were. Then when they are ready, I'll take you there. Okay?"

John nodded, satisfied. He ran out of the room with a spring in his step as Celia got out of bed.

She stayed indoors for most of the morning, spending some time with the boys. She briefly kept an eye on the television news, but other than a short announcement that a woman had collapsed at the library, she saw no sensational report. She kept the television on mute to avoid distracting the boys as she helped them work on a large jigsaw puzzle. Her mother had bought quite a big one, such that it covered a good portion of the living room carpet. It was a puzzle of a beachfront with a yacht on it. The boys had solved a quarter of the puzzle, and she proposed to help them get to the halfway point. This did not happen. In between their laughs and giggles as they worked together, she got a text from Melanie. She wanted Celia to join her at the library. Even though Melanie's text was brief, she could sense an urgency to it. She disliked the fact that something was pulling her once again away from her boys. She excused herself and drove to the library.

There were four grim-faced police officers in uniform near the entrance of the event space.

One of them stopped her from walking in.

"Excuse me, staff and detectives only," he said.

"I was working here last night," Celia said.

"Who do you work with?"

"Melanie Dawes. I am here to help her with the library situation," Celia replied.

After one of them went to confirm with Melanie, she was let in.

As she walked into the library, Celia had to find her way around crime-scene tape that surrounded the space. The place still looked disorganized, with rearranged chairs and tables. There was even some turned over furniture.

She found Melanie in the company of three detectives, led by Detective Bill Koloane. Other forensic detectives were powdering up pieces of evidence and checking every room.

Celia waited as Melanie listened to Detective Koloane explaining something that Celia couldn't quite hear. He occasionally glanced at Celia, but never showed any visible reaction to her arrival. Five minutes later, Melanie walked to Celia.

"Don't tell me it's what I think it is," Celia said.

Melanie sighed. "It is, unfortunately."

"The autopsy told them?" Celia asked. Melanie nodded.

Celia continued, "How did they do it so fast?"

"Apparently the pathologist was having a light night, so he started as soon as he received her."

"Wouldn't the family have wanted to be there?"

"Frank was there. He gave the go-ahead. He wanted it done fast too."

Celia was surprised. "Why did Frank want the autopsy done so fast?"

"Maybe he wants a quick funeral. I don't know," Melanie replied.

"So what did they find?" Celia asked.

"She was poisoned, apparently," Melanie replied.

"Poisoned? Are you serious?" Celia exclaimed. Her fears were coming true, "How did they do it?"

"He wouldn't tell me," Melanie replied.

"Wow. Crazy."

"Yeah. So you will give me a ride to the police station in a few minutes?"

"Why, are you a suspect?"

"We all are, Celia. You too. They are going to interrogate everyone afresh, so we are going to go there, eventually."

Sure enough, less than ten minutes later, Celia was driving to the station with Melanie in the passenger seat.

At the station, they sat in separate interrogation rooms. Two detectives attended to Celia; a Detective Dennis Browie and the familiar Detective Bill Koloane, who walked in carrying a cup of steaming coffee.

"Want one?" he asked, pointing at his cup.

"No thank you," Celia replied.

"So, we meet yet again, Celia Dube," Detective Koloane said. She did not know how to respond, nor was she eager to acknowledge this.

"Is there anything you would like to add to the statement you gave us about what happened that night?" he asked.

Celia thought for a moment before replying, "No, I think I told you everything."

"How long did you know Rachel Sablay?"

"Just two days. We met at the library and she asked if I could help out in the charity event," Celia replied.

Bill frowned.

"And did you see anything unusual that night? Think carefully."

Celia thought for a moment, flashing back on the events of the night. She did not think there was anything she had not told them.

"No, I didn't see anything. If I did, you know I wouldn't hold back," she replied.

"Fair enough," Detective Koloane said, closing his notebook and rising up from his seat, "you can go now."

"What do you have on the case?" she asked.

"You know I can't share any insight on the evidence we may have," he replied.

"At least tell me how she died."

"She was poisoned. I can't tell you what poison it is just yet. But that's what happened."

"And how was it administered?"

Detective Koloane hesitated and said, "Sorry, I can't disclose that right now."

Celia understood. When she walked out, she couldn't see Melanie. She sat on the bench in the lobby, waiting for her friend to emerge from her interrogation. She started studying arrested suspects being booked.

It was then that she saw Frank Sablay walking in. He headed right to the bench and sat next to her. He did not seem to remember her, because he did not greet her. He just sat there, staring at the wall ahead of him. He looked ruffled, with his hair slightly unkempt and his beard neglected. Celia deduced he had not slept very well the previous night.

"Mr. Sablay?"

He turned to look at her, "Yes?"

"I'm Celia Dube. We met at the charity event at the library. I'm so sorry for your loss,"

He shrugged. "I remember you now. I don't know what to say to that. I'm sorry too."

"Do you know how she died?"

"I guess I am about to find out," he replied, and with that he got up. Detective Koloane stood next to the door of the interrogation room. Frank walked in and Bill stood at the door for a moment looking at Celia. He walked over to her.

"What?" she asked.

"Don't do it," Bill said.

"Do what?"

"Don't play detective on this one. It won't end well," he said firmly, then went back to the room. The door slammed shut, and Celia wondered what he meant by that.

7

"I was in there for only five minutes. They kept you there for an entire hour, Melanie! My goodness, what did they want to know?" Celia exclaimed.

"Well, everything that happened. Minute by minute, everything I did since Rachel came to check out the place. But they were digging deeper, much deeper than the first interview. You could tell they were fishing for something," Melanie said.

They sat in a coffee house two streets from the police station. It was half-full, and ideal for conversation. They had just received their order - two apple pies and coffees.

"They were looking for a motive. A reason why someone would kill her. Or if you saw her killer," Celia said.

Melanie nodded. "Yeah, that and to see if there were any suspicious things that happened."

"What suspicious things?"

"Maybe suspicious things that killers do? I can't tell for sure. You know, for some reason today I can't come up with a conspiracy theory," Melanie replied. They both smiled.

Celia bit into her apple pie. It was a little drier than she liked, but still quite tasty. She enjoyed it as Melanie dug into hers.

"I still can't believe that I wasn't grilled as much as you," Celia said.

"You barely knew her."

"Yeah. Or maybe Detective Koloane already knows who his persons of interest are,' Celia said.

"I don't know about that. Sometimes, as they were questioning, it felt like they hadn't done their homework. But I hope they come up with a short list," Melanie replied.

"One of them could be Frank, her husband. After the argument we witnessed, those two didn't seem like best of friends, you know," Celia said.

"They will always look at the husband first. Did he look like… well, you know…," Melanie asked awkwardly, as if hinting at something.

"Like a killer?" Celia asked.

Melanie nodded.

Celia shrugged and continued, "No one looks like a killer, Melanie. Actually, I got that wrong. Some people definitely look like killers! Like that fellow Devreaux who came to the bay two years ago. He stayed here for three months, living on his expensive boat and having parties. He was just a high-spending tourist, people thought. Until they arrested him as he was about to kill someone and then discovered he was a serial killer. He killed five people in those three months, and no one knew! Sunshine Cove had never had a serial killer."

"Until then!" Melanie interjected.

"Yeah, but he wasn't really from Sunshine Cove either, right? If you saw him at the time, you would realize he was a beast just by looking into his dead eyes. There was something creepy about them. On the other hand, Frank is your regular 'he-wouldn't-hurt-a-fly' kind of guy," Celia said.

"But Frank was having an argument with his wife in the parking lot. Who knows what used to happen when they were at home?" Melanie asked.

"Exactly. There is no proof. For all we know, it was just a small disagreement that we got to witness."

"You can't say that without a shadow of a doubt, right?" Melanie posed.

"No, I can't," Celia replied. Her friend had a point. She remembered the sight of Frank looking spaced out, not a tear in sight, right after Rachel died.

"Did he ever go close to the body?" Melanie asked.

"I don't remember seeing that. He did arrive a few minutes after she died," Celia said.

"Arrive from where?" Melanie asked.

Neither of them knew. Had he stayed away from the moment it happened, to make it less devastating for himself?

"There was a man I noticed, who had a tweed jacket. He spent a lot of time talking to Rachel. Do you know him?" Celia asked.

"Oh! That is Rachel's business partner, Tim de Sousa," Melanie replied.

"They seemed to have a great working relationship," Celia said, remembering that Rachel always looked livelier when talking to Tim that night.

"From the little I saw, they looked like good colleagues," Melanie replied.

"Hmm. You know, I find it strange that Joshua left so early that night," Celia said.

"Oh, yes! I forgot to tell the cops that. Did you tell them about it?" Melanie asked.

"No, I didn't actually," Celia said. "Hopefully, we won't regret it."

"Why did he leave?"

"He seemed like he was going to let off steam. Something or someone had upset him."

"But why would he leave his boss alone?" Melanie asked.

"Good question. Did they have an argument? Did they disagree, and he was sent away? Or did he decide to quit?"

They both paused for a moment to think about the various possibilities.

Melanie sighed. "I need this case to end soon. The longer it's out there, the more it might hurt the library," Melanie said.

"Fortunately, there's been no crazy news report so far," Celia reassured her. She had told Melanie about the brief argument with the reporter. It was still a concern.

"That was before we knew that it was a murder. Now, things might be different," Melanie replied.

"You are right. It's possible that they will report it anew. But I wouldn't worry about it," Celia said, smiling.

"Fingers crossed," Melanie said as she held up her crossed fingers.

"That's the spirit!" Celia exclaimed, matching her friend's gesture.

"Meanwhile, I have to keep the library closed for a few days until the police finish their work."

"As it should. By the way, did Dani come for her stuff?" Celia asked.

Melanie nodded, "She did, but the police still stopped her from taking anything. She wasn't happy."

"I hope she didn't cause a scene."

"She pretty much did. I got the impression she's living on the edge. Her inventory must be pretty stretched."

"Could be. Do you think that Rachel gave her the vendor tent to help her get more business? If she was, then that was a kind thing to do. It's sad that the night ended that way. Her health food products looked good," Celia said.

"Yeah, they did," Melanie said, "I have to head out now. Can you drop me off?"

"Since you paid for my coffee, why not?" Celia said.

After dropping Melanie at the library, Celia drove home. It was already getting close to sunset, and she wanted to get home early in time for dinner. When she arrived, she found Mrs. Owens in the living room.

"They were not letting up, Audrey! They were making me look like some criminal from that TV show about the murderers. What is it called again?" Mrs. Owens said animatedly.

"I don't know the show you are talking about. There are so many these days!" Audrey replied.

Mrs. Owens turned to look at Celia, who had just stepped into the room.

"Cece, what's the name of that TV show, the one where they catch murderers?" Mrs. Owens asked.

"What are you guys talking about?" Celia said as she sat on the couch.

"Christine just got back from the police station. She tells me it's now a murder. You know about this?" Audrey asked.

"Yes. Yes, I do. I found out this morning. I was at the police station earlier," Celia replied.

"And you didn't tell me?" Her mother asked.

"Well, I just got home to tell you, but at least Mrs. Owens has told you, right? I went to the station with Melanie. I was only questioned for five minutes," Celia replied.

"Five minutes? Then why was I there for half an hour and I barely knew her?" Mrs. Owens asked.

"Mrs. Owens, you are one of the best storytellers in Sunshine Cove! Maybe the detectives did not want you to leave!" Celia said. Mrs. Owens laughed.

"You know what? You are right! They even brought me ginger tea and cookies. Did you get that?" Mrs. Owens asked.

"I would never get that. That's reserved for special guests like you," Celia teased.

Although the tone of the conversation had grown lighter, Celia knew her mother was troubled. Audrey excused herself to go to the kitchen. Keen to check on her, Celia headed to the kitchen too.

Her mother was prepping some meat broth and salad for dinner.

"Need some help with that?" Celia asked.

"Yeah. But first, tell me what's really going on," her mother said.

"What do you mean?"

"Why is it that you always seem to find yourself in places where murders take place?"

"This is only the second time it's happening, Mom. I meet many people. There's bound to be some repeat happenings," Celia said.

"Repeat happenings? Like what?" Audrey asked.

"Like I usually meet a conman or woman once a week without fail.

EYEBROWS AND EVIL LOOKS

They are out there posing as clients or investors, but I never tell you about them, right?"

"A con is not a murder, Cece," Audrey said firmly.

"And I don't find myself close to a murder every week, Mom. So this is actually an exception."

Her mother sighed.

"I just don't like the sound of it."

"It will be fine. I'll be checking in on Melanie from time to time until this blows over. She needs some support," Celia replied.

"You are not going to do anything crazy, are you?" Audrey asked.

"Nothing crazy, Mom. Come," Celia replied as she opened her arms for an embrace. She hugged her mother tight.

"Oh my God!" a shout came from the living room.

Celia and Audrey rushed there, worried.

Mrs. Owens stood on her own in the middle of the living room, staring at the television.

"What?" Celia asked.

Mrs. Owens simply pointed at the screen.

Playing on the screen was the interview of Mrs. Owens at the library. She spoke just as she had spoken that evening, and then Celia saw her worst fears materialize.

She appeared on screen, blocking off Mrs. Owens behind her and pushing back the reporters. Although her face appeared briefly, she looked angry and aggressive. At that moment, her hand came up to the screen and blocked it.

"Police say what was once thought to be death by natural causes is now a murder investigation. Are we witnessing an attempted cover up by the library management?" the reporter's dramatic voice filled the living room.

Celia's heart sunk.

8

Early the next morning, Celia got a call from Melanie.

"We need to talk!" Melanie said.

"You watched it?" Celia asked.

"No! But I woke up to so many text messages and missed calls, because I had decided to ignore the news. I had gone to bed early. What are we going to do?"

"Are you still home or heading to the library?" Celia asked.

"I am heading to the library. I need to be there," Melanie replied.

"All right, I'll meet you there as soon as I can," Celia told her.

Celia took a quick shower and freshened up. She was picking up her car keys from the couch when her mother came to her.

"Where are you headed?"

"To check on a client," Celia lied.

"Are you going to be spending another night here?" Audrey asked.

Celia realized the past two days had been so long that she kept returning to the house late each night. Going back to her place at those hours was impossible. It wasn't a problem, but she always tried to keep it from happening often.

"No, tonight I'll go to the house. I want to make sure everything is okay there."

"And the boys?"

"We can ask them in the evening when I am back. I want them to enjoy their holiday. See ya!"

As Celia drove while eating a sandwich her mother had quickly made for her, she reflected on the previous night. The news reports had been crazy, as she had feared, trying to portray the guests at the event as possible accomplices in a murder investigation. Although you couldn't see her face for too long on screen, she feared that someone who knew her might have recognized her. There had been a few text messages sent to her the previous night, asking her what was going on. Lies travel faster than the truth, and she hoped that this wasn't going to be the case, especially after she blocked off the camera with her hand.

She was more worried about Mrs. Owens, who was feeling guilty about doing the interview. It wasn't a long interview, and she had not said anything controversial. The issue was the news network's context was all wrong and thus colored Mrs. Owens' remarks in a bad light. She had left for her home in low spirits, and Celia felt sad for her. She had called her that morning to cheer her up and reassure her, but she knew it wouldn't be easy for a woman who wore her heart on her sleeve. It would be an interesting few days to come.

When Celia arrived, she was surprised to find Tim de Sousa, Rachel's business partner, standing in the library lobby. He was a tall man dressed in a pinstripe suit. He was talking on the phone as Melanie stood next to him. When Melanie saw Celia, she walked over to her.

"Thank you for coming," Melanie said.

"No worries. I am sorry about last night. How are you doing?" Celia asked.

"Let's talk about it over another apple pie. I know a place," she said with a wink.

"So, why is he here?" she asked, gesturing towards Tim.

"He says he's here to clear up any loose ends around the hiring of the venue, but maybe you can help me judge if there's more to it," she replied.

They walked over to Tim, who had hung up.

"Tim, this is Celia Dube, a friend of mine who was doing the makeup for the models."

"Hello. I am Tim de Sousa, Rachel's business partner," he said in a deep voice. His handshake was firm, and Celia felt taking charge of things came naturally to him, including simple conversations. "Rachel said good things about you."

"She did? After knowing me for only twenty-four hours?" Celia asked, puzzled.

"She was an awesome business partner," he said, "with a great eye for detail. She kept me updated on her plans for the event, so your name came up."

"Glad to hear I was able to make a positive impression while she was still with us," Celia replied, genuinely grateful.

They walked towards the event space. There were workers already taking out the hired seating and the stage. Crime scene tape was still visible.

"How was she as a business partner?" Celia asked.

"She's one of the best marketers and event organizers in town. I mean, she was," he said, pained by the correction he had to make. "We had worked for five years on this, building it and making it bigger."

"I saw you that night, talking together. I just didn't know who you were then."

"Rachel was taking the lead on this one. I came to back her up."

"How did you react when you saw her collapse?" Melanie asked.

Tim paused for a moment.

"I did not believe it at first. I thought she just tripped on her heel or lost her balance or something. I just rushed to her. Then when it was clear she was gone, I still did not believe it. I thought it was a dream. A bad dream," Tim said, his voice an octave lower for the first time.

Celia remembered him trying to give first aid to Rachel.

"About Joshua, Rachel's assistant. He left early that night. Do you know why?" she asked.

Tim shook his head.

"No, I did not even notice that he wasn't around. Joshua loves working behind the scenes. He sometimes keeps a low profile during events, so I hardly see him. I haven't spoken much to Joshua since that night other than checking on him."

"Oh. So he's okay?" Celia asked, curiosity getting the better of her.

"Well, I wouldn't say he's okay. He took the news pretty badly. He was actually supposed to be here with me today to sort things out, but he's still not in the right headspace. I let him stay home," Tim replied.

"But is it normal for him to leave events that early?"

"No, he's always with Rachel. The only other time that had happened was when he had the flu, and couldn't handle things. So she let him go. It's possible he was unwell."

"And he got along well with Rachel," Melanie said.

"Yeah, they had a very good working relationship. Her personal assistants tend to leave after a short period. Not Joshua. He stuck in for two years and was brilliant for us."

"Why did her assistants keep leaving?" Celia asked.

"Well, sometimes she can be very demanding. I used to call her the perfectionist, because she liked things done in a certain way. She can chase you out of town if you mess with her," he replied.

"We were at the police station yesterday after they said it was a murder investigation. I assume they called you in too?" Celia asked.

"Yes, last evening. That is what prompted me to come here this early. I really want to make sure that her family and her interests are taken care of, even though she isn't with us anymore. That's what she would have wanted."

"I hope they get a lead soon," Melanie remarked.

Tim forced a smile. "Same here. Did you two see anything odd that night?"

"No, other than Joshua leaving early, we didn't see anything unusual. It was promising to be a great night," Celia replied.

"It truly was," Tim agreed, "We had already raised quite a bit of money. Since her passing, more donations have come in through our office, more than we could have ever imagined. I hate to say it, but her loss is going to enable us to raise our biggest charity donation ever."

Tim got lost in his thoughts as he watched the workers carry out some more chairs. Celia was glad the event had raised a sizeable donation, but was equally sad about the circumstances that caused it.

"So, what information do you need from my agreement with Rachel?" Melanie asked.

Tim did not respond immediately. Melanie gently touched his arm. "Tim?"

Startled, he turned to them.

"Sorry about that," he said.

"I was asking what information you need from me about my agreement with Rachel," Melanie asked again.

"You know what? Let me come back tomorrow. I thought I was ready to be here, but I think I need to clear my head a bit," he replied. He turned around to leave when Celia threw in one last question.

"Sorry to push you, but do you think Rachel had any enemies?"

He paused.

"It's a tough business, and Rachel did not become one of the best by accident. She did not crush people from what I know, but there will be a few jealous people, I am sure."

"Does any name spring to mind?"

"Like I told the police, I don't think she really had enemies. But she had disagreements with a few people."

Celia could tell he was trying as much as possible not to name anyone.

"Did any of them attend the event?" she prodded.

He paused for a moment before responding.

"Yes. She had been having issues with a vendor who was here that night. Two vendors, actually. Martin and Dani. That is all I can say. Melanie, see you tomorrow."

With that, Tim walked off. Celia looked at Melanie. They both nodded in agreement.

It was time to find the Sunglasses Woman.

9

Celia read the text message with a smile on her face.

Cece, what happened to the face cream you were to drop at my house? I need to reduce breakouts. Add that new eyeliner too. Thanks. Don't make me have to call your mother.

Mrs. Owens did not miss an opportunity to be dramatic, she thought.

After Tim had left, Celia and Melanie had talked about Dani. Why did Rachel bring her to the event, knowing they did not get along well? Had they buried the hatchet, thus making it easy for them to work together again? They needed answers to these questions that only Dani could give. Strangely, she had not come for her health food products. When Melanie tried calling her, the call kept going to Dani's voicemail. Melanie sent a text instead, hoping that Dani would turn up during the day.

They then discussed what to do about the news reports. They agreed the best thing to do was to tell the truth, but limit any interactions with reporters.

"I don't want to do any interviews. I'll just draft a statement to tell the truth about the situation," Melanie said, and Celia agreed with this idea. Celia left soon afterwards to attend to a few client visits. She had an accumulated backlog of deliveries because of the time lost since the event and its aftermath. Now that Mrs. Owens had sent a text, Celia needed to restock. There were some bottles of face cream at her house, so that's where she headed.

She parked in her driveway, feeling a little strange because she had not been there for two days. She prayed no suspicious characters had noticed there was no one home, but she knew she was being a little too careful. She had installed a home security system with cameras since an attempted break in some months ago. In case someone tried to access the house while she was away, the security company got the alarm within seconds, and a team came in immediately. She would have also received a phone alert via their app. Just for good measure, a patrol vehicle kept base near her home, so she knew there was added security. This did not stop her from checking the CCTV camera footage stored on her home computer as she freshened up and packed more products for the afternoon delivery.

The face cream Mrs. Owens wanted was a good one, but Celia sometimes thought the products Mrs. Owens bought were more to appease her insecurities that come with age. She was still a beautiful woman, but she needed the actual reminder sometimes. Celia understood this and kept it in mind when she arrived at Mrs. Owens' house.

"You know, this cream is the perfect antidote for my spots. It adds a glow to my skin. Then that eyeliner can make people notice my eyes," Mrs. Owens said as she took the cream and applied it on her cheeks.

"Your eyes are one of your best features," Celia replied.

"You, young lady, know the secret to a woman's beauty. Her eyes are a treasure! They will tell you a thousand tales, they will make you swim across oceans, they will warm your heart and they will strengthen your frame. A woman's eyes are powerful," Mrs. Owens said animatedly.

"More powerful than her tongue?"

"More beautiful than her tongue, but not more powerful. The tongue is the ultimate weapon, with the power of life and death. Pass me the eyeliner."

Celia gave it to her. Mrs. Owens stood in front of her mirror, carefully thickening her eyebrows.

"See that?" Mrs. Owens turned to Celia, panning her face in each direction for effect. "I can already feel the glow. Do I look different?"

"Mrs. Owens, you always look beautiful," Celia reassured her.

"But I want to look different. I want to walk in the streets and have people think I am someone else," Mrs. Owens insisted.

Celia's eyes widened.

"Are you trying to disguise yourself?" Celia asked.

At this point Mrs. Owens was dabbing her face with some face powder.

"You know, an old woman like me can't wear a mustache or beard. Doing this is one of the ways to transform yourself."

Celia sighed. She knew this was about the news story. "Stop worrying about what people think. Just block it off," she said.

Mrs. Owens turned to Celia, "Cece, do you know how many phone calls and text messages I have received since yesterday? Over one hundred of them."

"Sorry about that, but you know you can just mute your phone."

"No, I must check a message! If it comes into my phone, I need to see what it says."

"All right, fair enough. How many of those were negative messages?"

"I don't know, maybe five. Some were pretty nasty."

"But if the majority were good, positive ones, then that's good! Let us not focus on the negative while ignoring the positive ones. It ruins our day and mood."

Mrs. Owens did not reply. Celia moved to her, standing behind her so they could see each other in the mirror.

"You need to relax. It will go away before you know it. Just don't react to anything. Okay?" Celia said.

Mrs. Owens' tense shoulders relaxed a little.

"You know, I worry about the library too. It seems like I brought all this negative publicity to them," Mrs. Owens said.

"It was already in the news before last night, remember?" Celia said.

"You know what I mean. Anyway, I have been thinking of doing something about it. That evening did not end the right way for any of us. I want us to do something that will bring back the joy into the place. The way it's supposed to be," Mrs. Owens said passionately.

"Wait, what crazy idea do you have?" Celia asked.

"The word is creative, Cece. I have a creative idea. Why don't we invite back all the models, but now make it more family-friendly? Then have a photographer take all our pictures in our fancy outfits, with all of us smiling?"

"You mean have a photoshoot?"

"Yes! A photoshoot on a sunny afternoon at the library. How about that?"

Celia smiled. "It isn't a bad idea but…"

Mrs. Owen was already out of the room, returning with a colorful outfit and a makeup set she had bought from Celia.

"I am already getting ready with my outfit and makeup. I suggest you do the same."

"As a model?" Celia asked. Mrs. Owens nodded. Celia laughed and turned towards the door.

"That's my cue to leave," she said.

"That's your cue to get that outfit ready. I am making scarves for this. Which color are you going with?" Mrs. Owens asked.

"I'll think about it, Mrs. Owens!" Celia said, smiling as she tried to get away.

"Orange it is! I'll get on with it as soon as possible. I'll be in touch with the dates and everything," Mrs. Owens exclaimed.

Celia found herself at the local supermarket, buying supplies for her mother's and her own house. They would usually shop together on such runs, but today she wanted to make up time. She also wanted to resupply her mother, whose supplies had run low since she had to host Celia's sons.

She was rolling a cart down the aisle when she almost bumped into another cart that suddenly appeared.

"Sorry, sorry about that," the man said to her. She recognized him —it was Frank Sablay.

"It's okay, Mr. Sablay."

She saw him smile for the first time since they met.

"We keep meeting in the unlikeliest of places. Are you stalking me?" Frank asked.

"Why would I do that, sir, considering we are all under investigation?" she replied.

She noted he looked polished this time. His outfit, a blue formal shirt with dark trousers and black shoes, was trimmer and he had a fresh haircut. He looked calm - maybe a bit too calm for someone who just lost his wife. His trolley was full of household goods and some snacks for a young child.

They walked down the aisle, him in the lead cart as she followed and chatted him up.

"How are you coping?" she asked.

"A day at a time. My focus is on taking care of our son."

"How old is he?"

"Six." Celia felt for him, remembering how her own sons had to deal with the loss of their father.

"I lost my husband some years ago. It wasn't easy to get my two sons to understand it as they were so young. But love always wins," she encouraged him.

"Thank you, and sorry for your loss. Our son means the world to us. We did not have a perfect marriage. You saw that on the day of the event," Frank said, "we were more similar than we wanted to admit. Sometimes when you have two alphas under the same roof, fireworks are bound to fly. Our son was the glue that helped us through those rough times."

"But you loved her?"

"I love her and miss her. I never believed in having a grocery-shopping list. I would simply take anything off the shelf! She was the one always keeping me in check," Frank said fondly.

"I understand. Why were you arguing that day?"

He paused for a minute, as if unsure of what to say.

"Heck, even the police know it already! Why should I hold on to it? This is the thing; I suspected she was seeing someone. So I hired a private investigator to follow her."

"You hired someone to snoop on your wife?" asked a shocked Celia.

"It isn't as bad as it sounds. I did it because I had to be sure. I did not want assumptions to cloud my judgment," Frank defended himself.

"What did you find?" she asked.

"Nothing concrete," he said, "but Rachel and Joshua did spend a lot of time together. The investigator did not get any actual evidence, but the signs were there."

"Signs that?" Celia prodded.

"Signs that there might be something between the two of them. As I drove her to the fundraising event, I confronted her. I tried to be as casual as possible, but she got angry. Then you saw our public argument at the car park," he replied.

Celia nodded. She did not blame Rachel, because she might have done the same thing.

"Tell me something, did you talk to Joshua at the event? Did you confront him about it?"

"No, I didn't. Why?" Frank asked.

"Because a few minutes after the event started, Joshua left. He looked like he had just come from an argument with someone."

"I can assure you, same way I told the police, that I did not talk to or confront him that night. I had other things to take care of, such as the well-being of my wife. And I failed on that part," Frank started tearing up, and pulled away from her to stand in front of the cold fridge where all the milk, butter and yoghurt was lined up.

She waited for him to compose himself, unsure if he was putting on an act. She believed he did talk to Joshua that night; the young man did not leave early for nothing. It was undeniable that Frank had the strongest motive for being the cause of it. Was he hiding something?

10

"Are you ready to go?" Celia asked her two young sons as she packed the final bag of four beauty product orders she would deliver that day.

It was eight in the morning, and she had decided that they were all going to have breakfast at their favorite family restaurant. James and John came running into the room, giggling with excitement.

"Yep! We are ready, Mom!" James said.

"Fix your brother's collar first. No son of mine is going out like that," she replied.

James turned to John and fixed his collar. Her mother, Audrey, sauntered into the room wearing a sundress and sunhat.

"Am I coming too?" Audrey asked.

"Come on Mom, did you forget we talked about this yesterday?"

"You said 'tomorrow I am taking all of you for breakfast' without mentioning names. How am I supposed to be sure?"

Celia knew her mother was teasing, considering she was dressed to go out.

"Well, your name is on the list. Unless you want to bail out last minute?"

"Never!"

They all got into Celia's Subaru station wagon and left. The drive to the restaurant was light-hearted, with Audrey leading them in singing nursery rhymes all the way. By the time they got to the restaurant, their voices were almost hoarse, and they were starving.

Celia loved taking the kids to takeout breakfasts because it was something she and Trevor, her late husband, used to do. Trevor had started the tradition when they were dating. When he started going for more military missions, they became more important. Whenever he was home, they tried to do it as often as possible. Now that he was no longer there, her mother Audrey stepped in from time to time, and Celia was grateful for it. Regardless of the weather, those mornings were always magical.

They were all having fluffy pancakes with maple syrup, sausages and tea.

As always, the boys were eating with excitement, occasionally bobbing their heads in happiness.

"Come on, keep eating before it gets cold," Celia encouraged James.

"These boys will be done before it gets cold, trust me," Audrey said.

"How sure are you?" Celia asked.

"I watch them every morning," Audrey replied.

"Ah, I see. If they do, then I'll buy you a milkshake," Celia said.

"Can I get a milkshake too?" John asked. Celia realized she had set herself up, because James joined in by raising his hand in support.

"All right! If you finish up before the food gets cold, you all get a milkshake," Celia said with a smile.

Suddenly, the boys' eating speed increased.

"Don't choke, boys!" Audrey added, amused.

It was at this moment that Celia looked towards the large restaurant windows and spotted him. He was walking past the restaurant, and she could see him through the large windows.

"Ma, look after the boys. I'll be back in a minute," she said.

Before her mother could raise an objection, Celia was already at the door. She turned right, just in time to see him go round the corner. She jogged lightly, her flat shoes helping her reach the corner.

A few pedestrians were between them, but she could see him over their heads. She walked faster, closing the distance.

"Joshua! Joshua!"

Joshua turned to look back at who was calling him. Seeing it was Celia, he stopped.

"Hey...," Celia started, "I saw you walking down the street and I just had to stop and say hello."

"Saw me from where?" he asked.

"From the family restaurant you just passed. I'm having breakfast with my kids there."

"Oh, I see. Cool, nice seeing you," he said as he turned to leave.

"Wait! I wanted to talk to you a little," she said, reaching for his arm. He stopped again.

"What about?" Joshua asked.

"Look, I was at the event when Rachel died and it was traumatizing for all of us. I just wanted to say I am sorry for your loss. I can only imagine what you are going through right now," she said.

He paused for a moment, studying her.

"Thanks. It's not been easy," he finally replied.

"How are you managing?" she asked.

Joshua took a deep breath.

"My friends and family have been with me. It's the reality of life, right? I have had to stay away from the office though. It's a bit...," his voice trailed off.

"Too much?"

"Yeah."

Celia's mind raced. She needed to talk to him. Should she ask him back to the restaurant to have some coffee?

"Um, I know you are in a rush. Could you give me your number? Then I could call you and we can talk about the whole thing. You know, just to decompress. I think that could help you. Or both of us," Celia said politely.

Joshua thought for a moment and then nodded. They exchanged numbers.

"One more thing, that evening I saw you leave a little early. Was everything okay?" Celia asked. She just couldn't let him leave without answering the question that had troubled her for several days.

"Yeah, everything was fine," Joshua replied, almost as if he knew this question was coming, "I had to go to the office and troubleshoot something. But Rachel was with Tim, so there was no problem."

"Oh, okay. And who…" Celia did not get to finish.

"Hello Joshua!" A voice boomed from behind the young man. Joshua turned to meet the approaching Detective Bill Koloane, who wore his usual long coat and a beaming smile. "I thought you said you were a minute away?"

"Yes, I just stopped to talk to a friend," Joshua replied. Detective Koloane saw that it was Celia, but acted as if he did not know her.

"No problem. Shall we? She can catch up with you once we are done," the detective said. Joshua nodded, and walked past him, headed to where an unmarked police car was parked.

Bill walked up to Celia briefly.

"Celia, we talked about this," he said.

"I am not doing what you think I am doing," she replied.

"My experienced eyes tell me that you are doing exactly that," he insisted.

"Then I think you need to take your eyes to the optician as soon as possible," Celia replied. "You are still doing interviews, I see."

"Yes. It's the nature of the beast. Two hundred people are a big number, and some of them take their time to come to us, like Joshua."

Celia was curious, "Have you narrowed it down to any key suspects?"

He laughed.

"You never give up, do you? You know I can't tell you that. The most you can know is that all options are open."

"What if I help you speed it up?" she asked.

"If you have any information, then share it. So long as it isn't a false lead. That won't be good for you. It might suggest motive," the detective said.

Celia nodded knowingly.

"Is there something you want to tell me?" Detective Koloane asked.

"Maybe you could look a little closer at her husband, Frank," Celia said.

"You know the first key suspect is always the spouse, right?"

"I know. Just saying you should check him out a little more," she replied.

"All right. I'll keep it in mind. For now, please avoid getting into trouble."

"How do you suggest I do that?"

"Avoid places where people suddenly die."

She would have laughed if it were not such a serious time.

"I hear you. It isn't something I am proud of. Maybe a crystal ball will help," she replied.

"Only if they worked. Anyway, in case you want to talk about it some more, then maybe we should do this over a coffee date," he said with a smile.

"Oh. Are you asking me out?" Celia asked.

"I already did."

"Well, I can only consider that once I am officially off the suspects list. I wouldn't want to jeopardize the investigation," Celia replied.

"I hear you. One more thing you can do is not play detective. It's a dangerous thing to do."

With that, he turned and headed to his car.

When she got back to the restaurant, her sons had eaten their pancakes, leaving their plates clean.

"Mom, we finished them!" James shouted, holding up his plate.

Celia smiled, "Good boys! Now, which milkshakes do you want?"

"Since I won the bet, I already made the orders," Audrey said, smiling.

"Great! Thanks," Celia replied.

"What was that about?" her mother asked.

"Sorry, I saw a friend and had to say hi," Celia replied.

"Who is this friend, if I may ask?"

"His name is Joshua."

"Joshua, huh? Let's hope you get in touch," her mother said, winking.

"We exchanged numbers, so we'll see," Celia said, glad to have dodged that bullet.

As she watched her sons jump with excitement, the reality of Detective Koloane's warning hit her. He was right. She was walking in the dark, and that wasn't a safe thing to do. It wasn't just about her personal safety, but that of her loved ones. Yet, she also knew that she wasn't going to back off. There were too many unanswered questions, and she wasn't going to sit around doing nothing about it.

11

Celia, her mother and sons, stood in the restaurant car park, taking in the morning sun. They were waiting for a taxi that would take them home while Celia went to meet her clients. Celia stepped away from them, and when she was out of earshot, she called Melanie.

"Guess who I just met? Joshua himself," Celia said.

"Wow. Where?"

"On the street. He was heading for his interview with the police."

"How is he? Did he tell you anything?" Melanie asked.

"Not really. We exchanged numbers so I'll get in touch with him at some point."

"Can I join you?"

"No, I don't think that will be a good idea. He might withdraw if he feels we're bombarding him."

"All right, cool. Well, maybe as you see Joshua, I can see Tim. I am due to take an invoice to his office."

"For that, we can go together, if you want," Celia offered.

"Yeah, why not? I don't like the corporate types. Are you available this afternoon?"

"I have four product deliveries, but I should be done by three," Celia replied.

"Great! I'll set it up for around four. Pick me up as usual."

Celia smiled. She found it interesting that Melanie was getting very comfortable being picked up. It seemed like they were now two partner detectives. She shrugged off the image. She didn't fancy herself as the sleuthing type.

As she walked back, the taxi arrived. Celia said her goodbyes, promising to see them that evening. The deliveries went well, and she finished up earlier than she thought. She managed to grab a quick bite before heading to the library.

Melanie was already standing on the sidewalk as Celia arrived.

"Hop in," Celia said, opening the passenger door.

Melanie quickly got in and they were off.

"Your car smells like fries," Melanie said.

"Oh, I got some takeaway on the way here,' she replied.

"Where is it?"

"I took a few bites and put it in the back. I can't drive and eat at the same time," Celia replied.

Melanie had already reached for the backseat and came back with the pack of fries and spicy chicken on her lap. She started eating it.

"Thank you," Melanie said.

"That's my lunch, Mel! Please don't finish it," Celia said firmly.

"Got it," Melanie said. She took a few more fries and then returned the pack to the backseat.

Tim's office was located in Kruger City, the nearby commercial city that was a forty-minute drive from Sunshine Cove. Celia did not like driving there because the place was hectic. Traffic was getting more congested as they got closer, with the landscape changing from peaceful tree-lined residential homes to commercial buildings. She could see skyscrapers dominate the skyline while greenery was scarce. She disliked the city because of this. Even at the best of times, it never had that serene vibe she got in her sleepy suburb.

The building with Tim's office was right at the outer edge of the central business district. It rose six floors up, with an all-glass exterior. Getting off the lift, they were met by the plush reception of the Gamut Ventures office.

The smartly-dressed receptionist told them that Tim was in a meeting. As they waited in the luxurious waiting area, they were given cookies and peanuts to chew on. Celia was impressed by the service and the classy office interior. Rachel had worked hard to build her organization.

Tim's door opened and a middle-aged man in a suit stepped out, with Tim following behind. Tim was dressed in black trousers, a white shirt and suspenders.

"Thank you very much, Gary, I'm looking forward to seeing you again," Tim said, shaking the man's hand.

"Until next time," the man replied. He walked off with a steady gait.

Tim walked up to the two women.

"Hello ladies! Sorry to keep you waiting. Come this way please," Tim said, leading them into his office.

His office's most standout feature was the large windows that went round two office walls, from floor to ceiling. They brought in natural light and gave a stunning view of the city and the distant coastline.

"Please, have a seat," Tim offered.

The two ladies sat on comfortable seats facing Tim's large ornate desk. He sat on an expensive-looking leather office chair.

"Welcome to Gamut Ventures. This is the company that Rachel built and that I was fortunate to join and expand."

"Nice office," Celia said.

"Thanks. This was actually Rachel's office. Everything in here is to her taste and style, except maybe the photos of my wife on the desk."

"You already moved in?" Melanie asked.

"Not really. This is temporary as I put things in order. She had her hand in a lot of things and I came in to try to piece them together properly," he replied.

"She had great taste," Melanie said.

"And a great vision," he replied, "she was one of the most driven people I know. She was the face of the company. The brain and the grit in equal measure. That is one thing that made me want to partner with her when she approached me. I knew that I would be working with a hard worker."

"A brilliant organizer too," Melanie said.

"One of the best. We were going to set up one of the biggest beach festivals later this year. It will be a big task to pull it off - I am not as good with people as she was. I don't know how I'll replace her, honestly," Tim said with a worried look.

"You will pull through. Make it happen. It's what she would have wanted," Celia replied.

Melanie took out the invoice and handed it to Tim.

"There's a breakdown of the costs. I decided to give a discount," she said.

"No need for that, we are going to pay you in full," Tim replied.

"But…"

"No buts. We want to keep our word with our suppliers," he said.

Just then, the phone rang.

"Hello Janet, I told you to… What? Where?" Tim picked up the cordless phone and walked to his window, looking down towards the car park. "Yes, what's she doing here? Where is security? Tell that security guard to get his legs moving, now!"

Agitated, Tim turned to them.

"I am sorry, I have to attend to something downstairs," he said, walking out of the office. Celia and Melanie walked to the window and saw a woman standing next to a tow truck.

"That's Dani!" Melanie said.

"We need to see this for ourselves," Celia replied.

They rushed downstairs to find Dani in the car park with a tow truck. She was overseeing as the driver hooked the tow cable to a high-end BMW saloon car.

"What on earth do you think you are doing?" Tim shouted at Dani and the tow truck.

"Taking what's mine!" Dani replied.

"You can't do this, Dani. Stop it!" Tim said. He turned to the driver, "Hey, you there! Stop that right now or I'll call the cops on you."

The driver stopped, waiting for Dani's instruction. Tim was now standing in front of Dani.

"What are you doing here, Dani?" he asked firmly.

"You know exactly why I am here. I am here to take what's mine," she replied with venom.

"That car isn't yours. You know that," Tim said.

"Then how am I supposed to get my money back, now that Rachel is gone?"

"That was an agreement between you and her. This is a company vehicle."

"Oh, shut up with that broken record excuse! I had an agreement with this company. You owe me money, and today it's time to pay up."

She turned to the driver and motioned him to continue. Tim grabbed her hand and held it back.

"You want to assault me now, Tim? Right here, in front of witnesses? You want to assault me?" Dani shouted.

"That's not what I'm here for!" Tim replied.

"Let go of my arm, Tim. Let go of my arm!" Dani cried.

Celia moved forward.

"Let her go, Tim, please," Celia pleaded. Tim let go.

"I am going to sue you for that!" Dani shouted. Celia turned to her.

"Dani, please. Let's solve this in another way," Celia said. Dani gave Celia one of the most intense stares she had ever seen.

"What other way, huh? What other way? Do you even know what they have done to me? For two years, two years, they have given me the runaround about my money. Sitting up there in that fancy office while denying me and my kids my money! How do you expect me to feed my kids?" Dani ranted.

"I understand that you are upset but..."

"No, you don't understand. You don't understand!"

Dani saw Tim on his phone calling the police.

"Oh, so now you are calling the police, are you sure about that? Are you sure you want all this to hit the newspapers? Because it will," Dani warned.

Tim lowered his phone. Celia turned to Dani again.

"Then let me talk to him. I'll find a solution for you. What do they owe?" Celia asked.

"Go check the books. They know," Dani hissed.

"Please give him some time," Celia pleaded.

"I'm giving him forty-eight hours. Give me my money or we go to court. And trust me, Tim, you don't want me to go to court," Dani said. She motioned to the driver to pack the tow cable. They then got into the truck and left.

Celia turned to Tim. "What was that about?" she asked.

"I can't talk about it. I have to call my lawyer," Tim replied as he walked back to the office building.

Celia and Melanie did not stay long after that. Tim said he would look into settling the bill the following week. As they drove back, Celia and Melanie kept recounting the incident.

"That was a surprise! It seems not all that glitters is gold. Did you see how mad she was?" Celia said.

"Yeah! She had what I call 'crazy eyes'. That level of anger is always intense," Melanie replied.

"Intense is the word! Dani has that look that could kill you," Celia remarked.

"Do you think she had a hand in Rachel's death?" Melanie asked.

"What would be her motive?"

"Revenge."

"But by killing Rachel she would never get her money back."

"She never got it when she was alive; why not try when she's dead?" Melanie said.

Celia's phone rung. She had connected it to the Bluetooth in the car to make it easier to talk to her clients while driving.

"Hello," Celia said.

A scrambled voice boomed through the car speakers, such that you couldn't tell if you were talking to a man or a woman.

"Listen, you troublemaker. You had better be careful."

"I'm sorry, who is this?" a bewildered Celia asked.

"I know exactly who you are, Celia Dube! Stay out of my business or you will get what's coming to you!"

Then the line went dead.

12

"Who on earth was that?" Celia kept saying repeatedly as she pulled over by the roadside. She put her hands to her head in disbelief.

Melanie was equally surprised, having heard the whole conversation.

"I don't know. Wow, can we check the number?" Melanie asked.

Celia grabbed her phone and checked.

"It was a private number. I can't believe this!"

"Check and make sure we are not being followed or something," Melanie said. They looked outside their windows and the rearview mirrors. Nothing looked suspicious.

"Who have we ticked off, Mel? Help me here!" Celia pleaded.

"I think you should relax. Take a deep breath first and calm down," Melanie urged.

Celia took three deep breaths and felt her heart rate slow down.

"All right, let's think through this," Melanie began, "We have Rachel's husband Frank, who you met at the supermarket, Tim her business partner, Dani who is owed some money and Joshua, who might or might not be connected with her death somehow. Anyone else?"

Celia shook her head.

Melanie continued, "All right. Out of those four people, who seems the most likely to do this?"

Celia thought about it for a minute.

"Dani seems to be the most unpredictable, so that's the first name on the list. I'll have to add Frank there. So it's between the two of them, because at this time I think either one of them had a hand in Rachel's death," Celia said.

"Great. So, I have to go to the library and notify security just in case they need to look out for something suspicious. I'll activate the cameras, then go home," Melanie said. "You, on the other hand, will drive straight home. Well, not really straight home. Keep looking in your mirror in case you are being followed."

"Wow, you seem to have this figured out," Celia said.

"I have watched too much television. I wish I had renewed my driver's license. Are you okay to drive?"

"Yes, I'll be fine. Already shaken that off," Celia replied. She lowered the handbrake and activated the indicator.

"This might just be a prank to get you to back off. Which means there's something we are doing right," Melanie said.

"That's a sure thing. We just need to find out what that right thing is," Celia replied as she put her foot to the pedal. The car jerked forward as she quickly accelerated into the evening traffic.

CELIA ARRIVED HOME to a carnival atmosphere. Soft music from the seventies was playing as Mrs. Owens and her mother danced away. They both wore brightly colored scarves, occasionally waving them in the air.

"Welcome home, Cece!" her mother said with a beaming smile as she danced to the tune playing over the loudspeaker.

As soon as she noticed Celia's presence, Mrs. Owens went to the couch and grabbed a bright orange scarf. She threw it at Celia, who caught it just in time.

"There's your designer accessory!" Mrs. Owens crooned.

Celia smiled at this.

"All right, you win," Celia replied, throwing the scarf around her neck. She suddenly did not mind the idea of the photoshoot, or the dancing taking place.

The three women danced graciously. Slow but soulful, in tune with the mid-tempo beat of the music. Mrs. Owens was clearly a great dancer back in her heyday, showing great technique to make her move changes and rope in her fellow dancers. Celia's mother was less gifted, but her adventure-loving spirit was always ready for a good time, so she was enjoying every moment. Celia was a decent dancer, and this reminded her of the nights out with Trevor where they would go for dancing-only dates. They would spend hours on the dance floor. They finally danced to their fill and settled down in the seats to catch their breath.

"That was fantastic. It took me back to the time I was in my twenties!" Mrs. Owens said. The other women laughed.

"You still have a lot of energy for a woman your age," Celia said.

"Are you trying to say I don't have the same energy?" her mother asked.

"Mom, you know I got my genes from you. You never missed a beat," Celia replied.

"Now, that dance mood is what I want to bring to that photoshoot," Mrs. Owens said.

"But I thought it was just getting a photographer and having people pose for the camera?" Celia asked.

"No my dear, it has grown wings. We are going to do a mini-festival. The kids will come, the women will come and there will be photos and dancing, and games all over the place. Your mom and other moms will prepare the best food, and we will all just have a good time and forget the dark times," Mrs. Owens said.

"Oh, wow! Sounds like quite the gig! Where do you plan to do this?"

"Where else? The library, of course! It's the perfect place," Mrs. Owens replied. Celia knew this might be a tricky suggestion to share with Melanie.

"I'm not so sure that's a good idea…"

"Why not?" Mrs. Owens posed, "We can't let death win. Let us show people the library is a safe place for our kids. Come on, lighten up! It will be a fun day!"

Celia's phone started ringing, and she paused to reach for it in her bag. She stared at the screen, hoping it wasn't the strange voice again. It wasn't. Detective Koloane was calling. Why was he calling so late?

Celia stepped out to take the call. It was a quiet night outside, with no clouds in the sky. Hardly anyone was out walking, and few cars were parked on the street.

"Detective Koloane."

"Hello Celia, how are you doing?"

"I am doing great. I did not expect you to be calling at this time," Celia replied.

He laughed. She liked his deep, gentle laugh, she realized.

"I wish I wasn't. Face to face would be better, but you gave me a difficult position," he replied.

"Well, it's a valid one, don't you think?"

"Yes, it is. However, I am calling about something else. Tell me something. Was there any confrontation between you and a lady called Dani Lepan sometime today?"

Celia was taken aback, "I wouldn't call it a confrontation. More of a situation where I managed to intervene and calm her down. Why do you ask?"

"I see. Well, I would suggest that you stay away from her because she has filed a restraining order against you."

"She what? Are you serious?" Celia's eyes were as wide as saucers.

"Yes, I am serious. So just make sure you don't break it, all right?" he said.

"That's no problem; I think it's unlikely our paths will cross again. I am just surprised. Why did she do this again?"

"Don't dwell too much on the reason, Celia. I am just looking out for you. Again, remember what I told you. Do not play detective. We don't know who's good and who's not," Bill replied.

"I heard you the first time. I'll keep my head low. By the way, did you get to talk to Frank today?"

"Were you suggesting that I talk to him or look into him? Because those can be two different things," he replied.

"I guess both?"

"Well, I'm looking into him. Let's leave it at that," he replied.

"Thanks for the… thanks for checking in," Celia said.

"You are welcome. Good night."

When he hung up, Celia stood there, thinking.

Was the phone call from Dani and was this restraining order one way of warning her to keep off? She wondered if there was a restraining order against Tim too. She made a note to check with him the next morning.

She was about to head back into the house when she noticed a faint glint and movement from inside a black saloon car parked across the street. Suddenly, she felt watched. Was she seeing things? Maybe. She turned to walk away. As she got to the door, she realized she couldn't shake it off. 'I have my loved ones in there, I might as well check.'

She turned back to the street and walked casually towards the car, trying to squint and see if she would see anything. There was a light tint on the car's windows, but the closer she got, the more her eyes seemed to make out movement in the driver's seat. She was now right on the tarmac, less than three meters to go. She was just about to close in when suddenly the car engine roared to life. The headlights came on and the car jerked out of its parking spot, rushing off.

"Hey! Who are you?" Celia shouted as she tried to reach for it, but she was an inch shy of the car. She watched as the red taillights disappeared into the night.

Dread filled her. Whoever it was knew where her mother lived.

13

"Cece, what's going on?" Celia's mother asked.

Celia, still standing on the dark residential street, turned to see her mother's head poking out of the house's front door.

"Nothing, Mom," Celia replied as she walked back to the house.

"But I heard you shouting," her mother said.

"I thought I saw someone. False alarm," Celia replied.

"Were they driving the car?"

"It was just passing by. Nothing to worry about," Celia said as she arrived at the door.

"Okay. We are just about to serve some homemade pie," her mother said.

"Yeah, just give me a moment, I'll come in. I didn't finish my phone call," Celia said.

"Okay. Don't make it a long one," her mother replied, closing the door.

Celia walked to where her car was parked and leaned on it. She didn't want her mother to get anxious or know that she had defied her request not to investigate Rachel's death. Yet, she didn't expect someone was watching her every move. After the threatening call, it was all becoming too serious now. Who was doing this? Was it Dani or Frank? Would the car return?

She was afraid, especially since her mother and kids were in the house. Her mother's house did not have CCTV cameras. They would have been safer at her house, Celia thought, but convincing her mother to leave at that hour would raise many questions. But she simply couldn't go to sleep without a plan.

She dialed a number.

"I thought this wasn't a good hour to talk," Detective Bill Koloane said.

"Well, the situation is slightly different. Something's happened," Celia said.

"What happened?"

"After we hung up, I noticed someone watching my mother's house."

"What?" Bill asked with concern.

"Yeah. When I walked up to the car, he or she drove off into the night."

"Did you get the plate number?"

"No, I... I didn't. I should have. I guess it threw me off a bit," she replied.

"You said this happened at your mother's house?"

"Yes. She lives on twenty-one Pembrook Road. Are you able to send someone to check it out?" she asked in her softest voice. "Or at least keep watch over the place?"

"I have a patrol unit in the area, they can drive by later. What was the color of the car?"

"Silver," she replied.

"All right. I'll let them know. They will just pass by," Bill replied.

"Thank you very much, detective," Celia said, relieved.

"In case there's something else, feel free to reach me," he offered.

"I'll keep it in mind," she replied.

She hung up and walked to the house feeling a little lighter. She took one final glance at the road before heading inside.

As soon as they had pie, the still jovial Mrs. Owens called a cab and left. Celia kept checking on her through phone calls until she arrived home safely. No one thought this to be unusual. However, Celia was unable to sleep for most of that night. Sleep came to her at three in the morning.

She woke up to the sound of her mother knocking on her bedroom door.

"Cece! Cece!" Audrey's muffled voice called. Celia walked to the door and opened it.

"Good morning!" Celia said, rubbing her eyes.

"What is a police car doing outside the house?" she asked.

"What police car?" a surprised Celia asked. They both walked to the living room window. Sure enough, there was a marked police car parked across the street.

Celia, who was inwardly pleased, said, "I have no idea. Maybe the neighbor is a police officer?"

"Actually, I went and asked them. Apparently, someone was watching our house last night. What's going on, Celia?" Audrey asked.

Celia braced herself for a difficult conversation.

"Mom, I don't know. But there was someone watching the house last night. I called the police to look into it," Celia said.

Audrey shook her head in disappointment.

"Why didn't you tell me the truth last night? Are we in danger?" she asked.

"I am sorry for that, Mom. I didn't want to worry you. So I just asked them to pass by. To be honest, I'm really glad they stayed longer!" Celia replied.

"Fair enough. So why is someone watching us?" her mother asked.

Celia sighed, "I honestly don't know. Maybe it's a reporter."

"A reporter?"

"Remember the news report? It could be paparazzi."

Audrey shook her head in disbelief.

"What will we do now?" she asked.

"I suggest you come over to my place. They don't know where I live. Even if they do, I have cameras and a regular patrol by the security company. We will be safer there," Celia replied.

"No, Cece! We don't have to do that," Audrey said, shaking her head vigorously.

"Mom, please. We don't need them digging into our lives. I think we should all move to my place for a few days until things cool down," Celia pleaded.

Audrey bit her lip and shrugged. "As you wish," she said, turning towards the kitchen.

"Thanks Mom! Let me tell the boys," Celia said, glad that it went better than she expected.

After they had breakfast, Celia and her two sons helped Audrey pack up a few of her clothes and belongings. It wasn't a lot, as Audrey insisted it would only be for three days. The boys loved the idea of their grandmother staying with them for a few days.

As they were leaving, Celia went to the police car.

"Thank you so much for looking out for us," she said to the lone officer she saw. He was young, probably in his twenties.

"You are welcome," he replied, "Celia Dube?"

"Yes, that's me."

The officer reached to his passenger seat and handed her a stapled letter.

"You have been served," he said. Celia opened the letter. It was the restraining order Detective Koloane had told her about. Celia was still surprised by Dani's action. She simply nodded at the officer. He drove off.

Celia drove to her house while constantly checking the rear-view mirror. She didn't want to be followed. Once home, she checked the home security system to make sure it was working and the CCTV batteries were powered up.

After spending a lot of time getting her family settled in, Celia postponed her client visits to the next day. Instead, she called Melanie for an afternoon coffee at their favorite coffee spot, The Pier. It was cozy, with jazz music playing in the background, and not too busy as usual.

"Your life is getting very dramatic," a wide-eyed Melanie said after hearing Celia's account of the night's events.

"Tell me about it. I feel like I have to keep looking over my shoulder," Celia replied. Her eyes darted around the restaurant once more. With several couples in view, nothing seemed off.

"If it's the reporter, then she's really trying to milk this story. But if it's Dani, then she's crossed a line here," Celia added.

"Why would she be so extreme though?" Melanie wondered.

"Do you know she's filed a restraining order against me?"

"What? For the drama at Tim's office?" Melanie asked, puzzled.

"Detective Koloane didn't say. Maybe there's more to the debt situation than Tim told us. I still don't get why she would have Rachel poisoned if it would put her money at risk," Celia replied.

"Unless she was fed up. Bitterness is a powerful thing," Melanie said.

"True. But it still doesn't add up to me," Celia said, "There's something missing. I wish I could talk to Joshua."

"You could call him. He might not answer, but it's worth a shot," Melanie replied.

"Wait, you have his number?" Celia asked in excitement.

"Sure! I got it when we were making plans for the event. I thought he was a little cute then," Melanie said as she scrolled through her phone.

Celia smiled. "He's still cute you know and I also have his number."

"Not making that move now," Melanie replied. Celia called him. He picked up the call, and Celia had a brief chat with him. She managed to get his home address: Glacier House, Portmorr Drive.

AN HOUR LATER, Celia arrived at Portmorr Drive, parking on the street next to Glacier House. It was a neighborhood where young families lived, which she found interesting because she didn't think Joshua fit in.

Glacier House was an old school style bungalow with cream-colored walls and brown highlights.

She didn't wait long after ringing the bell. When Joshua opened the door, he was looking a little ragged. He was in slacks, sandals, and a hoodie while his hair was unkempt.

"Come in," Joshua said, ushering her into his house.

"Are you sure? I can wait if you need a few minutes to freshen up," Celia said.

"This is my everyday look when I'm home. Please come in, you're welcome," he replied.

Celia walked in. His house was sparsely furnished but tidy, except for an old mug of coffee, a saucer with a half-eaten slice of bread and an open can of jam on the coffee table. She sat on the single seater, while Joshua sat on his couch.

"Would you like something, some water or juice?" Joshua asked.

"No thank you," Celia replied. Joshua went to the kitchen and returned, sipping a glass of milk. He lazily eased himself onto the couch.

"How did the police interview go?" she asked.

"I am surprised to be home right now," Joshua replied.

"Why?"

"They were treating me like a criminal," he replied with a shake of the head.

"What do you mean?"

"I mean, they were asking me all sorts of questions. Fishing for information," Joshua said.

"That's what the cops always do," she said.

"Yeah, but do they do it for four hours?"

Celia was surprised. They must be suspicious of Joshua.

"What was their most common question?" she asked.

"They kept asking me why I had left early, whether I had a fight with Rachel. That kind of stuff," he replied.

"I saw you leaving early. Why did you do that?"

"I was told to leave," Joshua replied, sipping his milk.

"By whom, Rachel?"

Joshua shook his head.

"No. Tim told me to leave."

Celia's eyes widened.

"Why would Tim ask you to leave?" she asked. Joshua shrugged.

"He thought I wasn't needed," he replied.

"But why? I mean, I could see there was a lot to be done."

"Tim didn't share your perspective," Joshua replied, shifting in his seat.

"How did you and Tim get along?"

Joshua took another sip of milk. "We used to. Then that changed when I started working closely with Rachel. Never understood why, because jealousy isn't a valid reason to make my life difficult."

"Did they disagree often?" Celia asked.

"Yeah, like all partners do. But they were a dynamic duo that made great business moves."

"Why didn't you leave like others before you?"

"I was learning a lot just by watching them work. I would pick the lessons and block out the tension," he replied with conviction.

"But it's not always possible to avoid the tension. Like that night."

"I guess so," Joshua said, taking the last sip of milk. He got up and walked back to the kitchen.

As she waited, Celia looked around the house. The walls were cream and bore the occasional framed photograph of a landscape and the Sunshine Cove harbor. Underneath it stood a small white cabinet. She got up to look at the photo of the harbor. Even as a still photograph, you could almost hear the waves crashing onto the shore. It was a relaxing piece.

Joshua walked back in, another glass of milk in hand.

"Who took the photograph?" Celia asked, pointing at it.

"I did," he said casually.

She remembered Joshua taking the photos of the library spaces, but he was clearly more gifted than she had imagined.

"This is beautiful," Celia said.

"Thank you," Joshua replied, heading back to the couch.

Celia's eyes then fell to the cabinet and saw a pack of syringes. She turned to him.

"Are these yours?" she asked, pointing at the pack of syringes.

Joshua shook his head.

"Those are Rachel's. I always carried them with me just in case," he said.

"For what exactly?"

He shrugged.

"She told me to keep them around whenever she was here and…" his voice trailed off.

"Joshua, you need to tell me the truth. How often was Rachel here?"

"Once in a while when work demanded," he replied.

"Were you sleeping with your boss?" Celia asked.

Joshua glared at her.

"How dare you! She's barely been dead a week and you come at me with this?" he raged.

"Joshua, calm down and answer my question," Celia said politely.

"Why should I? Get out!"

"Joshua, please…"

"Just get out!" Joshua shouted and marched to his door. He held it open, waiting for her to leave.

As soon as she stepped out, the door slammed behind her. She wasn't sure if she had just spoken to Rachel's killer, but she knew one thing; Joshua was the key to everything.

14

As Celia drove away from Joshua's house, she was wrestling with her thoughts. Why had she pushed him so hard? Could she have done things differently?

If he was having an affair with Rachel, would he have killed her? The syringes in his house were an interesting find, but she wasn't sure it meant much just yet. She needed to be sure before telling Detective Koloane.

She came to a stop at red traffic lights. As she waited, a familiar Panther SUV pulled up alongside her. As she studied it, she realized it was similar to the one Frank and Rachel Sablay drove, the same one seen at the library parking lot during the couple's argument. She inched her car forward slightly to get a better glimpse. Yes, it was Frank in the driver's seat!

Her mind raced as the lights turned to amber, then green. As his SUV lurched forward, she accelerated too. He was going straight down, while her route needed her to turn left. She changed her mind and drove straight after him, keeping a decent distance between them.

Celia did not know why she was following him – she had never done this before! She was reliving some TV shows she had seen; she thought. She might find something interesting, so it was worth a shot. He was still the first suspect in the case after all, yet she needed to know more about him. If he was the jealous type, which she suspected him to be, then he had every reason to kill Rachel. He knew her mannerisms, why she needed the syringes and might have poisoned her that night.

She tried to keep up with him and make herself seem normal by not driving too fast and allowing the occasional car to come between them. This hard work needed more concentration than she expected. This made her more nervous. She started humming to herself, resolving to drive as if there were no expectations. Actually, why pressure herself? She wasn't sure what she was going to see. After a few miles, it was clear they were headed towards the central business district. Was he heading to see Tim? That could be interesting too, she thought.

Her speculation soon ended.

Frank's SUV abruptly turned into an office block. The move surprised Celia, so instead of following, she slowed down and pulled over to a parallel parking spot. She watched Frank being checked by the security guard at the gate before he drove in, disappearing into the building's basement park. In a bid to see where he was going, she looked to the top of the building. It was the Marble Insurance building. He was in the real estate business so she knew he did not work there. Then it hit her. Frank was possibly about to cash out a life insurance policy following Rachel's death!

If that were it, then a lot would quickly add up. He had killed her for the money. She had heard about this kind of murderous plan many times, but had never imagined it would happen so close to home.

Celia believed she was onto something here, but she could only be sure if she could confirm the life insurance policy existed. She wasn't sure how to do that yet.

She was startled by a loud knock on her driver's window. She turned up to see a security guard in uniform staring at her.

Celia lowered her window.

"Is something wrong?" Celia asked innocently.

"You bet there is! You're parked in a loading zone! Are you blind?" the guard said in a scolding voice.

"I didn't see a sign...," Celia began.

The guard pointed to the sidewalk. "It's right there!"

Sure enough, on the sidewalk was a red and yellow sign with 'loading zone' and the picture of a truck on it. She had parked so fast she didn't notice.

"I'm so sorry! I didn't see that," Celia said. She put her car in gear and drove out. Looking at the time, she needed to get home. Just then, a call came in.

"Who is this now?" she said aloud.

As she had connected her car's Bluetooth system with her phone, she was able to check the number. It was her Maven Beauty Products boss calling in from headquarters. She quickly composed herself, then answered.

"Hello James," she said warmly.

"Hello Celia, how are you doing?"

"I'm fine. What's up?"

"I'm calling because you were supposed to confirm a restocking after you met some clients today. How many reconditioning products do you need?"

Celia gasped. She had not done a single client visit that day. Pursuing this investigation was making her business suffer.

"Um, well... Sorry, I didn't get to meet any clients today. I had to sort out an urgent matter. But I'll do that tomorrow," she replied.

"Please do before mid-morning. I don't want to send out the courier too late," he said.

"Great. Thanks, James!"

As soon as James hung up, Celia shook her head. For someone who was keen on hitting her daily revenue targets, this wasn't good. If she wasn't careful, her weekly report would fall short of its targets, and she would have to explain to the head office. This also meant that she would make less money, and that wasn't going to be good for her family. Was she letting this case take over her life?

Maybe her mother was right. She couldn't keep doing this and balancing her commitments with her kids. Once home, she checked on her boys and then went straight to the kitchen. She was preparing to bake when her mother came in. She had been tending to Celia's flowerbed and was still wearing garden gloves.

"What are you up to, Cece?" Audrey asked.

"Guess what, Mom? I remembered I had some maple syrup in the house that I got as a gift."

"What has that got to do with me?" she asked.

Celia smiled. "Well, maybe we should try it out as a sweetener in your lovely cookies."

Audrey smiled.

"Well then, let's get to it!" she said as she took off the gloves.

Later that evening they gave the kids a rare treat with maple syrup sweetened ginger cookies. The boys were excited. Celia smiled at the sight, her mind easing away from the day's concerns. The boys ate fast and were soon asking for more. Celia packed a few cookies into a takeaway pack. She knew they might not last the night, and she would need them to make peace with someone.

Celia woke up early the next day to go through her inventory of beauty products. She had to do it before sunrise because she wasn't going to let James and her clients down. After breakfast, she did her morning meetings with clients. By mid-morning, she had met five clients. She then gave James an accurate number for her re-orders. Having taken care of business, she had one more place to go: the police station. At the reception, she asked to see Detective Koloane.

Detective Bill Koloane, dressed as usual in trim shirt and trousers, walked up to her with a smile.

"Are you here to confess?" he asked.

"Not quite," Celia replied while returning the smile, "Can I see you briefly?"

He led her down the corridor and into his office. It was a small cubicle next to another. It was littered with papers and files, next to a computer screen and keyboard. It was in stark contrast to the detective's smart look.

"Sorry, this is how messy solving crime usually is," he said, pointing at a seat for her.

Celia sat down.

"I'm here to apologize for the other night," she said.

"No, its fine. My people came round, no?"

"Yes, but I know it wasn't the norm. My mother gave your officer a bit of a grilling too," she added.

"Hey, it happens sometimes."

Celia reached into her bag and took out a small home-wrapped package. She handed it to the surprised detective. He unwrapped it.

"Something smells good," he said, "Ginger cookies. How did you know?"

"I had a hunch," she said.

"I hope it's not a bribe," Bill said with a beaming smile.

"Now why would I do that, detective?" Celia replied with a matching smile.

The mood had softened just the way she wanted it.

"So, um. How's the investigation going?" she asked.

"It's making progress," he replied.

"Is it moving at a good speed?"

"It's always better if it moves faster. Why, do you want to give some information?"

"No information. Just an idea. I think you should check Rachel's call records," Celia said.

"We are already doing that," he replied.

"Oh? And any findings?"

"We are yet to get them from the mobile phone company. Even when they come, you know I can't tell you anything that we find," he said.

"Not even a little hint?" she asked.

"Not even a little hint," he replied.

She smiled to cover up the frustration she felt. She had hoped for more. Celia stood up.

"All right, I don't want to be the reason why the investigation is delayed," she said.

"Thank you for the cookies! Stay safe. Maybe next time we talk, it'll be over coffee," he said with a smile.

"I'll be looking forward to that," she replied with a smile.

As Celia walked into the sun, she had mixed feelings. She had wanted something more definite, to get an idea that would help her narrow down her thoughts about Dani, Joshua and Frank. Call histories can hide patterns, or reveal a frequency of communication that could mean something. Especially in the last hours of Rachel's life. Despite not getting a lead, Celia knew something would give. She just didn't know when.

She walked to her parked Subaru and from the corner of her eye noticed a head dip behind another parked car. Someone was watching her! Curious, she walked to the car and found the lady reporter crouching awkwardly.

Celia shook her head. The reporter straightened up.

"What are you doing here?" Celia asked.

"I could ask you the same question," the reporter replied.

"Have you been following me?" Celia asked, drawing closer to the woman, who seemed to be alone.

"I am not at liberty to confirm or deny that," she said.

"Were you stalking my mother's home the other night?"

The reporter's face adopted a puzzled expression.

"No! I may have my quirks, but paparazzi work isn't one of them."

Celia shook her head, noting the irony of the situation.

"How about your cameraman?" Celia asked.

"He loves his down time. Trust me, he would never do that. Do you see him here?"

Celia looked around and did not spot anything unusual.

"Stay away from me and my family!" Celia said, and walked towards her car.

"Are you trying to say your family is being stalked by someone? Do you think it's the killer?" the reporter shouted to Celia.

Celia kept walking. A further reaction wouldn't be wise for the story that might be coming. Yet, just like the reporter, she was wondering the same thing. It was now more likely that the person she found watching her mother's house was Rachel's killer. That wasn't good news.

15

The next morning, to her surprise, Celia got a call from Detective Bill Koloane. He wanted to meet her for coffee.

"Are you sure you have the time? You do have a case to solve," she said.

"I can spare an hour," Bill replied. "We can meet at The Pier."

"I love that place!"

"Good to know I have some good taste. Meet there at ten?" he asked.

"Sure!" Celia replied with excitement.

When she arrived five minutes before ten, she found him already waiting for her. After exchanging pleasantries, their coffee arrived with the day's special, an apple pie.

"I have been trying to get off coffee for a while. Doctor's orders. But I'll have a cup today," Bill said.

"No, you don't have to do that," Celia replied.

"But I know you are well versed in emergency procedures, so I don't have to worry," he said.

Celia laughed. "How do you know that?"

He looked at her knowingly.

"Ahh, yes. The cases," she replied, "The strangest way to meet someone."

He smiled.

"Since we are already talking about the case, I remember you said that Rachel was poisoned. How do you figure it happened?" Celia asked.

"Most likely through a puncture wound. She had a history of self-medication," he replied.

"She had a condition, right? What was it?"

"I can't tell you that, unfortunately. It's all confidential," Bill replied.

Celia sighed and then tried another approach.

"So, did you know that Frank and Rachel argued that evening?"

Bill sat up. "What do you mean argued?"

"Frank didn't tell you?" she asked. Bill shook his head.

"Well, they arrived late for the event. We were curious why. Then we found them arguing in the parking lot. It was heated."

Bill became thoughtful for a moment. "Interesting. He didn't tell me that. How were things between them for the rest of the evening?"

"Tense. I spotted Frank trying a few times to talk to her, but she wasn't up for it."

Bill rubbed his chin. She admired that it was clean-shaven and well chiseled.

"If you add to that the fact that Joshua left a little early...," she said.

"I know what you are suggesting," he replied. "He might have had a strong motive to do it. This is interesting information."

"So, any progress on the calls?" she asked.

"Tell me something, does this intense curiosity you possess run in the family?" Bill asked.

Celia laughed.

"It begins with me. But my late husband was a good teacher on how to observe details and question everything. He was in the military," she said.

"I know," Bill said. Celia figured that alongside revealing her marital status during the interrogations, he had done a background check on her.

"To answer your question about the call records... yes. I read them this morning, and I found some interesting things. But I can't disclose the details of an ongoing investigation," he replied.

Celia thought quickly.

"All right! Let's do it a little differently. I'll ask three innocent questions and if it's a yes, just nod. If it's no, then shake your head. Deal?"

"Celia..."

"Trust me. Please."

He leaned back in his seat. She took that as encouragement to continue.

"Were there many calls between Joshua and Rachel?"

Bill waited for half a minute, then nodded.

"Were many of them late calls?"

Bill nodded.

"Do you have access to their text messages too?"

Bill nodded.

"Are the text messages... you know... a little spicy?" she asked.

"That's it! You only asked for three," Bill said.

"That last one is a bonus!" Celia pleaded.

Just then, Bill's phone vibrated, and he checked it.

"Sorry. I'll have to cut this short. I'm needed at the station," he said in disappointment.

"That was a short one. I'm sure we have broken some world record with the duration of this date," Celia said.

"Duty calls," he replied, getting up and putting on his coat.

"Thanks for making the time," she said with a smile.

Placing a ten-dollar note on the table, he said, "You're welcome. And next time we do this, let's not talk about the case."

"I'll keep it in mind," she replied.

"Also, this chat was just for common knowledge. I hope you won't do anything silly?"

"I'll try not to, detective," she replied.

As soon as Bill had left, Celia got her phone out. She wanted to call

Joshua and ask him about the phone calls. But her first phone call was to Tim to talk about the restraining order.

"Yeah, I got one too. I told you that Dani is a little crazy," Tim said.

"I didn't expect her to go this far," Celia replied.

"If there's one thing I've learned, it's that people are full of surprises," Tim said.

After listening to Tim, Celia concluded she would need to use a process of elimination in order to figure out if Dani was the killer. This meant focusing on those she could get close to. Feeling lucky, she wanted to talk to Joshua again. Maybe she would be able to get him to say something. She was about to call him, then paused – what if he hung up? What would she do? A phone call was limited because she wouldn't be able to tell if he was lying or not. She needed to put her body language lessons to good use, and this was perfect for it.

"I think we'll be seeing each other again, Joshua," she said, picking up her bag.

* * *

CELIA PARKED across the street from Joshua's house. She waited in the car for a few minutes. His car was parked out front, so she knew he was home. She hoped he would open the door for her. It would be unproductive talking to someone across a locked door. She decided to sit and wait until he came out.

For the next two hours, she listened to two full Abba albums. She was just about to play them all over again when Joshua came out.

He looked better than the last time she saw him, wearing a t-shirt, jeans and sneakers. His hair was combed back, and he had shaved.

Celia quickly got out of her car and crossed the street. She went straight towards him, just reaching him before he got into his car.

"Joshua, I need to talk to you!" she said.

Joshua glanced at her, then dismissively opened his car door to get in.

"I told you to stay away from me," he said.

"You need to hear this. It's important."

"My life is important too," he replied, moving to get in. Celia held him back.

"Please get your hands off me," Joshua hissed.

"Look, I am sorry about our last conversation. I was out of line and should not have asked you that question," she said. He turned to her.

"What do you want now?"

"I was talking to a detective today, and it got me wondering if you and Frank ever clashed at the event?" she asked.

"Why would he talk to you about that?" he asked.

"Let's just say it was a followup interview. Anyway, he mentioned that they have been looking at her call history. Your name popped up a lot of times," Celia said.

"Of course, it would. We would talk about work anytime."

"Late into the night?"

"You're starting again," he said.

"Look, it may not mean anything. But I assume that if everything was transparent then Frank had no reason to be mad with you or his wife, right?" she asked.

"Right. There was nothing going on," he said.

"So, if they pull up the texts between the two of you, they won't find anything?" Celia posed.

"Wait, they can do that?"

"Yes, they can," she replied, studying his reaction. Joshua went quiet for a moment. He looked like he was reliving a moment in the past.

"Things get trickier when we talk about the syringes I saw in your house," she said.

"I told you she needed them! She said she had some condition. She would remind me to keep a pack just in case," he replied.

"So, you are telling me that after working for her for so long you don't know what she had? You expect me to believe that?" she asked.

Joshua sighed.

"You do know she died of poisoning, right?" Celia asked, "And if I told the police that you have a pack of syringes in your house…"

"Look, I didn't do anything wrong. I swear! I only kept them with me for her sake," he pleaded.

"What condition did she have?"

"She was diabetic. But she was managing it with the medication," Joshua said, a tear rolling down his left cheek. "All I wanted to do was make things easier for her. She deserved to have things easier."

Celia felt sorry for him. "Joshua, were you and Rachel seeing each other?"

He looked up.

"Yes… I was in a relationship with her," he admitted, "It was never meant to happen. But the more we worked, the more we just grew towards each other."

Celia now understood why he was struggling to deal with her death.

"This must be hard for you," she said.

Joshua simply nodded. She took a step toward him and let him cry into her shoulder.

Listening to his sniffles and feeling the pain he bore in his body; she knew he didn't do it.

16

Celia kept talking to Joshua until he calmed down. He was going to the shopping center to shop, which was probably a good thing for him to do. She was a fan of shopping therapy to help her feel good about the world again, and she hoped it would lift his spirits too.

After she watched him leave, she sat in her car for a few minutes, smiling. She had made positive connections that day, and this gave her a wholesome feeling. Her gut had always told her there was more to Rachel and Joshua's work relationship, and his admission proved it. At the same time, it meant Frank was justified to be suspicious. It did mean that Frank might have done something to his wife, but she wanted to be sure of this. The other intriguing detail was that Tim was no angel after all. As much as he had told them how good his work relationship with Rachel was, there were tensions. Sometimes tensions can turn deadly. She was keen to explore that some more.

"That's enough detective work for one day, Celia," she told herself. She dialed her mother.

"Cece, what time are you getting home?" Audrey's motherly voice echoed in the car.

"I'm on my way, actually. Is everything okay?"

"Everything's fine, the kids are fine too. They want chicken wings for dinner," Audrey replied.

"Why do takeaway when there's chicken in the fridge?"

"There's no chicken here, sweetie. I checked. When was the last time you did any shopping?"

Celia paused and realized that it had actually been it had been awhile since she did her major house shopping. This wasn't good, especially since she shopped together with her mother on those days.

"Now that you mention it... it has been a while," she replied.

"And the main reason is because you haven't had time to do our mother-daughter shopping trips," her mother asserted.

"I'm sorry about that."

"We can't go on like this, can we?"

"No, we can't. I miss bonding with you," she said.

"So when can we do it? Tomorrow?" Audrey asked.

Celia did a quick calculation.

"Why don't you make a short list of what we need and then we can set it up," Celia suggested, a way of buying time.

"All right, I'll hold you to that," her mother replied.

"Thanks Mom! I'll get you some chicken wings," she said.

"From Uncle Jerry's they said."

"Oh, they want those? Okay, I'll take care of it. Let me go now. See you soon."

Celia drove off towards Uncle Jerry's. It had become a favorite spot for chicken wings shortly after her husband's death. The owner, Jerry Meadow, was a kind man in his fifties who often came to the tables to talk to families that had visited his establishment. The chicken was prepared with that homemade kind of taste that kept people coming back. The kids quickly got attached.

She found a short queue at the popular place. A small family restaurant, it was nearly full of seated clients, which wasn't unusual at that time of the day. After some patience, Celia finally got herself chicken wings and French fries that could feed the whole family. She managed to wave at Uncle Jerry, who was in the kitchen overseeing things. She was walking towards the restaurant exit when she spotted a familiar-looking figure seated in a cubicle near the door.

She moved closer and confirmed that it was Frank Sablay. He seemed lost in thought, staring at the street outside. Celia wasn't sure if it would be a good idea to talk to him. Maybe he was waiting for somebody. Should she linger and see who he was going to meet? Her urge for a conversation won.

"Frank?"

Frank turned to her.

"Oh. Celia, right?"

"Yes. I didn't expect to see you here," she said.

"Well, yeah. I needed a break from the runaround," he replied.

"I was buying some chicken wings for my sons," Celia said, showing her package.

"Oh nice. I would have done the same, but my son is at his grandfather's. It will help him get his mind off things," Frank said.

"Can I join you?" she asked.

"Sure."

Celia sat opposite him. Frank looked polished, but a little sleep deprived.

"How are you coping?" she asked.

"Taking it a day at a time. Managing flashbacks isn't always easy, but you roll with it as it comes," he replied.

"Even after several years I still get flashbacks of my late husband, so I know what you mean," Celia said.

"Thank you for understanding," he said.

"I have been thinking about our last chat," Celia said.

"In the supermarket?" he asked.

"Yes. I found out something about the… about your suspicions."

He leaned forward. "Okay."

"You were right. Rachel was seeing somebody and I know who it is," Celia said, monitoring his reaction. He still looked composed.

"Who is it?" he asked.

"It was Joshua," she replied.

He gave a long wry smile before replying.

"I already knew. I always knew. I just didn't have the evidence."

"How do you feel about it?"

Frank shrugged. "I would want to kill him if he was right here, of course. When it comes to doing what's right, I don't mind using my hands to remind people. But what's the point? Rachel's already gone."

As Celia listened, she believed him. He looked like he could handle himself well.

"So, you have made peace with it?"

His voice started shaking.

"You don't make peace with loss. I lost her twice. When she was alive, sleeping with that young fool, and when she died. You don't get used to that. I'm not sure I ever will."

She couldn't tell if his shaky voice was due to anger or grief, but she had hit a raw chord for sure. Remembering how things went with Joshua, she didn't want to push too hard. However, she needed some answers.

"You've told me in another time and place, you would kill Joshua for what he did. I can only imagine what it felt like in that situation. Did you confront him on the night of the event?" Celia asked.

"No, I didn't. Why would I?"

"You had an argument about him with your wife, remember?" Celia posed.

"Yes, and I didn't want to have another one by going after him at the event! It would be a little too much, don't you think?" he replied.

Celia nodded, it would be a stretch, but people had done worse things.

"I hear you. When my husband died, it really helped me that he had life insurance. It's keeping the boys in school and helped me get back on my feet. Did… did Rachel have life insurance?" Celia asked.

Frank eyed her for a long moment with a steely gaze, the kind that could be an unspoken threat. It made Celia fidget a bit as she thought he was going to jump at her in anger, but he smiled instead.

"She did have life insurance. Three policies, actually. I should call it the lifesaver."

Celia raised an eyebrow. "Why lifesaver?"

"I have just discovered Rachel had quite a lot of debts, and her policies are going to help us clear those and take care of our son," Frank replied.

"Oh, so you have already talked to your insurance company to cash in?" Celia asked, trying to connect what he was saying with the day she had followed him.

"Yes. I needed to start the process early. It can take some time to get paid, so I didn't want to delay," he replied.

"You know what? I'll start calling it *lifesaver* from now on. Life insurance is too heavy on the tongue," Celia said with a smile.

"Should I ask for royalties to add to my son's college fund?" Frank joked.

Celia smiled. "Where do I sign, sir?"

Frank pulled out a paper towel from its stand and placed it in front of her. They both laughed.

Celia was glad she had navigated that conversation safely. Yet, even as she laughed with him, Celia couldn't shake off one thought; Frank had just admitted that the life insurance money was going to be a life changer.

17

Ten minutes later, Celia and Frank walked out of Uncle Jerry's while still laughing.

"Does your boy eat the entire week's shopping in three days?" Celia asked.

"He's a one-man army, he does it in two! And you could say he's very good at it!" Frank replied.

"Boys will be boys. I sometimes dread the day they become teenagers. I honestly don't know how I'll handle them," she said. She pointed at her car across the street, and he followed as she headed towards it.

"Well, there will need to be some adjustments. Different types of punishment, that sort of thing. Just keep doing what you are doing," Frank said. "From what you told me about your sons, they seem to be a smart pair."

"They are a cheeky pair, that's what! A very cheeky..." Celia didn't finish what she was saying.

She had gotten past a row of parked cars and into the middle of the street. Her focus was on Frank so she didn't notice a gray saloon car bearing down on her at high speed. She sensed the imminent impact at the very last moment and jumped back so fast that she bumped into Frank. Caught by surprise, he tumbled backwards and they both ended up falling flat on the pavement. As pedestrians stopped to see what was going on, the car's shrieking tires grew distant and disappeared altogether.

"Oh my God," Celia said as she recovered her bearings. She lay on top of Frank, who had broken her fall. She saw chicken wings sprawled around them.

"Are you okay?" Frank asked.

Celia moved her legs, then her arms.

"Yes… I think so…" she replied. With nothing broken, she rose slowly. Her heart was racing, her hair ruffled. Frank followed. They patted themselves down as they checked for bruises and brushed off dirt from their clothes.

"I didn't see it coming," she said.

"Neither did I. The crazy idiot driving that fast on this road should be arrested and locked up for a long time!" Frank said.

"Did you get to see the car well?" Celia asked.

"No, it happened so fast," he replied.

Celia's heavy breathing had eased slightly. She prayed this was just an accident, that it wasn't the killer after her.

"I'm so sorry for messing up your great outfit," Celia said as she looked at Frank's dirty trousers.

"Don't worry, I'll fix that at home," he replied.

He helped her pick up the chicken wings from the sidewalk and threw them in a trash bin.

"There goes our dinner," Celia said.

"Don't sweat it, I'll replace it," Frank offered.

"And I'll throw another couple of wings in," a voice said behind them. They turned to see Uncle Jerry at the restaurant door.

"Oh no, Uncle Jerry! It's fine!" Celia said.

"You're like a daughter to me, so you don't have a say in this!" Uncle Jerry said with a smile.

They all went back into the restaurant. Twenty minutes later, after thanking Uncle Jerry profusely, Celia had a bigger takeaway bag. Frank helped her carry it to her car.

"Thank you so much Frank. Really, this means a lot to me," she said.

"The pleasure is all mine. Get home safe!" he replied.

When Celia got home, the adrenaline in her system had lowered somewhat, and she wanted to hug her boys. After doing this, she watched them eat their chicken wings, despite the fact it was only four o'clock in the evening. She let herself forget the outside world and played some football with them in her backyard. She didn't tell her mother what had happened, as she knew it would worry her.

Suddenly, she heard her phone. She answered the call and pressed the phone to her ear.

"Hey Cece! What are you up to?" Melanie asked.

"Having some quality time with the boys," Celia replied.

"Great! Listen, I need your advice on something. Can you come over?"

"It can't be done on the phone?" Celia asked. The sun was about to set, and she didn't feel physically or mentally in the mood to leave home.

"Nope, not this time. If you can spare a moment, please," Melanie pleaded.

Celia sighed. "All right. I'll freshen up, then come over."

Celia told the boys that she had a last-minute call from a client and promised to see them before they slept. After a soothing hot shower and a fresh change of clothes, she felt energized. She kissed her mother's forehead and left for the library.

When Celia arrived at the library, it was closed, but Melanie had opened the side door for her.

"It's a little late to be at the library, Mel," Celia said as they walked to the reception.

"You know this is my sanctuary. If I could live here, I would," Melanie replied. At the reception, Celia spotted a tall vase full of fresh flowers.

"You are introducing flowers to your setup?" Celia asked.

"Nope. They just arrived," Melanie replied.

"You have a secret admirer suddenly," Celia said, smiling.

"I'm not sure about that, because they are from Tim."

Celia opened her mouth in surprise. "Tim de Sousa, Rachel's business partner?"

Melanie nodded.

"Why is he sending you flowers?" she asked.

"That's what I'm wondering about. Probably to buy time because he has yet to pay me for the location hire," she replied.

"He's sending you flowers to buy time for a debt? Don't you find that a little strange?"

"I do, but he told us he isn't good with people, so I am going with that as an explanation for his behavior," she replied.

"Well, if this is the advice you called me for, I'm not feeling like doctor love tonight," Celia said.

"He's not a secret admirer!" Melanie protested.

"If you insist. In other news, I had an unexpected chat with Frank today," she said.

"What do you mean by unexpected?" she asked.

"I was out buying the boys chicken wings. After I got my order, I saw him seated in one of the cubicles. So I went over to say hello."

"Uh huh, and?"

"Well, we got talking. Of course, I was fishing for information. After a bit of beating around the bush I told him that Joshua has been sleeping with Rachel."

"You what?" a shocked Melanie asked.

"I told him that Joshua and Rachel were seeing each other. I needed to see how he would react."

"Hold on. You're telling me you lied about their relationship to her widower to get a reaction? Isn't that going too far?"

"No, the info is true. Joshua admitted it to me," Celia said. Melanie's eyes grew bigger.

"Oh wow! And you are only telling me now? I thought we were partners?" she protested.

"In my defense, I have only known this for forty-eight hours," Celia replied, "Anyway, he got emotional, angry even. He always suspected something. Once he said that, I had to ask him if he confronted Joshua that evening. He says he wanted to, but didn't."

"What else did he say?" she asked.

"That he had nothing to do with his wife's death."

"Are you still suspicious of him?"

"Not really. He was genuine. We even left the place laughing," Celia replied.

"I love a happy ending to an interrogation," Melanie said with a smile.

"Don't be sarcastic now. I got so lost in the moment I walked onto the street lazily. I almost got hit by a car," she said.

"What? Are you okay?"

"I'm fine. It happened so fast, and I was too busy laughing to be more careful. It was my fault."

"Did you report it?" she asked.

"I couldn't. I have no idea what the color of the car was or the number plate. It's pointless reporting that. Though I wouldn't be surprised if it was the same car that was stalking my mother's house," she replied.

Melanie remained silent for a moment.

"You've gone quiet on me, Mel," Celia said.

"What if it wasn't your fault?" Melanie posed.

"It was. I walked onto the street without looking," Celia said firmly.

"But what was happening before?"

"A conversation."

"A distracting conversation with a suspect," Melanie said.

Celia's eyes narrowed. "Where are you going with this?"

"Listen. You've had someone make threatening calls, someone watching your house, and then somehow when you are talking to a suspect you almost get killed? Sounds suspicious to me," Melanie explained.

"I hear you, but I'm having a hard time believing Frank had a hand in today's near miss. He genuinely consoled me afterwards. Heck, he even bought my kids fresh chicken wings after the first ones landed on the sidewalk!"

"That's what he wants you to think, that he's genuine. But did he warn you about the car or pull you out of the way?" Melanie asked.

Celia thought for a moment.

"It happened a little too fast! I recall jumping back just in time. If he wanted me dead, he would have pushed me back onto the road, no? I don't think he had anything to do with it!" Celia said.

"Well, whether he had anything to do with it or not, someone tried to kill you today, Celia," she said.

Celia let the weight of what Melanie had just said sink in.

"Oh wow, you just made me relive it again," Celia said.

"I just know this is no accidental thing!"

"And I had just spoken to him about the life insurance…" she said.

"You think he killed Rachel for that?" she asked.

"It's possible. That means…"

Celia suddenly stood up fast, taking her bag from the table.

"Means what?"

"I have to find Joshua. If your wild theory is even forty percent accurate, then Joshua isn't safe tonight," she replied.

"Let me come with you!" Melanie said.

"No, I am just checking on him. I'll let you know if I get in trouble or something," Celia said as she walked fast towards the exit.

18

Celia drove her Subaru station wagon faster than she ever had. She didn't enjoy driving at night, let alone at high speed, so this made her nervous. But a life was possibly at stake.

She thought of calling Detective Koloane, but in her rush she had not put her phone on its stand in the car and it hadn't automatically connected with her car's Bluetooth system for some reason. She assumed this was because it was still in her jacket pocket. Reaching for it while driving would be unwise. She resolved to call him once she established Joshua was in danger. She didn't want to ruin any goodwill she had left in case she was wrong!

"Let him be safe and sound. Let him be home safe and sound," she kept saying to herself. She repeated it so many times it sounded like a chant.

As she came close to his house, she saw his car parked out front and was relieved. Then she saw its rear boot pop open as Joshua started loading boxes into it. Celia's car screeched to a halt by the side of the road.

She jumped out and ran towards him. Joshua was carrying what looked like a heavy box of books from the house and into his car's rear trunk.

"Hey! What are you doing?" she asked.

"What does it look like I am doing?" he replied.

"Moving out, running away? I don't know! You tell me what's going on."

"I have to leave. Now," Joshua said with conviction.

"Why?" she asked. He didn't answer, instead heading back to the house. He returned with another box.

"Why would you go into hiding if you have done nothing wrong?" Celia asked.

"To protect other people!" he replied.

"What if the other people want you to stay?" she asked.

"Then they lack wisdom," he replied.

"Has someone threatened you, Joshua?" Celia asked.

He ignored her and continued arranging his packages in the rear boot.

"Joshua, you can talk to me," she said soothingly.

"I don't want to talk about it," he replied.

Celia sighed.

"Look, I know I may not come off as someone who can help you in what you are going through. But I have a stake in this, too. No one else knows this, but someone has been stalking my family too. I fear for them every day because I don't know what's going on. But I also can't run," she said.

"I'm sorry to hear that. But what you have said is the exact reason why I have to leave. For people like you to have some peace. You have nothing to do with this. No one should come after you," he said.

"But that's how you let them win!" she said.

Joshua paused and thought about her words. He took in a deep breath.

"I appreciate your concern. I haven't had a lot of that lately," he whispered.

"I'm here for you, Joshua. Can you tell me who threatened you?" she asked.

"I still think it's better if you leave now for your family's sake," he said and went on arranging things in the boot. Celia was at a loss on what to do. Her mind raced in different directions.

"Why don't you come with me?" she suggested, "They don't know my actual house, just my mother's. No one will think of looking for you there. We don't have a connection. You can hide out for a few days and we'll take care of you."

"Are you crazy?"

"Hear me out! In fact, I have a friend of mine I can call to help us," Celia reached into her jacket's pocket for her phone.

"What friend are you talking about?" he asked quizzically.

Celia was still searching for her phone in her pockets. Where was it?

"He's a good guy. He's a detective," she replied.

"A cop? No! No cops, please!" Joshua said as he shut the boot and headed to the driver's door.

Celia realized she didn't have her phone with her, but she didn't have time to figure out where it was. She had to prevent Joshua from running off.

"Joshua, Joshua!" she said as she grabbed him and turned him around. "Please listen. Running away only makes it look like you're guilty and makes whoever was behind Rachel's murder win. Do you want that?"

"You need to leave now," he said.

"I'm not leaving you!" she insisted.

Suddenly they both heard a movement coming from the alley next to the house. The steady crunching of leaves. There were footsteps. A silhouette appeared from the shadows, and they couldn't make out who it was. It was a man, that's all Celia could tell.

"Who's there?" she asked in fear.

"You should have listened to him," the dark figure said to her threateningly.

19

Celia let out a low shriek as she took a step back. Joshua froze where he was, his eyes searching the darkness.

"Don't try to run and don't scream," the man said as he took a step towards them, "I wouldn't want to use deadly force."

The man was now standing in an area of low light, but they still couldn't make out his features. He was a tall man wearing a jacket and cap. His arms seemed to be in his pockets, but Celia suspected he was armed. She squinted her eyes to make out any details.

"We can't see you. At least tell us who you are," Celia said.

The man didn't reply, and this only heightened Celia's anxiety. Every part of her wanted to run, but her legs were as heavy as lead. Perhaps because of the fear she had, her mind was struggling to place the man's voice. No one was registering. She turned to Joshua, who was still frozen in place.

"Where are your car keys?" she whispered to him.

Joshua didn't respond or even turn to her. His breathing was fast and irregular, his eyes fixed on the man.

"Stop plotting a foolish escape. I can hear you from here," the man said.

"Tell us who you are, please," Celia asked again.

"You should know who I am," the man replied in a low drawl.

Celia turned to look at Joshua once more.

"Who is he?" she whispered.

"It's Tim," Joshua replied, his eyes still fixed on the man.

The revelation shook her. Tim de Sousa!

"Is that you, Tim?" Celia asked.

The man took off his hat, and although they couldn't see him, Celia could tell by the familiar outline of his head and physique that it was him.

"Whether I am or not, I think you can figure it out for yourself, no?" the man replied.

The voice fits, Celia concluded. However, this new knowledge didn't ease her anxiety. It fueled it, because now she had more questions.

"What's going on, Tim?" Celia asked.

"You are a smart woman. You tell me," Tim said as if mocking her.

"I'm not smart enough for this," she replied.

"Yes, you are! That's why you are here! To piece everything together into one neat ribbon," Tim said.

Celia gulped.

"I admire your drive to find out more," he continued, "It's a valuable asset in many fields. The only problem is sometimes when you try to save the world, you end up losing yourself and even harming the people you care about."

"What do you mean?" Celia asked, concerned.

"You should have stayed at the library tonight," he replied in a firm tone. Celia wondered how he knew about that.

"Have you been following me?" she asked.

Tim gave a short, humorless laugh.

"Let's just say that I knew you were coming," he said.

"How? Have you been tracking me?" she asked.

"Looking for a confession?" Tim asked in amusement, "I have my ways, Celia. Now it's my turn to ask the questions. What are you doing here?"

"I'm here to check on my friend," she replied.

"Your friend? Joshua is now your friend?" he asked.

"I consider him one. Yes," she replied. For the first time since Tim appeared, Joshua turned to look at Celia.

Tim laughed again. "Joshua must be quite the catch. It almost sounds like you are here to take Rachel's place in his life."

"It's not like that, sir," Joshua said, his voice shaky.

"And he finally speaks for himself, like a man! Bravo, Joshua, bravo! However, I have a word of advice; don't you think you should hang out with women around your age bracket? Because these older ones are bringing a lot of trouble into your life."

Celia interjected, "Tim, you need to show me some respect!"

"Shut your mouth, Celia, before I put a bullet in you!" Tim snapped.

Celia went quiet, keen to manage the situation. She felt like a fish out of water. She glanced briefly towards the street, hoping a passerby would see them. Strangely, there wasn't anyone walking about.

"Joshua, do you agree?" Tim persisted.

"Yes... yes sir," Joshua replied.

"If I was to let you leave this place tonight, where will you go?"

"To a place where I'll be hard to find. I want to start life anew," Joshua replied.

"But where exactly?" Tim asked.

There were a few awkward moments of silence.

"I'm still thinking about the best possibilities..." Joshua said.

"Ssssh!" Tim interrupted, "What is the first thing I told you to keep in mind when you joined the firm?"

"Planning is everything," he mumbled.

"There you go! Sadly, I can't let you go out there because you don't have a plan."

"Please, sir..."

"I wish things were different, son," he said.

Celia, worried that the conversation was coming to a fatal end, interrupted.

"Why did you have to do this?" she asked.

Tim sighed.

"You just can't help it, can you?"

"If we are going to go six feet under today, at least tell us what happened," she said, surprised at her own courage.

Tim took out a cigarette and lit it using a lighter. When the lighter's flame glowed, Celia caught a glimpse of his face. She saw pure evil in his eyes, for they were dark and soulless.

"It was never meant to end up with her dying. Some time off work would have been nice," Tim said, blowing out smoke.

"And now she's away from work permanently because of you," she said.

"There's no evidence that I had anything to do with that," he said confidently. Celia was tempted to agree with him – she had not seen this coming. But she wasn't going to do that.

"You're standing in front of me holding a gun. How much more evidence do you think they need?" she asked.

Tim shrugged and smiled. "I don't really care."

"You haven't answered my other question. Why would you do this? She was the brains behind your organization and she didn't deserve that," she said.

"Sometimes the founder's vision can get blurry, and if that happens some assistance is needed."

"You call what you did assistance?" Celia asked, shocked at his dark view of the world.

"I call it fate. There was no other way. The company needed to grow," he said casually. "It was going nowhere before I arrived. Everything was in shambles. I brought structure to the place. I brought the comfort and stability that enabled her to go and rub shoulders with the high and mighty. I made it possible for her to raise the money she did! I built her to what she was today! That company wasn't as strong or as prolific before I came!"

"Are you calling Rachel a poor leader?" Celia asked.

"I don't need to call her anything. You saw it for yourself when Dani came to the office to tow a company car. She was cutting deals and bringing in shady characters that were bad for business. Do you know how many news editors I had to convince to pull negative stories because of her stunts?"

Celia paused, reflecting on what he had just said. She finally saw the big picture.

"You had wanted to do this all along. Become her partner and take over the business. She just didn't see it coming," she said.

Tim smiled. "I knew you were a smart woman. As you can see now, hostile takeovers come in different forms. I think we have talked long enough. I was hoping that you wouldn't be here Celia, but since you are, I'll add you to the plans I had for Joshua."

Celia was about to panic. They needed to keep Tim talking.

"What do you mean you hoped I wouldn't be here? You were the one who almost ran me over today, weren't you?" she said.

"You are like a cat with nine lives. Your late husband would be proud," Tim said.

Celia wasn't surprised he had looked into her. "Why would you want my kids to grow up without their parents then?" she asked.

"Don't you understand? If you find yourself at the wrong place at the wrong time, the consequences can be quite tragic," he said casually.

He held it in his right hand, and their fears were confirmed. He had a gun.

In desperation Celia said, "Someone will hear the gunshots."

"It won't matter. I have the shadows on my side. Sorry it had to be this way," Tim said as he took aim.

Suddenly, another dark figure emerged from the shadows, moving swiftly towards Tim, tackling him to the ground. Celia didn't need to wait. She took hold of Joshua and they ducked behind his car. Celia peeked to see what was going on. The two figures wrestled. Then they heard loud sirens as the street was filled with approaching flashing lights. Four police cars came screeching to a halt in front of the house. Several officers jumped out with guns drawn, approaching the wrestling figures.

"I got him!" a voice shouted from the shadows. Three officers closed in on the two. Moments later, they walked out of the shadows, emerging into the light to reveal the already handcuffed Tim de Sousa. His face was angry. One of the officers was carrying Tim's gun. When they saw him in cuffs, Celia and Joshua stood up from their hiding place.

Detective Koloane walked up to the arresting officers and stared at Tim's defiant face.

"Tim de Sousa, you are under arrest for the murder of Rachel Sablay. Anything you say or do can and will be taken as evidence in a court of law," Detective Koloane read his rights.

Two police officers came to Celia and Joshua.

"Are you okay? Did he hurt any of you?" one of them asked.

"We are fine, just a little shaken. How did you find us?" Celia asked.

"Because I told them where you were," a voice said. Melanie walked up to them, smiling.

"Mel…" Celia said as they embraced.

"I had to do it because you forgot your phone," Melanie said.

"Thank you," she replied.

"It's over now," Melanie said, handing Celia her phone.

"I hope you are right," Celia replied.

20

"Watch it! That's a new sports jacket!" Tim protested as Celia watched him resisting the long walk to the police car.

"Shut up and move!" one arresting officer said, shoving Tim forward. They eventually got him to the car and placed him in the backseat.

Celia, standing on the street with Melanie and Joshua, wrapped the scarf Melanie had given her tighter around her shoulders to fight the growing chill of the night.

"Tim turned out to be quite something," Celia said.

"Here we were thinking Frank was the strange man," Melanie said.

"I think that's what Tim wanted all along," Celia replied.

"And you are right," Detective Koloane said as he walked to the two women. "He's always known that Rachel's husband would be the first suspect. So killing her on the evening they had a fight worked well for him."

"Do you think he planned it for that night?" Melanie asked.

"Maybe. I think he was always prepared. He just needed the opportunity. I have a feeling if we get to his house, we will get more evidence connecting him to the poisoning. I need to add that to the charge sheet," Bill replied.

"Wait. You are not arresting him for murder?" Celia asked.

"We have to search his house and trace other leads. For now, we are taking him in for threatening your lives and trespass."

Celia and Melanie looked at each other.

"Wow, I didn't expect that. He confessed to us just before you guys came in. I know that he killed her! Joshua and I'll testify!" Celia said, getting agitated.

"The two of you will definitely be called in as witnesses. But he hasn't confessed to an officer yet. Let's hope he does that at the station. But I need more evidence to convict. Good thing he'll be behind bars as he won't be able to interfere with the rest of the investigation," he said.

"I hope he never gets out, because he's a bitter man capable of anything," Melanie said.

"They always say never meet your heroes," Joshua said.

"He was your hero?" Melanie asked.

"He's the one who introduced me to Rachel and got me the job. I learned a lot from him," Joshua replied.

"Fortunately, not how to murder through poisoning!" Melanie said.

"Fortunately," Joshua replied, "I should have seen this coming. I let Rachel down."

Celia felt for him. "Stop beating yourself up. How could you have known?" she said.

"Maybe if we were not together, I would have seen the signs," he said with sadness.

"It's not your fault, Joshua," Celia said. "He's a very manipulative man who can blindside anyone. Tell me something: was it true, what he said about Rachel's plans for the company?"

Joshua nodded. "Rachel didn't want to expand and become big. She didn't want the company to lose its connection to the community. She obviously opposed his expansion plans. But things became a bit awkward when he found out she was secretly planning a big deal with another company."

"He had to plan a way to get back control," Celia said. "He wanted the whole thing for himself. Rachel's secret deal must have broken their relationship. It seems there was no other way than to get her out of the picture."

"He planned it for a while then, huh?" Melanie asked.

"He did! I believe when he sent Joshua home early, he was simply adding more smoke and mirrors to the investigation. If the murder charge wasn't going to stick with Frank, he had Joshua as a backup suspect," Celia said.

"He was the puppet master and none of the puppets had a clue," Melanie said.

"Why poison her?" Joshua asked. Before anyone could respond, a police officer walked up to the detective and whispered in his ear.

"To cover his tracks," Celia said after the police officer had walked away. "He chose something she did often as the means to have her murdered. He must have switched her vials at some point that night. She then injected herself with what she thought was medicine and minutes later she was dead."

"That's an interesting theory there," Bill said. "It's given me a few ideas for getting a confession out of him. Celia, give me your car keys. We need to search your car."

"Wait, why?" a startled Celia asked.

"Mel will tell you about it," he said. Celia handed him her car keys, and he passed them onto the officer. Celia watched a group of police officers surround her car. She turned to Melanie.

"Tim has been tracking us all the time," Melanie said. "Guess what I found among the flowers in the library."

"What?"

Bill held up an evidence bag. It had a short cable with a button-sized round microphone at the top.

"A listening device. He was eavesdropping on your earlier conversation with Melanie. That's why he was able to find you here just as you were talking to Joshua," Bill said.

"This guy is a sociopath," Celia mumbled.

"I hate to say it, but if we hadn't made it on time, I fear what he would have done to the two of you to cover his tracks," Bill said gravely.

Celia couldn't argue with that. She shuddered at the thought that her two sons would have spent the night not knowing where their mother was. She needed to call home.

"I'll need all of you to record your statements. Joshua, go over to that officer, she'll take care of you," Bill said, pointing at a female officer who was standing next to one of the police cars.

"Sure," Joshua said and walked to the officer. Bill turned to Celia.

"I know what you are going to say," Celia said.

"What do you think I am going to say?" he asked.

"Was it all really worth the danger?"

Bill smiled. "The first thing I was going to say is I'm glad we caught him before someone else got hurt. A big part of that breakthrough was as a result of your persistence."

Celia beamed. "Thank you."

"And then the other part is exactly what you thought I would say. Was it worth risking your life?" Bill asked.

Celia bit her lip. She didn't have a straight answer for him.

"I need to get home to the boys," she said.

"I understand. However, they are still working on your car. Plus, once the officer there is done with Joshua, she'll speak to you. I would suggest you call home and tell them you'll be running a little late. Same to you, Melanie," he said.

Celia and Melanie nodded. Celia moved a few steps away from them to call her mother.

"Cece, where are you?" Audrey asked.

"I'm going to be running late tonight," Celia replied.

"That's fine, but where are you?"

Celia wrestled for a moment about whether to tell her mother the truth or not.

"I need to tell you something, but I need you to promise me you won't get mad," she said.

"I'll not make such a promise. If you are going to speak, you better speak up like my daughter," Audrey said firmly.

Celia took a deep breath.

"Mom, I think you better sit down, because I have got a long story to tell you," she began.

21

It was a sunny Saturday afternoon at the library and, although she was trying to calm herself, Celia couldn't relax. Tim de Sousa was in jail but was eligible for bond unless the police found evidence that he murdered Rachel. This made Celia nervous, especially now that she and her family were attending a public event.

Mrs. Owen's idea had come to life. The garden outside the library was busy for a family fun day, with little tables, umbrellas, a bouncing castle for the kids, a deejay's booth, a food serving area and of course a red carpet and outdoor studio set up for the photoshoot. There was a bubbly crowd of families and residents of Sunshine Cove who were mingling and enjoying themselves. The red carpet was about ten meters long and was where Mrs. Owens wanted them to model their scarves. Celia had remembered to carry hers. When it was time to do the catwalk, Mrs. Owens went to the deejays booth and spoke into a microphone. Her charming voice boomed through the speakers.

"We are all here to bring the glow back to the library! We are here to show those news people that we love this place and we will keep coming back!" Mrs. Owens said. "And because Miss Rachel Sablay, God rest her soul, was doing such a good thing, we have to do a good thing too! We are going to raise some cash in her honor and share love with those in need. We are here to celebrate our community and to appreciate each other! Are you with me?"

"Yeah!" the entire crowd shouted in unison amid cheers and claps.

"Then put your hands together for our lovely models, who are all drawn from the community. Also, I made some lovely scarves so if you need some let me know. Enjoy the show!" she said with enthusiasm.

The catwalk started, with each model walking down to music. As Celia walked down the carpet with the other twenty-odd models, she had already abandoned her earlier misgivings about the idea. She was having fun despite the fact she didn't know how to catwalk like a supermodel, and the scarf became very bright orange in the sun's glare. The crowd was so enthusiastic and receptive she couldn't help smiling. Her sons jumped up and down as she walked past them, with their grandmother and Melanie clapping alongside.

The catwalk ended with Mrs. Owens' beloved photoshoot, where all the models did individual and group poses with their scarves as the prominent feature. When she took a glance, Celia saw Mrs. Owens beaming with joy.

After that, the crowd began to mingle. The adults talked and danced, food was passed around and the kids had fun in the playpen and bouncing castle.

Although she was more at ease, Celia kept looking out for the security people Melanie had hired to patrol the place. She spotted Melanie walking towards the deejay's booth and caught up with her.

"Hey Mel. Everything's alright?"

"Yeah. So far, so good. There's been no drama. I thought Frank was coming?"

"No, he wasn't ready to come by. But he sent his best wishes and supports what we are doing," Celia replied.

"That's a relief! I was worried that maybe he thought we were dishonoring his wife's memory."

"No, he's not that type of guy. So, the patrols are going well?" she asked.

"Yeah. The head of security is giving me regular updates."

"That's great," she said unconvinced, "I'm just worried about this Tim thing. I would hate it if he got out."

"Same here. But if Tim was released then the police would have called you by now," she said.

Melanie was right. It was a comforting thought, but that could change any moment.

"Let's try to forget that and enjoy the sun, shall we?" Melanie said, leading Celia to a group of friends. They were soon laughing.

Suddenly, the volume of the music died down. Celia and Melanie noticed the loud talking of guests die down too. They soon found out why. The crowd in front of them parted to reveal a posse of uniformed police officers, led by Detective Bill Koloane. He walked up to them; stern-faced. Celia wondered what was going on.

"Hello ladies. Seems like you are having a party," Bill said.

"It's more of a family fun day. How may we help you, sir?" Melanie asked.

"We received reports of a neighborhood disturbance. We are here to make sure it doesn't ruin your afternoon," he replied.

"So, you are not here to stop us?" Celia asked.

"Why would we stop this? We're here to celebrate with you," he said, smiling.

Mrs. Owens, who was listening in, suddenly shouted, "It's okay! They are here to join the party!"

There were loud cheers and claps as the party got back in full swing. The officers spread out to different areas.

"You chose a very dramatic way to make your entrance," Celia said.

"Official business tends to be that way sometimes," Bill replied.

"Is that what this is, official business?" she asked.

"Yes, since I'll have to hang around you and ensure things run smoothly," he replied.

"Well, I suggest you don't hang around me too long otherwise some people here will start getting ideas," she whispered.

"Before you two continue with your teasing conversations, I hope you are not here because Tim has been released," Melanie said to Bill.

Bill smiled, "He's not going to be out for a long time to come. We found the evidence we needed at his house. Syringes and a receipt he tried to hide for the poison bought just before Rachel's death. You can ease your minds now about that."

Melanie sighed in relief.

"Fantastic! Let me go and get you both some party favors before it finishes," she said, and disappeared towards the serving area.

Bill and Celia looked at each other with a knowing smile, before they continued watching her sons John and James dancing.

For the first time in weeks Celia felt light. As her sons danced away without a care in the world, her heart filled with warmth. Enjoying a sunny afternoon with her loved ones made everything beautiful again.

The End

NEW NAILS AND A NASTY NIGHTMARE

A SUNSHINE COVE COZY MYSTERY

ABOUT NEW NAILS AND A NASTY NIGHTMARE

Released: October 2020
Series: Book 3 – Sunshine Cove Cozy Mystery Series
Standalone: Yes
Cliff-hanger: No

Celia is a beauty consultant who loves making her clients look good and helping her friends get out of trouble. She also has a bad habit of poking her nose in some police investigations.

She's delighted when her dear friend announces that she'll be opening a nail parlor in the heart of town. Still, she's a little bit concerned about her friend's lack of business experience and the characters who'll be helping her in this venture.

Celia becomes a nervous wreck when she hears that there's been a death at the nail parlor and her friend is the prime suspect. Several questions race through her mind as she races to the scene of the crime like:

Who did it?

Was it one of the business owners?

Or her friend's competitor?

Or a disgruntled employee?

Celia doesn't know the answer to any of these questions yet but she's determined to find out. Will she be successful or ruffle too many feathers and become the killer's next victim?

1

Celia Dube enjoyed humming a happy song in the morning. She sometimes believed she gave the chirping birds a run for their money as she hummed. It energized her and set the tone for her day. Today, she was in tune with Miriam Makeba's famous song 'Pata Pata' as she hummed and danced on her bedroom balcony. This song brought with it a mixture of memories; which included joyful and painful moments.

She paused briefly to watch the ocean waters ahead of her slap against the rocks and sandy beach. This view was one of the reasons she had moved to Sunshine Cove with her late husband, Trevor. When they had seen this house and what it had to offer, there was no going back. This was where they'd raise a family. She loved the fact that she was just fifteen minutes away from the beach and the fine sand. In the midst of her hectic days, these moments made it worthwhile.

They used to hum together. It wasn't his type of thing at first. He was an army man, the type who was used to bellowing out orders. To him silence or subtle hums were meant for stealth, not joyful expression. Once he was converted, they would dance together on that very balcony, welcoming new days when he was home, or dancing under the stars.

"Cece, are you planning to leave or what?" a shrill voice shouted from below. Celia stopped her humming to look down at the speaker. It was her mother, Audrey Matinise and she didn't look too happy.

"I'm taking a break, Ma!" Celia replied.

"I thought you're supposed to be delivering some orders this morning?"

"Like I said, I'm taking a break before I finish up then head out."

"You're taking breaks and the day hasn't even started yet. What will happen by midday?" Audrey said.

Celia laughed. Often, the smallest pleasures rattled her mother. She was staying with them for the next couple of days and was always a big help. Celia had two boys to raise, and they were a handful as they were growing so fast. Motherly duties aside, Celia needed short breaks every now and then.

It had been an intense couple of days promoting a new line of Maven beauty products. As the lead Maven beauty consultant in Sunshine Cove, Celia had to ensure each of the new products gained traction in the market.

Sunshine Cove was your typical small coastal suburban town, full of tourists in shorts walking the streets, visiting gift shops, enjoying the cuisine at local seafood restaurants, wearing colorful casual wear and keeping a relaxed pace to life.

Celia knew her market and that one-on-one interactions with her clients helped to sell her products.

That's where Celia always shone. She had impeccable charming skills that won over even the toughest of clients. Although her years of experience gave her an edge over her competition, it was still a lot of work. Song and dance helped her fight the burnout that sought to slow down her endeavors.

She had several orders to make that day, and she wasn't done prepping the delivery packs. She worked from home, with one of the bedrooms specially converted to house weekly deliveries of stock that she received from the city headquarters. She knew she would have to give up the bedroom when her two sons got older. For now, it was there to build up funds for their future. If Trevor was still alive, he'd have approved.

She was finishing the last packs when her mother came in.

"Cece, have you seen the little dinosaur man?" her mother asked with her usual quizzical expression.

Although she was in her fifties, Audrey Matinise looked younger than her years. She claimed that spending time with her two grandsons was the secret to her renewed youthfulness, and Celia wasn't keen to argue with that.

"You can't use the Dinosaur Man anymore to charm the kids. It's been there for the last four years," Celia said.

"As the chief organizer of your kids' birthday parties, I know what works for them and what doesn't. Dinosaur Man is a popular feature," Audrey insisted.

Celia wasn't convinced. The Dinosaur Man was a life-size dinosaur head outfit with arms. You put it on and it covered the head, arms, shoulders and half the torso. The wearer became half human, half dinosaur. Admittedly, the boys loved it. But Celia felt it was time for a change.

"Have you considered that maybe the Dinosaur Man wants to retire?"

Audrey wasn't taking the bait.

"Have you seen it?" she asked.

"No, I haven't seen it. Even if I had, I wouldn't tell you where it was," Celia replied.

"Now why would you do something like that?" Audrey asked.

"I know why you're looking for it. You do this every year, Ma."

"What are you talking about?" Audrey asked.

"Stop acting all innocent. We're not doing that this year. We're celebrating James' birthday in a whole new way," Celia said emphatically.

"But I always make it a little different every year," Audrey said.

"It doesn't matter if you buy him a new set of clothes or a new toy or bake a different cake. For Frank, the main attraction is always the little dinosaur because you know he loves dinosaurs. But we need to show him a different experience this time, don't you think?" Celia asked.

"He's still a child. He has plenty of time to learn about those other things."

"He's turning eight in a few days. This is the best time to let his young, curious brain absorb every bit of knowledge about things. Let's show him a new side of Sunshine Cove," Celia said.

"Well, it just sounds to me like you're being a party pooper," Audrey remarked.

"What? Hear me out. I don't mind you planning the birthdays like you always have. But please, can you try something different this time?" Celia pleaded.

Audrey shook her head.

"Come on, Ma, you must have a few new ideas," Celia prodded.

"I can't promise anything, but I will give it some thought," Audrey replied as she left the room.

Celia smiled to herself. She knew this wasn't going to be a walk in the park for her mother but she was curious to see how it would go.

Celia's favorite coffee house, The Pier, was bought out recently and given a full facelift. Where formerly it had a finish similar to your regular city coffee shop with walls full of posters and flashy colors, the restaurant was now more homely. It had dark wood paneling inside and out that gave it that cozy feel. It's new owner, Festo Tshabalala, was a charming man. Stout and energetic, he wore smart casual suits and was always smiling at clients when they walked in.

Celia had a date with Melanie Dawes, one of her great friends. Melanie was a librarian with a vibrant personality, and Celia liked her curious nature. They met at least twice every week to connect and unwind from their busy schedules.

"Enjoying your visit, ladies?" he asked Celia and Melanie who were seated in one of the plush booths.

"We would be if our order was already here," Celia replied with a smile.

As if on cue, the waiter arrived with a loaded tray in hand. He served them their piping hot caramel tea and café mocha with two slices of carrot cake each.

"You were saying?" Festo asked, knowing he now had the upper hand.

"Yes, sir! We're now officially enjoying this!" Melanie replied. They all laughed.

"That's what I like to hear. If you need anything else, don't hesitate to let my people know," he replied, and moved to the next table.

"I'm going to fall in love with this place," Celia mused before she took a sip of the caramel tea.

"You and me both," Melanie replied. "So I have regular news and not so regular news that I want to share with you. Which do you want to hear first?"

Celia raised her eyebrows quizzically.

"Give me the regular news," Celia replied.

"Okay, here we go," Melanie said, taking a deep breath, "I'm opening a business."

"Are you serious?" Celia asked.

"Of course, I am. Are you saying that I don't look like a business owner?" Melanie asked.

"I didn't say that. I'm just surprised that's all. I mean, your passion and experience is centered around the library and I never pictured you in another place."

"You just admitted that I don't look like a business owner," Melanie replied.

"Oh, I did? I take it back. I'm sorry," she apologized.

"It's fine. Well, I can be full of surprises so don't be fooled," she said with confidence.

"I'll take your word for it. Tell me more about this new business."

"It's a nail parlor on Main Street. I'm talking manicures, pedicures and everything in between."

"A nail parlor? Wow, this keeps getting better. You know I'm in the beauty products business and you didn't tell me?" Celia protested.

"Hey, go easy on me! I'm telling you now, am I not?"

Celia shook her head.

"Anyway, the reason I'm telling you this is because I'm going to have a soft launch. Consider this an official invitation," Melanie said.

"Okay, sounds good. Tell me the date and I'll rearrange my schedule. I think I'll even come with a friend or two. Is that okay?" Celia asked.

"Sure! Just let me know who it is."

"Chloe Matthews. She's crazy about nails."

"Ah, our Chloe? Yeah, she's great company. The launch is tomorrow. You'll make it?" Melanie asked.

"Sure. Let me text Chloe right now," Celia said as she took out her phone, "I still can't believe you kept this bubbling under the surface all this time."

"I told you I was full of surprises," Melanie replied.

The two women laughed.

Celia was impressed. She admired her friend's new venture but wondered if she was biting off more than she could chew. She could tell it was not going to be a regular week.

2

It was a warm evening made for a night out, Celia thought as she walked down Main Street. Up ahead, she could see her destination.

The Afrostar Nail Parlor had a sizeable window front made of reinforced glass. While most of the upper part was clear such that you could see into the establishment, the lower sections of the window front had colorful stickers of two beautiful models showing immaculately done nails. Stylish and clean, it was slightly above the level of the other shops on Main Street.

It also had a neon sign in cursive font and gold lettering that had not come on although darkness had already fallen. Perhaps Melanie and her business partner didn't want to attract much attention from passers-by, Celia mused.

At the entrance, a large man in a tan suit confirmed her name was on the guest list and ushered her in. Inside, she was one of ten people present. Soft jazz music by Hugh Masekela filtered through the room.

The space was all white, with large mirrors along the longest walls. In front of the mirrors were customized leather seats for the customers. Next to each seat was a padded carpet. On the ceiling were miniature soft lights, which complemented the larger ones along the walls. It felt luxurious without looking out of reach.

"You look amazing," Melanie exclaimed as she walked towards Celia. Melanie was dressed in a long black and white satin dress that shimmered in the light.

"Why, thank you," Celia replied, gushing with pride. "It was a gift from a good client that I have never worn."

It was a mustard yellow evening dress with colorful patterns around her neck inspired by the Ndebele Isigolwani neck ring. She loved it. She'd never worn it because it stood out, and Celia usually liked blending into the background. Tonight was an exception.

"You didn't have to outshine us," Melanie said teasingly.

"Well, you said that you're launching your first business venture, and there was no way I was going to come here in anything less," Celia replied with a smile.

"Are you going to check mine out as well or the compliments are just reserved for Cece?" Chloe Matthews asked. She wore a fitting gray dress that accentuated her figure with black heels.

Melanie laughed.

"I was coming to you, be patient!" Melanie said, "You know that between the three of us you're always pulling out the classiest looks. You have not disappointed!"

Chloe did a little twirl. As the daughter of the clothing magnate Ezra Matthews, she was expected to look stylish. She did occasionally strut her stuff at events, but she loved blending in without the tag of a wealthy man's daughter. Her down-to-earth and relatable qualities were what endeared her to Celia. Over the past two years, they had built a great friendship where they could be open with each other.

"Of course, I haven't! I'm not here to attend. I'm here to enjoy the launch of what will be the best nail parlor in Sunny Cove," Chloe said.

"Amen! Thanks for your support Chloe. We're just about to start. We're waiting for two more people," Melanie said.

"You already have a decent crowd," Celia remarked as she scanned the room. "That fella catches my interest. Was he on your guest list or your business partner's?"

Melanie turned to see who Celia was referring to. It was a muscular man in a grey striped suit and slick hair. He looked polished, but seemed like a man who wouldn't be afraid to roll his sleeves and get his hands dirty.

"Both of ours," Melanie replied, "He's one of our big investors."

"Hmm. There's something about him I can't put a finger on," Celia replied.

"One day I'll tell you the story," Melanie said, "for now I have to go and open this event."

"Actually, I'll do that for you," a woman dressed in a silk dress said. She smiled and gave Melanie a casual wave as she walked up to the front where a simple glass stand was waiting.

"Who on earth is that?" Chloe asked.

"That, my friends, is Charlize Langa. My business partner," Melanie replied.

The music faded away. Charlize tapped a wine glass with a pen, producing that distinct clinking sound. The murmurs stopped and everyone turned to her.

"Esteemed guests, ladies and gentlemen. We are happy to have you here as our first visitors. We hope many more will walk through those doors for the next couple of years. My name is Charlize Langa. Some of you know me as an entrepreneur, business builder, PR strategist, and fixer. If you've been in the business circles in Sunshine Cove for the past five years then you have met me using one of those titles. I have them because I am a go-getter and I assure you we are going to make this nail parlor the best in town."

The guests clapped fervently. Celia nodded as she clapped. She had heard of Charlize, but didn't know much about her.

"Let me introduce to you my business partner who will say a few words before we get to the next bit of our program. Welcome, Melanie Dawes."

Charlize led the clapping as Melanie gracefully walked to the front.

"Thank you very much Charlize for the introduction. I'm not one to talk in public, but I have to show my appreciation. My gratitude goes to each one of you for supporting us this evening. We are hoping to form long-term relationships with you. I'm a librarian by profession but a business administrator by education. I have revamped and managed an institution, built a loyal community and my visionary mindset compliments Charlize's fantastic resume. Thank you and enjoy your evening," Melanie said with a broad smile.

The claps and cheers erupted as Melanie stepped back from the podium.

"Thank you, Melanie!" Charlize began, "I'm proud to count on you and I really appreciate the fact that you value our partnership. Now this wasn't meant to be a formal evening full of long speeches and boring anecdotes. We're here to celebrate! So, let's kick up the music, pass around the finger foods, have some wine and enjoy. Please don't dance too much. The floor might be slippery – and a little expensive."

Charlize gave a cheeky wink as the guests laughed. The music returned, louder than before.

Melanie walked back to where Celia and Chloe stood.

"That was beautiful," Celia said.

"Thanks, guys," Melanie replied.

"So why are you starting this business?" Celia asked.

"Well, its always been in the works. I can't just rely on one source of income. I need to fast track some of my goals. So here I am, diversifying my income," Melanie replied.

"Smart move," Chloe said.

An usher brought a platter full of steaming lamb sosaties, kebabs held on wooden skewers. It wasn't often you would find these at an event that wasn't a local backyard barbeque. They each grabbed one and dug in.

"Why the small splash?" Celia asked in between bites.

"What do you mean?" Melanie replied.

"Was it your idea to keep the launch small?"

"It wasn't. I believe in strong starts and building awareness as early as possible. Charlize had a different opinion and so we went with that," Melanie replied.

Just then, Melanie frowned. Celia followed her gaze, landing on a woman in a red dress with light tiger-paw patterns.

"What's going on?" Celia asked.

"I didn't expect to see her here," Melanie replied.

"Who is she?"

"I only know her first name. Patricia. She's the competition."

"Why would you invite your competition?" Celia asked.

"It's one of Charlize's philosophical stances. 'Know your friends but keep your potential enemies closer,' she likes to say," Melanie replied.

"That's a bold move," Chloe said.

"It's more arrogant, actually," Celia remarked.

"Well, I'll let Charlize handle it. I'm picking my fights tonight," Melanie said.

"And are you ok with that?" Celia asked.

Melanie shrugged.

"It will do for now. I just want us to focus on making it the best nail parlor this side of town. We have the next two months to do that," Melanie replied.

"Two months, you say?" Celia asked, "You're quite ambitious."

"Well Charlize and I have some pretty solid plans that we hope will come together."

"Enough about business! We need to catch up away from this work environment. It's been a while!" Chloe said.

"It sure has," Melanie agreed.

"You're not planning anything crazy, right?" Celia asked.

"Not really. Or even better, we could set up blind dates for each other," Chloe replied.

"Did you say blind dates?" Celia asked.

"Why not? I haven't heard a lot about you and Detective Bill recently. What happened?" Chloe asked with a wink. Melanie smiled.

"That's not going to be discussed here," Celia replied, her cheeks reddening.

"Chloe is onto something here. What's the latest on the handsome detective? You two had some amazing chemistry," Melanie said.

"I remember the sparks," Chloe chimed in.

"That were destined to be flames," Melanie added with a cheeky grin.

"Melanie, you of all people should be the last one talking about my dating life. Yours has been as barren as the desert for the last couple of months," Celia said.

"So, it sounds like all of us need a little excitement in our love lives," Chloe said. "I think I should find matches for each of us."

"Count me out because I'm not interested," Celia said.

"There's no way we are going to do it and leave you behind," Chloe insisted.

"Come on, Cece. Just a harmless night and we can each share our experiences after our dates. Lord knows I need an entertaining one," Melanie said.

"Moving on swiftly, you do remember that I supply beauty products, right?" Celia asked. "I have a few products in our line that could suit your establishment."

"Yeah, sure. Actually, I wanted to introduce you to Charlize," Melanie turned her head and signaled Charlize to come over.

Charlize excused herself from the group she was talking to and walked over to the three women.

"I hope you are enjoying the launch under Melanie's watch," Charlize said with a warm smile.

"She's doing an amazing job," Celia replied, returning the smile.

"I wanted to introduce you to my friends," Melanie said, "This is Chloe Matthews, the daughter of the man who owns the Matthews Clothing company."

"Nice to meet you, Chloe," Charlize said as she shook Chloe's hand. "I am honored to be in the presence of someone associated with a well-known and admired name in our community."

"I try to get out of the family shadow, but it finds me often. Congratulations on your launch," Chloe said.

"And then we have Celia Dube," Melanie continued, "She's a good friend of mine. We've done business deals together and organized events. She also happens to be the main distributor of the highly rated Maven beauty products."

NEW NAILS AND A NASTY NIGHTMARE

"Glad to meet you, Celia," Charlize said. "Melanie has praised your products so much that I was even thinking of getting one for myself!"

"You definitely can. What do you need?" Celia asked.

"I'll check my dressing table and let you know in due course. I hope you'll be coming to visit us as a client?" Charlize asked.

"Actually, that's one of the reasons I wanted you to meet her," Melanie said, "She would like to explore the possibility of supplying us with some of her beauty products."

"We have an amazing line of nail varnishes, nail polishes and so on in a wide range of colors," Celia said as she handed Charlize a glossy catalogue.

Charlize slowly flipped through the catalogue as she listened.

"Our distribution network is very good, and price point for the quality you get is quite a good deal especially for new businesses," Celia added.

Charlize began flipping through the pages slowly, with very subtle nods of her head. Celia's body language training kicked in subconsciously. She watched Charlize purse her lips. She could tell that she was wrestling with the idea. Charlize then handed back the catalogue.

"I think we'll pick this up later, okay?" Charlize said.

"So you're open to a conversation?" Melanie asked.

"I think you and I'll talk about this later. For now, let's just enjoy the evening," Charlize said with a forced smile. She then turned and left.

"Why did that feel like a blow off?" Chloe asked.

"Because it was," Celia replied.

"Guys, it wasn't a blow off," Melanie said.

"Sure felt like one," Chloe insisted.

"You could tell from her body language," Celia said. "I think she doesn't want to do business with me."

"Listen. I'll talk to her and fix this, okay?" Melanie assured her.

Celia shrugged.

"Good luck with that. I can tell a tough cookie when I see one," Celia replied. "I'm more worried about you. Knowing your personality, Charlize might give you a tough time here."

3

"How about we get a trampoline?" Audrey asked.

Celia sighed.

"The kids are too young to be jumping up and down. What happens if they break their bones?" she said.

"You were jumping on trampolines at their age, Cece. Stop being funny," Audrey remarked.

"Ma, have you forgotten the day I jumped too high and sprained my ankle?" Celia asked.

"That was nothing! A little herbal ointment and some rooibos tea had you jumping around again the next day," Audrey said.

Celia laughed.

"Before they jump on the trampoline, I would like to show them how to do it safely. Forget the trampoline," Celia replied.

"So what are these children coming here to do?" Audrey asked in frustration. "Planning a party is supposed to be fun and I'm not enjoying it this year."

"But you are being stubborn with ideas," Celia said. "You should try the internet. There're tons of ideas there."

"None of the ideas I came across interest me," she replied.

"It's not about what interests you, but what interests the kids."

"I could say the same thing about you and the trampolines," she remarked.

"It's not the same thing, Ma. Why don't you get in touch with Mrs. Owens? She could help you plan this thing. She loves the kids and is good with events," she suggested.

Audrey frowned. Celia knew this might get spicy. Mrs. Owens was a great family friend, and when she got together with her mother, it was usually a lot of fun. However, sometimes they had serious disagreements.

"Remember you're doing it for the kids," Celia said as she planted a kiss on her mother's forehead. "See you later."

THE SUNSHINE COVE Library looked immaculate in the afternoon sun. Its largely glass facade stood out in the midst of other older buildings.

Celia walked up to the library reception and found Melanie there, as usual. She was deeply engrossed, staring at her computer screen, which was hidden from view behind the counter.

"Hey, Mel," Celia whispered, keen not to disrupt the readers present in the space.

"Hey," Melanie replied without looking up. Celia rapped the countertop with her knuckles, startling her. Melanie shot her a look.

"Are you busy or can you have a quick chat?" she asked. Melanie's gaze softened.

"Sure, we can talk. I actually I need a break from all this. Are you willing to work part time?" Melanie asked.

"Here or at the nail parlor?"

"We can start with here. Right now. I just need a holiday or a getaway. Actually, we need to do that blind date soon," Melanie said.

"We killed that idea," Celia said dismissively.

"Come on, it will be fun," Melanie said, "Chloe thinks we should do it together."

"You mean at the same time?" Celia asked.

"Same time, same place. It will make you more comfortable. Just in case you don't like each other, we're your exit plan."

Celia shook her head.

"I am not going to join this bandwagon in a million years!" Celia insisted.

"Think about it for a minute," Melanie said as she turned back to the screen.

"I don't need to," Celia said with finality.

Melanie didn't reply. She was so engrossed in the computer screen, Celia got curious. She moved towards the side of the counter to get a better view.

"Is that the nail parlor you're looking at?" Celia asked.

"Yeah, it's a CCTV feed," Melanie replied.

"Why are you watching CCTV footage of your business from here?" Celia asked.

"I didn't realize how difficult it would be keeping up with a new business."

"Is it just the business you're keeping up with or something more?" Celia asked.

Melanie sighed.

"It's also not been easy to get Charlize to give me good updates about what's happening there. I mean, I can read the books of account and everything, but I need to know some of the things that happen when I'm not there. That detail just never comes out."

"You should get closer to the employees," Celia suggested.

"I'm working on that," she replied.

"How's it going with Charlize?" she asked.

"I'm managing. It's not a bed of roses, but I guess that's how things are when you're trying to get to grips with a new operation," Melanie replied.

"Did you talk to her about the proposal I gave?" Celia asked.

"I haven't really gotten time to do that. But I promise I'll do that later this evening, or at the latest tomorrow. Can you give me till then?"

"Of course I can, don't sweat it," Celia replied. "I think I'll be heading out now. I have one more delivery to make before I head home."

"Which direction are you headed?" Melanie asked.

"Towards the Farmer's Market."

"Which means you will be passing through Main Street. Fantastic! Can you drop this off for me?" Melanie asked as she handed over a cashbook. "We wanted one with our company logo on it."

"Sure! Should I give it to Charlize?"

"Yes, please. Just make sure you don't try to force the conversation again," Melanie teased.

"You have my word," Celia replied with a smile.

Some minutes after three in the afternoon, Celia arrived at the nail parlor. She found it busy with three clients, and the two staffers had their hands full. She could foresee they would need to hire new people to cover the demand.

She found Charlize attending to one of the clients who was waiting for their nails to dry.

Charlize walked up to her and smiled.

"Celia! What brings you here?"

"Hi, Charlize. Melanie asked me to drop off this cashbook," Celia said, handing it over.

"Thank you very much!" Charlize said.

"You're welcome."

Celia turned to leave and was about to step out when she decided to ask one of the employees a question. She walked up to Sarah.

"Hi, do you have silver nail polish?"

"No, we don't have it yet," she replied.

"So, how are you attending to clients who want it?"

Sarah shook her head. "We don't until Miss Langa brings it over."

After hearing this, Celia couldn't just leave. She walked back to the counter where Charlize stood.

"I wanted to get my nails done but apparently you don't have silver nail polish?" Celia said.

"Who told you that?" Charlize asked.

"One of your staffers. I can bring it in tomorrow if that's okay."

"You asked one of my staffers if they have silver nail polish?"

"Yes, I happened to ask as I was walking out," Celia said.

"Well, your concern is noted. But all bookings are done by me, so this is the right place to ask." Charlize stated.

"I didn't know that. But I'm here now."

"I would take it slow if I were you," Charlize said.

"Excuse me?" Celia asked, puzzled.

"You're pushing too hard."

"Am I pushing too hard? I was simply making an observation that could gain you an extra client."

"And I've taken it under advisement. Still, you shouldn't come into my store and start ordering us to do things for you," Charlize snapped.

"I was not ordering you to do things for me. It was a simple…"

Charlize interrupted.

"You made your proposal during the launch. You do not have to do it here when other clients are present."

"I didn't even raise my voice when I told you this. I am simply saying it would be nice of you to buy more stock. Melanie is my good friend and I would like her business to flourish even when she's not here."

"Are you trying to suggest that I don't know what I'm doing here?" Charlize asked.

Celia's phone started ringing. It was Melanie. Celia paused, then took it.

"Hey, Melanie. I delivered the cash book and…"

"Cece, I thought we agreed that you wouldn't talk to her about the deal?"

"I'm not talking to her about it."

"I can see what's happening right in front of me," Melanie replied.

Celia remembered Melanie had a camera feed into the shop.

"I hear you. I'm leaving now." Celia hung up and turned to Charlize. "I'm sorry for the miscommunication. I didn't mean to offend you."

"Thank you," Charlize said. She moved closer to Celia. "Just to make it clear: despite your friendship with Melanie, I am running the business. Please keep that in mind next time."

"I understand," Celia replied.

As she walked out, Celia couldn't help feeling something bad was about to happen.

4

Celia had just finished a client delivery when Melanie called. Stuck in traffic, she was tempted to use her actual mobile phone handset to take the call. Then she remembered that she'd recently fixed the Bluetooth system in her car.

"Hey, Mel! Talk to me," Celia said.

"Where are you?" Melanie asked.

"I'm caught up in traffic on the other side of town."

"Do you have any other deliveries on your schedule?"

"Not at the moment. Are you making an order?" Celia asked, smiling.

Melanie laughed.

"I am actually calling to say that we can meet you now. If you have a moment, please pass by the nail parlor," Melanie said.

Celia smiled.

"Are you sure? Charlize is okay with this?" Celia asked.

"I wouldn't call you if I wasn't sure."

"Great! I'm on my way. Give me about half an hour to weave through this traffic."

Celia was glad.

"This product is called Coral Smooth nail polish. It's a tribute to coral reefs which are endangered but still very important to our fishing communities," Celia said confidently.

As she spoke, she handed bottles of the nail polish for Melanie and Charlize to look at. They were seated on the leather seats in the service area. Sarah and Fidel, the two employees, had been excused for their lunch break so that the three women could talk in private. Celia had fifteen minutes to make her case, and she was giving it her best shot.

"So you're telling me it's made out of coral reef?" Charlize asked as she turned the bottle. She squinted her eyes to read the ingredients.

"Coral is not one of the ingredients. I think that would be illegal!" Celia said with a laugh, "As I stated earlier, our products are made from fully organic materials and are good for the human body," she confidently replied.

"So why would you call it coral and yet it's not made out of coral reef?" Charlize asked again.

Melanie cleared her throat.

"I think what Celia was trying to say is that Maven beauty products as a company are very environmentally conscious. So they have branded some of their products using the names of endangered species to highlight the causes behind them. I think that's good for our brand."

"Why don't you let her answer my question herself," Charlize said. Melanie frowned.

Celia was simmering with anger, wondering what she would say to Charlize that would not be disrespectful. She had a right to stand up for herself. She took in a deep breath.

"To echo what Melanie has said, Maven beauty products are fully organic and…"

"You said that already. Tell me something new," Charlize interjected.

Celia paused briefly before replying.

"We have a very good product that has won multiple international awards and you can use that angle to…"

Charlize put both her hands up. Celia stopped talking, disgusted by the gesture.

"Celia, with all due respect I am not here to listen to your company values. I'm sure they are of great benefit to your employees and shareholders. But right now I just can't see how bringing you on board is going to favor our nail parlor," Charlize said with finality.

Melanie was not amused.

"You're not giving her a chance to speak!" Melanie said.

"I've heard all I needed to hear. It doesn't suit my business," Charlize replied.

"This parlor is our business and I have a say in this conversation," Melanie exclaimed.

"And you have spoken. Need I remind you of the clause in our agreement that states we both must reach a consensus before any major decision? Nothing short of that can make us move forward," Charlize said.

Melanie bit her lip and went quiet, struggling to control her anger.

She exchanged a look with Celia, who was equally incensed.

"Unless there's something else that you'd like to say or show me, I think we're done here," Charlize said.

Celia shook her head. Charlize stood up and extended her hand toward Celia.

"Thank you very much for your time today, and I wish you all the best."

Celia stared at the hand for a few moments, resisting the urge to slap it away. She decided to take the higher road and shook it.

"Thank you for having me. I hope that sometime in the near future you will come around because I'm sure some of your clients will want to use our products."

Charlize smiled.

"We'll cross that bridge when we get there. However, if I were you, I wouldn't count on it too much," Charlize replied. She sauntered away, heading up the stairs to the mezzanine floor office.

"What the hell was that?" Celia asked, fuming.

"Trust me, I'm just as angry as you are. You warned me about how

NEW NAILS AND A NASTY NIGHTMARE

difficult she might be. I didn't know it would be this bad," Melanie replied.

"Hadn't you briefed her?"

"Of course, I had. I didn't set you up. I honestly thought we had smoothed things over, but she was clearly holding another ace up her sleeve," Melanie replied.

"I have met disrespectful people, but this was a stab in the back and one the worst interactions I have ever had!" Celia said. "I think you should reconsider this business partnership. It won't end well."

"Let me straighten this out. I'm not taking any more of this. I'm really sorry that it turned out like this."

"I'm sorry too," Celia replied as they both stood up.

Celia packed the beauty products she had laid out on the table.

Minutes later, she was ready to leave. She looked up to the mezzanine floor where the upper office was. Through its windows, she could see Melanie and Charlize having an intense argument. She couldn't hear what they were saying.

'That soundproofing must have cost a good amount,' Celia thought to herself as she walked out. It felt good to feel the afternoon sun again after the cold reception she had received. She needed to see her sons. They were the perfect antidote to the negative emotions she was dealing with.

"What do you mean, red in color? You know the boy doesn't like red."

Celia had just walked into an intense conversation between her mother and Mrs. Owens on speakerphone.

"Oh, but he is only turning nine years old! He can learn about new colors, you know! Also, how about throwing in a clown or two?" Mrs. Owen's voice crackled through the speakerphone.

"He's turning eight, Christie. You want to bring a clown? Have you seen James? He has never and will never like clowns," Audrey replied animatedly.

"Audrey, you need to open your mind to new things!" Mrs. Owens replied.

"No, Christie. We don't do red colored things or clowns here. Even

Christmas is just a regular day with a touch of smart clothes. No red in sight."

Celia listened, with her smile growing ever wider. She waved at her mother, who waved back and pointed towards the phone, shrugging her shoulders in wonderment at Mrs. Owens strange ideas.

"Maybe I should come over and we can talk better face-to-face?" Mrs. Owens suggested.

"No! Not now, Christie! The boys will be arriving soon from the school trip and I don't want them bogged down by our chat about this."

"It will only take a minute, Audrey."

"Tomorrow. Does tomorrow work for you?"

Mrs. Owens sighed. "Very well. Tomorrow morning it is."

"Perfect. They won't be around to hear our plans.

A horn sounded from outside. The boys had arrived.

"I have to go now, Christie. Enjoy your evening."

"Sure, and remember…" She didn't finish as Audrey had already hung up and was walking swiftly to the door.

"These guys are right on time!" Audrey said as she opened the door.

The boys barged in with their little travel packs, still buzzing with excitement.

"And then, and then we saw lions." James shouted.

"You saw a lion? Were you scared?" Audrey asked.

"No! The lion was locked in a cage!" he replied.

Audrey gave Celia a look.

"We have to change that image. You know lions aren't meant to be in cages," Audrey said as she led them to their bedrooms.

Alone now, Celia slumped onto the couch and it wasn't long before she drifted off into a deep sleep.

She was startled awake by a noise. She could hear the shrieks and laughter of the kids filtering in from the backyard garden. She couldn't believe they were still playing after such a long day trip.

She looked at the clock. It was five o'clock in the evening. The noise was still there. A buzzing sound. It was her phone, which was inside her handbag. She quickly searched for it and took it out. It was Melanie. Celia cleared her throat.

"Hello, Mel," she said.

"Where are you?" Melanie said.

"I am not coming if she wants to have another chat," she replied.

There was a brief pause. She could hear sniffling sounds.

"Are you okay, Mel?" Celia asked.

"Not quite. We won't be smoothing things over anytime soon, actually."

"She's that stubborn, huh?"

"Not that. Can you come over, please? Now?"

"What's going on, Mel?"

"Please come over. I need you, Cece."

"Can you tell me what's going on?" Celia asked as she grabbed her bag, put on her shoes and walked towards the door.

"Charlize is… she's lying on the floor. She's not moving. I think she's dead and I don't know what to do," a distraught Melanie managed to say over the phone.

Her words struck Celia like a thunderbolt.

5

Celia got to the nail parlor in less than thirty minutes.

Outside, the flashing emergency lights from an ambulance were lighting up the street. A small crowd was gathering outside as curious people wondered what was going on. Celia ran into the building and found Melanie confused.

"What happened?" Celia asked as her eyes took in the scene. In front of them, at the foot of the staircase that led to the mezzanine office, were two paramedics. Charlize's dead body lay in between them at the bottom of a staircase from the mezzanine floor. They were not conducting any emergency procedures, which was not a good sign. Celia looked around and saw the two parlor employees, Sarah and Fidel, who were in shock. What had they witnessed? she wondered.

Melanie was quietly sobbing, her hands clasped together as if in prayer for a miracle. However, Celia knew better, there was no way Charlize was rising again.

"Mel, you want to tell me what happened?"

Melanie nodded as she worked to compose herself.

"We were talking. Stuff about the business. Then she walked out and the next thing I know she was tumbling down the stairs."

"You saw her tumbling down?" the detective asked.

"I heard it first. It was like a rumble. At first, I thought the mezzanine floor was collapsing, so I ran out for dear life. Then at the top of the stairs I caught her taking the last few steps to the bottom." She paused. "I... I tried calling out to her. She wasn't moving. She wasn't breathing. I ran down and... I can't believe this is happening."

Celia massaged her back to comfort her friend, but it sounded to her like this was an accident. She could see both Charlize's heels were off, lying a short distance from her body. Had she tripped on one, missed a step?

She looked again at Fidel and Sarah, who were silently conversing. Maybe they saw more that could explain the situation.

"Let me ask your people," Celia said.

She was about to move towards the two employees when the police walked in. Two plain-clothes detectives followed two uniformed officers as they strode straight to where Charlize lay. Talking to the employees would have to wait, Celia resolved.

After conversing with the paramedics, the two detectives walked to where Melanie and Celia stood. The tall and hulky one took out a notebook and spoke while the slender one scanned the room.

"You're the lady who called?" the detective asked.

Melanie nodded.

"Your name, please, and your connection to the deceased?"

"Melanie Dawes. We're business partners," she replied. He quickly scribbled her responses.

The detective then asked for the identities of Celia and the two employees, which he also wrote down.

"Alright, tell me what happened here," the detective asked.

Melanie took in a deep breath then told him the same thing she had recounted to Celia.

"What were you talking about before the incident?" the detective queried.

"It was about a business deal that she wanted to make."

"What was the nature of the conversation?"

"What do you mean?"

"Was it cordial or more heated?"

Melanie hesitated, then responded. "It was more of an argument."

The detective's eyes narrowed. Then he wrote this detail down. Celia's eyes widened. Why had Melanie left out this detail earlier?

The paramedics had already left, and three forensic investigators had replaced them. They were taking pictures, samples, and looking for clues on the staircase as well as the mezzanine office.

"So, tell me again, why were you arguing?" the detective probed.

"It was something that happened often. You know, it's the norm in a business relationship," Melanie replied.

Celia wanted to pinch her now, because her responses did not sound very convincing.

"I know many business relationships where people don't argue much. Would you say you got along?"

"For the most part, yes."

"And for the other part?"

"It was…"

Melanie trailed off as she turned to look at Celia. Celia maintained a deadpan expression. She didn't want the detective knowing she was pinching her friend to keep quiet.

After a pause, the slender detective returned and whispered to the tall one. Celia would have wanted to do the same, but she feared that if the detectives saw any sign of scheming behavior, they might see Melanie in an unfavorable light.

It was too late, though.

The tall detective returned, handcuffs in hand.

"I'm going to take you into custody now, Miss Dawes," he said as he reached for her hands.

"Wait, what for?"

"You're under suspicion for the death of the deceased," he replied, locking both cuffs around her wrists.

Celia couldn't believe her eyes.

As they walked out into the street, the small crowd had grown larger. They saw Melanie being marched out, and it hit Celia what a spectacle it was.

NEW NAILS AND A NASTY NIGHTMARE

"Don't let them take me," Melanie said to Celia. "I didn't do anything."

"I know. I'm right behind you," Celia replied.

Melanie gave Celia one forlorn look as she was led to the police car. For Celia, the whole ordeal was surreal.

Celia quickly went into the parlor and told the two employees to monitor the place and the investigators until she got back. She then dashed to her car just as the police car sped off. As she fumbled to get her car keys out and start the engine, adrenaline was pumping fast in her system.

She followed them all the way to the station. While driving she kept trying to come to terms with the image of her good friend handcuffed and led out in public like a guilty criminal. It wasn't adding up. Maybe it was an accident. On the other hand, it was simply a case of being at the wrong place at the wrong time. But even Celia had to admit it didn't look good for Melanie. For now, all she could do to prevent the helplessness from paralyzing her was to show her support.

When they got to the station, Melanie was swiftly booked in and then led down the corridor to the interrogation room.

Celia waited in the lobby alone, seated on the wooden bench that had seen better days. She reached for her phone and dialed a familiar number.

"Hey Cecc, what's up?" Chloe asked on the other end of the line.

"Hey. Something's happened. Melanie has been arrested," Celia said.

"Wait, what?" Chloe asked in shock.

"Yeah. I'm at the station now, waiting to see what happens."

"How on Earth did that happen?"

Celia sighed, wondering whether to reveal the weight of the news.

"Something tragic happened at the nail parlor. Do you have a moment to come over?" she asked.

"Yeah sure, I'll be leaving in half an hour."

"Great. See you soon," she replied.

She lowered her phone, then stared at its screen.

"Is this the part where you call me?" A voice asked.

She looked up to find detective Bill Koloane staring down at her. Even in these testing times, she still found him disarmingly attractive. He was dressed sharply as usual with khaki pants, a striped long-sleeve shirt and brown shoes. His scalp shone under the glare of the house lights, and his beard had grown fuller.

She tried to smile back but didn't succeed.

"I don't think I'll need to do that now that you're here," she replied.

"Are you okay?" he asked.

"I'm not actually. You remember Melanie Dawes?"

"She works at the library, right?"

"Yes. Well, I'm here because she's been arrested for something she might not have done."

Detective Koloane sat down next to her. "How serious is this?" he asked.

"Her business partner fell down a flight of stairs and the police suspect that Melanie did it."

"Any special reason?"

"They had a heated argument before her fall. Melanie witnessed her fall."

"Hmm," Detective Koloane grunted, "That's serious."

"I am just trying to wrap my head around what happened."

"Was this a business dispute?" he asked.

Celia turned to him, wondering why he was asking her that question.

"Are you on the case?" she asked.

"I'm not at the moment. It hasn't been assigned to me. I have no idea what they're doing with her in the interrogation room."

"Then I hope you understand if I can't answer your question at the moment because I'm not sure it was."

"Fair enough," he replied. "Anything you want me to do to help?"

"Just go and check for me that she's okay and advise me on whether I should stay or do something else."

"Sure thing."

With that, Bill Koloane got up, walked down the hall towards the interrogation room, and disappeared around the corner.

One hour later, he returned. By that time, Chloe had arrived and was keeping Celia company.

"I'm being informed that after answering some questions, Melanie has decided to ask for a lawyer. So, she's going to the holding cell for the rest of the day until her lawyer comes over," he said.

"Has she made the phone call to the lawyer?" Chloe asked.

"I'm told that that has been done now though I do not know when he's going to come over. I would suggest that you leave, and I'll keep you posted on how things are going."

"Can I see her?" Celia prodded.

"Unfortunately, no. It's not allowed."

Celia thought for a moment. She turned to Chloe.

"I think one of us needs to stay here just in case something comes up. The other one needs to go and check on the nail parlor."

"I can keep watch over here. Run to the parlor and stay safe," Chloe said.

"Stay safe, too," Celia said.

"I'm at the police station. I'll be fine," Chloe said with a smile.

Then Celia remembered that Chloe was the daughter of one of the richest men in town. She wasn't going to be touched by anyone.

Celia stood up.

"Thanks for the help," Celia said as she turned to look at Bill. "Chloe will keep tabs on things."

Celia drove back to the nail parlor as promised. She found Fidel still there as forensic Detectives kept looking for clues around the staircase and the mezzanine office. Charlize's body had been taken away, leaving behind chalk marks to show where she had been found.

"They tell me they are just finishing up," Fidel said.

Celia nodded her head as she watched them finalize their investigation of the scene. They rolled out a fresh length of crime scene tape that blocked off the section leading to the staircase. She knew that she wouldn't be accessing that place anytime soon.

As the investigators left, one of them stopped to talk to Celia and Fidel.

"I would suggest that you don't touch anything around that area for the next forty-eight hours. We will know if you manipulated this place. Sorry for your loss."

Celia and Fidel exchanged looks after the detectives left.

"Hello, is everything ok?"

Celia turned to find Patricia Nesbitt standing at the entrance of the nail parlor.

"Can I help you?" Celia asked.

"I'm actually wondering if I can help you," Patricia replied.

"We are handling things, thank you," Celia replied, keen to make her leave.

"I'm not here to be a bother, and I'm actually the fellow business just down the street. I'm just here to show my support. Sorry for the loss of Charlize."

Celia nodded her head slowly.

"Life is short, isn't it?" Patricia said.

"Yes, it is."

"I mean, one minute you're gloating about running me and my business out of town and the next, you're lying dead on the floor. Such a pity."

Although she wasn't smiling as she said this, Patricia's words weren't exactly a show of sympathy.

"I'm going to ask you to leave now. Thank you for passing by," Celia said.

"Sorry to intrude, but I couldn't help coming. I'll be on my way."

Patricia turned to walk away and caught herself at the last moment.

"Just one more thing. I think we'll be seeing more of each other in the coming days. Just as a show of support," Patricia said with a wry smile.

She sauntered away with a spring in her step, confirming Celia's suspicions. This was definitely someone who had something to gain from the death of Charlize.

6

The next day, after she was done with her client visits in the morning, Celia went to check on Melanie at the station.

She had brought with her some muffins that her mother had baked, hoping that she'd be allowed to give them to Melanie. She was searched to ensure she didn't have any weapons. She had to leave her keys and other metallic objects in a safe. Surprisingly, the pack of muffins wasn't barred.

"Yes, you can see her," the officer at the desk said, much to Celia's relief.

She was taken to a visitors' room, where she waited. It was a drab place with grey concrete walls everywhere. A heavily grilled window was open.

Melanie walked in looking a little ruffled, but at least she had a smile on her face.

"It's so good to see you," Melanie said as she took a seat. A policeman stood at the door, watching them.

"How was your night?" Celia asked.

"I didn't sleep much. But I survived," Melanie replied.

"Chloe was here till yesterday evening, if it helps. We're here for you."

"For Chloe to stay that long, then I feel blessed. Thank you."

"I got you some muffins," Celia said as she passed the small pack to her.

"Hey, no. You can't do that here!" The policeman shouted as he marched toward them.

"Okay, sorry. I'll just take them back," Celia said as she reached for the pack.

"No, I'll take them now. Have to check," the policeman said as he grabbed the pack.

"Continue"

He moved back to the door.

"I hope he won't have eaten them by the time we are done," Celia said.

"I could have done with one of those! It was lukewarm tea and dry bread this morning. A fitting way to remember yesterday's interrogation."

"Did they question you for a long time?"

"When alone, it was short. Then I could remember you pinching me and I knew I shouldn't talk too much. I called my lawyer."

"Did they show up?"

"Yes. Later in the day. Then we did another session and my lawyer did most of the talking. I could tell they were a little frustrated," Melanie replied.

"Meaning they believe you did it."

"I may have been at the top of the staircase during the last moments of her fall, but I didn't cause it. But it's very hard to prove that without CCTV footage," Melanie replied.

"What do you mean? The cameras weren't working?"

"The cameras don't cover the top of the staircase, so you can't tell. You just see her tumbling," Melanie replied.

"We'll need to get that checked as soon as you get out."

Melanie shook her head, then buried her face in her hands for a moment. When she lifted her face back up, it was as if she had seen something.

"As hard as it is to say, I think either Charlize tripped, was unwell or... Or threw herself down the stairs," Melanie said.

"Threw herself? No, she didn't look like the type to do that," Celia said.

"But what other explanation is there?"

"There must be one. However, the suicide theory is outrageous," Celia replied firmly.

"Then help me solve this," Melanie said, reaching for Celia's hand, "Talk to Fidel and Sarah for me. I know they've talked to the cops. Find out if they saw something that could set me free."

Celia pondered this for a moment.

"Okay, I'll do that. Let's see what they have to say."

Later that day, Celia managed to call Sarah and Fidel to a meeting.

She had toyed around with the idea of meeting them at a restaurant for a more relaxed atmosphere, but she opted not to. She figured that it made more sense to talk to them together at the location where the tragedy happened.

Maybe the emotional gravity of the situation would clear their heads about what they saw at the time. It even gave the opportunity for them to walk through Charlize's last moments, a benefit of being right at the location. This way, she could spot any inaccuracies or blind spots in their stories.

She found them waiting for her at the entrance. She had taken the key from Fidel so neither employee could get in.

"Sorry to keep you waiting, guys," she said, opening the door.

Celia ushered them in and led them to the waiting couch. They sat next to each other with a pillow's width between them. She pulled a chair and sat facing them.

"As you both know, I'm Melanie's good friend, Celia. The last couple of days have not been easy for any of us I'm sure. Especially for you. You lost one of your bosses and it's not easy finding a new job in this town," she said as she cast an eye towards Fidel.

"It will be resolved somehow," Sarah said.

"That's exactly why I'm here. I'm curious to find out what

happened. So, feel free to share what you saw. We can start with you, Sarah. What did you see?"

Sarah took a deep breath.

"I was busy with a client at the time. I was fully focused on doing her toenails. So obviously, my whole attention was towards the floor. For some reason I turned around toward the steps, and that's the same time when I heard…" Sarah paused at this moment, as if she was remembering the trauma of what happened, "…when I heard her falling down the stairs."

"What happened after that?" Celia asked.

"Everything was crazy. By the time I figured out what was happening, Fidel was already next to her, checking her pulse and… and then he confirmed that she was gone."

"Who called for an ambulance?"

"Melanie did," Sarah replied.

Celia turned to Fidel, who was fiddling with his fingers as he listened to Sarah speak.

"Fidel, what happened?" Celia asked.

"I was with a client as well, just like Sarah. We were chatting a lot. You know, keeping her busy because that's what I do when clients come over. I keep them busy and happy with stories. I was also distracted just like Sarah and I didn't see what happened before Charlize fell down the stairs."

"But you responded faster than Sarah," Celia said.

"I guess I've got good reflexes," he replied.

Celia was not convinced.

"Were you in the army or special forces or something?" she asked.

Fidel shook his head.

"No, I've seen a lot of things in the street. When you grow up in a dangerous neighborhood, you grow up more alert than many people do."

"Fidel your reflexes were fantastic. I'm amazed that you were able to get there as soon as Charlize landed at the bottom of the stairs. Is there something else you might have heard or seen just before she fell?"

NEW NAILS AND A NASTY NIGHTMARE

Sarah and Fidel exchanged looks. Fidel turned to Celia, shaking his head.

"I wish I could say more but that's all I know."

"Since you were at the foot of the stairs first, where was Melanie at that time" Celia probed.

"She was standing at the top of the stairs, looking down on us," he replied.

"What was her face like?"

"She looked shocked. It's not something she expected, I guess," he said.

Celia was interrupted by a loud knock on the door. She looked up, puzzled. She wasn't able to see who it was because of the stickers on the window front. She just hoped it wasn't Patricia Nesbitt again.

"Any of you expecting someone?" Celia asked.

Fidel shook his head, and Sarah shrugged.

Celia arose and walked to the door. When she opened it, a tall graceful woman in sunglasses walked in. She stopped at the center of the room, looking around at the ceiling and the fittings and everything in between not saying a word.

"Excuse me, can I help you?" Celia asked.

The woman took off her sunglasses and smiled.

"I'm looking for Melanie Dawes," the woman said in a sultry, authoritative voice.

"She's not here at the moment. Who's asking?"

"My name is Gloria Langa, sister to the late Charlize Langa. And you are?"

"Celia Dube, a friend of Melanie's. Did you just say you are Charlize's sister?"

"Half-sister actually. We share the same father," Gloria replied.

"Sorry for your loss," Celia said.

"It shall be well, as they say. How do I find Melanie?"

Celia wondered whether to respond to her or just let it slide.

"She's with the police currently helping them with their investigation," she replied.

"I see. Well, here's my card. I would really like to talk to her. The moment you see her, kindly let her know. My family is very interested in the various pursuits she was involved in," Gloria said.

"Sure thing. I'll do that."

Gloria Langa smiled, put on her sunglasses, and cat walked away.

Celia turned to the two workers.

"Any of you saw her before?"

Neither employee had ever seen her. This thing was turning into a maze with hidden trap doors that she could fall through at any moment.

7

Having gotten nowhere the previous day, Celia decided to change her approach with the employees. She met them both for breakfast at the Pier, each an hour apart. She talked to Sarah first as she had her coffee and pancakes covered in maple syrup. It made her a little more forthcoming with information.

"Charlize was smart. Brilliant. She had an answer to everything," Sarah said in between mouthfuls.

"She was good with the clients too?" Celia asked.

"Yes, she was. She was very courteous and knew how to handle their issues. She added little perks, like giving them coffee or wine or even candy. She's the one who really taught us a new way of handling clients," Sarah replied.

"Was she strict?"

"Always. She kept time, always the first one to arrive and the last to leave. She made us keep track of all transactions. Our breaks were timed to the last second. She was a military sergeant, to be honest."

"What about her other side? Did she ever get angry?"

"Oh, yes. She had a short fuse. I think all perfectionists are like that. Very good at what they do, but if you fall short, they're like sharks. They can tear you to pieces," Sarah said.

"So, did she tear you to pieces often?"

"That usually happened if you really messed up. I think she gave me a talking to around thrice. It wasn't a pleasant experience. She made you feel small. If my mother had not taught me how to deal with negative comments, I'd be depressed right now," she said.

"I see," Celia said. If Charlize had flown off the lid and Melanie felt slighted, might she have acted in the spur of the moment, resulting in the tragic accident?

Celia caught herself. She couldn't believe that she was even thinking her friend might be guilty of something so hideous.

"After sleeping on it, do you remember something new about what happened that day?" Celia asked.

Sarah paused for a moment, her chin working as she enjoyed the last bite of her pancake.

"No, I'm sorry. It's the same recollection as yesterday. I wish I had more to say," she replied.

Twenty minutes later, Fidel sat in front of Celia. He was having porridge with a cob of boiled corn. A great meal that would keep you running for most of the day without hunger pangs. He was hungry and ate the meal ravenously. She let him finish first before they talked.

"You had a great night?" Celia asked.

He nodded.

"Yes. It was good. Short but good," he replied.

"Do you have a family?"

"They are not here. They live in the village. I wouldn't be able to afford to have them over."

"It makes sense. So, did you get to think afresh about what happened to Charlize?"

He shook his head.

"No, nothing new came to mind."

"Are you sure? Considering you attended to her pretty quickly. Maybe…"

"It doesn't change anything. I didn't see anything that could help," he replied.

Celia got the sense he didn't want to talk about it.

"Is this uncomfortable for you?"

"What?" he asked.

"Does talking about the event make you uncomfortable?" she asked again.

"Isn't talking about someone's death supposed to be? It's a hard thing. I'm not sure if I'll be fired tomorrow because of this," he replied.

Celia was surprised by this. She hadn't seen it that way. If he knew something, why would he incriminate his remaining boss?

"I understand. She's my friend too, you know. I'm just trying to help," Celia replied.

Fidel stared outside for a moment, then turned back to her.

"Sometimes, it's better to let things fix themselves. The universe won't fail her," he said.

Celia didn't understand him. There was a wall there. She had to find another way of reaching out to him.

During lunch hour, Celia was checking the equipment after the staff had left for their break when she heard the door open. A sharply dressed, clean-shaven man carrying a briefcase walked towards her.

"Hello there. I'm looking for Melanie Dawes?"

Celia braced herself. This trend of strangers looking for Melanie was worrying. She knew this was going to be another surprise.

"She's not here, Can I help you?"

"My name is Michael Nzomo. I'm Charlize Langa's lawyer. I'm here to discuss Charlize's will?"

Celia's antennas went up.

"What about her will?" she asked.

Michael handed her a piece of paper.

"According to her will, all the shares that she had in this business automatically come under my guardianship as her lawyer. Any proceeds of a sale, if it happens, will go to the family."

"Oh, wow," Celia said as she read the document. It was an official notice that simply stated his newfound status in the nail parlor.

"So, I wanted to come around and see what I'll be working with. I trust that you are going to be open tomorrow?"

"Yes, we shall be open tomorrow," Celia replied.

"Fantastic. Kindly inform Melanie that I'll be passing by."

As abruptly as he had come, Michael left.

Celia needed to see Melanie.

* * *

"It's starting to feel like you want to be in here with me," Melanie said with a smile.

"Why do you say that?" Celia asked.

"You have visited me every single day. That's impressive," she replied.

"Well, there's always something new in this story. I'm starting to feel like I'm walking through a maze," Celia replied.

"What did Sarah and Fidel tell you yesterday?"

"Nothing much. Neither of them saw anything before Charlize fell down the stairs."

Melanie shook her head.

"Fidel knows something. He may not be willing to talk, but I saw it in his eyes when he looked at me," Melanie said.

"Are you serious? What do you mean?" Celia probed.

"After Charlize fell, I was standing at the top of the stairs. He looked at me with the kind of look that said he saw something. At the time, I felt like he understood that I was not responsible for it. But now it feels like he's holding back for some reason," she explained.

"I see. But a look doesn't say much you know," Celia said.

"You need to do your thing, Celia. You're good at making people talk."

"I think you're overestimating my powers, Melanie."

"I know what I'm talking about. Remember, we solved the case together last time."

"I'm not promising you anything, but I'll see what I can do," she said.

Celia took out the letter from the lawyer and placed it in front of Melanie.

"Charlize's lawyer came by and left this."

Without responding, Melanie read the letter. Her rising eyebrows told Celia she was surprised by its contents.

"This is new. So, is he going to be coming to the parlor every day?" she asked.

"I don't know. However, he's coming in tomorrow. He's hoping to see you, actually.

Speaking of which, you should be out of here already. Forty-eight hours have passed. Have they set a date for a bail hearing or are they planning to release you?" Celia asked.

Melanie shook her head.

"I think you're overestimating the amount of luck I'm having right now. I'm not getting out, Cece," Melanie said.

"What are you talking about?"

"They've found some new evidence. Charlize had poison in her system when she died. It could have been administered by anyone two hours before she fell down the stairs," Melanie said matter-of-factly.

Celia was taken aback.

"If it was just a fall down the stairs, I was facing manslaughter. I'm looking at a murder charge now." Melanie said, breaking down in tears.

8

Celia woke up to high-pitched voices filtering into her bedroom.

At first, she thought it was part of a dream. But the more she strained her ears, the clearer the voices became.

"You have no clue why I am choosing purple. It is the color of nobility, luxury, power, and creativity. It's a good thing for the boy to make wishes with such a great theme color."

"But these are two boys! They need active intense colors like red and screaming orange!"

"The only screaming we need is that of joy from the boys, not the one you are doing right now."

"That's an insult now, Audrey. I didn't come all the way here to be insulted."

Celia tried to cover her head with a pillow, but it didn't help. She had hardly slept the night before, filling out transaction reports for the sales she had done that week. She then dropped the boys off at school and drove back home to sneak in a quick nap before starting her day. Now that she had been woken by the argument between her mother and Mrs. Owens, there was no way she was going back to sleep.

NEW NAILS AND A NASTY NIGHTMARE

When she walked into the living room, she found the two women seated opposite each other, in silent resignation.

"It's too beautiful a morning to be arguing" Celia said.

"Who said we were arguing?" Audrey asked.

"Ma, you woke me up from my nap. Now I have to endure sleep-walking for the rest of the day," she replied.

"Cece, you should weigh in on this. What color should we use for the theme party, red or purple?" Mrs. Owens asked.

"She doesn't need to vote," Audrey chimed in.

"But since we can't agree she can break the stalemate," Mrs. Owens insisted.

"No ladies, I will not be that person. I think this is a good time for you to find a way to meet halfway. You've been friends for too long not to figure this out," Celia replied.

"You're just going to leave us in limbo?" Mrs. Owens asked.

"It's only limbo if you let it," Celia replied as she turned toward the kitchen. "Oh, and you have till evening to agree. Otherwise I'll take over the planning."

* * *

THE POLICE STATION was busy that day. Celia counted fifteen criminals brought in within a half-hour period, the highest she had witnessed that week. There must be a crackdown of some sort, she thought.

She was seated on the old bench once again, waiting. The police station hallway had become all-too familiar by now. The noise of protesting suspects, phones ringing and chatter by detectives, slamming office and cell doors and footsteps all colored Celia's wait for Melanie to be released on bail.

The situation felt too real, almost as if it was Celia herself facing trial. If this was happening to her, it might have torn her to pieces because she would spend all of her time worrying about her boys.

She saw Detective Bill Koloane walking down the hallway with another detective, having a conversation. Impatient, she stood up and walked to him.

"Excuse me, detective," she said.

Bill turned to her and smiled.

"You're here for Melanie?" he asked.

"Yes. I'm hoping she's coming out soon?"

"They're just processing her. She should be out in about five minutes," he replied.

Bill waved off his fellow detective so he could spend some time with Celia.

"How are you holding up?" he asked.

"This whole thing is a bit unusual for me. I've never been to the police station this many times. I don't know what to say," she replied.

"There's no getting used to this kind of thing," he said.

"Do you like the gray walls that you see every day?" she asked.

"I enjoy imagining the number of colors I want to paint on them every day," he said.

They both laughed.

"Is that your version of hope?" she asked.

"Something like that," Bill replied.

Just then, Melanie came walking towards them, followed by a police officer. She was dressed in a fresh pair of clothes that Celia had brought for her previously. She still looked a little disheveled, but it was a blessing to Celia for her to see her friend walking freely again.

"I'll leave you guys," Bill said with a smile as he walked away.

Melanie and Celia embraced tightly.

"Thank you for coming to get me," Melanie said.

"That's what sisters are for. Come on, let's get out of here."

"Right now, I'm craving one thing: some chicken biryani."

"I'm sure we can take a detour on our way home."

"Let's not go home. After we get something to eat, I'd like to see the nail parlor," Melanie replied.

"Are you sure about that?"

"Positive."

After a hearty meal of chicken biryani, which was full of great rice and spicy chicken, they got to the nail parlor. Melanie walked around as if she was in a daze.

It looked like she was reliving everything that happened the day Charlize died. Celia was unsure whether to interrupt her or to let her deal with the memory.

"Are you okay, Mel?" she finally asked.

Melanie nodded and continued her walk around the space.

"Excuse me, is anybody home?"

Celia turned towards the door and saw Patricia already standing in the space. Melanie seemed to be oblivious to the new entrant. Celia walked up to Patricia.

"I thought we had an agreement that you wouldn't be coming here on short notice?" Celia said in a low tone.

"I saw Melanie coming in and I just had to come in and check on her," Patricia replied.

"She's fine, as you can see. Can you leave now?" Celia said, firmly.

"I actually wanted to talk to her because I had a proposition for her," Patricia said.

"I'm telling you that this is not the time to have that conversation. So, can you leave, please?"

"What conversation?" Melanie asked. Celia turned to find Melanie already standing next to her.

"Hello Melanie. I'm so sorry to hear what happened. I hope that this whole situation is resolved so that we can have you back on Main Street doing what you love," Patricia said.

Celia wished she could wipe the smirk off her mouth.

"Thank you for your kind words, Patricia. What's on your mind?" Melanie replied.

"Well, the main reason I'd like to have you back on the Main Street is so that we can have a very healthy conversation about your nail parlor. I'd be interested to buy it if it's on the market," Patricia explained.

"If it's on the market now? Why would it be on the market?"

"A nail parlor is not easy to run. Ask me, I've been doing this for eight years. I wouldn't want this fantastic establishment to just go to waste because of some challenges."

"What are you trying to say, Patricia?"

"Well, it's no secret that you're facing some legal challenges right now and so you're not able to run the business. Let me take it out of your hands so it you can focus on what's important and get your life back together," she added.

Melanie's eyes grew red with rage. Celia knew she was about to implode.

"I think this is your time to leave now, Patricia," Celia said as she gently pushed Patricia towards the door.

"At least tell me you'll give it some thought. I know time is not exactly on our side, but…"

Celia didn't let her finish. She ushered Patricia gently out, then closed the door and locked it.

"I'm sorry about that," Celia said.

"Has she been here while I was away?" Melanie asked.

"Yes, she has. Once. But I drove her out," she replied.

"They are hunting me down, Cece. And I don't know if I have the strength to keep running. You have to help me fix this," Melanie said, running her hand through her hair.

And at that moment Celia realized that she was possibly the only person who believed Melanie was innocent. But if Melanie didn't do it, then who did?

9

It was clear to see that Patricia's visit had triggered something on the inside of Melanie that she had been trying to suppress for the past few days.

Patricia had the kind of personality that was very hard to trust. She reminded Celia of those street moneychangers who dazzle you with their cards and take flight after making you lose all your hard-earned cash.

"I think we should just keep an eye on her and see what else she has up her sleeve. Right?" Celia said.

"Definitely. Now that I'm here, I'm feeling a heaviness about having it open," Melanie said.

"What's going through your mind?" Celia asked.

Melanie sighed.

"I'm not comfortable staying open until after Charlize's funeral."

"But I think this is what Charlize would have wanted. To keep the dream alive," she replied.

"I just feel it's disrespectful. Closing would be like flying the flag at half mast," she said.

"Sounds like giving up on the dream. You know how you can make it worthwhile? Put up a desk with photos of her and a condolence book. It would honor her memory," Celia said.

Melanie pondered this for a moment, then nodded.

"You're right. I like that. We can pay tribute to her," she replied.

"It will also be good for the clients who knew her," she added.

"I really need to find out what happened to her. Where was she poisoned? How did that happen?"

"I'm with you on that. Something sinister happened. The threat might be closer than it seems," Celia replied.

"What do you think we should do?"

"We should start with the guest list during your launch. It's possible that the person who did it was part of that event," Celia said.

"Got some time to help me with that?" Melanie asked.

Celia glanced at her wristwatch.

"No, I have an appointment with a client in an hour. I have to head out now. How about coffee later? Chloe wants to see you too," she said.

"Sure, we can do coffee," Melanie mumbled.

Celia smiled, then left.

* * *

LATER THAT DAY, the three friends, Melanie, Celia and Chloe, congregated at a local cafe.

"It's so great to see you out and free Mel," Chloe said.

"It's great. Although I feel like I constantly have to watch my back because I don't know who might come for me next," Melanie said.

"Who'll come for you next?" Chloe asked.

"The police. The person who did it. Who knows?" Melanie replied.

"Your recent experience has made you more cautious. Don't let it get to you, Mel. You'll get through this. Keep your head up," Celia said.

"That's easier said than done. Think about it this way: I have no witnesses or evidence to prove my innocence. The CCTV footage at the top of the stairs has a blind spot. How do I defend myself?"

"You have us Melanie, we're here for you," Chloe said.

"She's got a point there, though. The evidence is stacked up against her and I think it'll be a problem to make her case. You've got a great lawyer in Collins Rebbe," Celia said.

"Should I look for a proper criminal lawyer, though? This type of crime isn't his speciality," Melanie said.

"Don't change your lawyer. Stick with him for these two reasons: he's a great lawyer, and we'll help you find the evidence you need," Celia said.

"I agree with Cece. Collins has been great for us, even with some serious lawsuits that would have brought down our company. He'll raise his game," Chloe said.

"Alright. I'll keep my fingers crossed," Melanie said.

"Guys, why are we talking about depressing stuff? We should light up the place a bit," Chloe said, "How about we do that blind date?"

Melanie and Celia looked at each other.

"It'll be fine, Cece. It's just an evening out. Plus, if it doesn't work out, we can always call it an evening earlier than planned. You're game?" Chloe asked.

"Alright fine. There's no point of fighting it anymore. When do you plan to do it?" Celia asked.

"About this weekend on Saturday evening?" Chloe asked.

"Works for me," Melanie said.

"I'll make arrangements to have my mum watch the kids," Celia replied.

"Great! I'll keep you posted on developments," Chloe said.

"One more thing, Chloe. Your family is connected in certain places. What do you know about the Langa family?"

"You're talking about Frasier Langa, the real estate and timber magnate?"

"I'm not sure. His daughter is Gloria Langa."

"Yes, he's the one. He's got many children from several wives. It's an interesting situation, but he has the money to handle them, I guess. He's been part of quite a number of government deals too. Why?"

"Just curious. We happen to know one of his daughters. She's, as you say, quite interesting," Celia remarked.

"Has she done something crazy?"

"No, nothing. At least not yet."

"Alright. Sorry I don't know much more about them," Chloe said.

"I think we've got more than enough information to know who we're dealing with," Celia said.

It was late evening when Celia and Melanie got back to the nail parlor. They found Fidel and Sarah cleaning the place before they left for the day. Celia found it refreshing that the staff were managing through the difficult circumstances. It was a good sign that the business would bounce back.

Melanie was about to go up the stairs when a man came in. He was a very muscular man in a dark suit. He walked with a confident, agile gait. He had a neck tattoo that peeked from his shirt collar.

He didn't say a word. He simply walked straight up to Melanie as if he knew her. Melanie didn't flinch. He handed her a white envelope, then swiftly turned and walked out. Celia was intrigued.

"Who on earth was that?" Celia asked.

"No one you should know," Melanie said.

"Don't play games now. Who was that?" Celia insisted.

By this time, Melanie was already reading the letter. The more she read, the more her expression became grave. When she was done, she folded the letter.

"I'm waiting," Celia said.

"We took a loan for the business. Charlize made the deal. Now, the lenders want their money back," Melanie said.

"Who are these people you borrowed money from? Because that doesn't look like someone you should be making deals with," she said.

"It's a loan shark," she whispered.

"You took money from a loan shark? On a business that's hardly started building a client base?" Celia exclaimed.

"It was pretty stupid now that I think about it. Anyway, that's water under the bridge. I have forty- eight hours to come up with the money and I don't know how that's going to happen."

"So, what are you going to do?" she asked.

"I'm going to have to find it somehow or they might put a gun to my head," she replied.

10

"Have you made up your minds about this?" Celia asked. She stood at the end of the kitchen table, eating the last piece of buttermilk rusk, a tasty dry biscuit that she usually had with her morning coffee.

"Well, we're supposed to talk about it today," Audrey replied.

"But we agreed that if there was no progress by now, I would take over. Right? "Celia asked.

"That's true but…"

"No buts, Ma," Celia said.

Audrey stopped stirring the pot of tomato soup that she was making.

"You should understand that we're simply two passionate people working on this. So it will take us some time," Audrey said.

"Time's not on my side, Ma. We need to shop, send invites, decide on work to be done. If we want other kids to attend the party, we need to give their parents enough notice, don't you think?"

"We'll make the decision today, I promise."

"No Ma. I'll move ahead with the plan I have in mind."

"And what plan is that?" Audrey queried.

"You'll see it unfold very soon," Celia replied with a cheeky grin.

***

It was strange to walk up the staircase of Melanie's nail parlor, considering someone had died because of it.

Celia took one slow step after the other, keen to get through with it as she headed to the nail parlor office.

"You look busy," Celia said with a smile as she walked through the door.

She found Melanie deeply engrossed as she stared at her computer screen.

"Just reading our business plan a little as I try to stay on track with things," Melanie replied. "Is Fidel down there?"

"I don't think so. I didn't see him when I walked in. What's going on?" she asked.

"I'm wondering the same thing. He hasn't turned up for work today."

Melanie stood up and walked out. From the landing, she could see the expanse of the nail parlor.

"Has he turned up yet?" Melanie asked, calling out to Sarah below.

"He sent me a message some minutes ago. He's not going to make it today," Sarah replied.

"Why not?"

"He said he's handling a family matter."

"Is it serious?" Melanie asked.

Sarah shrugged and got back to preparing her workstation.

Melanie tried to call him on her cell phone.

"He's unreachable. I guess it's serious," she said.

"Let me know if he tries to get in touch with you again, okay?" she shouted to Sarah.

Sarah nodded.

Melanie walked back to the office, Celia in tow.

"Did you manage to talk to him the way we had agreed?" Melanie asked Celia.

"I actually didn't. He's a tough nut to crack, so I have to figure out another way," Celia replied.

"He hasn't said anything to me either. When he gets back, please talk to him. Like I told you, I think he knows something that could help me."

"Sure."

"I have another favor to ask you. Can you take me downtown?" she asked.

"What do you need to do downtown?"

Melanie sighed, then locked eyes with Celia. She immediately knew what Melanie was referring to.

"Do you think he'll listen to your case?"

"He has to because I need more time. Our projections and our reality are two different things. It'll take some time to pay him back. Besides, I need you to come with me because you're more persuasive than I am."

"You flatter to deceive, you know that?"

"I'm being honest," she replied.

"I have a question for you. What's your honest opinion about Patricia?" Celia asked.

Melanie thought about this for a minute.

"She clearly doesn't like the fact that we're running a business next to hers. She's got this scheming side to her, but I'm not sure she'd take the risk of getting Charlize killed just to get a piece of this business," she remarked.

"Stranger things have happened," Celia said, "Turf wars don't exist in the drug world alone, you know."

Melanie laughed.

"How's it a turf war and we'd only just began operations?"

"The turf war began the minute you decided to set this place up. Being a new place doesn't matter," Celia replied.

"I know what you mean but I just can't see how she would've done it."

"I think you need to keep an open mind about what could have happened," she urged.

"I'll make note of that. Right now, I really need a ride downtown. Are you in?" Melanie asked.

"Tell me something. How much did you know about this loan shark deal?" Celia asked.

"I honestly knew nothing about it. I didn't know the amount, the terms, the timelines. It seems Charlize was paying them off quietly. Until now," she said.

Celia had experienced loan sharks before, and they gave her goosebumps thinking about the experiences she'd had with them. As she was struggling to get her business off the ground, she needed to buy stock. It was brutal when she didn't pay on time, and she regretted every bit of it. She worried for her friend, because things could get complex quite fast.

"Mel, do you know any of these guys?"

"I know none of them. All I know is the name of the man I owe. Benji."

"Have they threatened you yet?" Celia asked.

"It hasn't gotten to that point yet. Why are you asking me all these questions?" she asked.

"I think you should simply not turn up. You didn't make the deal. Charlize did. She's passed on. They should discuss a new timeline for you."

"I don't think that is a safe bet. Remember, they know where the business is."

"This is going to get a little tricky for you, I'm afraid," Celia said.

"So, you're not going to take me downtown?" Melanie asked.

Celia sighed.

"You know me. There's no way I'll let you go into the lion's den without company," Celia replied with a smile.

They left together. Celia was keen to see what awaited them downtown.

11

Downtown wasn't the seediest part of the town, but it was one of the dangerous ones.

It wasn't a secret that this town had some gangs, and they operated much more freely in the downtown area. Some ran legitimate businesses, but most owned turf where they ran various devious schemes.

As Celia drove through the streets, she could tell her car was being studied by some groups that they drove past.

"Charlize drove down here to meet this guy?" Celia asked.

"I honestly have no idea if she did," Melanie replied.

"Maybe we should've asked to meet him at a restaurant," she said.

"He wanted it this way. So here we are," she clarified.

The address they were told to go to was a brick and mortar high-rise building on a busy street. To Celia's relief, it had a basement parking and she drove down into it. It was well lit, and most of the parked cars were more expensive than hers. This eased her concerns.

They headed to the third floor. The lifts weren't working, so the staircase was the only way up. It was full of human traffic, so it was slow going as they jostled and darted up the steps.

The corridor leading to the loan shark's office was full of small offices that ran open door businesses. They had stuck signs and placards advertising all types of services which included mobile phone repairs, a barbershop, electronics, cheap clothing, alcohol among others. It was a testament to the town residents' determined spirit to earn a living. Celia was impressed.

They got to a grilled black metal door. On it was the small piece of wood imprinted, *BCash Investment*.

Inside, a small reception area greeted them. The receptionist, a petite lady, ushered them into the larger office. A muscular man with slicked back hair, the man Celia had seen at the soft launch, was seated on a tall leather seat behind a shiny mahogany desk.

"Welcome, ladies. I've been waiting for this day for quite a while," the man said as he motioned them to take the cushioned visitor seats.

"Hello, Benji," Melanie said. "Thank you for taking the time to meet us."

"I always make time where my money is involved," he said with a wry smile.

"About that. I had a preposition. Can you give us two more months to get this off the ground? My co-founder recently passed on, and I'm trying to get the ship running again," Melanie said.

Benji leaned back in his seat and studied them.

"A deal is only as good as its word," he said.

"I know that, but…"

"There are no buts. You both made a deal."

"What she's trying to say is that she wasn't present at the time, and she might've made a more realistic projection of the timeline," Celia said.

Benji smiled.

"I can see you brought your public relations person to the negotiating table. It doesn't work, most of the time," he said.

"I'm just trying to help," Celia said.

"It doesn't matter. Maybe I wouldn't have listened to your realistic projections, anyway. For me, time is money. More time means I charge you more. Considering what you're saying, you might not be able to pay me more cash for more time," Benji said.

"I'll work really hard to make that possible," Melanie pleaded.

Benji shook his head and leaned forward.

"I don't work alone. I have people who need to eat too. This is how they eat; when clients like you repay on time. Understood?"

"Understood. But I can…"

"I said no buts. The best I can do for you is a twenty-four-hour extension. After that, I come for what's mine."

Melanie and Celia exchanged glances.

"What does coming for what's mine mean?" Celia asked.

"You'll know it when you see it," Benji said ominously.

Celia didn't like the sound of it, but knew the discussion was over.

As they drove back to the nail parlor, Melanie cut a frustrated figure.

"Charlize left me in this mess without telling me. I don't understand it," she said.

"She was ambitious, but this was a little rash on her part. Unless the cash was used for something else."

"It was used in the business. I checked the books just to be sure," Melanie replied.

"So, what are you going to do?"

Melanie sighed as she studied the traffic outside.

"I wish I could rob a bank, frankly."

They drove in silence for a few more minutes.

"What do you need that could boost the parlor's operations right now?"

"I need some product. I don't have the cash flow to get it."

"Listen. How about I supply you with the products you need on credit? Then we can agree on a good repayment plan."

"You would do that?" Melanie beamed.

"Yes, I would. It won't be on Benji's terms though."

"You're a lifesaver, you know that?" she said.

"Don't get too excited. We still need Benji's cash by tomorrow."

The drive became quiet again as they wrestled with the dilemma that was before them. There had to be a way out.

NEW NAILS AND A NASTY NIGHTMARE

* * *

"WHERE DO you want me to put these?" Chloe asked as she carried in two small boxes of beauty products.

"Place them at the corner there," Celia replied.

After placing the boxes as instructed, Chloe took a break.

"I don't know how you managed to convince me to come here, but it's breaking my back now," Chloe said.

"But I know that you have a thing for manicures and pedicures, so why not?" Celia said.

"You know me too well," Chloe replied.

They both laughed.

"Seriously, thanks for coming through. Melanie's a little stressed right now considering one of her employees has not turned up for the past two days."

"It's all good, I'm all yours. However, from tomorrow I'm only coming in the afternoon. Dad wants some help at the factory. Is that okay?" she asked.

"No problem."

The door opened, and Gloria Langa walked in. She looked graceful as ever, in casual top and khaki pants. She was in sunglasses, which she took off the moment she walked in.

"Hello, ladies," Gloria said.

Celia walked to her.

"Gloria Langa. I can see that you decided to visit us again," Celia said.

"I hear Melanie is back. Can I see her, please?"

"Sure. Let me take you to her office," Celia said.

Celia led her up the stairs to the mezzanine office. They found Melanie on the phone. They sat down and waited.

"Alright I'll get back to you in about half an hour. Thanks," Melanie said as she hung up.

"My name is Gloria Langa and I'm Charlize's half-sister. You're Melanie?" she said.

"Yes, I am. Celia told me about your visit when I was away."

"I was hoping we could talk about my sister, and what plans you have for this place," Gloria said.

"What would you like to know?" Melanie asked.

"There are many things, including how she worked. But the part I'm most interested in is the day she died. What happened?"

Melanie paused briefly.

"I'm also trying to figure out exactly what happened. She had just left my office after a conversation and the next thing I know, she was tumbling down the stairs," Melanie said.

"What kind of conversation did you have?" Gloria asked.

"Just a regular business conversation with a business partner," she replied.

Gloria nodded.

"I see. She didn't show any signs of strange behavior or illness?" she asked.

"No, she didn't. Like I said, I'm trying to wrap my head around what exactly happened that day as well."

"Interesting," she muttered.

"About the business, I believe that her lawyer is now the guardian of her shares. He passed by twice in the last two days to talk about it. I keep him posted about the day-to-day running as we work to get back on our feet," Melanie added.

"Yes, I'm aware. I talk to Michael every day as well. Is there anything you would like to let me know? Something you would like to get off your chest about my sister?" Gloria asked.

Celia was surprised by the question. Melanie frowned in puzzlement.

"I don't exactly get what you mean," Melanie said.

"It's my hypothesis that the conversation you had was a trigger to what happened to my sister."

"Look here, Gloria. I…" Melanie interjected.

"I'm not finished. I believe something happened in this room that day. I'll find the underlying cause of it. I suggest you start putting your affairs in order because you might not be running this business for very long," Gloria said with finality.

"I can assure you I had nothing to do with what happened to your sister," Melanie countered.

Gloria stood up to leave.

"And I can assure you that no one poisons my sister and gets away with it. I would say you can take that to the bank, but I know your financial situation doesn't allow you to do that. So, let's just say I will see you very soon," she said.

Gloria marched out of the office. Celia turned to Melanie, who was looking shell-shocked.

12

"I told you they are hunting for me," Melanie said.

Celia walked up to Melanie and hugged her.

"This is going to blow over. Trust me," she said.

"I did nothing wrong, Cece. Why can't anyone see that?"

Pulling out of the embrace, Celia and Melanie locked eyes.

"You have to believe something will come through. We just need to find the evidence to clear you," Celia said.

"What more evidence do people need? Isn't my word and my background enough?" she lamented.

"It sounds crazy, but your answers tend to add more doubt than clarity."

"What answers?" Melanie asked.

"Why didn't you tell me about the argument?"

"It wasn't important at the time."

"It wasn't important? Your co-founder died, and you didn't care to tell me you had an argument before the cops walked in?"

"I didn't think it had any bearing on the incident, that's what I meant," Melanie said.

"But as you can now tell, it did. I also know that she was giving you a hard time. Thankfully, your staff have not talked about that much."

"It was nothing I couldn't handle," she replied.

"And then there's the possible disappearance of Fidel, which only the two of us know about," Celia said.

"He's sorting out a family situation," Melanie said.

"You really believe that, or that's just a cover story," she posed.

Melanie took a step back, shaking her head. "Are you suggesting I've something to do with Fidel missing work?"

"I'm not suggesting anything. I'm simply saying a lot of things in your version of events aren't adding up."

Melanie stared at Celia. "You don't believe me, do you?"

"I'm not sure what to believe, Mel."

"You don't believe me. Wow."

"Mel..."

"No, it's fine. I just need some time to myself right now. So kindly leave," Melanie said.

"I'm still here working with you... working on this," Celia said, spreading her arms.

"Just go, Cece."

Celia lingered for a few seconds, then walked out of the office.

Before she left, she asked Sarah for Fidel's home address. She knew he lived across town but didn't know his exact residence.

As she walked out into the busy street, Celia knew she had to find Fidel. He knew something, and his disappearance only made this clearer.

When she got home, her argument with Melanie was still weighing on her.

"Why do you keep biting your upper lip, Cece? Is something the matter?" Audrey asked.

"It's a long story that I can't share right now," Celia replied.

Her mother wasn't the type of person to tell stories of her friend's ongoing involvement in a murder investigation. She'd end up worrying about Celia's safety.

"I have some news for you," Audrey said, "Christie and I finally agreed on a party theme."

"Oh, really?"

"Yes! And this is the list of things we will need to get to make the party work," Audrey said as she handed Celia a list. It was the longest list she had ever seen for a birthday party. They had gone with a blend of yellow and orange for the theme, and the total was double what she had ever spent.

"Ma, he's still a kid. We don't have to use our cash reserves to pay for a birthday party. This budget is insane."

"Who said you're going to pay for it?" Audrey asked.

"Ma, what are you guys going to do, swindle someone?"

Audrey took back the piece of paper.

"Christie and I will cover the costs. As far as we are concerned, you're just a guest," Audrey said as she walked away.

"But they are my kids."

"You're just a guest, Cece. Just a guest."

* * *

THE NEXT DAY, Celia struggled with her morning deliveries. Her clients noticed she was not upbeat as usual and wondered why. Celia knew the only way to ward off the cloud that was hanging around her was to talk to Melanie. She drove to the nail parlor after her schedule cleared, but it was closed.

She drove to the library and found Melanie at the reception desk, reading a book.

"Hey, Mel. Can we talk?"

"I don't think we need to do that right now," Melanie replied.

"I'm here to apologize about what I said earlier."

Melanie didn't respond.

"I was wrong. I know there are gaps in your account of what happened, but I had no right to accuse you. I'm sorry," she said.

Melanie closed the book and stood up.

"Come with me," she said as they walked outside.

They stood to one side of the entrance, where Melanie could at least see if anyone walked in or left.

"Don't you value our friendship?" Melanie asked. "Do you think that after all we've done together, including solving a case, that I'd do this? Don't you realize I have too much to lose? I've basically no one to turn to. You're the only person that I could talk to about anything in my life. To hear you say those words hurt me deeply."

"You're right. You have every reason to be disappointed with me. I'm here to apologize and say that I'm still in your corner. I'm still here to help you find out what happened to Charlize," Celia assured her.

"Are you sure being close to me won't cloud your judgment?" she asked.

"I'm here to find out the truth. It won't break this friendship," Celia said.

Suddenly Melanie's phone rang. It was Sarah.

"You need to come to the parlor right now."

"It's closed. What's happening?"

"I'm there right now and the door is open. They've come to take your stuff," Sarah said.

"Who are you talking about?"

"Some guys who look like bad news," Sarah replied.

Melanie lowered her phone slowly.

"It's Benji."

When Celia's car skidded to a stop outside the nail parlor, they found a bakkie, a light pickup truck, parked outside the door. Sarah was standing outside with a friend.

"They're inside. I don't know if they are auctioneers or…" Sarah said.

"I know who they are," Melanie said as she and Celia rushed in.

Inside, three men worked to disconnect beauty equipment. One was standing near the door.

"What the hell do you think you're doing? Put that stuff down!" Melanie shouted.

"We're here to collect what you owe," the man said.

"I said stop it!" Melanie shouted again as she tried to grab his arms. He pushed her off easily with his muscular strength.

"You can't do this, please. Please don't do this," Melanie said.

Celia was not going to stand back either. As one of the men tried to carry out a tray full of nail products, Celia stood in front of him. When he tried to move to the side, she moved with him.

"I don't want to hurt you. Please get out of my way," the man said.

"You heard her. You don't have to do this," Celia said firmly.

"If you don't pay, they don't stay," the man said.

"She's going to pay," Celia replied.

"That deadline lapsed. Today's collection day."

Celia braced herself, and then spoke, "I'll give you a choice: you either take those things or you give me twelve more hours to get your money. One of them is going to take weeks for you to make your money back and the other will take just twelve hours. What's it going to be?"

The man glared at her, wondering if she was pulling his leg.

"You realize you're making a deal with people you shouldn't cross, right?"

"I realize that," Celia said, pushing back the fear that was threatening to choke her.

The men exchanged glances.

"Twelve hours is twelve hours. Nothing more. If you dare cross that deadline, we have ways of finding you too, Celia," the man said.

Celia swallowed hard.

"See you tomorrow," the man said. He put down the tray and walked out.

The other men also sauntered out to their pickup truck, jumped in the back, before it sped away.

As Melanie and Celia watched the car drive off, they spotted Patricia watching things from across the street. She had a wry smile on her face.

"She seems to like a scene," Celia said.

"I'm telling you, Cece. Someone on the outside is playing games with us and I wouldn't be surprised if it has something to do with that woman who was staring at us right now," she said.

For once, Celia agreed with Melanie. It was time to find out what Patricia was really up to.

13

When Celia met Melanie at the café, she was a nervous wreck.

"I didn't sleep last night. I think for the first time in my life I got a panic attack," Melanie said.

"You should take some time out to forget about all that's happening around you. Maybe you should focus more time at the library," Celia suggested.

"The issue isn't where I spend time. It's the thoughts in my head. With each passing day I see new enemies and people I care about being sucked into this mess," Melanie lamented.

"You need to keep it together, Mel. For me and for other people who care about you," Celia encouraged her.

Melanie nodded.

"Drink your latte before it gets cold," Celia said. Melanie sipped on her drink.

"Do you think we can find Fidel?" Melanie asked.

"We'll find him, don't worry about it. I'm tracking down where he lives. He seems to be quite a secretive guy, no one seems to know."

"Maybe I should report him missing. I have a photo of him in my staff files," Melanie suggested.

"No, we can't do that. Let's give it till the end of the day. If I can't trace him and he doesn't show up somewhere, we can consider making a report."

"Why not now? Every minute counts, doesn't it?" Melanie said.

"I know you're worried. He might be the only witness who holds the key to your freedom. But remember you're still a suspect to the police. They might think you've got a hand in his disappearance," Celia said.

"You see what I mean? It just keeps getting worse and worse," Melanie wailed.

Celia reached out to hold her friend's hand and squeezed it gently.

"It will get better. One day, weeks from now, we'll look back and laugh about this. Trust me," Celia said.

Melanie nodded.

"One step at a time."

"Exactly," Celia replied, "For now we have a meeting with Benji to go to."

Melanie leaned forward.

"Cece, you've already done so much for me. You don't have to do this," she said.

"I want to do this. That's what friends are for," she replied.

"Thank you. I hope it's not a meeting downtown, like last time," Melanie said.

"No, thankfully. I asked him to meet us at the park."

"And he agreed to that?"

"He wasn't lying when he said he'll make time for his money," Celia replied.

* * *

THE BAY GARDENS Park was the town's best kept secret with a rich wealth of greenery and trees. It was perfect for those who wanted a quick relaxing stroll or for a romantic picnic.

Celia would have loved a picnic, as she watched a squirrel run up a tree. They were seated some meters from the entrance on a bench under the shade of a tree. It was cool and peaceful and even the sound of the highway traffic was filtered away by the lush surroundings.

"This was a good choice," Melanie said. Her eyes were closed as she breathed in the cool park air.

"I sometimes come here in between client meetings. It helps me clear my head and forget the madness of the world."

"It looks like I'll be borrowing that habit and making it my own," Melanie said.

Celia smiled.

Moments later, Benji walked up to them, accompanied by one of his men. The man hung back, scanning the area for any threats.

"Am I early?" Benji asked, smiling like an old friend.

"Not at all. Perfect timing," Celia replied. Melanie had bolted up and they all shook hands.

"I have lived here all my life and have never been to this place," Benji said.

"It does exist. Good for meetings and leisure," Celia said.

"I can see that. It's beautiful, but not my kind of thing. I'm more used to concrete and cash," he replied.

Celia was secretly happy that he wasn't in love with it. She would've never come back to the park if it meant bumping into the loan shark.

"Here's the cash as agreed," Celia said, handing him two thick stuffed envelopes. "All cash as requested."

Benji took the envelopes. He looked around, running his fingers across the edges of the envelopes as he toyed with the idea of counting the cash in the park.

"I trust it's all there. I wouldn't want to feel shortchanged," he whispered.

"I wouldn't do that to you. I'm a woman of my word," Celia reassured him.

Benji smiled.

"Great. It was a pleasure doing business with you. All the best with your parlor. And my deepest condolences on the loss of Charlize. She was quite something," Benji said.

Melanie took a step forward.

"Tell me something, Benji. How did the two of you meet?" she asked.

"I don't remember. I'm not good with that bit of things. She had my number; I had the money she needed."

"Anything else that stood out to you about her?"

Benji smiled.

"You're fishing for something. You won't find it with me. Have a great day, ladies," Benji replied. He walked away quickly, his henchman following closely behind.

Melanie turned to Celia with a tear in her eye and said, "Thank you."

When Celia got home, her mother met her in the driveway. She was holding some balloons in her hand.

"This is your ticket into the house. We've just started," Audrey said.

"What's this?" Celia asked.

"It's a balloon halo," Audrey replied.

Celia was confused. "Who came up with this?" she asked.

"Just wear it and enjoy the party," Audrey said.

Celia obliged, squeezing the chicken wire halo that held the two balloons onto her head. It fit just right. She walked into the house.

The living room was yellow nearly everywhere and packed with kids in all manner of joyful states. There was chatter, laughter, shrieking, arguments and other displays of innocent child energy. It was infectious. Celia felt more alive than she had felt for most of that day.

Mrs. Owens and Audrey had put together a very lively birthday party full of all kinds of food and snacks. Instead of Dinosaur Man, they had brought in an actor with a full Minion mascot outfit in yellow and blue. The kids kept adding the mascot in most of their activities, and Celia knew the actor would be exhausted at the end of it all.

On top of all the usual cakes and tasty bites, Mrs. Owens had made low sugar snacks and juices to keep things healthy. Her other high-

NEW NAILS AND A NASTY NIGHTMARE

light was seeing Mrs. Owens and her mother sipping juice while seated together as they enjoyed the kids having fun.

Celia spent a lot of that time serving the children and ensuring her sons were as happy as could be. She was enjoying the distraction. It was a nice break from all the tension. She got her son, the birthday boy, his favorite football team's kit from head to toe. He had recently become very passionate about playing it at school and she wanted him to know he had her full support.

Early the next day, Celia went to see Melanie with a slice of cake from the party. She wanted to check on her before heading for her client delivery trips.

Melanie was starting her day at the library, so Celia drove there. She had called in advance and found the front door open. Melanie was performing her early morning duties.

Celia held up the cake jar and waved it at Melanie as she approached. "I've brought the sugar rush you need for today," she said.

Melanie smiled. "I hope you have more because that jar might not be enough for me," she replied.

"My Mum makes heavenly cake. You only need this one because it packs a punch," Celia said.

As Melanie ate the piece of cake, Celia told her how the birthday party went. Then, Melanie's phone rang. It was Patricia.

"I don't need her to ruin my appetite so early in the day," Melanie said.

"We need to know what she's up to. Talk to her. Only this time, string her along," Celia said.

"String her along?"

"Yes. Make her believe you want the deal."

Melanie nodded. She took the call, putting it on speakerphone.

"Hello, Melanie. How's it going this morning?" Patricia asked.

"I'm fine, thanks. What's on your mind?" Melanie asked, trying her best to be civil.

"You know I'm still thinking about the offer I made you. I want to sweeten the deal a little more. How about I add two thousand dollars. Would that make you reconsider?"

Melanie paused, as if doing a mental calculation of exactly how much investment she had put in.

"You know what? If you double that I might actually be open for conversation," Melanie replied. Celia gave her the thumbs up sign.

"Let me get back to you on that but I'm happy that you're coming around to the idea. I'm confident that we can come to an agreement. I'll be in touch," Patricia said.

When Melanie hang up, Celia was excited.

"Nicely done. Very believable," Celia said.

"You think she'll buy the place?"

"I think she'll have the money. Once we start talks with her, we can dig into her a little more," Celia replied.

"What if I actually want to sell the place?" Melanie asked.

Celia frowned.

"Are you serious about that?"

Melanie sighed.

"Maybe it's too much trouble to keep the business," Melanie said gravely, "I wouldn't want to end up like Charlize."

"Why are you saying that? Did someone threaten you?"

"Because it might be time to let it go," she said.

"What happened, Mel?" Celia prodded.

"I can't talk about it right now. Thanks for the cake."

With that, Melanie walked off, the echo of her footsteps sounding hauntingly in the large space.

14

Celia didn't see Melanie for the next two days. They had brief chats on the phone, checking in on each other. Melanie never mentioned if she was in fear for her life, or whether Patricia had called back. Celia judged that her friend needed some time to think. For those two days, the nail parlor was closed. This worried Celia slightly, but she understood. However, if it went on for longer than necessary, she would have to do something to get Melanie back to herself again.

That particular morning, Celia slept in. She had been doing more client visits than normal to make up for the days she had spent attending to the nail parlor and Melanie.

She was woken up by her alarm clock. When she grabbed it to stop its incessant ringing, she was surprised to discover that it was midday. For some reason the clock had rung later than it usually did. She made a note to have it checked in case it was faulty. Checking her phone, she saw a missed call from Detective Bill Koloane.

She hoped it wasn't something to do with the case. She called back.

"Good morning Celia, did I call at a bad time earlier?" he asked.

"Not really. I was asleep, though. Not intentional," she replied.

"Then it was a bad time. I was wondering if you were open for coffee later today," he said.

Celia almost choked. He was finally asking her out. She did a quick calculation of her day. She had already lost a couple of hours. It would be a tricky fit.

"I would've loved to, but I need to catch up with the day. Let me take a rain check on that one," she replied.

"At least I tried. Have a great day and hope to see you around sometime," he replied.

"But not at the station," Celia added.

"Of course. No stations involved," he said with a chuckle.

As she got ready for the rest of the day's activities, she realized she loved the fact that he had called. It had made her day more exciting.

"Get a grip on yourself, Cece," she said to herself.

A few hours later, she was glad to see the transformation in the face of a satisfied customer.

"You always bring me the best these days. Thank you!" Flavia said as she took her delivery.

"These days? I've always brought you the best, Flavia," Celia protested.

"I know that. But if I tell you that every day, it will go to your head," Flavia countered.

Celia laughed. She probably had a point.

"You're always welcome. Next time, let me know what you need a week early," Celia said.

"You can count on that," Flavia replied.

Celia drove out into the light afternoon traffic. She decided to head to the Pier for a quick lunch before planning her afternoon.

She had just taken a seat when she received a text.

'Are you free?'

It was Melanie.

'For about an hour. Why?' Celia texted back.

'I need a ride. Can you come over?'

'Where are you?'

'At Charlize's funeral. Westmore Cemetery.'

NEW NAILS AND A NASTY NIGHTMARE

Celia wasn't aware that the funeral was happening that day. She was more surprised that Melanie attended, considering she was one of the suspects in Charlize's death. She hoped that her friend was okay.

'Heading there now. Stay safe.'

* * *

WESTMORE CEMETERY WAS the only prestigious burial ground in the area. Usually, the well-to-do were laid to rest there. It had well-manicured lawns, elaborate graves with fancy tombstones, and was well spaced out.

When Celia got there, Charlize's burial seemed to be the only one taking place that day. It had already ended. Mourners had gathered in small groups, talking, while others got into their cars and were driving off. There was a long procession of cars parked close to the burial site.

Celia found Melanie standing near the large oak tree at the corner leading to the burial site. She was dressed in black from head-to-toe, including a pair of dark sunglasses.

"Thanks so much for coming. You're a lifesaver," Melanie said as she got into the car.

"You have to stop saying that," Celia said.

"Alright, I'll remember next time," Melanie replied as she took off her sunglasses.

"I'm surprised that you're here, considering Gloria is not exactly a big fan of yours."

"I know. I'm still innocent till proven guilty, though. I kept my distance from the immediate family. Charlize was my friend, despite all her flaws and the tragic way she died," she said.

"Where to now?" Celia asked.

"You can drop me at the library. I'm still not ready to go to the nail parlor right now."

As Celia drove off, she had to pass by the mourners lined up on either side. It was slow going as they snaked their way through.

As they were just about to go past the last group of mourners, a woman in black wearing a wide-brimmed hat, sunglasses and a dark veil over her face walked onto the road and stood in front of Celia's car. It was Gloria.

Celia and Melanie exchanged glances, wondering what was going on.

Gloria walked to the passenger side of the car. Melanie rolled down her window.

"I just wanted to say thank you for coming," Gloria said.

"You saw me?" Melanie asked.

"Of course. It's a very open space here," she replied.

"I just came to pay my last respects," Melanie declared.

"I would like us to have a chat sometime, Melanie. How about tomorrow?" Gloria asked.

"Ummm, sure. Would you like us to meet at a restaurant or something?" she asked.

"We'll meet at the nail parlor. I think that works best for both of us. Say one o'clock?" Gloria said.

Melanie nodded.

"Great, see you then," Gloria said, stepping back.

Celia saw her watching them drive off from her rear-view mirror.

"That was interesting," Melanie said, "Good to see that she didn't take it to heart that I was at the funeral."

"Again, I'm surprised that..." Celia didn't finish her statement.

"Wait, wait! Stop the car," Melanie exclaimed.

"What's going on?"

"Just stop the car, Cece!"

Celia braked hard, relieved that no one was behind her.

"Behind the trees there. Do you see what I see?" Melanie asked.

Celia squinted her eyes.

"It's a guy walking. Wait, is that..."

"It's Fidel. It's him! Come on, let's catch up with him," Melanie said.

Celia quickly turned to the left, away from their driving path out of the cemetery. She joined a narrow lane. As she got closer, Fidel heard their car approach. He started running.

NEW NAILS AND A NASTY NIGHTMARE

Melanie got her head out of the passenger side window.

"Fidel, please don't run. Don't run!" Melanie shouted.

Just as they lined up with him, he ducked behind a line of trees and disappeared from view.

"Stop the car!" Melanie screeched.

The car had barely stopped when Melanie jumped out and ran towards the crop of trees where he had disappeared. Celia followed closely behind.

When they got to the line of trees near the ridge, Fidel was nowhere to be seen.

Like a ghost, he was gone.

15

"Where did he go?" Melanie asked.

"He must know his way around this place," Celia mused.

They had just spent another fifteen minutes looking around the area to see if they could spot him. His footprints disappeared after the line of trees, masked by the dead leaves spread all over the ground. It would have been easier to track him with a search dog, Celia thought. He was not up in the trees either.

"Let's go. We won't' find him here," Celia said.

They walked back to the car and settled into their seats.

"Let's assess this for a minute. Fidel goes missing. He can't be found. No one knows where he lives. Even on the records you have, right?"

"Right," Melanie replied.

"Okay. So the question is: why did he attend the burial?" Celia asked.

"He was doing what I was doing. Paying his last respects."

"But why was he hiding from the crowd? Just like you?"

"I can't tell," Melanie said.

"Just like you, he's taking precaution. I don't think he was hiding from you. Just like me, he'd be surprised to see you here. There's someone he fears in that group of mourners. Someone close to Charlize. The question is who," Celia said.

"It could be Gloria, other business associates..."

"Or Patricia," Celia said.

"Of course. Patricia," Melanie said.

"Something doesn't add up here," Celia said.

"I got a note the other day."

Celia turned to her.

"What note?"

"It was more of a threat. Or a warning," Melanie said.

"Where is it?"

"I tore it up. I found it at the parlor. Just before I opened the place. Whoever put it there knew what time I opened the place. It simply said that I should stay away from Patricia."

"What does stay away mean? It could be anything."

"Yeah, but I can't take risks to find out what anything means," Melanie replied.

"Is that why you've kept the place closed for the last few days?"

"It's one of the reasons," Melanie replied.

Celia pondered this revelation.

"You told me that you had a photo of Fidel in your staff records, right?" Celia asked.

"Yes. Why? We don't need to report him missing, at least we know he wants to hide," Melanie replied.

"We don't need to do the reporting," Celia said, "I have a better idea."

*   *   *

MELANIE WAS APPREHENSIVE, Celia could easily tell.

Whenever Melanie got nervous, she rubbed her wrists. If it was mild, she'd rub her wrists gently and slowly. When it was high level, she'd vigorously squeeze or massage her wrists as if she was trying to wipe off a stain.

They were seated in the nail parlor's mezzanine office. Gloria was sipping on a mug of takeaway coffee that she had come with. Celia was standing next to the windows listening to the conversation.

Celia could also tell that Gloria didn't want her in the room as she talked to Melanie, but Melanie had insisted. She wanted to study her body language and step in if Melanie got overwhelmed. Gloria had obliged.

"I know I came off pretty strong the first time I was here. I hope you can forgive me. I was quite emotional after losing Charlize, so I hope you understand where I was coming from," Gloria said.

"I understand. Grief is a difficult thing to navigate," Melanie replied.

"I'm hoping that we can all recover from this loss," Gloria said, "I know that she played a big role in setting up this business. The two of you working together was going to be very successful."

"Thank you for the kind words," Melanie replied.

"How are you planning to continue the business?" Gloria asked.

"Well, I've got a plan and so far, it's working. Of course, the pace has been slow as we readjust. When I get another partner, it will be a great thing," Melanie replied.

"So, you're looking for another partner, right?" Gloria asked.

"Yes, but I'm not in a hurry at the moment. I want to pick the right one. We'll make do with what we have in the short term," Melanie said, briefly nodding at Celia.

"That's good to hear. I was going to say that instead of getting a partner, you could actually consider selling off the business perhaps?" Gloria casually said.

Melanie clasped her hands together tightly.

"I don't intend to sell the business," she said firmly.

"I hear you. I just thought that it'd be a great way to honor my sister's memory."

"Why would it be so important to sell it in her memory? I mean, if the wrong person buys it, they'd kill the business," Celia chimed in.

"It was just a suggestion," Gloria said, smiling, "You can actually ignore it. Let's talk about something else."

NEW NAILS AND A NASTY NIGHTMARE

Melanie smiled back, but it was one borne out of suppressed anger.

"I believe in the business," Melanie said, "It's very important to me, the same way it was important to Charlize when she was alive."

"I don't doubt that. My only concern is you are a library person. This beauty industry business isn't a walk in the park."

"What are you trying to say, Gloria?" Melanie asked.

"Focusing on what you're good at is usually a great way to attain success." she said.

Melanie laughed aloud this time. Again, Celia could tell it was a way of suppressing her anger.

"I'm not interested in having a conversation with you if all you're going to do is insult me. We're done here," Melanie said.

"At least think about it," Gloria said as she stood up and left.

Melanie banged her hands on the table as soon as Gloria was out of earshot.

"What's wrong with that woman? Can't she just grieve in a normal way?" she raged.

"What she said wasn't driven by grief," Celia said.

"What was it driven by?"

Celia pursed her lips. She had keenly studied Gloria's body language throughout the exchange. She knew the weight of what she was about to say.

"Gloria wasn't here to offer you any advice or to make amends. She's still declaring war. Considering this is the second time she's doing this; you need to watch your back."

16

"There's a saying that goes 'if two elephants fight, it's the grass underneath their feet that suffers.' You now have two big elephants circling around you. They will crush you if you let them," Celia said.

"But they're not fighting each other," Melanie said.

"Not directly. They both want you to sell the place for different reasons. Patricia wants the whole of Main Street to herself. Gloria… Gloria maybe needs the money for some reason."

"She doesn't look like it."

"She doesn't have to. Since the proceeds go to the family, she seems primed to be a beneficiary."

"Good thing Charlize and I did the fifty-fifty split."

"You told me you might consider selling it the other day. Then today I saw a side of you that's passionate about the place and I wondered what changed?" Celia said.

"I was at a low place then. But I want to put up a fight. I've been warned about Patricia. I don't know why they warned me about her. I'm not comfortable dealing with her. Gloria's motives are unclear. Maybe a different buyer would sway me more," Melanie said.

"So, what are you going to do?" Celia asked.

"Hold out until I can't anymore."

"I expect them to try to force you into a deal."

"They just might."

"Then we'll need to prepare for them. Meanwhile, give me Fidel's file. I need to check it out."

"How long do you need it for?"

"Not long. Why?"

"I'm taking the afternoon off, and so will you. Our date is happening this evening," Melanie said.

"Are you serious? Chloe never sent the invite."

"I'm the invite, because we're going there together."

* * *

CELIA NEVER EXPECTED to be listening to a band on a weekday evening.

Of course, she'd done it before, when Trevor was alive. It was their second wedding anniversary. He'd taken her to their favorite restaurant at the time, the *Grass Whisperer*. The band played so beautifully that if he'd proposed to her a second time, she would've said yes. It was one of her favorite memories.

The band playing this evening mixed instrumental songs with acapella versions seamlessly. It was magical, and instantly ushered in a relaxed, carnival atmosphere.

Celia was feeling nostalgic as she sat next to Chloe and Melanie. They each sipped glasses of fruit wine, compliments of the restaurant as they waited for their three dates to arrive.

"Why are we the first ones to get here? Ideally, the men are supposed to be waiting for us," Melanie asked.

"Well, this was a way of throwing them off. They'd have to bring their A-game now when they know we've been waiting for a while," Chloe replied.

"I'm not sure that's a wise decision, but I guess it's never too late to try out something new," Celia remarked.

"That's the spirit," Chloe said with a smile, "Cece is ready to take on the challenge. You should warm up to things, Melanie."

Melanie shrugged.

"One thing that will warm me up right now is some roasted steak and potatoes," Melanie countered.

"Be at ease, the wait is ending now," Chloe whispered.

Sure enough, two men approached their table. One was dressed in a navy merino zip neck jumper and khaki pants while the other wore a black shirt with gray trousers. Both looked well-groomed and smiled as they got closer.

They greeted the women warmly and took their seats opposite to their dates, Melanie and Chloe.

"Ladies, this is my date Casper. He's a programmer," Chloe said as she pointed at the zip neck jumper guy, "This other gentleman is George, he's an interior designer."

"Nice to meet you all," George said as Casper waved.

Celia leaned over to Chloe.

"I can safely say that I'm solo, right?" Celia asked with a smile.

Chloe giggled. "Your date is five minutes late, but he's on his way," she said.

Celia didn't have to wait long. Emerging from the shadows, a familiar figure walked to the table.

Celia didn't want to believe her eyes, but when he finally stood opposite her, she couldn't help blushing.

"I apologize for being late, but I think I could get a warmer greeting," Detective Bill Koloane said, smiling broadly.

Without answering him, she gave him a warm hug.

"You could've warned me it was you," she whispered into his ear.

"I'm just as surprised as you are," he whispered back.

They settled into their seats. When Chloe tried to make conversation that would involve everyone, Celia and Bill inevitably ended up talking to each other more than they did to the rest of the group. She learned a lot about Bill that night: his love for long drives, going outdoors, cycling, traveling, his love for children, his upbringing in a broken family and his love for pastries. Melanie and Chloe occasionally gave Celia knowing looks and winks as the evening wore on.

During dessert, Celia leaned over to Bill and whispered, "Not to be rude, but I honestly wish that we'd go somewhere else and just talk."

"You read my mind," he replied.

Their inside jokes continued for most of the night. By ten o'clock, they were all full, cheerful and ready to go home. Bill insisted on following Celia's car until she got home. When they got to her house, they stood next to her car watching the stars.

"We finally did this," he said.

"I didn't think that it would take Chloe to convince you to make time," Celia replied teasingly.

"I've learned my lesson and apologize."

"I think a true apology involves changed behavior. Can I expect a different approach?" she asked.

"You'll definitely get a different approach," he replied.

They turned to each other and looked into each other's eyes for what felt like an eternity. She wanted to kiss him, but it felt too soon.

"Have a beautiful night," she said, embracing him.

"Sweet dreams, Cece. I can call you Cece now, right?"

"Yes, you can," she said.

As she walked to her front door, she felt like she was walking on a cloud. She heard him drive away and already missed his presence. It then hit her she was falling for a detective. Was she crazy? Trevor was an army man, a man of danger. Bill was a cop, another man of danger. What did that say about Celia? Was her love for dangerous men a good thing or a flaw? She didn't really want to know, not at that moment. This felt good, and she was enjoying every minute of it.

It was when she inserted the key into the lock that she saw the note. It was taped on top of her door. At first it looked like something the boys would've done. When she took it, she unfolded it to see if there was something written inside.

'Stay away from the Melanie situation. It won't end well for you.'

Cold shivers went up her spine and replaced the warm fuzzy feeling she'd enjoyed all evening.

17

Celia was torn.

Part of her wanted to open the door as quickly as possible and lock herself in the house. The other part wanted to search around the house, because whoever had taped the note might be watching. She went with the latter, scanning the dark shadows around her home. She was hoping for some movement, but she spotted none. All she could hear were crickets, the occasional rustling of leaves and passing traffic.

Who was this? How did they know her house? Who was trying to warn her and Melanie and why?

She had many questions as she got into the house. She fastened all the locks and set the house alarm, just in case. Without switching on the house lights, she went to the window and spent another ten minutes watching the shadows outside. Maybe the intruder would feel safe and make a mistake. Again, she spotted nothing.

When Celia got into her bedroom, she saw the feed from her CCTV camera. She rewound the footage for the evening and studied it.

Her mother drove in.

She played with boys in the driveway.

NEW NAILS AND A NASTY NIGHTMARE

They got back into the house at seven.

At nine o'clock, a dark figure appeared.

The intruder was wearing a hoodie and a facemask, so she couldn't make out who it was. The figure kept close to the house, so it was hard to know their walking style. With no clear identifiers, she knew it was a lost cause. At least she knew what time they'd made their move.

She went into the kitchen where she could switch on the lights and examine the note a little more. It was written using a biro pen, and the handwriting was easily readable. She couldn't tell if it belonged to a male or female, but it was definitely an adult. Then she realized it was written on a store receipt. The receipt date was for the previous night! It indicated the purchase of Swiss roll and a pack of sausages. This was a clue she could use. Most likely the writer of the note had made the original purchase.

She went to her bedroom and switched on her laptop. She searched for the Dully store on the receipt. She watched the mouse spin. Then a list of locations emerged. However, there was only one she reckoned it could belong to - the Dully Corner store across town.

Early the next morning, after dropping the boys in school, she drove across town. She had never been to the Dully district of the town in a long time, and yet it had hardly changed. There were a few modern buildings, but most of the locals kept their simple homes and compounds in the same style from twenty years ago. It was still very relaxed and far removed from the high-traffic areas.

The Dully corner store itself was one of the more modern buildings. Sitting conveniently at the junction of two streets, it had a sizeable car park on its front, which was where Celia parked her car.

She walked in like a regular shopper, scouting the place in case she saw a familiar face. It was well stocked with all kinds of essential items, the kind of store that had one or two attendants manning it. She was also checking to see if they had CCTV cameras. They did.

Armed with her can of baked beans, she went to the counter. It was not a busy morning, which was a good thing. After the cashier had checked her out, she made her move.

"Sorry to bother you, but I was here last evening and there's a gentleman who pickpocketed my purse. I only realized this later that night. Could you help me find him?" Celia asked.

"I'm sorry, lady, it's against company policy to do so," the cashier replied.

"Please. He took some cash that I needed to pay for my son's treatment. I know the money will never come back, but at least let's get him off the streets,' Celia pleaded.

There was no one else in the store, and after a moment, the cashier caved in.

They went to a desk close by which had a computer monitor showing the various cameras inside the store.

"You were here at what time?" the cashier asked.

"At seven-o-eight in the evening. Check the counter cameras, because I think that's when he took it," Celia replied.

As they skimmed through the footage, she prayed she would see him without a hoodie. It wasn't likely he would have one considering it would be suspicious in a store, but the skeptic in her wouldn't give herself too much hope.

"There you go," The cashier said, "Did you say seven-o-eight?"

"Yes. Is that him?"

"I don't think so. That's just Fidel, he comes here all the time. It can't be him because I know him."

"You say he comes here all the time?" Celia asked.

"Every evening. Pretty cool guy. Are you sure you were pickpocketed at the cashier's? Because I can't see…"

The cashier turned around to see Celia dart out of the door, heading fast to her car. As she got in, she could hear him shout at her. He wouldn't call the police, she figured. There was nothing really to report there. Just a confused woman who distracted him.

But she had gotten what she wanted. She had seen his face. It wasn't covered by a hood.

It was a familiar face.

It was Fidel!

As she drove away, Celia called Melanie.

"I've found him," Celia said, excitement etched in her voice.

"Found who?" Melanie asked.

"Fidel. I've found him!"

"That's great! Where is he? Have you talked to him?"

"He's not here physically but I know how to get him."

Celia was already thinking of how she would confront him. She needed to do it soon.

"Can I tag along?" Melanie asked.

"Not on this ride, but I'll keep you posted," she said.

"Please do. I'm trying to get Patricia off my back. She has the money and wants to close the deal."

"String her along as much as you can," Celia said.

"I've got to. Thanks for the good news."

As she hung up, Celia knew she only had one shot at this. She would have to make her move that very night, lest he disappeared again.

* * *

"You know this isn't an actual date, right?" Celia said as she grabbed another beef biltong, the dried meat snack of choice in her town.

She was seated in Bill's police car, interrupted by the occasional chatter from the police radio.

"But it's a sign of changed behavior," Bill said with a smile, "There was no time to ask you out considering the nature of what I do. So here I am."

"I appreciate the effort," Celia said, "although it danced on the edge of reason."

"How so?"

"You saw me in traffic and pulled me over," she said.

"I didn't use my siren. I asked you like any regular guy would. By flashing my headlights."

"Regular guys pick up girls using their headlights?" Celia asked.

"You'd be surprised by what happens in the real world."

They both laughed.

"I just never expected to eat a meal in a police car. At least that's a new memory."

"Which other crazy car have you eaten in?"

"An army tank."

"You're kidding, right?" he exclaimed.

"No, I'm not. I was married to an army guy, remember?"

"Of course. You had some good times, I can imagine," he said.

"Yes, we did. This is a good time too," she said.

"I'm here to create more good times. If you'll be open to that possibility," he replied.

Celia smiled. She understood now. She liked the idea of dating someone who looked for answers, just like she did. It wasn't really about them being a detective or army guy. They looked for answers through the lens she did. This was what attracted her to Bill. She had tried dating two years after Trevor's death, but this was the closest she had come to actually liking someone romantically. It felt like she was twenty-one again.

"I think there's some room for exploration," Celia replied.

"That's sounds like music to my ears," Bill said.

They talked for close to an hour. When it was finally time to go their separate ways, neither of them wanted to say goodbye.

It was almost sunset when she completed her last delivery. She would normally head straight home afterwards, but Celia had some unfinished business.

She had parked some distance from the Dully corner store. She was staking out Fidel. She kept looking at her watch as she counted down towards seven o'clock.

It was soon dark, and the streetlights and car park lights illuminated the area around Celia's car. She was glad.

At quarter past seven, she spotted Fidel's dark, familiar form as he walked into the store. He looked calm and relaxed. This was clearly a place he felt safe. He even didn't feel the need to change his regular routine every evening. She felt lucky. She'd played out the scenario in her mind several times during the day and hoped it would work.

NEW NAILS AND A NASTY NIGHTMARE

Ten minutes later, he got out of the store. He was biting into a hotdog as he walked.

"Fidel, we need to talk," Celia said as she suddenly appeared in front of him.

He lost grip of his hot dog, almost dropping it before catching it just in time.

"Please don't run this time. I got your warning note on my front door. I need you to tell me what's going on," Celia said.

Fidel composed himself.

"I shouldn't be talking to you and you shouldn't be here," he said.

"I need to know what's going on, Fidel. Please," she persisted.

Fidel sighed as he tried to think of what to say to her.

"We can't talk here," he finally whispered.

"I've got my car with me. We can drive to wherever you need us to go," she offered.

He hesitated, then nodded.

"Okay. But prepare yourself mentally. It's going to be a long drive."

18

Driving at night was not something Celia enjoyed very much. Especially when she didn't know where she was going or how long the trip would take.

They had driven out of town and were now on the highway parallel to the beachfront. It did offer great views of the city lights in the distance, but this wasn't that kind of drive.

Fidel kept looking over his shoulder to see if they were being tailed. She found it a little over the top, but she didn't know what story he was about to spill. Maybe the precaution was justified.

They drove for half an hour before he instructed her to take a side road. It was a gravel road with a harsh ride due to the potholes, but she kept going. As she drove, her phone started ringing. It was her mother. She had left her in charge of the boys, knowing it might be a late night. She always told her where she was going to be, but tonight she hadn't. She knew her mother was worried.

"Hey, Ma. How are the boys?" Celia asked, speaking through the Bluetooth in the car. It allowed her to focus on the road.

"They're fine. They just had dinner."

"Great. Tell them I'll be coming in later. If they sleep before I get there kiss them goodnight for me."

NEW NAILS AND A NASTY NIGHTMARE

"Where are you, Cece? It sounds like you are driving in a rally or something."

She hadn't realized the road was making the car shake and rattle so much.

"I'll update you when I get to my destination."

"You promise to let me know?"

"I promise, Ma."

When she hung up, there was a brief silence before Fidel broke it.

"We're here."

They stopped at the edge of a little township. You could see it in the valley below from where they had stopped, with little lights coming through the widows.

"Where are we going?"

"To have dinner," Fidel said.

"Is the car safe here?"

"Once you've come this far, no one can touch you," Fidel replied.

A short walk from her car led them to a little restaurant that served local cuisine. It was made of recycled wooden pallets taken from freight containers. This gave its exterior a distinct style, although she couldn't appreciate it fully since it was nighttime. On the inside, the decor was simple. The pallets were everywhere, from the chairs to the tables, to the wall art.

"What is this place?" Celia asked.

"It's a hotel. Or as you call it in your side of the world, a restaurant," he replied.

"I mean this whole area?"

"It's called Diskerp. Don't look for it on a map, you won't find it. It's what we call off the grid."

"It can't be really off the grid. I could see those little lights in the township valley."

"Solar power. We have our own solar farm some meters from here. It's dark, so you can't see it"

"Are you serious?"

"Very serious. This is home."

"You commute from Main Street all the way here, every day?" Celia asked.

"No, I have a second home closer to the office. But this is where I call home," Fidel replied.

The waiter, a burly middle-aged bearded man, walked up to them.

"I think I'll order a bunny chow for both of us. You must be hungry."

"I sure am, but I wouldn't finish a full one. Besides, you just had a hot dog not too long ago," Celia said.

"Quarter loaf it is. One each. Thanks," Fidel said.

"And some mineral water, please," Celia chimed.

Fidel smiled.

"You can take chicken broth instead? It's a good substitute," he suggested.

Celia hesitated.

"Alright, with some broth," she said. The waiter nodded and left.

"Why do you love this place?" Celia asked.

"Because there are no CCTV cameras around and they have great food," he said with a smile, "Keeping my tracks invisible doesn't mean I can't have some of the best local food in town."

The food didn't take long. The waiter was back with the bunny chow made out of hollowed out bread filled with curry and strips of chicken. The broth came steaming, ideal for the chilly night.

"First we eat, then we talk," Fidel said.

True to his word, the bunny chow was delicious. It was rich with flavors as if made from the love of a mother for her children. By the time she was on her last morsels, she was too full.

"That was quite something," she said.

"It's the ultimate soul food, I believe," Fidel said, smiling with pride.

Celia noted that this was the most open, sincere version of Fidel she had ever met. Still, she knew he possessed some facts that could just be the key to unlock this murder mystery and reveal who Charlize's killer was. She just hoped she had the right skills to elicit this information from him.

"So, tell me, why did you look for my house and put a note on it?" Celia asked.

"I wanted you to be safe from them. I wanted to stay anonymous, too," he said.

"Who are them?" she asked.

He cleared his throat and spoke.

"I used to work for Patricia Nesbitt, the lady who owns the other nail parlor down the street."

Celia almost choked on her broth.

"You what? For how long did you work for her?"

"Two years," he replied.

"Did Charlize and Melanie know about this?"

"Charlize did. She's the one who hired us."

"So why did you send a note warning Melanie about Patricia? How is Patricia connected to what you want to tell me?"

"After I left, I kept in touch with my colleagues who still work there. They tell me Patricia has been saying a few suspicious things about Charlize's passing."

Celia's eyebrows went up.

"What kind of things are you talking about?" she asked.

"She's saying that she knew that Melanie's nail parlor wouldn't last. She wanted to buy it out. That it was only a matter of time before something tragic happened. You know, crazy stuff," he said.

Yet, to Celia, this didn't sound like something sinister.

"Is there anything else that she said?" she asked.

"After the boss fell down the stairs, she kept telling her staff that Charlize was poisoned. They came and told us."

"But this was already after the police came, right?" Celia asked.

"No, this before the cops came to tell you or Melanie. This was the very day she was poisoned," Fidel said.

This revelation lit a bulb in Celia's mind.

"That's definitely suspicious. Sounds like she knows something we don't," she mused.

"That's exactly what I thought," he said.

"So why did you go into hiding?" Celia posed.

"I needed to. Something my boss didn't know about me is that I've been locked up before," Fidel said.

"You mean…"

"Yes, I've been to prison before. I did three years for vandalizing someone's property. I was part of a wrong crowd back then, and we did a few things I'm not proud of. But I thought that the moment the police knew that I, an ex-con, was working at the parlor, they might suspect me. I don't need that kind of attention in my life right now," Fidel replied.

Celia took a moment to take in all the things he had said.

"But you're a good man, Fidel. You're clearly looking out for me. You tried to save Charlize. You even warned Melanie about Patricia."

"Maybe she thinks it's a prank or something," he said.

"She didn't. Especially after you sent me a similar message as well."

"I just did what I had to do. There are some evil people out here. You never know who's aiming for you," Fidel said.

"You believe Patricia knows something about Charlize's death?" Celia asked.

"When Patricia speaks, she's looking to light a fire. She's not speaking from a rumor mill. She knows something because she was already talking about the poison thing even before the police had announced it to anybody. I would have loved to find out more, but I can't put myself in a situation where I'm digging up that information. I may get myself in trouble," he said, looking around to see if anyone was eavesdropping on their conversation.

Celia listened, dumbstruck that all the things he was saying seemed to be legitimate. She needed to crosscheck his records. But so far, he sounded authentic.

"What if I helped you avoid that trouble? Would you help me find out more from Patricia?" she asked.

"How are you going to do that exactly?" he asked.

Celia smiled. "Fidel, I was able to find you from a store receipt. A receipt, of all things. I didn't even use fingerprints or tracking your mobile phone. I know you're taking precautions with avoiding CCTV cameras, but if I could find you from a receipt, then they can find you just as fast. I've got a friend in the police department who can help us. But I need you to take a risk," she said.

Fidel pondered for a moment. "If I do this, then I have a lot more to lose," he said.

"We both have a lot to lose. But we're here in a wooden restaurant talking about doing the right thing. We can't hide in fear, because this isn't going away if you don't do something. We already lost Charlize. We don't have to lose Melanie or anyone else."

Fidel nodded. "Alright. Let's get them," he said.

19

Celia got out of Diskerp with Fidel in the passenger seat and dropped him off when she had reached a safe distance.

"If you weren't with me, I wouldn't be able to guarantee your safety," Fidel said.

They agreed to keep in touch. He gave her a mobile phone number that he'd only switch on at midday every day, if she needed to reach him.

"Let's keep doing this until we've resolved the situation," he said.

Celia drove as fast as she could, heading home. Her mother was still awake, and Celia had let her know that she was safe and on her way. This wasn't enough for Audrey, so she kept calling every ten minutes for an update.

When she finally did get home, some minutes after midnight, her mother was full of gratitude.

"I thought we talked about this. You're not supposed to be sending me to an early grave, Cece," Audrey lamented as Celia settled in, taking off her jacket and scarf.

"We said that I should keep in touch. You know that it's not always possible to send you my exact location," Celia said.

"Why not?"

"Don't worry, Ma. I'll always be here when you need me, okay?" Celia said. She kissed her mother on the forehead.

They soon bid each other goodnight and retired to their beds.

However, Celia couldn't sleep. Her head was buzzing with ideas. The more she replayed what Fidel had told her, the stronger her resolve became. The wheels in her mind began hatching a plan that might just work.

* * *

CELIA SCHEDULED ONLY one delivery of the new nail polish brand the next morning. After it was done, she called Melanie.

"Tell me something happened," Melanie began.

"Something did happen. I met him. We talked about many things. I can tell you this as fact: he gave us the ticket to clearing your name."

"Yes! I knew it. Tell me more. When is he coming over to talk to the police?" Melanie asked.

"That's the tricky part. He's not going to do that."

Melanie went quiet for a brief moment.

"Why not? How is this supposed to help me?" she asked.

"Calm down, Mel. This situation affects other people too, including Fidel. That's why he went underground. He needs us to help him," she said.

"What do we need to do?"

"I want us to go together and have a chat with our suspicious friend, Patricia Nesbitt," Celia said, "Are you free right now?"

"I'm always free where clearing my name is involved," Melanie said.

"Where are you now?"

"At the nail parlor," she replied.

"Wait for me, I'm on my way there," she said.

She hung up and stepped on the accelerator.

When Celia arrived at the nail parlor, she quickly parked her car and ran inside.

She found Sarah alone.

"Where's Melanie?" Celia asked.

"She left ten minutes ago," Sarah replied.

"Where did she go?"

"She didn't say. All I know is she left in a hurry."

Celia took out her phone and tried calling her. The phone rang, but she wouldn't take it.

"Which direction did she go? Was she in a car?"

"She was on foot. She headed to the right, down the street."

Celia immediately knew where Melanie was headed.

"Oh no, Mel. You're not supposed to go there alone," Celia turned on her heel and dashed out.

She walked past her car, walking briskly down the street. Three minutes later, she stood outside Bittos, Patricia Nesbitt's nail parlor. She had never paid attention to it until now. Even as she rushed to get inside, she couldn't help noticing the red facade with the name emblazoned on top of the door. It felt like a nightclub rather than a nail parlor.

When she walked in, it was reasonably busy. Staffers in red branded shirts were attending to clients. It was definitely a busier morning than AfroStar was having.

One of the staffers available approached Celia.

"Hello ma'am. What kind of service would you like?" she asked in a sweet voice.

Sorry, but I'm not here to get your service. I'm here to see Patricia Nesbitt, your boss," Celia said.

"She's in a meeting right now. Can I ask you to wait or leave a message?"

"I can't wait nor leave a message. I need to see her. Now," she insisted.

"I'm sorry, I can't let you do that."

"Where is her office?" Celia asked as she walked towards the back of the establishment.

"I'm sorry I can't…"

"Tell me, where is her office?" Celia prodded.

The woman pointed towards the left, where there was a brown metal door.

Celia walked to it. As soon as she got to the door, she could hear the sound of shouting coming from inside.

She felt the knob, and it turned. She barged in. She found Melanie and Patricia glaring at each other. It was clear that they were in the middle of an argument.

"I hope you've come for your friend here, because she's trying to get herself in trouble," Patricia said.

"The wicked run even when they're not being pursued. Do you have something to say to me, Patricia?" Melanie raged.

She was spoiling for a fight. Celia knew a buildup of frustration had led to Melanie's rash action, but she had to find a way to use to it to their advantage. Celia shut the door behind her.

"Even if I had something to say, you're the last person I'd tell it to," Patricia said, holding firm.

"That wasn't a problem when you wanted to buy my parlor, was it?"

"Enjoy saying that because things are changing very fast. You won't see what hit you when it comes," Patricia said.

"Ahh. What are you planning next?" Melanie asked as she stepped up to Patricia.

Celia decided to speak.

"The two of you need to ease off each other," she said.

"No easing off here, Cece. She knows more than she's telling us. I'm here to make sure that she talks," Melanie said with conviction.

"I'm not telling you a single word," Patricia countered.

"We could've done this the easy way, but I guess we'll have to do it the hard way," Melanie hissed.

With that, Melanie grabbed Patricia by the neck and pushed her towards the wall at frightening speed.

20

In a fraction of a second, the story of the cornered cat flashed across Celia's mind.

The cat could be taunted, but it always made an effort to avoid confrontation. However, when it was pushed to the wall, with nowhere to go, it became vicious.

As she watched Melanie drive Patricia towards the wall, she knew that the cat in this case was Melanie, not Patricia. She had watched her life crumble around her for the last couple of weeks, and she was being pushed to a corner. Now that she had no options left, she had become vicious.

With quick reflexes, Celia pulled off Melanie from Patricia, separating the two women. Thankfully, Patricia didn't' move to attack Melanie in retaliation. It would've overwhelmed Celia.

"Calm down or else you'll lose it all," Celia urged Melanie.

"You have no idea what's at stake," Melanie said.

"I know exactly what's at stake. Now you'll either let me help you or go to prison. What's it going to be?" Celia asked.

She could feel the fight leave Melanie's body as her breathing eased.

"Thank you. Now, let me do the talking from here onwards, okay?"

Melanie nodded.

Celia turned to Patricia, who was standing as she massaged her bruised neck.

"Before you get any ideas, we need to talk."

"I said I'm not saying a word," Patricia replied.

"It's not a request," Celia said. She pulled over one of the visitor chairs and pointed at it.

"Sit!" Celia ordered.

Patricia gingerly eased herself into the seat.

"This isn't an interrogation. This is a conversation. We're not interested in violence, despite my friend's passionate reaction. We just want honest answers to simple questions. Fair enough?" she said.

"I'm going to do a lot of listening. I'm not interested in…"

"Why did you tell your staff that Charlize had been poisoned before the police even knew it?" Celia asked.

"What? She knew that?" Melanie asked.

"Be calm, Mel," Celia snapped. Melanie retreated.

"I don't know what you're talking about."

"Are you sure about that? Because as it stands, Charlize died. No one knew it was because of poisoning except you. What do you think the detectives will say?"

"I didn't do it," Patricia protested.

"It doesn't matter, does it? All they need is to connect these bits of information to its source. You."

"You can't make it stick," Patricia said.

"True, that's not my job. My job here is nearly done. All they need to do is arrest you. Guess who you'll see on the witness stand that day? Five of your employees. Some of them are still working here, but they can't stand for an injustice. You still think I can't make it stick?"

Patricia began visibly sweating. Celia had her where she wanted her.

"We're waiting for your decision," Celia said.

"I'm not the one who did it. But I know the person who might know about it."

"Who?"

"Will you protect me?"

"It depends if you're lying or not. Who?"

Patricia was clearly struggling to say the truth. But she also wanted to save her own skin. The ultimate dilemma.

"Gloria knows something about it."

"Her half-sister?" Melanie asked.

"Yes, her half-sister."

"Stop being outrageous," Melanie said.

"Let her speak, Mel. Tell us what you mean," Celia breathed.

"I don't know much. Just that Gloria knew her sister would be poisoned," Patricia said.

"Who did the poisoning? Where and when did it happen?" Celia asked.

"I don't know!"

"This isn't looking good for you," Celia said.

"That's all I've got to give," Patricia replied.

"So, what's the connection between you and Gloria?" Celia asked.

"She's a silent partner."

"Partner in what?" Celia probed.

"In several businesses, including *Bittos*,"

Celia chuckled.

"Hold on. So you're telling me you've been trying to buy our nail parlor on behalf of Gloria?"

Patricia hesitated, and then nodded. Celia and Melanie exchanged looks.

"Suddenly a lot of things make sense. Maybe one more thing that could help you is if you take us to the ringmaster," Celia suggested.

"What do you mean?" Patricia asked.

"Take us to Gloria. Let her speak for herself."

"I can't do that. No way."

"Shall we make the case against you or her? Because we'll win either of those cases. Your choice," Celia said.

Patricia rubbed her eyes. Celia wasn't sure if she was wiping off crocodile tears or real tears.

"Alright, I'll do it. On condition that I'm protected."

"On condition that we find the real murderer, the possibilities remain open."

"I'll give you who you want."

Celia's heart skipped a beat. She couldn't wait to see and hear from Gloria Langa.

A few minutes later, Celia was driving with Patricia and Melanie in the backseat.

Celia preferred it that way because Melanie could keep an eye on Patricia, just in case she tried something funny.

Patricia would occasionally give directions as they headed towards Gloria.

According to Patricia's directions, they were heading towards Gloria's house which was in the Neddle suburb. It was quite a wealthy neighborhood with high gates, electric fences and trimmed hedges.

After forty minutes of driving, Patricia said, "We're here."

To the side of the high brass gate was an intercom system to alert the owner of the house that there were guests at the gate. Patricia spoke into the system.

"Hello, Pat! What brings you here?"

"Sorry to bother you, Glo, but I had something really urgent to discuss."

"It's that serious, huh? Okay. But the automatic gate has a problem so my grounds man is coming to let you in," Gloria replied.

"Sounds good," Patricia replied.

Two minutes later a scrawny young man in a straw hat opened the large gates and they drove in. Celia drove down a driveway that wasn't too long as she could see the main house ahead of her. A well-manicured compound flanked it, with tall majestic trees lining the driveway. Gloria clearly lived well.

The main house was equally majestic, with marble walls and wrought iron windows.

Gloria herself emerged to welcome them. She initially looked surprised, but quickly composed herself.

"It's lovely to have you," she said as she led them in. A tall hallway with art pieces along the walls welcomed them at the door.

Her living room had a modernist take to the furnishing. It had modern Scandinavian style seats with trim finishes that gave the room a simple yet sophisticated feel. Celia loved it.

Once they were all seated and served with fresh orange juice, Celia remembered to discreetly turn on her phone audio recorder.

"So, what brings you here?" Gloria asked.

"I think you're aware I've been pursuing a business deal with…," Patricia began.

"We've come to talk business," Melanie interjected.

"Are you talking about the nail parlor?" Gloria asked.

"Both nail parlors," Melanie replied.

Gloria looked at Patricia quizzically.

"They know, Gloria," Patricia said.

"What do you mean they know?" Gloria asked.

"They know that you're my silent partner."

Gloria let out cheeky laugh, as if Patricia had said a stale joke.

"So what does that have to do with your visit? Because I don't see how that's anyone's concern. Why have you brought them here?"

"Because she had to," Melanie said.

"Last time I checked, Patricia was a free-thinking person. Why is Melanie replying on your behalf Patricia?"

"This is bigger than her. This is about your half-sister, the dear friend that I lost," Melanie said.

"She was my sister, so I lost someone who might matter more to me than to you," Gloria countered.

"Did she really matter to you Gloria?" Celia asked.

"I beg your pardon?"

"Charlize. Did she really matter to you?" Celia asked again.

"She was my half-sister, why wouldn't she matter to me?"

"Because I'm sitting here wondering why you would poison your half-sister," Melanie replied.

Gloria's demeanor changed to a more serious and grave expression.

"Are you listening to yourself? Have you come here to insult me in my own home while drinking my own juice?" Gloria fumed.

"She simply asked a very straight forward question which all of us would like an answer to. Did you poison your sister?" Celia asked.

"I did no such thing. I don't know who'd do such a thing," Gloria replied.

"Then why is it that the day after you had an argument at a family meeting about how well she was doing with the nail parlor, she suddenly turns up dead two days later?" Celia posed.

"What happens in my family is none of your business. I'm actually about to have all of you thrown out of my home," she said.

"Patricia told us that Gloria didn't like the fact that Charlize opened the nail parlor on Main Street."

"It was my street. The street with sufficient traffic to cater to one nail parlor. Not two. It didn't make business sense for her to open a competing parlor so close to the one we had started," Gloria explained.

"And that's why you're angry," Celia said.

"Of course, I was angry! It was a silly business decision."

"Where were you the morning Charlize died?" Celia asked.

"I was horse riding at a nearby ranch," Gloria replied.

"Do you have evidence of this?"

At this point Gloria went quiet as she glared at the three women.

"You're really asking me for evidence?" Gloria asked.

"Yes! If it's not too much to ask," Celia replied.

Gloria stood up.

"I'll get you the receipt that I was given that day."

She marched towards the corridor, her footsteps disappearing into the expanse of the house. It was after two minutes that Celia got the gut feeling that Gloria wasn't coming back.

Celia got up and followed the route Gloria had taken down the hallway. She was passing one of the big windows when she spotted Gloria's form running towards the garage.

"She's getting away," Celia said as she dashed to the front door.

She eventually caught up with Gloria, who had just opened the garage door to reveal three luxurious cars.

"I didn't do anything!"

"Then why are you running? Celia asked.

"You can't arrest me, so leave me alone!"

"She can't arrest you, but I can," Detective Bill Koloane emerged from one end of the garage with two other officers.

"Who are you?" Gloria asked.

"Your ticket to justice," the detective replied firmly as he took out his handcuffs.

21

The Pier was buzzing that afternoon.

It was packed with clients looking for good food and an easy time with their company. Celia, Chloe and Melanie were part of the crowd, talking through how events unfolded.

"She might get bail, but she'll have to put up a strong case for it to be approved. She tried to run," Celia said.

"But she didn't escape," Chloe said.

"It's the intent sometimes," Celia replied.

"But why did she do it?" Chloe asked.

"I think it's easier to ask how she did it."

"Alright, let's go with that," Chloe said.

"Gloria found out that Charlize was opening a nail parlor on the same street. These two sisters never got along since childhood, and that has spilled over into their adult lives. Gloria hated this. She bought some poison, put aside a lethal dose. She then went ahead to ask for a coffee date with Charlize."

"So, she started this plan some weeks before the nail parlor was launched?"

"Yes. She wanted to apologize for the painful memories they shared and the pain they caused each other. Charlize thought it was worth a shot to repair their relationship. But when she went to the washrooms, Gloria placed the poison into her drink. After sipping the drink, she only had two hours to get the antidote."

"Two hours she didn't have," Melanie said.

"Is all this based on what she said?"

"Not entirely," Celia said, "They found CCTV footage from the restaurant where they met. You can see Gloria putting the powder into Charlize's drink."

"So, it caused a heart attack after I stressed her with an argument," Melanie said.

"She was going to have one, anyway. The truth is that by the time she fell down the stairs, she was already dead," Celia replied.

"She's going away for a long time," Chloe said.

"Cece, I wanted to ask you something," Melanie said.

"Sure. What's on your mind?" Celia asked.

"I'm really grateful for all the times you came through for me during this crazy ordeal. You're the true friend that I never thought I needed. Thank you for standing with me," Melanie said.

"Like I said last time, that's what true friendship is all about. Standing in the gap, right?" Celia replied.

"Exactly," Melanie replied. "So, when I say this, I'm not trying to burden you with more responsibility or trying to get off mine. Would you like to be my partner in this business?"

"You're talking about the nail parlor?"

"What other business do I have? The money you gave to pay the loan shark can be considered equity invested. Unless you have misgivings about that."

Celia thought for a moment.

"It was part of my family savings," she said.

"I can understand if you still want it back, but of course we'd have to discuss a payment plan across the next couple of months and…"

"Wait, I wasn't finished. Despite that, I still have an interest in investing part of that money and this could be a good start."

"Is that a yes?" Melanie asked.

"Yes Melanie Dawes, I'll be your business partner. You need to talk to that lawyer though."

"Don't worry. All that has been arranged."

"Fantastic!"

"Why are you using my words?" A voice said.

Celia turned to see Detective Bill. He was holding a bouquet in his hand.

"Hello, detective," Melanie said with a smile.

"Hello, Melanie. Sorry to interrupt you, but I have a package for someone."

Bill handed the flowers to Celia. It was a healthy bunch of red Barberton daisies. Celia was simply astounded.

"I hope you're not allergic to these," he said.

"Not at all. I love flowers," she replied.

"Great. Then you'll like the second gift too."

Celia's eyes widened.

"What second gift?" Celia asked curiously.

"The gift of me. Will you go on a date with me?" he asked.

Celia heard the hushes and giggles around her as her friends watched.

"Yes, I'll go on a date with you, Detective," Celia replied, smiling.

"Drop the name 'detective' as a change in behavior. Deal?" he said with a grin.

Celia chuckled. She liked where this was going.

The End

HIGHLIGHTERS AND UPHEAVAL

A SUNSHINE COVE COZY MYSTERY

ABOUT HIGHLIGHTERS AND UPHEAVAL

Released: November 2020
Series: Book 4 – Sunshine Cove Cozy Mystery Series
Standalone: Yes
Cliff-hanger: No

What happens when a very expensive piece of artwork is stolen at a private event?

And someone close to the owner of the artwork is found dead.

Are the two misfortunes linked or coincidental?

Celia Dube, Sunshine Cove's resident beauty consultant and part-time amateur sleuth, was one of the guests at the event. She's determined to find out who did it, even if she gets on the nerves of the local law enforcement personnel and attracts the attention of people linked to both misfortunes.

Will she be successful in her sleuthing endeavours or become the murderers next victim?

1

Celia Dube wasn't suicidal.

However, for a fleeting moment, she wished she could go on a free fall from the fifteenth floor of the skyscraper she sat in.

"Cat got your tongue?" the tall bespectacled man asked her as he leaned forward from behind his polished mahogany desk. Richie Butt was in his early fifties, clean-shaven and wearing a pinstriped suit. He looked more like a banking executive than the chief executive of the successful Maven Beauty Products.

Celia blinked several times as she gathered her thoughts. She was dressed more officially than she usually did. She had a dark trouser suit on, matching shoes and freshly done hair. She looked good, but wasn't feeling good. Her lips felt dry, so she licked them. She then reached into her bag and frantically searched for clear lip balm.

She found it and applied it, avoiding eye contact with him. She heard him crack his knuckles.

"Well?" he asked.

"Not really, sir. I was thinking of a suitable, factual answer," she replied.

"Did you find the numbers you were looking for?" he asked, his eyes narrowed.

"Well, it's true that the sales for the past four weeks have dwindled consistently by around five per cent each week. I adjusted my distribution routine slightly, but this should pay off in the coming weeks," Celia replied.

"How have you adjusted your distribution?"

"I got into partnership with a local nail parlor that recently opened. It's been getting good traffic, and I secured a space within the establishment to set up our Maven products. They've started picking up pace," she replied.

This was true. But what she didn't add was that she co-owned the nail parlor with her best friend, Melanie Dawes. Running the place had been eating into her time; affecting her targets. Stating this could be detrimental. Perhaps when the numbers were back up again, she would find a clever way of breaking the news.

Richie took off his glasses. He let out a pronounced sigh and then sat back into his cushioned leather chair. He rocked slightly as he studied her. The silence was only broken by the muffled sound of street traffic below.

"You're one of my best people. You've had an amazing run here, and your sales have never fallen consistently for a four-week period. Is there something else that's been taking your attention? Maybe at home?" he asked in a conciliatory tone.

Celia wasn't keen to give him any more excuses. "Things are fine. I know what's ailing my distribution plan and I'll get it back on track," she said.

"I hope so, because I have a new product that needs to launch."

She sat up in her chair. "What kind of product?"

"It's a new brand of highlighter. I'd like to sell it as an alternative to the rest. It's got a great formula that's kind to the skin. I'm keen to sell it to women over thirty. I know many of them live in Sunshine Cove," he said.

Celia nodded in agreement. The beautiful suburban town along the coast had a close-knit population full of people over thirty with families as well as retirees. It also hosted tourists across the year due to its great weather.

"I can do what's needed to make it catch on. I've done it before," she assured him.

"I know. Something interesting I've probably never told you before: you're unique. I've got distributors in major cities across South Africa who run a more structured delivery set up. You're the only one who does personalized delivery in the entire network. And you kept beating their numbers."

"I can only credit my clients. They helped me understand their needs," she replied.

"That's good. But these recent results aren't good. Maybe their needs have changed," he said.

Celia's eyebrows furrowed. "What do you mean?" she asked.

Richie leaned forward. "Maybe your distribution approach, which has worked for so many years, needs to change."

Celia clenched her jaw. She knew what he was alluding to. Maven would bring in some of their representatives and open stores in Sunshine Cove. She'd be forced to get a lower commission and possibly be stationed at one of the stores. It would deprive her of the profits she got directly and tear down the distribution system she had built. She didn't want that.

"The system works just fine. My customer relationships are fantastic. I just need to step up a gear," she replied.

"You're one of the few distributors I trust. However, I need assurances that this won't fail," Richie said.

Celia put a hand across her heart. "I give you my word, I'll make this work. What's my target?"

"Two thousand units in fourteen days," Richie said calmly.

Celia's jaw dropped. "That's a little tight, don't you think?"

Richie smiled.

"If you can rediscover your previous high sale numbers, you might pull it off."

It was a test, Celia thought to herself. He knew what he was doing. Her whole operation was at stake.

"Check your numbers. It might be a tight squeeze, but you can actually do it," Richie added.

Celia took a deep breath and stiffened her shoulders.

"Alright. I'll go for it," she said as she pursed her lips.

Once she got back to Sunshine Cove, Celia dropped off five hundred highlighters at her home. The headquarters was sending the rest of the batch the next day by van. She then headed for the nail parlor. Driving to the Afrostar Nail Parlor had become a daily routine for Celia ever since she bought a fifty percent stake in it. Owning it alongside Melanie had been an eye-opening experience. They both had to adjust their schedules to ensure the place was running well every day. They hired a new manager, Persha, to oversee things, because Melanie still had to run the library and Celia needed to run Maven's distribution network. However, Celia was the one who spent the most time at the place these days, because she could see its potential. She'd been stocking Maven products on a display shelf installed at the parlor for this purpose, and they were going well. But she now realized it couldn't replace her delivery runs.

Celia walked into the parlor. It was spacious and clean, with leather seats for clients and a white finish to the walls. It was half-busy. That's how it was most mornings, before picking up late in the afternoon. By the time night fell, they usually had a healthy number of clients. They hired two more nail technicians to handle the extra workload.

Today, Melanie was around, engrossed in her laptop in the mezzanine office.

"This is a surprise," Celia said with raised eyebrows. She leaned on the doorframe.

Melanie looked up, and her face beamed.

"Is that meant to be a dig at my lack of frequent visits here lately?" she asked.

"Not at all. But if you see it that way, who am I to deny you the guilt trip?" Celia replied with a cheeky grin.

"It's a good thing I have enough good spirits to allow some guilt as well," Melanie replied with a wink.

HIGHLIGHTERS AND UPHEAVAL

"How's it going?"

"Persha is keeping the place running along just fine. I don't even have to look over her shoulder anymore," Melanie replied.

"After the morning I've had so far, that's music to my ears," Celia said.

Melanie stood up and walked to the front of the desk. "Tell me more," she urged, folding her arms across her chest.

"Well, I had an intense meeting with my boss at Maven today. I had to defend my recent performance. Sales have gone down the last four weeks," she explained.

"Wait. But some products have been moving fast on the shelves here," Melanie said.

"Yes, but the model I had was to deliver a lot of products to the customers. I eased that part of the business, hoping that this would eventually take off to cover the difference. It hasn't panned out that way," Celia replied, shrugging.

"Sorry that this place has affected your distribution. You can fix that just by refocusing, right? You've got a great network in Sunny Cove, I don't think you've lost it in four weeks."

"You're right. I just need to plug into it again with the same intensity. There's only one catch: I've got to launch a new product at the same time. That's never easy. And I only have fourteen days to do it."

"Whoa! Got a target to hit?"

"Yep. As always. Need to move at least two thousand units of stock in that time."

"You can't do that alone," Melanie said.

"See what I mean?"

Melanie suddenly smiled and clapped her hands together. "I've got just the solution for you. It's something I've been thinking about for some time."

Celia straightened her stance. "What?"

"We came to own this place off the back of a tragedy, when my former co-owner died. In the spirit of a fresh start, I was thinking: why not change the name, the branding? It would be awesome. Then we can launch your product at the same time. Perfect match!"

Celia shook her head. She also wanted to rebrand the place, as she didn't like the color scheme. But that was as far as it went. The main issue she had with Melanie's idea was that it was bad timing to launch two brands at the same time. Her extra-curricular course on marketing had taught her one thing: never re-launch a brand off the back of another launch. One was bound to suffer. Both would be time intensive. Getting the official documentation from the local authorities processed, overseeing the rebrand, then planning the launch, marketing it, changing the look of the parlor... it was all too much. It would dig her into a deeper hole.

"With all due respect, Mel, that won't work," she replied.

"Why not?"

"Too many variables taking our energy. I was thinking of changing the color scheme and logo, but a full rebrand with name and everything will be too much work. Then we'll be back at the same place talking about how I dropped the ball. Let's hold off on that."

"But I really think the place needs a fix."

"I hear you, but not now. Let's make a deal. If you help me hit my sales target in fourteen days, then we can have another chat about the branding."

Melanie smiled and nodded. She stood up and walked up to Celia. They shook hands.

"Looking forward to doing this business with you, Cece."

As Melanie went back to her computer, Celia smiled. She knew Mel didn't understand the gravity of the situation, but admired the drive she had.

Celia hoped nothing would derail her efforts, because she would have to muster all her marketing and distribution powers to make it work.

2

Later that night, Celia sat in her bedroom, with her laptop on her lap. She wracked her brain about her plan for the next two weeks. She'd already bid the boys goodnight. They were both so tired after dinner that she didn't need to read them a bedtime story.

She dug up her full client list. It had over six hundred names on it. Some of them were no longer her clients, but she saw a chance to revive those relationships. But she knew that even if she got a good response, she might only be able to bag four hundred sales at best. She needed a new way to reach people.

Early the next morning, Celia packed the first delivery packs for clients she was meeting that morning. Each client was going to hear about the new product, whether they wanted to or not.

As she made their morning bacon and eggs, her son James walked up to her.

"Mum, why aren't you humming today?" he asked.

"Huh? What do you mean?"

"You always sing when you're making breakfast."

His eye for detail warmed her up, and she smiled.

"I'm looking for a new song to hum. I promise I'll do that tomorrow, okay? Give me a high five," she said, opening her palm low enough to reach him.

"Yes!" James exclaimed, his hand meeting hers.

Her scurried back to his brother John who was watching cartoons.

After dropping them off at school, she went for her first delivery. It was to Emily Villiers, a real estate agent who lived in the Cape Heights, a middle-class neighborhood popular with singles and divorcees.

After ringing her doorbell, Emily appeared at the door. She was a tall woman in her thirties, with long flowing hair that always fascinated Celia. Fortunately, her fascination had made Emily trust her with her shampoo supplies.

"Great! Always on time," Emily said, smiling broadly.

"Is there any other way to do it?" Celia asked.

"I hope not because we wouldn't be meeting now!"

Celia passed on the customized gift bag to Emily.

"Everything's in there: your shampoo and conditioner."

Emily took out the two bottles, checking their seals.

"Looks good. I might need an extra bottle next week. My mother has fallen in love with this stuff," Emily said.

Celia's eyes widened.

"Has she? Just send me the order and I'll drop them off. Also, I think you should try out something new."

Celia showed her the box with the highlighter.

"It's our latest addition to the list of products we offer. It's got its own brush in there too and is dermatologically tested," Celia said, her words rolling off her tongue.

Emily frowned.

"I honestly don't use a highlighter, never really seen the need," Emily replied.

"But you've got such great cheek bones. I think you should give it a go, honestly. It's only going for twenty-five dollars."

Emily checked out the pack as she weighed her options.

"You'd be my first customer. Also, it helps hide wrinkles, especially if your lovely mom wants to look more ageless than she already is," Celia added.

Emily chuckled.

"That's a good one. You know what? I'll buy it. I'll let Mom try it and let you know how it goes!"

"Sounds perfect!" Celia said, beaming.

Emily handed her the cash for the products.

Celia almost jogged back to the car. Making a first sale always excited her.

Her next drop off was at Christie Owens house. She was a retired nurse and midwife, as well as a close friend of Celia's mother. Since she was in her sixties, Celia wanted to pitch the highlighter for her wrinkles as she dropped off her eye shadow and lipstick.

"Who's there?" Mrs. Owens' muffled voice came from behind her front door.

"It's your daughter," Celia replied. Celia sometimes said this because Mrs. Owens had actually been her mother's midwife when she was born. This had always been the special bond between their families.

Mrs. Owens opened the door and Celia smiled at what she saw. Mrs. Owens was wearing a shower cap and had applied a gray facemask that made her look like a ghost.

"You're never late are you?" Mrs. Owens asked, trying to move her mouth as little as possible.

"Good morning to you too, Mrs. Owens. What kind of face mask are you wearing?"

Mrs. Owens shrugged. "I can't remember the name. I got it from the supermarket. It claimed it could relax my skin. You should come in," she said as she led the way into her home.

Inside, Mrs. Owens' living room had hardly changed from the last time Celia saw it. It was still colorful, and a little cluttered. She had the immaculate seats from years ago. But the main highlights of the space were the various souvenirs she had gotten from her travels.

They included postcards, statuettes, artworks and even steel weapons from different parts of the world.

"Make yourself comfortable while I get you some tea and a sarmie," Mrs. Owens said.

"Actually, kindly allow me to say no. I'm in a bit of a rush. I've got such a busy morning of deliveries to do," Celia said.

"You're developing a bad habit now, turning down my tea and sandwiches. Don't you like them anymore?" Mrs. Owens asked.

"I always have, and I'd love to. Just bear with me this time. Besides, the steam from the tea might mess up your face mask," Celia said. Mrs. Owens nodded, reluctantly buying into Celia's argument.

Celia laid the eye shadow and lipstick on the coffee table. She then held up the highlighter.

"Also, I think you should try this once you're done with the mask."

"Is it on offer?" Mrs. Owens asked, nearly breaking into a smile.

"It's not. Cash only. By the way, you still owe me for the last delivery," Celia said.

"Oh? I didn't settle that? Well, give me the next few days to get the money together from the bank. I'll send it to you."

"You always say that. Could it happen sooner? Like right now?"

"I wish I could, my dear. What I've got can't settle that balance. Good thing is I always pay, no?"

This time Mrs. Owens gave a half-smile and a wink. Celia tried her best not to shake her head in disdain.

"So, tell me about this product," Mrs. Owens said as she took the box.

"It's a highlighter. You apply it sparingly on your cheekbones and around your eyes. It's especially good for hiding wrinkles."

"Aaah! Just what I need. You're going to show me how to apply it?"

"I wish I could. But by the time you've removed the face mask, I'll already be late," Celia replied.

"Fair enough. Tell you what, because you've extended me this kind gesture to make me look good, I want to give you one in return. Do you still love art?"

"You mean like visual art? Of course. I've never stopped. Why?"

"Well, I've got a rich friend, Betty Mihlali. She inspired me to start this art collection spree. But she was much better at it. She has an amazing art collection. She's hosting a private exhibition sometime this week. I could get you in."

"Really? Sounds interesting. Is it a long affair?" Celia asked, concerned it might take her away from her targets.

"Not at all. I don't have the full details, but I'll fill you in the next time I meet you. Which could be as soon as tomorrow, since I'll be coming to see your mother."

"Alright, sounds good. See you then," she replied, smiling. Moments later, she left.

As she got into her Subaru Impreza station wagon, she checked the clock to see how much time she had before the next client. Fifteen minutes for a drive that needed thirty.

"Let's hope there are no speed guns along the way," she said as she revved the engine.

* * *

THE MEZZANINE OFFICE was decked out with flip chart paper on its walls. Scribbled on them were notes about the marketing campaign for the launch of the new highlighter. This wasn't Celia's regular approach to this kind of campaign. Usually, just a few notes in her notebook would be enough. But she wasn't doing it alone this time—she needed Melanie to understand the scope. To do this, she talked her through it, and they brainstormed various ideas. Slowly, Melanie was getting the hang of it. It would be easier to leave her to run some parts of the sales while Celia dealt with the rest.

"It seems we should sell more than the highlighter, right?" Melanie asked.

"Yeah, we can push several brands at the same time. I always try to close one sale with another. If I deliver two products to a client in the same package, that's a win for me," Celia replied.

"I now know why you're so highly rated. That's a great strategy," Melanie said with a smile.

"Just sharing nuggets of what's worked for me!"

As they kept planning, it became clear that one of the best ways to sell would be to have a mini event. They just needed to figure out which kind. After several ideas, they were drained and frazzled.

"Why not do an open day, here? We could put out flyers on the roads and other social spots to get the word out," Melanie suggested.

Celia shook her head.

"No, that would mean we should cater to a large crowd in here. This place is not built for crowds. Then some people would be put off by that," Celia replied. She stood up and walked to one of the papers.

"There must be somewhere we could do this," Celia wondered.

"How about here?" a male voice bellowed.

Celia turned round to find a huge bunch of flowers staring back at her. It was so big; it was half the size of an average adult.

"What's this?" Celia asked, a puzzled look spread across her face.

A beaming Detective Bill Koloane poked his head over the flowers. He had walked in so silently she hadn't heard him.

"Is this big enough for whatever you're planning?" Bill quipped.

Celia put her hands to her face as her ears reddened.

Melanie, on the other hand, had stood up and was smiling too.

"I like me a consistent man," Melanie teased, winking at Celia.

Celia lowered her hands and smiled. "You're doing too much, Bill. I could get bored fast if you keep sending flowers every week," she said.

"Well, we'll cross that bridge when we get there, won't we?" he replied, handing her the flowers.

She gazed at them in wonder. She had two more of his bouquets at home, which had not dried out yet. Her two sons could think she was redoing the interior in bits. This one was the biggest one yet.

"Thank you very much, Bill. As Mel said, I salute the consistency," she said.

Bill nodded slowly. "You're welcome," he said, his eyes falling on the walls, "I can see you've been busy.

"Yeah. Got to launch a new product. Mel is helping me plan. It's a tight schedule with a huge target," she replied.

"Anything I can use? I can move a few hundred bottles," he offered.

Celia shook her head. "Not unless you're a cross dresser, then no. You can't use highlighter on your skin!"

Bill moved closer to her. "You don't win if you don't take a few risks," he quipped.

"I think we'll take a rain check on that thought," Celia said. She had to get through with the plan.

"So, can I steal you for a coffee?" Bill asked.

"Not even a stick of chewing gum can get me out of here," Celia replied.

Bill sighed and lifted both his arms in surrender as he backed away. "Alright. At least I gave it a shot. I'll leave you to it," he said as he headed to the door.

"Thanks, Bill. I'll make it up to you sometime," she said.

"I'll look forward to it. Take care of her, Mel," Bill said as he blew Celia a kiss.

"Am I getting one?" Melanie asked teasingly.

Bill obliged, blowing her a kiss too. Melanie put her hands to her face, mimicking Celia's earlier blush.

"Oh, thank you, Bill! This makes me feel less of a third wheel," Melanie said.

"I'll catch you all some other time," he said and left.

Celia placed the flowers to the side and turned back to the walls. She exhaled and placed her hands akimbo.

"It's time we saved my job," Celia declared.

3

"No, that can't work, Mel," Celia said, shaking her head vigorously.

"Why not?" Melanie asked with her eyebrows raised.

"Because we don't have the budget for it," Celia replied.

They were seated at The Pier, their go-to restaurant where they would unwind, or like today, brainstorm. It had a cozy, welcoming feel with its wood finish interior and spaced out seating. The well-designed cubicles were ideal for discreet conversation with business partners and couples. Celia had noted a few as they walked in, which was interesting for a weekday.

"We can find a way around it. Hire volunteers or something. The point is, you need to be able to cover more ground, faster. We can't sell these things from your car and the nail shop alone," Melanie said.

"I hear you. But remember, I don't have a huge margin on these products. It's very easy to go over budget and end up in a hole. Besides, I used quite a bit of cash investing in the parlor. I haven't broken even yet, so I don't want to load on more debt," Celia replied.

Melanie pressed her lips together and then shrugged.

"It's your call. I'm just saying from the numbers you're doing every day, you won't hit your target," she replied.

Celia exhaled. "There's got to be another way."

"Got any ideas?"

"Maybe another coffee will unlock my mind, because I've got nothing," Celia said.

She knew she couldn't keep it that way, because the clock was still ticking.

* * *

When Celia arrived at her mother's house, she found Mrs. Owens already there. The two women were talking animatedly.

"And you bet he wasn't going to take it lying down," Mrs. Owens quipped.

"He must have come out with guns blazing," Audrey Matinise, Celia's mother, said.

"Of course! There's no other recourse."

Seeing none of them had turned to look at her when she walked in, Celia cleared her throat. The two women turned their gaze to her.

"Can I get an intro to the story at least?"

Mrs. Owens waved her hand in disapproval. "No, that's not possible. We're already an hour into the story, a rewind will take too long. Besides I need you to give me a lift back home," she said.

"But I just got here, ladies," Celia protested.

"I know, an emergency has come up," Mrs. Owens said.

"What's going on?"

"Betty needs one of my rare pieces for the opening, tomorrow evening. She's sending someone to pick it."

"Oh? It's just art. I thought someone was ill," Celia said, setting her bag down.

Mrs. Owens stood up. "Now, that's one of the things you need to change before you come for the event tomorrow. Art is life, and this is a very unique piece," she said.

"Sorry, I didn't mean to trivialize it. So, it's happening tomorrow?"

"Yes. I already told your mother everything."

"Ma, you're coming?"

"I thought my daughter needed a date," Audrey said with a broad smile.

Celia sighed. She knew her mother was actually disinterested in art, so it was going to be a long night trying to explain what each piece symbolized. "Alright, let's go Mrs. Owens, before you enlist my kids too," she said.

*　*　*

THE LADY CAUGHT Celia's eye the moment she saw her. She was prim and proper, standing upright with a sharp gaze.

"She looks well put together," Celia remarked as she parked in front of Mrs. Owens' house.

"Trust me, you don't know half of it," Mrs. Owens replied.

They shook hands with the lady.

"Mary Sakayi, personal assistant to Betty Mihlali," Mary said in a quick and efficient manner, with a smooth accent Celia couldn't place.

"Celia Dube, beauty consultant," she replied.

"Nice to meet you," Mary said, before turning to Mrs. Owens "Is the piece ready for collection?"

"It's just in the usual spot; I was too lazy to put it in a box."

"That's fine with me, I'll handle that for you," Mary said.

As they walked into the house, Celia was even more intrigued. If this was how Betty's personal assistant carried herself, then Betty would be quite the enigma. This intrigued her.

Celia decided to head home. The beauty of living in Sunny Cove was she didn't need to worry about traffic. It was always light, which meant she could get across different neighborhoods in good time. She barely lamented about the robots, the local slang for their traffic lights system.

As she drove, she remembered she needed to call Bill. She dialed him up using the Bluetooth system in her car.

"Hello, beautiful," Bill's voice boomed over the car's speakers.

Celia smiled as she felt her cheeks redden. "Hey yourself. Are you a fan of art?" she asked.

HIGHLIGHTERS AND UPHEAVAL

"What kind of art are we talking about?"

"Well, abstract. Paintings. Sculptures. Rare art."

"Um, not really. Tell me what's on your mind," he replied.

She pursed her lips. Why didn't he like art as she did? "I wanted to invite you to a little event I'm going to. A friend of a friend is opening her expensive art collection for viewing to a limited audience. I'm on the list and was looking for a date. Are you free tomorrow night?"

Bill exhaled. "Nope, I actually have to do our monthly security meeting. Sorry."

Celia wore a half-hearted smile. "It's okay. No problem. Maybe next time.

"Yeah, maybe. Have fun on my behalf!" he said.

When he hung up Celia let out a pronounced sigh. She was eager to see him again, but also realized they had different tastes. She made a mental note to ask him more about his likes and hobbies. They'd never really talked about it. She hoped they weren't too different from hers.

* * *

"Does this look too loud for an evening?" a smiling Audrey asked as she walked into the living room where Celia was. She held up an orange dress with burgundy highlights.

Celia's eyes widened.

"It's screaming 'look at me, I'm a work of art too', but not in a nice way," Celia replied.

"Are you serious? I thought it matches the theme of the event," Audrey said, holding the dress away from her and studying it from top to bottom.

"It will only cause chaos."

"Well, Betty Mihlali is used to a little chaos," Audrey replied with a coy smile.

Celia cocked her head. "What do you mean?" she asked.

"With the divorce and family feud going on in her family, this dress won't shake her up one bit," her mother replied.

"Tell me more, please," she said, her eyebrows furrowed in curiosity.

"You'll have to talk to Christie about all that," her mother replied, referring to Mrs. Owens. "So, you're saying this doesn't blend in?"

"It's actually competing for attention. If they pinned you to the wall as a painting, it would make sense. Walking around with it will not get you the kind of attention you want," Celia advised.

Audrey snorted. "I'll have you know that it got me the right attention at the Sunshine Jazz Festival five years ago," she said.

Celia rolled her eyes. "You're making it worse now, Ma! Five years ago? Please, show me something else. I want you to look beautiful."

"Something like what?"

"How about the blue silk dress?"

"The one with beads on the hem?"

"Exactly! It's subtle, but the beads are a nice touch. Try it."

Audrey glanced at Celia. She then walked off to the bedroom again. While she waited, Celia wondered what kind of chaos her mother had referred to. It made her even more intrigued to attend the event. She knew if she talked to Mrs. Owens, she'd be more than willing to share what she knew.

When she returned, she was holding the blue silk dress.

"You know I don't like this dress so much because it reminds me of Trevor. He used to love it," Audrey said.

Celia bit her lower lip. Her mother had once attended a family dinner wearing the dress. Celia's late husband Trevor had complimented her about it and she had treasured it ever since. Celia hadn't remembered this precious memory.

"I'm sure he would want you to wear it, because you look stunning in it," Celia replied.

"You're probably right," Audrey said as she gently caressed the fabric.

As Audrey went back to the bedroom a happy woman, Celia turned to look out the window. She realized Bill's unavailability was a blessing in disguise. Recently, her mother had been hinting that it wasn't worth dating someone in law enforcement. She expected a big argument if that happened, but Celia was determined to keep the news away from her mother for as long as possible.

4

Celia couldn't tell the size of Betty Mihlali's home as it was nighttime when they arrived. However, she knew it was an expansive property in HillBend, a highly priced neighborhood. The driveway wasn't as long as she expected it to be. The main house looked palatial, with high walls, large windows and a gray stone finish.

When they arrived, they had to go past a security checkpoint where their names were checked against a list. Mary was there as she kept a watchful eye on the security staff.

"Is she a jack of all trades?" Celia asked Mrs. Owens once they'd been let in.

"Mary is Betty's shadow in every way. If you want to know Betty's next plans and biggest secrets, Mary's the one to go to. Of course, she'll never tell you. She's loyal and organized to a fault. I don't think Betty can operate without her," Mrs. Owens said.

"She sounds like she makes everything move," Audrey said. They were led by a chaperone who took them down a long hallway.

They were ushered into a ballroom filled with piano music and the chattering of guests. Celia could see some of the faces were of the notable people in Sunny Cove; the mayor, several company executives and some wealthy landowners. As they mingled, Mrs. Owens took the time to point out two notable attendees.

"You see that young man holding a glass of vodka?"

"The one in the checked jacket and the sullen face?" Celia asked.

"Yes. He's Tony, Betty's son. He's a quiet but rebellious one," she said.

"He doesn't look too happy," Celia observed.

"Large crowds aren't his thing, I believe," Mrs. Owens replied.

"And where's the daughter?" Audrey asked.

"She must be somewhere chatting up a man. She's been known to be overtly flirty. Let me look for her," Mrs. Owens said as she scanned the room.

As they waited, Celia noted the walls were filled with artworks of all kinds. Paintings, sculptures, or charcoal drawings. She was impressed that this collection was worth millions of dollars. Small groups of people gathered in front of each piece to study and talk about it.

Mrs. Owens tapped Celia's shoulder.

"Before I leave you, let me show you Isabella. She's the one wearing the flower dress with the fresh rose stuck above her ear," Mrs. Owens said.

Isabella was beautiful and carried this fact with an elegant charm. She smiled and chatted up multiple people. She was clearly enjoying it, a clear contrast from her brother.

"I have to leave you now. I need to attend to Betty. I want her to use a little of that highlighter you sent me."

"What's her skin like?" Celia asked.

"A little darker than mine."

"Then you can dab a little more on her skin. Not too generous though," Celia advised.

"I'll try," Mrs. Owens said with a smile. She left them.

Celia and her mother kept busy, checking out the art works in between nibbling the tasty bites passed around on platters.

"Ladies and gentlemen, may I have your attention please," Mary's eloquent voice said.

The chatter in the room died down as everyone turned to listen. She stood in front of the slightly raised platform near the large sliding door. Next to her was an object, possibly a sculpture, draped in a satin cloth.

"We're all grateful to have you here. In the next five minutes Miss Betty Mihlali will be coming to give her brief remarks about why we invited you here today. I wanted to personally thank you for gracing our occasion. We'll be taking reservations for visits to the collection that will be open for the next seven days. We'll also have a special gift for each of you at the end of the event later tonight. Thank you for your patience," Mary said with a broad smile.

Celia watched her strut off, heading towards one of the long hallways in the house, presumably to find Betty.

Sure enough, five minutes later, Betty herself stood in front of them. She wore a shimmering silver dress that occasionally blinded you when light fell on it at the right angle. Her face was beaming, and she had applied a tad too much makeup. When Mrs. Owens reappeared, she seemed undisturbed.

"Did you apply all that?" Celia asked.

"You told me to put it on generously," Mrs. Owens replied.

Celia put her hand to her cheek, her mouth agape. "No, that's not what I meant. You're supposed to check if it suits her skin first," she whispered.

"Well, it's too late now. Although I wouldn't worry too much. She's wealthy enough to survive it," Mrs. Owens said with a nervous smile.

Celia sighed and chose to focus on what Betty was saying.

"And that's why I'm sharing these pieces with you tonight and for the next seven days. Only recommend your close friends and associates. I'm not opening up my home to the whole world. This is my haven and a family space. So appointments for visits will need to be made in advance. Speaking of family, I'm glad my son and daughter are both here," Betty said as her eyes searched the crowd.

Tony, who had a fresh glass of wine, made a half-hearted wave to the guests, while his sister Isabella made a more enthusiastic wave.

HIGHLIGHTERS AND UPHEAVAL

"I'm honored to have their support. In line with that, I have a special piece I wanted to share with you. I know you must be wondering what this is next to me," Betty said as she turned and pointed at the satin-covered object. "It's a piece that's special to me. I got it from my great grandfather, and it's been passed down through my family. It carries a lot of memories, prestige and value for us here, and..."

Betty stopped talking. She leaned her head to one side, a quizzical expression on her face.

"Is that someone screaming?" she asked.

Celia pricked her ear. Yes, there was the sound of a faint scream. It came from outside. Then it grew into a loud, terrifying shriek.

"Can someone help check what's going on," a concerned Betty said, "Where's Mary? Mary, can you check who that is?"

Celia's eyes moved around curiously. Mary didn't reply, but several murmurs went up.

"I'll go find her," Isabella's voice rose over the din as she dashed out.

"What's going on?" Audrey asked Celia.

"I don't know, but I'm going to find out," Celia replied, already turning to follow Isabella.

Celia soon found herself walking behind Isabella, down the winding path leading towards the expansive back lawn of Betty's home. The pathway was lit with small lights that offered some illumination for the dark night.

Celia saw Isabella suddenly stop, as if she had been struck by lightning. Her eyes widened with horror. She'd clearly spotted something as she put her hands to her head.

"Oh, no!" Isabella shouted. She kicked off her heels and started running. Celia upped her walking pace.

She temporarily lost sight of Isabella around a hedge. When Celia cleared it, she saw the dark form of a now stationary Isabella next to a gazebo, leaning forward. Below her was what looked like someone's unmoving form. The night shadows were hiding the complete scene, so Celia started running towards her.

As she got closer, Celia could clearly tell that it was a woman on the ground.

"Is she okay?" Celia shouted.

Isabella didn't answer. Instead, she fell to her knees, sobbing quietly. When Celia got to her, she understood why.

Lying with her hands askew was Mary. There were noticeable bruises around her neck. Celia kneeled down and felt for a pulse. Mary's body was still warm, but she wasn't breathing. There was no pulse either. Her glazed eyes were open, facing the sky. Celia briefly turned to look at the sky.

It was a clear starry night, a thing of beauty, and possibly the last thing Mary had seen during her final moments. Celia exhaled as it dawned on her that someone in that compound was a cold-blooded killer.

5

Celia immediately called the police.

After the call, she was at a loss on what to do. She decided to pull away the crying Isabella from Mary's lifeless body. Other guests started approaching the area.

"Hang back, Hang back! There's a body back there!" Celia shouted at them, hoping they wouldn't get too close and disturb the crime scene.

Betty approached in panicked haste. "What's happened?" she asked.

"She's dead Ma, she's dead," Isabella wailed as she fell into her mother's arms.

"Who's dead? "Betty asked Celia.

"Mary," Celia replied.

Betty's eyes welled up as she hugged her daughter tightly.

Sirens could be heard from a distance. Celia wasn't surprised they were coming so fast. Wealthy neighborhoods tended to have better emergency response times. When the police and paramedics arrived, they immediately cleared the area around the gazebo and cordoned it off with yellow crime scene tape. Three large portable lights were strategically placed to illuminate the scene.

Small groups of guests whispered to each other as they watched from a distance. Celia comforted the still distraught Betty and Isabella before moving to the edge of the cordon so as to see what the police were doing. She was joined by Mrs. Owens and her mother.

"Eesh. Who could have done this?" Audrey asked.

"Some lunatic who doesn't care about human life," Mrs. Owens replied.

"It must be one of the guests, right?" Audrey said.

She exchanged looks with Mrs. Owens, and Mrs. Owens looked at Celia.

"It's possible," Celia said, "No one's left the compound and I don't think anyone here could dare jump over the electrified fence. That's why the police aren't allowing anyone to leave just yet."

Sure enough, the police had started conducting interviews of every guest. Celia watched as Tony and an older man were approached by two policemen for questioning.

"Who's the man standing with Tony?" Celia asked.

"That's his father, Caleb Khoza. Betty's ex-husband," Mrs. Owens replied.

Celia's eyes widened. "Betty invited her ex-husband to the event?" she asked.

"They get along. Don't ask me how," Mrs. Owens replied.

Tony and Caleb were separated for questioning, both looking troubled.

Celia turned her gaze to other people in the small groups. They were clearly discussing what had just happened. From the corner of her eye, she saw a man sporting a tuxedo and slicked back hair walk up to Betty and Isabella. He hugged them affectionately as he whispered words to them. He thereafter stood next to them as a show of support.

"What about the man in the tuxedo standing next to Betty?" Celia asked.

Mrs. Owens craned her neck. "That's Liam Turnton. He owns a successful private gallery. He's been a good family friend for years," she replied.

Just then, Celia spotted familiar head bobbing over the small crowds. Detective Bill emerged and was about to walk past them when Celia tugged at his coat.

"Hey Bill," Celia called out.

Bill turned, then smiled. "So this is the party I missed out on?" he asked teasingly.

"Hush! Are you here to take on the case?" Celia inquired as she glanced around her quickly.

"Looks like it," Bill said, "I thought we agreed we wouldn't be meeting like this?"

"As soon as we find the killer, we'll make sure he gets the memo," Celia said.

"Sure thing," Bill said as he bent over slightly and lifted the cordon over his head. He then walked slowly to where Mary's body lay covered in a white sheet.

Several things happened in the following half hour. Celia and most of the guests were interviewed by the police, and had their fingerprints taken. Understandably, everyone present was a suspect, and this truth still made Celia shudder. She could've rubbed shoulders with the anonymous killer, who most probably didn't look like they could harm a fly.

After her interview, she went back to watch the detectives processing the scene. Mary's body had already been placed on a stretcher and was being wheeled toward the waiting ambulance. The detectives were doing their final touches. Celia then spotted Bill and a fellow detective walk towards her.

"How's it looking?" Celia asked when they got close.

Bill shook his head, "Tough."

"What do you mean?"

"Whoever did it chose a great spot. Hidden in the shadows, all witnesses were inside. No traces of foreign fiber or hair on her. No finger prints," he replied.

"What about footprints?"

"I've got no idea what type of grass is on this lawn, but it's like a thick carpet. Shoes don't leave imprints like they normally would.

Plus, I think a lot of guests walked around the body too, so it would've been hard to figure out the killer's prints."

Celia sighed. That's not the news she wanted to hear.

"We do have one last roll of the dice: the CCTV cameras," he said.

This didn't pay off either. Three days earlier, a problem arose with the wiring and some cameras in the system stopped working. The maintenance crew were due to fix it the next day after receiving the necessary parts. The team in the camera monitoring room were crippled. The gazebo was one of the areas where the cameras were dead.

"It should've been fixed sooner," Betty rued as she walked with Celia into the ballroom where the launch event was taking place. There were some jackets, sweaters and coats lying on tables and chairs.

"I hope no one forgets anything. Otherwise I'll have to set up a lost and found desk now that Mary..." Betty's voice trailed off.

She stopped walking. Celia held her as she cried for a few minutes. When she had composed herself, they continued looking around the room. Then Betty let out a shriek.

"No, no...." Betty said as her eyes bulged out of their sockets. Celia followed her line of sight, and her eyes fell on the stand that once held the satin-covered sculpture. It was no longer there. Celia rushed to the stand. She circled it once, then looked around. Next to it was the satin cover lying on the floor.

"Did you ask one of your people to keep it safe while we were outside?" Celia asked.

Betty, with both hands on her cheeks, slowly shook her head.

"They've taken it," Betty then mumbled.

"Wait here, I have to tell the officers before they leave," Celia said as she rushed outside. The parking lot was largely empty as almost all the guests had already left. She slowed to a gentler pace, realizing it was a lost cause. She found Bill and his team as they were just about to head out.

Bill, who was talking to a junior officer, saw her approach and walked towards her.

"Are you okay?"

"No, I don't think that's possible, considering what this night has turned out to be. And now Betty's sculpture is gone," Celia said.

Bill raised an eyebrow. "Sculpture?"

Celia nodded. "She had a rare sculpture she was due to unveil before we heard Mary's scream. It's gone now, without a trace. I was hoping we could stop the guests from leaving, but.." her voice trailed off as she pointed at the parking lot in frustration.

Bill's eyes narrowed. "This is a development I didn't expect. Take me there," he replied, motioning for an officer to follow him.

As they walked to the house at a brisk pace, Celia felt her stomach churn. Someone was playing a game of chess, and she had a strong sense that they were just getting started.

6

Celia watched Bill and his colleague examine the area around the sculpture stand. They took photographs, wiped the stand for finger prints, checked for footprints and placed the satin cloth into an evidence bag.

"Where are Tony and Isabella?" Betty asked. When Celia went to check on them, she discovered that Tony had left. Isabella, on the other hand, was nowhere to be seen. Since Celia didn't know the layout of the house, she gave up her search. As she walked swiftly back to the ballroom, Celia's mind raced. Was the thief an opportunist who took their chance after Mary's death? Or were they more diabolical, killing someone in order to steal the piece?

When Celia got back, Bill had already finished gathering evidence. He walked up to Celia, shaking his head.

"There's nothing to be found there. No visible footprints or fingerprints."

"From that alone, do you think we're dealing with the same person?" she asked.

"Possibly. They know how to cover their tracks well. And from what I can see, there are no cameras on the inside. I saw some cameras facing the driveway were working. We can have a look at those. But first, what sculpture are we talking about here?" Bill said.

Celia nodded. "Let's go ask her."

They both walked up to where Betty was. She sat still in a red velvet Victorian era style sofa. Despite her eyes being squeezed shut, she still looked regal.

"Ms. Mihlali," Celia began, "the detective is wondering what type of sculpture it was."

Without moving or opening her eyes, Betty began speaking. "The Imvunulo sculpture. It shows a Zulu woman performing the dance in celebratory traditional clothes. It's the only one of its kind," she replied.

"It's worth a lot?" Bill asked.

"Depends on your understanding of a lot. This piece goes for over eight hundred thousand rand," Betty replied.

"That's a good sum," Bill conceded, "We need to check the cameras again."

Betty opened her eyes slowly, as if waking up from a nap. "Of course."

Betty led them down the hallway to a small room. Inside were eight flat screens neatly arranged next to each other along one wall. The screens showed most of the exterior of the home. Seated in front of the screens were a young woman and a man. They both turned to see the arriving party and instantly stood up when they realized it was their boss.

"Sipho, the police need to see the footage again," Betty said.

"Again? They were here some minutes ago," Sipho replied.

"We're here for another incident. A sculpture has been stolen," Bill replied. Sipho looked around him quizzically.

"What time did it happen? Because we just restarted the system ten minutes ago," Sipho replied.

"What for?" Betty asked.

"We decided to do a quick audit of the systems after that last wiring fault. But we can take a look, let's hope we find something."

Sipho tapped his colleague's shoulder and she quickly went to work, rewinding the footage back to the time it was restarted. As they went through the various cameras, Celia tried her best to use her knowledge on body language to pick out any strange movement. The fact that the exterior wasn't flooded with lights didn't help much, giving the cameras a grainy look. But Bill's more experienced eye came to the fore once again as he pointed at the screen showing the one corner of the parking lot.

"Stop it right there," Bill said. He then craned his neck closer to the screen, squinting as he tried to make out what he was looking at, "What are those two up to?"

"That's your son Tony, isn't it Betty? Who's he talking to?" Celia asked.

Betty moved closer to the screen. "That's Liam Turton, he's an art gallery owner."

"It looks to me like they are arguing about something. Can you zoom in a little?" Bill instructed.

Sipho adjusted the angle and zoomed into the two men. Celia noted that the two men were right on the edge of the screen so you couldn't see their full bodies. Occasionally, they would drop out of frame.

"Rewind slightly," Bill instructed.

The image rewound, then played again. You could see the two men move into the frame, then disappear as the boot door came up. When the boot closed, the two men stood next to the car and started arguing. It didn't last long, and ten seconds later, Liam got into the car and drove off.

"Where did Tony go?" Celia asked.

Just then, another car, a modern Mini Cooper, drove off into the night.

"That's Tony's car," Betty said.

Bill grunted. "I'll need to take this with me," he said.

"What do you think they are doing?" Celia asked him.

"It's possible they both carried the sculpture to Liam's car and then drove off together," Bill turned to Betty, "Ms. Mihlali, what kind of man is Liam?"

HIGHLIGHTERS AND UPHEAVAL

"Um, well. He's a good family friend… I don't think he would steal it," Betty said.

"Why not?" Bill asked.

"He's not that kind of man," she replied.

Bill nodded. He turned to Sipho and gave him a flash drive. Celia went closer to Betty.

"Ms. Milahli, how about we head out back to the living room? I think we can leave them to do their jobs."

Betty obliged, and they walked out. They went to the living room and Betty motioned to the head server, whose team was wrapping up for the evening.

"How much food was left after tonight?" Betty asked.

"Quite a lot. It's all in the kitchen, though. We're simply packing our gear and heading out."

"Can you come over tomorrow?" Betty asked.

The head server was puzzled.

"Tomorrow?"

"Yes. I'd like you to help me take the good food to some kids I work with. Kindly ensure its stored well in the freezer before you leave. I'll pay you for it."

The head server smiled. "Thank you for your kindness. I can come with a small team and we can do it on the house, considering tonight's events."

Betty shook her head. "No, I'll pay you for it. That's what will make me happy. Don't suffer on my account. Be here at eight," she said.

The head server smiled "As you wish Ms. Mihlali."

"Oh, and kindly bring me one of those biltongs. I feel like biting into one right now," Betty said.

"Sure."

The head server headed out as Celia and Betty settled in to the space. Betty let out a pronounced sigh.

"What a night! The sad thing I've learned in all these years on this earth is that sometimes when it rains, it pours," Betty said.

"I can only imagine what you're going through right now," Celia said. Betty glanced at her.

"Mary wasn't just my employee. She was my second daughter. My confidant. You must be wondering why I'm not in tears right now. It will come. After you all leave this place, I'll break.

Betty paused to compose herself. A tear snuck out of her eye, and she quickly wiped it off with a finger. "And then tomorrow morning, regardless of whether grief allowed me to get some sleep or not, I'll embark on the task of finding the person responsible for this darkest of nights, and I'll make them pay for it with their lives," she said menacingly.

7

As Celia listened to her, a shiver went down her spine. Holding Betty's intense gaze, she knew she meant every word.

In a bid to deflect from the gravity of the statement, Celia tried to change the topic.

"Has your family always been passionate about art?" she asked.

Betty smiled as her mind flashed back to a memory. "My grandfather used to work at a museum. He quit that job because he got bored with the silence you tend to find in museums. He then joined a tours company and started going on travel expeditions. He connected with tourists who gave him small art pieces as souvenirs. One even did a pencil portrait of him. It's in here somewhere. Anyway, from then on he became a collector. He passed that on to my father and here we are," she elaborated.

Celia nodded in approval. "Did the art bring you into wealth?"

"In some ways, yes. You could argue my grandfather became an art broker of sorts, well into his eighties. It's during those days that he came across this sculpture that was taken today. It's not just an aesthetic or cultural investment. It holds a lot of meaning for the family, symbolic of when this whole journey began. My life is a complex yet simple one, and not many understood it the way Mary did," Betty said, going into a reflective mood.

"Where did Mary live?" Celia asked.

"She had an apartment not far from here. I didn't want her to commute from too far. It's on Creek Road. A nice place. She had a roommate. Bilha, I forget her second name," Betty replied.

Celia's ears pricked up. "Could you find her details for me?"

"Of course, give me a moment," Betty said as she got to her feet.

"And Betty, could you please get me a copy of tonight's guest list too?"

Betty nodded as she left.

Celia was curious to learn more about Mary. Talking to the roommate was a good place to start, as it might shed more light onto why someone wanted her dead. On the other hand, the guest list was going to help her narrow down possible suspects. She knew one of those names would lead her to the killer.

When Betty got back, she handed Celia a printed guest list. "This is the crosschecked one. Those who attended are marked, those absent are unmarked. Give me a notebook so I can write Mary's address," she said.

Celia reached into her bag and took out her notebook. Betty wrote down the address and handed it back to Celia.

"I also included her phone number, so you can call in advance and plan," Betty added.

"Thank you so much," Celia said. Betty handed her the notebook. Celia noted Betty's clear, cursive handwriting.

"I don't think you're with the police, but I assume you're asking for these because you want to find the tsotsis behind this, right?" Betty asked.

"Yes, I do," Celia replied.

"Good. I need more people in my corner. We can't let these thugs rest," Betty replied.

* * *

HIGHLIGHTERS AND UPHEAVAL

WHEN CELIA GOT to the nail parlor, she found Melanie conducting interviews for sales people.

Perturbed, she pulled her aside.

"What's going on, Mel? I didn't give my go ahead for this," she said in a hushed tone.

"Well, I thought we'd start somewhere. You need sales agents, and time isn't on your side," Melanie replied.

"Our budget is also not on my side. I hope you've not hired any," Celia replied.

"Not many."

"How many, Mel?"

"Just six," she replied.

Celia rubbed her temple. "That's three too many! Please, just freeze any hiring until I say so," Celia said as she turned to leave.

"Where are you going?" she asked.

"For a drive," Celia replied as she headed back to the sunny street outside.

* * *

CELIA DROVE her Subaru Impreza station wagon towards Fall Pier. It was a small private boat dock used regularly by the wealthy in Sunshine Cove. She was driving on a road that was adjacent to the shore. It was a picturesque driving experience, and she slowed her driving pace slightly to take in the view. Celia could see the open ocean, and in the distance were the small forms of ships. As she got closer to the dock, she could clearly see the yachts, speedboats and jet skis moored near the dock.

She managed to find a parking spot outside a beach bar. Her destination was just five minutes away, and she opted to walk there and get a better sense of the place.

As she walked up the narrow-cobbled street, she passed tourists and locals in shorts, flowery shirts, tops and sunglasses. She turned into a short driveway which had three houses facing the ocean. They were all made of stone cuts and were all bungalows. She wondered if it was because of a building law or individual preference. She arrived at the third house, which had a short wooden fence, and she could easily see the open garage door facing the street. Parked in it was a Mini Cooper with its bonnet open. Tony was hunched over it as he seemingly worked on the engine.

Celia walked up to him. He spotted her before she got there, but kept working on the engine.

"Hi Tony," Celia said, smiling.

"That's a rare first. You already know my name," he replied without looking up.

Celia's eyebrows narrowed. "What do you mean?"

"I saw you at the launch last night. I didn't think you'd move this fast," he replied.

Celia frowned. "You actually think I'm here because I'm interested in you?" she asked.

Tony straightened, placed the spanner on top of the radiator. He took a cloth and wiped his hands while giving her the once-over. "So, you're saying you're not interested in me?"

Celia shook her head. "I'm interested in you, but not in that way. Never in that way." she replied.

Tony chuckled. "Izzit?" he said, "You have no idea how many times I've heard that."

"I'm here to talk about Mary Sakayi's death last night," Celia said.

Tony shrugged, then reached to his side. He grabbed a large mug and took a sip from it. As he lowered it he looked at her. "You want some stew? It's proper lamb potjie," he said.

"No, thanks."

"Are you the police?"

"No, I'm not. My name is Celia Dube. I know your mother. I'm here on her behalf. Can we talk about last night?"

"We already are, although I'm wondering why I should talk to you, you're not a cop,"

he said, looking down at her.

"You left pretty early yesterday. Why was that?" Celia asked.

"I didn't leave early. I left right after the police finished with us."

"I mean, as a family member, I thought it would be prudent to stay and offer support to your mother and sister."

Tony scoffed. "I offered them what I could. We all have different ways of processing grief," he replied.

Celia raised an eyebrow, surprised by his indifference. "So you were pretty close with Mary?" she asked.

Tony took another sip of the meat stew. "We were as close as professionally possible. I hope you're aware she was my mother's personal assistant, right?"

"Yes, I am. You said you were troubled when you left. Is that why you drove out with Liam Turnton?

Tony pursed his lips. "He's a good family friend. He took me out for a couple of drinks, that's all," he said.

"You're sure that's all?"

"Yes, that's why I'm having this soup. It's mathi after last night, the perfect tonic for grief and a hangover. But it seems to me that you're trying to suggest something else," he replied.

"I'm sure you already heard the sculpture was taken."

Tony wrinkled his nose. "The cops were already here searching for it and found nothing. I had nothing to do with it."

"Does Liam have something to do with it?" she asked.

Tony rubbed the back of his neck. "I think you're asking these questions to the wrong person. I have no idea what caused last night to happen and you're here interrogating me?" Tony protested.

"It's not an interrogation, it's a conversation."

Tony laughed. "I didn't think that moving here would give me such rich conversations. Thank you for the exposure, I'll keep it in mind," he said as he put aside the mug, grabbed the spanner and went back to work.

Celia knew he was blowing her off. She looked over the place. It was a nice, well-kept house. Next to a small pile of tools in the garage was a 'for sale' sign.

"How long have you been here?" she asked.

"A little over a month," he replied.

"Nice. Not many young men in their early twenties can afford such a place."

"Don't worry, I don't need any more of my mother's money to keep myself going. You can let her know that in case she's wondering," he replied.

"That's not my intention."

Tony straightened. He cocked his head to the side. "I've not done my house warming party yet. In case you want to check out the inside, come over next week."

Celia clenched her jaw. Why would he want to hold a party in the midst of a tragedy? She shook her head.

"I think I'll be leaving now," she replied. She was about to take out her business card, then realized he wouldn't use it. He was more likely to discredit her by virtue of her Maven title on the card. She needed to make new ones for such assignments.

"Suit yourself," he snapped, then went on with his work.

Celia scowled, turned on her heel and marched to the gate. As she walked down the cobbled street, she reflected on the fact he was willing to suggest a housewarming party, yet a close family acquaintance had just died. It was all too casual.

He was masking something else, and she intended to find out what it was.

8

When Celia returned to the nail parlor and found Melanie briefing the six new hires, she didn't feel rattled. The combination of the drive and getting started on the quest to find Mary's killers had given her renewed focus.

Melanie walked up to her. "Are you okay now?" she asked.

Celia smiled. "Yeah. How's the briefing going?"

"Almost done. They know everything they need to do to push the highlighters."

Celia sighed. "I hope you didn't forget that I can only afford to work with them for three days," she said.

Melanie smiled. "There's no 'I' here. We're in this together. We'll do five days. We can manage that. Okay?"

Celia nodded. "Thanks for the help with this. If we're doing two more days, do you think we can use them for the closing weekend?"

"What's the closing weekend?" Melanie asked.

"It's the weekend we're going to sell out what's left of this batch of highlighters. It's all hands on deck," Celia said.

Melanie nodded. "It sounds like a challenge. I like those," Melanie replied.

"Then let's get it done," Celia said with conviction.

* * *

LATER, Celia met Isabella at a café she had never been to before, the Red Chimney. It was made of red brick from top to bottom, with black tiles at the top and white wooden window frames breaking up the brick dominance. The place was half full and playing some Afro jazz instrumentals, giving it a laid back feel. It had outside seating with large umbrellas that face the street, and this is where Celia found Isabella waiting for her. Isabella wore a sundress, sunhat and dark sunglasses.

"You're good with time," Isabella remarked with a half-smile. Celia settled in, placing her handbag on an empty seat.

"It's a habit. Good to see you're here already," Celia replied.

"Well, count your lucky stars because it's just by chance. I'm a perennial late comer to most places, a downside that comes with the family name. Most people are waiting for me, and not the other way round."

"So, what made this meeting different?" Celia posed.

Isabella giggled. "Yussus, you're putting me on the spot now?" Isabella said. She then leaned forward and whispered, "I've never been to a meeting where a murder is being discussed, so I have slightly more motivation than usual."

She then leaned back and winked. Celia found this odd. Isabella waved at a waiter. The waiter, a tall lanky young man wearing a spotless white shirt and dark trousers, hurried to their table.

"Could you kindly bring me a cappuccino and a tasty curried mince vetkoek please," Isabella said.

The waiter, who had scribbled some notes in his tiny notebook, then turned to Celia, who was fidgeting as she couldn't see any menu on the table.

"Where's the menu?" she asked.

"We have no physical menus anymore. I could bring you the tablet so that you can scroll for what you'd like to have," the waiter replied.

Celia shook her head. "Just get me some house coffee please," Celia replied.

"You're not eating anything?" Isabella asked.

"I'm not keen on feasting at the moment," Celia said with a smile. The waiter left.

"Now I'm feeling a little guilty for making that order," Isabella said.

"No, no! You shouldn't. That's just a personal choice and has nothing to do with what we'll discuss," Celia replied.

"Good. Because I find food to be a coping mechanism. I eat a lot when I'm stressed," she said.

"What's stressing you?" Celia asked, seeing an opening to start her questioning.

"Everything. Mary's death for starters, the publicity around this whole thing," she touched her hat as if to indicate she was in disguise, "the things we need to do, the sculpture being missing, taking care of my mother. It's all a little overwhelming, frankly."

"Were you close with Mary?"

"We knew each other pretty well. She was very focused and clear about the work she's doing. So we couldn't hang out on a Friday night, although I tried. But she was great for us, especially for Mum. She knew everything that made Mama tick and exactly how to get them to her," Isabella said.

"So you could say that other than doing her job well, she also knew some family secrets?"

Isabella paused for a moment as the waiter brought their orders. The coffees were both steaming hot, and the vetkoek looked appealing with a side of salad. Isabella took off her sunglasses and bit into the dish. She closed her eyes as she chewed slowly.

"Yebo, it's a good one," she remarked. "Sorry, what did you ask again?"

"Did Mary know some family secrets? Sensitive ones?"

Isabella twisted her nose at this as she mulled over the question.

"She knew things about my mother's dealings that even I didn't know about. So there's definitely something there. How much she knew only Mama can tell you."

"So, you weren't jealous about this?"

Isabella leaned back, looking puzzled.

"Me, jealous? Nah, I was just happy she found someone to help run things smoothly. Before Mary came, we struggled to balance things out. Too many projects and investments to run. When she came, everything lined up perfectly. So I'm actually crushed because where do we find another Mary? She was one of a kind," Isabella replied.

Celia sipped her coffee, which was still too hot to handle.

"I met your brother. He told me he moved out a month ago. Was there a family-related reason for that?"

Isabella shrugged. "I wouldn't know. He can be quiet with his motivations sometimes. So I can't be sure. It's typical for a man of a certain age to want to be independent," Isabella said.

"You don't want to be independent either?"

Isabella laughed. "I enjoy the perks of living with my mother. Trust me, it's worth it. Plus, I'm also a romantic free spirit. I want to be taken from home by my groom once I convince myself that marriage is worth it. At the moment, it just looks like a prison that ends up being hell. I've lived it."

Celia paused, intrigued by the statement. She had loved her marriage, but was losing Trevor a sort of hell? It had been for a few years. But she didn't feel the same way about marriage. Not yet, anyway.

"What about your brother? Did he like Mary?"

Isabella put her hand halfway up as she chewed another mouthful. Celia waited.

"Tony is a different kettle of fish. He wants to run things. A lot of things, despite being quieter than I am but very ambitious and driven. He's been increasing his involvement in the family businesses, and maybe they had a few run ins. But he would never do something like this."

"What run-ins are you referring to?"

"Well, small arguments that would find their way to Mama's lap. Twice they argued in her office and she had to intervene."

"I see. Is Tony close to your mother?"

Isabella smirked. "That's the irony. They're not close at all."

"So why does he want to run her businesses?"

"He claims he's learning and can separate personal differences in the business setting. But I can bet he's doing it all because of Dad."

Celia frowned. "How does that work?"

Isabella leaned forward. "Tony and Dad grew really close after the divorce. It was a messy one, and Dad ended up worse off than he expected. So it always seems to me that Tony is trying to help him out in some way."

"Help him do what?"

"Recover. Get back on his feet."

"Revenge?"

Isabella almost spat out her cappuccino. She shook her head. "I didn't say that."

"But there's bad blood between your parents, no?"

"You're beginning to sound like the cop that interviewed me," Isabella said.

Celia frowned. "What did he say?"

"He had strange questions like yours. Good thing he was handsome. If he wasn't a cop named Bill, I'd date him," Isabella joked.

Celia almost choked. "You say you were interviewed by a detective called Bill and you find him attractive?"

"If he wasn't a cop with that name, you bet I'd date him."

For some reason, Celia felt that was a compliment to her, for her taste in men.

"So, bad blood?"

"I wouldn't phrase it that way. Call it differences," Isabella countered.

Celia nodded slowly, then studied the street for a moment. "It sounds to me like you're trying to be in everyone's good books. You're the only one in this family without an axe to grind," she replied.

Isabella shrugged. "I don't look for trouble. I try to help out where I can, put out fires and then relax to some good food. Playing my cards right is not really a disadvantage in a family like mine. It brings peace of mind," Isabella explained. She grabbed her mug and took a few sips.

Celia nodded. To her, Isabella always wanted to play it safe, because she loved the comfort and rocking the boat wasn't her style. This wouldn't make her a good killer.

But then again, it was too perfect. She was clearly good at manipulating those around her to see her in good light, and this could be an asset for a killer to use to hide in plain sight.

Celia needed to keep an eye on her, in case Isabella showed her darker side, a side she believed exists in every human being.

* * *

"ARE WE DOING THIS AGAIN?" Audrey asked Celia.

Celia had arrived home five minutes earlier and had just plopped herself on the sofa next to her two sons before her mother called her to the kitchen.

Celia looked at the food Audrey was preparing, some mealie pap and wors.

"You want me to order in?" Celia asked.

"I'm not talking about dinner, Cece. Christie tells me you're digging into the death of that lady," Audrey said.

Celia sighed. "With all due respect, Mrs. Owens should slow down with the gossip."

"That's beside the point. Are you?"

"Ma, I'm simply helping make sense of things."

Audrey shook her head. "We talked about this and you said you would stop going after these things. The last time you did this, we had strange cars parked outside the house!"

"Please keep your voice down, Ma. Look, that's not going to happen again," Celia replied.

"How sure are you it won't?"

Celia tried to hold her mother's gaze, but ended up looking away. Audrey sighed.

"Just as I thought. You're not sure. Just like that time you were dealing with a killer. For once, think about your kids, that's all I ask," Audrey said, before turning back to the check on the wors.

Celia lingered for a few seconds before walking out. She understood what her mother was saying, but she had already set her sights on meeting the gallery owner the next day.

It had just hit her that Mary's murder was possibly used as a distraction to aid the killers in the theft. That way, the two crimes were connected. The other alternative was that when Mary had been murdered, the thieves saw a surprise opportunity to steal the sculpture. Both versions suggested she was looking for evil people who hide in plain sight.

She intended to know if Liam Turnton was one of them.

9

As Celia approached the entrance of the Masava Gallery, she felt like she was walking on hallowed ground. It had a cobbled driveway that was lined by well-manicured bushes. Its facade had the refined look of a stately home from the early 1900s, but it had been built only five years ago. Two tall columns flanked each side of the high, double door entrance she walked through. In another time, it could easily be repurposed as a cathedral.

Inside, there were tasteful hanging lights to complement the natural light coming from the large glass windows. The large spaces were cream or off-white except the floor, which had a black and white pattern akin to a chessboard. Spaced out along the walls were paintings from different times in South African history, regions and artists. There were also a few international works on display.

Celia loved visual arts, but in-between work and taking care of her sons, she hardly got enough time these days to attend any art-related events. So being here gave her guilty pleasure.

Occasionally she came across a sculpture in the middle of the walkways, and Celia found herself gravitating towards them. She liked the fact she could walk around and explore them from different angles.

HIGHLIGHTERS AND UPHEAVAL

Part of her also imagined the far-fetched possibility of bumping into the stolen Imvunulo sculpture. She didn't expect a great art thief to display their winnings, but her dramatic side couldn't help imagining it.

She studied the bust of Ameria, a once popular folk musician who crooned her way to the presence of kings and queens alike in her day. It was a marble statue, and it fascinated Celia that although her eyes were unmoving, she could see the immense joy captured by the artist.

"It's quite a beautiful piece," a female voice behind Celia said.

Celia turned around to see a well-dressed, bespectacled woman smiling at her. Celia was surprised she hadn't heard her approaching.

"It sure is," Celia replied as she studied the woman. She then saw the small badge on the left side of her chest. Curator. "You've put together quite the collection here."

"We try to bring in as much quality work and share it with our esteemed visitors such as yourself. I'm glad you're enjoying your tour. Is there any piece you fancy?"

Celia frowned. "You mean to buy?" she asked.

The curator nodded.

Celia smiled. "You know what? I think I have. But I'd like to speak to the owner of the place so that I can learn more about the story of the particular piece."

"Although he comes here occasionally, he's such a busy man. That's why I'm here to assist you," the curator replied politely.

Celia had seen his car parked outside, so she knew he was in. She decided to push further.

"Well, I always enjoy talking to the gallery owner. Sometimes the journey to make these spaces viable is just as important as that of the art work itself," Celia added.

The curator gave it a brief thought. "You know what? Let me have a chat with him and see if he can come see you. Who do I say it is?"

"Celia Dube, a friend of Miss Betty Mihlali. He'll know," Celia said.

"Thank you, Miss Dube. Excuse me, I'll be back with you shortly," the curator said. She then walked away, the click-clack of her shoes echoing through the space.

Five minutes later, she returned.

"I'm sorry, but Mr. Turnton is unable to see you at the moment. He's quite held up," the curator said.

Celia cocked her head to the side. "He's too busy to meet a cash-paying client?"

"It's the nature of his work, nothing personal."

"Did you tell him that I'm Betty's friend?" Celia asked.

"Well, he says he doesn't know you, so he can't come to talk to you without a formal appointment."

Celia knew it was a less than subtle blow off by Liam. "Tell him I'll see him soon," she said as she walked off toward the exit.

***

"You should have seen them light up a place. They were magical," Mrs. Owens said. She was seated on a couch in Audrey's living room. On a single chair was Celia listening. After hitting a dead end at the gallery, she ran a few errands before learning Mrs. Owens was at her mother's house. She took the chance to pass by and talk about The Khozas.

"You attended the same events?" Celia asked.

Mrs. Owens laughed. "You children of these days think I didn't have fun when I was younger, eh?" she replied.

"I'm just curious," Celia said.

"I was older than many people in that room, but I had fun anyway. Then I met Betty and Caleb. After I was introduced to them, we started talking and hit it off."

"How were they together?" she asked.

"They looked happy together. But they also loved attention, so sometimes part of me thinks they were too open with everybody. It's good to be called approachable, but with them they were taking it too far."

Celia smiled as she pictured it.

"One thing I noticed, though. Caleb had a very smooth tongue. He could talk you into doing anything for him," Mrs. Owens replied. Celia's eyes widened.

"What did you do, Mrs. Owens?" Celia asked with a cheeky grin.

Mrs. Owens smiled. "I was a good dancer, always have been. But I never danced with men in public. The one man who managed to get me to do it was Caleb."

Celia's smile broadened. "Did you enjoy it?"

"It was too short a dance, less than ten seconds. Betty came and made it clear she didn't want him dancing at the time," she replied.

"I'd do the same thing," Celia said.

Mrs. Owens gave her a surprised look. "You're supposed to be on my side."

Celia chuckled. "Tell me something. When you say he had a smooth tongue, you mean Caleb was a hit with the ladies?" Celia asked.

Mrs. Owens nodded. "Well, it looked like that. There were a few rumors going round in the tabloids, as always. Many were fabricated. After that dance incident I apologized to Betty and we became good friends," she replied.

Celia leaned back and smiled. Either Mrs. Owens was being modest or she really didn't know much about him. Despite this, Celia needed to find a way to talk to Caleb Khoza. Isabella would've been the easier route to him considering neither Betty nor Tony was willing to make an introduction.

However, Isabella said they were not exactly on speaking terms after a short argument before Mary's murder. She didn't even know where he lived, as he had moved to a new address recently. She did mention that he liked to hang out at the local golf club, where he often struck business deals. Short of stalking the place, Celia would have to figure out other time-friendly ways of tracking him down.

She decided to go to the easiest place to start: a simple search on the internet. Despite being a resident of Sunshine Cove, Celia didn't look out for celebrity gossip and buzz. The closest she got to it was through her clients, some of whom were living in that world. Although she had heard of Betty and Caleb, she'd never really known much about them. She was lucky that they were quite visible when they were married. She found articles, photographs, and magazine profiles done on them when they were together. This was intriguing as she was able to learn about their marriage a little more.

Considering the proliferation of tabloids and gossip blogs, she had to read and crosscheck certain facts and storylines. Soon, she could sift the consistent truths from the hyperbolic and sensational.

When they got married, Caleb was a fast-rising entrepreneur in the field of media and artistic production. He was raised in a middle-class family while Betty came from a wealthy family. They fell in love and were married for thirty years before it all fell apart.

The change in coverage was drastic. Happy photos and aspirational pieces gave way to hit pieces where Betty complained of mistreatment while Caleb did the same. It was a messy, year-long divorce process, majorly because a lot of the wealth they had as a couple was going to Betty. It was implied that Caleb had cheated on her repeatedly, and a lot of the property they owned as a couple was actually in Betty's name. Caleb argued he'd bought most of them, which included land, hotels, businesses and art works. Betty on the other hand had the evidence of the deeds and documents needed to prove ownership. One of the best lawyers in town managed to secure her a large portion of the wealth.

"He must have a bone to pick with her. A big bitter bone," Celia said to herself. But was it strong enough for him to kill?

News reports after the divorce showed Caleb was rebranding himself. He had set up a thriving production company that rolled out high end ads and worked with some top regional talents. He was being talked about again in the right circles and didn't look like he had a begging bowl. He even did a video interview where he talked about 'moving on because life is too short'. In the video, he wished his wife well, and pledged to make it work for the kids and our loved ones.' There was simply nothing to show that he had sour grapes.

Curiously, Celia noted that Tony retained the Khoza surname, while Isabella went by her surname, Nene. It was more evidence to show that Tony leaned toward his father's side, while Isabella was keener to sit on the fence.

Were Tony and Isabella wrong to suggest Caleb had issues with his wife? It might be the regular impassionate distance, which is expected anyway. She wasn't convinced he was bitter about it.

To prove this, Celia had to see him face to face. He had an office at the Weterveld Office Park. She deduced it might be easier to find him there, because she couldn't afford to waste time stalking the golf club. She still had the highlighter stock to keep pushing. In all the articles and reports of their divorce, one thing stood out: no one knew the real reason for their separation. There was a lot of rumor and speculation, but nothing concrete. Which implied there was a secret.

Celia loved unearthing secrets. She was curious about how dark Betty and Caleb's secret would be.

10

As luck would have it, the chips fell towards another visit to Liam Turnton's gallery. Celia had gone to visit Betty briefly and learned she had just left for the Masava Gallery. Unable to resist the temptation, Celia drove fast towards there. In her mind, Betty could introduce her and she would finally have a chance to ask Liam a few questions.

When she got there, she parked near the main door of the gallery. As she walked towards it, she saw Betty and Liam talking next to one of the tall columns. She hastened her steps, putting on her warmest smile.

"It's great to find you two here!" Celia said as she closed in on them.

A shocked Betty turned to look at her. Liam looked perplexed.

"Celia? What are you doing here?" she asked.

"I was coming to see you at home. Then I was told you had gone to the gallery and here I am," Celia replied. She waited as Liam and Betty exchanged awkward glances.

"I've got to be going now, Betty. It was nice seeing you," Liam hurriedly said, before pecking her cheek. As he turned to leave, Celia caught herself before she audibly protested. She watched him walk into the gallery and turned to Betty.

"What was that about?"

"We were just catching up. He wanted to know how things are going since the incident," Betty replied.

"I would like to talk to him. An introduction would've been nice, you know," Celia said.

"Today's not a good day for that," Betty replied.

"But it would be great to talk to him now, since I'm here," Celia insisted.

Betty shook her head, taking Celia by the arm and leading her towards the exit.

"I don't think you need to talk to Liam. I already talked to him and frankly he doesn't have much to say," Betty replied, "You drove here?"

"Yes, I did. Why?" a puzzled Celia asked.

"I didn't, so you're luckily going to be my ride home. Let's go," she said.

As they rode in Celia's car, Betty kept fidgeting in the passenger seat.

"Can this seat lean back?"

"Sure it can," Celia said as she pointed towards the seat, "To the other side of your seat, at the corner you'll find a small lever. Just pull it and you'll get a good angle."

After two awkward attempts, Betty figured it out and tilted the backrest as far as she could. She now looked like she was in a pool chair.

"This is more like it. Sorry, I'm a little spoiled. I'm used to a little button on the armrest doing the job for me," Betty said with a relaxed brow free of frown lines.

"It's fine. This car of mine is a little old school, but she does the job," Celia replied.

"It sure does. It rides well too."

"Does your husband drive something else?" Betty asked.

Celia paused as her smile waned. "My husband died a couple of years ago. He was on duty in the military when it happened," she replied.

Betty gawked, then put her right hand over her heart. "Oh, my! I'm so sorry, I didn't know."

"It's okay. It's the ups and downs of life," Celia said.

"Yes. The ups and downs," Betty remarked, then went silent as she stared out of the window.

After about a minute's silence, Celia decided to revive the chat.

"Do you miss it?" she asked.

"Miss what?"

"The ups and downs of marriage."

Betty took a deep breath. "Sometimes. I had great times with Caleb. Actually, really fun times. I've never had as enriching a relationship as that one. Every day was an adventure. We were truly soul mates."

Celia smiled. "You guys were truly living the life. Appearing on magazines and other publications. Being guests for social events. That must have been fun."

Betty's faced lit up, and there was a glint in her eyes. "We were one of those couples that were the toast of the party, I won't lie. And although we were both very private people, we couldn't run too far from the cameras. So instead of fighting them, we decided to constantly shape the narratives."

"Wait, what do you mean by shaping the narrative? Were you…"

Betty shook her head. "No, not like that. We never paid off a single reporter. Well, maybe gave a few gifts here and there, but never bribed anyone to tell any story. We didn't need to. They were always hungry for stories and new angles to old stories. So we began appearing at certain places for certain reasons, and also 'leaked' little juicy stories to keep the tongues wagging," she replied with a cheeky wink.

Celia frowned at this.

"It was the way of increasing, or simply influencing your social capital in certain ways. And it worked. It still works to this very day," Betty added.

Celia cleared her throat. "Then what led to your separation?"

Betty let out a pronounced sigh. "I'm still not ready to talk about it. If I've never told any of my people, then know it's one of those things we don't feel will add value to our lives. So it's best to just keep moving on," she replied.

"But I'm not a journalist," Celia said.

"I know. But you might be the anonymous source that they need. I don't think we need to give you another job description, you have enough of those I'm sure."

Celia shrugged. "How do you feel about how it's affected your son and daughter?"

"I think they're handling it pretty well. Everyone has their own way of dealing with things."

"Do you get along with your son?"

Betty shot Celia a look, "We're not a split family. We have our personal differences, but we're all family. I need you to remember that."

Celia nodded, realizing she was beginning to rattle her. "I understand. Pardon me if I was a little abrasive."

"Don't worry. I know everything about being abrasive. Trust me, that's even close to what I used to do when I was your age," she said.

"Talking about ages, you still haven't told me the story of the art piece."

Betty laughed. "Once you get me home in one piece, I might consider doing that."

Celia laughed, but she realized Betty was stonewalling her. Had she pushed too hard and now the rapport was gone? It sure felt that way. She already knew Betty was an expert at blowing off people with a smile. You felt good about being cut off or rejected in an actual social setting. Was it happening now?

Her hunch was confirmed when they arrived at Betty's expansive home. Once the car came to a stop, Betty turned to Celia.

"How much was that?"

Celia was puzzled.

"It was on the house, you don't have to pay me anything," she replied.

"No, I insist," Betty said, reaching into her purse. She took out a two hundred rand note and handed it to Celia.

"You really don't have to," Celia still said, knowing even if it was a cab ride, it was at most an eighty rand trip.

"I do. Whatever it takes to make you comfortable matters to me," Betty said as she placed the note atop the center console. She made a move towards the exit when Celia tried to stop her.

"Can we continue our chat?" Celia asked.

Betty paused with the passenger door ajar. "No, I don't think so. I'm developing a headache, so I'll go have a siesta. That usually does the trick. Maybe next time, when we meet in a more causal setting," Betty replied.

Celia forced a smile. Betty shut the door and sauntered to the house.

Celia exhaled. She now knew it might be tricky to meet Betty again and get anything from her. She determined to be more cautious and deflect the conversation if she ever found herself in the same room with her.

"Those walls of Jericho are up and running," Celia mused as she squared her jaw.

She was convinced that someone in the family was involved in Mary's murder and the theft. Intrigued by her reflections on marriage, Celia now needed to talk to Betty's ex-husband, Caleb.

There was a strong possibility that he would help bring the freshly built walls of Jericho tumbling down.

11

Back at the nail parlor, Celia found herself on the whiteboard. Instead of drawing the next marketing strategy, she drew a link chart of all the possible suspects and persons of interest. She wrote their names, then connected them with lines where needed. She had seen it done on a TV show once, and since she had mapped out a great marketing strategy, why not map out her suspects too? She felt it might help her think more clearly.

Pretty soon, she had all the key names she had a hunch about. As she stared at her handiwork, Melanie walked in. She froze as she studied the chart. She then looked at the friend quizzically.

"Have you gone crazy?" Melanie asked.

"No, why?"

"I only see these things when they're looking for serial killers on TV. Are you looking for one?"

Celia smiled, then shook her head. "Now you're the one who sounds crazy. I'm doing this to see if I'm missing something. What do you think?"

Melanie stared at it again. "I can't make sense of it. What's the connection between Tony and Liam?"

Celia smiled. "They were seen driving off together that night.

Before then, they'd possibly carried the sculpture to the car together," she said.

"But did you see it on the cameras?"

Celia shook her head. "They were not clear on the frame for us to tell if it was the sculpture they were carrying or not."

"That's not a strong link at all. Why would they do it?" Melanie asked.

"Liam owns an art gallery. The sculpture is a rare one that can make him good money at an international auction. Eight hundred thousand rand or more. If he's greedy enough, he's got a motive. Liam also has a record. He's been arrested twice. Jailed for a year for selling forged artwork. The other time he was arrested was for a fight with Caleb."

"Wait, they fought? About what?"

"The papers said it was over a business dispute. I think otherwise," Celia replied.

"How's Tony connected to Liam then?"

"Tony's reason is a bit weaker. Maybe he was swayed by Liam, considering he's an influential family friend," she explained.

Melanie scowled. "You linked Tony to Caleb, too. Father and son?"

"Yeah, it sounds like a stretch. But think about it. Most of the wealth after the divorce went to Betty, not Caleb. He wouldn't be happy about that. In fact, he could be very bitter about it. So what if it was a revenge plot that involved his son?" Celia asked.

"Does Tony hate his mother that much?" Melanie asked.

Celia scratched the back of her head. "It doesn't look like he does. But you do realize most killers don't look like they could kill someone. The only issue with that is Tony was in the ballroom when the murder happened."

Melanie curled up her lip. "On your chart, Isabella isn't connected to anyone. Why?"

"I can't think of where she fits. She's a fence sitter. The problem with her is she would be easily swayed by someone on the rest of this chart to do their bidding. So long as at the end of it all she benefits," Celia said.

Melanie's eyes narrowed as she studied the names. "That makes Isabella more dangerous if she's manipulated," she said.

"Perhaps. But I think she's a masterful manipulator herself, although I'm yet to confirm that."

"Betty's also on the list?" she asked, glancing at Celia.

"Just keeping my mind open. It could be part of an insurance scam or something," Celia said with a pronounced sigh.

The two friends stood in front of the whiteboard in complete silence for another minute. Melanie then turned to Celia.

"I know, I know," Celia said while nodding slowly.

"I take my words back," Melanie replied, "This isn't crazy. This is good for you. Because it shows you that you need hard evidence or a confession to make any sense of these connections. I know you have a good eye for these things, but you can't just rely on your gut feeling, Cece."

Celia bit her lower lip. Melanie was right, and that truth was in itself a punch to the gut.

* * *

CELIA KEPT CHECKING HER WATCH. Bill was supposed to be picking her up that afternoon so that they could go for a chilled late lunch, ending it at around four in the evening. They hadn't done that in a long time, and she was eager to catch up.

He was running late, so she called him.

"Hey there! How's it going?" he asked.

"You tell me, it's three o'clock. How far are you?" she asked.

"Oh."

As soon as she heard that, she knew it wasn't happening. She shook her head.

"Sorry I've gotta go and follow up a possible lead in the murder case," Bill said.

"What kind of lead?" she asked, her ears pricked.

"I've got to go and talk to one of the witnesses urgently. It seems their brain fog cleared or something."

"Ah, interesting. Which witness?"

"Isabella," he replied.

Celia's eyes widened. She was now really curious.

"You say her brain fog has cleared about the night? What do you think she's going to tell you?"

"I have no idea. But I hope it will be a good break. On my way to her place now."

"Alright, great. Say hi to her mom for me," Celia said.

"I don't think I'll see her at the apartment," Bill replied.

Celia raised her eyebrows. "Apartment? What apartment?"

"Isabella's apartment."

Celia's mouth gaped in amazement. To her recollection, Isabella said she didn't have another home. Where did this apartment come from?

"Look out for her. She's not what she seems. Also, check her place for clues. You never know. But why doesn't she just come down to the station and do this?" Celia replied.

"I wouldn't know, but hey, I gotta go now. Talk later."

Before she could interject, the line went dead.

Celia gritted her teeth, wanting to call him back. Had Isabella lied to her, or was she lying to Bill?

Celia paced. Then an idea came to her. Over their restaurant meeting, Isabella said she found Bill handsome enough to date. Now that she'd invited him to her secret apartment, was Isabella trying to seduce him?

12

"Are things moving or not?" Richie asked.

Celia hadn't given her manager an update in days about the sales of the beauty products and frankly didn't want the pressure it brought. But he'd called, and she wasn't going to ignore his calls.

"It's coming along nicely. We're just over the halfway mark with the sales, so we're right on track," Celia replied, trying to sound as enthusiastic as possible.

She stared across her bedroom at the delivery packs for that morning. She had packed four instead of seven; three clients had canceled their orders the previous night. True, they were just over the halfway mark. But she had to increase her momentum.

"I'm glad to hear that. The only thing is you're already into the final week. The deadline is getting closer, although I'm rooting for you," he said.

"Here I was thinking you'd be so impressed you'd give me an extension," Celia teased.

"There's no need for an extension when it comes to you. I'm sure you'll pull something off to beat the deadline. I'm looking forward to it," Richie said.

They kept discussing a few other work updates. After he hung up, Celia fell back into bed.

As she stared at the ceiling, she slowed down her breathing to calm herself down. She didn't want to start the day under pressure.

Her mind drifted to her first impressions of Mary. Eloquent. Focused. Organized. Driven. Even though Celia had only interacted with her briefly, Mary had left a mark. Maybe that's what thriving looks like, Celia thought; other people noticing the strength of your purpose just by watching you.

How did she get that way? What was she like away from the run-around?

Then she remembered Betty talking about Mary living with a roommate. What was her name again? Celia reached for her notebook and flipped through it.

Bilha Ledisi. 121 Creek Road.

Celia exhaled. Once her deliveries were done, she'd pay Bilha a visit.

* * *

"So, you lived with Mary for how many years?" Celia asked.

She sat in a bucket seat inside the sparsely furnished but colorful apartment that Mary used to share with Bilha, her roommate.

"Around five years," Bilha replied. She was short and plump and wore spectacles. She had a nerdy look which, to Celia, complimented her social scientist career.

"So, you got to know her well."

"Yes, we grew close in recent years. It wasn't that easy at first."

"How come?"

Bilha smiled sheepishly. "Well, Mary was a force of nature. She was one of the most focused and organized person I knew. I'm pretty organized myself, but she was top tier. That's one of things that made us great roommates. We liked the peace and clarity that organization and efficiency brought."

Celia couldn't agree more. The apartment was well spaced out and painted in shades of yellow and white to create a sense of tangible warmth and cleanliness.

"However, she had a serious case of tunnel vision. She could cut off the people around her easily when she was set on a goal. Although she was working on creating a balance for this, it was a tricky trait to get used to. But once I got to know her, I realized she's quite an empathetic person and a joy to live with," Bilha replied.

"That's great to hear. Was she seeing someone?"

Bilha sighed. "No. She had two more years left in her grand plan before she started dating seriously. She always said she wanted her next man to be her husband. It's sad that's not going to happen. Whoever was going to marry her was going to be one lucky guy, I can say that for sure!"

Celia smiled. Bilha was so genuine as she marveled at the thought of Mary in full flow.

"What was the one thing she could never leave behind?"

"Her phone, obviously," Bilha said with a chuckle.

"And her notebook, too. Although for the night of the event she had just bought a new one," Bilha replied.

"Oh. Is the old one still here?"

"One of the old ones, because she has whole cartons of notebooks she's used for years. I don't know why she used to keep them because she hardly went back to read any of them."

"Maybe they were a progress marker or something," Celia remarked.

"Yeah, maybe you're right."

Celia leaned forward. "Would it be too much of a hassle to see the latest one she had?"

"Sure, let me see if I can get a hand on it," Bilha replied as she got up and went to the bedroom.

Bilha soon got back with the book and Celia immediately started poring through it.

There were shopping lists, meeting notes, to do lists and also addresses that she saw as she leafed through the book. Every page was scribbled with stuff, and a few had doodles and inspirational quotes.

It's the to do lists and addresses that Celia was more keenly interested in. She narrowed down to one entry that had the date before the murder.

'Meet Tony and Mr. C. at the club. Three sharp sharp!'

Celia deduced who Tony was. But who was Mr. C? And what significance did that have?

"Allow me to go with this so that I can look at it a little better. Maybe it can offer clue on what happened."

"Anything that will help us find out what really happened to her. I really miss her."

"I can feel your pain. Let's hope the truth comes out soon," Celia replied.

Bilha escorted her outside. As they waited for the lift to come up to her floor, Bilha said, "You know, she used to support a little girl from one of the townships. She'd been paying her school fees for the past three years. Mary really wanted her to become something. Her sudden death has hit the girl hard."

"Oh no, sorry to hear that. Are you in touch with the girl?"

"Yeah. I'll help her get through it, and I'll even pick up from where Mary left off. The girl is going to finish school," Bilha said.

Celia felt the weight of the loss that Bilha carried engulf her. She didn't know what to say.

The lift arrived and the door opened. It was empty. Celia got in and turned.

"Thanks for everything."

The door quickly started closing. Suddenly, Bilha poked her arm in between the doors and they reopened.

"Don't let the killer win," Bilha said with tears rolling down her face.

Celia, stirred by the powerful words, nodded.

She clutched the notebook tightly in her hand as the doors slid shut. The lift hurtled towards the ground floor.

13

The following day, Celia was up before sunrise. She had tried reading the notebook the previous night, but was too exhausted. She had to make time to look into it before the day took over. As she flipped through the pages, she kept an eye out for meetings and such.

Mary clearly liked lining up most of her meetings from mid-morning to mid afternoon, and had the resilience to do back-to-back meetings. Celia admired this, as she knew how hard it can be. She often had to deliver her beauty products to multiple clients in succession, and a simple delivery could quickly develop into a long crisis-filled day if the clients are difficult.

After reading through most of the notebook, Celia resolved she would pay Tony another visit after she had finished her morning deliveries. She was glad that she had several orders for the highlighters. They had also started moving faster off the shelves at the nail parlor, another good sign. However, she knew that she still needed the sales weekend to push all the units out.

It was some minutes past midday when Celia finished up with her morning deliveries. She had delayed at the last house call, as the client seemed to be going through a rough time in her marriage.

"You know that you can't make a man happy, right, Cece? It doesn't matter if you cook his favorite meals, keep him cozy, keep his laundry spot on and bear him children. He'll always be looking for the next option," Sasha lamented as she sipped a mug of green tea.

Celia had heard Sasha narrate this story before, but in different words. She could tell where it was going.

"Who did he cheat with this time?" Celia asked.

Sasha snorted. "Some college girl living in the township. Can you believe it? Leaving me for a township girl?" she replied.

Celia didn't agree with the suggestion that young women from low-income neighborhoods were not good quality women. It was more likely that her husband was using his wealth to take advantage of the college girl. But she didn't want to antagonize her client by putting it bluntly.

"You don't want to leave him yet?" Celia asked.

Sasha shot her an angry look.

"For who? So that another woman can pick him up? No way, I'll stay right here."

Celia shook her head. She had tried many times to advise Sasha. The concept of boundaries and self-worth never really caught any traction, though.

"So how will you sort it out now?" Celia asked.

"That's why you're here."

"Excuse me?" Celia asked with raised eyebrows. She wasn't ready to do give any more advice. She knew it would be disregarded.

"You should give me ten of those highlighter bottles," Sasha said. "Some impulsive retail therapy on his tab will be quite handy."

"You don't need all this right now. What if he acts up?"

Sasha chuckled, "He doesn't even know what highlighter is. So let me handle that. We'll call it planning for the future."

That's how Celia managed to make double the sales she expected to have that morning.

Celia would've felt guilty, but she didn't take advantage of Sasha and swindle her into buying more highlighter make-up. Buoyed by this unexpected sale, she decided to check on Tony.

HIGHLIGHTERS AND UPHEAVAL

As she parked in front of Tony's gate, she was relieved to see the car in the garage, a telltale sign of his presence.

She knocked on his front door and waited. After what seemed like five minutes of waiting, the door opened. He was scraggly-looking with unkempt hair, a vest and shorts. He didn't look like he was planning on leaving or receiving visitors. He definitely wasn't embarrassed.

"You again" Tony said.

"Missed me?" Celia asked.

Tony snickered. "What do you want this time?" he asked, rubbing his left eye.

"I learned recently that you met with Mary two days before the event. What was the meeting about?"

Tony sighed. "You couldn't find anything from the night of the robbery, now you're searching in reverse?" he posed.

"Just answer the question. You've got nothing to hide, right?" she said.

"We talked about the event. Logistics, budget, the programme, the works."

"Just the two of you?"

"Yeah."

"Then who is Mr. C, who was also supposed to be at the meeting?" she asked.

Tony rubbed his left forearm.

"I have no idea what you're talking about," he replied.

"Was it your father, Caleb?"

Tony guffawed. "Haibo, you're doing too much. I have no clue what you're talking about," he replied.

Celia nodded slowly. "I assume the police told you they have all CCTV footage from the night," Celia said, "It showed that after the murder, you and Liam Turnton carried something bulky to his car. Then you both drove off. Is there anything you want to tell me now?"

Tony itched through his unkempt hair as if he was being ravaged by mites.

"I don't remember everything about that night. I already told you I spoke to Liam, and drove out with him, but I... I mean, we didn't take that sculpture," he replied.

"Are you sure this is the hill you want to die on?"

"Why would I steal from my own mother?" Tony asked, crossing his arms and leaning his left shoulder on the wall.

Celia stared at him, trying to read his eyes. He didn't flinch as she expected him to.

"You know, it would be a shame if it came out that the one person you look up to has set you up for a long stint behind bars. Should he suffer the same fate as you?" Celia asked.

"Who are you talking about?"

"Your father."

Tony shook his head. "You're confusing me. One time you say it's Liam, the next question you say it's my father. Tell me, which of the two is my partner in crime?"

Celia studied Tony's face. It was twitching slightly every few seconds, like he had a system glitch. She came to understand he was irritated when he reacted this way.

"You tell me, Tony. You. Tell. Me," Celia said, saying the words slowly for maximum dramatic effect.

Tony's face twitched some more, then he shrugged it off.

"You can call me anytime you want as you think about it," Celia said, handing him a slip of paper with her phone number. She hadn't got round to printing new business cards, so pieces of paper would have to do the trick.

"Don't hold your breath," he said with a sly grin. Celia turned and walked towards her car.

His body language confirmed to her that he knew more than he was letting on. She'd pushed him a little more than last time. Was it enough to spur him to make a mistake? Time would tell.

* * *

CELIA WALKED into The Pier restaurant to get a quick bite and ease her mind.

HIGHLIGHTERS AND UPHEAVAL

In recent times she had been scrutinizing herself for inefficiencies. She had realized that prolonged hunger was her enemy. Previously, she never used to care about food when she was deeply engrossed in her work. These days she could hardly function well if hunger was on hand. Her decision making slowed, and her reactions became labored.

Her dilemma was more complex than that. She found it amusing that when she had a brief dalliance with intermittent fasting a few weeks earlier, her alertness and concentration levels increased. The fact that hunger was now slowing her down was a fascinating realization about how her body worked. She needed to do some more reading and experimentation to see which state would give her the best results.

For now, all she craved was a bunny chow.

She sat at a corner that offered a good view of the whole restaurant without making her conspicuous. She enjoyed studying people, and could see who was coming in and going out.

As she waited for her order, her phone rang.

"Hello Cece, I was thinking about you," Mrs. Owens crooned into Celia's ear.

"Are these happy thoughts or dark thoughts?" Celia asked.

Mrs. Owens chuckled. "I would never share with you dark ones, my child. Those I carry alone, never to burden you. I do have an idea for your event."

Celia rubbed her temple. She knew what was coming. Mrs. Owens was an idea factory, and if you didn't rein her in things could get bent out of shape.

"Tell me about it."

"Well, I was talking to Melanie, and she seems to be getting young models, which is of course sensible. But aren't you worried you're cutting off another section of the market?"

"Erm, for starters, they are sales agents, not models. That aside, which market do you feel I'm cutting off?" Celia asked.

"Eish, Cece. I'm talking about people who look like me. We're the golden girls who want to age fine like wine, so we should be represented in your promotion. So, I think you should try to include some models around my age too."

Celia bit her lip. She knew this was more than just an idea.

"You've already taken your models to her, haven't you?" Celia posed.

"Well, you know I move fast, right? I only showed her the list of models."

"How many?"

"A good number."

"How many, Mrs. Owens?" Celia insisted.

"Just twenty. That's quite a decent number, right?"

Celia sighed. "No, it's not. It's more than we can handle. Remember, I want to pay everyone I'm working with on this."

"Oh, some of them are coming for free and don't need to be paid," Mrs. Owens said.

Celia shook her head. "No, it would also mean I need more handlers to attend to them. That's too much. Reduce them to three."

"Three? Why are you being so ruthless?" Mrs. Owens protested.

"I'm actually making it easy for you."

"Make it seven."

"Three is the best I can do."

"Five and let's call it even. Alright? They'll not burden your team. I promise."

Celia closed her eyes. "Alright. Five. No more than that. Give the names to Mel and I'll crosscheck them."

"That's my little biscuit! I knew you'd come round. Have a lovely afternoon," Mrs. Owens chirped with joy.

As soon as she hung up, Celia checked on Melanie and informed her of the new quota. She was finishing her call when her eye was drawn to the restaurant entrance.

The familiar lean form of Liam Turnton walked in. She studied him as he talked to a waiter. From his body language, she could tell he wanted something and wasn't sure the restaurant would provide it. She silently prayed that he wouldn't leave so that she could avoid confronting him in the parking lot. It gave him more options of escape. If he stayed in, stuck with a plate of food in front of him, she had a more controlled setting to make a move.

He turned as if about to leave when the waiter made a suggestion that halted his step. He smiled, then allowed himself to be led to the other side of the restaurant, away from Celia's line of sight.

A sly smile formed on her lips as she embraced the opportunity. She wolfed down the remainder of her chicken bunny chow, enjoying the taste of the soft hollowed out bread stuffed with chicken. She was glad that it wasn't too spicy. She then gulped down the fresh orange juice.

Satisfied, she took out her hand mirror and checked her teeth and lips for any crumbs. After applying some lip gloss, she stood and casually strolled until she could see where Liam sat. He was still alone and had been served with soup as a starter. After slightly adjusting the hair that fell on each side of her face, she continued her walk to his table. She arrived there just as he was about to down a spoonful of soup.

"Mr. Turnton?"

His hand froze mid-air, and he looked up quizzically. Wearing her broadest smile, she continued.

"I'm Cece. I'm sure you remember my face from the museum? I'm here because we have something important to talk about," she said as she eased herself into the seat across from him.

"I'm having my lunch and I don't have time for…"

"Oh, I don't have to take too much of your time if you don't want me to. But your freedom depends on it. So you'll talk to me here and now for your own good, kind sir," she interrupted with a confident swagger.

14

He stared at her in disbelief, and she held his gaze.

"A fine gentleman like yourself shouldn't mind some lively conversation," Celia said.

A vein pulsed on Liam's temple as he slowly shook his head.

"It sounds like you're propositioning me. I'm not interested," Liam replied, holding up his left hand to show a silver wedding ring.

Celia would have laughed out loud if the suggestion wasn't so condescending. He was showing her spite, and was clearly not going to give her an easy time. Celia sat back briefly, watching him down his soup faster than he had started.

"You own Masava Gallery, one of the most coveted private galleries in town. Yet you don't seem to like talking to your clients," Celia said.

Liam went on eating his soup in silence. Soon, the spoon was clinking the bowl as he cleared its contents. Liam pushed the bowl to the side and waved to the waiter, indicating he was ready for the main course.

"Silence, in this instance, isn't golden, Mr. Turnton. Especially when it's suspected you witnessed a robbery and murder."

HIGHLIGHTERS AND UPHEAVAL

Liam gave her an icy stare, his eyes narrowing with mild contempt.

"Unless the police interrupt regular people's lunches these days, we have nothing to talk about," he replied.

Celia leaned forward and smiled. "Call me a friend of the police and the family. I think you're a friend of Betty's too, no? I'm sure you'd like her to get some peace of mind in this matter."

"Of course. But in the right way."

"There's no right way in this, sir. Someone innocent was strangled that night, and a sculpture stolen as well. Nothing about those two incidents was done the right way," she said.

They paused their exchange as the main course arrived. He was having a spicy lamb curry and fried rice, the kind of dish that one would relish in Durban. Although they weren't in Durban, Celia appreciated the restaurant's handiwork in delivering a delicious-looking meal.

Liam began eating, showing a high level of excellence in using a fork and knife. He was clearly used to dining with the high and mighty on a regular basis, the moneyed buyers of his art.

"What did you see that night?" Celia asked.

"I already told the police everything I know," Liam replied as he went for another mouthful.

Celia wasn't getting anywhere, so she changed her approach.

"I read something about you. You used to do art auctions for a couple of years. Why did you stop?" she asked. He ignored her, slicing through his soft lamb meat to get a smaller piece for his fork.

"You once had a run-in with the police about some forged art. You spent a year behind bars. I'm sure not many people know that. But here you are, living the good life once more, a changed man," she said.

Liam paused, staring at her as he chewed slowly.

"It would be a pity if the police found out you have some more forgeries in your gallery collection right now," Celia added.

Liam stopped chewing, then swallowed hard. It was a gamble, but it seemed to have struck a chord. "What do you want?"

"Tell me what you saw."

"I didn't see the murder. I was inside, just like everybody else."
"But did you know about the murder and robbery plot?"
Liam shook his head, "No."
"Although you might know who did it, right?"
Liam clenched his jaw.

Celia leaned forward a little more, then whispered. "You were once close friends with Caleb and Betty. When they were married. The other day at the gallery, I could see how she looked at you, how you talked, how you were gentle with her. What's going on between the two of you?"

Liam curled his lip. "I like her."
"As friends?"
"We've known each other longer. Now we're more than friends."
Celia's eyes widened. "Aah. Was the fight you and Caleb had once because of this, or a business disagreement?" she asked.
Liam glanced away, then nodded. "He didn't like how I associated with her."

Celia leaned back. Betty had got fed up and cheated on Caleb. Sitting across from her was the real reason why the couple divorced. It was clear to her that there was unresolved animosity between Caleb and Betty, despite their attempts to mask it.

"Where's the sculpture, Liam?" she asked.
"I have no idea about that," Liam replied.
Celia sighed. "Thank you for your honesty. Let me excuse myself, I wouldn't want to ruin your lunch," Celia said as she got up. "I hope the next time we meet you might be more willing to talk about how the sculpture got out of the compound."

* * *

CELIA DROVE into the Sunshine Cove Police Station parking lot, which was fuller than she expected. She had to drive around just to find a parking spot. She managed to get a spot right under a tree. It was a tight fit, but her station wagon was able to nimble its way into the space and still give her enough room to squeeze out of the car.

She had just stepped out when she spotted them. Bill was laughing, clearly amused by the animated Isabella. They were standing next to one of the police cars.

Celia frowned. The two looked like old high school friends catching up on good memories. Celia stiffened her shoulders and walked over to them.

As she got closer, Bill noticed her and his smile eased slightly.

"Look who's here," Bill said. "We were just talking about you."

Celia's eyes narrowed. "Oh? I never thought I could inspire such humor," Celia said with a forced smile.

"Actually, I was laughing at myself," a jovial Isabella said, "I was so nervous when we met, I tried to wear that silly outfit as a disguise, remember? Bill was just pointing out that it was totally a waste of time for a trained eye," Isabella gushed.

Celia shrugged. "I'm not a trained eye and could tell who you were the moment I laid my eyes on you."

"That's the result of hanging out with me," Bill said with a chuckle.

Celia would have bantered to this, but at the moment she found it colorless.

Isabella glanced at her phone. "My cab is here, so I'll leave you to it. Thanks, Bill, for the help," she said.

She then left. When she was out of earshot, Celia stepped up to Bill.

"What was that about?" she asked.

"I just brought her in for some more questioning," he replied.

"Have you brought in Tony or anyone else for this?" she asked.

Bill crossed his arms. "What are you getting at, Cece?"

"I'm just wondering why she's the only witness you're questioning multiple times. To the best of my knowledge, she doesn't have much to say."

"Sometimes it's not about what a suspect says. It's about what they do, and finding the weak link," he said.

"It sounds to me like you're trying to confuse me, Bill, and I'm not buying it," Celia snapped.

Bill rubbed his chin, like someone trying to control his temper. He stepped closer to her and looked her in the eye. His gaze was intense.

"This is why I'm a detective, and you're not. Let me do my job, and I'll let you do yours."

"Are you sure you're doing your job, Bill?"

"We're on the same side, Cece."

"I'm not so sure about that anymore," she replied.

Bill stepped back. "I'm going to go now, got a case to clear off my desk. Have a nice day," he said.

With that, he marched off towards the station building.

Celia felt the cords in her neck tighten as she held back an explosion of words. Words she couldn't take back. Instead of blurting them out, she clenched her fists as she watched him go.

15

Later that evening, Celia wasn't in her best spirits. She prepared dinner in silence and served her sons and mother Audrey with minimal conversation. After she had tucked them into bed, she went to fold the laundry.

Audrey waited until the kids were asleep to approach her.

"Had a long day?" Audrey asked.

"Kind of," Celia replied.

"Wanna talk about it?"

Celia was tempted to spill her frustrations about Bill to someone, but it wasn't going to be her mother. She didn't want her to know that she was dating a police detective. After losing her husband Trevor while on duty during a military tour, Audrey didn't want her to date someone who faced that kind of danger every day. Bill was in that high-risk partner category.

But Celia seemed to be attracted to this type more than any other. She had tried other options. This, for some reason, was the type that always had the last man standing. She understood the risks that came with it, but she couldn't deny it either. On a night like this, she didn't need a lecture from her mother about it all. Especially when things were already hitting a rocky patch.

"It was just a long day," she replied, "I'll sleep on it."

Audrey shrugged. "Alright. I can finish that folding for you if you want to catch some sleep."

"No, it's fine. This is me counting sheep with each fold. I should be blacking out the minute I hit the bed after I'm done."

"I love the optimism. Have a goodnight, Cece."

"Goodnight Ma."

Celia didn't sleep well that night.

* * *

THE FOLLOWING morning's fair weather didn't lift her mood.

"Someone's in the trenches today," Melanie said, seated across from her in their mezzanine office.

"Is it that obvious?" Celia asked, avoiding eye contact by focusing on her computer screen.

"Your energy in a room is too strong not to notice when it changes. Is everything okay at home?"

"No issues at home. Maybe I should go do some field sales. Get my energy back up," Celia replied.

Melanie gave a quizzical smile. "I don't think doing more sales will fix it. Besides, we're supposed to be partners here. We practice ubuntu. So tell me what's up," she said.

"You're throwing ubuntu as a philosophy now?" Celia asked, half-smiling.

"I am because we are. Something tells me you like it, too."

Celia sighed, then rubbed her temple with her hands. "It's Bill. I don't understand what's going on with us," she said.

"What do you mean?"

"I went to see him at the station yesterday and found him talking to Isabella. Actually, let's just say they were openly flirting."

Melanie's eyebrows went up. "Are you sure they were flirting?"

"I saw how they looked at each other. How they laughed. Everything I learned in that body language course was right there before me. I know it when I see it."

HIGHLIGHTERS AND UPHEAVAL

Melanie winced. "Did you confront him about it?"

"On the spot. He shut it down as if nothing happened. Shame!" she hissed.

"Do you want me to give my opinion?" Melanie asked.

Celia nodded as she checked her phone. "Go ahead."

"He's being disrespectful. The least he could do is allow you to share your thoughts on it and then give his side of things. Shutting you down is a red flag," she said.

"Go on."

"So, I would say cut him off. Hang him out to dry until he comes to his senses. Focus on your other interests, like hitting these sales targets," she suggested.

Celia leaned back in her chair. "You know the most annoying thing about it? He's doing it with a suspect in the case. Why would he do that?" she posed.

"Sounds hectic to me," Melanie said.

"Dodgy and hectic. It won't end well. And it might mess up the case," Celia added.

"Like I said, cut him off. You don't want him feeding your leads to her."

Celia smiled. "Why are you giving me relationship advice when you're not in one yourself?" she asked.

Melanie lifted an eyebrow. "Don't look down on the single just because your king has revealed himself. I'm biding my time," she quipped.

"The king part sounds a little ambitious right now," Celia said as she glanced at her phone again. No text had come in.

"Cece, get off your phone and do something productive," Melanie admonished, "Forget about that man. When he needs to call you, you bet he will."

Celia sighed and put her phone back into her bag. This kind of thing never bothered her before, but it now did for some reason. As if she was worried.

That's it. She was worried. About what? About Isabella. She scoffed at the thought and vowed to banish it. Insecurity of that kind had no business being in her emotional space. It would only serve to derail her.

Celia stood up. "Alright, I'm off. I have some deliveries to make. If something comes up, call me," she said.

"Sure thing," Melanie replied.

Celia drove to three homes after that, dropping off shipments of assorted products while also pitching the highlighter to secure sales. She managed to sell ten of them, as two clients wanted to share them out with close relatives and friends. That delivery run made her smile.

Having completed her run with two hours to spare, she decided to drive to Caleb Khoza's office. She had been postponing this encounter as she looked for a window that wouldn't clash with her sales targets. He was possibly a man on edge, so she had spent time thinking of ways to approach him that would make it less confrontational. She needed a ruse that might help along. She believed she had come up with the right one, borrowing her experience working at a TV station in her younger days.

She had purchased a new notebook, and downloaded an app onto her phone that gave her better sound recording. She had even gone as far as finally printing a hundred business cards. If her proxy identity worked this time, she might try to use it more often.

Part of her questioned the morality of her deception, but she found it mild in the sharp light of tracking down a killer. The end justified the means. She had then set up an appointment with Caleb. He was going to be part of a short interview for a fictional Cape Town magazine. Hopefully, it would get him to warm up to her faster.

Live in the moment.

This was the thought running through her mind as she walked confidently into the office of Khoza Entertainment.

* * *

"You look familiar," Caleb said.

"Yes, I think we saw each other at Betty's launch," Celia replied, masking her unease.

"Oh, yes! You were there to cover it?"

"Yes, I'm a correspondent at large for the magazine, writing about the art scene here. So that event was right up my alley," she replied.

Caleb nodded, one hand resting on his chin as he studied the business card she had handed him. "So, what would you like to know Eunice?"

"I just had a few questions about you and your company. It's no secret that you've been quite involved in various artistic productions over the years, and I thought you'd be interesting to profile. As an emerging voice," Celia said.

Caleb grunted and wrinkled up his nose. "I'm not really an emerging voice, am I?"

"Sorry, let me rephrase. You're rebranding, showing the world a new side of you. The kind of thing my readers will find interesting," Celia replied, as she took out her phone and placed it on the table.

His eyes narrowed as she did this.

"I'd like to go on the record, it's easier considering the time constraint," Celia said with a smile.

Caleb shrugged, then nodded. "Sure."

"So, tell me a little about your interest in the media and arts."

Caleb smiled. "I've always loved art. Grew up with a few paintings in the home. Taken to the theater often by my father. Became a television extra on a few television shows in my early twenties. So the bug caught on, and after university I started my first production company. The rest is history," he said.

"Seems the path to this success chose you. Did you become an art dealer at some point?"

Caleb cocked his head to one side. "Not really. I was tempted to do it, but it takes time to build trust in that market. I prefer this, which has more regular returns. Adverts, plays, television shows are more exciting to work with," he replied.

"Interesting. If you don't mind, allow me to touch on your marriage briefly. Did your divorce affect your trajectory?"

Caleb adjusted his seating position. "Well, we were quite active in the social scene as a couple. So understandably, when it ended, there was a period of reflection. I thought it wise to, as you call it, rebrand with a new outfit. We're currently doing well."

"Good to hear. Have your kids followed your footsteps?" Celia asked with a smile.

Caleb laughed. "I'm not sure I would want them to. Tony is mildly interested in the arts though, but Isabella is a free spirit. I think she's still figuring out who she is at the moment. That's all fine, you never want to box your kids in a corner."

"So you could say Tony is closer to you than Isabella?"

Caleb shook his head. "I wouldn't say that. I play no favorites," he replied with a half-smile.

Celia grinned. She wished he knew what she had learned from her earlier chats with Tony and Isabella.

"I think you're quite the revolutionary, keeping a loose rein on your kids and letting them flourish on their own terms. Some of us didn't get that," Celia said.

"Your parents were stricter?"

"Slightly. When the cash is tighter, your path is sometimes dictated to you. But I was lucky because my parents came round to support me later."

"The thing with parenting is there's no manual. You have to do what feels right then hope they turn out right," he replied.

"I couldn't agree more. One last question. I've scoured all sorts of news reports and was wondering if you could shed some more light on this. What led to your divorce?"

Caleb leaned forward, his eyes narrowed, his lips in a tight line. "What happened is knowledge that belongs to only myself and my ex-wife. It's not for public consumption."

"Did she cheat on you?" Celia prodded.

Caleb smashed his hands on the table, startling her. She impulsively grabbed her phone, fearing he might go for it.

"Didn't you hear me? That's none of your business. I think your time is up now," Caleb snarled.

"Sorry. I didn't mean…"

He tossed her business card toward her. "Just get out of my face!" he bellowed.

Celia quickly stood up, grabbed the card and walked out as fast as she could. She didn't even take the lift, choosing to dash down the steps. It was only when she got to her car that she stopped to catch her breath. Then she checked her phone. It was still recording.

She smiled. She survived. Even better, she had never thought going undercover would be so satisfying.

16

On her drive to Betty's Mihlali's house early the next day, Celia had come up with the questions she needed to ask her about the affair with Liam. Betty was a smart woman, and would try to dodge the issue just like Liam did. If she had managed to keep this secret from the press for so long, then she was well-versed in the art of dodging questions and giving vague answers. Celia didn't want to leave empty-handed, but also hoped at the end of it all she would still have some level of access to Betty instead of being banished for being too nosey.

That was the delicate balancing act.

But as she sat across from her in the garden, she suddenly realized there was no guarantee it would work. They sat in garden chairs with a small round metal table between them. Atop it were two glasses of chilled water.

"You should bring a few of your products over so that I can try them out," Betty said after they had been discussing the benefits of sunscreen.

Betty loved sitting outdoors in her garden, and she had a great view to look at. There were a host of different trees that added beautiful colors during flowering season, namely rusty-red colored bougainvillea and the purple-flowered jacaranda trees. Thick, lush grass covered the garden like an expensive carpet. This was great for relaxed walks. As Celia had recently learned, it was bad for murder investigations where clear footprints were needed.

"I'll look at what I have and share it with you next time," Celia replied with a smile, "Guess who I bumped into while having lunch."

Betty shrugged as she sipped her water.

"I met our gallery owner friend, Liam," Celia said.

Betty stopped drinking her water, placing the glass back on the table. "I thought we talked about you not going to see him?" she protested.

"I didn't. We bumped into each other at the restaurant. So technically, he came to me."

"You didn't need to talk to him, Celia," she said, her tone getting icy.

"Why is that, Betty? Please, feel free to tell me."

Betty glared at her. "Through your confident questioning, I can tell you learned something new. The reasons families like mine keep their position in this fickle world is because we remain true to each other, regardless of the storms we face," she said, "I expect the same loyalty from you."

"I'm listening," Celia said.

Betty crossed her legs. "My marriage wasn't perfect. It had fantastic moments, as I told you before and as I'm sure you've seen on the tabloids. Behind all that, we're human beings with fears, dreams and ambition. I'm ambitious. Caleb wasn't as ambitious," she said.

"When you say that, what do you mean?" Celia asked.

"He couldn't look at the big picture and make sacrifices to bring those big dreams to life. He loved living in the moment. That's why when a beautiful woman in a skirt appeared at his productions, he stopped thinking with his brain and let his short-term desires take over," she replied.

Celia's eyes narrowed. "So you're saying he cheated first?"

"He was always a ladies' man. He still is, don't be fooled. He just knows how to play the game so well you won't really notice. After fighting him on this and catching him with several women, I realized I needed to value myself more. He was dragging me to a level I didn't want to be in, frankly. I think the day I stopped fighting for him was the beginning of the end for our marriage."

Celia detected a hint of sadness in Betty's voice, as if a part of her had died with that decision.

"The kids had grown up and were making their own decisions. We had no glue left to hold us together except our public lives. So we kept it together for the cameras. I must say during those years of pretense, I learned a lot about manipulating the media and controlling your narrative. It's a very valuable skill, so I guess there's a silver lining in all of this," Betty said with a short giggle.

"Did this rift make your children take sides?" she asked.

Betty thought about it for a moment. "I wouldn't say that. I think Tony and Isabella aligned themselves according to their personalities. Tony doesn't mind being decisive and aspires to be the man of a house someday, so naturally he's taking his father's side. We bond, of course, but I know where he can be swayed. Isabella is a fence-sitter, a clever one at that. Sometimes this reality worked in my favor, sometimes it didn't. I still love them both because, we're all flawed humans at the end of the day," she said.

Celia was intrigued listening to this as it confirmed her earlier assessments. But it was time to pull the trigger.

"What brought you and Liam together?" she asked, going for the tamer version of the obvious question.

"You're quite diplomatic," Betty said with a grin, "He was ambitious just like me. He sees the big picture."

"Sees?"

"Yes, my use of that tense is deliberate because we're still seeing each other. We're partners, if you want to call it that."

As much as Betty was confident, Celia wasn't so sure about Liam's loyalty to her.

"What happened when Caleb found out you were also having an affair?"

"He threw a fit and then we officially split. Weeks later, I asked for a divorce. I learned a lot about him during that process. He came up with a lot of schemes to prevent him from losing out in the property split. But like I said, he never thought of the big picture. That's why he ended up with the short end of the stick," Betty said with finality.

Celia's suspicions were confirmed. Caleb's claim that he had moved on wasn't true. He still had unfinished business with Betty.

"Thank you for the chat," Celia said.

Betty smiled. "I always have time for a cautionary tale."

* * *

CELIA DECIDED to take a walk to the park. It was a sunny weekday, and not many people were about. She enjoyed taking a stroll there once in a while when she needed to think.

Tony was erratic in his behavior and what he was letting on, but it was clear he had a connection with his father Caleb that he didn't want his mother to know too much about. Was he working for his father and trying to find a weakness that his father could exploit? Did he know more about Mary's death than he was letting on?

What was Liam's involvement in this whole thing? As much as Betty loved him, he had a shady side that meant Betty wasn't being wise, placing a lot of trust in him. He also had the network needed to offload the sculpture once it was taken.

It had become clear that Betty had more skeletons in her closet other than the fact she was possibly the cause of the divorce. Celia was convinced now that those skeletons were responsible for whatever happened that night. Celia knew Isabella lied to her about not having an apartment, but what else was she lying about? Also, was she trying to manipulate the investigation? Was Bill able to see through her wiles?

What if the murder and the robbery of the art piece were not connected? What if none of these people were the killer?

She sighed. She had established a lot of truths and lies in these relationships, but she didn't seem closer to solving the murder and robbery. What was she missing? The one thing that she hadn't explored in-depth was the sculpture. The key still lay with the sculpture. She really needed to talk to Bill. She not only missed their conversations, but she needed to run her theories by him. His experienced detective mind might help her past her blind spots.

Celia took out her phone and dialed his number. The phone rang.

"Bill's phone," a female voice filtered through the earpiece to Celia's ear. She froze.

Why was Isabella answering his phone?

"Is that you, Isabella?"

"Oh, hey Celia. Sorry, Bill is driving at the moment. Can I take a message?" Isabella asked.

"He's driving? Driving to where?"

"Oh. We just came from the police station, so he's dropping me at my place. He says he'll call you once he gets there in around twenty minutes. That's okay with you?"

Celia went quiet. Her throat tightened, and she didn't know what to say.

"Celia?"

Celia lowered the phone and cut the call. A tear rolled down her left cheek as she walked to the nearest park bench. She slowly sat on it and watched two gray ducks swim in the small park pond.

As much as she hated to admit it, her insecurity was justified.

She bit her lower lip, hating the fact that she had to cast out another potential partner from her life.

"Toughen up, Cece. We've got a case to solve," she told herself. She would find a way.

17

As she sat in her office, Celia stirred a fresh pot of coffee as she stared at the computer screen.

Betty had told her about why it was important to her family, but Celia didn't know much about the stolen sculpture. Looking it up online didn't reveal a great deal other than confirming it was called the Imvunulo sculpture, after the Zulu dance that was done to show off the attire of Zulu men and women. The reference images she saw were of Betty's piece as it was the only one in existence. She was about to log off when she came across a blog that made her curious.

It claimed that there were supposed to be two, and not one Imvunulo sculpture. The second sculpture had gone missing decades ago, but the blog claimed it had resurfaced with an anonymous owner. This baffled Celia, because one dancer performed the dance at a time, not two. Therefore, it made sense that only one piece existed.

The possibility intrigued her. The story of their separation and reunification alone was worth six figures. If someone had already found the missing one, it would motivate the thieves to steal Betty's sculpture. As much as it sounded outlandish, she couldn't dismiss it outright. Getting both would mean double or even triple the cash the single sculpture could fetch. It was worth exploring and eliminating if it wasn't true.

Celia had just stumbled on a strong motive. She found herself rocking in the chair with excitement at the prospect. She was tempted to call Bill and ask for help in exploring this possibility. He might even have the resources through the police network to confirm if there were two sculptures. But she was still angry with him.

"Hey, Cece. Did you get a call from Eva?" Melanie asked as she abruptly opened the office door.

This startled Celia and she almost spilled her coffee. "The girl you sent to deliver the box of highlighters? No, why?"

"I hear they want another box, and we are short on those. How many more do you have?"

Celia smiled. She had thought selling them off in singles was the way to go, but this was the second order of a whole box she was getting.

"I'll need to drive home and bring some more from the store," she replied as she stood up.

"I think you should. In fact, bring around five boxes. Let them hang around just in case," Melanie suggested.

Celia didn't like a lot of inventory hanging around the parlor for security reasons, but Melanie's suggestion made sense.

"Five boxes it is!" Celia said as she grabbed her car keys.

She was just about to grab her phone when she saw it vibrating. A text message had just come in. She checked, thinking it might be Eva. Instead, it was Bill.

"Hey, Cece. Sorry I couldn't answer your call while on the road. Wanna catch up over some slap chips? Let me know."

She scowled, and Melanie noticed this.

"Someone annoy you?" Melanie asked.

"No one of importance," Celia said dismissively. Celia threw the phone into her bag and headed out.

* * *

WHEN SHE GOT BACK to the nail parlor with the cartons, she sent out a few more deliveries. As they approached the close of business, she had sold two more cartons. To catch a break, she went through the guest list from Betty's launch. Questions started popping into her head.

Who was at the party who might have known the actual value of the sculpture? Caleb, Liam, Betty, and possibly Tony and Isabella.

Other than the obvious names, was there someone else?

She went through the guest list again. Each entry had ticks next to them to confirm that they attended the event. After reaching the end of the list, her list of suspects was still the same. What was she missing?

She bit her lip as she mulled.

It was on her second run that she had a brainwave. She had been spending all this time looking at the names of those who attended the event. What about those who didn't attend?

She started going through the names without check marks, indicating they were absent. She listed five names. She grabbed Mary's notebook and searched through each page of handwritten notes. She wanted to see if any of the five had met Mary before the event. Ten minutes in, her heart leaped. Only one name popped up. Franco Duvall.

Mary had made an entry two days before the event, scribbled at the bottom corner of a page cluttered with notes.

'Meet Franco Duvall at 10 a.m. Discuss program.'

Who was Franco, and why had Mary met him to discuss the event program?

Celia stood up and paced with excitement. Why hadn't he attended the event? She had several other questions she needed to ask him, but she needed to find out who he was and where to find him.

Her phone vibrated. She looked at the screen and frowned. It was Bill. She ignored the call and went on pacing. She stopped in her tracks as an idea came to her. She rushed to her laptop, and changed the entry in her search bar. *Frank Duvall art.*

The results were still bland as far as information was concerned, but two entries came up that she hadn't seen before. She had found him. Franco C. Duvall. Wealthy art dealer. Her eyes glinted as she smiled.

She leaned back, satisfaction filling her so well that the renewed vibration of her phone couldn't catch her attention. Bill would have to wait. Could Franco have known what was going to happen that night? Was that why he stayed away, to eliminate himself from scrutiny as his people did the dirty work? He knew the event programme, so he could time his men to strike at the right time and he wouldn't be there. It was a smart move as it gave him a strong alibi, and none would be the wiser. It also meant the killer was still on the guest list. If she could find Franco, then he could lead her to the killer he sent.

The phone vibrated again. She ignored it.

Her focus was on finding Franco.

18

She sought more information on who Franco was.

A simple internet search showed he didn't have a large digital footprint to follow. From the few articles she found, she gathered he was a rich man who had several businesses in town. It was a little difficult to find articles that elaborated on the businesses he invested in. Then she found a short article that mentioned he ran a 'variety of businesses including loan sharking'.

She leaned back in her chair. From her recent experience with the dark side of loan sharking, she suspected it might be one of his highest earners. She also suspected he ran other underhand businesses. Loan sharking was a murky world, and she would need to be more cautious when dealing with him.

The fact he was involved in that line of business meant one of her recent acquaintances would know him. She took her phone and dialed.

"Hello Benji. How's it going?" Celia asked.

She had met Benji, a loan shark, after he came to collect cash that their nail parlor owed. After paying him off, Celia had kept his contact details just in case. She hadn't expected to call for his services this soon.

"I'm sharp. You need a loan?" Benji asked in his deep guttural voice.

"No cash. But I need a favor. Before I state what it is, how well do you know Franco Duvall?" she asked.

Benji paused briefly. "I know him. What do you want from him?"

Celia smiled. "I need to meet him. Can you make it happen?"

"You haven't answered my question."

Celia cleared her throat. "Well, I'm looking into something. A friend of mine had something valuable stolen from her. I was curious if he might have heard about it, since he was a guest but didn't show up."

"If he didn't show up, why would you tie it to him?"

"My friend met him before the robbery."

"Then let your friend do it."

"She was killed during the robbery."

"Oh."

Benji was quiet for a brief moment. "There's no way you're meeting him without my being there. He's not the kind of man you should meet," he said.

This sent a shiver down Celia's back, but she wasn't backing out now.

"Sure. Let me know when we can do it," she replied.

"I'll call you," he said, and then hung up.

* * *

"You'll let me do all the talking," Benji instructed as they walked up the dark steps to the third floor. He was a hulk of a man, so big he almost filled up the whole staircase with his frame. Celia followed close behind.

"I'm not here to set off fireworks," Celia replied.

"That may not be your intention, but it doesn't take much to mess things up with this guy," Benji said.

"Alright. You're the boss," she said.

They went one more floor up, which was the topmost. The

building wasn't an old one. On the ground and first floor was a lounge -, a place where those who love their drink, music and women would come to party. The third floor had business stalls and offices. Franco himself took up the fourth floor. It seemed Franco, who apparently owned the building, liked everyone to subscribe to his philosophy of fitness. He had built it with no provision for lifts, so you had to use the stairs each time to access a floor.

They walked through a short, carpeted corridor. At the end of it stood a large man in a dark suit. He stood in front of a brown oak door.

As they got closer, the man put forward his right hand. The two visitors stopped a metre away from him.

"Howzit? We're here to see the boss," Benji said.

"Who's talking?"

"Just tell him it's Benji. He'll know."

The man put up his left hand to reveal a small walkie-talkie nestled in his palm. He tried to keep his voice low but Celia found it futile. They were close enough to hear everything.

"Yeah, let them through," a voice crackled over the walkie-talkie.

"Roger that."

The man turned to his side and reached for a small screen console. He held up the palm of his hand and it was scanned instantly. The lock on the door opened with a large click sound.

The man pushed the door open.

"You may see him," he said.

"Thanks," Benji replied.

Celia and Benji found themselves standing on even thicker carpet. The place had cream walls. Brass was nearly everywhere: at the reception, on visitor seats, down corridor walls railings.

"Please come with me," a smartly dressed lady told them. She walked with vigor as she led them down the corridor. Celia felt watched and spotted CCTV cameras along the way. They passed two more security men before reaching the end of the corridor marked by another oak door. The lady scanned her palm on the console and the door unlocked.

They were ushered into a well-furnished office with oak from top to bottom. The only thing that wasn't oak was the thick red carpet they stood on, and the leather seats. Behind a large polished table sat the fifty-something year old athletic form of Franco Duvall. He had a graying beard and hair, freshly combed back despite his receding hairline. He wore a black half coat and trousers with a white shirt. He had taken off his tie, which lay on his desk, looking out of place as the only thing that wasn't well-arranged. He was alone.

"Benji!" Franco bellowed as he stood up, a broad smile oozing warmth as he approached them.

The two men embraced.

"It's been a minute, brah," Benji said.

"A long one too, brah. Howzit?" Franco countered. "We used to run into each other in good ways."

"Sometimes rotating in the same orbit causes problems," Benji replied.

"Wise words," Franco said as he laid his eyes on Celia.

"This is Celia, a friend of mine. She has a unique problem that I feel we can help her solve," Benji said.

Franco shook her hand. "Welcome to my lair. Please, have a seat," he offered.

The two visitors settled into low leather seats as Franco went back to his large leather armchair. Although she couldn't see them, Celia detected the faint, musk smell of cigars.

"How may I assist you?" Franco asked.

"We're here because of the Imvunulo sculpture," Benji said.

Franco raised an eyebrow and leaned back. "The one that was taken from Betty's place? A pity. Along with the other tragedy. Sometimes I'm grateful I don't attend some of these events. You just never know," he replied.

Celia frowned at his reply, as she felt it showed a self-righteousness he didn't deserve.

"Heard anything about it on the streets?" Benji asked.

Franco rubbed the back of his neck and then shook his head. "Nah. Nothing that you don't know."

Celia clenched her fists, because she could tell from his body language that he was lying.

"Why didn't you attend the event?" she asked.

Benji shot her a look, which she could see by the corner of her eye but ignored it.

Franco grunted. "Like I said, I did it because you never know with these things. I don't need a spotlight on me right now," he replied.

"Or maybe you knew something would happen?" Celia posed.

Franco's eyes reddened. "You speculate boldly," he said to her, his intense gaze meeting hers.

"It was actually a question," she clarified.

"Did I know what was going to happen that night? No. Have I heard of something possibly related to it? Perhaps."

Celia's ear pricked. "What have you heard?" she asked.

Franco leaned forward. "I heard rumors there's a second piece."

"Go on," Celia urged, "Someone told you they have the other one?"

Franco nodded. "He wanted me to buy it, but I held off on it. As I said, I didn't want a spotlight on me at the time."

Celia's eyebrows furrowed. "At the time?"

"There may have been a follow up proposition made," Franco replied.

"And suddenly your concerns are thrown out the window?" Celia asked.

Franco wore a sly grin. "There is no such thing as morals in business. Only self-interest, deals and profits."

Celia and Benji exchanged glances.

"Are you going along with this?" she asked.

"I think that's none of your business," Franco replied. He leaned back and turned his gaze to Benji. Benji stood up.

"Thanks for hearing us out, Franco. We'll leave you to it," Benji said.

"But..." Celia began, but Benji held up his right hand to silence her.

"It's done. Let's go."

"Good chat as always Benji. Let's game and deal one of these days," Franco said.

"I'll keep it in mind, my friend," Benji replied.

As Celia and Benji walked down the stairs, she was agitated.

"Why did you cut me off?" she asked.

"I told you to let me do all the talking!" he said.

"But we were getting nowhere with it!"

He stopped abruptly and grabbed her shoulders. She could feel the power in his grip.

"If you push him too far, he doesn't forget. And you don't want someone like that coming after you. Even I can't protect you."

"Why not?"

"Because it's going to be settled between the two of you. That's the way it is."

As they got into Benji's SUV, Celia exhaled.

"Tell me something, when you used to do deals with him, where would you meet?"

Benji thought about this for a moment. "Mostly at casino poker rooms," he replied.

"Why there?"

Benji shrugged. "I wondered the same thing. But he always said that's the only place he liked doing deals."

Celia's eyes glistened. "I think we need to find the next poker tournament in Sunny Cove. That's where the sculpture deal will be happening and we have to be there, Benji," she said with conviction.

19

"Where would you meet him?" Celia asked Benji as he drove.

"I only met him thrice. Like I said, Franco has an odd way of doing this kind of thing. He never strikes deals in offices. If you want to meet him, you do it at the casino. Plus, it was always after gambling on the poker table," Benji replied.

"He would make you play?"

Benji shook his head. "Maybe others, not me. I have no interest in poker, but he loves it. So he would play the game as I watch. Then once he gets eliminated, we would meet."

"Wait. So he wouldn't win any of those games?"

"He won none. He makes small bets at tables, then usually gets eliminated in the early rounds."

Celia furrowed her brows. "Why would he love the game when he never wins?"

Benji shrugged. "Gambling is a strange thing. I didn't mind watching though."

"Where would he take you?"

"We would go to an adjacent room and make the deal."

Celia nodded slowly as she digested the information. Franco saw deals as gambles, and the setting set the mood for this. She knew there was a small but growing gambling community in Sunshine Cove. The three casinos open were run by hotels, but she needed to find out which ones hosted poker tournaments.

"Where do we look?" she asked.

"They used to have poker rooms at some hotel near the harbor, but they shut it down. I met him there twice. These days the poker rooms are at the Leafy Sands," Benji replied.

Celia smiled as she stared out the window. She was no stranger to the Leafy Sands hotel. It was time to revisit the place.

"Could we stop over at the mall?" Celia asked.

"Why?"

"There's a small gift I need to get for an old friend," she replied.

* * *

As CELIA WALKED through the lobby of the Leafy Sands towards the reception, she felt like she was going back in time. The set up still looked the same as it had close to a decade ago when she first walked in there fresh out of college.

At the time she was looking for a job in the make-up department at a television station, but she hadn't gotten leads yet. Sunshine Cove was smaller in those days, so such opportunities were rare. She later had to move to Johannesburg to secure her first TV gig. But before she figured that out, she worked at the Leafy Sands hotel as a server at the hotel, before being moved to the casino. That's where she truly cut her teeth. Working as a server was a tough job. She had to wear short outfits and walk in heels for ten hours a day, smiling at gamblers as well as spectators. She remembered days when temperatures would drop, and she would suggest coffee or tea to clients instead of alcohol so that she could carry something warm in her hands.

She wanted to work her way up and started learning how to be a dealer. She had shadowed a pro for a few weeks after her shifts before she decided she would enroll for the six-week course. It started out well, but a week later the call from Jo'burg came in. She dropped the course and left town to pursue her dreams. Although they were still friends, she hadn't seen the Manager, Davie Sanders, for several months. One of the receptionists led her to his office.

"You don't seem to age," Davie joked as he walked up to her with a broad smile.

"Is that supposed to be some form of flattery?" Celia asked as they embraced.

He had visibly added more girth, and it made him look shorter than he really was. He had also let his beard grow fuller, giving you the impression he was a younger version of Santa Claus without the red costume.

"It's been a long time. What brings you here?" Davie asked.

"I wanted to say hello and see how things are going," Celia replied.

"We're still running, haven't slowed down yet," he replied.

"I wouldn't want it any other way. You gave me a chance to grow and I'm grateful for it. Actually, that's one of the reasons I'm here," she said as she handed him a small box.

"You bring gifts as usual. No cookies this time?" Davie said.

"It was a little short notice, so I came up with the next best thing," she replied.

Davie put the box aside without opening it.

"In that case, I'll open it when you're gone in case I'm disappointed," he replied.

They both laughed.

"How are things at the casino?" she asked.

"While others are closing their rooms, we're getting good traffic. It's been good so far. Why? Finally want to be a dealer?"

Celia chuckled.

"Not really, but I wouldn't mind being in the room to watch and learn a little more. Just to refresh the memory," she replied. Davie narrowed his eyes.

"You don't look like you need a career change. So what's this about?"

"I need to meet someone, and I've got a feeling he'll be at the tournament this weekend. All I need you to do is allow me to watch things and if he comes around, I'll be able to meet him."

Davie shook his head.

"Who's this person?"

"Sorry, I can't tell you."

"Then that's a little tricky for me. You already know watching as a spectator is free," he said.

Celia shook her head. The spectator sections were elevated above the playing tables, and this would hinder her from being able to follow Franco if he made a move. She needed to be closer.

"Dave, I would never try something fishy in your place. I'm not looking to play or place bets. Just to talk to him. He's a little slippery to get, just like many chronic gamblers. This is my chance to reach out to him."

"So, it's someone with a problem?"

"Yes, you could say that."

Davie stroked his beard as he gave it some thought.

"Alright. Then just turn up and wait to see if he shows up," he said.

Celia cleared her throat. "Is it possible to get a door pass too? It would be great to just blend in with the staff," she said.

"You're pushing your luck here, Celia," he said.

"I know it's a huge favor. But I have to look a little official for this. You know me. Have I ever let you down?" she asked.

"You let me down when you left for Jo'burg," he replied.

She half-smiled, while also looking at him with puppy eyes. Davie held her gaze, as if looking for any sign of deceit.

"I'm a little short on game supervisors. The job is to simply look around the room, that's all. I might need one for a night or two during the tournament," he said with a cheeky grin.

Celia smiled, "I'm in."

20

Two nights later, Celia walked up to the Leafy Sands Hotel Poker room. It was ten-thirty, and she had left her two sons at her mother's house for the night. She wore a white shirt, a black half coat, as well as black trousers and shoes. Her outfit was slightly different from that of the staff, who wore a similar outfit but with red highlights. She liked it because it helped her blend in.

She had put her badge pass in her trouser pocket just in case she needed it.

Before the first day, she had kept checking in with Davie, hoping to find out which players had placed buy-ins for the Saturday poker tournament. Players signed up using their initials, and only a few had done that in advance. None of the initials fit Franco's. By Friday evening she knew she would have to wait for him on the material day.

When she got to the entrance of the poker room, she found a small group of about fifty people made up of some players and spectators, milled outside making conversation. She made her way to the whiteboard standing just outside the door. She saw the initials of the signed-up players for each table. She noted that two initials at tables one and three matched Franco's. She would be keeping a close eye on those.

Celia walked into the poker room. It was different from the one she had worked in years ago, and much better. It had red floor carpeting, with green tables that were lined with wooden edges. The room housed four tables, and she figured Franco would be on one of them.

She saw four dealers on standby at each table. At one corner of the room stood the Shift Manager, who ensured games ran as they should. She walked over to him.

"Hi. I'm Celia, sent here by Davie to look into things. How's your day going?"

The man half-smiled, his eyes wary.

"I'm Nelson. Shift manager. What exactly will you be doing again?"

"Just observing on behalf of Davie," she replied, taking out her badge pass, labeled 'supervisor.'

Nelson studied it for a short while, before lifting his head and nodding in approval.

"Welcome to my room, Celia. You have a spot you would like to take?"

"I think I can stand next to you, if that's fine with you?" she suggested.

"That's okay. I don't have an extra seat though," he replied.

"Don't worry; I've been on my feet all night before. I'll be fine," she replied with a smile.

The games were starting at half-past eleven. Franco walked in five minutes before it started. He had an unlit cigar propped in his teeth, and wore a leather jacket, khaki shirt and jeans. He was attempting to dress down, but he still looked polished, Celia thought.

He settled at table three without noticing her, and she kept her eye on him from then on. The games started. As Benji had indicated, Franco didn't last long. He went all in during the third round of betting, something that you didn't usually do unless you had a strong hand. But Franco knew he didn't, yet took the risk. Inevitably, he was eliminated. He wasn't dramatic about the loss. He simply adjusted the cigar in his mouth, got up and walked out.

"I'll be right back," Celia said to the shift manager.

She walked out and saw Franco going down the stairs. On the

lower floor were the slot machines. Franco walked in between them, slowly looking to his left and right and he walked by. Was he looking for someone, she wondered?

At the end of the line of machines was an empty one, which Franco promptly sat in. Celia was some distance back, so couldn't see him clearly. She couldn't get too close either, in case he spotted her. So she stopped and waited. She pretended to oversee one gambler's game as they played the slot machines. She then spotted Franco getting up. Two other men in the adjacent slot machines promptly followed him. They walked towards the back of the room. Celia stepped up her pace as she sought to catch up with them. At the same time, she took out her phone and dialed.

"We're heading to the back, at the other end of the slot machines," she said.

Franco and the men disappeared through a door that was guarded by a security man. Celia slowed down. Shortly afterwards, Benji appeared behind her.

"Where are they?" he asked, looking around.

"Follow me," she replied.

They walked up to the door. The security man stopped them.

"You need authorization to pass," he said.

Celia took out her pass, which he examined, then returned to her.

"Sorry, Miss Celia," he said as he opened the door. She stepped in, but the man blocked off Benji.

"He's with me," she said.

"He needs his own authorization."

"Are you sure you want me to call Davie and tell him you're harassing your fellow employee and a potential client?"

The security guy grunted and stepped to the side.

"Thank you," Celia said as Benji stepped in.

They walked down a long, well-lit corridor that turned left. When they made the turn, it led them to a door at the far end. When they opened it, they emerged at the rear of the casino. It was dark, with lights from the overhead casino rooms adding illumination to the place. They could see some large trash bins hidden by the shadows.

Two hundred meters to their right was what looked like a large store. They could see Franco and the two men arriving at the store entrance. Parked outside the store was a dark van.

"We need to get closer," Celia said.

"It's your turn to follow me. Keep to the shadows," Benji whispered as he started inching forward.

She followed him closely.

They got as close as eighty meters away, hiding behind a pile of discarded wooden crates. Through small gaps in the pile, they followed the proceedings. Franco stood with his legs apart, flanked by the two men on each side. He had lit the cigar and was smoking it.

"Are you going to do it or not?" Franco asked, sounding agitated.

Celia, curious about his irritation, tilted her neck to get a better look.

She saw the people Franco was addressing, two men donning African traditional masks made out of plastic. She found this odd. Who comes to a meeting in masks?

"This is how we want to do the deal," the Leading Masked Man replied.

Franco shook his head.

"That's not how I work," he said, turning to leave.

"Hold on!" the masked man replied.

Franco turned back to him.

The Leading Masked Man slowly started taking off his mask. Celia held her breath.

21

He stopped halfway.

"If I take this off, you have to add a hundred thousand rand to the rice," the Leading Man said.

Franco snorted. "What for?"

"For the risk I'm taking. Both these pieces will get you upwards of two million rand. Sounds fair to me," the Leading Man replied.

Franco glanced at each of his henchmen, as if seeking their approval.

"Come on. Make him take it off," she whispered as she wiped her brow.

"I said both masks off," Franco said.

The Leading Man shook his head. "We keep both. My partner doesn't need to do so. You're negotiating with me," he insisted.

"So, what is he here for?" Franco asked.

"He's my handyman. He lugs around what I tell him to lug around."

There was a pause as both men sized each other.

"Alright, where is it?" Franco finally asked.

The Leading Man motioned to his partner, who went to the back of the van. He walked back carrying a weight wrapped in a cloth.

When he got to the Leading Man, he placed it on the ground and unwrapped it.

It was the Imvunulo sculpture, showing a single dancer frozen in the middle of a move. It glowed when streaks of light struck it.

"Bring it closer," Franco said.

"I need to see what you have first," the Leading Man replied.

Franco turned to one of his men. He walked off to the right, rounding the building. Moments later he returned carrying a suitcase. Behind him was another man carrying the second sculpture.

Celia gasped. "It actually exists," she said.

The Leading Man moved closer to inspect the second sculpture as Franco stepped forward to check the first. They both inspected each other's sculptures. Satisfied, they stood eye to eye.

"How much would you sell both for once they are yours?" he asked.

"You should take the suitcase and let me worry about what I make of it," Franco replied.

The suitcase was handed to the Leading Man, who opened it to check. The other masked man came closer and shone a torch on its contents.

Celia couldn't tell, but she assumed there was a large amount of cash in it. She moved forward. She lost, then regained her balance, bumping into a crate. This triggered two loose crates on top of the pile to start teetering.

"Don't you dare," Celia hissed as if the crates could hear her.

The Leading Man shook Franco's hand. "It looks like it's all there. Shall we…"

He stopped talking as the sound of one of the crates, smashing into the ground, interrupted their conversation. Celia and Benji froze and held their breaths as they watched Franco, the Leading Man and their men turn toward them.

Franco's henchmen took out their guns.

"Did you come with friends?" Franco asked.

"You tell me. That's the same direction you came from," the Leading Man replied.

The two men with guns pointed them towards the pile of crates.

"Come out of there before we come for you," Franco shouted.

Celia and Benji glanced at each other. Benji shook his head. They were staying put.

"Did you hear me?" Franco asked again.

Silence.

"Suit yourself," Franco said as he motioned his men to walk to the pile, "They're coming for you."

Celia started trembling as the men came closer.

"What do we do?" she asked in a shaky whisper.

"Wait," Benji replied. He was crouched, ready to pounce on the first man to appear.

As the footsteps reached them, the place was suddenly flooded with a blinding light. Celia closed her eyes. Then she heard the sounds.

"This is the police! Put down your weapons and put your hands up!" a voice bellowed over a megaphone.

Celia tried to open her eyes. Then the gunshots began, and she threw herself on the ground under a hail of bullets.

2 2

When the shots stopped, Celia kept hugging the ground, terrified. She heard running footsteps all around her but didn't dare move. Then someone put a hand to her shoulder.

"Celia, you can to get up now. It's over," Benji said. He slowly helped her sit upright. "Are you hurt?"

She shook her head. "What on earth happened?" she asked.

"The cops took them out," he replied.

"What do you mean took them out?" she asked.

He then pointed behind him, and she caught a glimpse of the body of one of Franco's henchmen.

"Everybody?" she asked.

"Not everybody," another voice said. It was from the approaching Detective Bill.

Celia didn't say a word.

"Are you okay?" Bill asked.

"She's fine. Just a little shaken," Benji replied.

Bill gave him a cursory glance, then turned back to her.

"What about Franco? Who were the masked men?" she asked.

"We've arrested Franco. For the masked men, maybe you need to see them for yourself," Bill said.

Celia's eyes widened.

"Did he force you down here? Because you know you shouldn't have been here," he said, giving Benji a disapproving look.

Celia forced a smile. "Doing this was my plan. The question is, how did you find us?"

Bill crossed his hands. "Well, considering you weren't answering your phone, I had to track you down," he said.

Celia didn't know if she was relieved, offended or attracted to him by this revelation. It felt like all three at once.

"Just get me somewhere I can rest, will you, Benji?"

"Sure," Benji said as he helped her to her feet and they walked past the perturbed Bill.

Later, she sat at the back of an ambulance, sipping bottled water after surprising paramedics with how dehydrated she was. From where she was, she could see the buzzing crime scene in front of her. Several police cars bathed the scene with flashing lights. The two henchmen's bodies were still on the scene, covered up with white cloths as the scene was processed. Yellow tape cordoned off the area and detectives were taking all sorts of forensic and material evidence they could find.

The police had talked to Benji and Celia, who recounted how they had found themselves as witnesses to the chaos that ensued. Benji left afterwards, while Celia hung around as the paramedics attended to her for mild shock.

"How are you feeling now?" the paramedic asked.

"Like hundreds," Celia replied with a smile.

"Good, because I think he's coming to get you," the paramedic said. Celia followed his gaze and saw Bill approaching with two coffees in hand.

"I thought you might be feeling some of the night chill and got you a cup," Bill said as he extended one of the cups toward her.

Celia took it.

"I hope you secured the two sculptures," she said.

"It's already boxed up and ready for the evidence room. Are you sure they are worth one and a half million rand?" he asked.

"On the international market, which is where Franco would be taking them, you could fetch much more than that. The story of those two will raise its value," she replied.

"I can see the motivation to steal them."

"Who are the masked men?"

"Look behind me, they should be coming up any moment now," he said.

Sure enough, two familiar heads flanked by two policemen were marched towards two waiting police cars.

Celia's jaw dropped. She saw the forlorn faces of Caleb Khoza and his son Tony. They were placed in the back of separate police cars, which sped off immediately with blaring sirens.

Celia sat silently, trying to digest the sight she had witnessed.

"They made it hard to catch them," she whispered.

"It's hard to catch evil sometimes," Bill replied.

"I bet they stole it together. Tony carried it with Liam, so you should send officers that way. About the murder, I'm not sure who did that. Frankly, that's the part that disturbs me the most in all of this," she said.

"None of them have talked. But I'm sure once I get into a room with them at the station, we'll get to the bottom of it," Bill remarked. "You're not drinking that?"

Celia looked down at the cup of coffee she was holding in between the palms of her hands.

"The coffee is giving me the heat I need right where it is," she replied.

Bill glanced at the paramedic. "Could you give us a minute?"

The paramedic nodded and walked away to his colleague. Bill moved closer.

"Before I head out, I wanted to apologize. I know you're angry about the whole Isabella investigation I was doing," he said.

"It looked to be much more than an investigation to me," Celia replied.

"It was meant to look natural."

"Natural? Flirting with a suspect is natural?"

"Lowering her guard. Learning her weaknesses. Playing along – with boundaries of course. That's all I was doing," he replied. "I didn't mean to disrespect you."

Celia smirked. "Too late for that, don't you think?"

Bill sighed.

"Was it worth it? Did you get the leads you hoped for?" she continued.

"In hindsight, it wasn't one of my finest ideas," he conceded.

Celia shook her head. "It's unbelievable to me as well. So I'll let it sit with you for a while," she replied.

"What's that supposed to mean?" he asked.

Celia gave him an intense stare.

"It means you need to reflect on what you really want out of our interaction. Because I know what I want and what I don't want. And what you did, is definitely not welcome here," she replied.

They held that gaze for a few more seconds, before Bill looked away.

"Fair enough," he said as he turned to leave.

"But please, do me one favor: let me know who confesses," she said.

Bill kept walking, and lifted his right hand to give a thumbs up.

23

"I'm not ready for this," Celia said.

Celia was seated at her office desk, her head propped by her hands.

"The whole setup is great, and we already got a few clients buying stuff. We're ready for you," Melanie said.

She was wearing a bright yellow t-shirt, which was part of the renewed marketing effort.

Celia hadn't worn hers yet. It lay folded on the table, right next to the laptop she was using.

"I hear you. I'll be down in a minute. I just needed a moment alone, that's all," Celia replied.

Just then, her mother Audrey, also in a yellow tee, also walked in and stood next to Melanie.

"Cece, we're waiting for you. Are you coming down?" Audrey asked.

Celia forced a smile. "Yeah, Ma, I'm coming. Why are you guys acting up?"

"We're acting up? No, I think you're talking about yourself. Today is the first day of the sales weekend and our founder is not here? No way. We've got some highlighters to sell!" Audrey said animatedly.

Celia slowly stood up and reached for the t-shirt. She held it reluctantly.

"Caleb did it," Celia said, feeling the t-shirt in her hands.

"What?" Audrey asked. Celia looked up at her.

"I just got off the phone with Bill. Caleb confessed to killing Mary," Celia said.

Audrey froze. "But how? We saw him at the event, right?"

"He was there moments before. His son Tony covered for him. Caleb waited for Mary to step out as she answered a phone call and followed her. He lured her to the gazebo under the pretext he had something important to tell her. He then strangled her," Celia said.

"But why?"

"He claims he only wanted to make her pass out so that a search would begin. He wanted to create a panic. It gave him and Tony the chance to steal the sculpture. But I know he wanted to kill her. He wouldn't get away with it if she lived," she replied.

"But how did he get back to the house so fast?" Melanie asked.

"You forget Caleb used to live there before the divorce. He helped design the house, so he knows it inside out. An under-used side door exists that leads to the washrooms. After killing her, he used it to get back into the house as everyone else went round the long way to reach the gazebo."

The three women stood in silence, digesting the news.

"I can see why your shoulders are drooping," Audrey said as she walked over to Celia.

They embraced.

"Not a great way to start the most important sales weekend of my career, huh?" Celia said.

"Look on the bright side. They caught him," Audrey said with a smile.

"I still don't get it. What led him to this? Did he hate his wife this much?" Melanie asked, frowning.

Celia sighed.

"He says it's because of a gambling debt he has. But I think he's been bitter since the divorce, and he was plotting how to hurt Betty in a big way. This was his revenge," Celia explained.

"So he manipulated his son to hurt her," Melanie said.

"Exactly. Got the son into a huge case he doesn't need. But his mother is trying to get him out."

"Can she do that?"

"Eish, where are the lady bosses of this place?" a loud female voice shouted.

They all turned round to see the smiling face of Mrs. Owens. She had applied a little too much makeup, and as a result looked much younger than usual.

"I'm waiting to start my photo sessions with the models. Are you coming?" she exclaimed.

"Sure, we're coming!" Celia replied.

Mrs. Owens beamed. "Great! Just checking. Oh, and I hope we've got some snacks around. I can see myself needing an energy boost in about an hour," she said with a wink, before heading back down the stairs.

Celia whispered to her mother, "Don't tell her just yet."

She knew if Mrs. Owens caught wind of the news, it would definitely affect the day's event.

"Don't worry about it. This and the thing you're having with the detective are safe with me," Audrey said.

Celia's eyes widened.

"Yes, I've known about it. You know how I feel about you dating people in the disciplined forces. I don't want you to go through another Trevor season again," Audrey continued.

Celia smiled as a tear rolled down her cheek.

"You don't have to worry about that. I've taken a little break from it all," she said.

"Are you sure? Because I've noticed how you pick his phone calls and read his texts," Audrey teased.

"I'm not falling in love with him," Celia said, smiling as she held up the t-shirt. "Now if you don't mind, I'm going to slap this on and join you in a moment."

"You don't have to. You're the best seller I know, even without the t-shirt. Let's go sell the hell out of this thing," Melanie said.

Celia smiled. "I like the sound of that. Let's do this," she said.

The three women marched out together, ready to take on whatever the day would throw at them.

The End

CHRISTMAS CAROLS AND LIPSTICK PERILS

A SUNSHINE COVE COZY MYSTERY

ABOUT CHRISTMAS CAROLS AND LIPSTICK PERILS

Released: December 2020
Series: Book 5 – Sunshine Cove Cozy Mystery Series
Standalone: Yes
Cliff-hanger: No

Everybody's looking forward to Christmas but not Celia.

Why?

Because she's been making promises all year that she can't seem to keep.

Promises to take her young children on a luxurious holiday.

Promises to her clients to make them look like a million bucks over the holiday season.

Promises to a friend to sing Christmas carols.

Celia knows if she can work a bit harder, maybe, just maybe, she'll be able to fulfil her promises.

She's in for a shock when a client dies at one of the corporate functions she's a part of. The incident seems coincidental until someone else dies at another corporate function. It seems Celia is the common denominator at both murder scenes.

Celia's blood pressure goes through the roof when she's identified as a person of interest by the police. She feels the world closing in on her and wonders if there's anyway out.

Christmas is meant to be the most wonderful time of the year but it seems Celia's living in her worst nightmare. Will she piece the clues that'll lead her to the murderer or become the killer's next victim?

1

Although there were exceptions, Celia Dube had always considered most Black Friday offers to be a well-marketed swindle. However, on a bright December morning, as she walked side by side with her mother, she expressed her reservations. Her mother wasn't impressed.

"You can't be like this. This is not how you get into the Christmas season," Audrey Matinise said to her as she fiddled with the rose tucked above her ear. Dressed in a light blouse, sunglasses balanced on her forehead, long denim shorts, and sandals, her mother was already in holiday mode. A wide-brimmed sunhat would complete the look, Celia thought.

Celia couldn't blame her. The weeks leading up to December always had carnival weather: the sun shone round the clock and flowers bloomed in colorful celebration. Celia herself wore a plain green t-shirt, jeans, and sneakers, and wished she had dressed down some more. For her, the warmth of the sun's rays on the skin was a natural tonic. They were at the newly opened supermarket in Sunshine Cove, the largest in the town. It was a fancy place, mirroring those in the big cities with wide aisles, numerous goods, brightly lit interiors, and polished floors. The aisles were filling up with other shoppers every minute.

"You know what I'm saying is true, Ma," Celia replied. "They're pretty good at making you feel good about it."

"But aren't you supposed to feel good when buying things? It's a beautiful day, in a beautiful new store, and I plucked a beautiful flower and added it to my beautiful self. Just to enjoy this shopping experience. Isn't that something nice?" Audrey said.

Celia shrugged. She wasn't surprised by her mother's reaction. It was the manifestation of a contradiction in her personality. Her mother was a famed frugal spender for most of the year. Celia had seen her in action from her childhood and could certify that her mother was a master who could teach classes on the subject. However, when Christmas approached, she loosened her stance and became a champion of commercialism.

"Each year you create a new speech about this. You should write poetry," Celia said as she pushed the half-full trolley down the aisle.

"These Ebenezer Scrooge vibes you've got made us miss so many offers during Black Friday. Now, you should let it go. We're not going to miss the good Christmas offers," Audrey replied. As if in silent support of her, several posters announcing discounts on products were on display everywhere they turned.

An instrumental version of *Jingle Bells* played from overhead speakers. The relentless marketing drive compelling shoppers to part with their hard-earned cash impressed Celia. As a beauty consultant and make-up distributor, Celia knew the tricks of selling. She wasn't falling for the ruse because she had other pressing needs.

"They're all offers for Christmas decorations. We've got a lot of those from last year!" Celia exclaimed.

Audrey threw her hands up dramatically. "Remember, the Christmas tree is going to be at my place this year. I need fresh decorations."

"Ma, we haven't voted yet. You know we've got to vote and decide which of our houses will put up the tree."

Audrey grunted in disapproval. "Maybe we should change that

rule. Christmas trees shouldn't be held hostage by the flip of a coin. We should simply rotate every year."

"Where's the fun in rotating? They flip coins in soccer all the time before a game starts. I mean, you said Trevor was a genius when he came up with the coin toss vote, remember?" Celia said.

In past years, Celia had found it nearly impossible to bring up the name of her late husband Trevor during Christmas. The pain of his sudden death while on military duty had been too hard to bear, especially with two young boys to raise. Now, she loved saying it with fondness, especially when it brought up such happy memories.

"He was a genius alright. However, you won't put me on a guilt trip with that. I won't be dishonoring Trevor by changing the rules a bit," Audrey said.

Celia chuckled. "Sounds like you're the real Ebenezer Scrooge in this scenario."

"And there they are - my two lovely angels!" a voice boomed behind them.

Audrey and Celia turned around to see the seventy-something-year-old Mrs. Christie Owens flanked by two other women her age. Each one had a small, empty shopping basket in their hands. They looked regal in their flowery dresses. Mrs. Owens tended to affect those around her with her love for flowers. Whether intentional or not, her influence showed in other women's clothes, which fascinated Celia.

"Christie!" Audrey exclaimed as she embraced Mrs. Owens. They had been family friends for years, and Audrey considered Mrs. Owens as the elder sister she never had.

"I can see you're also in the Christmas spirit," Mrs. Owens said as she also embraced Celia.

"Some of us are," Audrey said, shooting a stern look at Celia.

"Mrs. Owens, even you would have to agree with me that the Christmas buzz comes a little too early these days, right?" Celia asked.

Mrs. Owens frowned. "It's never too early for Christmas. Don't you go down that rabbit hole of indifference, my child. It doesn't end well," Mrs. Owens replied.

"What brings you here, Christie?" Audrey asked.

"Oh, shopping for treats for our fellow choir members. We've started rehearsals for this year's Christmas carol concert. We've been waiting for you to join us," Mrs. Owens said.

Audrey shook her head. "I'd love to, but we have other plans. Celia promised to take us on a little travel holiday."

Mrs. Owens beamed. "Oh, my! That's so sweet of you, my child. Appreciating your family like that."

"It's just a little trip, nothing too fancy," Celia said, rubbing the back of her neck.

"Nothing is too little. Don't try to be modest here. I'm sure the boys are excited."

"Oh, they already are. They keep talking about it every evening," Audrey quipped.

"Have you picked a holiday destination?" Mrs. Owens asked.

"I've got a few secret options. But I'm open to suggestions," Celia said, keen to move the conversation in another direction.

"Planning a surprise. Great! I think it's time I came for a visit, Audrey," Mrs. Owens said.

"Definitely. I'll be waiting for your call," Audrey replied.

Mrs. Owens gave a light nod as she and her entourage went on their way. Celia and Audrey continued down the aisle.

"You shouldn't have mentioned the holiday trip," Celia said, frowning slightly.

"Why not?"

"You know how Mrs. Owens can be when she gets hooked to an idea."

Audrey kept scanning the shelves. "You're the one who said you're open to options. She's going to go on a treasure hunt just for you."

Celia sighed. "I know. I'm not proud of it."

Audrey stopped walking and reached for something on the shelf. "Tough times don't last. Christmas lovers do. So, you're still against these lovely bulb lights?"

Resigned, Celia shook her head.

"That's the Christmas spirit!" Audrey remarked as she placed them in the basket.

Celia gave a half-smile. She wanted to finish shopping and then head to the beach to bask in the hot sun. She considered the mild burning sensation on her skin as a reminder that things could be worse.

She needed it because she was struggling to swallow a bitter pill. The holiday trip that her family was so excited about was unlikely to happen, and she was the only one who knew it.

2

Celia needed to catch up with business. After they finished shopping and had lunch, she went on her delivery run. She had a few Maven beauty products to deliver, which now came packed in Christmas-themed delivery bags from the head office. Celia arrived quickly at her first client's house.

Andrea Wester lived close to the beachfront where one was more likely to encounter throngs of tourists rather than car traffic. As Celia cruised through the streets packed with strolling holiday-goers, she guessed that more people were taking out their pending leave days before the year ended. However, she knew many international tourists had escaped their cold winters for Sunshine Cove's warmer climes.

Andrea's house sat on a one-acre compound and access to a private beach. She didn't have to worry much about bumping into the crowds, Celia mused.

Celia drove up to the tall red gate. She reached for a short, mounted console outside the gate and pressed a small button with her index finger.

"Who is it?" a female voice crackled from the small intercom speaker on the console.

"It's me. I've got your products here," Celia replied. She wondered why Andrea was asking for her identity, yet she could see the car from the camera mounted above the gate. Seconds later, the gate automatically opened and Celia drove in. The driveway was a short one. Nestled under the shade of the tall trees surrounding it, the two-story house was inviting. In front of it were an SUV and a sleek sedan.

Celia parked the car and walked up to the front door. She was three steps away when the door opened and a smiling Andrea appeared.

"You look dashing," Andrea said.

Celia smiled. "Are you trying to get a discount from me with that compliment?"

"Is that possible? It would help me during my trip to Dubai," Andrea replied. "Come in."

They walked down a short corridor and emerged in a living room with a sunken profile. People sat lower than the actual ground level. Celia found this creative and to her taste, although there was little chance of replicating it in her home.

"You're heading to Dubai for Christmas?" Celia asked.

"Yes. I've been meaning to do it for quite some time, actually," Andrea said.

"But are you going to enjoy it? I mean, I only know Dubai for the shopping malls, fancy buildings, and hotels. Sounds like a business destination rather than a holiday one."

Andrea laughed. "It's so much more than that. I'm especially looking forward to the Desert Safari. Also, a change of pace is always nice."

Celia nodded. For a moment, she flashed back to the holiday trips she'd taken with Trevor. They were always a blast. She wouldn't mind a change of pace either.

"How much would it cost to go there? The bare minimum, of course," Celia asked.

"Well, we're going for two weeks. I'm not sure about the exact figure, but it's over a hundred and fifty thousand rands."

Celia whistled. "That's… a lot," she said as she reached into the gift bag as she took out Andrea's package.

"I guess it is. You can get cheaper packages. It just depends on where you're going to stay and for how long. You plan to get out of town too?"

"It's something I'm working on. Let's see how it goes," Celia replied, hoping her smile masked her anxiety. She handed Andrea the package.

"Don't wait till everything's perfect. Life's too short," Andrea remarked as she opened the package.

Celia bit her lip. Life was short, but at that moment, her aspirations needed an urgent meeting with her reality.

An hour later, Celia got to the nail parlor. She met a sight she had grown to love.

Located on Main Street, Afrostar Nail Parlor was still getting used to the large volume of business it had been getting in recent weeks. Every workstation had a client, with the staff attending to at least two clients at a time. As she walked towards the back, Celia waved at Sarah Wena and Fidel Nzomo, their nail technicians, while they hurried around.

"Hello, Celia," Persha, the parlor manager said from behind the reception counter.

"Hey, Persha. Everything's good?"

"Everything's hundreds," she replied with a smile.

Celia loved the fact Persha adeptly handled the day-to-day running of the place. It helped her and her partner handle their other jobs. The fact that Persha addressed her by her first name was deliberate–no *Miss Dube* here. Communication lines needed to be free of haughty titles.

Celia climbed the short flight of stairs that led to the mezzanine office. Inside, she found Melanie Dawes hunched over her laptop. She was wearing a bright yellow sweater with a green decorated Christmas tree on its front. Celia raised her eyebrows as she concluded that even Melanie had caught the festive fever.

"I thought you'd be at the library today," Celia said.

"I was going to. But Carol told me she's going to take care of things," Melanie replied.

Celia took a seat at her desk. She frowned. "Carol?"

Melanie looked up from her screen. "Oh! I forgot to tell you. I got an assistant."

"Since when?" Celia asked.

"It's been two months now," Melanie replied.

"You kept this from me for two months?" Celia asked.

"Technically, I didn't. If you'd have dropped by, you would've met her," Melanie replied.

Celia smiled. Melanie had a point. Celia hadn't passed by the library for a long time now.

"I'll try to do that. I'm famished! Can we order some takeout?" Celia asked.

Melanie shook her head. "Not for me. I just had some salad," she replied. She then leaned forward with a sly grin. "What happened to the free lunch our handsome detective used to order for us?"

Celia shrugged. "Things change."

"Hmm. Ever since Benji helped you on the last case, I've not seen sparks flying between you and Bill. You want to talk about it?" Melanie prodded.

Celia scrolled through her phone. "You're being nosey today. What did you put in that salad?"

Melanie chuckled. "You're seriously not going to tell me anything?"

"Nope."

"Not even tomorrow?"

Celia put down her phone. "Look, whatever's going on between Bill and I is a little different now. That's all. I'm not going to talk about it because it's not a priority."

"As you wish, my dear friend. As you wish," Melanie replied.

Celia cleared her throat. "Tell me, how are we doing with the numbers?"

Melanie leaned back in her seat. "You mean the profits?"

Celia nodded.

"Well, they've been consistent since we broke even last month. So, week on week, we're doing well," she replied.

Celia twiddled her thumbs. "Would you say we've accumulated enough for me to take out some cash?"

Melanie's eyes narrowed. "What do you mean by taking out the cash?"

"You know, to pay ourselves better like we said we would when we bought the place," she replied.

Melanie shook her head. "The profits are good, but not that good. We need to keep it going for another six months before we talk of a reasonable margin to work with."

"Six months?"

"Yeah. It's tough growing a business, and the cash we have now is a good reserve in case something goes south. Besides, I've still got the library gig and you've got the beauty products gig to keep us going. Unless there's something that's come up?"

Celia shook her head. "No, it's fine."

Melanie leaned forward. "Cece, I can tell when something's eating you."

After a brief pause, Celia spoke. "I was due to take the family to Mauritius for Christmas. A lot of the cash for that was from my savings. We both know I used it to invest in this place. So, I'm very short right now."

"That's hectic. Why Mauritius?"

"New country. Warm, beautiful beaches. Affordable. I found some great deals. However, biggest of all, I was looking forward to this. It's supposed to be my first holiday trip with the boys in a long time. It hurts to think that I'm going to break their hearts."

Melanie sighed. "Wow. That's pressure, huh? We can do a loan or something, you know."

Celia shook her head. "Never. In my book, loans and holidays don't mix."

"So, what are you going to do?" Melanie asked.

Celia stared blankly at the ceiling. "If only robbing banks was allowed for certain situations. Doing something illegal doesn't sound so bad right now."

Melanie stared blankly at her friend, knowing Celia meant every word. "Are you willing to take that risk right now?"

Celia shook her head and stood up. She started pacing.

"Something different is on my mind. Maybe we should lease out a corner of our nail shop?" Celia suggested.

Melanie frowned. "To sell what?"

"Um, I don't know. Christmas decorations?"

Melanie shook her head. "*Haibo*, no way! You are now stretching it, Cece."

"Okay, what on earth should I do that makes me some good money in less than four weeks?"

Melanie tapped the top of the table with her pen. "How about you get a short-term make-up contract?"

"We live in a small town, Mel. There are no TV stations here that can give me that kind of contract," Celia replied.

"That's not what I mean. Many end year office parties are coming up in the next couple of weeks. I know some of them hire make-up artists for the day. Why not try those?"

Celia stared out the office window briefly and then started nodding slowly.

"You've got a point. They do take many pictures there and the female employees do like to have their make-up done. But companies are going to be closing in the next two weeks. I'll run out of time looking for those leads," Celia replied.

"Not if you work with Fezile Radebe," Melanie said.

Celia's eyes narrowed. "Fezile the photographer?"

"Yeah, he's the one. He's the most booked photographer in Sunshine Cove for those gigs. I'm sure you'll earn a pretty penny if you worked with him."

Celia shook her head.

"Why not?" Melanie asked.

"I just can't. Not with him."

"What's wrong with him?" Melanie asked.

"I didn't say there's anything wrong with him."

"You should call him. He's the lifeline you need," Melanie said.

Celia didn't agree with Melanie. The last time she worked with Fezile, things ended very badly.

Was it worth the trouble to tempt fate one more time?

3

"The Good Book says 'as a dog returns to its vomit, so does a fool return to his folly,'" Celia said. "Been there, done that. It won't work."

"You can use all the expressions in the world. All I know is that there's something you're not telling me," Melanie replied.

Celia turned to her. "Listen, we have some history. We're oil and water. We don't blend."

Melanie wore a cheeky smile. "What kind of history?"

"Not that kind of history. We worked on something some years ago and it didn't go well. I'll leave it at that," Celia replied.

"Well, it was some years ago. I assume both of you are at different stages in your careers," Melanie said. "I'd consider rebuilding that burnt bridge. The word on the street is that he's looking for a make-up person for his corporate shoots."

"Who told you this?"

"His current make-up person, Maria. She's in her last trimester and has eased off her schedule. He's been working with a few part-timers. None of them are as good as you, that's for sure. I can ask her to put in a word for you."

"You're serious?"

Melanie was already dialing her phone. "Watch me."

After a few minutes of conversation, Melanie hung up. "She's going to talk to him."

Melanie took a sticky note and scribbled on it. "Here's his number. Call him after half an hour." She held out the note to Celia, who hesitated briefly before taking it.

Half an hour later, Celia had a short phone conversation with Fezile. To her surprise, she managed to set up a meeting for later that evening. After getting more encouragement from Melanie, Celia left the office and headed for her mother's house. She arrived just in time for afternoon tea.

"You always come running when you know I'm making masala tea," Audrey remarked as soon as she walked in.

"That's a good thing, Ma. It means you make the best tea in town," Celia said.

"She's using my recipe, you know," Mrs. Owens bellowed as she strode in from the kitchen with a kettle.

Celia laughed. "I didn't expect to find you here, Mrs. Owens."

"I'm not a visitor, you know," Mrs. Owens quipped as she took a seat at the dinner table.

Celia's sons, John and James, having heard their mother's voice, rushed in from the rear garden and embraced her. They'd recently closed school, and Celia was happy that her mother was able to watch over them when she was working. The boys quickly took their seats at the table. Laid out before them were their mugs and a plate of rusks, so she knew they couldn't be kept waiting. Celia and her mother took their places.

"Who's going to say grace?" Mrs. Owens asked the boys. The two brothers glanced at each other and John took the responsibility. Celia and Audrey exchanged knowing looks as the young boy prayed with gusto.

As soon as he was done, the boys jumped for the rusks.

"Watch it!" Celia exclaimed, "If you drop a single one, you're not going to have more."

The boys slowed down, keen to make their happy hour last longer.

"Let's talk about holiday locations. What are you looking for?" Mrs. Owens asked.

"I already had a place in mind," Celia replied. She was trying to discourage Mrs. Owens from rambling out a list of possible destinations. It would be tiring to listen to.

"Yeah? Where?" Mrs. Owens asked.

"She won't say because it's supposed to be a surprise," Audrey chipped in.

Mrs. Owens' eyes glinted. "Those are the best, by the way. They feel random, but you have so much fun!"

Celia nodded. She dunked a rusk into her tea then popped the soggy sweetness into her mouth.

Mrs. Owens wasn't done yet. "Not that I want to intrude on your plans or anything, but if you haven't booked hotels or anything, you should maybe consider Egypt. You can have the kids check out the pyramids that they see in comic books. Alternatively, go to the Maasai Mara in Kenya. I was once there some years back and witnessed the great wildebeest migration there. It's truly one of the wonders of the world," Mrs. Owens said.

"It sounds interesting," Audrey said.

"Oh, it gets even more interesting. You can go to the Tsavo and see the descendants of the man-eating lions prowling the savannah," Mrs. Owens said in excitement. John and James' eyes widened as they heard this.

Celia frowned. "Mrs. Owens, we have children at the table."

"What's wrong? They'll hear about such lions when they go on a safari anyway, right?"

Celia shook her head. "Well, that just strikes fear into their hearts."

"Bah! They're growing into men. That won't phase them. I mean, instead of them learning about the big bad wolf eating little red riding hood, it's better to hear African stories like this one. The man-eaters of Tsavo are something they can handle."

Celia had to smile. The analogy made sense, and she was being a touch too sensitive. "I'll think about it," she replied.

Later that evening, Celia drove to *the Pier*. It was her favorite restaurant not just because of the well-made, authentic South African food, but because the rustic wood finish, the music they played and its affable manager made it feel comfortable. A homely feel was a major deal when going out. It was also the reason she'd asked Fezile that they meet there. The relaxed setting would help her handle any awkwardness that might come up.

However, she soon realized this wasn't entirely true.

"I've been waiting for your call for the last two years," Fezile said.

They sat in one of the private cubicles within the restaurant space that offered good privacy for dates and conversations such as this.

Celia's frowned. "Excuse me?"

"You're going to apologize first?" Fezile asked.

Celia gulped. This was unexpected. "I'm not here to apologize, Fez. You know what happened that day."

Fezile gave a guttural laugh that irked Celia. "Then why should I do business with you? As far as I'm concerned, we still have some old unfinished business to settle before we can do any new business."

He crossed his arms and eyed her. He looked like a smug mafia boss waiting for one of his henchmen to confess to a misdeed before he meted out a violent punishment.

She returned his gaze and wondered why he seemed so confident. What did he have up his sleeve?

She knew she might eventually honor his request, unnecessary as it was. It might massage his ego into hiring her, but it would also give him license to take advantage of her. If she got into a compromised situation with him, she knew one truth: he wouldn't protect her.

4

Celia clenched her fists under the table.

"What happened wasn't my fault," she said matter-of-factly.

"Oh, but it was. If you'd just paid me at the end of the event as agreed, what took place would never have happened," Fezile retorted.

Celia glowered at him. "Really? You're not responsible for shouting down the artist manager and threatening to break their equipment?"

"I was expressing my displeasure at the mistreatment shown to me," Fezile replied.

"You were causing an unnecessary scene over a debt. Do you realize I paid you out of my pocket?" she said.

"After two months of waiting!"

"What did you expect? I had to find the money somehow. I may delay, but I keep my word."

"The delay did its damage. And you ruined my reputation with artists," Fezile said.

Celia massaged her temple in frustration. "You did that to yourself. Anyway, if saying it will end this discussion, then I'm sorry."

Fezile smiled. "Thank you. You could say it was a blessing in disguise. After I switched, the corporates showed me the love I needed, and the pay is better."

Celia wished she could scold him, but she needed him. "I'm glad that it's working out for you. Can we put that behind us and work as friends?"

"We're not friends," Fezile stated.

Celia sighed. "Alright. Can we work together as professionals then? Because word on the street is you need a make-up person who can handle the elite companies you're working with. I can do that."

"What makes you think so?" he asked.

"A lot of my existing clients are from the affluent neighborhoods. I know how to handle rare tastes and high expectations. I'm sure Maria told you that herself. You need me now just as much as I need you," she said.

Her eyes searched his face, which was contorted with doubt.

After a brief silence, Celia instinctively reached for her bag as if about to leave. Seeing this, Fezile cleared his throat.

"I have four corporate clients about to hold their office parties. It's mostly an afternoon or evening of speeches, strange gifts, and bad dancing. However, our job is to make them feel and look good. The jobs happen within the next two weeks. Are you up for it?" he asked.

"I wouldn't be here if I wasn't. You know my rates, right?"

Fezile nodded. "You're pricey, but I've seen your recent work."

"Let's get to it then," she replied as she took out her notebook and pen.

For the next half hour, she scribbled away. The clients were an oil distribution company, a branding company, a girl's empowerment NGO, and a property management firm. She noted the number of staff expected to be at each party. Fortunately, they were not as many as she thought they'd be, with the oil distribution company being the largest with fifty, and the property management the lowest with ten. She made notes of each date the events were taking place, the physical address of each location, and the contact person they were to engage with. The level of detail would help her plan her movements for the next two weeks.

Fezile grew less confrontational the more he talked and was now addressing her like a peer rather than an adversary.

"So, we start with Dune Oil tomorrow evening. Any questions?" he asked as he finished.

"It has fifty employees. How many women are there and do the men need touch-ups too?" Celia asked.

"Female employees are only fifteen. So, your workload is a little light there. The men don't need any touch-ups. The women are always the camera lovers," he said.

Celia nodded. "I'll carry some lip gloss for the men, just in case. I've got a new lipstick line I want to use on the ladies. Maybe they can buy a set or two. It has different shades of red: matte lipstick, gel lipstick..."

Fezile put up his hand to stop her. "I don't need to know the details. That's for the ladies. Are you planning to cold sell? I'd rather you didn't," he said.

"Well, I won't have to if I got a strategically placed stand next to my workstation."

Fezile shook his head. "I can't promise that."

"Alright. I'll work with what I have. I'm not here to mess you up," Celia replied.

"Good," Fezile said as he took out his wallet to attend to the bill. "Sounds like we're done here."

"One more thing," Celia said, "Can we square out any of our differences away from clients?"

"Just do your job and we'll be fine," he remarked. He then stood up and left.

Celia waited for a waiter but didn't see any. She grabbed the bill book, walked over to the cashier, and settled it.

When she walked out into the street, darkness had fallen over the streets of Sunshine Cove.

Once she got to her mother's place, she talked her into being her subject as she tested a faster make-up routine.

"What's this for?" her mother asked.

"Just practice. It's good to stay sharp," Celia replied as she applied foundation.

"Suddenly, you're keen to keep up with the competition."

"Some would argue I don't have any competition," Celia said tongue-in-cheek.

Audrey grunted. "That's your comfort zone talking. Don't listen to it."

"This is me not listening to it, Ma," Celia replied with a smile. "Tilt your head up for me, please."

She was able to do it in ten minutes, which was a decent pace. She would try to shorten that time. She promptly helped her mother take it off as they prepared for bed.

After tucking in her boys, Celia retreated to her room. She took her bag and reached inside for her notebook. It wasn't there.

"Where did I put that thing?" she asked herself.

She searched the whole bedroom. Nothing. She retraced her steps across the house, mirroring her movements that evening. She couldn't find it.

Celia grabbed her car keys and went to the car. She searched the seats, floor, everywhere. Nothing.

The notebook, with all her detailed records about the gigs, was gone.

5

Celia had always been as stubborn as a bloodhound. Once she set her mind on a task, she kept going at it until she completed it.

Searching for her notebook was no different. She retraced her steps three more times until her brain was frazzled. The only place left to look was at the restaurant, although she could've sworn she left with it.

"Mental blind spots," she whispered to herself as she drew her blankets. It took a while for sleep to come.

The next day, she made breakfast for her family and thereafter left for *the Pier*.

When she arrived, they hadn't opened yet, but there were workers inside. She knocked on the locked front door and waited.

Moments later, the manager walked up to the door. Festo Tshabalala was a stout, charming man who always wore his trademark smart casual suits. Recognizing her, he smiled as he unlocked the door.

"Celia, we're not open yet, you know," he said.

"I know. Sorry to bother you by coming this early. I was here last evening and I might have left my notebook in one of the cubicles," she replied.

"Oh, that was yours? The one with the brown leather cover?" he asked.

"Yes, you found it?" she asked eagerly.

"Yeah, just give me a second."

Festo walked back into the restaurant. Celia could see a cleaner mopping the floor. Moments later, he returned with the notebook.

"I didn't look inside, so couldn't tell if it was yours. I would've texted you about it," he said.

Celia smiled as she took the book. "Don't worry. Where did you get it?"

"It was handed in by someone who found it in the cubicle," he replied.

"That's a kind soul. Thanks again and have a good one," Celia said.

"You're welcome."

Celia exhaled with relief. She could now focus on the first gig which was only hours away.

She made a few deliveries before heading back to her place in time for lunch. Since the boys were at her mother's, she could prepare a quick meal of chicken bunny chow and eat it on her own without a hassle. It was something she looked forward to. To clear her mind, she played some of Hugh Masekela's jazz tunes. She started preparing for the gig. She was going to dress in a trouser suit, which would be formal but give her the flexibility to stand and move around.

At four o'clock, Celia left for the oil company. She was intrigued it wasn't located in Kruger City, the nearby commercial city that was a forty-minute drive from Sunshine Cove. Yet, she understood that having offices outside the hustle and bustle of the concrete jungle had its advantages.

She arrived in forty minutes. The Dune Oil offices were housed in an ultra-modern complex with vast swathes of greenery around it. The compound had little flower gardens and manicured hedges. She noticed that the main building was fitted with solar panels.

She went up to the third floor of the building. The party was taking place inside the open-plan office, with one section rearranged to accommodate the mini stage, a deejay's booth, a dance floor, and a food service area.

Fezile, who had already arrived, was patrolling the office, possibly looking for the best areas for different kinds of shots.

Upon seeing her, he walked up to her. "One of the things I like about you is that you're always early."

"This is me behaving," Celia replied with a wry smile. "Where do I set up?"

"This way," Fezile replied as he led her towards a corner that was opposite the dance floor. It had a leather seat, supposedly taken from one of the managers' offices. Next to it were two small tables.

"This is all for you," he said, pointing out the section. "I hope you brought your mirror."

"Always."

"So you'll work on one at a time. One of the side tables is for your working kit and the other is for the lipstick line you talked about," he said.

Celia smiled, surprised by his effort. "Thank you."

"Nothing crazy on their faces, even if they ask for it," he warned. "Let them get angry here rather than after the party when they wonder why you messed up their faces."

Celia nodded. She understood this very well. Years ago, she once worked on guests at an office party and the staff came up with the impromptu idea to do a Halloween-themed look. Celia regretted it when complaints came in that their 'office party was ruined by rogue make-up.' She had no evidence showing who told her to go in that direction. She became the scapegoat. She made amends by giving a free make-up session to all aggrieved workers.

As darkness crept in, she started applying make-up on the female employees. She noticed that only three women working at the oil company were over the age of thirty. This intrigued her. On further investigation, she realized most of them were young engineers and technical professionals.

She couldn't resist chatting them up as she worked on their faces.

Her standout conversations were with Fridah who was in her second year there and due for a promotion to become a Distribution Supervisor; Angela who was the transportation manager; Lizzy, the Contract administrator, and Mphokati, the vice-president of operations.

By the end of the make-up session, she was so inspired that she realised she'd hardly pitched the new lipstick line to any of the fifteen women. She needn't have worried because as the evening wore on she received seven orders. A great start.

Fezile had set up a portable studio along one of the walls fitted with his lights and other props. It had a green screen background, which Celia knew he would use when editing the photos later. She observed that he was wrong about the photo lovers being women only. The male employees clamoured for time in front of the lens just as much as the women did.

The manager announced the Secret Santa gift-giving session. Each employee had selected random names and bought a gift for that person. After you received your gift, you had to guess who bought it for you. Celia watched in amazement as people got microwaves, televisions, shopping vouchers, while others rued their luck after receiving relatively mundane things such as skipping ropes. The fact that many of those present were intoxicated meant that the reactions were light-hearted, and the guessing games even more hilarious. Of course, those who bought bare-minimum gifts such as skipping ropes hardly revealed themselves.

"So far, so good," Fezile said as he stood next to her, wolfing down some meat samosas.

"Yeah, it's been very good," Celia replied.

"For business?"

"Yeah. I also got to bond with some women working here. I mean, they were…"

Celia's words trailed off as she spotted three employees rushing to one of the office stalls. As the music kept playing, she saw another man move quickly through the crowd. He arrived at the deejay's booth and told him something. The music stopped. A voice crackled over the microphone.

"Guys, something's up with Lizzy. Does anyone here know first aid?"

The whole room fell quiet as Celia ran to the office stall. When she got there, she found another employee already performing CPR on Lizzy.

Lizzy had just unwrapped her Secret Santa gift, which contained a crystal ball that now lay beside her. Fifteen minutes later, her hand was still limp, with the gift-wrapping paper in its grasp. Her chest was unmoving and her skin increasingly cold.

Lizzy was dead.

6

Celia watched with silent shock as four paramedics lifted Lizzy's body onto a stretcher and covered it up with a white sheet. They wheeled her away as the rest of the office watched. A somber mood hung over the place as two policemen interviewed the members of staff closest to the incident.

The management talked to each other in hushed tones. Staffers were in tears. Mphokati and Angela were locked in a tight embrace. Fridah, who stood alone, occasionally dried her eyes with a handkerchief.

As soon as the police had left, employees moved away in different directions. Those with their own offices locked themselves in, while others went to the spacious boardroom for a cry. Others went to the balcony, and a few left for the washrooms. Everyone took a moment to grieve, Celia observed. She walked over to Fridah, who was still standing alone.

"I'm sorry for your loss," Celia said.

"It just shouldn't happen," Fridah replied as she dabbed her eyes once more.

"If you need to talk, I'm here," Celia offered.

CHRISTMAS CAROLS AND LIPSTICK PERILS

"I mean, she had the sniffles last week. But that's just the sniffles. It's not supposed to end this way," Fridah continued.

"Would you like to take a walk with me?"

Fridah shook her head. "I think I'll head to the washroom. Sorry, I ruined the make-up you did so perfectly," she said.

"Don't mention it. Honoring your colleague is way more important to me," Celia replied.

"Thank you. Please excuse me," Fridah said as she walked off towards the washrooms.

Celia walked back to Fezile, who was packing his camera gear into his bag.

"That's pretty sad," she said.

"Yeah. I've seen a lot of things at these parties, but this is a first," Fezile replied.

"What kind of things have you seen?"

"Fights, arguments, embarrassing episodes. Only one fainting. This is the first death I've seen at one of these functions," he replied as he neatly placed a camera lens into its designated section.

"You seem pretty composed for it to be the first time. Are you okay?" Celia asked.

"Me? Of course, why wouldn't I be?" he asked as he zipped up the bag.

"I mean, just checking. We have different ways of coping with death," Celia replied.

Fezile slung the bag over his shoulder. "Exactly. It's the circle of life."

"True. Do you want to debrief now? I can quickly pack up my stuff."

"No debrief. I didn't drive today, so I'm going to catch the metro. Later." With that, Fezile walked towards the exit.

"Hey, are you forgetting something?"

Fezile stopped and turned. "Get home safe." He then disappeared through the doors.

Celia wasn't amused. "This is supposed to be teamwork. You pack your stuff, I pack mine. We leave together," she muttered.

She trudged to her workstation and started carefully packing her products.

It was almost midnight when Celia got to her mother's house. Her sons were already asleep, but her mother was still up, watching a Christmas movie.

"You're home a little later than I hoped," Audrey said.

"These things tend to go past their set end times," Celia replied. She glanced at the TV screen as she took off her coat, "Haven't you watched this movie fifty times?"

"You can never watch it too many times. They rerun it every year to set the mood. It's a classic. Did it go well at least?" Audrey asked.

"Events can pull surprises on you, but it went well for the most part," Celia replied as she planted herself on the couch.

"Great! I'll warm up the dinner we had," Audrey said as she got up from her chair.

"No, don't trouble yourself. I'm not hungry," Celia replied.

Audrey raised her eyebrows. "It doesn't look like you had a feast there."

"I'm just not hungry," she replied.

"Let me get you some broth at least," Audrey replied as she walked off to the kitchen.

Minutes later, she returned with a steaming bowl of chicken broth. Even though she didn't feel hungry, Celia couldn't resist the enticing aroma. Her mother's cooking was tingling her taste buds and warming her soul at the same time.

"I don't know how you do it," she said, licking her lips. "Are you going to give me the recipe sometime?"

Audrey wore a smile that stretched from one ear to the other. "You'll have to earn it."

Audrey didn't get to finish the movie, considering she knew almost every actor's lines. The predictability made her eyelids heavy. They both turned in an hour later. Celia was glad that her mind had relaxed to a level that allowed her to quickly find sleep.

The next morning, Celia was woken up by the sound of laughter. She covered her head with a pillow as she tried to catch another few minutes of sleep. However, the laughter and talking voices were too intrusive.

Still in her pajamas, she ambled to the living room. As she got closer, the chatter and laughter grew louder.

"There she is!" a cheery Mrs. Owens said as soon as she noticed Celia. "I hope we didn't wake you?"

Celia squinted as her eyes fought the bright sunlight that lit up the room. She could make out that Mrs. Owens was seated on the couch next to Audrey. They both had mugs of masala tea in their hands.

"Well, you did. Hello, Mrs. Owens," Celia said.

"I'm so sorry, my child! I got a little caught up in the mood," Mrs. Owens replied. "Shall I pour you some tea?"

Celia didn't need to reply, as Mrs. Owens was already pouring the tea. Celia gingerly made her way to a chair and sat down.

"Your mother has this lovely recipe for making masala tea that she's been hiding from me for years," Mrs. Owens replied as she handed Celia a mug.

"There can be only one queen of masala tea in Sunshine Cove, Christie," Audrey said with a sly grin.

"You're the queen of masala tea, and I'm the queen of carols. Speaking of which, I just reminded your mother how you used to sing so well when you were a child," Mrs. Owens said.

Celia forced a smile. "That was over twenty years ago."

"That may be, but the love for carols is a lifelong thing. Look at me," Mrs. Owens said, and then she proceeded to croon out *Joy to the World*. A smiling Audrey joined in the singing. Celia watched in amazement.

"Join in," Mrs. Owens urged in between lines.

Celia was still warming up to the day. She shook her head and sipped her tea instead.

The two older women went on singing and got so enamored by it that they stood up and became more animated. When they were done, they high fived each other.

"Now that's what I call getting in the mood," Mrs. Owens said with a beaming smile. "I'm starting rehearsals at my house this week, Cece. You should join us after work."

Celia rubbed her brow. "I wish I could. I have a pretty crazy week with the events lined up. I don't think I'll make it."

"I'll keep a slot open for you. Plus, I'm getting a few more holiday destinations lined up. I'll tell you about them the next time we meet," Mrs. Owens said.

"Alright, thanks," Celia replied. "I should get ready for work."

After an hour of grooming, Celia left for her briefing meeting with Fezile. She arrived at *the Pier* ten minutes early but found him already waiting for her, working on his laptop.

"Good morning, Fez," Celia said with a smile.

"Good morning," he replied without taking his eyes off the screen.

Celia eased into the seat opposite him. "I hope you got some sleep."

"*Yebo*. I slept like a baby."

Celia nodded. She ordered some coffee from a passing waiter.

"So, where do we start?" she asked.

"We talk about the event. What worked, what didn't, and then see what we can do for the next gig," he replied.

"Great. I think things went smoothly except for the sad incident at the end," she remarked.

Fezile nodded. "Anything else?"

"I wish we could've done something more for them," she added.

Fezile raised a brow. "Done something more? Like what?"

Celia shrugged. "I think we could have taken more initiative in the rescue."

Fezile straightened his shoulders as he stared at her. "We're there to do our jobs and leave. Nothing more, nothing less."

"And if our client is in distress?"

"They have systems in the organisation for that."

"So, you'll sit there and watch?"

"Exactly. Do you realize if something goes wrong while we're trying to be heroes, they could sue us?"

Celia shook her head. "That won't happen. I've saved people in trouble before. I wouldn't let it happen on my watch."

Fezile laughed. "You see, that's the issue here. This is not your watch. It's mine. We're not partners. You work for me. So, what I say goes."

Celia swallowed hard. She'd hoped this would go better. The next gig was just a day away, and she dreaded it already. With Fezile dictating things, things could only go one way.

Downhill.

7

Celia turned up at the Reddi Agency offices an hour and a half early, keen to ensure that she had already set up before Fezile arrived. The branding company offices were spacious and open plan as well, in addition to some standalone offices for the managers. It was a very colorful office, with different copies of their award-winning branding work gracing the walls.

Staff dressed in casual wear and had access to an office bar. A section of the office also had gaming tables for playing pool and foosball. To the outsider, these perks created the impression that the company cared for its employees' welfare. While it was true to some extent, Celia had come to learn that such trappings were a sign of an overworked staff. The management provided recreation facilities to discourage people from leaving the office. It was clever, but ultimately restrictive.

Celia quickly struck a rapport with the office manager, Clarise, who helped her find an empty office to use as her working space.

By the time Fezile got there forty-five minutes later, she was ready to go.

"You stepped up. Impressive," Fezile said as he unpacked his gear.

"I always step up, Fez. It's just my thing," Celia replied, keen to let him know that she was capable of taking care of business. She was still smarting from his rebuke when they last met.

The party got underway at four in the evening, with the dancehall music tempting people out of their workstations. Many headed to the bar as others gathered in groups for jokes and conversations. A few were already at the gaming tables. Soon the atmosphere was filled with merry and cheer.

Celia did the make-up for most of the women, while a few opted to do it for themselves after alleging they weren't used to someone else doing their make-up. She didn't argue with them, but hoped it wouldn't mean a reduction in her flat fee rate. The initial hours of the party were the busiest for Celia. Once she completed her tasks, she was able to relax and watch Fezile work.

He admired the space, with its high roof, large windows, and colorful walls. He took numerous pictures with the staff in various positions, and Celia knew he was having a blast.

Celia took a short break and went outside to call her mother. She let her know that she might be home earlier because she didn't intend to stay till late.

As she walked back, she spotted two staffers arguing in the corridor leading to the lifts. She slowed down as she got closer. From their exchange, she quickly learned their names were Matt and Henry.

"You crossed the line," Henry said. "You don't see me getting any of your stuff, do you?"

"It was just *biltong*. I already said I'd pay you for it."

"It's not about the *biltong* or the cash. You've been working hard to tick me off all year. What problem do you have with me?" Henry retorted.

"You're blowing this out of proportion. You buy those at the restaurant downstairs every afternoon. All it needs is to take a lift to the ground floor. Is that so hard?" Matt replied.

Henry grabbed Matt by the collar. "Listen. I need you to start respecting me and my stuff."

"Excuse me, is everything okay?" Celia said. She wasn't keen on watching a fistfight.

The two men glanced at her, then back at each other. Henry let go of Matt's collar.

"Everything is fine," Henry said.

"Sharp. Everything's okay. Do you need help with something?" Matt asked her.

"I'm looking for Clarise. Could one of you help me find her?"

"Sure," Matt replied as he walked back to the office. As Celia followed him, she could feel Henry's eyes boring through her.

After Matt had tracked down Clarise for her, he disappeared into the crowd of dancers. Celia simply gave Clarise an update of how things were going, then went back to her workstation. She watched as the party got livelier. The agency boss gave a hearty speech that had everyone in stitches. He then had gifts distributed. For a short while, everyone tossed around wrapping papers as they unboxed the gifts they had received.

Five minutes after the music and dancing resumed, Celia noticed people had formed a circle around the dance floor. She moved closer and saw Matt at the center of the circle. He was dancing the *Vosho*, which involved squatting and straightening back up to the beat of the music. Although he had a stocky frame, his movements were swift and energetic. Celia also knew that, like her, most of those around the dance floor couldn't risk killing their knees by doing the move. They danced vicariously through him, praising his performance with whistling, cheers and claps.

He was holding one of his squats as he shook his shoulders when he clutched his chest. His eyes rolled back into their sockets as he fell to his side. People were still clapping at the strange move when his head hit the floor. The thud as it made contact with the floor and Matt's stillness brought a quick hush to the watching crowd. Two colleagues rushed to him. Celia's view was blocked as other employees jostled to see what was happening.

"Someone call an ambulance!"

Celia heard someone screaming. Another colleague walked off fast as he furiously pressed his mobile phone. Celia managed to push through the crowd. Matt lay unmoving on the floor with his eyes were closed. They were trying to resuscitate him, but Celia could tell it wasn't working.

She wanted to jump in but she remembered Fezile's words and held back. At least she could tell his two colleagues were doing the right thing.

However, twenty minutes later Matt was still lying flat on the floor, lifeless. The paramedics arrived and confirmed that Matt was dead. Around the room, the laughs had been replaced by sobbing and shocked faces. The regular police were present. They were recording statements and taking pictures of the scene.

"I can't believe this is happening," Celia remarked.

Standing next to her, Fezile simply grunted in reply.

Celia took out her phone. "Let me call Bill, he might be able to help out here."

Fezile shot her a look. "Who's Bill?"

"He's a cop friend of mine. I'm just going to ask him to follow it up, in case there's something fishy," Celia replied.

Fezile shook his head. "But you can see the police are already here."

"He's in the homicide division. They look into suspicious deaths," she replied.

"*Eish*, what's suspicious here? Let these guys do their own work. We can't put ideas in their heads," Fezile replied.

Celia frowned. "Does this look normal to you? People collapsing at our gigs?"

Fezile grabbed her phone-holding hand and lowered it. "It's none of our business. Stay out of it."

"Are you serious right now?"

"You're working for me. Be smart and let them handle it," Fezile replied curtly. He kept his eyes trained on Celia until she put her phone back in her bag.

Later that evening, Celia was still restless. She texted Bill, and he agreed to meet her.

The next morning, Celia drove to the police station. She found him at his cluttered office desk. It was always buried under a pile of files and papers. As soon as she sat down, two cups of coffee were brought in.

"Sorry it's not as fancy as a restaurant," Bill said. Detective Bill Koloane was bald and sported a beard that was more rugged than usual. He wore a navy blue shirt instead of the usual white ones. He had loosened his tie and rolled up his sleeves. Next to him, a fan whirred.

"It's not supposed to be a date, so no pressure," Celia replied.

"I know. You didn't tell me why you wanted to meet. Is this about us or something else?"

"It's about something else. I'm not ready to have that other discussion," she said.

She narrated what had happened at the two office parties. Bill nodded as he listened.

"So, you're telling me these two people have died in two consecutive events you've worked in?" he asked.

"Yes. I thought the first one was natural. But a second one after that? I'm here because it sounds like too much of a coincidence," she replied.

"Tell me more about how they collapsed."

"It was seemingly out of nowhere. No one hit them, nothing odd to my eye anyway. It just happened and I don't know why. Anyway, what I'm suggesting is you could look into both. Maybe the post mortem results will tell you something," she replied.

"What if there's no connection?" he asked.

Celia shrugged. "Well, then I'm choosing the wrong events to work in."

Bill slowly tilted his head as he gazed at her. "Some might say you have some experience in that."

"Don't start."

"I'll leave it at that. So what stopped you from calling me earlier? I would've liked to check out the scene."

Celia let out a pronounced sigh. "I was discouraged by my colleague. He thinks I'm overthinking it."

"Which colleague?"

"He's a photographer I'm working with at the events."

"Why would he stop you?"

"He's concerned that it will affect his business prospects if we call in the police," she said.

Bill leaned back and stroked his beard as if he wanted to straighten it out. "He thinks he'll get a bad reputation?"

Celia nodded. "I can understand where he's coming from. If we don't intervene, we avoid a lawsuit. But I don't understand the lack of empathy. He believes people die if needed."

"Does he react when the deaths occur?"

"Not really."

"Doesn't seem like someone motivated by the welfare of his clients," Bill said.

"You can say that again," Celia replied.

Bill crossed his arms. "You two don't sound like a good fit. You have your other businesses. Why are you working with him?"

Celia forced a smile. "I have my reasons. You could just question him, you know."

"I can't. Everything you've told me is speculation. It doesn't work that way. But if I were you, I'd keep an eye on him."

"Why?"

"He sounds more detached than normal. Maybe he knows more than you think. He does move around and interact with everyone during the event, right?"

"Yes, he has to."

"That's a good way to find his victim, blending his mission with the nature of his work," Bill said. "I'll look into the post mortems and see what I can find."

Celia nodded slowly as she realized what he meant. "I'll look for something to connect him. Which would mean I'm working with a murderer, right?"

"You *might* be working with one. Remember, you're still speculating. But if you're right, you should be smart about it. You don't want him to know that you suspect him."

"But why would he do it?" she asked.
"That's for you to find out," he replied.

8

After making deliveries for most of the day, Celia arrived at the nail parlor later that afternoon. When she entered the mezzanine office, she was met by an excited Melanie.

"Did you hear about the Bay Gardens Park newest attraction?" Melanie asked. She knew it was one of Celia's favorite spots due to its abundant greenery and trees.

"No. What's going on there?" Celia asked.

"They've set up a play park in a small section of the place. They've got slides, tree houses, trains, swing horses, the works. They're going to be running every weekend until Christmas day. It's perfect for the kids and family," Melanie said.

"Well, good for them," Celia replied.

Melanie frowned. "Wow, good for them? That's it?"

Celia eased into her seat. "Okay, I might check it out at some point. But for now, I'm just staying focused on what each day needs."

Melanie walked over to her and placed her hand lightly on Celia's shoulder. "How did it go with Bill?"

Celia sighed. "It was a start, nothing much."

"He's going to look into it, right?"

"Nope, he needs more evidence. But he'll follow up on the post mortems."

"And how are you handling that?" Melanie asked.

"I'm trying to wrap my head around it all. But it's all a blur right now," she replied. "What if it's Fezile?"

Melanie's eyes widened." Are you trying to lose your gig?"

"Hear me out here. For both deaths, he was extremely indifferent. Not a hint of emotion or empathy. Not in his words or speech," Celia explained.

"People handle grief differently," Melanie remarked.

"That's what I thought too until he admonished me for wanting to call the cops."

"You called the cops on him?"

Celia shook her head. "No, I wouldn't do that unless I had some evidence. But I did suggest to Bill that the two deaths aren't natural."

"And why did Fezile tell you not to call the police?" she asked.

"He gave the lame excuse that it might ruin the business," she replied.

Melanie paused to think, then nodded. "It makes sense to me."

Celia leaned forward, her mouth agape. "What?"

"I mean, why draw attention to the business when you're just service providers?"

"And what if it's a very convenient way of ensuring he keeps doing it?" Celia posed.

Melanie shook her head. "You're overthinking this now. I thought you had let go of whatever disagreement you had with the man?"

"I did. This is different," Celia replied.

"Why are we talking like this? There's been no mention of foul play from the families of the victims. You need to clear your head before you meet Fezile again. Don't mess up a good gig over something you're not sure about," Melanie said.

Celia stared at her computer screen for a few minutes, then sighed. "You're right. There are just too many theories flying around here. Let me make a call."

She took her mobile phone and dialed.

"Who are you calling?" Melanie asked. Celia motioned at her to wait.

"Hello?" Bill's deep voice came through the earpiece.

"Hi. Have you got a minute? I just wanted to know if you got any feedback on the post mortem results."

"Not yet. Lizzy's family had already done the first one, so they are getting a second opinion done. Matt's results are being relayed to the family at some point today. I might have something tomorrow," Bill replied.

"Oh, great. You're not going to watch them do it?" she asked.

"I can't go there on a hunch, Celia. I'd rather examine the findings then recommend something. Trust me, I'm following this up," he replied.

"Okay, sorry for being a bit too nosy there. Thanks for the effort. I guess I'll call you tomorrow?" she asked awkwardly.

"Sure, but only in the afternoon. I've got a crazy morning."

After she hung up, Melanie stared at her with a cheeky smile. "At least I can see you're on talking terms again."

"It was a professional phone call. Nothing to read into it."

Melanie laughed. "Have you seen yourself when you're on the phone with him? Your facial expression says a lot, that's all I'm saying."

"Oh, cut it out now," Celia said. Just then, her mobile phone rang.

"He must be calling back to ask you out," Melanie teased.

"It's not him," she quickly replied as she answered the call. "Hey, Fez."

"Where are you?" Fezile asked.

"At my office. Why?"

"I need to meet you," he replied.

Celia glanced at her watch. "I'm heading to do a delivery in ten minutes, can we do it after that?"

"No, we need to meet right now," he insisted.

"Is everything okay?"

"Stop the funny questions and tell me if you're coming or not," he snarled.

"Okay, I'll talk to my client and push it forward. Where do I find you?"

"At our usual meeting spot. I'll be waiting," Fezile replied as he ended the call.

Celia took the phone off her ear and frowned.

"What's up?" Melanie asked.

"I don't know. Something's going on with Fezile," Celia replied.

"What does he want?"

"He wants to meet me immediately. I've got to delay Marge's delivery. She won't like it," Celia said as she rose from her seat.

"Good luck with that."

"I'll need it. He didn't sound like a happy man," Celia said as she walked out.

9

"It's not what you think," Celia said.

"Oh? Tell me, what is it supposed to be?" Fezile asked as he flared his nostrils.

Celia squinted. The only time she'd seen him in this state was when they had their last falling out. "I didn't call the cops," she said.

"Then how come the police paid another visit to the oil company and started asking questions?" he asked.

"They did? When?" she asked, wondering why Bill hadn't told her about that.

"This afternoon. They only return if they suspect funny business. When they get to us, we can kiss the other contracts goodbye," he ranted.

"But I didn't call them."

"Then who did?"

"Just because I wanted to do it doesn't mean I was the only one thinking it. Besides, every death needs to be reported at the police station. It could be the bosses or even her family who told the police," Celia replied.

Celia had to lie. If he was involved in the deaths, telling the truth would put her in grave danger. If he wasn't involved, she would lose an income source. Lying was the safest option.

Fezile shook his head in disgust.

"But why should you be worried if they interview us? We have nothing to hide, right?" she asked.

He stared back at her. "No, we don't. But we shouldn't meddle with this."

"Fez, is there something going on that you want to tell me?" Celia asked.

Fezile stared at his twiddling thumbs for a short moment, then took a deep breath. "Look, I was once caught up in a false accusation thing. Two friends fought at a club, I tried to break it up. One died from a blow but I was arrested for his death although I didn't even hit him. All I wanted to do was help."

"Are you serious?" Celia asked, wide-eyed.

"Yes. I was behind bars for a month. I was released when they cleared me. But a month is a long time to be locked up. That's why I avoid getting mixed up in these kinds of things. Trouble might look for me again," Fezile replied.

"But you weren't convicted. That means you don't have a record," Celia said.

Fezile tapped the side of his head. "The record is here, in my mind. I have to keep an eye over my shoulder. The two deaths are strange, but we shouldn't interfere."

"Are you suggesting that these deaths aren't natural?"

Fezile shrugged. "Well, that's a possibility."

Celia smiled. "Here I was thinking that I was alone."

"I have my opinions. But I just watch and stick to my business."

"But these deaths are affecting your business. What are we going to do?" Celia asked.

"We? We are not doing anything. As far as I'm concerned, it could even be evil spirits playing tricks on us."

"Evil spirits?"

"I do have enemies, Celia. Don't think I've become this successful without a few people hating my guts. I would've even suspected you if I didn't think you needed the money," he replied.

Celia held her head in her hands. "Unbelievable. So, what now?"

"We do what we always do. Plan for the next gig. We have a week to go. But this time, we lookout for things that are out of place," he said.

"But that means we should try a few things we don't usually do."

Fezile shook his head. "No. I'm only talking about keeping our eyes open. We can't change how we work. Like I said, if the cops come in and notice we changed our way of working, they'll focus on us. We don't need that."

Having resolved that, they went on to discuss the plan for the following week.

Later that evening, Celia arrived at Marge Thobiso's store. She found her busy attending to a customer and waited for her to finish. She walked around window shopping. It was a little gift shop that had all kinds of affordable gifts, from dolls to miniature trains and gift cards. Celia realized she hadn't even thought about buying any small gifts for the family. Getting cash for the trip had absorbed all her focus.

"Cece! Howzit?" Marge said as she approached.

"It's good. Sorry, I was late with this," Celia said while handing her the package.

"At least you made it. I ran out of the lotions this morning, so this is a godsend. The new lipstick range is in here too?"

"Of course. I think they'll do well on your thick lips."

Marge smiled. "You're trying to flatter me so that I don't complain. This is the third time you've pushed your delivery in three months. I'm beginning to feel unappreciated here."

"You know I appreciate you, Marge—don't I always come through?" Celia said with a charming smile.

"*Eish*, but why is this pack of lipstick so pricey? For twelve hundred rands? You didn't even wrap it in a Christmas-themed pack. It would've warmed my heart a little. I think a discount can help me feel better."

Celia wasn't amused. "I'd love to give you a discount, but I can't at this time."

"But it's Christmas, Cece. I've just given a discount to the customer I was talking to."

Celia fidgeted. "I'd love to. But you've got a great deal for six shades of lipstick. That's our lowest introductory price. How about I give you a discount in January?"

Marge shook her head. "Tomorrow isn't promised. Today is all we have."

Celia sighed. She realized she wasn't going to win this. Marge was one of her most reliable clients, and she didn't want to lose her.

"Alright, you win. I'll give you ten percent off."

"Twenty."

"Marge, you run a store. You know how important margins are. The best I can do is fifteen," Celia replied.

Marge beamed. "I'll take that. Let's go to the counter and I'll pay you."

They walked up to the counter, and Celia took payment for the goods.

When she got back to her car, Celia was drained. It was going to be a slog keeping her margins healthy. She turned on the radio and switched stations. All of them were playing Christmas songs and she didn't want to listen to any of them. She landed on one playing some South African house music and turned up the volume. She was soon drumming her hands on her lap.

Her mind wandered to the deaths. As much as they could be a coincidence, her gut feeling told her otherwise. Now that Fezile agreed with her, did it exonerate him? She couldn't let her guard down as he was smart enough to put up an act. But who else could be a suspect? She recalled Matt having a tense conversation with Henry. There was a sinister tone to how Henry talked to his colleague that Celia couldn't ignore. Maybe one of the deaths was natural while the other one wasn't. She decided that it might be a good time to talk to Henry. She would do it without alerting Fezile.

Her mobile phone vibrated. It was a text message. She read it and she scowled.

Remember the time you licked the bottom of the shoe?

The text came from a strange number. Who was this, and how did they know about that? It was one of Celia's crazy memories from high school. Being bullied in her first year was a rite of passage, and she had endured some unpleasant experiences. Licking the bottom of her shoe had been one of them.

No one thought she would do it when the burly older girl had told her to. But Celia took the shoe and licked it. Twice. She was shockingly calm while doing it, even as those watching were grossed out despite the fact it tasted like mud following the rains that day. Instead of receiving a dressing down, she was gifted a pack of cookies for her troubles.

'Sorry, who is this?' Celia texted back.

Moments later, the reply came in.

I'm someone you need to remember urgently. If you don't, you'll pay a heavy price.

10

Celia tried calling the number that texted her, but the call didn't go through.

She decided to view the texts as a prank. Only someone who knew her very well, either from her close family or former high school mates, knew about that incident. She only wondered where the prank was leading.

So she had started inquiring from the people around her to find out who was responsible.

"I hope this is not some treasure hunt set up to get me excited for Christmas. Because you know I love treasure hunts," Celia said.

Her mother stared at her with a puzzled expression. "Why would I prank you, Cece?"

"Because you've done it before. Remember the time in my teens when you tricked me into various house chores with the promise of getting a bike?" Celia asked.

Audrey laughed. "That was a good one. But you did get the bike."

"After a whole year of chores, Ma. That was a long wait."

"Well, bikes were not cheap those days, so I needed to save up. Besides, you were getting dangerously lazy, and I wanted to make sure you grew into a responsible woman. I'm glad it panned out," she said.

"So you're telling me this is not a Christmas prank? I'd understand if you don't want to admit to it, but why use my high school memories?"

"It's not me, Cece. But I wish it was. Sounds like a fun way to get your mind working towards a surprise Christmas gift," Audrey replied with a smile.

"Do you think it's Mrs. Owens?" Celia asked.

"Mrs. Owens wouldn't know about it. You never told her about those things when you were in school," she replied.

"But you must have told her, since I shared everything with you," she remarked.

"It's possible, I can't deny that. But it was so long ago."

"You're right. I've got too many other things on my mind. I'm turning in," she said.

"Good idea. Be patient. I'm sure the prankster will one day get tired of all the run-around and just surprise you," her mother said with a wink.

The next day Celia made sure she met all her delivery targets that morning before she drove to the Reddi Agency offices. She was determined to talk to Henry but didn't want to walk through the office doors and cause a stir.

She recalled that during their argument, Henry and Matt had mentioned a restaurant in the same building where Henry bought his *biltong*. She walked into Jazz's Skewer, which was located on the ground floor. It was a cozy little place with wooden tables and chairs, and a menu filled with predominantly South African meat snacks and dishes.

She picked a table where she had a good view of the door, ordered *biltong* to see what it tasted like. It was well flavored and meaty. She enjoyed each bite. It was better than many she had eaten.

She was sipping her fresh grape juice when Henry walked in. She quickly walked over to the counter and convinced him to join her. She bought him a glass of mango juice as well to sweeten the offer. They were now seated opposite each other.

"Why are you so curious about what happened?" Henry asked.

"It's my way of processing things. It affected me considering I saw him dance, then suddenly he was gone. I've never seen someone so vibrant go in such a manner," Celia replied. "How are you all coping with it?"

"Coping as well as we can. Most people are still coming to terms with it," he replied. He sipped his mango juice.

"What about you?" Celia asked.

"And…?"

"Are you also, trying to make sense of it all?" she prodded.

Henry shrugged. "We'll all die one day you know."

"Yes, we will. But he was a colleague. It's Christmas time. It's not the time of the year to encounter a sudden death," Celia replied.

Henry shrugged. "We didn't get along that well. I think you can attest to that by the argument we had. So, it might sound strange, but I don't miss the guy."

Celia pursed her lips. His lack of emotion surprised her. "You don't even feel sorry for his family?"

"They'll get over it," he replied.

Celia frowned. "Had you been feuding for that long? Because it looked to me like there was a build-up to that argument."

"We had several run-ins before, of course. The man had no honor in him. Taking credit for work he didn't do, back-stabbing. To me, the guy was a jerk on most days and I don't get along well with jerks," Henry remarked.

"Did it ever get physical?" Celia asked.

Henry chuckled. "Beyond what you saw? No, and I'm glad it didn't get that far. I would have lost my job. Anyway, it was only a matter of time before one of us left that space. But I guess he had it coming, considering he collapsed and died for nothing."

"So, you believe it was a natural death?"

"Of course. Nothing else can explain it. It might be because of a condition in his family or something," Henry replied. "Look, I've got better things to do than talk about the past. Enjoy your drink."

With that, Henry got up and left.

Celia was still puzzled. Henry was odd, but not in the way she expected. He had issues relating to Matt on a personal level. Office rivalries exist. Was he callous? Yes. But was he murderous? She doubted it.

She wanted to find out more about the actual victims and the companies they worked for. It meant, at some point, going directly to them with her queries. But she wasn't sure this was the best way to find evidence that the deaths were connected.

Back at the nail parlor office, Celia researched the oil company. Dune Oil had been in existence for twenty years. Although it was initially fully owned by a South African magnate, he had recently sold a stake to a British investor. The investor came in with a good cash injection that had financed their expansion, including the new complex built on the outskirts of Sunshine Cove. There had been a raft of new appointments in recent years, with younger faces replacing the old hands in several departments. However, as much as the oil business could attract controversy, Celia didn't find any alarming story that could raise her suspicions.

Another half-hour of research didn't show any connection between Dune Oil and Reddi Agency. They had never worked together, and as far as she could tell, none of their employees had worked for both companies.

'What was she missing?' she asked herself.

Resigned that she had hit a dead-end, Celia left for her briefing meeting with Fezile.

"So, the next client is a girls' empowerment NGO, and they want something different," Fezile said.

"What do you mean by *different*?" Celia asked, opening her notebook.

"They want a white Christmas theme to their party."

Celia frowned. "But we're in Africa. Snow isn't our thing."

"It's an office thing, don't go all politically correct on them," Fezile replied.

"But I'm not. I mean, creating that look isn't a big deal. I've done it before. I was thinking, why not blend that with some African vibe to it? We can pick Ndebele or Zulu beadwork as inspiration for something."

Fezile leaned back in his seat and nodded with a smile. "I like the sound of that. Some bright colors too."

Celia froze as a new thought came to her. "You know what? Let's use Xhosa face-painting as an inspiration. *Umchokozo* would look great."

"*Umchokozo* can work?" Fezile asked, puzzled.

"Yeah, why not? I'll put patterns of white dots on their faces along the bridge of the nose, above the eyebrow or along the cheeks. It will look great, trust me," Celia replied, smiling.

Fezile leapt in his seat. "Forget the other idea. *Umchokozo* is the one we go with. My mother used to rock that look."

"Judging from your reaction, you're going to pitch it to them?" Celia asked.

"Of course. The only question is are working with the same budget you shared?" he asked.

Celia lightly tapped her pen on the table as she considered his question. "Erm, this will mean a tiny increase in the budget. I'm bringing a mix of two different looks. Never seen them done before at an office party, have you?"

Fezile shook his head.

"Well, that should be value for money. Besides, I need to buy a few extras to add to my make-up kit to pull it off. So the extra cash isn't just profit," Celia replied.

"By how much is it going up?" he asked.

Celia pondered for a moment. "Thirty percent."

Fezile whistled softly. "They'll fight that one."

"Twenty-five percent then. The product I'm getting for the face painting is top grade."

Fezile wrung his hands. "I hope you're not setting me up a dud gig here."

"I can handle it. You'll just have to trust me on this," she replied.

"Alright. I'll pitch it to them and let you know," Fezile replied.

"Nice one, Fez!" Celia said as she added a note to her book. "On another note, what's the plan with Lizzy?"

"What do you mean?" he asked.

"Any news on the funeral arrangements and so on?"

"They're having an office vigil today in her memory. I already sent them a card," he replied.

"We're going for the vigil, right?"

Fezile glanced at his wristwatch. "It starts in twenty minutes. We won't make it."

Celia shook her head and closed her notebook. "We're going there. Now."

"We agreed that…"

"No. This isn't one of those. Let's go." With that, Celia stood up and headed out.

She sat in her car and waited to see what he would do. If he was putting up an act, this would be a good test. After a five-minute wait, she wanted to drive out. Then she saw him exit the restaurant. He got into his car and they drove off together.

They arrived at the Dune Oil offices after an hour and found the vigil underway. The open-plan office that had been full of Christmas decorations a few days earlier was now draped in black cloths. Lit candles were strategically placed on workers' desks.

Seats were arranged to face the mini-stage that was used during the party. Some staffers were dressed in black, but most dressed in their regular outfits. Celia and Fezile took two empty chairs at the back and listened as one of the bosses gave a moving tribute to Lizzy's work. Sniffles punctuated the air every so often.

Ten minutes later a break was called, and tea was served to everyone. Celia spotted Fridah and went to talk to her.

"She was a gem, that's for sure," Fridah said as she massaged the mug of tea in between her palms.

"I only spent a few minutes with her and she left a strong impression. You said she had the sniffles that day. You mean she was unwell the previous week?"

Fridah nodded. "She had a regular cold. Nothing serious. She was always in good health."

"How was she in the office? Did she have any disagreements with anyone?" Celia asked.

Fridah shook her head. "None that I know of. She was a model employee, frankly. Although she was one of the younger ones, she was mature beyond her years. She was more of a peacemaker than a rabble-rouser. That's one of the things I liked about her."

"She was due for a promotion. How did everyone else feel about it?" Celia asked.

Fridah smiled. "She was competitive, that's true. But if she was going to compete with anyone then it would be me. We were both eyeing the same position. One of us was going to get it and she came out on top."

"How did that make you feel?"

Fridah sighed. "Disappointed, of course. But it wasn't the end of the world."

"That's a good mantra to live by. Are you lined up to take up her place now?" Celia asked, watching Fridah's reactions keenly.

Fridah sighed. "You know what? It's too early to think about that. Right now, I just need to mourn a dear friend."

To Celia, Fridah seemed genuine in her grief. There wasn't a single sign of deception.

"I understand. Sorry for your loss," Celia replied.

"Thank you," Fridah said.

Celia didn't see the need of mingling too much with employees she didn't know, so she looked for Fezile. She spotted him standing on the balcony.

Sensing her arrival, he turned to her. "There you are. I'm leaving now. I think we've done enough consoling for one day."

"I think I'll hang around for a few more minutes. Thanks for coming out," she replied.

"Thanks for pushing me. I'm normally not comfortable with these types of things. See you soon," he said and left.

Celia stood at the balcony, watching the shimmering sun fall towards the horizon. Next to her, a few employees were fixated by the sight.

There was a faint vibration in her bag. She unzipped it and took out her phone.

Remember the time you were told to harvest darkness?

Another text. Once again, it was a memory from her first year in high school. She was still being broken into the system. The harvesting darkness prank was one of several that happened. It involved the task of filling a bucket with darkness and delivering it to the bully that sent you. Obviously, no one could execute such a task, leading to other dehumanizing punishments. However, this didn't last long. Six weeks later, the girl was expelled after Celia reported her antics. For a long time, those memories were left in the past. But with these reminders, she realized they were still vivid to her. Although she wasn't that victim anymore, someone else was determined to revive them. But why these memories? Why not the happier ones?

"Is this a prank? Tell me who you are or stop sending me these texts," Celia said to herself as she typed the same. She sent the message and waited. The reply came fast.

My texts are important. I hope you don't realize this when it's too late.

Celia winced. This wasn't a riddle or a clue that would be ideal for a treasure hunt.

It was a warning.

11

This stranger wasn't giving her a fighting chance. Who did she need to remember? Celia asked herself.

The beautiful view before her suddenly became cold and unimportant. As much as she wanted to believe it, this wasn't a prank. Celia couldn't shake off the thought that the texts were connected to something more sinister.

She quickly left the vigil. Throughout the drive, she tried to keep her mind off the texts by listening to her curated mix of music. She didn't want to get to her mother's place in a worrisome state. It did help, as she arrived home in a better mood.

"Ah, just the person I was waiting for!" Mrs. Owens exclaimed as Celia walked into the living room. Mrs. Owens stood in front of the television and Celia's mother lay on the couch.

"What's going on here?" Celia asked.

"Oh, we're just warming up for a little rehearsal," Mrs. Owens replied.

"But I thought those were to happen at your house?" Celia said.

"I do special sessions for your mother here. She needs some extra help. I also need to coach myself since I'm the choir leader. But first, I got you some more holiday destinations. Have you booked your flights yet?" Mrs. Owens asked as she rummaged through her handbag. She took out three glossy brochures and handed them to Celia.

"How did you get these?" Celia asked.

"I know a friend with a travel agency. She had some pretty interesting packages, I tell you. I was even tempted to take one myself. You'll find her contact details at the back of the brochures."

Celia perused the brochures. They were for trips to Madagascar, Morocco, and Zimbabwe.

Mrs. Owens came closer to Celia. "I picked the ones I liked. Morocco caught my eye because of the city of Tangier. I've read captivating novels about the bohemian cafes and how much like Europe it is today. It's a nice way to experience another continent without going too far, don't you think? Oh, and Madagascar will be a hit with the kids. They'll be thinking of all the sights and sounds from the cartoons, but then you surprise them with the stunning beaches and the boat rides they will take. Then Zimbabwe has the spectacular Victoria Falls. I was there twice when I was in my forties and it was simply breath-taking. You should trek up there during sunrise. It's an easier trek to get up there. Plus, Zimbabwe is a closer holiday destination than the rest. It might be a pretty good bargain."

Celia stared at Mrs. Owens, amazed that she had become an impromptu tour guide.

"You're spending a lot of time on these. Please, these are enough for now. Thanks a lot for the effort," Celia said.

"The pleasure is all mine. Are you joining us?" Mrs. Owens asked.

Celia shook her head. "I've got a few other things to get out of the way."

"Did you find the prankster?" Audrey asked.

"What prankster?" Mrs. Owens asked.

"Cece believes you've been pranking her the last few days with strange text messages," Audrey replied.

"I didn't say those exact words, Ma," Celia protested.

"Is that so? What messages are these?" Mrs. Owens asked.

"Someone's been sending me texts of high school memories. And I did say if it's one of you then you can reveal yourself now," Celia said as she eyed her mother.

"It's not me, Cece. I told you," Audrey said.

"I'm too old for pranks these days. I prefer carols," Mrs. Owens replied.

"Why don't you talk to Rosie Williams? You were both pretty close in high school," Audrey suggested.

"Funny you should say that because I was going to call her today," Celia replied.

"She might have the answers you're looking for."

"Thanks, Ma," Celia said as she walked to the bedroom.

"We're still holding the slot in the choir for you," Mrs. Owens said.

"You'll be waiting a long time," Celia whispered to herself as she shut the door.

She immediately called Rosie Williams. Her mother was right, she might have the answers. But Celia didn't plan on stopping with Rosie. She needed to find out who else from her high school was still in Sunshine Cove. That was one way of narrowing down the person responsible.

Surprisingly, Rosie was open to having a chat that very evening. Celia freshened up and left for her date with Rosie.

They met at Lily Dhow restaurant, which overlooked the beachfront. The sun had already set, but they chose to sit on the balcony since there was a soft breeze that evening. Soft jazz music filtered across the place to create a very relaxing ambience.

Rosie still looked youthful, with her colorful evening dress and ponytail hair. Celia had donned a gray maxi dress that did the job without being attention-grabbing.

"I'm glad you called, Cece. It's been a while," Rosie said as they looked through the menu.

"Yes, it has. How's it going with the family business?" Celia asked.

"It's doing quite well, thanks. I've gotten used to the pace in Sunshine Cove again," Rosie replied with a smile. She had a maturity and calmness about her that always intrigued Celia. Maybe it came with the exposure to wealth since Rosie came from a well-to-do family. She had moved back from Johannesburg to help run the family business.

Although they had been high school mates, their friendship began while in primary school after they met at a local debate club competition. They struck a fast friendship and they would often meet at debating events.

"It's funny how life becomes a maze when we grow up. We can't do the casual meets like we used to," Celia remarked.

"What do you call this? I mean, we're meeting less than two hours after you asked for the date. I think that's progress," Rosie replied. They both laughed.

"Speaking of childhood, how much do you remember about our time in high school?" Celia asked.

Rosie raised a brow. "Which part of high school are we talking about?"

"Well, the first year," Celia replied.

"I do remember we didn't compete with each other as much as we did in primary school. You always used to win those debates."

"You beat me twice, though," Celia chimed in.

"But you were a legend in the world of debating. That was a fact. Anyway, I remember that our friendship didn't gel that well in the first year of high school. But I remember quite a bit. Why do you ask?"

"Why do you think we didn't keep nurturing our friendship that first year?" Celia asked.

"If I told you I'd have to kill you," Rosie said in a conspiratorial tone.

"Do you mean that?" Celia asked.

"Mean what?"

"You'd kill me if you told me?"

Rosie chuckled. "I'm joking! Why would I do that about childhood memories?"

"I'm just curious," Celia replied.

The waiter interrupted them and took their orders. When he left, Celia found Rosie staring at her with a quizzical expression.

"What? "Celia asked.

Rosie's eyes narrowed. "You took that seriously for a reason. Why?"

"Someone's been sending me strange texts with stuff about high school. I was wondering if it was you."

"Oh. Wow. I wouldn't do that. Texts about which high school stuff?"

"Just some stuff that I did. I'm pretty sure I shared some of those memories with you," Celia said, "If you're behind it you can tell me now."

Celia didn't want to tell Rosie the exact nature of the texts, just in case she knew more than she was saying.

"This is beginning to feel like an interrogation," Rosie commented.

"I'm just asking a straight question. You have my number. You know me better than most people. Are you sending me those texts?" Celia asked.

"I swear if it was me I would. I would only do that if it was a prank, and I'm not up for that this Christmas," Rosie replied.

Celia gave a shaky smile. A few seconds of silence passed between them.

"I'm sorry about that. I overstepped a bit. Let me go freshen up. I'll be right back," Celia said. She quickly left the table.

While in the washroom, Celia looked at her reflection in the mirror as she cleared her head. Was she normal? Why would she bring an old friend and put her on the spot like that? She calmed down and realized while her approach may have been not as smooth as she would've liked; it was justified. She needed answers, and she was asking one of the people likely to have the answers.

She walked back wearing her warmest smile, determined to liven up the evening. However, as she got to their table, she noticed that Rosie looking spaced out. In her hand was Celia's mobile phone.

"You forgot your phone, and a text came in," Rosie said.

"Why are you reading my messages after what we talked about?" Celia asked.

"I was curious. I was wondering what's bothering you."

The awkward silence returned as they held gazes. Rosie's eyes flashed with fear.

"What does the text say?" Celia asked.

Rosie handed her the phone.

The text read: *Remember me yet? The key to a saved life or certain death is in your hands.*

12

"You shouldn't have looked in my phone," Celia said to Rosie.

"As I said, I was just concerned about you."

"What else were you checking for?" Celia asked.

"Nothing, that's all I saw," Rosie replied.

"Give me your phones," Celia said, holding out her hand.

"Cece, what's this about?"

"Prove to me you're not a part of this. Show me your phones."

Rosie reached into her bag and took out her three mobile phones. They were all high-end smartphones. Two had facial recognition locks, and the third used a fingerprint lock. Rosie unlocked them.

"I only need to check your call logs and message outbox," Celia said as she scrolled through the first phone.

Five minutes later, she was done. She handed the phones back to Rosie.

"I told you I had nothing to do with it," Rosie said.

"I'm sorry. It's just that this is starting to get to me a little bit."

"Don't let it. It's already clouding your judgment," Rosie advised.

"Look, it was nice seeing you, Rosie. But I've got to go. I'm not myself tonight. I'm sorry," Celia said as she took her bag.

"Where are you going?"

"To seek the help of a friend," she replied.

An hour later, Celia sat opposite Bill in his office. He was working late, and she took the chance to pass by. There were other officers around that night, but it was less busy.

Bill was reading the texts on her phone. "Why didn't you come to me earlier?"

"I thought it was a prank. So, I didn't make much of it," she replied. "Now I think they might be coming from the killer."

He looked up from the screen. "The killer?"

"The two deaths that happened at the offices?"

Bill leaned back in his chair. "I've not received the results of those post mortems yet. They're still testing for some substances. So you can't say they were murdered just yet. This might still be a prank."

"It's not. Trust me," she replied.

Bill held her gaze and then went back to check the messages. "Each text came from a different number. These types of numbers are hard to trace because they are computer-generated. This person could pretend to be from anywhere in the world."

"But computers are interconnected. There has to be a way to trace them," Celia said.

"There's a young kid here who's part of our Computer Fraud division. They've handled cases that used these kinds of numbers. I'll ask him for a favor," Bill said as he stood up.

"Please ask him to try his best. It's driving me crazy," Celia said.

Bill walked to the door. He paused and turned to her. "If this isn't a prank, I hope you've thought about someone in your childhood who might be doing this."

"I'm still working on it," she replied.

"Work harder, just in case," he said and left.

Celia sighed. She was too tired to start digging the past for possible names.

Ten minutes later, Bill returned. "He's going to give it a shot. Now we wait and see."

"What's the probability?" Celia asked.

"Ten to twenty percent. It's a well-designed system to mask the source. But as they say, nothing is foolproof," Bill replied.

Just then, a detective holding a brown envelope appeared at the door. "Sir, the post mortem results just got dropped off."

"Finally," Bill said. The detective gave the envelope to Bill, who immediately tore the seal with a letter opener.

He took out two different sheets of paper and held them side by side. As he read the results, his eyes widened. He kept shifting his attention from one document to the other.

"What do they say?" Celia asked.

Bill didn't respond, checking the results on each document one more time. He then slowly lowered the documents and looked into her eyes.

"Traces of poison were found in the internal organs of the two victims. You might be right. You've been exchanging texts with the killer." Bill said matter-of-factly.

13

"*I* might be right?" Celia asked. "We just confirmed they were murdered. Isn't that sufficient proof that I'm right?"

"You're right about the murders. It's now a case under my docket. I can now rally my team and resources around this. However, we're yet to connect the texts to the killer. Whoever is texting you needs to say something incriminating. Otherwise, it could still be someone with a dark sense of humor who knows you've been to these office parties," Bill replied.

"I'm beginning to sound like a broken record, but it's not a prank, Bill," Celia said.

"As I said, cases rely on strong tangible evidence, not theories. What connects the poisoned victims to the texts? What connects the victims? How are they connected to the killer? These are the questions we have to answer," Bill replied.

Celia went quiet. Bill was right, but she didn't want to hear more doubt or uncertainty.

"Alright then. You'll visit the victims' offices and interview the staff as well? I think some of your men did this earlier," Celia asked.

"They did, but now we go in proper. Naturally. I want to piece together the events leading up to their deaths."

"Are you going to at least let me know if there are patterns?" Celia asked.

"And you'll be interviewed as a witness. If there's anything else that might influence you, I'll let you know. But only as much as is needed. Nothing more," he replied.

"That doesn't sound as reassuring as you want it to," Celia remarked.

"You need to always remember you're a civilian, Cece. It will protect you," Bill said.

Just then, her mobile phone vibrated. She glanced at the screen. She bit her lower lip.

"What does it say?" Bill asked. When she didn't respond, he took the phone from her and read the message.

What is invisible and you only get to see it when it's dipped in the mud?

"What's this supposed to mean?" Bill asked.

Celia walked over to the window and stared outside.

"Celia?"

"I usually get very straightforward texts. This one is more abstract. It's a riddle," she replied.

"You're sure?"

"Yes. I'm expected to answer or else I won't get the next clue."

Bill sighed. "As you figure out the riddle, let me give this new number a shot. Might get lucky," he said. He jotted down the number in his notebook, placed her phone on top of his desk, and left.

She thought about the riddle, but nothing came to mind. It didn't trigger any memories about high school. Maybe it was a sign that this was a treasure hunt.

"I've got to take a walk," she said to herself. She grabbed the phone and walked out of Bill's office. Outside, it was a warm summer night. She walked slowly to her car. When she reached it without any new ideas coming to mind, she decided to call her mother.

CHRISTMAS CAROLS AND LIPSTICK PERILS

"Ma, what's invisible and you only get to see it when it's dipped in the mud?" Celia asked.

"Are you trying to make me age faster? How am I supposed to know?" Audrey asked.

"We always solve riddles together."

"The only thing that comes to mind is glass."

"Hmm. Glass. You might be right. Thanks for the chat, Ma," Celia said and hung up.

Celia quickly replied and waited. Moments later, the reply came in.

You're smarter than I thought. Do you remember now?

'You need to give me a more specific clue to remember you,' Celia texted back.

I'm right here in Sunshine Cove. It shouldn't be hard.

Celia's mind was still too tired to start thinking of all the former high school mates who were still in town, or how many they were. Other than Rosie, she wasn't in touch with any of them.

'At least give me your initials,' Celia texted back. The reply was prompt.

Too bad. You could've saved a life if you tried harder. Goodnight, Celia.

14

Celia banged on the roof of her car. The palm of her hand stung a little, and she acknowledged that it wasn't a good way of expressing her frustration.

She knew she had work to do before the next office party, which was a few days away. She needed to build a list of former high school mates who were still in Sunshine Cove. Hopefully, by elimination, she would find the person behind the text messages. If she didn't do this, the killer would wreak more havoc at the next office party. She had to stop it.

"Did you find anything?" Celia asked as she walked back into Bill's office.

Bill looked up from his desk. "Nope. The trail keeps bouncing off different computers around the world so it may take a while."

Celia sat down. "A while means an hour or two?"

Bill shrugged. "Hard to tell at the moment. Are you okay?"

"Yes," Celia said, "Why?"

"You just look a little more flustered than you were earlier."

"I do? Oh, it must be because I was talking on the phone for a bit there."

"Who were you talking to?"

"Erm, a difficult client. Dealing with unusual demands isn't easy," Celia replied.

Bill's gaze lingered on her face for a few more seconds.

"What?" she asked.

"I hope this stuff isn't getting to you," he said.

"Well, it's not the greatest feeling in the world. But I'll have to find a way to cope," she replied.

"I think you can spend time with your family. Bond with them a bit. Forget about work and this other stuff. It'll refresh you," he advised.

Celia cocked her head to one side. "You're right. I should go and get some downtime." She stood up. "You'll let me know how it's going with the tracking, right?"

Bill nodded. "Sure."

Celia drove to her mother's house. This time, she wasn't surprised to find her watching another late-night Christmas movie.

"Ma, do you still have my yearbook from high school?" Celia asked.

"I'm sure it's somewhere in my bedroom. Why?" Audrey replied without shifting her gaze from the TV screen.

"I just want to check out my yearbook, that's all," Celia replied.

"This is about the prank texts, isn't it?" Audrey asked.

"It's triggered a few memories I want to revisit. My mind has been a little foggy about some of them."

"You don't have to go back to the past, you know," Audrey said as she got up.

"Don't worry, I'll be fine," Celia replied.

Her mother went into her bedroom and ten minutes later walked out with the yearbook. Celia could tell it had been well looked after, as the hardcover was in pristine condition.

Celia sat down and studied the cover.

"You want some masala tea with that? Looks like you'll be turning the pages for a while," her mother asked.

"Yes, please," Celia replied with a smile.

The yearbook cover had the name Blue Wave School embossed on it. Around the edges were fading stickers they used to buy from the shop.

On the second page, Celia read the different messages written by her classmates on the last day of high school. As she read them, she smiled. They were all surprisingly confident and inspirational instead of sad and melancholic. She remembered how hopeful they all were that they would end up in the same universities afterward. The reality check came soon enough as they got to the real world. Celia had quickly made peace that life has seasons, and she would never see some of her classmates again.

Although all the thirty classmates she had at the time left messages in her book, what she was most interested in were those she used to hang out with the most. They were not necessarily a clique, but they were the most likely to know a bit more about her personal experiences. Most of them had become her best friends after she survived the bullying during her first year.

Many left Sunshine Cove after high school, but a few had stayed over the years. Of those who had stayed, she wasn't sure who was still around, as she had only maintained regular communication with Rosie for most of her adulthood. She felt slightly embarrassed at this. She was sure Rosie met some of them on her own volition, but Celia hadn't taken much interest in pursuing those old connections. Life was a funny thing. The older you got, the more you drifted away from your formative years. Life has different seasons and perhaps holding on to the connections might have hindered her development into the woman she was today.

She singled out the most personal messages written on the page. She took out her notebook and started writing down the names of those she considered her closest friends at the time. Angela Mbeki, the deputy-mayor's daughter; Tshala Nketsi, her nemesis- turned-friend; Sally Khumalo, who always wanted to be a singer; Anna Pumzile, the multi-talented one; Zandiswa Lebohang, who was shy but the smartest of her friends at the time; Rehane Vander, her proud former neighbor who always dreamed of traveling the world; Megan Botha, who came from a rich family and always shared out her treats;

Faith Sakayi, the gossip who always had a story to tell; and Tumiso Zondi, the tomboy who kept them in check.

After listing them, Celia flipped through the pages and checked the photos of each name. People do change their looks over time, but some distinct features can stand the test of time. She found herself smiling, appreciating the innocent-looking faces. When she saw hers, she was surprised at how she still had puffy cheeks.

She then went to the address book and started getting their home addresses. She couldn't trace most of them, but all she needed were some contacts. She was confident she would be able to track down the rest.

When she was done with her shortlist, it was way past midnight. Her mother had already turned in.

She gave the yearbook one more pass before she closed it for the night. She hovered over the innocent, smiling faces. They had all taken different paths in life.

One of them had chosen murder.

"I'm coming for you, whoever you are," Celia whispered.

15

"Stop everything you're doing, Mel. I need your help with something," Celia said as she strode into the nail parlor's mezzanine office the next morning.

Melanie, who was working on a proposal, looked up from her computer. "Good morning to you, too."

"I'm sorry. Good morning," Celia said as she took out her notebook. She walked to the whiteboard and listed the nine names of her former schoolmates.

"Are those clients?" Melanie asked.

"Suspects" Celia replied.

"Suspects of what?"

"The texts and murders. These are my former high schoolmates. They were the ones most likely to know or have an idea about some things I've been getting in the texts," she said.

Melanie stood and walked to the whiteboard. "So, they're all living in Sunshine Cove?"

"I'm not sure they are all here. I don't have some phone numbers and addresses, but it's possible," Celia replied.

"This might take some time and we have a business to run, you know," Melanie replied.

"Mel, I know that. But I also don't have any peace of mind knowing there's someone out there playing a sick game while killing innocent people around me," Celia replied.

"*Eish*. You make it sound so dark. That person must be carrying some strong evil inside them," Melanie remarked.

"Trust me, I'm still coming to terms with it. What I'd like you to do is help me call these people up. The first phase is to find out who still lives in Sunshine Cove. Nothing more."

"I'll be honest. I think we're doing something crazy, but I'll help you," she said.

"Thank you. Let's do it within the hour and see where it gets us," Celia said, reaching for her mobile phone.

They spent the next hour making phone calls and, where necessary, searching online. After an hour, they had narrowed down their list to five names: Angela Mbeki, Anna Pumzile, Tshala Nketsi, Rehane Vander, and Faith Sakayi. Megan, Zandiswa, and Tumiso had immigrated to Europe. Sally died in a road accident three years earlier.

They both stared at the shortened list. Next to each name was an address and phone number.

"What do we do now?" Melanie asked.

"We call them. You take three, I take three," Celia replied.

"Wait, a minute. Before we even think of that, you've never bumped into any of them in recent times?" Melanie asked.

Celia shook her head. "None in the last three years. I bumped into Rehane at the mall once, with her rich fiancé. I also met Tshala. We chatted a bit, and that was it."

Melanie stared. "That's a surprising record. You had no disagreements with any of them?"

Celia laughed. "That's a part of childhood. But nothing serious. The only one who fits that category was Tshala. But she was my enemy before we became friends."

"But when you met, you didn't talk much."

"No, it wasn't out of spite. At least I don't think it was. We were just two awkward adults with nothing to talk about," Celia replied.

"Let's get to work."

Melanie put her hand up. "Wait, we're not just randomly calling them. You were their former classmate. I'm just a stranger. What do I say?"

"Tell them you're my assistant and are confirming who they are and that I'd like to talk to them," Celia suggested.

Melanie chuckled. "You're becoming good at this deception thing. I'm not sure if that's a good thing or a bad thing."

"Mel, I'm still me. This side of me is not for the people I care about," Celia replied.

"If you say so," Melanie replied as she reached for her phone.

After a few phone calls, Celia eliminated both Angela and Tshala. The latter now ran a children's home on the outskirts of town and had her hands full raising a generation of orphaned kids. On the other hand, Angela got married and had moved to Johannesburg a month earlier.

Celia focused on the remaining three. She wanted to set up a meeting with each of them. With her training in reading body language, she knew a face-to-face encounter would help her identify odd behavior. She spoke to Anna Pumzile, who ran several businesses in town. She didn't promise a meeting but asked Celia to check in later. Celia couldn't reach Rehane on the available number, and she assumed that she had changed it. She had a physical address as a backup. Lastly, she had a brief conversation with Faith, who was running to court to represent a client in a case. She promised to call back.

"How about you arrange a mini-reunion for just the four of you? It might be a good way to get all of them in one place and chat them up," Melanie suggested.

Celia shook her head. "It feels a little too soon right now. I don't know the history they have with each other. The safest bet is to meet them individually. I can get a better feel of who they are."

"Who are you going to meet first?" Melanie asked.

"Let's start with the one who seems the hardest to get," Celia replied.

That afternoon, Celia drove up to the Craven Residences neighborhood, passing several high gates until she came to house number seventy-two. It had a tall, wrought-iron gate. The gates opened as soon as she got close to it, which surprised her.

She soon understood why. As much as you could get past the front gate, there were two more barrier gates along the one-kilometer road leading to the house. She was stopped at the first one after three hundred metres.

A man wearing a well-pressed security guard uniform walked up to her and leaned into the driver's window.

"Hello, Madam. Who are you here to see?" he asked.

"Hello. I'm here to see Rehane Garber," Celia replied.

"Do you have an appointment?"

"No, I don't. I just thought I'd drop by and see an old friend," she replied.

The guard shook his head. "It doesn't work that way. You need to set an appointment."

"Now that I'm here and I don't have her number, can you call her and set it for me? Just give me a date and time," Celia suggested.

The guard straightened, then walked to the guardhouse. She saw him use the landline phone to make a call. Minutes later, he returned. "Miss Garber has set your appointment for right now," he said. He walked to the side and raised the barrier.

Celia smiled as she drove through. As she approached the second barrier after three hundred more metres, it was raised before she got to it too. She drove through and noticed the line of tall trees that emerged on either side as she got closer to the house. She soon saw the imposing facade of a palatial townhouse.

She parked in the sizeable parking space in front of the house. Although there were no other cars visible, Celia noticed the three-car garage. She was pretty sure there were some pricey vehicles behind the rolled down shutter doors.

She walked to the solid wood front door and rang the bell. As she waited, a gentle breeze caressed her face.

The door opened, and a tall woman with long black hair opened the door. Wearing a bright yellow sundress and jewelry, she looked like a princess.

"Well, look what the cat dragged in," Rehane said as she stared down at Celia.

16

"You're not addressing me, right? Because it might not end well," Celia replied, giving Rehane an icy glare.

The two women stared at each other for a few seconds before bursting out in laughter. They embraced.

"It's so good to see you, Cece," Rehane said.

"Am I the only thing you're missing in this fancy house you live in?" Celia teased.

"That, and maybe a pet tiger for my amusement. Come on in."

Rehane led her down the hallway. Inside, its high ceilings and white walls gave you the impression you were in a castle. In a way, it mimicked Rehane's personality.

Unless you knew her, you'd always feel smaller around Rehane and it wasn't due to her height. She had a way of making you feel smaller, even from a stare. It had been this way since they were children. They were neighbors while growing up. Rehane had always spoken about flying to other countries, visiting exotic beaches, and living a life of fun and adventure. Her ambitious daydreams usually made you wonder if you needed to revise your own.

After high school, Rehane's parents moved to another neighborhood, and they lost touch.

But when Celia had bumped into her at the mall some years back, Rehane looked happy. She was arm-in-arm with a rich man who looked ten years her senior.

They walked through a door leading out into the sun-bathed garden. It had green, luscious grass that was being watered by a sprinkler. Fruit trees dotted the landscape. Out of the corner of her eye, Celia saw a Boerboel dog amble towards them.

The dog wagged its tail as Rehane patted it. Celia froze, surprised by how big it was.

"Don't worry about him, he's a gentle soul," Rehane said. The dog came to Celia, and she patted it as well.

"He's a good sport, "Celia remarked.

"He loves most visitors," Rehane said. They sat down under the verandah. "So, what brings you over?"

"I have been getting flashbacks lately about our high school days. So, I decided to touch base," she said, watching for Rehane's reaction.

Rehane adjusted her hair. "Have you now? What kind of flashbacks?"

"You tell me," Celia said.

Rehane raised a brow. "I have no idea what you're talking about."

"Are you sure? You've not sent me nostalgic text messages about the good old days?"

Rehane shook her head. "I avoid my phone like the plague. If I need to use it, I usually call. You'll never find me texting."

"Did you change your number?"

"I'm always changing my number. There are a lot of strange people out there," Rehane replied.

"I know what you mean," Celia replied.

"Sounds like someone is trying to reach out to you for some reason," Rehane remarked.

"That's what a friend of mine is saying," Celia said. She looked around her. "This is a pretty nice place. How's your husband doing?" Celia asked.

Rehane wiped her nose. "He's not around anymore."

"What do you mean?"

"He died last year," Rehane said, lowering her eyes.

"Oh my. I'm sorry to hear that. You two looked so good together when we met," Celia said.

"Thank you. Life has its ups and downs," Rehane replied.

"I know what you mean. If you don't mind me asking, how did your husband pass on?"

"I'd rather not talk about it. It's still a sensitive subject for me," Rehane replied.

"I understand. I lost mine a couple of years ago. It still lingers to this day. Listen, would you be open to meeting again with maybe two other people from our high school days? Just to do lunch or dinner and catch up sometime?" Celia asked.

"Who else do you have in mind?"

"Just Anna Pumzile and Faith Sakayi."

Rehane frowned. "I'm not sure about that. This quiet life away from the masses is kind of good for me. I have my small circle of friends and I'm content with that. But I don't mind meeting with you again."

A butler brought a bottle of grape juice and two glasses. He poured the drink into each glass before excusing himself.

"To good memories?" Rehane asked as she raised her glass.

"To good memories," Celia replied. They clinked glasses.

Celia spent the next two hours with Rehane, talking about many other things in life. She learned that Rehane stayed at home most of the time unless a business engagement came up. She didn't have a child during her marriage, so when her husband died, she inherited his estate and businesses. She was set for life, so long as she kept the businesses and investments healthy.

When she left Rehane's, Celia couldn't help feeling a sense of sadness. As much as she was living the lifestyle of her dreams, Rehane wasn't happy. There was an emptiness that Celia couldn't explain. She had the feeling that Rehane was hiding behind her reclusive nature. She also wondered how Rehane's husband met his death.

Celia drove towards town. She had called Anna earlier, and she had told Celia to pass by anytime. Celia drove up to Anna's Delights, a bakery on the edge of the town's business district. It had a colorful exterior. A life-size caricature of a woman holding up fresh loaves of bread stood at the front of the shop. Celia walked in. It looked like a mini-supermarket with low shelves across the space. Celia walked over to the counter to talk to the cashier.

"Excuse me. I'm looking for Anna Pumzile," Celia said. She had just finished her query when Anna walked into the store with another lady.

Anna smiled when she saw Celia. "Hey, Celia!"

"Hey, Anna, how are you?" Celia replied as they shook hands.

"I'm well. Wow, you just popped in," Anna said.

"You did say I could walk in anytime, right?" Celia said.

"Yes, I did, I can't deny that. However, I'm going to a meeting right now. Can you come tomorrow evening, say at five?" Anna asked.

Celia nodded. "Sure, I can do that. I'm meeting Faith Sakayi tomorrow as well."

"That's super," Anna said. "She's a lawyer now. She helped me on a case not too long ago."

"Thanks for that tip. I look forward to meeting her." Celia replied.

As Celia exited the shop and walked back to her car, she wondered why Anna needed Faith's services. Faith was, for all intents and purposes, a criminal lawyer.

When she got back to her mother's house that evening, Celia was exhausted. After dinner, she somehow found the strength to listen to her boys tell stories about the man-eating lions of Tsavo. They had pressured her mother to get them a book about the lions from the local library. Their excitement about it was palpable as they both shouted at the top of their lungs and made wild gestures with their arms and faces.

It was almost seven o'clock when there was a knock on the door.

"Sorry I'm late, Audrey. I got caught up talking to some choir members," Mrs. Owens said as she casually entered the house. John and James ran to hug her. They were both rewarded with a lollipop each.

"You look like you got hit by a train," Mrs. Owens said to Celia.

Celia half-smiled. "If I had known you were coming, I would've tried to freshen up."

Mrs. Owens laughed. "Well, I've got something that will cheer you up," she said as she reached into her large handbag. She took out several brochures and held them out with a sparkle in her eyes. "I've found you more great places to check out!"

She walked up to Celia and placed them in front of her.

Celia's tired eyes widened. "Why are you doing this?"

"I simply want you to have a fantastic vacation," Mrs. Owens replied.

"I'm not sure that's what we really want. I told you not to spend so much time on this," Celia replied.

"Well, she's simply trying to be helpful," Audrey chimed in.

"No, she's not. She's trying to control what we do," Celia said.

"I beg your pardon?" Mrs. Owens asked.

Audrey turned to the boys, "John and James, go and play in your room for a few minutes."

The boys lingered for a few seconds before Audrey got up and led them to the bedroom.

"What's troubling you, Cece?" Mrs. Owens asked once the kids had left.

"You keep coming here every single day with brochures and ideas about destinations that no one can visit even in a year," Celia protested.

"I know a few people who travel to these places every year."

"Well, we're not one of them," Celia replied.

"I know, child. But you can at least look at the brochures and find one location that works for you," Mrs. Owens said.

"There's no point in it."

"Why not?" Mrs. Owens asked as Audrey returned to the living room.

Celia exhaled. "I don't have the cash needed to go on holiday. We'll spend Christmas here."

Audrey and Mrs. Owens exchanged glances.

"But what about the boys?" Audrey asked.

"We'll make it up to them later," Celia replied.

"What happened, Cece? I don't understand this," Audrey said.

"You'll hate me for it, but that's just the way it is. I just can't afford it," Celia replied.

With that, Celia walked out the front door, leaving Audrey and Mrs. Owens struggling to digest the news.

17

Celia walked up and down the street for half an hour. The night was warm but windy this time. She rarely took such walks, but tonight she needed a breather. There was hardly anyone else walking at that hour, so she had the road all to herself and her thoughts. She'd wanted to keep fighting the reality, hanging on to an outside chance that she'd make enough money before Christmas. But it wasn't adding up. She realized she'd not only been worried about letting her family down but also about not being able to recover fast enough. She'd even viewed the nail parlor investment as a mistake. The walk helped her accept that she had done the right thing. She now acknowledged it as a sacrifice that was starting to pay off.

The wind grew stronger and kicked up more dust and sand, which she took as her cue to return home. Her mother and Mrs. Owens were talking when she came in. They went silent.

Celia cleared her throat. "I'm sorry about my earlier outburst. I didn't mean to talk to you that way."

"It's fine, Cece. We were just a little shocked that you were carrying that burden alone," Audrey said as she walked over to her. She stood next to Celia, with an arm around her shoulder.

"I didn't want to let you down. But here we are. Sometimes you attract what you fear the most," Celia remarked.

"You haven't failed us. You're an amazing daughter, a fantastic mother who fights for her sons no matter what. I'd rather have that than anything else," Audrey said.

"I'm with your mother on that one. You're a powerhouse. We'll be here to make it a great Christmas for you and the kids, even if you're not traveling," Mrs. Owens said.

"I'm glad to hear that," Celia said with a half-smile.

"But there's a catch. I need a different kind of apology from you. I've talked to your mother, and we agreed you'd both attend the Christmas carol practise tomorrow," Mrs. Owens said.

"Do I have to?" Celia asked.

"Do you want to make amends for the outburst? This is how you do it for me," Mrs. Owens said with a cheeky grin.

Celia slowly nodded. "Alright. I'll be there."

Mrs. Owens pumped a fist in the air. "That's the spirit!"

The next day, Celia woke up early and made several deliveries to some of her clients. Once done, she drove to Regent Court, a block of apartments converted into offices. She walked into the offices of Provost Law that were located on the first floor.

"Hello. I'm looking for Faith Sakayi. Is she in?" Celia asked the receptionist.

"Have you booked an appointment?" the receptionist asked.

"No, I haven't. I had tried calling her, but she didn't answer," Celia replied.

"Unfortunately, she's not in. May I ask who's looking for her?"

"I'm Celia Dube, an old schoolmate of hers. When will she be back?"

"It's hard to say. She's usually in court at this time," the receptionist replied. "You could leave your details and I'll have her call you back."

Celia left her phone number and proposed an appointment for the next day.

Celia strode out of the building's front door and into the afternoon sun. To her surprise, she was able to recognize Faith, who was approaching the entrance in the company of a bald man. She was dressed in a full black skirt suit, while the man wore a gray suit.

"...and thereafter we'll follow it to trial. I hope it gets fast-tracked because sometimes the court schedules can have a massive backlog," Faith said to the man.

"Sounds like a plan," the man drawled.

"Faith Sakayi?" Celia said.

Faith stopped to look at her. "Yes?"

"It's me, Celia. We went to the same high school?"

Faith's face came alive. "Oh, yes! Wow, it's been a while!"

"Yes, it has. I was actually coming to see you. Anna Pumzile sent me, she told me you handled a case for her."

"Oh yes, yes. Let me just finish off here and I'll be with you in a minute," Faith said as she moved aside with the man. Celia watched Faith talk to the man animatedly as he nodded throughout. She employed her body language skills, taking note of highlights such as the scar on the man's face, the expensive wristwatch, and the fact he kept glancing towards her occasionally. He was a man of means with high situational awareness. This man was ready for anything at any time, she mused.

Faith said her goodbyes to the man, who walked towards a high-end SUV. The driver of the SUV got out; a hulking, mean-looking man wearing sunglasses. Celia had seen the type and knew their job wasn't just playing chauffeur. It reinforced Celia's earlier assessment: the bald man wasn't just a wealthy client, but also a dangerous man. It made her wonder what sort of cases Faith was handling for men with an intimate knowledge of the underworld.

Faith walked back to her, beaming with a smile. "Again, this is quite a surprise. A blast from the past. How are you?"

"I'm great. It looks like you're doing very well for yourself," Celia replied.

"I try. We've got to keep chasing our purposes in this crazy world. You're looking pretty good yourself," Faith replied.

"You think so? Thanks. In my field it can be a bit more grueling to the skin," Celia said.

"Oh? What do you do?"

"I'm in business. I'm the sole distributor for a major beauty products company. However, I also run a nail parlor in town. You should visit us sometime," Celia said.

"Now that you mention it, I've been thinking of a spruce up soon. But you're asking me to cheat on my salon," Faith replied.

"Is it cheating if it's on the house?" Celia asked. They both laughed.

"What brings you over?" Faith asked.

"Anna told me you're a lawyer. I didn't know you handled all types of clients," Celia said.

"Oh, you're talking about that guy? He's not a client. He works for me."

Celia's jaw dropped. "Are you serious? Working for you as what exactly?"

"He has a special set of skills that suit a business that I run,' Faith replied.

"I'm intrigued. Do you mind if I ask what kind of business it is?"

"I run a chain of nightclubs that tend to attract some big spenders. I need smart people who can handle both the civil side and the not so civil side of things. Especially security," Faith replied. "It goes with the territory."

Celia slowly nodded. "It sounds like a tough business."

"It sure is."

"He and the driver look formidable. Together they can handle all sorts of dirty business," Celia remarked.

Faith's eyes narrowed. "You're a curious one, aren't you?"

Celia smiled. "Guilty as charged. I'm just wondering how they do their thing, frankly."

"If I told you I'd have to kill you," Faith said with an unflinching gaze.

Celia felt her smile fading. She'd heard those words before, but for some reason, they sounded more sinister when Faith said them.

Her words were laced with violence.

18

Celia pursed her lips as she looked into Faith's intense eyes. "Excuse me?"

Faith's smile grew wider. "It was on a light note. I get told that a lot in my line of work. So I find it interesting to say it to other people and see how others react. I think I've grown a little numb to it, but your reaction was the most genuine I've seen in a while."

Celia smiled nervously. "Your delivery was too powerful to ignore."

"I'm sure you experience a little dark humor in your line of work."

"I do, but you face higher stakes," Celia replied.

"What's life without a little risk?" Faith replied. "Let's go talk in my office."

They took the stairs to the first floor. Faith's office wasn't particularly big, but it was well furnished. A copy of her law degree and other certifications hung on the wall. Her polished desk was neatly arranged, with a desktop to one corner. A big shelf filled with books and thick files stood to one side.

Celia sat in one of the two visitor chairs as Faith eased herself into her leather seat behind the desk.

"Tell me what's on your mind," Faith said.

"I wanted to get a better understanding of criminal representation. I'm trying to figure something out. Anna told me you're a criminal lawyer?" Celia asked.

"Yes, I am. Are you in trouble?"

"I can't say much at the moment. Do you enjoy your work?"

"Well, it has its moments," Faith replied.

"I always pictured that it must take quite a leap to defend criminals," Celia said.

"My clients aren't criminals unless convicted by a court of law. Until then, they are just regular citizens like you and me."

"Well, don't you think calling them regular citizens is a stretch?" Celia asked.

Faith's lip twitched, and she leaned forward. "What exactly are you getting at, Celia?"

"I'm not getting at anything. I'm just saying most of the time your clients are actual criminals. Right?"

"That's true at times, yes."

"That's all I was saying."

"Within contexts of their accusations, we always look at them with a clean slate unless we know otherwise," Faith replied.

"And it's worked for you just fine. You've won a lot of cases," Celia remarked.

"I don't blow my own *vuvuzela,* but my record speaks for itself," Faith replied.

"Was Anna's case a criminal one?" Celia asked.

"I can't talk about the details of my clients' cases."

"Understandable. Tell me, would you be open to a meetup with a few girls from our high school years? Maybe me, you, Ann, and some other girls still in Sunshine Cove?" Celia asked.

Faith drummed her fingers on her desk. Celia noted that her short nails were well-polished.

"I guess it's a possibility. When did you want to do this dinner?" Faith asked.

"Oh, I'm just getting to see if people are interested first, then I might plan something," Celia replied. She had found Rehane's reaction to the question interesting and decided to pose it to Faith too.

Faith frowned. "Okay. I'll consider it."

"Great," Celia replied as she stood up. "I don't want to take too much of your time. I'll be in touch."

"You have my number?"

"Yes, Anna gave me your card," Celia said, flashing it.

"Oh. I see," Faith said with a quizzical expression. "Yeah, drop me a message sometime and we'll look into it."

Celia turned to leave.

"Was that all, or did you have another reason for coming?" Faith asked.

Celia turned back to her.

"Oh, I had one more question. When you win a case, let's say you get a murderer off the hook, do they sometimes offer you a reward?"

"What do you mean by reward?"

"Well, do they offer to do something for you as a show of gratitude, separate from your legal fees? Especially things that might not be legal," Celia said.

Faith leaned back in her chair. "If I told you...," she said, her voice trailing off.

Celia understood.

She drove back to the nail parlor, her mind mulling over what kind of power Faith wielded over her criminal clients. When she arrived, she found Melanie attending to a distressed customer.

"It's not the nail technician's fault," Melanie told the customer, a fashionable woman in her twenties.

"Of course, it is!" the woman countered, "my nails have never reacted this way."

Curious, Celia drew closer and looked at the nails the woman was flashing. They were discolored.

Melanie noticed Celia and whispered. "Help me here, what is this? She got her nails done here a couple of weeks ago."

Celia smiled at the woman. "Hi, there. I think you're having an allergic reaction. That's not the fault of the technician, as we use some of the safest products in the market. Have you ever had a manicure before?"

"No, this was my first," the woman said.

"This is something new for your nails and you might be allergic to them. I can give you the name of a good doctor who can attend to you," Celia said.

"Are you serious?"

"I'm simply looking out for you," Celia replied. She wrote down the doctor's number and gave it to the woman. Celia spent a few more minutes reassuring her that she would be fine, and then the woman left.

Sarah Wena, the nail technician who had served her, looked shaken.

"Don't worry about it, Sarah. She'll be fine. Relax," Celia said. Sarah half-smiled and nodded.

Celia and Melanie went up to the mezzanine office.

"Thanks for stepping in. None of us knew what was going on with her. I was just bluffing," Melanie said. "I take it the drive wasn't fruitful?"

Celia shrugged. "Not as I would've liked. Faith's smart and good at what she does. But I didn't get a strong sense that she had a bone to pick with me."

"She might be a good actor."

"I thought the same thing about Rehane. Her husband died mysteriously, and she lives a reclusive life. Something's missing in her life, but she's got a lot of resources if she wanted to pull this off," Celia said.

"What resources does Faith have?"

"She has access to a good roster of criminals to choose from to pull off the murders. But I'm sure there are more efficient ways to kill people rather than poisoning. Why not use guns or something?" Celia asked.

"It's not about who dies. Whoever is doing this wants you to suffer," Melanie said.

Celia pondered this for a moment. "Which means how I react to what happens is important to them. Why?"

"Maybe they want you to be troubled? Or they know you'll be curious and go after them like you're doing now," Melanie said.

"That's a morbid treasure hunt idea," Celia remarked.

"This world is a strange place. The question is, are they watching your reaction from inside or outside the office party?" Melanie asked.

Celia stared at the ceiling as she thought about it. "Definitely from the inside," she replied.

"It's a possibility. What about Anna?" Melanie asked.

"We didn't meet. I'm running out of time before we do the next gig," Celia said.

"Can't you push the gig?"

"You know how it is with Fezile. He doesn't want to shake things up with his client. I don't blame him. What would he say anyway? He's just a service provider," Celia said.

"You can come up with something creative?"

"Nothing short of *'Hello, we'd like to advise you not to do this because one of you might die'* will work," Celia replied.

"You make it sound dramatic," Melanie said.

"Because it is! Watching random people die belongs to the movies, not real life," she said.

Melanie walked up to the whiteboard. "Maybe it's time for that reunion dinner?"

Celia sighed. "Maybe. Only Rehane didn't seem excited by the idea."

"She's a curious one. She's the only one among the three who already has someone close to her die under mysterious circumstances," Melanie said.

Celia nodded slowly. "I'm not saying she killed her husband, but someone that's killed before finds it easier to kill again and again. Until they are stopped. We need to be careful."

19

Celia didn't want to do it, but she had no choice.

"You've got to try it out one more time. Don't let that talent go to waste," her mother said as she got into the passenger seat of her car.

"That was a long time ago, Ma," Celia replied.

"Well, it's never too late to start over," Audrey said, smiling.

Celia started the half-hour drive towards the Amzizwe Theatre that was located near the Macan Residences. It was the quiet semi-posh neighborhood where Mrs. Owens lived.

Celia had left the nail parlor and picked her mother up from home as she thought about Rehane's involvement. They had many disagreements while growing up, but she couldn't pinpoint any that might trigger any bitterness. If she was involved, she had someone else committing the crimes for her. When she found the time, Celia needed to track down the familiar faces that attended both parties.

"You should pass by the store to buy some cupcakes for the choir," Audrey said.

"Are you serious? I'm sure Mrs. Owens has them well-fed," Celia replied.

"It's not about that. We need to make a good impression," Audrey said.

"Alright. But the store is going to be out of our way. There's a restaurant up the road with some decent ones we can buy," Celia said.

She stopped over at the Yellow Cherry restaurant. Her mother waited in the car as she went in. She ordered forty cupcakes. The server looked at her in surprise as they didn't have enough of them available. She asked Celia to wait for fifteen minutes until another fresh batch got out of the oven. Celia didn't mind it—anything to delay her arrival for the rehearsal was welcome.

She sat at one of the tables as she casually scanned the interior. The aesthetics were simple. It had sky blue walls, with yellow cherries painted on them. The floor tiles were all white, while the layout was a mixture of tables and booths. It had your typical fast-food restaurant feel.

Then she saw them. Seated in one of the booths were Anna and Faith. They were so deep in conversation they hadn't noticed her.

"This is an interesting coincidence," Celia whispered to herself. She had time to kill, so she walked over to their table.

"Got room for one more?" Celia asked with a cheeky grin.

The two women looked at her with shock etched on their faces.

"*Eish*, Celia. What are you doing here?" Anna asked.

"I'm on my way to rehearse some Christmas carols. I just passed by to pick up some cupcakes. I'm surprised to find you guys here," Celia said.

Anna and Faith exchanged hurried glances.

"We do coffee dates once in a while," Anna said. Faith nodded in agreement.

"Is it a serious meeting or…" Celia asked.

"Semi-serious," Faith said.

"Yes, semi-serious," Anna chimed in.

"So, can I join you? I'll only be here fifteen minutes as I wait for those cupcakes," Celia said.

"Sure, why not?" Faith said as she gently patted the sitting space next to her. Celia sat down.

"It's safe to say it's not just court cases that bring the two of you together," Celia said.

"It was only one," Anna replied, "And she did a splendid job."

"I'm sure she did. I was impressed when I met you, Faith," Celia remarked.

"Were you now? I got the impression you were fishing for information," Faith said.

"Fishing for a good lawyer is more like it," Celia replied as she twiddled her thumbs.

"You've got a case that's going in that direction?" Anna asked.

"An old friend does. Pardon me for asking this Anna, but was your case of a criminal nature?" Celia asked.

"Celia, I thought we talked about this?" Faith said.

"That's why I'm politely asking your client. You don't have to answer me, Anna, if it's uncomfortable for you," Celia replied.

Anna fidgeted. "I've never been convicted."

"That's a little different from what I asked," Celia prodded.

"You've always been quite obnoxious, Cece," Faith said.

Celia raised a brow, "Always?"

"Yes. I remember we used to argue a lot in those days. You haven't changed a single bit. One would think that being a make-up professional would have you show a humbler disposition," Faith continued.

Celia's eyes flashed with anger, but she bit her tongue. Faith was belittling her, but Celia didn't think lashing out would help her quest. She chose to overlook it.

"Oh, I never thought of it that way. Our days in the debate club were heated, but in a good way," Celia replied.

Faith smirked. "They were heated. There was a time I even despised you. But having you as a competitor made me work harder during the debates. When I look back, I learned a few tricks there that led me down the path of becoming a lawyer."

"So it's a fond memory?" Celia asked.

"Perhaps. Would you rather it wasn't?" Faith asked with a smile.

They locked eyes for a few seconds before Celia softened. "I'd really like to have more of this. We have a lot to talk about. I'm trying to find other people from our time to join in."

"How about Bontle Garber? She's back in town," Faith said.

Celia frowned. "Bontle? Who is she?"

"She was in our class. A quiet, shy girl. Always in the background of everything. I bumped into her three weeks ago at the mall," Faith replied.

"I don't remember her," Anna said.

"Neither do I," Celia added.

"She gave me her address," Faith said as she opened her purse. She took out a piece of neatly folded paper. "I've never gone there."

"Why not?" Celia asked as she took the paper.

"I didn't have the time. We never talked much while in school, and I don't force conversations. But you're pretty talented in that area," Faith said.

Celia looked up from the paper and caught the faint glint from Faith's eye. There was an unmistakeably pleasure Faith was deriving from having an upper hand in their interaction.

A bell from the counter chimed. The cupcakes were ready.

"This was interesting. Looking forward to meeting again," Celia said as she got up.

"Yeah, it was insightful. Take care of yourself," Faith said.

Celia nodded and walked to the counter. She carefully picked the two boxes of packed cupcakes and headed to the car. Her mother helped place them in the backseat. When she got into the driver's seat, Celia glanced at the window where her two former schoolmates sat. They were staring at her intently. She waved through the windscreen. They waved back.

"Who are those?" Audrey asked.

"I thought they were old friends. Now I'm not too sure," Celia replied.

"Why not?"

"They can't be trusted," Celia replied as she started the car.

20

They arrived at the Amzizwe Theatre ten minutes later than the agreed time. It was a design marvel in the area, with its imposing facade, wide foyers, and well-equipped auditorium. Celia and her mother walked to one of the spacious rehearsal spaces. Inside, they found a group of thirty women, huddled in little groups, having a chat as they sipped tea. Around them were neatly arranged seats that covered a third of the room, leaving a lot of walking space. It was an ideal rehearsal space.

"Perfect timing for the cupcakes," Audrey said with a gentle nudge. "You should put your phone away."

"I will. I'm just reading this," Celia replied, staring at her phone. Bill had just texted her.

We can't trace the origin of the texts. Back to square one.

Celia put her phone on silent mode and shoved it into her bag as Mrs. Jones walked up to meet them.

"Welcome to the Sunny Carol Choir," Mrs. Jones exclaimed. She went on to introduce them to the rest of the choir members. Audrey took the chance to pass the cupcakes around the group. Celia observed that most of the attendees were in their fifties or older, although she spotted two women who were close to her age. There were five men and two teens present. Three of the men were seated and looked like spectators. Celia assumed they were the husbands of some of the women.

"Alright, let's get down to it," Mrs. Owens said. The group moved like a colony of penguins on a beach as they rearranged themselves to suit their voices. Two lines were formed, all facing Mrs. Owens and Flora, the designated choirmaster.

Audrey and Celia stood to the side, waiting.

Mrs. Owens walked up to them. "What are your singing voices?"

"You tell us. You've heard me sing before," Audrey replied with a smile.

"Alright! So, do this after me. Ahhhhhh," Mrs. Owens said, warming them up for a quick voice range test. They spent the next minute doing this. Once they were warmed up, Flora took them through a series of high and low note singing exercises to test their voice range.

Two minutes later, she whispered into Mrs. Owens's ear.

"I have my answer," Mrs. Owens said. "You're both mezzo-sopranos, so stand on this line."

Celia and her mother went to join one of the forward lines.

"You need to watch your voice. Don't growl," Mrs. Owens whispered in Celia's ear.

Celia looked puzzled. "I'm growling?"

"Yes. Listen to your singing," Mrs. Owen replied and went to stand next to Flora.

Now set, the choirmaster took them through a voice warm-up for five minutes.

Celia struggled to keep up the pace, already self-conscious after Mrs. Owens's remarks. She varied the pitch and speed of her singing as she tried to match those around her.

They started singing *Angels We Have Heard On High*. As they kept singing, hitting higher notes, Flora angled her ear from one end of the choir to the other. She suddenly stopped where Celia and Audrey were and pointed at Celia with a disapproving stare. Audrey nudged Celia.

"Are you okay?" Audrey whispered.

"Yeah, Ma. Just trying to find my feet," Celia replied. This was true, but there was an additional distraction. She was thinking about the upcoming office party gigs. What was she going to do to delay it?

"Let's go once more. Gloo—oo--," Flora shouted to the choir as she walked up and down the front of the choir, listening.

She walked from this side to that, listening to the voices. As she got closer to the mezzo-sopranos, she frowned. She lingered there for a few minutes then ordered everyone to stop.

"This line only. Sing," Flora instructed Celia and Audrey's line. They sang for thirty seconds before she stopped them again. Flora pointed at Audrey and Celia. "Just you two."

Audrey glanced at Celia, who fidgeted slightly. They belted out the first line before Flora shook her head.

"Are you guys really singing?" Flora asked.

Audrey frowned. "Of course, we are. What do you mean?"

"Alright, do it one at a time."

Audrey went first, then Celia.

Flora moved closer to Celia. "You're very off key. Slow down and stop growling."

"How am I growling?" Celia asked.

"I don't know how. Can you fix it?"

"No. I can't sing," she replied.

"What do you mean you can't sing? You've been singing since you were five," Audrey said.

"But I'm in my mid-thirties now, Ma," Celia replied.

Flora had Celia do it one more time. By the end of it all, there were frowns, puzzled expressions, and sheepish smiles.

"I've never heard someone so off-key in a long time," Flora remarked.

"Cece, you can sit this one out. I'll make you some ginger-lemon water to fix it later," Mrs. Owens chimed in.

Other than temporarily becoming a public spectacle, Celia didn't mind being removed from the choir. As she watched them sing, she plotted how to catch the office party killer by surprise. However, she needed to convince Fezile to help her execute it.

Would her plan fall on deaf ears?

21

The coffee was bland, but Celia drank it. Fezile had suggested they meet at his favorite café for breakfast, a little place that had seen better days. However, it had a charming ambience that captured the mood of the nineties. Celia liked that, along with the fried eggs.

"So, what do you think?" Celia asked.

"There's nothing to think about. The answer is no," Fezile replied as he scooped another spoonful of mielie pap porridge.

"Why not? It would help us plan better," she replied.

"We don't need to check out the place in advance. It's never been a problem for me. Why start now?" he asked.

Celia leaned forward. "It's standard practice in video productions to do a recce of the location before you do the job. Why not here?"

"That's for video, not photography. I don't need too much prep unless it's a product shoot in a studio. In the field, you work with what you get. So long as I have my full kit, I'm good to go," Fezile replied.

Celia let out a pronounced sigh. "Aren't you worried about this happening again?"

"It won't happen again," Fezile replied.

"What makes you so confident?"

"Lightning doesn't strike the same place twice. Or in this case, thrice."

"It actually can. There's been research about it. One finding showed it struck the same spot eleven times," Celia remarked.

"That's a rare instance. I don't think it will happen here," he replied.

"Fez, hope is not a strategy," Celia said.

"Who said I'm living in hope? I talked to someone, and they told me it won't happen. The police are on the case now, so maybe the person responsible will back off," he said.

"You talked to someone? Who's this person?" Celia asked.

"A former *sangoma*."

Celia almost spilled her coffee. "A former *sangoma*? They retire?"

"Anyone can retire, including traditional healers."

"He might be one of the fake ones. Sorry, we have to be serious about this Fez. Please hear me out. We're talking about lives here. Let's try it out once. If it doesn't work, that's fine. We can map out entrances and exits, and we'll be better prepared for whatever will happen. Plus, it might make the client feel extra special because of it. Even if you don't need to do it, it will make you look detailed and professional," Celia said in her softest voice possible.

She watched Fezile as he stared at his nearly empty bowl of porridge. After a few seconds, he lifted his head. "We'll only do this once."

"That's all we need," Celia replied with a beaming smile.

The ZW Girl offices were located in Fairdale, a residential part of town. It was one of several neighborhoods where old houses with spacious compounds were being sold and replaced by modern office blocks. Celia estimated that within five years, the place would have more office blocks than houses.

They pulled up to a twelve-story building with a futuristic design that mimicked a honeycomb. Its facade was filled with large windows. On the third floor, they were met by Joy, the charming media relations officer.

"This is where we're holding the party," she said, showing them a medium-sized space that could hold a hundred people. There were a few seats present, while all the walls except one were windowless. The walls had catchy murals of smiling girls and positive messages.

"I love the space," Celia said, grateful that this party wasn't being held near people's workstations.

"It's one of our favorites too. We hold mentorship sessions here with girls from difficult backgrounds. And when we need to unwind from a hard week's work, this is where we screen films or have customized mini-concerts with artists," Joy replied.

"The lighting works for me during the day. I can tell that the sunset can be seen from here, right?" Fezile said as he walked to the large window. It ran from the ceiling and just stopped short of the floor level.

"Exactly. The sunset always adds a different hue to the space in the evenings."

"That's perfect for a photo-shoot. Sunlight paints surfaces like nothing else. Can we push the start time to four in the evening?" Fezile suggested.

Joy cocked her head to one side. "I'll not promise you that, as my bosses have a few things to do before then. I'll sell them the photo-shoot idea and we'll see."

Celia pointed at a closed door along one of the walls. "Is that the door service providers will use?"

"No, that's the fire escape. They'll access the space from the lifts and the stairs," Joy replied. "This space is separate from the office side, so they can work without clashing into employees."

"You finally got to meet them? "Fezile asked.

"Yes, thanks for the link-up. We already agreed on a menu and the price. Let me leave you to it, you can call me when you're done," Joy said. She left.

Celia moved closer so that she could whisper. "Hold on. Are we talking about the same service providers from the other office parties?"

Fezile nodded and whispered back. "My clients often don't have caterers in mind, so I recommended the one I've worked with to come in. I get a cut and everyone's happy."

"So across the three parties, the same company has been working with us?"

"Yes, they have," Fezile's eyes narrowed as he quickly read her mind. "They've got nothing to do with the other stuff. The cops already checked them out."

"I've not denied that. But do you know the people working there every week?"

"I know the owner and that's all that matters. She's someone I trust," Fezile replied.

"Someone is killing your clients at these office parties using poison. We need to vet her people," she said.

Fezile shook his head. "Are you crazy?"

"I could ask you the same question. Why would you oppose this?"

"Because the cops already cleared them."

"Why are you fighting this, Fez?" Celia asked. "Are you trying to make sure another client dies in your hands?"

Fezile glared at her. "You're really messed up if you think I'm behind this."

"Then prove it. Let's vet the caterer's team before the event," Celia said.

"If I don't?"

"Then I'm not going to work on this anymore. I can't let another person die while we just watch," Celia said.

Fezile leaned in until they were eyeball-to-eyeball. "The last time you messed up my gig, you disappeared. Try it this time, and I'll make sure you regret it."

22

Celia paced around her office for twenty minutes before Melanie protested.

"Why are you pacing around?" Melanie asked.

"So now I can't pace in my own office?" Celia asked.

"Not if it affects your co-worker. You're not sure quitting the gig will work, are you?"

"No. Fezile is a free spirit. He moved on the last time we broke ties, he'll move on again if I do the same thing," Celia replied.

"So did you quit or not?" Melanie asked.

"I put him on notice. I didn't confirm it. Yet."

"So what will help you confirm it?"

"Tracing the killer. After checking out the location, the killer can use two ways to get there. If the killer is an outsider, he or she can easily enter the office from the lift or the stairs. I don't think they'll use the fire escape. However, I'm certain they're not an outsider. I think the killer is part of the catering team," Celia said.

"Then why don't you get to know the team?" Melanie asked.

"I've been hesitant to approach our previous clients because of Fezile, but after our argument, what have I got to lose?" Celia asked. "I'm calling Fridah."

Five minutes later, she had an address scribbled in her notebook. She grabbed her bag and headed for the door.

"You can just call them," Melanie suggested.

"I don't want to warn them I'm coming," Celia replied.

Half an hour later, she was at the reception of Imaze Catering Company. It was a small ground floor office. From the waiting bench she sat on, she could see two vans with the company logo parked outside.

"Miss Dube?" the receptionist asked. "She'll see you now."

Celia was led down a narrow corridor. At the end of it was a door with a small plaque engraved 'CEO'. Celia entered the office and saw a smartly dressed woman seated behind a curved table. She stood up.

"Gloria Jackson. Please have a seat," the woman said, smiling.

"Thank you, Gloria. You're the owner of the place?" Celia asked as she took a seat.

"Yes, how may I help you?" Gloria asked.

Celia cleared her throat as she got into character. "There's a small private party I want to do for my family and friends, and I was wondering if that's a service you can handle."

"Of course. How many people are we talking about?" Gloria asked, her pen ready to jot down.

"Let's say fifty to seventy people," Celia replied.

"That's very manageable for us. Which dates are you looking at?"

"Erm, I was thinking of the twenty-third of December."

Gloria whistled. "That's close to Christmas day."

"Will that be a problem?" Celia asked.

"Yes. A good chunk of our staff will be gone for the holidays by then."

"Oh, I see. How about I bring the date earlier?" Celia said.

"Well, if it's a date before the twentieth that can work."

"The nineteenth," Celia said. Gloria scribbled the date.

"Do you have any particular preference as far as meals are concerned?" Gloria asked. "You can take a look at our diverse menu."

Gloria handed Celia a catalogue. It had pictures of different meals, their prices, and recommended menus. Celia studied it for a few minutes.

"Yes, I think we'll do a lot of meat. And some vegetarian dishes," Celia said.

"That sounds good. We can customize a menu for you," Gloria said, smiling.

"Do you also have a catalogue showing your catering team?" Celia asked.

Gloria wore a puzzled expression. "No, we don't. Why?"

"I usually like seeing the people I'll be working with before I hire them," Celia replied.

Gloria exhaled. "Why would that be necessary?"

"Because I….," Celia's voice trailed off as she sought the right words. "I want to match them with a certain theme of dressing for that day."

Gloria forced a smile. "We come with our well-pressed uniforms."

"Don't get me wrong, I'm not saying your clothes don't work. I'm saying I had a theme in mind for the party and I wanted to do some fitting. So that we know everyone's size. It will add a little light touch to things," Celia replied, smiling.

Gloria balled her fists. "We don't do that here. For security reasons, I prefer all my staff to be dressed in uniform. No compromises."

"So I won't be able to see them?" Celia asked.

"That's not going to happen, unfortunately. Even if it were possible, most of them are off today. Do we go on or do I cancel this?" Gloria asked.

Celia paused for a moment, her mind racing.

"Let me take a rain check on that. I'll talk to my husband and get back to you," Celia replied.

Gloria opened her cardholder and gave her a business card. "When you get round to it, there's my number."

As Celia walked out of the offices, she took a cursory glance around the place one more time. There was no sign of busy activity, so Gloria wasn't lying about her staff being away.

When Celia got into her car, she opened her bag to stash Gloria's card. She saw a neatly folded piece of paper inside and quickly remembered her encounter with Faith and Anna. She unfolded the paper, read the address, and placed it on the passenger seat. She started the car and drove away with the new destination in mind.

She entered the Mpule district, which was a lower-middle-class area with old tenements. As she drove down the street, fruit and food vendors waved their wares at her, hoping for a sale. She stopped outside the Swavi Apartments, which was written across the building in faded paint. She compared it to the address on the paper. Certain it was the right place, she parked next to the shell of an abandoned car.

Two men in their forties were seated outside the apartments' main gate on plastic chairs. One man was sipping something from a soda bottle wrapped in newspapers. Celia assumed he didn't want strangers to know the bottle's contents. The other man lazily slouched on his chair with one hand on his chin.

"Howzit, gents? I wanted to see the caretaker," Celia said.

"You're looking at him," the man holding the bottle replied.

"Great. I was looking for an old friend of mine. I was told she lives here. Her name is Bontle."

"Bontle who?"

"Bontle Garber," she replied.

The caretaker shook his head. "There's no Bontle Garber here. There was a Bontle Madimise, but not Garber."

"There was?"

"Yes. She moved out last week," he replied.

Celia frowned. She might be using an alias. "Where did she move to?"

"We tend not to ask tenants where they are going when they leave," the caretaker said. The other man grunted in approval. The caretaker took another sip from his bottle, leaving a thin liquid film on his upper lip.

"I see. I was wondering, do you have a picture of her in your records?" Celia asked.

The caretaker's licked the film off his upper lip. "We tend not to ask for that when tenants are moving in."

"That's a strange thing to do. You should have proper records," Celia commented.

"You are asking strange questions, madam. Who are you?" the caretaker asked.

"As I said, I'm an old friend."

"If you're an old friend, how come you need a photo to recognize your old friend? Don't you know what she looks like?" he challenged.

Celia gritted her teeth. "She's a childhood friend. People change as they grow up."

The caretaker chuckled and pointed at his slouched companion. "This here is my friend Vusi. We've known each other since we were ten years old. The only thing that's changed is he has gray hair and a few more wrinkles now."

The caretaker starting laughing, and the other man joined in.

Celia exhaled and reached into her bag. She took out a hundred rand note. "This can add an extra bottle of whatever you're drinking."

Her statement caused the slouched man to take a peek.

The caretaker took the note. "You're very generous for someone with a poor memory."

"So, can I have her picture please?" she asked.

"As I already told you, we tend not to do that," the caretaker replied nonchalantly.

Celia exhaled. "So I take it you won't help me?"

"Today's not your lucky day, madam. I have nothing to give you. Not even some of this stuff. It's not good for you," the caretaker said. He then burped loudly. The other man nudged him playfully, and they laughed.

Celia spun on her heels and marched to her car. She drove off fast, kicking up as much dust as she could.

She felt like she had been set up. Was this a distraction by Faith to unsettle her? She tightened her grip on the steering wheel and stepped on the accelerator a little more.

Fezile hadn't informed her that he had called off the party, so it was safe to assume it was going to happen the next day. It dawned on her that quitting the gig wasn't going to stop the killer, whoever it was.

Her only option was to catch the killer red-handed, preferably before the next victim breathed their last.

23

On the day of the office party at ZW Girls, Celia's eyes kept darting around the room. She was ready for anything.

It was mid-afternoon and *Felis Navidad* was already playing off the speakers around the space as employees mingled around. The space had been transformed since Celia and Fezile did their recce.

The room's walls were covered in Christmas decorations depicting winter landscapes and starry night skies. The sun rays streaming from the large window painted the room in an orange glow and soft shadows. All the chairs had been taken out. Bales of hay were strategically positioned around the space as seats. Cocktail tables were also added. There was an open area near the window which acted as the dance floor. To one corner was a table with a sound mixer, microphones, and a laptop. It was a modified deejay's booth.

Celia had noted that while the catering supervisor had arrived, most of the catering staff, including the chef and servers, hadn't arrived yet. She was informed they were on their way.

She had called Fezile to confirm her attendance the day before, and he looked more relaxed. He walked around taking pictures, maximizing the warm, orange hue from the sun.

Celia had set up her station along one of the walls, between the fire escape door and the main entrance, with two bales of hay marking her territory. It wasn't ideal for visibility, but at least she had a good view of both exits. She'd already worked on two people to gauge whether her new approach was working, and she liked the results. She had incorporated the usual make-up with the *Umchokozo* face painting. She added various styles of white dots onto the employees' faces, and it delivered a beautiful aesthetic. Joy loved the look. As a bonus, Celia gave each employee a red and white Santa hat. She knew they would catch the eye of those who were still hesitant to visit her workstation.

She didn't have to wait long. She was soon serving a queue of employees who were, keen to get their pictures taken before the sunset. She worked as fast as she could, especially since most of the employees at ZW were women. But she enjoyed every minute of it.

When she was done, Joy came over to her. "You're doing some of the best work I've ever seen, and I'm not just talking about parties. We get to keep the hats, right?"

"Yes, of course! It's all part of the make-up budget," Celia replied.

"Fantastic! I might call you in to talk a bit more about make-up once the holiday season is over. A lot of us are fans of your work," Joy said.

"I'd like to hear about it later. I'll help you market it to my colleagues," Joy replied.

"By the way, I've got a new lipstick line you can buy," Celia said.

When she left, Celia punched the air. This was the kind of feedback that made her job worthwhile. She enjoyed the euphoric feeling for about five minutes before she quickly calmed down when she remembered her other mission. She started keeping an eye out for the unusual. She saw people grooving on the dance floor, as others sat in pairs on the hay bales and chatted. Others stood around the tables as they talked. The party was buzzing with music and chatter.

Celia's eyes started paying attention to the servers, who moved around with food platters or delivered various beverages.

Something from the main door caught Celia's attention. Two staffers pushed in a customized sleigh stacked with gifts of all shapes and sizes. It was padded with velvet fabric while having wooden top rails and handlebars. Its long runners were fitted with small wheels to make it easy to move around.

Celia had a broad grin. She didn't believe in bucket lists. However, she'd never seen a reindeer, elf or the real Santa Claus in South Africa. At least she could now say she'd seen a sleigh.

"Have you seen that thing?" Fezile said.

"These guys are going all out with this party," Celia remarked.

"I think I'm going to enjoy this one," Fezile replied as he moved away to take more pictures.

As the sleigh made its way slowly towards the dance floor, it caught the attention of other employees who started clapping and cheering. Celia saw Kelly Thobiso, who she learned was the CEO while doing her make-up, walk up to the front of the room with a microphone in hand.

"It's that time of the year again, Team ZW!" Kelly said, eliciting more cheers.

Two staffers positioned the sleigh in the center of the dance floor, in between Kelly and the gathered workers.

"It's an honor to say thank you to all of you. You've worked so hard throughout the year. You have done so much to make the lives of girls in this country better," Kelly said, "You've been a valuable treasure to their lives. Team ZW!"

"Team ZW!" the workers said in unison.

"Santa's sleigh is here, and I think everyone has a labeled gift. We have two members of our team who will do the duty of passing along the gifts to their rightful owners," Kelly said. The two staffers began handing out the gifts to different employees.

Celia kept looking around to see if any of the servers were out of place. However, they were all standing in their positions, looking immaculate in black and white uniforms. Each server was focused on their tasks.

Celia turned her gaze back to the gift-giving. Then it hit her.

Lizzy died with a gift wrapper in her hand.

Matt collapsed after the gift-giving session.

The gifts. That's how the killer was poisoning them.

Instinctively, she jumped up from her position next to Fezile and ran towards the employees who were eagerly receiving their gifts.

"Cece!" Fezile said behind her.

"Keep an eye on the serving team!" Celia said without slowing down. With no regard for dignity or space, she hit any gift box off their hands.

"Drop your gifts! Please drop your gifts!" Celia shouted. "They are poisoned!"

"What's going on back there?" Kelly asked as she craned her neck for a better look.

"Don't open a single one, please!" Celia urged as she kept swatting them off their hands. Sounds of smashing glasses and ceramics filled the place as boxes fell to the floor.

Celia got to Kelly and snatched the microphone.

"Listen to me," Celia said while breathing rapidly, "one of the boxes you're holding has poison in its gift wrapper. I'm not lying to you, you'll have to trust me on this. Please don't open your gift box. Place it on the ground and step away from it."

Celia handed the microphone back to Kelly. "Sorry about that."

"Cece!" Fezile shouted. Celia turned just in time to see Fezile standing in the lift bay. "She took the lift!"

He then dashed down the stairs in pursuit of the killer.

24

Celia slowed down by the lifts. She could see that the lift the killer was in had stopped on the ground floor. She started running down the stairs. Craning her neck over the railing, she saw Fezile's figure taking the last steps to the ground floor.

"She got out on the ground floor!" Celia shouted to him.

Fezile disappeared, and she tore down the steps to catch up. When she hit the ground floor landing, she turned to the receptionist. "Which way did they go?"

The receptionist pointed to the right and Celia sprinted out the front entrance. To her right, she saw nothing beyond the pedestrians walking outside. Except one of them was staring down an alley. She ran toward him and ducked into the narrow alley.

Ahead of her, she saw the familiar form of Fezile running. She couldn't spot the server but assumed she was ahead of him. She pushed on, dodging two trashcans and other trash lying around. Her flat shoes gave her the stability she needed. Her shins caught the splash of cold, stagnant water, but she didn't care.

She heard the sudden screech of tyres and she looked up just in time to see the server fall onto the tarmac. Celia noted that she was wearing a white and black uniform. The server got up and kept running. Fezile emerged from the alley, jumped over the car's hood, and disappeared from view. By the time Celia got to the road, and the cars were moving again. She held up her hand until they stopped. She got across.

On the other side, she entered a day market. It was full of stalls filled with products of all kinds: shoes, belts, jackets, dresses, and any other clothing accessory you could think of. It wasn't thronging with people, so Celia could see through the narrow passages in between the stalls. She couldn't see the server and Fezile. She paused, her chest heaving as her eyes darted in different directions.

"Where did they go?" Celia asked a stall owner. He pointed to his left, but she couldn't see anything to indicate where the two had disappeared. She started moving through the passages, taking a pause when she arrived at a junction

She caught sight of Fezile several stalls away. He was walking with his eyes darting in different directions, clearly searching for the server. Celia started walking towards him. As she did this, she bumped into a woman draped in a gray shawl. She had covered her face such that only her eyes were visible.

"I'm sorry," Celia muttered. The woman said nothing and hurried past her. Out of curiosity, Celia turned. She saw the black shoes and trousers. The woman was limping. It was her.

"Hey!" Celia shouted. The woman started running and ducked into a passage to the right.

Celia gave chase. The woman was several paces away. Celia hoped for a lucky break and she soon got one. As the woman was about to cross a junction, Celia saw Fezile's speedy form emerge from the right. He slammed into the woman's midriff, sending the two of them straight into a pile of clothes.

"*Aweh!* What are you doing?" the female stall owner protested. She had barely finished speaking when the stall's support poles and canopy collapsed on them.

25

"Fezile!" Celia exclaimed as she rushed to the collapsed stall.

The pile of fallen canopy and poles started moving from side to side. The poles fell to the side as Fezile and the woman got to their feet, still covered by the canopy. Although she could only see their feet peeking under the material, Celia could tell Fezile was trying to subdue the woman. Fezile managed to uncover himself as they wrestled and quickly gained the upper hand by grabbing hold of the woman's swinging hands.

"Stop moving!" Fezile ordered. The woman kept trying to wriggle free of his grip. As this went on, Celia took out her phone and called Bill, giving quick directions to where they were.

By the time Celia finished the call, the woman had stopped fighting and seemed to be struggling to breathe under the canopy. Fezile quickly released one of her arms and threw off the canopy from her head. They stood facing each other, and he quickly restored his hold on both of her arms. A gasp left Celia's lips as she looked at the short-haired woman.

"Who are you?" Fezile asked.

The woman shot him an angry look, then resumed her quest to get her arms free. Fezile did his best to maintain his hold without hurting her. He decided to turn her around so that her hands would be behind her back. The battle for control had them shuffle their feet on the earthy ground, and soon a cloud of dust surrounded them.

Fezile succeeded in turning her. With her hands behind her back, it became slightly harder for the woman to put up a fight.

Celia stepped closer to get a closer look at the woman's face. "Bontle?"

The woman stopped moving and turned her bulging red eyes to look at Celia.

"You know her?" Fezile asked.

Celia recognized her. She was the slim girl who used to sit in the back of the class. Shy, and always following. She never spoke much and chipped into whatever adventure they had. During that first year of high school, they were bullied together. But after they graduated into the second year of high school, their circles changed and Celia didn't interact with her much.

"Bontle, you look… different," Celia said.

Bontle started laughing. It got louder with each breath she took.

"I remember you," Celia said. "I remember you."

Bontle eased down her laughing spasm and looked up at Celia once more. She smiled like a crazed maniac, sending shivers down Celia's spine.

"You remember me, you say," Bontle whispered. "Tell me, what do you remember exactly?"

Celia rubbed her palms together. "I remember the times we would go to the neighboring school to watch the boys play football. I also remember that time we created our little class magazine by tearing off pages from our exercise books. You'd go and distribute the five copies we created to as many students as possible," Celia said.

Bontle sneered. "Is that it? The activities where I was always in the background? What about the other memories I sent you?"

"I also remember that first year," Celia replied.

"I knew you would. Do you know that our short friendship during that year is what helped me keep going?" Bontle asked.

Celia nodded. She understood why. She had spent a lot of time alongside four other students, encouraging each other to stay strong. "I know. We kept each other strong."

"And then as soon as we got to the second year, you joined a clique and cut me off," Bontle said. "That hurt, you know."

Celia licked her lips. "Bontle, we weren't friends at the time. We never were. We just found ourselves going through the same thing, and we helped each other through it."

"Who was I to you?" Bontle asked.

"As a person?"

"Yes, as a human being. Who was I?" she asked.

"You were my classmate. Shy, smart, a team player, and…" Celia's voice trailed off as Bontle started laughing again.

"Can you stop that and hold still?" Fezile said.

Bontle angled her head towards him, her laughter reduced to a giggle. "You're charming, aren't you?"

"Are the cops on their way?" Fezile asked.

"I always wanted to work in forensics, you know," Bontle said. "I never made it. But when I read in the local papers that you had helped the police solve a murder; I was impressed. I've always looked up to you, Celia," she said.

"What are you talking about?" Celia asked.

"I'm trying to appreciate you, Celia," she replied.

"Why did you do this, Bontle?" she asked.

"If I told you what I know, will you remember me?" Bontle asked with a wry smile.

"This isn't a game. How did you know about the office parties I was working in?"

Bontle exhaled. "You were a little careless with your notebook. I learned so much about you while reading it. It was an honor."

Celia froze. The notebook she forgot at *the Pier*. It had all the details about the gigs. Bontle found all the information she needed to plot her path to Celia.

"You've… you've been following me for some time, haven't you?" Celia asked.

"Just like high school. Always in the background. I was doing it all for you," Bontle said, giving Celia a lingering gaze.

Fezile turned to Celia with a puzzled expression. Celia didn't have the answer to the question his eyes asked her. The wailing sirens of approaching police cars got closer.

"Why the killings, Bonnie?" Celia asked.

"You called me Bonnie. Just like the old days. Maybe there's some hope for your memory," Bontle said to her, then turned away. She started humming a strange tune. Her voice became drowned out by the loud sirens of arriving police cars.

Aware that the police had arrived, Bontle started wrestling again, to Fezile's annoyance. He did his best to hold her wrists from slipping. Frustrated, Bontle started kicking backward, and Fezile moved closer to her to limit her striking range. Still, Bontle managed to kick him twice before he got the right pose. The dust rose again. One of the watching vendors started coughing.

"You despise me, don't you?" Bontle asked Fezile, giving him a sidelong glance.

"I don't want to hurt your arms, so please stay still!" Fezile said.

Two uniformed police officers appeared with guns drawn.

"Step back from the lady and put your hands up," one officer ordered.

"If I do that, she'll kick you in the teeth. Just bring the cuffs," Fezile replied.

"I said step back and put your hands up!" the officer repeated.

"He's not the criminal, she is," Celia chimed in.

The officer shot her a look. "Be quiet, lady."

Fezile let go of her hands and moved a step away from Bontle. Without warning, Bontle swiftly spun around and punched him in the gut. Fezile groaned in pain as he went down on one knee. Bontle, with bulging, crazed eyes, turned to face the police officers.

26

Celia had expected Bontle to cause some drama, but this had surprised her.

"Put your hands up!" an officer shouted at Bontle.

Bontle didn't seem to have heard him. She glanced at Celia, then started running towards one of the passages.

"Stop!" the officer shouted.

Bontle didn't stop. She bolted past some vendors who, perhaps fearing what she would do, stepped aside. However, she didn't get past the third. A hulking man halted her run. He held onto her until the two police officers reached them and handcuffed her.

Celia ran to Fezile. He was still groaning while lying on the ground in a foetal pose.

"Are you okay?" Celia asked.

Fezile shook his head. "Just give me a minute," he murmured.

Celia turned to the officers. They were struggling to move Bontle, who was refusing to walk.

The approaching sound of sirens meant other officers were arriving. One officer spoke into his radio, directing the arriving officers to where they were.

Moments later, detective Bill Koloane and his team of investigators appeared.

Two detectives went to help the arresting officers. With Bontle proving to be stubborn, they resolved to half-walking and half-carrying her towards the waiting police car.

As they did this, Celia moved in. Her movement attracted Bill's attention.

"Stay out of the way, lady!" an officer ordered.

Undeterred, Celia walked alongside them. "Why did you do it, Bonnie?"

"Not now, Celia. Can't you see I'm leaving this place?" Bontle replied while panting.

"I need to know. Why did you kill those people? They were innocent," Celia said.

"Were they really innocent?" Bontle asked.

"Just answer the question," Celia insisted.

Bill pulled Celia away. "We'll have plenty of time to do this later," he said.

"I want to know right now," Celia protested as his sturdy frame halted her forward movement. She watched the detectives take Bontle further away from her.

"Promise me you'll visit, Celia? I'll give you my answer as a Christmas present," she heard Bontle shout as she and the officers disappeared between the stalls.

Celia knew it wasn't over yet.

27

Days later, Celia's sons jumped and clapped while standing outside their home as their Christmas tree was offloaded by two delivery men. Celia, her mother, and Melanie watched. Covered in netting, the Grizzly Peak tree was nearly three metres high.

"You got the one I've always wanted," Audrey remarked.

"Come on, Ma. What stopped you? "Celia asked.

"You know, the ceiling in my house is lower than yours. How would it fit?" Audrey asked.

"By trimming the tree?" Celia teased.

"That's a waste of a good-sized tree," Audrey replied.

With Celia playing the role of spotter, the delivery crew eased the tree through the front door. They positioned it in the corner adjacent to the largest window in the house. The delivery men left. Celia and Audrey studied the tree as John and James searched a box of decorations that sat next to it.

"Why would you put it there instead of your favorite corner near the television?" Audrey asked.

"I think it would be magical to see the lights shining from outside," Celia said.

"That's an awesome idea," Melanie remarked.

Audrey beamed. "Can we now say the holiday bug has caught up with you?"

"Yes, we can safely say that," Celia replied, smiling.

"I'd better help those boys. Things are getting out of hand," Melanie said as she moved towards them. They were now struggling with the Christmas light wires. The more they tried to figure them out, the more tangled they got.

"You know what? Let's start putting up the decorations," Celia said.

They lost sense of time as they worked around the tree, placing in the colored balls and the little ornaments. They had even added a twist, using traditional beads on the trees, which added a dash of color. Melanie managed to untangle the lights. Soon after, the Christmas lights were twinkling on the tree.

"What about this?" Audrey asked. In her hand was the Christmas tree topper, a large gold-colored star. Celia took it.

"We're supposed to mount it up there?" Melanie asked. They instinctively looked at the top of the tree.

"We don't have to. The gap between the tree and the ceiling will be too small."

"But the tree is not a tree without the star on top," Audrey said.

"Who said so?" Melanie asked.

"We do it every year. It's one of our things," Celia replied. "We do have a ladder for this."

Audrey shook her head. "I'm not going up that ladder."

Celia laughed. "This is one of those times where Trevor would save the day."

The doorbell rang.

Audrey walked to the door. "Look who's here, Cece."

Bill and Fezile walked in with bags in hand.

"We thought you might need some help with the tree. I can see we're too late," Bill joked.

"This was your idea, Mel?" Celia asked. Melanie gave a wink.

"Merry Christmas," Bill said as he handed his bag to Celia.

"Thank you. What is it?" Celia asked.

"You'll find out soon enough," Bill replied. "But Fezile here has something else too."

Fezile stepped forward and took out a gift box from his bag. "This is from me to you."

Celia stared at the box. "Is this deliberate? After the office parties, I don't want to touch a gift box wrapped like that."

"Don't worry. I checked it myself. It's safe," Bill said, smiling.

Celia took it and set it aside. "I'll open it later when I'm a little more confident."

Fezile laughed. "Thank you for everything. For all the good you did at work. I should've listened to you when you warned me."

Celia pressed her hands to her cheeks. "I don't know what to say. Thank you, too."

"Oh, one more thing," Fezile said. He took out a thick, white envelope from his inner coat pocket. "Joy and Kelly from ZW Girls wanted you to have this."

Celia took the envelope. "What for?"

"The forensics team found traces of poison on the wrapping of Joy's gift. Bontle would switch the original wrappers during the events. You saved Joy's life," Bill said.

Celia opened the envelope. Her eyes widened.

"*Eish*, are these air tickets?" she asked.

"Did I hear air tickets?" Audrey said as she homed in on Celia. She took the envelope and looked at it. "*Aweh*! Is this for us?"

"It's for all of you," Fezile replied.

"Heee!" Audrey exclaimed as she did a little jig.

"Who told them about Mauritius?" Celia asked.

"I had to get some help from Melanie," Fezile said. "She told me what's been going on with the holiday trip situation. The staff at ZW raised cash and paid for it," Fezile said.

Tears rolled down Celia's cheeks. She hugged Fezile. "Thank you for this, you don't know how much this means to me."

"*Ube neKrismesi emnandi*," Fezile said.

"Merry Christmas to you too," she replied.

Fezile eased the embrace. "Maybe we should work together more often."

Celia chuckled as she dabbed her eyes. "Is it worth the risk?"

"At this point, I'm ready for a few more surprises," he replied.

"Cece! Have you seen the dates?" Audrey shouted from across the room. "We fly out on Boxing Day and return in the New Year. You know what that means?"

"What does it mean?" Celia asked

"It means we're going to be caroling on Christmas Eve. Let me call Christie to confirm," Audrey said as she reached for her phone.

"Don't call her, Ma. We already know I won't be singing," Celia replied.

"Who cares what you sound like? You'll make a joyful noise," Audrey said with a sly grin.

Celia laughed. Bill leaned in. "Celia, can we talk for a minute?"

They moved to the kitchen, which had the lingering aroma of masala tea.

"I'm going to be doing my first interrogation session with Bontle today. She's cooled off now. I was thinking that you could come and…" Bill said.

Celia shook her head. "I don't want to watch it."

"Why not? We already know she did it. We searched her apartment, found the poison and gift wrappers. We've matched it to the poison that killed Lizzy and Matt."

"What about the caterer?" she asked.

"They hire new people often. After Bontle read your notebook, she must have started snooping on how Fezile works. She then applied for a job in the catering company and was hired," Bill replied.

"Sounds like you've got a strong case already," Celia said.

"We do. Only one thing is missing. Her motive."

"I think she needs a mental assessment first. Something's wrong with her," Celia remarked.

"That's already done. She passed. That's why we need a motive. She said she wants you to visit. To get your Christmas gift," Bill said.

"I know what she's going to say. She'll claim I inspired her to kill so that she can watch me solve the investigation. That's why she was sending the clues. She turned the whole thing into a game," Celia said.

"You may be right, but I still need her to say those things. We need a confession from her, and you can help us get that. You're still up for it?" Bill replied.

Celia stayed quiet for a moment. She nodded. "Yes, I'm up for it."

"Good. I'll set it up," Bill said.

"But she's wrong about one thing. What she wants to tell me is not my Christmas gift. It can never be," Celia said, glancing around her living room. "This right here is my Christmas gift."

"I hear you. Listen, I know you and I haven't had the best interaction for the last couple of weeks since… since the Benji situation. I overreacted then, and I apologize," Bill said.

"Apology accepted," Celia replied.

"When you get back from the vacation, let me know. I'd like to take you somewhere as we usher in the New Year."

"Where to?" Celia asked.

Bill broke into a grin. "That would ruin the surprise, wouldn't it? Let's just call it the first step toward a fresh start."

Celia showed him the gold star. "Our Christmas tree isn't done yet. Do you think you can help put this up?"

Bill smiled. "I'll give it a shot if you tell me what you feel about my offer."

Celia flashed a dimpled smile. "I don't mind a fresh start."

The End

FOUNDATION AND TEMPTATIONS

A SUNSHINE COVE COZY MYSTERY

ABOUT FOUNDATION AND TEMPTATIONS

Released: April 2021
Series: Book 6 – Sunshine Cove Cozy Mystery Series
Standalone: Yes
Cliff-hanger: No

When did looking good cause so much trouble and a murder?

Celia loves her job. Seeing people look good after applying her makeup products gives her great satisfaction.

She can't believe her luck when the wife of a famous sports star employs her services for a celebrity event.

However, she's left speechless and confused when this client is found dead at the after party and Celia is identified as the prime suspect.

As she delves deeper into the victim's life, she discovers that there are many people who wanted to take her place as the wife of a celebrity. But who wanted it bad enough to have wanted to kill her?

Celia knows she has to think outside the box and follow her instincts, otherwise she might end up behind bars or worse, the killer's next victim.

1

Celia Dube didn't believe in creative accounting, but the interrogation that morning seemed to suggest that she did.

"Was it a vacation or a work trip?"

"It was a work trip," Celia replied, shifting in her seat. Her Ankara dress didn't fit as well as it had several months ago, and this brought her some discomfort.

"Then where are the receipts?" Sarah Gaines asked. She was a slender, bespectacled woman in a tight-fitting gray suit. They hired her to come round every six months to check the company books. Sarah brought to the office a renewed sense of order. Not that Celia and her business partner Melanie Williams didn't champion the ideal. However, Sarah came to ensure it was happening. Her presence often came with demands for reports, receipts, and other evidence that company cash was spent as recorded. Finding them wasn't always a walk in the park.

Celia and Melanie had run the Afrostar Nail Parlor for close to a year. They'd become well known for the head-turning styles that inevitably caused a buzz in the small seaside community of Sunshine Cove.

Like bees to honey, their clientele list grew. With that came the need for outside help, and Sarah ran a tight ship during audit week. Masala tea and chocolate chip cookies were a running theme when she was around.

The business partners loved and loathed audit season in equal measure. However, they knew how important it was to understand the health of their business.

When Celia arrived that sunny morning - later than usual after her car battery died and she had to get her two sons to school - she'd found Melanie leaving.

"I'm headed to the library," Melanie said. "I've done some of the treasure hunting. Now it's your turn," she said, brushing past Celia towards her parked car.

"Wait, how many receipts are missing? I mean, we were pretty careful this time around," Celia replied.

"You remember the trip to Dar? Well, we need to prove it wasn't a vacation," Sarah said.

"But it wasn't."

"That's where you have to find the missing evidence, Cece. Godspeed," Melanie replied with a wink as she got into her car.

The nail parlor was full of activity. All the client stations were occupied. Fidel Nzomo and Sarah Wena, their hardworking and trusty nail assistants, had their hands full attending to each client. Their manager, Persha, smiled at Celia and confirmed that the auditor was upstairs, waiting.

As Celia trudged up the stairs, she felt the tiredness in her limbs slow her down. She hadn't slept in three days as she juggled keeping the kids active at home, fulfilling orders for her Maven Beauty products, and running the parlor.

She found Sarah going through a file.

"Good morning, Sarah," Celia said as she set her bag down.

"Good morning. I trust Melanie has briefed you about the receipts I'm looking for today?" Sarah asked.

"Yes, the trip to Dar. I'm sure the receipts are in here somewhere," Celia said.

Sarah smiled. "Look, I've never had an issue with you guys, so I'm sure there's an explanation. I'm just asking the same questions a regulator would ask. If you can answer them, you'll be fine."

"I hear you. Give me a few minutes please," Celia replied. She took a deep breath and strolled to a shelf stacked with files. She started rummaging through them. Sarah settled back on her computer, neat rows of files and receipts surrounding her workspace.

Five files later, Celia was still hunting. She had laid a file on the table, slowly leafing through its pages, when a woman sauntered into her office. The woman's hair caught Celia's attention first: her dark hair stood proud and tall, an afro that had been nurtured and tended well. In her freshly manicured hands was a pair of designer sunglasses. The nails matched her outfit, a stylish sage dress with glitter highlights over her comely figure.

"Hello, may I help you?" Celia asked.

The woman turned slowly, like a former runway model would in the real world.

"I'm looking for Celia Dube," the woman asked with the calm, well-articulated delivery of someone who knew her power in the world.

"Yes, you're looking at her."

The woman stretched out her hand in greeting. Celia met it.

"I'm Mika Kanene-Motsepe, and I'd like you to do a job for me."

Celia raised a brow. "What kind of job?"

"I'm having an event in three days. My husband is receiving an award, and I'd like you to be our make-up person for the day," Mika replied.

Celia's mind instinctively felt heavier as it resisted the idea of new work.

"I'm not sure I can honor your request. I've got a lot going on this week. Would you mind if I gave you a recommendation?" Celia asked.

"You already come highly recommended. Sorry, I'm not keen to go elsewhere."

"Mrs. Motsepe…" Celia said.

"Call me, Mika."

"Mika, I'd love to work with you. But the way my week is currently set up, I have to resolve a few issues here."

"How much?" Mika asked.

"Excuse me?" Celia asked.

"How much will it take for you to become available in three days?" Mika asked.

Celia was jolted. She hadn't expected the pushback. "I'd have to think about it."

Mika reached into her purse and took out a business card. "I'd like that. However, get back to me as soon as you can. The event is still going to happen. I'd like you to join us. Have a great day."

Mika twirled and strode out, her cushioned flats, barely making a sound on the metal floor.

Celia placed the card on her desk and resumed going through the open file. After half an hour of searching and fielding other business calls, she only managed to find two receipts from that trip. However, she was confident there were receipts at home that would vindicate her.

"Is this a bad time?"

Celia lifted her head and saw Detective Bill Koloane standing at the open door. He smiled at her. Her heart got fuzzy whenever she saw him these days. In recent weeks, it had become clear their interactions while solving cases had given way to a strong mutual attraction. Bill had asked her on more dates, and she was willing to explore where they would lead. She was enjoying the ride.

"Hey. Um, no. Come in," she replied.

Bill walked up to her, a small bouquet in hand.

Celia smiled feebly. "You didn't have to."

"Oh yes, I did. The last time you got these was when?"

Celia squinted in thought. "Hmmm."

"Choose your words carefully."

"Last week, I haven't forgotten."

"One every week is the rule, and I'm a man of my word. So, are you ready?" Bill asked.

"Ready for?" Celia asked, puzzled.

"We had a lunch date, remember?"

Celia put a hand to her forehead. "Oh, yes! I'm sorry. Let me get my bag."

As she left, she alerted Sarah. "I'll be here waiting," Sarah said.

They drove to the Orchard, a quaint little restaurant not far from the nail salon. They served local and Caribbean dishes, both of which Celia loved. At least she could tell he was paying keen attention to her. However, when it came to the menu, she felt bewildered. She kept scrolling up and down the pages, unable to settle on an item.

"Are you ready to order now, madam?" the smiling waiter asked for the third time, notebook in hand. He wore the standard white and black uniform, with an orange collar line to make the outfit unique.

"Nope. I don't know what to eat," Celia replied.

"You can try the lamb curry? It's pretty good here," Bill suggested, as he dug into his *bobotie*, a tasty dish of spiced minced meat baked with an egg topping.

"I'm not sure I want something local right now."

"Why not try something new?" Bill suggested.

She shook her head.

"You could have a look at our snack menu. You might find something light, but interesting there," said the waiter.

He directed her to the page with the list of snacks, which Celia tried to peruse as fast as possible.

"Erm, maybe get me a slice of carrot cake," she said.

"Will you have it with a drink?" the waiter asked.

"Yes, just house coffee. Single," Celia said.

"House coffee it is," the waiter replied, taking the menu off her. "I'll be with you shortly."

Bill gave her a lingering look as the waiter left.

"What?" she asked.

"You're doing all that slaving at the office and don't want to eat?" he asked.

Celia was tempted to lie that she had a heavy breakfast, but a homemade ginger cookie wasn't a convincing argument.

"I'm just not that hungry, actually. I don't know why. But I'm sure it might kick in later today," Celia said, feigning a smile.

Bill shrugged. "As you wish. Just make sure you get something before the day ends."

"Sure. How's work?"

"Let's not talk about work," Bill said as he cut a piece of meat. "I'm glad we got to connect before the holidays ended officially."

Celia's eyes twinkled as she smiled. After Celia and her family had returned from a fully paid holiday trip over Christmas, Bill had taken her on a three-day hiking trip to Cape Town. Each day, the stunning beachfront and views gave her reason to go on an adventure. They toured sites, hiked up mountains, and strolled the sandy beaches barefoot, the waves massaging their feet. She had her doubts before the trip. However, Bill was a gentleman throughout. It turned out to be a fond memory.

"Yes, thanks for the treat. I didn't expect it," Celia said.

"That was just the beginning. Ready for the next adventure?" Bill asked.

Celia smiled. "Sure, I would. I just wish…"

Bill interrupted her. "Don't say the word *work*. Take it out of the equation."

Celia nodded. "Yes, I'd love to do the next adventure."

They went on chatting for the rest of the hour. As he dropped her off at the nail parlor, he handed her a gift-wrapped box.

"That's for you. To make your day a little lighter."

Celia beamed and unwrapped the box. Out came a silver necklace bearing a pendant with her initials.

"You're spoiling me, Bill," she said.

"Is that the new version of thank you these days?" he asked.

Celia blushed. "Thank you, kind sir. I pray that you have a great day."

"Same to you, beautiful."

Celia got out of the car and walked away with a spring in her step.

As soon as she settled at her desk, she got buried again in customer queries, searching for receipts and following up orders.

She couldn't wait for closing hours. However, each workday has its surprises. Five minutes to closing time, Persha came up to the office. "Celia, we may need to push for another two hours."

Celia, who was writing on the whiteboard, turned to her.

"Ms. Lily isn't here yet?"

"She's here. She just wants the extras. I tried to ask if she could come in tomorrow and she said no," Persha replied.

Celia sighed. "She loves the last-minute appearance."

"It comes with the job."

"Thank you, Persha," Celia said as she went to lean on her desk.

"I'll let you know when we're done," Persha said as she turned to leave.

Celia walked back to her desk but didn't get there. Her legs suddenly buckled under her. The world swam around her as she fell to the floor. Then everything was engulfed in utter darkness.

2

"What's wrong with me?" Celia asked. Her throat felt dry.

"You're going to be fine," Doctor West said as she lifted her stethoscope off Celia's chest. "Your breathing seems normal and your heartbeat is regular now. Please lie down."

As Celia slowly lowered herself until she was lying flat on her back. She shifted uneasily in the uncomfortable hospital gown. "How long do I need to stay?"

"We'll know when I get back the test results. Excuse me," the doctor replied and walked out.

Celia's mother, Audrey Matinise, who was standing near the door, moved closer to the hospital bed.

"How many tests is she talking about?" she asked.

"I'm not sure, Ma. All I remember is they took my blood and did a scan. So I'm guessing they'll be checking for various things with the samples they have," Celia mumbled.

Audrey had received a call from Melanie when it happened. Celia's staff at the parlor rushed her to the hospital. When she arrived, she was still unconscious. Doctors attended to her until she regained consciousness before running other tests.

"You don't know what they're checking for? What if they're doing ten tests and you only need to do three?" Audrey asked.

"But isn't that how it's supposed to work? Then they eliminate all possibilities?" Celia asked.

Audrey shrugged. "I just don't trust them if they leave things that open to interpretation."

Celia sighed. Her brain still felt foggy, and she wasn't keen to analyze things right now.

An hour later, Doctor West returned. She wore a beaming smile. "You're in luck. Everything checks out fine. Your vitals are okay, but your blood pressure has been slightly high recently. Have you been taking a lot of coffee lately?"

"Just one cup a day. Nothing too serious," Celia replied.

"That shouldn't be a problem. How many hours of sleep do you get versus the work hours you put in?"

"I sleep for six hours."

Audrey chuckled.

Celia shot her mother a look. "What, Ma?"

"Six hours? Have you forgotten we live in the same house?" Audrey asked. She turned to the doctor. "She does four hours at best. On most days. I don't think she's slept for the past three nights."

Celia's forehead furrowed. "Ma, that's unnecessary."

"The truth is necessary. The doctor needs to know," Audrey replied.

"Is that true, Celia?" the doctor asked.

"On some nights, yes. I work for an average of twelve hours a day."

The doctor shook her head. "That's not a good balance. I can tell that you're fatigued."

"She's also not been eating well," Audrey chimed in.

"Ma, please. Are you trying to be Mrs. Owens?"

Audrey put a hand to her forehead. "*Haibo*! I forgot to call her and let her know."

"That's another red flag," the doctor said, shaking her head. "You must get a lot of rest for the next week. That's an order, not a request.

No going to the office or else your body will shut down on you. Okay?"

"But I have a lot of work to get through," Celia said.

"No buts, Celia," the doctor interrupted. "Eat often, but avoid junk food. Healthy meals are key. You might need to shed some weight too through exercises. Come by regularly so that we can review how your blood pressure is doing. Another thing: when you came in, there was an issue with your insurance cover."

Celia's eyes widened. "What?"

"The cover you have is for outpatient only. It limits access to some services. You should add an inpatient cover to it," the doctor replied.

"Hold on. What are you talking about?" a puzzled Audrey asked.

"That's the policy she has," the doctor replied.

"But I'm not spending the night here, am I?" Celia asked.

"No, you're not, fortunately. But my advice is to get an inpatient cover or change policy providers," the doctor replied.

After the doctor stepped out, Audrey looked at Celia. "You took out a comprehensive cover for me and the kids and not yourself?"

"Ma, it's expensive. Sacrifices have to be made," Celia replied.

Audrey shook her head vigorously. "No, no more of that. We have to get you on comprehensive."

"That will cost me more money, which I don't have."

"We'll find a way. We always have," Audrey replied defiantly.

Silence descended as they soaked in the situation.

"Pass me my phone, Ma," she said.

"What for?" Audrey asked.

"I need to make one phone call," Celia replied.

"The doctor said you shouldn't be working."

"He also said that I need to bump up my insurance cover. Are you going to cover that for me?" Celia posed.

Audrey hesitated for a moment, then handed Celia the phone.

"*One* phone call only," Audrey said.

Celia dialed Mika's number.

"I've been wondering when you're going to call," Mika crooned.

"I'm sorry Mika, I had a few things that I had to attend to urgently."

"My proposition is pretty urgent too, seeing as the event is only days away," Mika replied. "Have you made a decision?"

Celia inhaled. "Yes, I have. I'm going to work with you."

Mika's smile was audible. "Fantastic! I'll be sending you the schedule later today. You can let me know what time you'll come in so that the driver can pick you up."

"The driver?" Celia asked.

"Of course. Do you think I'm going to let you drive here on your own? You're part of my entourage now," Mika said.

Celia's eyes glowed.

"What's going on?" Audrey interrupted her conversation.

"That sounds good. Thank you," Celia replied.

"I look forward to seeing you soon," Mika replied, then hung up.

Audrey held out her hand. "Phone."

"I need to keep it close. Sorry," Celia said, tucking the gadget under the covers. Audrey shook her head.

An hour later, Celia was back home. She spent the rest of the day propped up on the couch, watching television. The only interruptions she got were her sons checking on her, and her mother bringing in regular fruit cuts of mangoes, bananas, apples, and avocados.

"You need the energy for your body to recover," Audrey said.

"This will make me bigger, Ma. This is all fructose you're feeding me. Perhaps a change in diet will be a better option?"

"Funny you should say that. Mrs. Owens is coming up with a diet for you," replied Aubrey.

Mrs. Owens had been their family friend for years. In her days as a nurse, she helped deliver Celia into the world. Now comfortably retired and enjoying her hefty pension, she often came for visits to bond. She could be a handful sometimes, and Celia was wary of this.

"Here we go again," Celia said.

The next day Celia woke up fatigued. She made a feeble attempt at exercise using an online video but didn't make it past five minutes.

"You should ease off for another day or two," Audrey said as she served up a red-brown concoction.

"What is this?" Celia asked as she studied the glass quizzically.

"It's an herbal drink," Audrey replied. "Ginger, lemon, some beet, and honey."

Celia took a sip and shivered as the bitter taste shot through her.

"I thought you put honey in it?" Celia asked.

"Just a drop," Audrey replied with a cheeky smile.

After she'd somehow finished the drink, Celia spent the rest of the day indoors. Her state of inertia was broken by a one-hour afternoon stroll in the sun.

On the day of the awards, Celia woke up with the sunrise and made the boys' breakfast before they left for school.

"We agreed I was going to do that this week," Audrey said after Celia returned from dropping the boys at school.

"Ma, it's the day of the event. I like building my rhythm early," Celia replied. "Besides, making breakfast isn't heavy work."

"And dropping the kids off? I'm only trying to help you," Audrey said.

"I appreciate it, Ma. In that same spirit, can you drive me to the nail parlor?" Celia asked.

Audrey shook her head. "No way. We said no work."

"I'm not going to work," Celia said, raising her hands. "Can you see how bad my nails are right now? I can't claim to run a business yet my nails look like this."

"I can do those for you," Audrey offered.

"Ma, let my people do it. Let's make it a date. You and me getting our nails done," Celia said, flashing her most charming smile.

Audrey looked at her nails. "Now that you mention it, they need some attention."

Two hours later, they were both seated in the cushy chairs at the nail parlor, getting the full manicure and pedicure service. Afterward, Audrey drove Celia back to her house to freshen up.

At exactly two o'clock, a dark SUV with chrome wheels rolled up the driveway. Celia and her mother both heard its big engine rumble and watched it arrive through their living room window.

"That's my ride," Celia said as she picked up her purse, took hold of her suitcase containing a dress and makeup kit, and headed for the door.

"You didn't tell me they were going to pick you up," Audrey remarked.

Celia smiled. "You don't have to worry about anything."

"You're forgetting something," Audrey said as she dashed to the kitchen. She returned with a lunchbox. "Remember to eat."

"Ma, I'm sure they've got plenty of food there."

"I wouldn't be your mother if I don't think of everything," Audrey said.

Celia gushed. "Thanks, Ma," she said as she walked out the door.

Nothing could've prepared Celia for the Motsepe home.

Tall wrought-iron gates opening like the gates of heaven into a long driveway, the well-trimmed hedges and greenery built her anticipation for what the house would look like.

Sitting at the far end of the expansive compound, the big house was nestled among trees. It had several balconies, a three-car garage, a gazebo, and tall windows. You could only dream of bigger things if you lived there.

A butler met her at the door and led her down the hallway. Mika appeared through one of the large oak doors with her arms outstretched.

"Welcome home, Celia," Mika said. She took Celia's arm and led her up the winding flight of stairs to the first floor. They walked down another hallway until they got to a well-lit room with tall windows that overlooked the massive lawn. The room's set up resembled a lounge, with three blue-satin settees and a large dressing table to one end.

"This is my retreat room, but for today it's your working room. It's got everything you need. If you open that little side door," Mika said, pointing to one end of the room, "you'll access a bedroom. You can freshen up there if you need to, as it has its bathroom. Once we're done tonight, you can sleep there and leave tomorrow morning."

"Thank you very much, but I think I'll head home after we're done," Celia replied.

Mika scoffed. "Nonsense. It will be late and your kids will be asleep, anyway. Feel at home."

Not wanting to rub her client the wrong way, Celia smiled. "I appreciate it. Oh, I got you something." From her suitcase, she took out two cases of the new Maven beauty foundation. "Something you can use even when I'm not around for such nights."

Mika smiled. "I don't use new products often, but with you I'll take a chance. Thank you." With that, she turned and left.

Celia walked to the windows and took in the serene sight of the gardens before she started unpacking. She had just finished setting up her make-up workspace when Dean Motsepe appeared. A tall, athletic man, he looked as fit as a warrior from Shaka Zulu's kingdom. He smoothed out the front of his t-shirt as he gave her the once-over.

"You're Celia?" he asked.

"Yes, I am. You're Dean?" she asked, although she didn't need to. Everyone knew who the former rugby captain was.

Dean smirked, possibly due to her feigned ignorance. "Yes, I am. Are you ready to start?"

"Yes, just give me five minutes."

"Alright. Get comfortable. I like your outfit, and I'm looking forward to our session together," Dean said in a slow drawl.

"Excuse me?" Celia asked, quickly staring at her form-fitting dress.

Dean laughed and then winked at her. He slowly backed away and disappeared down the hallway.

Celia stood there, suddenly unsure if she should be in a room alone with him.

3

"Have you ever been to Paris?" Dean asked as she powdered his face.

"No, I haven't. How is it?" Celia asked. She had welcomed his return with minimal fuss and wanted to keep it civil. She kept the door ajar, just in case.

"Well, the answer to that question depends on which version of me you want to narrate the story," Dean replied with a cheeky smile.

"Which versions are there?" Celia asked.

"Which versions do you see?" he countered.

Celia knew he was testing her. She didn't want to speak her mind, although she already had three versions in her mind. The man who lived the good life unapologetically; the man who was loyal to those he loved; and the man who could lead you to war. All were flattering but came with flaws that she wasn't interested in exploring.

"I'm not very good at guessing," she replied.

Dean laughed. "You're too modest for your good, Celia. But in a good way. You blend into any space you get into, and that's a quality I like."

"Thank you for the kind words. Please tilt your head back slightly, and try not to smile," Celia said.

"Oh, sorry. I get carried away," he remarked.

"You were telling me about Paris," she reminded him.

"Ah, yes. The city of love, so they say. I've come to appreciate the power of consistent marketing. I think after the Romanticism movement of the 18th century celebrated love through artworks, the city latched onto that and never let go. But is it really the city of love?"

Dean paused briefly as Celia dabbed around his mouth. Once done, he continued.

"In comparison, our city of love is probably Cape Town. Or maybe Durban. Sunshine Cove comes close because of its small size and charm. We have a sense of community that those big cities just don't have. That's why I'd rather live here and experience love in its purest form. *Eish*, we have many beautiful places here. But I would still go with Cape Town. You enjoy the sparkling waters along the beaches, go whale watching, and then enjoy a sundowner at a winery. Perfect love spot. What do you think?"

Dean was about to break into a broad smile, his cheek muscles bunching up and his lips parting, when he caught himself and quickly relaxed again. Celia made her final touches, silently considering her answer.

"I didn't consider you a romantic," Celia said.

"I'm not. Just an observer. Maybe an artist. Speaking of artists, I must say you're one of the best if not the best person who's worked on my face," he said.

Celia raised a brow. "How can you tell? You haven't looked into the mirror yet."

"Your hands glide over the face like a feather," he remarked.

"Thank you. I think we're done now," Celia replied, stepping back. "You can check yourself in the mirror."

Dean stood and walked up to the full-length mirror that stood along one wall. He moved his head this way and that, angling his face for the best light and visibility.

"Interesting," he mumbled, moving closer to the mirror until he was inches away from it. The overhead strobe light hit his face, enhancing his features. "You're nothing like Paris. You're the real deal. Sunshine Cove love. I've got no fear of those stage lights now!"

"You'll be looking great," Celia said.

Dean turned with a cheeky smile. "That's the first time you've acknowledged my impeccable looks."

"I'm just confirming what you said," she replied. She wasn't keen to go down the rabbit hole he was opening.

His phone rang. He took it out of his pocket, glanced at the screen. "Excuse me, I'll be back."

"Sure."

As he stepped out into the hallway, she heard him say. "Hello, princess."

Celia fiddled with her make-up set but couldn't resist the urge. She could still hear his voice murmur indelibly in the distance. She slowly made her way to the door and stepped out into the hallway. She followed the sound of his voice and finally arrived at a door that led to his study. It was slightly ajar. She scanned the hallway to make sure no one was close by and then craned her neck to listen.

"You went where again?... I told you that's not possible... Baby, get serious. I've got an event tonight. I'm pretty sure you will miss me if you get on that plane without me... Alright, alright. I'll add you to the list. Okay? Yes, I'll see you tonight. I promise."

Celia stepped back, believing she'd heard enough. As she turned to walk back, the nonchalant face of Mika met her.

"Sorry, Mika," Celia said in a panicked whisper.

Mika shushed her with a finger over her mouth and then smiled. "I was looking for you. Ready to work on me?"

Celia nodded, and they walked back to the workroom.

"You're a curious cat," Mika said as she settled into the chair.

"I was simply checking on him," Celia replied as she wrapped the make-up bib over her bosom.

Mika chuckled. "I check on him too. I used to do it every night. We'd fight and ruin our evening dinners often. Then I realized that skipping dinner was making me lose a lot of weight, and I didn't need that."

Celia pursed her lips, unsure of what to say.

"Trust me, it's not worth it. It's a much better life if you simply let him play with his toys," Mika remarked.

Celia paused and then took her brush. "Close your eyes."

Later that afternoon, they left for the event in a two-car convoy of sleek sedans, with the Motsepe's in the lead car while Celia rode in the second car. Celia found it intriguing that they didn't want to use one car, but she didn't mind feeling like royalty for one evening. She managed to chat with the driver on their way there, an ex-military man with a love for conspiracy theories.

At the awards event, the layout mimicked that of the Oscars. There were all sorts of celebrities, long red carpets, cheering fans, flashing lights blinding your eyes, genuine joy mixed with flashes of insincere admiration. Inside, Celia sat in the same row where Dean and Mika were, a perk of being part of their entourage. A hefty man who introduced himself as Khaya Ndlovu, Dean's former teammate, and best friend, joined them.

As the ceremony went on, Celia kept glancing at Dean and Mika. The two exchanged whispers now and then, punctuated by warm smiles where necessary. When Dean's name was called, Mika stood up to clap, joined by Khaya and many other people in the audience. Celia had to follow suit.

Towards the end of his speech, Dean looked to his wife. "And finally, to Mika, for all the good and hard times we've had, you've never wavered, never faltered, never let me down. You've been my rock and always will be. Thank you."

Celia immediately glanced at Mika, who mouthed a 'thank you' back to Dean. She clapped with a beaming smile.

Dean strode back to his seat, a gold-plated statuette in hand. He embraced Mika with a long, passionate hug as cameras flashed around them.

After the ceremony, various interviewers seeking a sound bite crowded around Dean. For the first three, Mika stood by his side in support. However, she slowly slinked away as more reporters lined up. Dean wasn't showing signs of turning any of them down.

Celia wanted to follow Mika as she left for the cars, but Dean called out to her for a touch-up. Celia obliged and hung around him for the next half hour as he espoused to different outlets about his career and opinions on nearly everything. Both sides were milking the moment unabashedly.

When he finished his final interview, they walked back to the car together. As they exited the auditorium, a tall shapely woman with long dark hair walked up to them.

"Congratulations, tiger," the woman said, smiling.

Dean laughed and gave her a hug that nearly lifted her off the ground. "I thought you decided to skip it."

"And miss out on your greatness? How could I?" the woman said, her voice cultured yet sultry.

"Are you coming to the after-party?" Dean asked. "I think we need to catch up a bit."

"Sure," the woman said. Dean gave her hand an affectionate squeeze, and the woman left.

Dean turned to Celia. "That remains between us."

"What are you talking about?" Celia asked.

"The person who just greeted me."

"I didn't see anything," Celia replied.

Dean smiled. "I like you. Let's talk about your remaining installment and bonus after the party."

"Sure," Celia replied as she headed to her car.

"One more thing. My friend Khaya didn't come in his car today, so he's going to ride with you. Are you okay with that?" Dean asked.

Celia frowned. "He's already in the car?"

"Yes, I think so. I hope that's fine with you?" Dean asked.

Celia wasn't comfortable with it. If Khaya was anything like Mika's flirting husband, it would be an uncomfortable ride.

Celia sighed. "I'll be fine."

"Great! See you at the party," Dean replied.

Inside her car, Celia was surprised to find Khaya seated on one end of the backseat. She had secretly hoped he would sit next to the driver.

"We meet again," he said, the white of his teeth catching the glow of the roof light.

Celia sat on the opposite end of the back seat, ensuring there was as much room between them as possible.

"You sure you want to sit that far away?" he asked.

"I'm seated where I was when we drove here. It was a little quieter then. I'd like to keep it that way," Celia quipped.

Khaya frowned. "Your loss."

She didn't respond, for her mind had already moved on to other, more curious things. As they drove off, she wondered about the tall, shapely woman.

4

Celia didn't consider going out to party as a form of entertainment, but she got a good sense of the club scene through conversations at the nail parlor.

The after-party location was the Heartland Lounge, a high-end establishment. While others used the word 'club' for any entertainment spot, this was truly a club. It had a dress code, and only guests on the list were allowed in.

Celia walked closely behind Dean and Mika, with Khaya hanging in the wings.

Once they got in, a chaperone led them to their VIP area, which had comfortable leather seats, and a large white table decked with snacks and bites. The wall had a banner emblazoned 'Congratulations Legend!'

Celia sat next to Mika and Dean as the other seats around them filled up with former teammates, executives from their businesses, and friends.

The music mix was a wonderful blend of old-school house music and current hits.

"Are you comfortable?" Mika asked.

"Yes, thanks. I just haven't been in such places in years," Celia said, struggling to speak over the loud music.

"Welcome to my world," Mika said.

"You come here often?" Celia asked.

"Not here. But I used to party every weekend. These days I only go out when celebrating something," she replied. It appeared that none of the people in the VIP area were from Mika's friendship circle, Celia observed.

"How about Dean?" Celia asked as she watched him and Khaya talking animatedly.

"You'd think it's his bread and butter. He hits the town at least twice every week," Mika replied.

Just then, Khaya and Dean got up. Khaya led him out of the VIP area.

"Where are they going?" Celia queried.

Mika sipped her juice before replying. "To meet and greet. There are a lot of fans here."

"How do you cope with all the attention you both get?"

Mika smiled. "I used to be a TV presenter back in the day. So I'm used to it. All you have to do is to be yourself and avoid the snakes who might be coming after you."

"Snakes?" Celia asked with a frown.

"There are always snakes looking to cut down a famous figure," Mika replied.

As a waiter started serving alcoholic drinks, Mika tapped Celia's forearm. "Let's get a table."

Celia wore a quizzical look. "Why?"

"Do you drink?" Mika asked.

Celia shook her head.

"Neither do I, so let's go," she insisted.

Outside the VIP area, they realized that although the place was full of people, there were several empty tables. They took one near a corner, away from the crowd.

As she sat, Celia could see Dean talking to two women. They giggled at what he was saying and occasionally touched his arm. She knew from their body language that they were captivated by his charm.

"Mika…" Celia started.

"Don't worry, I can see them," Mika replied in a monotone.

"Why are you so comfortable about this?"

Mika raised a brow. "Comfortable? What makes you think that?"

"I'm sorry if that came out wrong," Celia said. "But you're not reacting to it. It doesn't seem to affect you."

Mika chuckled. "Dean's an entertainer, always has been. He can dance with them, take them for concerts and boat rides, the works. Underneath his large frame is a shy man who's never really grown up. They see his fame, I see his frailty."

Just then, the bartender walked to their table.

"Hello, ladies. I've got a special delivery for you," he said. He had two tall glasses filled with fresh juice cocktails. He served each of them to the two women. "For you, Mrs. Motsepe is the Caribbean mix; and for you, beautiful lady is the Tropical blend. Both fantastic cocktails. Enjoy."

He took away their previous glasses and left.

Celia was puzzled. "That's the first time I'm getting served by the actual bartender."

"Welcome to my world. This is either Dean's or Khaya's doing," Mika said as she sipped her drink. "It's pretty good."

Celia sipped hers. The rich, pleasant flavors surprised her. "You're right. That is good. Anyway, allow me to ask this. Earlier today, when you found me in the hallway, you made me wonder. Is he doing more than entertaining?" Celia asked.

"He's got a girl or two on the side. That's true, nothing to hide there. I've even met them," Mika replied.

Stunned by the statement, Celia hit Mika's glass by accident, spilling some juice onto her dress. She quickly grabbed the glass and steadied it before it spilled all its contents.

"Oh, shucks! I'm so silly," Celia said. She scrambled for some serviettes, dabbing the left side of her outfit.

"That caught you off guard," Mika remarked as she watched. "Nothing a little water won't fix if you attend to it now."

Celia shook her head. "This should do it. We should get you another drink."

Celia noticed Mika looking at her at her glass. After her mishap, it was now half-full.

"This is perfect. The glass is half-full. Why would I waste all this goodness? Forget it. I'll finish it and then we'll get another," Mika said.

"Fair enough. So, why did you meet them?" Celia asked.

"They say keep your friends close and your enemies closer. I need to know whom my husband is seeing, and they need to know that I exist. And then we came up with an agreement," Mika said.

Intrigued, Celia asked, "What kind of agreement?"

"If I told you, I'd have to kill you. Let's just say things are much more peaceful now," Mika said playfully, running a finger across the breadth of her glass. "You really should get some water to rinse off that stain. Take it from someone who understands that fabric."

Celia relented, excusing herself to go to the washroom. Once there, she did her best to wash off the juice from her dress. The most affected part was on the lower left side. After ten minutes, she believed she'd done her best.

While leaving the washroom, her phone rang.

"Hey. I've been trying to reach you," Bill's deep voice said.

Celia cupped her hands over her phone to limit the external din. "Sorry, it's been a busy night."

"Sounds like you're having a good time," he replied.

"You can hear that?" she asked.

"Clear as a whistle. So I can assume it's going to be a late night. So I can't steal you away for a breakfast date tomorrow?" he asked.

Celia paused for a moment. "Yeah, I don't think we'll do breakfast. This will end late. How about lunch again? I'm taking the day off, anyway. I promise I'll have an appetite this time."

"I'll hold you to that. See you at lunch tomorrow. I'll pick you up." He hung up.

Celia sighed as she made her way through the partying crowd to her table. As she pushed through small groups of chattering friends, the drunk rapper and the occasional bad dancer, she affirmed that she was too old for this.

"This place is packed!" Celia exclaimed as she took her seat. Next to her, Mika was silent. She sat hunched over as if she was taking a nap.

"Mika?" Celia called, putting her hand on Mika's shoulder. She shook her. No response.

Celia stood up, took hold of both of Mika's shoulders, and lifted her. Mika sat up, her head flipping to one side, her eyes wide open.

"No, no, no, no..." Celia said, her heart racing. "Somebody help me!"

People around her turned to see what was going on.

"Is she okay?" someone asked as Celia checked Mika's pulse.

"No, she's not okay. She's dying!" Celia said, her voice choking.

Someone screamed.

5

"Somebody help me!" Celia shouted as she tried to hold up Mika's limp body. Different revelers were drawn to the commotion. The music in the club went to a barely audible level. Two people ran to her and, together, they eased Mika to the floor.

A bouncer arrived, with two others following closely behind.

"What's going on here?" the first bouncer asked.

"Call an ambulance!" Celia said as she positioned Mika for mouth-to-mouth resuscitation. The lead bouncer motioned to another behind him, who took off towards the entrance.

Celia started pressing Mika's chest. From the corner of her eye, she caught sight of Dean and Khaya emerging from the crowd of onlookers. They looked stunned.

The two bouncers returned with a stretcher. A third man, in white gloves and a white shirt, accompanied them.

"Are you a paramedic?" Celia asked.

"Yes. I'm the club paramedic. We need to take her to the ambulance," the third man said.

Celia stepped back. She watched with amazement the speed and care they used to place Mika onto the stretcher. In about twenty seconds, they had her strapped down. The two bouncers lifted the stretcher and headed towards the exit with the paramedic behind them. Celia followed.

"She needs oxygen. Do you have some in the ambulance?" Celia asked.

"We have everything one would need if unconscious. Please stay back," the paramedic replied as they got to the ambulance. Inside, the ambulance looked well equipped. Once she was inside, the paramedic resumed CPR. The doors closed, and the ambulance sped away, its lights flashing.

Suddenly Celia felt an eerie silence around her. Then a hand grabbed her upper arm. "Let's go back in," the bouncers said.

"Do you need to hold me that way?" Celia asked.

"Yes. We need to keep you here until the cops come," he replied.

Then it dawned on Celia. They thought she drugged Mika.

"I was in the washrooms when she collapsed. I don't know anything about this," she said.

"Tell that to the cops when they get here," the bouncer replied.

As they got back to her table, Dean and Khaya walked up to her.

"What happened there?" Dean asked.

"I don't know. I got back from the washroom and found her unconscious," Celia replied.

"You think we're foolish? Did you drug her?" Dean asked, getting too close for comfort. For the first time, she began to feel intimidated by Dean's towering presence. Celia leaned back as a bouncer came between her and Dean. Khaya held back Dean. They started retreating.

"You better hope she lives!" Dean shouted.

"Sit," the bouncer ordered Celia. She sat down, her mind racing. Why was this happening?

"Stay where you're seated!" someone shouted.

Celia craned her neck and saw three policemen moving through the crowd of revelers. One of them walked to where Celia stood.

"Who was with her?" the policeman asked.

Celia raised a hand. "I was."

The policeman gave her the once over. "What's your name?"

"Celia Dube," she replied.

"What's your relation to the victim?"

"She was my client. I'm a beautician and do make up for my clients," she replied.

"Alright. Stay there. Detectives are on their way," he replied. He then went on to stand next to the table Mika and Celia had sat in less than an hour ago.

He stood there until the crime scene detectives arrived. For Celia, seeing them gave the whole incident a chilling finality. Mika was truly gone. Her heart sank as she pondered the vulnerability of human life. Celia had hoped she'd see Bill. He would understand how she felt, but he wasn't there.

Celia observed as the detectives with their gloves on, with accompanying fingerprint powder, went over the scene meticulously. They placed the glasses they had drank from into an evidence bag.

Celia then recognized Detective Reuben, whom she had seen with Bill several times. He walked up to her.

"Hello, Celia," Reuben asked.

"Hello, detective. I'm sorry we've met in such instances several times," she said.

"Well, this life is a strange thing. You were with the victim?" he asked.

"Yes. I returned from the washroom and found her unconscious. I honestly don't know what happened while I was in the washroom," she replied.

"No problem. We'll see if there are any witnesses who saw anything. We'll also have a look at the cameras. However, I'll need to ask you a few questions," Reuben replied.

"Is Bill coming to join you?" she asked.

"Not today. He's caught up on another case. I'm the lead on this one, but he'll listen in where needed," Reuben replied.

He took out a notebook and started asking her questions, focusing on the events before, during, and after Mika collapsed.

He was winding up when Dean appeared. He looked tipsy.

"What did you put in her drink?" Dean asked.

Celia's eyes widened. "I didn't put anything."

"Liar! You sat with her all night," Dean frothed. He turned to the detective. "Why isn't she in cuffs?"

"She's still a witness," Reuben said.

"But can't you see she's the only one who was closest to Mika?" Dean asked.

Celia bit her lower lip. Dean was trying to pin it on her, and she didn't have a defender. She once again wished Bill was there.

"I don't tell you how to do your job, don't tell me how to do mine," Reuben replied.

"They'll do a chemical test to see if it was me. I doubt they'll find what you think they will," Celia replied.

Dean paced. "Who sent you? Who sent you to ruin my day?"

"No one did. At this rate, I'm beginning to wonder why you're so eager to have me arrested. Are you afraid of something?" Celia posed.

Dean leaned over until they were eyeball-to-eyeball. "If it's proven that you did this, you'll have a very hard life ahead."

Celia swallowed hard. Reuben put an arm in-between them. "Alright, that's enough."

Dean backed off and walked away, stomping his way through the crowd.

The detective went and talked to one of his colleagues briefly. He then walked back to Celia.

"I need you to accompany me to the station," Reuben said.

"Am I under arrest?" Celia asked.

"That depends on what you say next," he replied.

Celia held her chin up. "I didn't kill her."

The detective's right arm reached for the cuffs on his waist. "You're under arrest for the murder of Mika Motsepe. Anything you say or do can and will be used against you in a court of law."

Celia didn't hear the rest. Instead, the sound of her pounding heart filled her ears.

6

"What's the real reason you left Mika alone at that exact moment?" Detective Reuben asked.

He sat across from Celia in a gray-walled interrogation room. The lone light above them made the shadows around the interrogation room more ominous.

Celia swallowed hard, her lips dry. "I needed to go to the washroom after spilling some juice on my dress."

"Your dress looks pretty stain-free," he remarked.

"I washed it off. That's why I went to the washrooms. I didn't want to, honestly. But Mika herself insisted I do. She loved the dress and didn't want it ruined," she replied.

"For how long were you gone?" Reuben asked.

Celia paused before responding. "About ten minutes."

"Then she had already collapsed by the time you got back?"

"Yes," Celia replied.

"Was she dead?"

"She had a weak pulse. So, she didn't have much time," Celia said.

"So, you were seated with her all night, you drank juices with her and you had access to her drinks. Then after you left, she falls unconscious. Is it possible you gave her something before you went to the washrooms?" he posed.

"I know how it looks, but I'm not responsible," Celia said.

"You're making it difficult to believe you."

"What do I need to do to prove it?" she asked.

"Tell us why you did it," he said.

"But I didn't do it!" she retorted.

"Then who did?"

"I don't know!"

The detective leaned back in his chair, tapping his notebook with a biro pen.

"You're not getting out of here with that approach," he said.

Celia sighed. "I'd like to speak to my mother and lawyer."

"You can only talk to one. Which one will it be?" he asked.

"My mother," she replied.

Detective Reuben grunted. He closed his notebook and stood up.

"We're not done yet, so sit tight," he said. He walked to the door, pressed his thumb on the biometric scanner to unlock it, and left.

Ten minutes later, he returned. He placed her phone on the table.

"One phone call," Reuben said as he stood waiting.

Celia called her mother. The phone rang a few times before it was picked up.

"It's a little late to be calling," Audrey said in a sleepy voice.

"Hi, Ma. Something happened. I'm at the police station. Could you call Harry and tell him to come down?" Celia asked.

"Are you okay?" Audrey asked.

"I'm fine. Just tell Harry, okay?"

"Okay. We'll be there together," Audrey replied.

After the detective left, Celia put her head in her hands. She reflected quietly for the next two hours. She kept replaying her conversation with Mika where she had declined to attend the after-party. Mika's persuasive nature won her over, but Celia now wished she had held her ground.

She then heard footsteps approaching the door and lifted her head off the table.

The door swung open. In walked a suited man with a briefcase. It was Harry Smith, a lawyer who had represented Celia's family over the years in various legal matters. She never thought one of those *matters* would include a criminal case.

"Hello, Celia." he said as he planted himself on the opposite seat. He beamed at her, placing the briefcase on top of the table.

"Welcome to my latest scenario," Celia replied.

"You make it sound like we do this every week," Harry remarked.

"Fortunately, we don't," she said.

He popped open the briefcase. He took out a notebook and a small portable audio recorder.

"Your mother's waiting for me outside. Have they been good to you?" he asked.

"As best as they can," she replied.

He eyed the handcuff tying her to the table. "Tell me what happened."

Celia recounted what transpired from the time she met Dean and Mika to the time she was arrested.

"So, you didn't notice anything or anyone suspicious before you found her dead?" he asked.

"I've wracked my brain about it and I spotted nothing overtly suspicious. I tend to believe I'm pretty good at spotting such stuff these days, but this one flew right by me," she said.

"I know what you'll say, but I still have to ask this: do you have anything to do with Mika's death?" he asked.

Celia sighed. "No, I didn't kill Mika."

Harry scribbled down a few more notes before quickly scanning through them.

He winced. "The circumstantial evidence points to you, of course, which is the basis of their current suspicion. If they strengthen their case using forensic evidence, this could go down to the wire."

"But I didn't do it!" she protested.

"And I believe you. I'm just saying let's hope someone isn't trying to frame you," he replied.

Inside Celia's mouth suddenly felt parched. "You think someone is trying to box me in?"

"It's possible. So that they, the real killer, can get away with it. If I were the sinister individual, I would go for that option too. It covers my tracks," Harry said.

Celia clasped her palms together and stared at the table.

"So, what next?" she asked.

"I'll have a chat with the detectives about this," he replied.

However, it soon emerged she'd have to attend a court hearing to post her bail. The next day, she was arraigned in a small, packed courtroom alongside other accused people. The judge, a bespectacled woman in her sixties, listened to every charge before quickly handing her decision.

Celia had never been in the dock before, and this bothered her. However, it was over as fast as it started. She was granted bail.

Later, Celia walked up to her mother in excitement.

"They let you out, my baby," Audrey said.

"It's going to be fine, Ma," Celia replied.

"What are we going to do now?" her mother asked.

"Find a way to clear my name without getting into more trouble, Ma," she said.

7

Although the plan was to get home and relax, that was hardly possible.

The moment they got home, Audrey got to work in the kitchen, prepping a feast as if it were Christmas. The only different thing was that she avoided most of the fried dishes she loved making, boiling them instead. She also left out foods containing wheat, all in the name of helping Celia get on a different diet regime.

By the time Celia had freshened up, her mother had decked out the dining table. The result was a sizeable portion of mashed potatoes, boiled chicken, and plenty of steamed vegetables. A side of fruit salad completed the ensemble.

"This is not our usual feast, but we have to give thanks for today's victory," Audrey said.

After they ate to their fill, Celia's phone started ringing. First, it was Melanie.

"Hey. I just heard the news. You were doing something for that rugby legend's wife, right?" Melanie asked.

"Yeah. It was a crazy night," Celia replied.

"Are you okay?"

"I'm better now," Celia replied. She didn't want to tell her she spent the night in a cell.

"That's great to hear. I hope they catch whoever did this," Melanie said.

"You have no idea how badly I want that to happen," she replied.

"Take care and let's talk soon," she said.

Celia was soon fielding calls from three reporters, who somehow got her number. She declined to talk to them. The last call she took was from Bill.

"I heard you visited last night," Bill said.

"Too bad you weren't there," she said.

"I had to be somewhere else. Are you okay?" he asked.

"Yes. I had nothing to do with it," Celia said.

"I believe you. Just keep your cool. Keep your nose out of trouble. You know what I'm talking about," Bill advised.

"I hear you loud and clear," Celia replied.

Afterward, Celia felt a wave of drowsiness hit her. She'd been up all night, so this wasn't a surprise. She returned to her bedroom and fell into a deep slumber. She woke up hours later to the excited sounds of her sons arriving from school.

"Grandma told us you went on a work trip," John said with a beaming smile.

Celia cast a knowing look at her mother. "Yes, it was a busy workweek. Did you miss me?"

"Yes, we did. Did you get us souvenirs?" James asked, hugging her for the umpteenth time.

"Oh my. I was so busy that I forgot. But I'll get you something on my next trip," Celia replied.

"Will you be going to the same place?" James asked.

Celia paused. "No, not the same place. Another better place."

She played with them for a short while before they went for their evening baths. Thereafter, they spent the evening watching animated movies until it was bedtime.

The next morning, Celia slept in. She didn't even hear the kids leave for school. She hadn't expected her exhaustion to linger for that long. She woke up some minutes before eleven and struggled to get her body out of bed. She washed her face and ambled to the dining table, still wearing her pajamas.

"You slept like a log. That's a first," her mother said as she served her breakfast. "Guess who's here?"

"Who?" Celia asked.

Mrs. Owens waltzed in from the kitchen, donning an apron, a chef's hat and holding an egg whisk like a microphone. She sang it in Xhosa.

I'm here to tell you that you need to wake up.
And dance a little more.
Shake off the weariness of yesterday.
Take charge of a bright new day!

Mrs. Owens sang this a little off-key while doing a light jig around the breakfast table. Celia resisted the urge to cringe at the performance by smiling in mild amusement. Mrs. Owens must have composed the song, for Celia had never heard it before.

"*Eish*, isn't she something?" Audrey asked, grinning.

"Isn't it too early for a sugar rush?" Celia asked.

"It's never too early for a little dance. Get on your feet," Mrs. Owens said.

"No, you can't force this," Celia said, but her protests were cut short by her mother and Mrs. Owens. They both led her to the carpet and danced some more as Mrs. Owens crooned away.

Soon they were out of breath, and Celia retreated to finish her breakfast.

Afterward, the two older women wanted to go to the spa and unwind, but Celia was restless. She couldn't truly relax until she erased the questions in her mind. Who wanted Mika dead? Was she being framed? Why did they do it in such a public place? Are the police moving fast enough? She felt a strong urge to make things happen, but she remembered Bill's advice. *Stay out of trouble.*

"Let me go outside and get some sun," Celia said. She stepped out into the front driveway. It was sun-bathed and the traffic on the road was modest. She leaned on her parked car and called Bill.

"How's the case going?" she asked after the usual pleasantries.

"I'm not sure I can tell you that. It's an active investigation being led by another detective. You're a suspect. It would look a little inappropriate to give you that kind of information," he replied.

"Are you serious?" she asked.

"Very serious," he replied.

Celia massaged her temple. "This whole thing is like a dark cloud hanging over me. A cloud I didn't ask for. It's driving me a little crazy, to be honest."

"I can imagine your mind is a little jumbled up. But trust me on this. I'm only trying to protect you, and to protect myself," Bill said.

"Alright. I guess I'll have to figure this out on my own," she replied.

"Did you listen to what I just said? Don't try anything with this one, Cece. Just hold out and the evidence will speak for itself," he advised.

"What if the killer is trying to frame me? What then? They could have planted the evidence to make me look guilty," she said.

He paused. "You could be right. We'll have to prove it beyond a shadow of a doubt."

Celia laughed painfully. "You're trying to humor me?"

"Hardly. I suggest you hold back on anything your mind tells you to do," Bill said. "Let the cops do their job."

Celia sighed. "I'll try."

"Please do. I'd hate if you made it worse for yourself," he said.

"It's already pretty bad. I don't want it to get worse. Thanks for listening," she said.

When she hung up, she stepped back from the car and pondered her situation. She was innocent. She didn't know any witnesses in the case, and she wouldn't need to threaten anyone. She could still go to places and have simple conversations without stirring trouble. That's what she'd call it. Simple conversations. It was time to head back to the club.

During the day, the Heartland Lounge still looked impressive from the outside, unlike most nightspots.

Its facade appeared flashy with its colored windows and neon sign. Shiny silver tiles accentuated its whitewashed walls. To her relief, there was no security at the entrance. She walked in, down the dimly lit corridors, and emerged in the well-lit bar area. A few tables had chairs on top of them. There was soft house music playing - so soft one could only hear the beats. The counter was empty, with no bartender in sight. A lone cleaner moved around the space, taking the chairs off the tables and arranging them neatly.

Celia walked over to the cleaner.

"Excuse me. Are you open?" Celia asked.

The cleaner turned and flashed a tired look. "Yeah, we can serve you drinks. What do you want?"

"Just a glass of juice. Is the bartender around?" Celia asked.

"Which bartender?"

"The one who usually serves here. I was here two nights ago," she replied.

"Well, the night shift hasn't started and one of them was fired. But I can serve you," the cleaner replied.

Celia frowned. "Wait, which one was fired?"

"One of the night ones. It was after some lady died during the night shift. I don't know the whole story because I wasn't there," she replied.

Celia's mind raced. "Is the manager around?"

"You want to complain to the manager about that?" the cleaner asked, eyebrow raised.

"Nope. Maybe I want to see if there's a vacancy," she said.

The cleaner gave her the once-over. "You don't look like the bar tending type."

"I know. This is for my brother," Celia said, thinking on her feet.

She smiled, but the cleaner didn't look impressed. She pointed towards the first floor, to what looked like an office.

"That's the boss's lair. You're lucky because he usually arrives at this time," she said.

"Thanks," Celia replied and made her way to a carpeted flight of stairs.

She arrived at the office door, finding it slightly ajar. She knocked.

"Come in," a male voice bellowed from inside.

She pushed the door open and stepped into the room. It was a stylish office, with all three chairs and a couch made out of leather. The office desk had a glass tabletop. Lighting brackets on the wall provided relaxing illumination. The walls had teak-brown wallpaper from ceiling to floor, while the floor carpet ran from wall to wall.

A short, heavy-set man stood in front of the desk, studying a document. He wore a grey suit that bulged at the seams. He turned to look at her.

"Can I help you?" he asked.

"Yes. I was looking for the manager," Celia replied.

"I'm the owner of the place. The manager comes in later. What do you need?" he asked.

"Oh, I see. I'm Celia Dube. I was wondering if I could…" she began.

"I know you," the man interrupted. He placed the folder on the desk and stepped up to her. "You're the woman who wants to bring down my business."

Celia frowned. "Bring down? What do you mean?"

He stood directly in front of her, his fiery eyes boring into hers. "You're the woman who was arrested the other night. Looking for your next victim?"

"I didn't kill anyone," she said.

"One rule I have here: If anyone wants to destroy my business, I usually destroy them first. Tell me why you deserve to walk out of here alive," the man snarled into her face.

8

Celia pursed her lips as the man's hot, angry breath hit her face. She took a step back.

"I'm here to find the killer. Someone is destroying my life too, and I want to know why. Killing me won't solve that," she said.

The man's angry gaze lingered before he suddenly broke into laughter. A loud, grating laugh. He turned on his heel and walked back to his desk. He eased into his leather chair.

"Are you going to stand there as we talk?" he asked.

Celia hesitated and then sat in one of the visitor chairs. It was comfortable, but she was on edge.

"Who's destroying your life?" he asked.

"Can I get an introduction first?" she asked. She needed to know who she was talking to, just in case.

"I'm Robert Zungu. I own the place. That's all you need to know for now. Now, who's trying to destroy you?" he asked.

"As I said, I don't know. That's why I'm here," she replied. "I was hoping you'd allow me to see the CCTV footage from that night."

Robert chuckled. "Show them to a suspect? Are you insane?"

"I didn't do it," she said.

"That's what they all say. I can't show you anything as I haven't watched all of it," Robert said.

Celia frowned. "But you recognized me. How is it possible you've not watched the footage?"

"You didn't understand me. I watched the bit where you were caught. But I haven't studied all of it. Only my manager has done that. Anyway, there's a copy with the police and I'm sure they'll do a better job with it," he replied.

Celia found it hard to believe his claim. "Why did you fire the bartender?"

"I was informed he wasn't doing his job."

"In what way?"

"How we rank performance is not information we share with the general public."

"But it happened right after the incident. Was your decision influenced by that?"

"Anyone who tries to destroy my business can't be allowed to stick around. No one gets drugged in this place, and no one has ever died in here. We had to re-evaluate things. It is what it is. Everyone who comes to work here knows this," Robert replied.

"Did you know Dean and Mika personally?" Celia asked.

Robert leaned forward. "Everyone knows the Motsepes. They are valuable patrons when they behave."

Celia's eyes narrowed. "What do you mean by when they behave?"

He grinned. "You'll have to ask around town. I'm not a tabloid to give you information that's public knowledge. All I'll say is Dean loves a good party, whether it's in the club, at his house, or on his boat."

"Did you get along with them?" she asked.

Robert twiddled his thumbs in irritation. "I already said they were valuable patrons."

"It's not the same as getting along with them," she replied.

"I don't have to get along with any patron, let alone be their friend. This is a business, not a social network," Robert quipped. "So are you going to tell me who is trying to destroy you or not?"

Celia paused. "When I find out, you'll be the first to know."

Robert leaned back in his seat. "Spare yourself the trouble. The next time you walk through my doors, you won't leave. I'm not interested in the energy you bring here, so please, make a point of staying away."

With that, Robert took the document and started studying it again. He didn't move when she stood up.

Celia left his office. She went down the stairs and saw a waitress wiping down the countertop. Celia walked up to her.

"Hi, I was looking for the night shift bartender," Celia said.

"Which one? The new one or the old one?" the waitress asked.

"The one who was fired the other day," she replied.

"Oh. He's not coming back here," the waitress said.

Celia nodded. "I know that. But do you know where I can find him?"

The waitress paused and gave Celia a quizzical look. "Who are you again?"

"I'm planning to open a bar and I liked the job he was doing. I'd like to offer him a job," she lied.

The waitress hesitated, then reached for her phone. "I know he lives on the east part of town, near the rail tracks. But I don't know where exactly. You call him and ask. His name is Lawrence."

The waitress gave Celia his number.

Celia reached into her purse and handed her a note. "Thanks. Split that with the cleaner you're working with."

Celia stepped out into the sun-drenched car park and called him.

"I'm aware that you recently lost your job?" Celia said. "I'd like to make you an offer."

"Who are you?" Lawrence asked.

"Someone who wants to make your life better," she replied.

Lawrence went quiet for a moment. "Alright. We can meet."

"Where?" she asked.

"I'll text you the address," he replied and hung up. Celia smiled. She got into her car.

Without a second thought, Celia found herself calling Bill. If she couldn't get through to the bar owner, maybe he could.

"Hi, Bill. How's the day going?" she asked.

"So far, so good. That sounds strange to say when you've made a couple of arrests. Headed to a briefing meeting. What's up?" he replied.

"You know the club where... um, where Mika died? I was wondering if the detectives have gotten round to talking to the owner? You know, getting the camera footage and so on."

"I can't tell you that. I'm not aware if they have. I'm not leading the investigation."

"I know it's Detective Reuben. Maybe you can whisper in his ear," Celia said in her softest voice.

"Hmm. Although he consults with me from time to time, I'm not sure what this is about. What's going on?" he asked.

Celia gripped the steering wheel. "Well, I just think you should check on the club owner. You know how they usually know about the celebrities who patronize their establishments. He might be able to give insights into how Dean and Mika behaved in the club. I'm just trying to offer ideas that get you closer to clearing my name," she replied.

"Well, you need to be patient. The truth always rises to the surface. If you had nothing to do with it then there's nothing to worry about."

"Yeah, I know. I just felt a funny vibe when I talked to him. So I..."

Bill interrupted. "Hold on. You went to talk to him?"

Celia tapped the steering wheel. She'd slipped up.

"Um, yeah. It was just a casual conversation. Nothing serious," she replied.

"When?" Bill asked.

"A few minutes ago."

Bill let out a heavy, angry sigh. "Celia, you should know better than spending your time talking to witnesses, especially when you are a murder suspect."

"But I didn't know he's a witness," Celia countered.

"No buts! Get the heck out of there, and for your sake stop making the case complicated. Stay away from witnesses!"

Celia felt small. "I'm sorry."

"You need to be more careful, for your own sake. This can come back to bite you. If you're still there, you better leave. Now." He hung up.

Celia inhaled deeply. What was she supposed to do? The idea of someone gleefully framing her while she sat back filled her with helpless anxiety.

"Lord, grant me the grace," she mumbled as she turned on the car. She had already agreed to a meeting with the bartender. There was no point in canceling now.

When she arrived at the Bludsloo Township, she parked at the market centre where he said he would find her. She had texted back that she was driving a blue Subaru Impreza station wagon.

The market centre was made up of several freight containers that had been converted into shops. They sold household items, groceries, alcohol, and electronics. There were weather-beaten wooden benches in front of one kiosk, where men sat drinking sodas as they debated the day's political news.

For some reason, this image made her think of Dean. It still confounded her he thought she killed his wife. Was he the one framing her?

But what if he was not involved? She wondered how he was dealing with the loss. Did he feel a lingering emptiness? Did he regret organizing the after-party? She could relate to the loss of a spouse, having lost her husband Trevor several years ago. Maybe she would get the chance to help him grieve if circumstances changed.

Twenty minutes went past. He was running late, and Celia was beginning to attract the attention of three young men who had walked past her car thrice already.

When she saw them in her rear-view mirror for the fourth time, she already had her hand on the ignition. One of them broke off from the group and approached, his right hand hidden behind him. She started turning the key when the bartender emerged and stopped the intruder.

They had a hushed conversation. The intruder placed whatever weapon he was carrying back into his jumper pocket and walked away. The bartender walked up to the Subaru's passenger door and got in. She reached for her small audio recorder on the center console and pressed the record button.

"You should be more careful next time," Lawrence said.

"But you told me to wait for you here. I didn't know they would come for me," Celia protested.

"There's always a way around things," he replied. "What do you want?"

Celia eased back in her seat. "Thanks for coming over. You remember me, right?"

"You're the lady they arrested the other night. I guess this isn't about a job offer," Lawrence said.

"No, it isn't. Unfortunately. I didn't kill Mika. She was a good client. I'm trying to find out who did. Can you tell me your version of what happened?" she said.

"I don't remember everything," he replied.

"What do you remember?" she asked.

"Just serving you the drinks under special order. When I served you the cocktail juice, I went back to the counter," he replied.

"It's kind of unusual for a bartender to serve tables?" Celia asked.

"That's not for everybody. That's a special service requested by a client," he said.

"And who requested it?" she asked.

"A man called Khaya told me to make it for you on behalf of Dean," Lawrence said.

"Was he there as you made them?"

"Yes. He gave me the glasses to be used. He called them celebration glasses," Lawrence replied.

Celia's mind raced. Had Mika's glass already been laced by poison? Or was Lawrence part of the plan too?

"That's interesting. Our table wasn't far from the counter. Surely you saw something when I was away at the bathroom," she prodded.

He shook his head. "I didn't see any of that. I was busy serving customers. The last thing I saw was the commotion. Nothing in between."

Celia didn't believe him, so decided to change tack. "Did you see anything unusual with Dean?"

"You mean other than his mistresses?" Lawrence asked.

Celia's eyes widen. "You saw his mistresses?"

"Yeah, he had three women in there," he replied.

"Which ones? Do you know their names?" she asked.

He shook his head. "Nope. I just know their faces."

"So, you can't help me identify any of them?" she asked.

Lawrence shook his head. "Unless you have their pictures."

"So why were you fired that night?"

"Who told you I'm fired?"

Celia tilted her head in surprise. "The owner of the club told me."

"Oh," he said, nodding knowingly.

"Oh?" she said, mimicking his head movement. "Is that all you can say to that?"

Lawrence went quiet.

"If you're not fired, what's going on?" she asked.

Lawrence didn't respond. His eyes studied the men outside the kiosk.

"Are they paying you to keep quiet?" she prodded.

"I think I've said enough. Stay safe," he said. He quickly opened the door and exited.

"Hey!" Celia shouted as she watched him disappear.

As she started her engine, she knew he was hiding something.

9

While she drove away, Celia's phone rang. She'd connected her phone to the car's Bluetooth feature, so the ringing came through the car speakers.

"Hey. Are you still roving around hunting for witnesses?" Bill asked, his loud voice filling the car.

Celia winced. "Um, no. I'm driving."

"Good. I'm just looking out for you. I know you can be a little stubborn, sometimes," he said.

"Sometimes facts can be a little stubborn in the face of me," she said with a light giggle. "Did you find out if they got the footage?"

"They are going through it right now," he replied.

"Oh! Great. Are you going to be there with them?" she asked.

"It's not my case, Cece," Bill said.

"But you said they consult once in a while. You could pop in for a few minutes, you know," Celia said. She knew if the suspect was caught on camera, she wouldn't need to drive around talking to people. The case would be solved overnight.

"Look. Instead of talking about the case in every conversation, how about you come over to my place for dinner?" he offered.

"Is this a sneaky way of having me visit you for the first time?" she asked.

"Well, it's a different approach to helping you. Plus, you can finally see how I live," he replied.

"Sounds like a plan," Celia replied, smiling. She silently hoped that he'd have an update on the footage by that time.

Celia soon arrived at her destination, the nail parlor.

She got in. It wasn't busy as only one station was taken. Melanie stood next to the reception counter having a chat with their manager, Persha. When Melanie saw her, she began waving her hands like an air marshal guiding a plane to its parking. The only difference was that Melanie wasn't welcoming Celia.

"No, no, no! Go back!" Melanie said.

"What's wrong?" Celia asked.

"You're not supposed to be here, and you know it. What did the doctor tell you about going to work?" Melanie asked.

Celia grinned. "But he did say I can do light activity."

"Coming to work isn't a light activity," Melanie said.

Celia smiled. "You're right. I'm not here to work. Today, I'm one of your clients."

"Well, if it's getting your nails done, then I have no objection. Let's shower you with some TLC!" Melanie said as she led Celia to one of the unoccupied workstations.

Celia spent most of her afternoon there. After her nails were done, she chatted with her staff for another hour since no other clients came in. She caught up with the goings-on in their lives. No one worried about her case. They knew who she was, and this helped her relax. She didn't touch a single file or notebook.

"I'll be heading out now," Celia said, smiling.

"You're required to stay away from work for one more week. I hope you've got things to keep you going," Melanie replied.

"Don't worry, I've got a lot of other things on my plate," she replied.

"Those nails look good on you. You should wear that more often and have it seen by the world," Melanie remarked.

"Funny you should say that. I've got a dinner date at the mister's place. Let's see what he thinks," Celia remarked.

Melanie gave a cheeky wink. "Ohhh. Our favorite detective is pulling all the stops this time around, huh?"

"It's getting more interesting, I must say. But don't overthink it. It's just a simple evening," Celia replied.

"Well, better get moving and have fun," Melanie said.

Celia arrived at Bill's house just before dusk.

He lived on Shore House Street, a series of identical two-bedroomed bungalows within a gated community. They were old buildings from the seventies, but the occasional coat of paint rejuvenated the outdated design.

"Glad you could make it," he said as he let her in.

Celia walked into a neat living room with a faded three-seater couch, two single-seaters of a different design, and some art prints on the walls. There were a few small carvings on the two stools in the room. Other than that, it was quite austere. Soft jazz played from a radio that Celia couldn't see.

Bill didn't have a television set but had a work desk with a computer in one corner of the room. The desk lamp was lit, illuminating the stick board just above it. The board had various sticky notes and newspaper cuttings. If this was material from cases he was pursuing, then he probably didn't bring many visitors home, Celia mused.

"Nice place," she said as she sat on the couch.

"Thanks. You can tell it misses a woman's touch. It's not fancy but very practical," he replied. From the kitchen, he came in with two fast food delivery bags. "They just got dropped off, so the food is hot."

After bringing two clean plates and some cutlery, he served the meal: French fries, glazed chicken, and a tub of spicy sauce. They ate as they talked about how their days went. However, Celia was keen to find out about the footage.

"I didn't mean to push too hard about the footage. But you know how it is. I want to know," she explained.

"I hear you. But I never joke about that kind of stuff. You know me by now. My principles aren't the only thing that I abide by. Legally speaking, I would be committing an offense by showing a suspect a piece of evidence that could be presented to a court of law," he replied.

"But you're not the investigating officer in the case," she said.

"That's even worse. It might be said that I'm willingly obstructing or compromising the case of a fellow officer. In both cases, it makes you look guilty, and I'll have a case against me as well, apart from being dismissed from the force," he said.

Celia sighed before biting into the last bits of her chicken.

"Fair enough. Can you at least tell me what you saw then?" Celia asked.

"I'm not supposed to tell you that either. I'm sure your lawyer is going to get in touch with you to let you know," Bill replied. "But that also depends on if you're the only suspect in the case."

"Am I the only suspect?" she asked.

"You know the husband has to be considered too. Then we rule out one after the other," he replied.

"Bill, please. No details, just the major hints. Does the footage show the killer?" Celia asked.

"No, it doesn't. At least there's nothing conclusive right now. I didn't see all of it, but I know the camera facing you was in an awkward position. You can't see the heads of anyone who sat at your table," Bill said.

Celia put her hand on her chin. "That's no good. Because I have a feeling that someone came to our table while I was in the washroom."

Bill shrugged. "Well, they know she was poisoned. They're focusing on the murder weapon, which was the glass and its contents. It's a matter of narrowing down to the people who touched her glass. You were one of them."

"I touched it by accident. I was simply clumsy, and it spilled slightly," she said.

"That's your version. The video shows that you touched it," Bill replied.

Celia went quiet for a moment. "What does that mean, Bill?"

"It means you had the opportunity to place something in her drink before you left for the washrooms. It doesn't look good, Celia," he said gravely.

10

Celia stood up and paced the room.

"So, you're saying the case could go all the way," she asked.

"Yes. Unless they find a more credible suspect that's going to be pinned by strong evidence," he replied.

"But how can you guarantee that? I feel useless with a noose hanging over my head if I don't do something about it. I want to seek out the truth," she said.

Bill sighed. "The truth is, if you chase down the case, then it puts you in jeopardy if you can't find the truth. The safest bet is for you to prove it in court. Your fingerprints and Mika's are the ones prominent on the glass. You're the prime suspect at this moment. Dean is also there, but in second place for now."

"What about the bartender's fingerprints? He made a cocktail for her," she asked.

"That would mean he's also in consideration. They have to find cause and motive for him. I think there's also one more unidentified person who came to hug Mika before she took her last sip," Bill said.

Celia grew wide-eyed. "Who's the person?"

"Unknown. The problem is, why did they come when you had left?

Was it the opportunity presenting itself, or had you excused yourself so that they could move in and do your bidding?"

"You think I'm guilty."

"No. I'm trying to explain to you how the investigators will look at it. No one wants to spend years chasing red herrings. They'll work with the best bet. Right now, that bet is you and probably Dean," he replied.

Celia sat back down.

"Where did they take her when the ambulance came for her?" she asked.

Bill raised a brow. "Are you trying to change the subject?"

"No. I'm trying to think of the whole situation differently."

"They took her to Trinity hospital."

Celia tilted her head to one side. "Trinity? That's half an hour away. Why do that when Guada Hospital is five minutes away?"

Bill shrugged. "Good question. It's possible the detectives already have the answer to that one."

"But as detectives, you must ask the club owner. Because they own the ambulance and decided to take her there," Celia asked.

"Celia, I think you need to slow down," Bill said.

"What do you mean?" she asked.

"You're asking me a lot of questions about this case. It's all a bit too much. I wanted you here for a quiet evening, that's all."

"Bill, I'm trying to clear my name!"

"You're doing it wrong. You're not a detective. I'm not going to execute orders just because you say so," he replied.

Celia paused, her eyes welling up. "You don't want to help me, do you?"

"I am helping you," he replied.

"Then why don't you just check in once in a while and share some information that might help me?" she asked.

"Because my hands are tied. I've got to obey the law or else we're both screwed," he said.

Celia shook her head. She stood and reached for her bag and jacket. "Thanks for the food."

With that, she headed for the door. Bill followed her, not protesting her departure. As she walked to her car, part of her wanted him to run after her and reassure her of something, anything. But he didn't. He watched her drive off.

Celia drove home with tears in her eyes. Sleep was hard to come by that night.

The next morning, she woke up early and dropped her kids at school. When she got back, her mother was waiting.

"I heard you crying last night," Audrey said. "Everything okay?"

"We cry all the time, Ma. That's how its always been when life gets to us," she replied.

"Are you sure it's not something you want to talk about?" Audrey persisted.

Celia feigned a smile. "I'll take care of it."

Half an hour to ten, Celia drove to the Heartland Lounge car park and waited. She remembered her conversation with the cleaner about the time Robert arrived at work, which was often by mid-morning.

She bit into the vegetable sandwich her mother had made for her.

'It has fewer calories and no dangerous cholesterol,' her mother had said.

It tasted bland to Celia, but she powered through it hoping it would eventually become an acquired taste.

Sure enough, some minutes after ten, Robert's sleek SUV drove into its designated parking spot. He alighted, dressed in a cream suit, white shoes, and a white fedora hat. He did look like a rich mafia boss.

"The only thing missing is a shiny cane and a cigar," Celia whispered to herself.

Celia quickly got out of her car. She caught up with him just before he entered the club.

"You're looking very sharp today," Celia said.

Robert turned and glared at her. "I thought I told you not to come back here. Mkwazi!"

"I wouldn't do that if I were you," Celia warned. "Especially because your ambulance didn't take Mika to the closest hospital.

Especially because you're paying off the employees that you supposedly fired."

"You don't know what you're talking about," Robert said.

"Oh, I do," she replied. She raised her phone and played back a bit of the recording of Lawrence talking. "I've backed them up in case anything happens to me or them. Imagine the police getting their hands on them."

Robert's stare softened. At the same time, a hulk of a man appeared in the doorway. His muscles rippled underneath his black t-shirt.

"Yes, boss," Mkwazi said.

Robert delayed his response by a few seconds as he studied Celia's eyes. She held her gaze.

"Nothing. Go check the tire pressure on the car," Robert said, handing the man his car keys. Mkwazi took them and walked past them, towards the car park.

"What do you want?" Roberts asked.

Celia decided to go with one of her theories, hoping it would stick.

"I'm told Dean had at least three of his mistresses here that night. And he's paying everybody, including you, to make sure that story doesn't get to the papers or the police. Is that true?" Celia asked.

"I'm only protecting the interests of my establishment. I'm not interested in rumors," he replied.

"But it's one of your employees that told me this. Are you calling them liars?" Celia asked.

"Lawrence is no longer an employee here," Robert said.

"But he told me you didn't fire him. Who's telling the truth here?" she asked.

Robert chuckled. "Listen. I don't have any knowledge of their claims about people being paid off to keep quiet. However, if someone works for me, they deserve some compensation."

"Okay. Tell me this, then. Did Dean have three women he's seeing in the club that night?" Celia asked.

Robert nodded. "Yes, he did have three women in here."

"When we say three women, are we including Mika?" Celia asked.

"No. His wife is his wife, not his mistress. When I say he had three women, he had three women he was catering to that night," he replied.

"Who were these women?" Celia asked.

"I only know two. Lynn and Martha. The third one is new. It was the first time she was here, and he kept hiding her in some corner," Robert said.

Celia frowned. "Hiding her? Why?"

Robert shrugged. "Who knows? People sometimes don't want everyone else knowing there's a new catch. He didn't want her to be seen, or to be connected with her."

This intrigued Celia. Who was the mystery woman, and what was her mission that night?

"Lastly, who is Khaya?" Celia asked.

Robert smiled at her. "Are you trying to find him too?"

Celia frowned. "What do you mean, find him too?"

"He's been missing since the day after Mika died. No one knows where he is. He can't be reached on the phone. It's like he vanished into thin air," Robert said.

11

Listening to some *Kwaito* music while driving to the doctor's office was the only way Celia could liven up the experience. She generally didn't like hospitals. Other than the time she was giving birth to her sons, she was glad that she'd never been admitted for an overnight stay. Although she didn't like visiting hospitals, this was the one way to ensure she was getting back on track with her health.

As she drove, her mind kept mulling over her conversation with Robert. It was becoming more apparent that Dean had something to do with Mika's death. The fact that his third mistress was such a secret added to the intrigue. And where was his best friend, Khaya?

When she arrived, Doctor West already had a patient, so she waited. She watched a whole episode of a soap opera before the doctor called her in.

"How have you been coping with the changes?" Doctor West asked.

"Are you doing tests or just asking questions?" she asked.

"For now, I just need your responses. Depending on what you say, we'll see if you need a test or minor checkup," she replied.

Celia told him about the dietary changes first. She was having some vegetables now with each meal and had cut down on sugar and other carbohydrates. She still ate chicken, beef, and lamb, but hadn't had fish in a while. However, her hardest task was taking more water. She constantly forgot to stay hydrated.

"Are you working out?" she asked.

Celia shook her head.

"Well, you need to do that otherwise you'll take ages to see any changes. Let's see how much you weigh," she said.

Celia got on the weighing machine.

"You've only lost a kilo since the last visit. I expected you to have lost much more by now," Doctor West remarked. "At this rate, it will take you five years to achieve the targeted weight."

Celia chuckled. "You're exaggerating now, doctor."

"I'm factoring in relapses because your diet hasn't changed that much. The discipline that working out brings will help you see faster results. Right now, you're too comfortable," she said.

You're too comfortable. Those were the same words she told herself every day since Mika died.

"Okay. I hear you now. So, I have to crank it up a notch?" she asked.

"Two notches. Diet and exercise. We need you to lose weight faster and build that discipline. Do you get any discomfort in your joints?" Doctor West asked.

"On some mornings. It's mostly fatigue though," she said.

"Do the exercises. Start walking every day. If you get used to that, start jogging as well. Just make sure you have a regular workout schedule," she suggested.

"I'd love to join a gym, but my schedule is not the greatest," she said.

"Then work out at home. Start small and build from there. We'll do a review soon. I hope there will be at least five kilos off," Doctor West said.

"Sounds good. Thank you, doctor," Celia said.

As she drove away from the hospital, she craved some bone broth. The best she knew about was at *The Pier*, her favorite restaurant. It was a homely, relaxing space with dark wood paneling that rejuvenated her. She decided to pass by.

She was walking to the restaurant after parking her car when a man stepped out from behind an SUV. They bumped into each other.

"I'm sorry," Celia said as she stepped back.

"Oh, it's you," the man said. It was Dean.

Celia composed herself. "I'm sorry for your loss."

"Are you?" he asked.

Celia frowned. "Yes, why wouldn't I?"

"You know you killed her, right?" he asked.

"I didn't do it. Look, could we have some coffee and talk about this?" she asked.

"I've never had coffee with a criminal, so that's tempting. But unlikely," he said.

"I'm innocent. The proof will come out one of these days," she replied.

"Stop preaching to the choir. You will get your dues, sooner or later," he said.

"Tell me something. Where did Khaya go?" she asked.

Dean froze. "I'm wondering the same thing."

"I find it strange that your best friend can disappear without a trace the day after your wife died," Celia said.

"Khaya has his issues. I can't speak for him. I'd like the answer to the same question you're asking," Dean replied.

He got into his SUV and drove off.

Celia stood there for a minute, gathering her thoughts. If his head had been in a different space, she'd have loved to have a chat. She would've gotten a better sense of who he truly was.

At the restaurant, she ordered her bone broth. She ate it slowly as she plotted her next move. Robert had given her Lynn Tebogo's number. She was one of Dean's mistresses.

"Once you speak to her, she'll give you Martha Mimi's number. The two mistresses know each other, although I don't know how Dean keeps them content," Robert had said.

Celia called Lynn. They had a short but pleasant conversation.

Lynn agreed to meet Celia. At her house, a middle-class apartment block.

Lynn was busy feeding her nine-month-old son when Celia arrived.

"Don't mind him, he'll be done soon," Lynn said as her son ate with relish.

"He loves his potatoes, huh?" Celia asked as she settled in.

Lynn grunted. "His love for food comes in waves. Last week it was rice and beans. Now it's mashed potatoes. I'm not looking forward to what it will be two weeks from now."

They laughed. After she had fed him and lulled him to sleep, Lynn returned and sat across from Celia. In her late twenties, Lynn was beautiful and looked more mature than her age.

"So, what did you want to know?" Lynn asked.

"You don't remember me? Because I remember you," Celia said.

Lynn squinted as she tried to remember Celia's face. "Remember you? From where?"

"The night Mika died," she said.

"Oh. That. That was one crazy night. But I didn't pay a lot of attention to the whole drama around that time," Lynn said.

Celia raised a brow. "She was Dean's wife. Why didn't it bother you?"

Lynn shrugged. "As you said, she was his wife. I had no other reason to get close to her nor care what happened to her."

"You do realize that you have a son with a married man, right?" Celia asked.

"Are you trying to shame me?" Lynn asked, her eyes bristling.

"No, I'm not. Sorry, I didn't mean it that way. What I meant to say is what happens in his marriage affects you in some way. Even his wife's death," Celia clarified.

"Fair enough. But when we met, I didn't know he was married. It only came out two months into my pregnancy. Then the drama started," Lynn replied.

"What drama?" Celia asked.

"Mika was interesting. She sent people to follow me. I received strange texts warning me to stay away from Dean or else I would get physically hurt. Just crazy stuff. And it was all coming from her," Lynn replied.

"Did anyone hurt you?" Celia asked.

"Thankfully, no. She somehow learned I was pregnant, and we met face to face. She offered me cash if I agreed to terminate the pregnancy and move elsewhere. I was offended and walked out on her. After the baby came, she congratulated me by sending a gift hamper and a shopping voucher that's valid for two years. I thought she had come to her senses," Lynn replied.

"You're still using the voucher?" Celia asked.

"Yeah, why not? My son needs things," Lynn replied. "I think it was the only thoughtful thing she did for me."

Celia leaned forward. "Dean isn't helping?"

"You see, that's where the problem is. He hasn't been able to do as much as he used to. You may not know this, but she ran nearly all his businesses. So, I'm guessing she controlled quite a bit of his cash flow. After she sent the voucher, she told him not to send me money. Isn't that twisted?" Lynn asked.

"And how has your relationship with Dean been after that?" Celia asked.

"Dean has always had my back, even when things were a little sketchy between him and his wife. To be honest, at some point I thought he would leave her and we would raise a family together. Especially since they don't have children of their own," Lynn said. "He always makes time for his son."

Celia realized she had never thought of asking Mika if she had kids. It just never came up. This new knowledge raised more questions in her mind about Dean and Mika's relationship.

"Dean doesn't seem like the type to settle for one woman," Celia remarked.

"Tell me about it. I was in my final trimester when Martha appeared. That's when I knew who he was," she replied.

"Did Mika's behavior make you bitter?" Celia asked.

Lynn pondered for a moment; her eyes trained on the ceiling.

"What she did was stupid, and maybe callous. It still rattles me when I think about it. Is that bitterness? I'm not sure. Did I wish her well? I would have if she did the same for my son," Lynn replied.

"Did the anger you felt drive you to want her dead?" Celia asked.

Lynn shook her head vehemently. "No way! I can't be taking such risks when I've got a son to take care of. I'd rather avoid such drama and just live."

"So, who do you think did it?"

"I'm not snitching or anything, but have you met Martha? Once you meet her, you'll maybe have your answer."

Celia raised a brow. "Why do you say that?"

"Just meet her. Anything I tell you might cloud your judgment. Do you have her details?" Lynn asked as she reached for her phone.

"No. I'd appreciate it if you could share them," she replied.

"Sure," Lynn said. She read out Martha's number. "She lives in a better hood than I do. A proper country house."

"Paid for by Dean?"

"You'll have to ask her that. But rumor has it that she doesn't work much, so the money must be coming from somewhere."

"I also learned that there's a third woman. Do you know anything about her?" Celia asked.

Lynn shook her head. "He's already onto the third? I'm not surprised."

Celia smiled. "Thanks for the chat."

"You're welcome. If you need to have another one, let me know," Lynn replied.

As soon as Celia got back in her car, she called Martha. It didn't go through. Instead, she heard a different message.

"Thank you for calling Martha. Depending on the message you leave on this voicemail, you'll either be alive or dead tomorrow. Please leave your message after the tone."

Celia hung up.

12

Martha's house was not as ominous as her voicemail, but it had a unique look compared to those in the colorful neighborhood.

It was a country house on the outskirts of Sunshine Cove, where some of the town's well-to-do lived. It had black roof tiles. Its black gate was made of wooden planks instead of wrought iron like that of the neighboring homes. A small sign *'Drive slow. Furry cat on the prowl'* hung from the gate. As soon as she drove up, a guard started opening the gate. It wasn't automatic, but it was efficient.

After Celia had parked and stepped out of her car, she stopped to stare at the other car in the lot: a white BMW sedan with black trim. It was a pricey model that needed deep pockets to maintain, the kind that turns heads. Something rubbing on her leg startled her. She looked down and saw a furry cat next to her. It was gray with white circles around each eye. It made a decent panda impression.

"Welcome to my home," Martha said as she walked to Celia. She wore a flowing white robe with black patterns along the hems. The black lipstick on her thick lips matched the long dark hair that fell on her shoulders. Her makeup was minimalist but tasteful. Celia could tell that she stocked lots of dark-colored products to enhance the mystic aura about her.

"Thank you for making time. You've got a nice home here," Celia said as they took their seats in a garden gazebo.

"We make the most of this short life we have on this planet," Martha replied. "You wanted to talk about Dean and Mika."

"Erm, yes. I did. I know you're familiar with both of them," Celia said.

"One more than the other. I'm Dean's mistress," she replied.

Celia raised a brow. "You're quite open about it."

Martha shrugged. "What's there to hide? I like him, he loves me. He takes care of me and I elevate him. It's a win-win situation."

"Is it really? You do know Mika died, don't you? I wager that you were there that night," Celia said.

Martha swept her hair over her shoulder. "Yes, I'm aware of that. Tragic event. But she's gone. Life moves on."

Celia's eyes narrowed. "You didn't like her, did you?"

"The feeling was mutual. If I had died, she wouldn't have mourned me either," Martha replied.

"Did you ever meet and talk?" Celia asked.

"Twice. Our last one didn't go well. We had a little argument."

"What was it about?"

"She wanted us to sign an agreement that outlined our roles in Dean's life and her role in his life. Any breaches in the contract would incur penalties," she said.

"What penalties?" Celia asked.

"You'd pay cash. Or disappear," she replied.

Celia's eyes narrowed. "For what kind of transgression?"

"Slander. Espionage. Getting pregnant. That kind of stuff. I have to say, if I was in the same position, I would've done something similar. It was all-encompassing, but her approach had no benefits for me. I refused. We exchanged words. After that, I stayed out of her way. Until that night."

"And were you out of her way that night?" Celia asked.

"I didn't kill her if that's what you're asking. If I did, I might just tell you,' Martha said with a smile. "Frankly, if I did it, I wouldn't have used poison."

"What would you use?" Celia asked, intrigued that Martha was considering it.

"A sniper. A cut brake line. Something more dramatic but distant from me. Poison has to be administered up-close, and that wouldn't suit me. As you can see, I'm very recognizable," Martha replied.

"So, you wanted her dead, but you don't like how it was done?" Celia asked.

"Exactly. It's okay if I say that, right?" Martha said.

Celia smiled out of sheer surprise at her audacity. They went on talking, changing the subject from murder to makeup, a topic that Martha was knowledgeable about. The conversation was so engaging that Celia offered to supply her with foundation, but only after the investigation was over.

As Celia drove away after the meeting, she was still in awe at the strange aura Martha had. Martha was the type of person who could talk about death for hours. But did that make her sinister enough to hire someone to do it for her? Was she being open to cancel herself from suspicion? Or did she believe she was too smart to be caught, so it didn't matter, anyway?

Sometimes killers dare you to find proof of their misdeeds, Celia thought to herself.

When she got home, Celia found Mrs. Owens and her mother sitting on yoga mats in the middle of the living room. Oriental instrumentals played softly in the background. They had their eyes closed, seated on the floor with their backs upright and their legs pulled towards their bodies. But it wasn't comfortable, as they both fidgeted in the struggle to hold the pose.

"Breathe slowly. Don't rush it," Mrs. Owens said as she popped open one eye to see who had come in. Celia stared at them in fascination. She'd never imagined she would see her mother and Mrs. Owens practicing yoga.

"Alright, let's shift position to the chair pose," Mrs. Owens said as she got to her feet. Audrey heaved herself slowly off the floor as if she'd broken a bone.

"Hey, Cece. You wanna join in?" Audrey asked.

"Don't ask her. She should join in. You're going to be doing this even when I'm not around," Mrs. Owens replied.

"I'm not sure I should be doing that in a dress," Celia said.

"Then go and change. We'll be here waiting for you," Mrs. Owens said.

Celia went to her bedroom. She returned after a few minutes in loose-fitting pants.

"Alright. Let's go into the chair pose," Mrs. Owens said. She put her hands together in front of her and slowly bent her knees to simulate a sitting position. "Come on, I'm not supposed to be doing this alone."

Audrey and Celia followed suit, lowering themselves.

"My knees are not going to be happy here," Audrey said as her legs started shaking.

Celia felt the strain, but she kept going. When they each had their knees at nearly forty-five degrees, they held it there.

"Keep steady and breathe slowly," Mrs. Owens said. Celia glanced at her and noted her knees were shaking too. Suddenly, Audrey lost her balance and fell backward onto the floor.

"Oh my," Audrey exclaimed.

Mrs. Owens looked to her side, lost her balance, and fell over. Celia laughed as she got back to an upright position.

"I thought this is supposed to be relaxing?" Celia said.

"It is relaxing. We just need to get used to it," Mrs. Owens said as she caught her breath.

"I don't think we need this pose. Do you have another one?" Audrey asked.

Mrs. Owens was already standing. She placed her right foot in front of her left. "We can do the high lunge."

She lifted both hands straight above her head and bent her right foot while keeping her left straight. As she lowered herself, her legs started shaking again, and it wasn't long before she fell over.

Celia shook her head. "How are we supposed to do this on our own when our instructor can't?"

"Hush! This is all about patience and humility," Mrs. Owens retorted.

Celia laughed. "But I won't be able to know when I'm doing it right if I keep falling over."

"She's got a point, Christie," Audrey said.

"You two just want things easy. The good book says don't despise humble beginnings!" Mrs. Owens replied.

Celia was in mid-laughter when her phone rang. Still trying to contain herself, she took the call.

"Is this Celia?" a voice asked.

"Yes, it is. Lawrence, is that you?" Celia asked.

The voice paused. "I'm ready to talk about that night."

Celia punched the air. "When do you want to meet?"

"Can you come right now? I'll send you the location," Lawrence replied.

After he hung up, Celia headed for the bedroom.

"Hey! "We're just getting started," Mrs. Owens said.

"Sorry, I'm already done!" Celia replied.

13

The Filale Coffee House was an ordinary restaurant with one unique feature: there were traditional Zulu shields everywhere. Not the actual shields, but printed ones. They were all over the walls, seats, and tables. Napkins and staff uniforms had miniature shields printed on them. It was a little overboard in Celia's opinion, but they won her over with their quality food served in generous portions.

She was halfway through her lamb stew while Lawrence was nibbling the last pieces of his pap with grilled chicken.

"How does Dean treat women," Celia asked.

"He gets a lot of attention, so sometimes you'll find him talking to women he just met as if he'd known them all his life. But the women he keeps close to him were three," Lawrence replied.

"So, the special service you offered was Dean's idea?" Celia asked.

"Yes, and the club owner and manager played along. Dean picks a favorite waiter or bartender to take drinks to his women. I thought it was because he wanted the ladies to feel special, but it's simply a security precaution. This way, he can control the flow of information. He doesn't tip me for this service. He pays me to do it," Lawrence said.

"How many of his mistresses did you serve that night?" Celia asked.

"Three of them," he replied.

"Do you mean his wife and two others?" Celia asked, just to be sure Mika was not on his list.

He shook his head. "Mistresses only."

Celia's forehead furrowed. "Who's the third one?"

"She's new. That was the first time I saw her there. She sat with two of her friends at one end of the counter for most of the night. Dean would order drinks for them, and I'd deliver," Lawrence replied.

Celia tried to reexamine her memories of that night, but couldn't recall a young woman at the counter. "What was she wearing?"

"She wore a black jacket with a butterfly pattern. I'd never seen one like it anywhere. Maybe Dean imported it or something," Lawrence replied.

"And she was seated in a blind spot, so there's no footage of the area where she was seated?" Celia asked.

"You won't get any clips of that section," he replied.

Celia nodded quietly. It seemed Dean was determined to keep this new woman a secret.

"Has he threatened you since it happened?" She asked.

Lawrence thought about it for a moment. "Dean doesn't threaten. You just know he's going to make your life difficult if you cross him."

Lawrence ate up the last bit of his dish.

"I've said enough. I need to go," Lawrence said, downing his glass of tonic water. But Celia had one question she had to put to him.

"Lawrence, Mika's drink had poison in it. You came to our table with Khaya to serve the drink. He told me he didn't make you do it, he was only escorting you. So, the question is: Did Dean send you to add something to Mika's drink?"

Lawrence's eyes reddened with anger. He stood up and straightened his collar.

"I came here to talk about the mistresses, not your suspicions of me. I think we're done here," he said. "Tomorrow's not promised. Stay safe."

Lawrence sauntered off. She watched him, knowing that he had once again held back. She wasn't sure she would see him again.

Instead of going back home, Celia decided to surprise Bill at his police station office. She stopped at the bakery to get his favorite chocolate doughnuts.

When she got there, she found his office door open. Bill was deeply absorbed by something on his computer screen.

"Hello, there," she said, smiling.

Startled, Bill lifted his eyes and smiled back. "What are you doing here?"

"I'm allowed to check in on you, right?" she asked.

"Yeah, sure. Come in," Bill said. Celia walked up to him, handed him the doughnuts, and sat down.

He chuckled. "You're here to fatten me up?"

"Since I can't eat them, one of us has to," Celia replied. "Why do you look so serious?"

"So serious?" he asked.

"You were riveted to the screen when I came in," she replied.

"Oh. Just checking out some case stuff," Bill said with a dismissive wave of the hand.

"Alright. Anything to do with Mika's case?" Celia asked.

He shot her a look, and she got the message.

Celia raised her hands in mock surrender. "Yes, I understand. Sorry for pushing."

"You need to unlearn that," Bill advised.

"I agree, sir. Totally," she said.

Just then, there was a knock on the door. It was Detective Reuben. He glanced at her.

"Hello, Celia," Reuben said.

"Hello, detective," Celia replied.

"Everything okay here, Bill?" Reuben asked.

"Yeah, everything's okay, buddy. What do you need?" Bill asked.

"Can you come over for a second? I've got something I need you to help me figure out," Reuben replied.

"It won't be a long one, will it?" Bill asked.

"No, just five to ten minutes," Reuben replied.

Bill turned to Celia. "Are you in a hurry?"

"No, I can wait," she replied.

Bill grunted, grabbed a doughnut, and strode out as he sunk his teeth into its juicy goodness.

After he had left, Celia tried to resist the urge but gave in after a minute. She stood and went to check Bill's computer screen. He hadn't locked it. On the screen was a video playing. She clicked the play button and quickly realized it was the CCTV footage from the night Mika died.

"Oh, my word," Celia muttered under her breath. She checked the folder containing it. There were several other clips, all totaling ten gigabytes. She thought quickly. She didn't have a flash disk. Where to put it?

Then she remembered. Her phone. Its SD card had enough space to hold the footage. She quickly got her phone out of her purse and turned on the Bluetooth function. She then sent the file from the laptop to her phone. It indicated seven minutes of copying.

"I hope you can do this fast before he gets back here," she whispered. She went back to her seat and monitored the copying progress from her phone.

Thirty percent. Her fingers rattled the table.

Fifty percent. Her foot started tapping the floor.

Eighty-three percent. She could hear Bill's voice in the distance. He was having a lengthy conversation in the corridor.

Ninety-five percent. She heard Bill walking toward the office. She crossed her fingers.

Bill strode in, sighing. "That was interesting."

"What was? Tell me all about it," Celia asked eagerly, keen to distract him from the computer.

"A traveling forgery syndicate came into Sunshine Cove. Then some killings started, targeting electronic stores. They've been buying out these stores after their owners die," Bill said.

"How do they connect electronics with forgery?" she asked.

"The electronics stores are fronts. Fraud and forgery are where the money is," Bill said. "We're putting together a case before doing a raid soon."

"It sounds like a sane plan in a crazy world," Celia replied. She checked her phone. The transfer was successful.

"It's always been crazy. It just keeps bringing these surprises, though. So, what did you want to talk about? "Bill asked, leaning back in his seat.

"I was just checking in, to see how you're doing. And I brought you some doughnuts to cheer you up. I think it was a good idea, don't you think?" Celia replied.

"That's it?" he asked.

"That's it. Now I've got to go. I'm going to be meeting Melanie shortly," Celia said as she stood up. "We'll talk later, right?"

"Yeah, sure. Thanks for the sugar rush," he said.

"Anytime," Celia replied, smiling. She blew him a kiss and left.

She drove to the Glendale Park car park. She was an hour early for her meeting time with Melanie. She went through her phone and opened the video file she had downloaded from Bill's computer. It started playing. She watched it for a while before she spotted something.

She saw a woman wearing a black jacket with butterfly patterns. The grainy image wasn't helping much. She studied it some more but couldn't tell who it was. The camera's angle only captured a sliver of the jacket. The woman stood next to Mika, possibly having a conversation, while Celia was in the washroom.

This footage both excited and frustrated Celia. It confirmed Lawrence wasn't lying about the jacket. But it also wasn't useful because the jacket owner's identity was still a secret.

When Melanie arrived, they went inside the park together. Glendale Park was a cozy little paradise of greenery on the edge of the city. Its tree-lined walkways and picnic sites were a favorite with locals over the weekends. On a weekday, it had fewer people and was perfect for a relaxing conversation.

They sat on a bench overlooking the pond where a raft of ducks swam.

"It's been crazy handling the audit, but it's finally over now," Melanie said as she reached into a bag of birdseed. She tossed a few towards the ducks, which quickly swam to the shore.

"You miss me. Just admit it," Celia said, smiling.

"Isn't what I said the same thing?" Melanie asked.

"No, it isn't," Celia said.

"Well, we'll wait for next time then. You look happier than usual. What's going on?" Melanie asked.

"I got some good news," Celia replied. "A lead in the case."

"You haven't been taking time out, have you?" she asked.

"And let the wheels of justice crush me by accident? No way. I have to fight this charge somehow. I'll sleep on a hammock when this is all over," she replied.

"What's the good news?" Melanie asked. Celia told her about the footage.

"Just when I thought the smile had something to do with Bill, you tell me how you lifted footage from his computer. Don't you want to find lasting love?" Melanie asked.

"He doesn't need to know," Celia said. "Are you going to sell me out?"

"Of course, I won't. But you need to do things that draw him closer to you," Melanie said.

"I bought him doughnuts," Celia said. "To make up for an argument, we had the other day."

"You argued?" Melanie asked.

"Yeah. It was a small argument about the case. I felt he wasn't fighting for me," Celia replied.

"What do you mean?" Melanie asked.

"He kept discouraging me from pursuing the case, saying it might hurt me in court. But at the same time, I can't sit back," Celia said.

Melanie frowned. "Did you listen to yourself as you said that? You sound very entitled."

"It's not what it sounds like," she said.

"But that's what it *sounds* like. That's a dangerous place to be. I think Bill is right. He's playing it by the book so that you don't land yourself in trouble. I've solved cases with you, so I know you've got the gift of seeing things many people don't. But you need to hold back sometimes," Melanie replied.

Celia sighed. The words stung.

"Perhaps I've been a little overbearing," she muttered.

"And you're lucky he's there to show you what to avoid. And I'm worried about you the same way he is,' Melanie said.

"What are you worried about?" Celia asked.

Melanie remained quiet for a moment as she watched the ducks in the pond. "Something interesting about a duck is its feathers are waterproof. If it dives underwater, it will come up again and the feathers underneath will be totally dry. You aren't a duck. I fear that at some point, you'll either clash with the cops or with the killer. When you do, you'll not come out of it high and dry."

14

Instead of trying awkward yoga stretches that she knew nothing about, Celia started the next morning with a long walk. She had bought a decent pair of sneakers and trainers. She thought of getting herself some earphones and headbands as she had seen on other people, but she wasn't at that level yet. Headbands were for the fitness addicts; earphones connected to her phone, would only distract her with its music. For now, she wanted to hear and feel her surroundings until she got comfortable.

Her route wasn't long. She played it safe by going right after sunrise. Most people she ran into were either runners or heading to work. She only spotted two walkers, an elderly couple on the opposite side of the road. Maybe walking isn't the most energetic way to start the day, she mused. Immediately, she started plotting how she would graduate to running.

When she got back home an hour and a half later, her sons had already left for school. She was sweating after walking the four-mile route without stopping. She was proud of that. She drank two liters of water afterward, just as the doctor ordered.

"You look like a spring chicken," her mother joked as she served up a pancake and milk.

"I'm supposed to be cutting down on the carbs, Ma," Celia said as she stared at the meal.

"That's why I'm serving you one pancake and not five. It's just a pancake. It's got a little flour in there, but it's mostly eggs. Eggs are good for you, no?" Audrey asked.

"You've got a point there, Ma. Thanks," Celia said as she dug into her light breakfast.

"When you're done, we can go shopping," Audrey suggested as she folded some laundry. "We're running short on a few things soon and there's a sale going on."

Celia shook her head. "Sorry I can't make it."

"Why not?" Audrey asked.

"You know our shopping trips last for nothing less than three hours," Celia replied.

"It's not three hours," Audrey said.

"It's a minimum of three hours. It can go higher," Celia teased.

"And that's a perfect time killer. You're not going to work at the nail parlor, nor are you making any deliveries. Why not go shopping? It's therapeutic for us. Remember?" Audrey said.

Her mother was right. Celia did find it therapeutic most of the time.

"I'm just not in that space today, Ma. Also, I need to run an errand, so that will affect things. Maybe another day," Celia replied.

"When this house runs out of things, don't complain about it," her mother replied.

Celia appreciated the warning. But she had other, more exciting things occupying her mind. She wanted to understand Dean a little more, and she knew a straight-talker to help her with that. She wanted to find a strong motive that would lead him to kill his wife. Everything suggested he might've hired someone in his circle to do the deed.

After she had showered and freshened up, she went to her balcony overlooking the ocean. She made a call.

"Hey, Martha. It's Celia here. I was wondering if you wanted to grab a coffee? I had a few more questions that I know you can help me answer," Celia said.

The line remained quiet for a few seconds. "Hello?" Celia asked.

"I'm here. I'm listening. I was checking my schedule. I'm open, but I usually don't leave my house unless it's super important," Martha said.

"This is super important," Celia said.

"I know. The issue is what you want to talk about has dark energy around it. I handle dark energy often, but I try to keep days like today free of that," Martha replied.

Celia almost rolled her eyes. Where was this coming from?

"Erm, Okay. Is there a place you want to go to that has *light energy*?" Celia asked.

Martha laughed. "When it comes to energy for me, it's just dark or good, not heavy or light. Talking about places, there's a great restaurant we can go to. Lots of good energy that outweighs the dark. You'll love it. We can meet in two hours?"

"Perfect. See you then," Celia said.

Celia met Martha at the fancy *Captain Harro* restaurant overlooking the Zeze River. The restaurant's interior was themed around a ship, with oars and ship's wheel designs dotted the place. Even the table mats had images of boats on them.

"I've gone on two cruises with Dean and they were some of the best memories of my life. Needless to say, when this restaurant opened it became one of my favorite spots," Martha said as she ate her prawns.

Celia wasn't a big fan of seafood and had ordered a chicken salad. She craved a plate of French fries but had to remind herself that she was on a diet.

"You met Dean as he was dating Lynn, his other mistress. Right?" Celia asked.

"Well, she got herself pregnant. That's unfortunate," Martha replied.

Celia raised a brow. "What's that supposed to mean?"

"She lost her spot because of that. The thing with these boys—I'm talking about men like Dean—is you need to stay fresh and sprightly. Weighing yourself down with pregnancy isn't going to cut it. Sometimes it works, and they settle with you. But most times it doesn't," she replied.

"Do you like children?"

"I love children. When they're not mine, of course. I'm not ready to carry anyone's seed. I just want to live my life with freedom."

Celia smiled. "You know that Mika and Dean didn't have children."

"I know that."

"Maybe he started straying for the same reason," Celia said. "So painting Lynn's pregnancy as a mistake may not be the case. What if Dean wanted the baby?"

Martha laughed. "Is that what Lynn told you?"

"I'm a mother and I happen to know the life-changing effect they have on their fathers," Celia replied.

"Well, more power to Dean if that's the case," she said.

"Have you discussed children with him?" she asked.

"Yes, but nothing serious. The usual stuff. I told him I'm not ready for it," she replied.

"Is that why he may have a new catch?"

Martha put her fork down and wiped the sides of her mouth.

"I know what Dean is, so it wouldn't be far-fetched to hear this. But I know what I offer him," she replied.

"Do you want him all to yourself?" Celia asked.

"In a perfect world, why not? We would travel the world together without the other hang-ups of life," Martha replied. "But Dean is slow to go for his freedom."

"What do you mean, his freedom?" Celia questioned.

"It's no secret he wanted to be free of his marriage. He told me that he and Mika discussed a divorce several times," she replied.

"But you couldn't get him to pull the trigger and serve the divorce papers."

Martha frowned. "I have to admit that was one area where he didn't play along."

"Or maybe he's already pulled the trigger differently. Do you believe he had something to do with Mika's death?" Celia asked.

Martha flashed her dark smile again. "Like I said last time, if it were me, I'd find a way to end things. Maybe I'd be a little neater in my craft." There was a twinkle in her eye as she spoke. Perhaps Martha was toying with her once more, Celia thought.

"What were you wearing on the night she died?" Celia asked.

"A purple dress," Martha said.

"Did you have a black jacket with you?" Celia followed up.

Martha laughed. "I have a love for black, but strangely enough no black jackets. I should change that though."

"Okay. Did you see any young woman with a black jacket that night?"

"No, I don't recall that," Martha said. "This woman you're asking about is the new catch, right? You think she did it for him?"

"I can't say. Enough of that, let's finish this food. It's pretty good," Celia remarked.

"I knew you'd love it. Please come with company next time. Three isn't always a crowd," Martha said with a wink.

As Celia walked to her car, she felt the same way about Martha: she had enough drive and mental strength to commit the murder, especially if it meant getting more benefits from Dean. Behind the scenes, Dean pulled the strings to get her to do his bidding. If Martha didn't do it, then the third mystery woman seemed the likely suspect.

She was driving home against the traffic, so the roads were clear. She was on the two-lane A8 that led to the highway when she saw the pickup behind her. It was a wide and raised vehicle, with thick wide tires. It had its headlights on, which she found strange on a sunny afternoon. As it got closer to her, it indicated as if about to overtake. However, even when there wasn't oncoming traffic, it retreated.

Then it started tailgating her. It would speed up to within millimeters of her rear bumper before backing off. She tried to see who the driver was, but its tinted windshield didn't help.

She accelerated, her Subaru picking up speed with minimal effort. But the more powerful pickup kept up with her.

It suddenly overtook her and then slowed down while still on the oncoming lane, such that they were side-by-side. Its windows were up so she couldn't see who was driving, but she could hear the faint bump-bump of loud music that was playing inside it.

"Cursed kids," Celia muttered under her breath.

Without warning, the pickup veered towards her, smashing into her side. Celia gripped the steering wheel with all her might. The car weaved slightly but managed to stay on the tarmac.

The aggressor wasn't done. The pickup came alongside her again and struck her side with more venom. The Subaru swayed, and Celia couldn't whip it back onto the lane. She felt the sudden drop off the road and into the gravel as she hurtled fast toward a clump of trees.

15

Celia braked hard, banking the car to the left as hard as she could. It turned to her will, but only just. It skidded on the gravel, its two right wheels lifting off the ground slightly, nearly going into a spin. The hard turn slowed its forward momentum, though. It came to a halt just before it hit a tree, landing on its four wheels.

As the dust settled around her, Celia found her bearings. She unfastened the seat belt that had pulled tight around her torso. The scene cleared in front of her. She could see a car slow down on the road and stop. The pickup was nowhere to be seen.

A man emerged from the stopped car and ran to hers. He knocked on her window twice before she reacted. She unlocked the door. He tried to open it, but it was jammed. He motioned her to move to the other side. There, the door opened.

"Are you okay?" the man asked.

"Yes... yes, I'm fine," she replied as she put her foot on the ground. He held her as she carefully stepped out. She moved slowly, keen to sense if any of her limbs were in unusual pain that might be a sign of injury. She was glad to feel no discomfort other than a dull pain in her chest caused by the seatbelt.

She walked around to shake off the fog in her mind and to slow her heart rate. Once she was more composed, she looked at her car. The side that took the pickup's hits was severely dented, jamming the doors. The rest of the car looked intact.

"You're lucky," the man said. "Do you have someone you can call?"

Bill. She needed to call Bill. She walked back to the car, got her phone, and called him. He promised to call an ambulance. In less than half an hour, he was on the scene. By then an ambulance had arrived and Celia was receiving first aid. They discovered she had a small bruise on her forehead, close to her hairline. She found it odd, for she couldn't recall hitting anything.

"I'm glad to see you in good shape. Did you see who it was?" Bill asked.

She shook her head. "The windows were heavily tinted. I could hear music playing though."

"What kind of music?" he asked.

"I'm not sure. I just got the sense it might have been some wild kids. The pickup was being driven erratically," Celia replied. She described the pickup in more detail.

Thereafter, Bill sent a call out on his radio, alerting road patrol units to be on the lookout.

He walked Celia to his car after the paramedics gave her the all-clear.

"Are you sure it has nothing to do with the Mika case?" he asked as they got into the car.

"I'm not sure of anything at the moment, Bill," Celia said as she closed her eyes. "I just need a rest."

"Alright. I'm glad you're okay. I know I can't stop you from trying to clear your name. Lord knows I've talked to you about it. But whatever you're doing, this is a sign that it's not a game. Someone's sending a message," Bill said as he started the car.

"Yeah, you're right. Thanks for the concern," she replied. "In such cases does insurance cough up the money for the repairs?"

"It will take some time to process. It's a hit and run, you know," he replied.

Celia gave a feeble smile. "Just what I need. A tight budget and car repairs."

"You'll pull through. You always do," he reassured her.

She asked him to drop her off a block away from her house. She wanted to avoid what she considered a *dramatic entrance*. She didn't want to shock anyone.

Celia slowly walked home as if she were taking a stroll. However, this act didn't fool her mother.

"You've got a bandage on your forehead. What happened?" her mother asked.

Celia had forgotten about it. There was no point hiding it now.

"A minor accident, don't worry," Celia said as she eased into a chair.

"Where's your car?"

"Somewhere waiting to be fixed. It got damaged pretty badly, but I'm okay. By the way, I'm going to be borrowing yours once in a while. Just like the good old days," Celia said with a smile.

Her mother grunted. "You shouldn't be thinking of driving. Get some rest first."

Celia went to sleep early that day, as the events of the day had drained her physically and mentally. She woke up early the next day. She considered going for a walk but decided against it. Instead, she searched online clothing stores and brands for the black jacket with butterfly patterns. Nothing came close to the image she had of the jacket.

There was a knock on her door. Before she could answer, it flew open.

"Good morning, darling. Are you going to stay in all day?" her mother Audrey asked. In her hand was a box of cereal.

"I thought you wanted me to take it easy?" she replied.

"Not when you're finishing all the cereal and refusing to go shopping with me," Audrey said, holding up the empty box.

Celia sighed. "Alright. Guilty as charged. I'll take you shopping."

"Thank you! We leave in ten minutes," Audrey said as she left.

"Ten minutes? That's too short!" Celia protested, knowing she needed to prepare.

"Fifteen then!" Audrey replied.

At the supermarket, Celia found herself gravitating towards the clothing section. Her mother kept hovering in the household section. The trolley was already half-full.

"Why are you going in a different direction?" her mother asked.

"I'm curious about changing my look a bit," Celia said.

"You don't even wear half the clothes you have. What's the point of looking for more?" Audrey said.

"To replace the ones I'm already wearing," Celia replied. They both laughed. Celia loved these moments of random, senseless amusement while they shopped.

While her mother was distracted at the vegetable section, Celia went up the escalator to the next floor to another clothing section. There, she went straight to the aisle with the ladies' jackets. She combed through them meticulously, at times going through hanger by hanger. She found no sign of the jacket with butterfly patterns.

When she returned, she found her mother chatting with Mrs. Owens. Standing next to them was a tall man with one of the longest beards she had ever seen.

"Celia, this is Teacher Mfosi. He's recently become a very good friend to me. Teacher, this is Celia, my daughter from another mother," Mrs. Owens said.

"Nice to meet you, Celia," the man said in a softer voice than she expected.

"Are you dating?" Celia asked.

Mrs. Owens laughed while Mfosi smiled sheepishly.

"No, this is my teacher, Cece. He's a great teacher. He can offer you a lot of great lessons about the mind," Mrs. Owens said.

"Body and soul too," Teacher Mfosi added. "I've heard a lot about you, Celia."

"Good things or bad things?" she asked.

"Good things. Of course, there are a few things that I can help you with to achieve your full potential," Mfosi replied.

Celia quickly glanced at her mother and Mrs. Owens. "Is this what I think it is?"

"We just want you to get better and healthier," Mrs. Owens said. "He has classes twice a week at his studio. You should come."

Celia couldn't believe it. She shook her head slowly as she backed away.

"You know what? I've just remembered I've got a meeting," Celia said.

"Wait, we aren't done shopping," Audrey said.

Celia reached into her bag and took out several notes.

"Can I borrow your car?" Celia asked.

"But you already have the keys," Audrey replied.

"Yes. However, it's important you permit me to take it away," Celia said.

"Sure, you can take it," Audrey said.

"Super. Call a cab and I'll pay for it. Thanks!" Celia said, blowing a kiss as she walked fast down the aisle. She couldn't believe they staged a mini-intervention. The gall of it all is what surprised her. She didn't need it at all.

She drove her mother's car and parked on the street overlooking Dean's house. The advantage of staking out this time was that she had never used this car. She was more confident that she would avoid detection.

It was two hours later when she saw Dean's car. But it was arriving, not leaving. Her heart sank. However, she needn't have worried. Twenty-five minutes and a fruit smoothie later, Dean drove out again.

She drove behind him at a steady pace and decent distance, keen not to stand out.

He stopped over at the liquor store before going to a mall. There, Celia waited for him. When he returned with a trolley full of shopping, she saw her opportunity. He opened the tailgate of his car and started loading the boot with shopping.

Celia walked up to him with her phone in hand.

"Hello, Dean," she said.

Dean looked up and frowned. "I thought we're not supposed to cross paths."

"We're not crossing paths. This is pure coincidence," she said as she raised the phone's screen to his face. On it was the freeze-frame image of the black jacket.

The moment he saw it, his face softened.

"Do you want to talk now or do I have to talk to her first? Because if I talk to her first, it might not go well for you," she said.

Dean pursed his lips and nodded. "Let's talk."

16

Celia rested her head in her hands as she listened intently to Dean, intrigued by how he described his new mistress.

"She's probably the love of my life," he said.

"I'm not saying love doesn't exist. But you're twice her age, Dean," Celia said.

"Does it matter? I think what's important is the value each person brings to the table," he replied.

"Do any of the other mistresses know her?" she asked.

"They're smart. They know of her but don't actually know her. And I like it that way," Dean replied with an assured swagger. He loved this idea of controlling his relationships, Celia thought. It was probably something he didn't experience with Mika.

"Why the secrecy?" Celia asked.

"I was still assessing her. Gauging her character, goals, and abilities. Right now, she's close to the real deal," he said.

"And you bought her the jacket?" she questioned.

He shook his head. "I never shop for her clothes. That would defeat the purpose of secrecy, right? She does her shopping."

"I see. Can I meet her or see a photo?" Celia asked.

Dean shook his head. "That's how leaks happen. Then before you know it, I'll be fighting salacious falsehoods in tabloids. Over the years, I've had enough of the back and forth," he said.

"So, she remains a little secret?" Celia prodded. "For how long?"

"For as long as she behaves. Although I think she might just be the one to stop me from looking for more," he replied with a cheeky grin. "She's so bloody smart, it always surprises me."

"Did your wife know her?" Celia asked.

"Maybe. Mika had access to my phone records. If she didn't know, she had a way of knowing. I never announced any of my women to her. She'd just come up to me with a full dossier on who they were. But she understood me, and let it be," he replied.

Celia nodded thoughtfully. Although Mika had said she was used to his philandering ways, she must have carried some pain.

"You know, I lost my husband a couple of years ago. He was a military man. He died on duty. It filled me with an emptiness I couldn't understand. It's taken me years to get around it," Celia said.

"I'm sorry for your loss," Dean said.

"How are you handling the death of your wife?" she asked.

Dean pondered for a moment, probably measuring the weight of his words. "I'd be lying if I said a veil hasn't lifted. It has."

"Oh. Okay. We all grieve differently," Celia said.

"There's no grief. Not really. Our marriage died a long time ago. I will miss her expertise in managing my businesses, but that's it," he said in a monotone.

Celia paused to digest his response.

"Now that Mika's gone, what happens to the mistresses?" Celia asked.

"Nothing. None of them can take Mika's place. It could've ended in a better way, but this is the version that came. So, we work with it."

"You talk as if you knew what would happen," Celia said.

"What's that supposed to mean?"

"Did Khaya kill her for you? Is that why he can't be found?"

Dean clenched his fists. "I'll advise you to look up Khaya's record. It's a colorful one. It's very possible that after Mika died, he did the math and decided not to attract attention to himself from the authorities. It won't be the first time."

"I see. Please understand I'm not saying that you paid him to do it. But I've been told you wanted to divorce her. Since that didn't happen, did killing her cross your mind?"

Dean's expression darkened further. "You may think this line of questioning is smart, but it's clear that you have a sinister agenda. I think our chat ends here."

He got up and strode away.

Celia watched him leave, fascinated. He believed in keeping secrets because it gave him the illusion of control. That was his weakness, and she needed to think like him. There were going to be more skeletons in his closet. She could feel it. For starters, if she was Dean, where would she hide a mistress?

She mulled over this as she drove to the police station where Bill was waiting for her.

"Are we having lunch at the police canteen for once?" Celia asked with a cheeky smile.

"Nope. I've got something better in mind," he replied.

He took her on a drive. They ended up at Glendale Park.

"You spoke fondly about this place," Bill said.

"Aren't you going to run late for work? Because when I come here, I spend nothing less than an hour," she replied.

"I think I need the relaxation too. I want to know what's so special about this place," he said with a smile.

They went to the wide tree-lined pathway. It had people doing various things like strolling, walking pets, and sitting on wooden benches along the stretch.

They bought some ice cream and walked slowly, talking and laughing. They stopped by a man playing the saxophone and listened for a while. Celia rested her head on Bill's shoulder as the soulful tunes floated towards them.

They continued walking, going on a much narrower path that had fewer people.

"This was a great idea. Why have we never thought of it?" Celia asked.

"I guess sometimes you don't know what you're missing until you try it," Bill replied.

Celia chuckled. "Someone's sounding very smart today."

"Oh? I've not been smart on other occasions?"

"You've been surviving on a shoestring budget of witty lines."

They teased each other some more until they had run out of jokes.

Bill held her hand as they walked. For the first time in ages, Celia felt truly safe and connected with someone she was attracted to.

"Thank you for being there for me, although I'm a little hard to handle sometimes," she said.

"Yeah, you make things harder than they're supposed to be," he replied. "But I like that side of you too."

"It's not been an easy road since Trevor died. I never thought I could open myself up to someone again. I'm like my dented car in some ways," she said.

"Quit talking like that. You're sounding very…" Bill said but didn't finish his line as something whizzed past his ear.

"Get down!" he shouted as he violently pulled Celia to the ground. She landed awkwardly on her stomach, inhaling the dust on the ground.

"Keep your head down. Someone's shooting at us," he muttered under his breath.

17

The shooting stopped. Bill quickly got up and gave chase. He moved in a zigzag fashion to make it harder for the shooter. Celia watched him disappear into the bushes. At the same time, she noticed movement higher up. She guessed that there was an incline because a man emerged at the top of the crest. A car screeched to a halt next to him. Celia heard the opening and slamming of the door as he got in. The car's wheels screeched some more as it pulled away. Seconds later, Bill reached the crest. The shooter was gone.

Celia got up and dusted herself off. Her outfit had dirt all over its front, difficult to remove when the fabric was white.

"Well, someone burst that beautiful bubble," she whispered to herself. Two passersby approached to check on her. She assured them she was fine.

Several minutes later, Bill emerged at the bottom of the incline. He was searching the ground for shells or footprints, Celia figured.

Bill walked back gingerly, his suit ruffled by the leaves and branches he had powered through moments ago.

"Are you okay?" he asked.

Celia nodded. However, her hands were trembling. It was begin ning to dawn on her that she could have died. He noticed this and hugged her.

"Looks like one of us is making someone angry," he said. He pulled back from the embrace and looked at her. "Is there something you want to tell me?"

"Nothing I can think of," Celia replied. She wasn't keen to revisit the conversation.

"I'm just making sure that you've not flown too close to the sun. If someone's after you, I need to know. If someone is coming after me, it's easier," he replied.

"How is it *easier* for you?" she posed.

"What I meant is, I can handle myself. If they're coming for you, then I need to know."

Celia considered this for a moment. She knew if she told him what she'd been up to, it would sour things. She didn't want to risk that. Also, what would she tell him? That it was Dean?

"I've got nothing to share. Honestly," she said.

He looked into her eyes. He already knew. They spent another hour at the park as other detectives arrived to investigate the shooting, take their statements and collect samples.

"Let's get you home," Bill said after they had done their part.

The drive back to her place was a quiet one. People talk about trauma bonding, but Celia felt the incident had created some distance between them. She knew that she'd have to take the first step to fix it, but she wasn't ready to do that just yet.

When he dropped her off, Celia found Mrs. Owens in a deep conversation with her mother.

"I was wondering when I would see you today," Mrs. Owens said.

"What happened this time?" Audrey asked, noticing the dirt stains on Celia's clothes.

"I had a fall. It's nothing," Celia replied. "Why did you want to see me, Mrs. Owens?"

Mrs. Owens stood up and headed to the kitchen. "Because I've got something for you."

Moments later, she emerged carrying a plate with an apple pie on it.

"This is my apology for the supermarket incident," she said.

"Oh my. You shouldn't have," Celia replied as she took it.

Mrs. Owens handed her a fork. "Taste it."

Celia took the fork and cut out a piece of the pie. She chewed the piece slowly, savoring the rich flavors.

"Mmmh," she hummed with joy. "This is good."

Mrs. Owens beamed. "I'm glad you like it."

"I told you she would," Audrey chimed in.

"This is sweet. But you're still blindsiding me," Celia said.

"I know. But this is better than the supermarket thing. I'll do better next time," Mrs. Owens said.

"I'm sorry too for leaving abruptly. But it was a little overwhelming," Celia said.

"Well, that's in the past now. I had an idea for something. Can I share it with you?" Mrs. Owens asked.

Celia wanted to say no, but it would be rude. "Sure, let's hear it."

"I know you're taking up walking and maybe jogging now. I thought of a nice route we could take together. It would be perfect for you," Mrs. Owens said.

Celia shook her head. "Sorry, I've already chosen a route and a running buddy."

"That fast?" Mrs. Owens asked.

Celia shrugged. "Yes. I already started my morning walks. Ask Mum."

Celia shot a look at her mother.

"Ahh yes, she has. Sorry Christie," Audrey said.

"Oh, well. At least I tried," Mrs. Owens said.

"I love the pie. Thanks for this. I needed the lift," Celia said. "I'll finish the rest later."

She went and stored it in the fridge.

Celia freshened up and later left to meet Melanie at *The Pier*, their favorite local restaurant. She found it only half-full, which was ideal for a conversation.

"I'm so glad that you're not hurt," a stunned Melanie said after Celia recounted the shooting incident.

"I'm still shaky about it," Celia said, lifting her left hand. It trembled slightly.

"Do you think it was Dean?" Melanie asked.

"It's possible. We had a spicy conversation just hours before. All he needed to make was a phone call. I suspect it could be the same guy who ran me off the road," she replied.

"Who's this guy?"

"My current theory? Khaya, Dean's good friend, disappeared after Mika's death. It could be him doing all his dirty work."

"If he wasn't silenced for something else."

"Yes. Too many variables," Celia said.

"What's the plan now?" Melanie asked.

"To keep my eyes open. Anything could happen. But even more importantly, I need your help with a clue that's been bothering me here," Celia said. She took out her phone and showed her the freeze-frame of the woman in the black jacket. "I don't know how to find this person."

Melanie studied the freeze-frame for a moment. "Have you tried a reverse image online search?"

Celia shook her head. "How does that work?"

"I guess it works the same way as you'd search for a word. You'll upload the image into the search bar and it will look for similar results. However, it might not work in this instance because it probably needs to exist somewhere else online. But what have we got to lose?"

Melanie took out her laptop, and they did an image search. The results came up empty.

"Let's try out a regular search." Melanie said as she typed *custom black jackets*.

Several online stores later, they came across a small business that made the exact jacket. Celia was elated.

"It's near the marina on the East part of Sunshine Cove," Melanie said. "A lot of rich folks live there."

"Dean can afford an apartment there, I'm sure. One of those deluxe ones. He said he never shops for her clothes, so it makes sense she would buy clothes from the shops closest to her. I guess that his new mistress lives in that neighborhood," Celia said.

"Possibly. Or not. But how would you be able to find her?" Melanie asked. "It's not exactly a small place, is it?"

Celia drummed her fingers on the table. Then an idea hit her. "Did you say it's near the East End marina? That place has berths for boats, right?"

"Yes."

"Mika and the club owner once mentioned that Dean loved going on boats. Does he own a boat? Could you search for a news article about him buying one?" Celia asked.

Melanie keyed into the search engine and waited. Several results showed up and her eyes lit up. "You're smart. He did buy a boat last year. *The Tempest.* It's smaller than the average yacht, but it's still a capable vessel. It looks great."

Celia punched in the air. "She might not be living on the boat, but we now know where we can search for her. Dean loves secrets, and this sounds like the perfect spot to keep her under wraps but still have a little fun."

"Are you suggesting a stakeout?" Melanie asked.

"Well, there's only one way to find out, isn't there?" Celia said. "We have to go to the marina and check it out. So, stake out it is."

"Now?" Melanie asked.

"It's now or never," Celia said as she got up.

18

Once they arrived at the East End marina, it didn't take them long to find *The Tempest*.

They initially thought they'd have to ask someone. But as they walked along the boardwalk, they quickly recognized her. She was slightly smaller than the other yachts that were there, but still exuded opulence. It was a lustrous white color, with thin gold-colored lines running along the hull. The name itself was printed on both sides of the stern in cursive lettering.

"It's a beautiful luxury," Melanie remarked.

"You sound like you want to get on board," Celia said.

"I think that would be trespass," Melanie said as she looked around them. There weren't many people around.

"Do you think there's someone onboard?" Celia asked.

Melanie did a quick scan of the vessel. "I can't tell with the naked eye. I wish I carried the binoculars."

They walked past the boat two more times. Spotting nothing, they retreated to the car and waited.

"I told Mrs. Owens that you're my running buddy, just in case she asks," Celia said.

Melanie shot her a look of irritation. "You're joking."

"I'm serious. We might need to go jogging together. Can we do it tomorrow morning?"

Melanie shook her head. "Not happening."

"Come on. At least think about it."

They waited for another hour.

"We should get some sandwiches. This might go all the way to sundown," Melanie said.

"I don't think that's going to be necessary," Celia said.

They both looked towards the boat. A young woman in her early twenties got off the boat. She wore a t-shirt and shorts as she walked on the boardwalk with the casual nature of someone who'd been there for a long time. She disappeared around the building.

"That's her," Celia whispered.

"Are you sure?" Melanie asked.

"I'm not because I've never seen her face before. I just have a gut feeling," she replied.

"What now?"

"We wait for her to return," Celia said. "Then we can take her some sandwiches as good neighbors do."

"Neighbors?"

"Yeah. We've got to weave a story, don't we?" Celia said with a wink.

Fifteen minutes later, the woman returned to the boat.

"Ready?" Celia asked.

"We don't look like boat owners," Melanie said.

"How do boat owners look like?"

"Sunglasses, shorts. Maybe a flowery top."

"Then let's buy some sandwiches and sunglasses," Celia said as she got out of the car.

After they made their purchases, they strolled to the yacht donning sunglasses, trying their best to blend in.

Celia got on the boat first, calling out. "Hello? Anybody home?"

At first, there was silence. She called out again.

Then the sliding door opened. The young woman peeked through the door.

"Can I help you?" she asked in a soft voice.

Celia smiled. "Hey there. Sorry to bother you. We saw you earlier and thought we should introduce ourselves. We live two boats away."

The young woman frowned. "You live here?"

"Yeah! I know it doesn't look like it, but business meetings call sometimes. I'm Celia, and this is Mel," Celia said.

Melanie waved at the woman.

Celia handed her the sandwiches. "These are for you."

The young woman hesitated at first, then took them. "Thanks."

She was about to shut the sliding door when Celia stepped closer. "We're also here to talk about the lady who died at the club. You heard about it, right?"

"Yeah, what about her?" the woman asked.

"I saw you on the CCTV footage. You wore a black jacket with butterflies on it. Right?" Celia asked.

Fear flashed in the young woman's eyes. "I didn't do anything."

Celia smiled. "I know you didn't. But you can help us find out who did."

The woman hesitated and then stepped back from the door. "Come in."

The interior of the yacht's cabin was simple, clean, and luxurious. Save for the circular porthole windows, it felt like a fancy living room. It had four plush seats made of exotic fabrics, the wooden panels reflected the light and the finishing was immaculate. The colors were a blend of gold-brown for the wood and white or silver for the furniture, walls, and fittings.

Once they sat down, Celia went straight to the point. "Are you Dean's girlfriend?"

The woman shrugged. "Kind of? We're still in the early stages of seeing each other."

"Yet he's allowed you to live here," Celia said.

"He's that kind of guy," she replied.

"What's your name?" Celia asked.

The young woman inhaled deeply before answering. "Winnie."

"Nice to meet you, Winnie. I'm Celia and this is my friend, Mel. How long have you been dating Dean?" Celia asked.

"Around three months," Winnie replied.

"And do you know he's… he was married?" Celia asked, correcting herself.

Winnie shook her head. "I found out after that night. The night that his wife died. It caught me off guard."

"Are you saying that if you knew it earlier, you wouldn't have dated him?" Melanie asked.

"I wouldn't. I wasn't raised that way," she replied.

"But you're still here," Celia said.

"Breaking up with a grieving man isn't easy. He needs me right now."

Celia found Winnie's youthful innocence disarming. She sounded too simple to have done anything to Mika, but she hadn't ruled her out yet. Human beings are full of surprises.

"What did you wear that night?" Celia asked.

"A black jacket," Winnie said.

"Can I see it?" Celia asked.

Winnie left them, went into an inner room, and then returned moments later with the black jacket in hand. "It's custom made."

Celia studied it. It was made of khaki and felt supple in her hand. It was definitely the one from the footage. She tried to mask her excitement. "You like them rare?"

Winnie nodded.

"Have you spoken to Dean about that night?" Melanie asked.

"Yeah, but not much. He likes to talk about other things to dull the pain," she replied.

"He has been acting strange?" Celia asked.

"Not really. But he's stopped taking the anxiety medications I used to get for him."

"What medications?"

"I don't know the name. But I used to just go with a prescription, and I'd get them over the counter."

Celia and Melanie exchanged glances.

"Which chemist is this?" Celia asked.

"Wimbledon Chemists. It's just ten minutes from here," Winnie replied.

Celia smiled. "Could you direct us there?"

Winnie sketched out the simple directions. As they left, Celia thanked Winnie and told her to keep their visit a secret from Dean.

"We need to go to the chemist. That may be where he was buying ingredients for the poison," Celia said when they got back to the car.

Melanie took off her sunglasses. "Let's go."

"Change the look back to the former. We'll need another story," Celia said, ditching the sunglasses.

Wimbledon Chemists was a small establishment with a facade full of advertisements. The door jingled when they entered, announcing their arrival.

A small, wiry man in a white overcoat smiled at them from behind the counter.

"Hello, how may I help you?" he asked.

"We're from the Sunshine Pharmacy board doing a study about people who send third parties to pick their subscription medicine," Celia said. She had already noticed the forms and prescription notebooks on the counter. She understood why Dean would send Winnie to this pharmacy. The man looked impressionable, and he still kept his records the old school way.

The man frowned. "Oh. Is that a thing?"

"Is what a thing?" Celia asked.

"Checking that out? I thought it's pretty normal," he replied.

"Well, it is, and it isn't. We're constantly looking at ways to improve service delivery in the community," Celia said with a smile.

"What do you need?" the man asked.

"Could you give me a tour of the shelves? We first want to establish the ease of access," Melanie said.

"Sure, sure," the man replied. He walked from behind the counter and led Melanie across the room. As he did this, Celia reached for the large notebook that lay on the counter.

She leafed through the pages as quickly as she could. It didn't take long for her to realize she wouldn't find any records of prescriptions in it. She was tempted to go behind the counter, but Melanie and the man returned.

"I'm not so sure I can help you much with the prescription stuff. I've got to check with my superior before I can give you that information," the man said.

Celia smiled. "No problem. We can come back another day in the week. Have a great day!"

As they walked out, Melanie tugged at Celia's sleeve.

"Why did you bail?" Melanie asked.

"It wasn't going to work," Celia replied. They reached the car and leaned on it.

"Let's regroup," Celia said. "Winnie said Dean sent her for anxiety medication. If this is true, these are just regular medicines. Mika wasn't killed using anxiety drugs."

"Maybe he bought the poison elsewhere," Melanie said.

"Or he had someone else get it for him," Celia added.

"Or he bought it off the shelf," Melanie said.

Celia's eyes lit up. "You're onto something."

"Wait. So now Dean's the main suspect?" Melanie asked.

Celia nodded. "The more I think about it, the more it becomes apparent. Mika died the other day, and he's still taking care of his women. If you meet him, he doesn't look like someone in mourning. I know these aren't concrete reasons, but that's my gut feeling."

"What if you're wrong?" she asked.

"Well, I guess we have to push the envelope until something gives. Either he did it, or he hired someone to do it. If he finds out that we know where he's hiding Winnie, he'll come for us. And we'll be waiting," Celia said.

19

The next morning, Melanie and Celia met for their morning jog around the beachfront. Celia had managed to convince her with the promise of a hearty breakfast. As they ran, they kept an eye out for strange people along their path.

The previous day's conversation was still fresh in their minds. Celia was still apprehensive that the shooter could make another attempt on her life. They made slow but steady progress, with Celia unable to push hard because her lungs were not used to the strain. Occasionally, they would slow down to a walk so that she could recover.

After a half-hour of running, they got to the elevated lookout point near the fort. It had a stunning view of the ocean, and one could see the ships sailing in the distance.

They did some light stretches and were about to run back when a familiar figure approached.

"Do you know… how fast… you're running?" Mrs. Owens asked as she hauled herself up the incline that led to the lookout point.

Celia put her hands on her hips. "How did you know we were here?"

"I was on my morning walk when I saw you pass me. I decided to join you," she replied.

"We can safely say that we can't look out for ourselves if we didn't see her at all," Melanie whispered to Celia.

"I have to agree with you on that one," she whispered back.

Mrs. Owens eventually reached them and leaned on the railing. "That was a proper one. Whew!"

Celia smiled. "We've just finished our stretch and want to head back. Should we wait for you?"

Mrs. Owens shook her head and waved them away. "No, no. You go ahead. My run ends here."

The run back was even harder for Celia as her body grew fatigued. By the time she got back home, her legs were sore. She had a hearty breakfast with Melanie before freshening up.

"Is your car still getting fixed?" Audrey asked.

"Yes, Ma. I've not raised all the cash I need to finish it up," Celia said.

"Well, let's hope you do. I miss mine," Audrey said. "Take care of it."

Celia and Melanie left, going separate ways. Melanie was headed to the nail parlor while Celia was headed to see Dean. She had spoken to Martha and Lynn. They both confirmed that he sent them at least once to the chemist to buy medication. Only Martha had been sent to buy rat poison.

Lynn added an interesting anecdote. When she asked if he would leave his wife for her, Dean joked that he'd only leave Mika 'if someone poisoned her.'

This had strengthened Celia's resolve. If he was pulling all the strings, she needed to pose a few tough questions to him. It was much better than waiting for him to do something bad to her.

When she got there, she was kept waiting at the gate as the security team checked if he wanted to see her. Several times they came to ask her purpose for the visit. Each time, she answered, "he's a client."

However, when they came up to her for the umpteenth time, she said something else.

"I have a prescription for him."

Five minutes later, the gates opened.

"I hope whatever you're about to say is useful," Dean said as he led her down the hallway.

"I'm not sure if it helps you or not," she replied.

He stopped walking and turned to her. "Let me be the judge of that."

"I heard that you've been taking out a few prescriptions. What are they for?" Celia asked.

"For my anxiety. I've had a few attacks recently," he said.

"What about the rat poison?" Celia asked.

"Oh, that. That was for a sick dog that needed to be put down," he replied. "I wanted to give it a more humane send-off."

"I'm not sure using rat poison on a dog is humane," Celia replied.

"I've done it before without any qualms," he replied.

Celia studied his expression as he said this. He was indifferent, as if it were a passing cloud.

"So you never bought poison from any of the chemists?" she asked.

"Never."

"Have you ever joked with anyone about poisoning your wife?" Celia asked.

Dean's eyes narrowed. "You're barking up the wrong tree."

"I'm just letting you know that if I can hear about it, then the police eventually will," Celia said.

She started leaving, then stopped.

"One more thing. They're closing in on the person with the black jacket. The one with the butterflies on it. I'm sure you know who that is, right?" Celia said.

The color left his face. As she walked back to her car, she was confident she'd planted seeds of doubt in him. He'd make a mistake anytime now, and she'd be waiting to follow the trail.

She drove out of his large compound, went around the block, and drove back to his street. She parked some cars away from his gate and waited. She wanted to be there when he made his move.

Two hours later, a taxi drove past her and stopped at Dean's gate.

To Celia's surprise, Winnie got out of the taxi and walked to the gate. She talked to the security men briefly, and they opened the gate for her. Winnie jumped back in the taxi and the gates swallowed it.

Moments later, the taxi drove out. When it went past her, Celia noted that it was empty.

A few minutes later, Dean's gray SUV drove out. Its windows tinted, Celia couldn't tell if Winnie was inside. She put her car into gear and started following him.

20

Celia struggled to keep up. Her mother's car wasn't as powerful as her damaged Subaru.

She kept pushing the accelerator to the floor as much as she could while keeping sight of Dean's SUV. Fortunately, another sedan stood between her car and the SUV, so she had a good view of them. She stayed alert, just in case they branched off to another road.

Celia believed they were headed for the highway leading out of town, but it soon proved otherwise.

They branched off to another road that led to the marina. They were heading to the boat.

The road was busier than the others, and she eventually lost sight of them.

Then it hit her. Were they were planning their escape? Leaving by boat wasn't out of the question. Her heart rate went up. She needed to get there fast. She decided to do something she had never done in her life—drive like a crazed lunatic.

She drove as fast as she could over the curbs and road reserves as she sought to catch up with them.

Twenty minutes later, she arrived at the marina. She was relieved to find Dean's SUV parked near his boat, which was still docked.

She thought quickly. Should she call Bill? Alert the Coast Guard? But they hadn't left the berth, so both options sounded premature. She moved closer to the boat, walking along the boardwalk. As she got closer, she heard shouting.

When she went aboard, it appeared the shouting was from the cabin. She slid open the door and entered. She couldn't find anyone, but she could still hear them. Through one of the porthole windows facing the bow, she saw Dean and Winnie standing on the bow of the ship. They looked like they were sparring. Winnie held a short knife in her hand, while Dean held a skewer.

"You lied to me," Dean said.

"We lied to each other. We're now square," Winnie replied.

Celia quickly made her way out of the cabin, walked to the side of the boat, and appeared on the bow.

Neither of them had noticed Celia's presence. She thought of shouting at them, but this might startle one of them and lead to a bloodbath. She approached cautiously, making sure she was in a position where both of them could see her.

"Guys, don't do this," Celia said.

Winnie glanced at her, then returned her gaze to Dean. He didn't flinch a muscle.

"Stay out of this, Celia," Dean hissed.

"What are you planning to do here?" Celia asked.

"Whatever it takes to get my life back. This woman is a witch I wish I never met," Dean replied.

Winnie scoffed. "It takes one to know one, doesn't it?"

Celia noticed that Winnie's stance and voice were more assertive than the first time she met her. She was surefooted and arrogant, and this was a surprise to Celia. All the naivete she had seen when they first met was gone.

"Winnie, you know I've wanted to help you since we first met," Celia started.

"Save your breath, Celia. I've been watching you for the longest time. I know why you're here," Winnie replied.

Celia, caught off guard, tilted her head to one side. "Why am I here?"

"To get one of us behind bars. It's not going to be me," Winnie replied.

"You deserve to be behind bars!" Dean exclaimed.

"Do I? Or do you? Because as far as I'm concerned, you've got a paper trail that leads the poison back to you," Winnie replied.

"You're trying to frame me!" Dean said.

"I don't try things. I do things," Winnie said.

Judging from the exchange and body language, Celia could tell that Winnie had the upper hand.

"What things have you done, Winnie?" Celia asked.

Winnie chuckled. "You think you're so smart. Coming here to save us. You should try saving yourself first."

"Did you send someone to shoot me?" Celia asked. She looked around her at the other boats, wondering if the sniper was hiding somewhere, waiting for the right moment. She saw nothing like that but spotted two onlookers standing on the boardwalk who were pointing at the boat. She hoped they'd call the police.

"Alright, we can't do this all day. I'm sure you got on this boat to head somewhere," Celia said.

"I want her off my boat," Dean said.

"How will you do that?" Celia asked.

"Watch," Dean said. He suddenly lunged, catching Winnie off-guard. Despite this, Winnie stepped back just in time, and the skewer fell short by inches. However, she stepped awkwardly on a roll of rope that was lying on the deck. She lost her balance. With flailing arms, she fell backward, hit the railing, and toppled into the waters below. A splash followed.

"Don't come back!" Dean shouted as he dropped the skewer.

Celia rushed to the railing. Below, she saw Winnie flapping frantically while gasping for air. There was no sign of the knife.

"She can't swim," Celia said to herself. She looked about to find a spot where she could dive into the water when she spotted one of the onlookers already swimming towards Winnie. She urged him on as he closed in on the young woman.

Celia searched for a life jacket around. She couldn't see one.

"Where are the life jackets?" she asked Dean.

"She's not getting one from my boat," he replied.

Celia turned back in time to see the onlooker wrap one arm under Winnie's armpit. Through a gap in between the boats, he swam toward the shore while tugging her along. The other onlooker stood on the boardwalk with an inflated tyre tube connected to a rope. He threw it at them.

Relieved, Celia turned to Dean. "Where's your soul?"

He chuckled. "I'm not here to save those who want to ruin my life. And I can ruin yours too. Right here, right now."

As he said this, he started walking towards Celia. She could see the anger in his eyes. She then felt a knot in her chest, and the world started spinning. She couldn't believe it was happening again. She fell onto the deck. In the distance, she could hear sirens. Her clouded mind hoped it was the police, but all her senses soon faded as the world disappeared around her.

21

Celia woke up in the ambulance before it left the marina. She tried feeling her body but there were tubes stuck into her arm. It was medication and some glucose.

"You're very low on energy," the paramedic said.

"Are the police here?" Celia asked feebly.

"Yes, they arrived as soon as we did," he replied.

"Did they arrest anyone?" Celia asked.

"I think I saw that famous rugby guy in handcuffs. I'm not sure he was arrested," the paramedic said.

"What about the young woman?" Celia asked.

"We already rushed her to the hospital. She's going to be okay, I think," he said. "You, on the other hand, need to relax. We're taking you to hospital."

It felt like a long ride for Celia, with a lot going through her mind. When she arrived at the hospital, she opted to walk on her own into the doctor's room.

Doctor West smiled. "When they told me you were coming in an ambulance, I got worried again. You don't look too bad."

"I hope I'm not. I've not fainted in years. And now I do it twice in a few weeks?" Celia said as she took a seat.

"Let's do a quick check and see how everything's going," she replied.

The doctor checked all her vitals, as well as conducting a blood test. Celia was lying on the bed when the doctor returned after an hour.

"Frankly, I think everything's okay. The test results look fine. I know the paramedics gave you glucose for a reason. So, I've only got one question: when was the last time you ate?" Doctor West asked.

Celia pondered it for a moment. "Honestly, I don't remember. Oh, yes. I had a good breakfast with my friend Melanie."

"Are you doing exercises?" she followed up.

"Yes, I've been going for runs with a friend of mine," Celia said.

"And what do you eat afterward?" the doctor asked.

"A health sandwich," she replied.

The doctor shook her head. "I don't know what a health sandwich is, but you've been eating less than you need and doing high-energy activities. You need to eat more."

"But if I eat more, I'll add weight," she said.

"Not necessarily. If you stick with the diet you told me about, but add more portions of vegetables and some meat, you'll be fine," he replied.

"Great. So, can I go now?" she asked.

"Of course. Just eat better and avoid stressful situations," the doctor replied.

"I can do the first, but I'm not sure about the second," Celia said with a chuckle. "Thank you, doctor."

As Celia walked down the corridor, she saw three men walking towards her. One of them was a familiar face.

"Bill?" Celia asked. He looked up and smiled.

He went to her. "If they told me you were also here, I would've come to find you."

"I'm fine. They've just discharged me, although I need to pass by the pharmacy for some medication," she replied.

"This is becoming a thing," he remarked.

"I won't let it become a thing. I've been making good progress," Celia replied.

"I know you'll progress. But what were you doing on the boat?" he asked.

"I had to find out the truth," she said.

"And die in the process? Why didn't you call me and let me know?" he prodded.

Celia sighed. "I was worried you would stop me."

Bill shook his head. "Let's talk about it later."

He continued his walk towards the wards.

After she picked up her medication from the pharmacy, Celia was on her way out when her phone rang.

"I don't usually do this, but Winnie is also admitted here and wants to talk to you," Bill said.

"We were brought to the same hospital?" Celia replied.

"Come to Ward F4 Room 3," he said.

When she got there, she found Winnie lying in bed. She was the only patient in the room. Her left arm was cuffed to the bed railing. Next to her stood Bill and Detective Reuben.

"She was asking for you," Bill said.

"Hey, Celia," Winnie said.

"Hey," Celia replied. "Better now?"

"Yeah. That fall was quite something," she said.

"Yes, it was. Why did you ask for me?" Celia asked.

"I just wanted to say I respect you. You survive everything life throws at you," she said.

Celia looked at her in bewilderment. However, she could tell from Winnie's eyes that there was an element of sincerity.

"Are you willing to tell them what happened?" Celia asked.

Winnie tugged at the cuff. "Do I have a choice?"

Celia shrugged. "Yes, you do. I hope you make the right one."

She turned to leave.

"I also wanted to apologize for the shooting incident," Winnie said.

Celia looked at her again. Winnie had a wry grin of contentment.

Suddenly, she didn't see a young woman. She saw a ruthless opportunist.

"You did that?" Celia asked.

"I can tell them who did. If you do me one favor," Winnie replied.

22

Celia agreed to Winnie's request but didn't know how to do it.

As she waited in the visitor's lounge, she paced back and forth, hoping that Winnie was holding her end of the deal.

Forty minutes later, Bill came out of the room. He was smiling.

"I hope she talked," Celia said.

"She did. She's one of the smartest and conniving people I've ever met at that young age," he remarked.

"I know what you mean. What did she say?" Celia asked.

"From her account, she killed Mika. However, she didn't get into a relationship with Dean with murder on her mind. The more she heard Dean talk about his failing marriage, the more ideas she developed in her head. At first, she wanted Mika out of the picture so that she could have him all to herself."

"So she started using his habits against him, right?" Celia asked.

"Dean has an addiction to certain medication, and she used that against him. She did her research on the poison to use. She forged some of his prescriptions to get the blend she needed. She'd also been pressuring him to buy some assets in her name, and even proposed marriage once," Bill said.

"She's a visionary. She wanted it all," Celia said.

"One way or another, she was going to get away with some or all of his wealth. But Dean's commitment issues made him slow in some of these decisions."

Celia shook her head. "In the end, she became a victim of her desires. Dean found out about the fake prescriptions and realized her end game. That led to the incident at the boat. Did she say explicitly that the idea to kill Mika came from her conversations with Dean?"

"She said he talked about scenarios of leaving his wife. One of them was an accidental death. He never specified what that was, according to Winnie. But she started thinking about it. I think she wanted to prove herself," Bill said.

"Does it mean Dean has some questions to answer? Because at times I think he played a part in it, and other times it sounds like Winnie did it on her own," Celia said.

"She did it on her own. She even gave us the number of the gun-for-hire who shot at you, but it's not working. It's likely he used a fake name and can't be found easily, but we'll look into it," he said.

"I have a feeling the man you're looking for is Khaya. He's been missing for a while, but I suspect he helped her do this. Once Dean knows his best friend was involved, he might help lure him to you," Celia said.

Bill nodded. "That sounds plausible. But she insists that she did all the plotting. But we have to talk to Dean about these strange things he's been saying to her."

Celia sighed. "It's a crazy world out here."

"Are you going to pass on her message to him?" Bill asked.

"I'll have to, if only to see his reaction," Celia replied.

"Are you going to call him?" he asked.

"This one has to be in person," she said.

"How are you getting there? I can give you a ride," he offered.

"It's not too crazy for a cop to drive me around?"

"It's my car. Let's go," Bill said as he led her to the car park.

He drove toward the marina. However, when they got to the T-junction, he got a call from one of his colleagues.

"I have to take a slight detour here," Bill said, turning left instead of right.

"I can't believe we're going to a crime scene," Celia remarked.

"Who said it's a crime scene?" Bill asked.

"It isn't?" Celia replied.

Bill chuckled. "Lower your expectations. It sounds like a minor disturbance."

They drove on for another ten minutes before they entered a car wash.

"Are you going to stay in the car or coming with me?" Bill asked.

"I'm coming with you. I want to see what being on the beat is like," Celia said with a smile.

When they walked into the car wash offices, they found a male customer arguing with one of the employees. He accused the employee of damaging his car. It looked like it could get physical quickly. Bill calmed them down and asked to see the damage on the vehicle.

They walked towards the back of the carwash, and Celia froze. She put her head in her hands in disbelief.

There, in shiny new paint and mint condition, was her Subaru station wagon.

Suddenly she was surrounded by cheering and clapping as the customer and employee became friends again. They were all in on the plan to surprise her.

"You deserve to get your car back," Bill said as they hugged.

From elsewhere, Audrey and Mrs. Owens emerged.

"Finally, I can have my car back!" Audrey joked.

The employee handed the car keys to an emotional Celia. She took them and was about to get into the car when she noticed the keyholder had a silver ring with a sapphire stone fitted on it.

She spun and found Bill on bended knee right behind her. She gasped again.

"Don't faint on me now," Bill said. The onlookers laughed. Celia's eyes welled up.

Bill continued. "I've been wrestling with my thoughts about you for a long time, trying to solve the mystery of why I find you both annoying and lovely at the same time. Then I realized there's a lot of you in me, and there are other things about you that make me want to be a better man. So today, I'd like you to join me on the beat. Officially. Celia Dube, will you marry me?"

Celia didn't remember saying yes. Her lips moved, and the tears took over. She floated toward him and fell into his arms. There, she felt a happiness she thought she'd never experience again.

The beginning of an adventure she hoped would never end.

The End

THANK YOU!

Thank you for reading the first six stories in the Sunshine Cove Cozy Mystery series. I really hope you enjoyed reading it as much as I had writing it!

If you have a minute, please consider leaving a review on Amazon.

It doesn't matter how long or short it is as other cozy mystery readers will find value in what you liked about this book.

Many thanks in advance for your support!

NEWSLETTER SIGNUP

Want **FREE** COPIES OF FUTURE **CLEANTALES** BOOKS, FIRST NOTIFICATION OF NEW RELEASES, CONTESTS AND GIVEAWAYS?

GO TO THE LINK BELOW TO SIGN UP TO THE NEWSLETTER!

https://cleantales.com/newsletter/

Printed in Great Britain
by Amazon